The Steerswoman's Road

By Rosemary Kirstein

The Steerswoman's Road

ROSEMARY KIRSTEIN

BALLANTINE BOOKS
NEW YORK

A Del Rey® Book
Published by The Random House Publishing Group

Copyright © 1989, 1992, 2003 by Rosemary Kirstein

Library of Congress Control Number: 2003106448

www.delreydigital.com

ISBN 0-345-46105-3

Text design by Kris Tobiassen

Map by Rosemary R. Kirstein

Manufactured in the United States of America

First Trade Paperback Edition: July 2003

10 9 8 7 6 5 4 3 2 1

These books are dedicated to

INGEBORG KIRSTEIN
who traveled far, to a very strange land indeed,

and to

BRIAN BAMBROUGH
one good wizard

and most importantly, most especially to

SABINE KIRSTEIN
*who taught her little sister the music of language,
and the dance of ideas.*

ACKNOWLEDGMENTS

The author wishes to thank the following people, whose assistance helped make this book possible:

Ingeborg and Willi Kirstein, for food, lodging, and financial assistance; Brian Bambrough, for emotional support, gainful employment, and advances upon wages; Shelly Shapiro, for artistic perceptiveness, professional dedication, and personal encouragement; Lisa Bassi, for providing intelligent critiques and poetic inspiration; all my other friends, for their encouragement, comradeship, and patience; and

Sabine Kirstein, for everything mentioned above, and much more.

Umber

Lake Aizi

Terminus

Lake Cerlew

The Wulf

Logan Falls

Kirawan

The Wulf

Shore Road

Wulfshaven

The Islands

The Crags

Inland

(ships vanish)

Shoreline Unknown

Southport

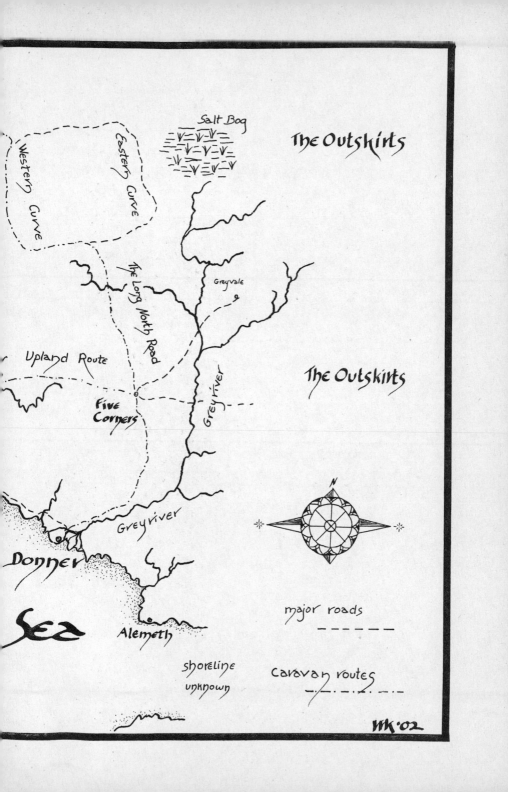

BOOK ONE

THE STEERSWOMAN

1

*T*he steerswoman centered her chart on the table and anchored the corners around. A candlestick, a worn leatherbound book, an empty mug, and her own left hand held the curling parchment flat. The lines on the paper seemed to be of varying ages, the ones toward the center drawn with cracked, browning ink, those nearer the edges sharp and black. Extent of detail also showed progression. A large body of water, labeled "Inland Sea," dominated the central portion. The northern shore was depicted with painstaking precision. Farther north and farther east lines became more general, and there was a broad blank space on the right-hand side of the map.

The innkeeper regarded the woman a moment, then turned his attention to the chart. "Ah, look at that, now, all laid out just like we were birds and all." He tilted his head for a better vantage. "Here we are, then." He placed a chubby finger down on the parchment, on a spot north and east of the sea, midway between precision and vagueness. "Here's this very crossroads, see, and the town, and the tavern itself." The last was not depicted. The steerswoman made no comment.

The finger moved northeast, leaving a faint, damp mark. "There, that's where me and my brothers used to live. Right there; I know that river, see."

"And that's where you found the jewel," Rowan the steerswoman said.

"Yes, lady, that's right. Felling trees, these great big ones here." With a sweep of his arm he indicated a vast supporting beam visible in the ceiling of the narrow sitting room. "There we were, cutting these great things down—they did the worst of it, I'm not so strong as my brothers." The innkeeper was an immense square block of a man, of the sort whose padding generally concealed considerable muscle. "So I spot this smaller one, more in my range, like. And I heave back my axe, give it one great bash—and there it was."

Rowan reached across the table and picked up the object that lay there, an irregular lump of wood about the size of her two fists. As she turned it over in her hands, something glinted inside the hollows and depressions carved into its surface: rich colors that fractured and shifted as the light shifted, opalescent—now blue-black, now sky-blue, now a flash of purple, recalling amethyst. The surface was laced with tiny veins of silver. Rowan touched one of the visible faces and found it perfectly smooth, far smoother than a jeweler could have cut it, and with a faintly oily feel.

Putting the object down on the chart, she reached into the neck of her blouse and drew out a small pouch, hung by a leather cord. She slipped the cord over her head, opened the pouch, and slid its contents out onto the table.

The innkeeper smiled. "Ah, you've got one, too, though not so large and fine as mine." He picked up the blue shard, about half the size of the thumb he rubbed across it. "Oh, it's the same, yes." But it seemed less a jewel than a slice of a jewel. It was flat and thin as a knife blade. Only one surface showed, the other sheathed in some rough-textured, silver-colored metal, as if it had been pulled from or broken from a setting.

The steerswoman made a vague gesture. "We can't tell how large yours is, imbedded in wood. All the others I've seen are like my own, small and one-sided. I suspect that what you have is actually several jewels, nestled together." She turned back to the map. "Can you recall which side of the tree it was found in?"

He was surprised. "Side? No side, lady. It was inside like I said."

"Yes, but wasn't it closer to one side than the other?" She tapped the object. "It wasn't directly in the center, or the pattern of the grain would run around it in a circle. It was off-center. I need to know in what direction."

"Ten years back? Who can tell one side of a tree from another, ten years back?"

Rowan leaned back in her chair, contemplating a moment. She was an unprepossessing figure, of average height, and of average build for her height. Her traveling clothes, a rough linen blouse and trousers, were dusty and perhaps a bit tattered. Her hair, cut short for convenience, was the color of dark wet sand, save where the sun had bleached pale streaks. She possessed no outstanding beauty, and yet her face fascinated, not by any great perfection of feature but by its intelligent, constantly shifting expression. It seemed as if the actions of her mind were immediately reflected on her face, giving her a strange air, part vulnerability, part arrogance. One could not tell if she was helplessly incapable of guile, or if she simply considered it beneath her.

"The jewel showed at the first strike of your axe?" she asked the innkeeper.

"Yes, lady."

"Which way were you facing? Were there landmarks about? What did you see?"

"See?" He was blank a moment, searching his memory; then his face lit up. "I saw the Eastern Guidestar. The sun was just setting, see, the stars just showing, and as I get ready to swing, I look up and see the Eastern Guidestar shining through the branches like an omen. I remember thinking that."

Rowan laughed, slapped her hand down on the table, and rose.

"Does that tell you something, lady?"

"Indeed it does." She had gone to where her pack lay against an armchair, and was opening her tubular map case. She pulled out another chart, smaller than the first, and brought it back to the table. "Here." She pushed the lump to one side and spread the new chart on top of the first. "Do you see that this is a more detailed map of this small area?" She indicated the land around his finger-smudge.

"Yes . . ."

She nodded. "Here's the river, as you said, and it must have been around here that you felled the tree."

He squinted along her finger. "Could be, yes . . ."

"Were there any other landmarks? What did you pass on the way there?"

"We crossed a brook. . . ."

"Could it be this one?" With a series of questions she narrowed the possibilities until both she and the innkeeper were satisfied. She marked the position with a small star. Next she questioned him closely about the terrain and the other types of vegetation nearby, adding symbols and notes. At last she said, "And you were facing the Eastern Guidestar, which is southeast from there," and drew a small arrow by the star, pointing southeast. The innkeeper saw that there were per-

haps a dozen such stars on the map, three of them accompanied by arrows. All the arrows pointed southeast.

The steerswoman picked up the wooden shape again, giving her
attention not to the jewels but to the wood itself. She ran her fingernail lightly along the grain. "Did you use the tree that held this in
constructing any part of this building?"

"Why, yes. The great mantelpiece over the fireplace in the common room."

She tossed the lump to him. "Show me." The terse command was
tempered by her evident delight. The innkeeper could not imagine
why the prospect of examining a mantelpiece would please her so. He
led her down the short paneled corridor, passing a wide-eyed chambermaid who hastened to get out of their way, either out of respect for
her master, or for the woman who followed him.

The common room was a wide low chamber that ran the entire
length of the inn. In the far corner, a door led to the kitchen and service area, with kegs of various brews and wines nearby. Rowan and the
innkeeper entered from another door in the same wall. A massive
fieldstone fireplace filled the area between the two doors. The opposite wall held the entrance and a rank of windows, all flung open to
admit the weak spring sunlight. As an attempt to dispel the native
gloom of the chamber, this was a failure, and only served to offset the
dark comradely warmth that prevailed.

The confluence of several bands of travelers had provided the inn
with a crowd of surprising size. In one corner, a caravan guide was re-
galing a merchant who had three lovely young companions—daugh-
ters, by the merchant's evident disapproval of their bright-eyed
attentiveness. Nearby, some of the other caravan members were conversing with five soldiers in red surcoats, apparently in the service of
some or another wizard currently aligned with the Red. Close by the
fire, a group of pilgrims were receiving an impromptu lecture from
their leader; a local wag stood close behind his chair, parodying the
man's pontifical gestures and expressions, while the pilgrims watched
in a dumbfounded fascination that the unknowing leader seemed to
attribute to his own rhetorical brilliance.

Far to the left of that group, Rowan identified a band of no less
than a full dozen Outskirters. War-band size, she realized with some
concern. But they seemed, at the moment, cheerful and unthreaten-

ing, oblivious to the ring of silent watchfulness around them, a ring that was slowly being frayed by the friendly, the brave, and the simply curious.

Seeing that nothing undue was about to transpire, she turned her attention to the fireplace and the mantelpiece, which was high up, safely out of casual arm-reach. It held a display of oddments and fancy mugs.

Rowan found a tall stool by the fire. She tested it with a fingertip, and it wobbled perceptibly. Seeing her intent, a local farmer leaped up. "Here, lass, I'll give a hand." He moved it to where she indicated and patted the seat, saying, "Up you go, lass, be glad to hold you," with a grin and an overly familiar wink.

"A little respect, man. That's a steerswoman," the innkeeper protested. The farmer backed off in surprise.

"It doesn't mean I couldn't use a hand," Rowan said, half annoyed, half amused. She climbed to the top of the stool while the farmer carefully steadied it, his friends chortling at some expression on his face, invisible to Rowan.

Ignoring them, she turned and carefully examined the squared-off end of the mantel, her face close to the wood, her hands moving over the grain.

The innkeeper watched in perplexity, then eyed the group around the fire, as if debating whether to betray his ignorance with a question. His quandary was solved by a serving girl, who, bustling by, noticed the steerswoman for the first time. "Here, what are you doing?" she called.

Rowan looked down. "Counting rings," she said with a grin, then returned to her work. The innkeeper's flapping gesture sent the girl back to the customers, and then he cleared his throat experimentally. His comment was forestalled by an explosion of loud voices from the near corner, and heads turned in the direction of the Outskirters.

One of the barbarians, a particularly burly specimen with a shaggy red beard, had risen and was leaning across the table to reply to a local who had joined the group. But he spoke with laughter and had leaned forward to pour more wine into the man's cup. "Ha! Stories! We've tales enough, and more than enough. I shouldn't wonder you'd ask, living in these soft lands. Sit in a tavern with good wine and good ale, and hear someone else's miserable adventures."

The band of Outskirters was becoming more infiltrated as surrounding people edged a little nearer at the possibility of a story.

"As for us," the barbarian continued, sitting down, "when we want something unusual we come to small taverns and sit under dry roofs, drink wine, and gawk at the local dullards." He spoke good-naturedly; certainly none of his comrades seemed to find the present company objectionable. One Outskirter woman at the end of the table sat shoulder-to-shoulder with a handsome field hand. He spoke to her in quiet tones; she gave occasional brief replies, a small smile on her face, eyes looking now to the left, now to the right.

"We'll bring a goblin, next time," a second barbarian volunteered, speaking around a mouthful of roast venison. "He'll have stories, or perhaps he'll do a clever dance."

"I've seen the goblins dance," said a farmer with brooding eyes. "I don't care to make closer acquaintance."

"Nasty beasts," the first Outskirter agreed. "Singly and in troops. Only last month our tribe was beset by a troop, and at night, too, the worst time to deal with them. Garryn's pyre, remember?" His friends nodded. "We had to burn him at night. Ha, there's a story—" He received a shove from his comrade. "What!"

"Let Bel tell it."

The man was outraged. "I was there!"

"For only part."

"I never left!"

"You slept."

"Never! Well, yes, with the help of a goblin's cudgel . . ." But the cry had been taken up by the other Outskirters. The woman at the end of the table rocked indecisively a moment, then rolled her eyes and got to her feet. Somewhat shorter than expected, she climbed to stand on her chair so she rose above the listeners, her head up near the low rafters.

She gazed up at the air for a while, as if choosing her words. Though small, she looked strong and able. She kept her balance on the chair easily, feet planted wide in shaggy goatskin boots which were met at the top by leather leggings. Her sleeveless shirt was equally shaggy. Her cloak was made of the unmatched skins of seemingly dozens of very small animals, crudely stitched together. Rowan wondered if she was not too warm.

With a gesture that commanded instant silence, the barbarian began to speak.

> "Silence and silence; the battle stilled.
> The outcome delivered, foes dispersed:
> Garryn's gift. His was the guidance,
> Warrior's wisdom, and heart of wildness."

Distracted, Rowan returned to her counting. The innkeeper finally spoke up. "What does it tell you, lady?"

"A moment." She finished, then gestured for him to pass the wooden lump. She placed it on the edge of the mantel and turned it this way and that, comparing it to the beam. "It tells me the age of this tree."

"The age?"

A grizzled elderly local spoke up. "One ring every year, on a tree." He was seated on a stool by the hearth's edge, his hands busy knitting a large square of off-white wool. Beside him, in a deeply cushioned armchair, an even older woman worked at needlepoint, her near-sighted eyes perilously close to the flashing needle. The old man grunted. "Don't need a steerswoman for that. One ring a year." The woman nodded, her work nodding with her.

"You can see the center of the tree, here. I can count all the way out to the edge: forty-three rings." The innkeeper and the farmer peered up. "And this—" She turned the glittering wood object again. "See how close the grain is? It came from about this area. Where the tree is perhaps fifteen years old."

Across the room, the quiet grew deeper as more people turned their attention to the Outskirter.

> "The sun sank, urging us speed,
> For in deep darkness, fire calls to Death,
> To furies fouler, more fearsome than Man—"

Goblins were attracted by fire, Rowan remembered, only half listening. She clambered down from her perch, thanked the farmer, then settled on a lower stool. "Forty-three years old when it was cut down, ten years ago. And the jewels appeared at the fifteen-year mark, about.

Roughly, then, thirty-five years ago, these jewels and the tree came to-gether."

"Came together? But surely they grew there, magic and all?"

She smiled. "Possibly they grew there. Likely they were put there, that is, driven into the bark, just at the surface. Later, the tree grew outward, and the wood engulfed the jewels."

"The tree didn't grow them, then?" The farmer spoke up, indicating the innkeeper with a thumb gesture. "Like he's always telling?"

Rowan looked apologetic. "I have one, found in a spadeful of dirt from an irrigation ditch, far from any tree. If trees grow them, then the earth does, as well."

The old man spoke to the farmer. "She's going to find out about them. That's what they do, you know. Always asking questions, the steerswomen."

"I thought they answered questions."

"Of course!" He laid a finger aside his nose. "You and me, we ask the steerswomen. And they ask themselves. Answer themselves, too, they do, in the end."

Rowan made to speak to the innkeeper, but found him distracted by the Outskirter's poem. Apparently the goblins were attacking:

"The cries of the crazed ones, hefting cudgels,
Driving from darkness, drawn by fire,
Hunting heat, and knowing no hindrance
Of men, matter, arms, or means . . ."

The steerswoman went to the innkeeper and got his attention. "Might I possibly borrow this piece of wood for a time? It would be good if I could show it to some people at the Archives."

He was dubious, but reluctant to deny her. "Well, lady," he said, "I'd hate to part with it. I mean, how I found it and all . . . I'm sure it must be magic, and as it hasn't done any harm yet, I suppose it must be doing some good."

"I don't really need it," she admitted. "But it would be helpful." A change in the reciting Outskirter's voice made Rowan glance her way.

"Faltered finally, felled by this sword—" Bel stood straight and slapped the hilt with a gesture that tossed back one side of her cloak.

Her movement revealed, below the edge of her shaggy vest, an eye-catching belt of silver, decorated with flat blue gems.

Rowan handed the jeweled lump back to the innkeeper blindly and forgot about the man as completely as if he had vanished. Edging her way through the tables, she approached the crowd around the Outskirter woman.

"—held by this hand. So passed horror."

Bel paused, then shifted her weight slightly, and the informality of the movement made it clear that the tale was over. There were murmurs of appreciation from those gathered and some table-pounding on the part of her Outskirter cohorts. She hopped down from the chair, with an unnecessary but clearly welcome assist from the field hand. He made a comment that Rowan could not discern but that made Bel laugh with plain happiness.

Rowan approached them, torn by reluctance and necessity. "Warrior?" she called, using the barbarians' preferred form of address. The woman turned to her, curious, not annoyed by the interruption. "Might I speak to you?"

"You're doing it."

"I'm curious about your belt."

Bel looked down at it herself, appreciating it afresh. "My father made it himself, a long time ago. So, there's not another one like it, if that's your interest."

"Not quite. I wonder about those jewels, where they came from." She saw suspicion rise in the other's eyes. "I'm a steerswoman," she hastened to explain.

Suspicion changed to interest. "Ha! I've heard of such before, though I've never met any. It means I can ask you anything I please, can't I? And you have to answer?"

"If I know the answer, I have to give it," Rowan admitted.

"That's not always sensible. There are some answers one may need to keep to oneself."

Rowan laughed. "The situation arises less often than you might think. Still, I'll answer anything you like, but I'd first like to ask, if I may. Can you—" She tried not to glance at the field hand. "Can you spare some time?"

The barbarian considered, weaving minutely. Then, with an apologetic look toward her friend, she led Rowan to a table to one side.

Rowan briefly recounted her interest in the jewels and displayed her own shard. "I noticed the first as a charm in a witch-woman's hut in Wulfshaven. She told me where she'd found it; I was only interested because of its beauty. But when I came across another, in some arid farmland on the western curve of the Long North Road, I became more curious. There's no similarity in the types of terrain where they're found, as there ought to be. And they're never found in a natural state; always polished, with some metal setting."

Bel listened, then, with a new curiosity of her own, removed her belt and studied it. Rowan leaned forward.

The belt consisted of nine jewels shaped as rough disks, thickly edged with silver and connected by large silver links. The whole was finished with a heavy clasp in back. The jewels themselves varied more widely than any Rowan had seen before. Some had silver veins running from a central vein, as a leaf might; others had the same fine parallel lines as Rowan's. There was one type totally new to her: not blue at all, but a solid rich purple, with rough veins so thick as to stand in high relief on the surface. "How old is the belt?"

The Outskirter calculated. "My father gave it to me some ten years ago, when he joined a war band in another tribe, for love of the woman who led it. I heard he was killed in a raid later. But he had it before as long as I can remember, which I admit is not many years. Twenty-one." Something occurred to her. "No, here; there came a man looking for my father some years ago. He named him as the Outskirter with the blue belt, and said he'd heard of him from a tribe we had passed." She paused, then shook her head. "Many years ago, well before I was born, my kin told me. So that he had it twenty-five, perhaps thirty years ago."

"Did he say where he found the jewels? I have some maps; perhaps you can point it out?"

"I'll be glad to try."

Rowan led the barbarian back to her chamber, then drew out and displayed her charts. The small-scale map proved useless, as no part of it was familiar to Bel. The large-scale map was of limited use.

"My father told me he found them on Dust Ridge, out on the blackgrass prairie," the Outskirter said. "But I don't find that here."

"What direction does it lie from where we are?"

"Due east. At a guess, I'd say three months' march."

Rowan measured out a distance with calipers. The location was situated in the vaguest part of the map, solidly in the Outskirts. She had no information about the area.

She sat back, silent. Bel watched her with interest, making no comment. "I'll have to go there," Rowan said finally.

"My war band returns tomorrow, in that general direction. They won't take you all the way, but you'll do well to travel with them as far as you can. It's no place for casual visitors."

Rowan proceeded to put away the charts. "A good idea, but I have things to attend to first." She gave a small grimace. "I'll have to return to the Archives and tell the Prime my plans. I've neglected my usual route as it is, following the lead on that charm the innkeeper keeps."

"This Prime is your leader?"

"Not in any usual sense. She doesn't command. She's . . . central. She keeps things in order; she's a final source. Her opinion carries weight, and her suggestions are usually followed. But she doesn't completely control me, or any steerswoman. Still, I don't think she'll be happy to hear I want to spend all my attention on this one problem . . ."

Bel watched as Rowan organized her possessions with practiced efficiency, packing away those things not necessary in the morning. Presently the Outskirter spoke. "Where do these Archives lie?"

"West," Rowan said. She discovered a clean mug and with a gesture offered Bel some wine from an open jug. "North of Wulfshaven." She poured for herself also, and sat. It came to her that Bel probably had no idea where Wulfshaven was, or what lay to the north of it. "I'm sorry, did you mention that you had a question?"

"Yes," the Outskirter replied. "You're going back? Farther into the Inner Lands?"

"That's right. Four weeks' journey, perhaps, considering the spring rains I'm likely to meet. Or, I may do better to go south on the Long North Road, to the sea. I can halve the time, if I happen to meet a ship traveling in the right direction."

The Outskirter sipped. "I've never seen the sea." She raised her cup a little. "Nor tasted wine as good as this. None has made it out as far as my tribe's lands." She looked at Rowan, her head tilted to one side. "What's it like, the sea?"

Rowan settled herself into an explanation. "Large," she began, but Bel spoke again before she could continue.

"May I travel with you?"

Rowan was taken aback. "That's not your question?"

"No. I'm curious, the Inner Lands sound so different. I was going to ask you what life is like there, but if I travel with you, I'll find my own answers."

The steerswoman looked at her again, studying her anew. Dark eyes, large eyes full of intelligence. An Outskirter with curiosity.

Rowan considered her usual displeasure in traveling with company. She had done it before, for convenience or added protection in difficult regions, but she had never found it comfortable. There were always compromises, the need to consider the other's personality and quirks. Such things tended to accumulate, eventually requiring major adjustments in Rowan's natural behavior. It became irksome.

But this barbarian, this warrior, seemed somehow cleaner, more direct than other people Rowan met. But not uncomplicated, not without depth. Rowan considered the improvised poem. A woman with such a talent was certainly no common barbarian. Also, she seemed genuinely friendly and was manifestly no fool . . .

Her request made sense; an Outskirter, even traveling alone, would be considered a threat by any people she might meet. Steerswomen, on the other hand, were usually welcome everywhere.

Rowan found herself intrigued, interested, and suddenly pleased with the idea. "We leave in the morning."

Bel laughed happily, an honest, cheerful laugh. They spent the evening discussing routes.

In the morning the innkeeper breakfasted with them, resting from the duties that had roused him well before dawn. "Feast or famine, see. A week of good business, then they all leave at once. Those barbarians were out early."

"It's a long march back to the Outskirts," Bel said, examining her gruel as if she had never before seen the like. "It's best to cover as much ground in the morning as possible. It makes for a longer rest in the evening." With a discerning eye she studied the row of little condiment jars on the table, experimentally combined two on her meal, and seemed pleased with the effect.

"Did everyone leave?" Rowan asked the innkeeper.

He jerked his head in the direction of the back rooms. "The pilgrims are snoring—and making an unholy racket of it, as well. The caravan was gone before light, and the soldiers just left. Scattered every which way, they did, on some wizardly errand, I suppose."

They stood at last before the door. The air was cool with mist, and the sky was white with the cloud-diffused sunlight. The road south was deserted, the few shops and houses just beginning to come to life. The jingle of a donkey cart could be heard, hidden by the mist, and the air was still in the way that always presaged furious heat for the afternoon.

The yawning serving girl handed them packages of trail food, and Rowan reached in her pocket for some coins for the innkeeper. He pushed back her hand. "No, lady, business has been good; and I'd have to be doing poorly indeed to make a steerswoman pay for lodging."

Embarrassed, she thanked him quietly and put her money away. She was always disturbed by such moments, always gratified and always vaguely ashamed. She felt she would never get used to it.

Bel stood expectantly silent a moment under the innkeeper's gaze, then resignedly pulled out a small silver coin and handed it to him. "Tell your cook to put tarragon in the stew," she advised, then ambled off without a backward glance. Rowan hurried to catch up, then fell in step beside her.

2

Bel and Rowan had chosen to travel south from the inn at Five Corners, down to the mud flats and the dreary port of Donner on the mouth of the Greyriver. The road was broad and well established, as it represented the southern end of the Long North Road, one of the few major caravan routes. It was presently deserted, and the travelers walked alone as the darker north forest gradually gave way to a wood of silver birches, bare but for handfuls of tiny bright green leaves at the very ends of the branches. The Outskirter watched everything about her with lively interest.

"Is this very different from the land where you live?" Rowan asked.

Bel nodded, a broad movement. "Mostly in the color. The farther into the Outskirts you travel, the duller the colors grow. Trees are green, while they last, but they thin out quickly. And the animals are fast to find any greengrass that makes its way that far."

A clearing appeared on the left-hand side of the road, and they found themselves passing a meadow aburst with dandelions. On the far edge stood a small cabin, a corral nearby holding a crowd of white goats.

There was a faint rustling in the greengrass nearby. The movement caught Bel's eye. "Ha!" A stone was in her hand and out of it in an instant; it contacted with a faint thump.

She went to the spot and came up with a small rabbit. She waved it happily at Rowan and laughed. The steerswoman found herself laughing, also; Bel's pleasure was neither innocent nor childlike, but it was wonderfully direct. They continued on, Bel expertly gutting their dinner as she walked.

"What kind of dangers do you meet here?" the Outskirter asked.

"Wolves," Rowan said. "But they're not common, and they tend to stay clear of the road, save at night. On the other hand, bandits are attracted for the same reason the wolves stay away. The road's not well traveled this time of year, so we've less danger of bandits."

"But more of wolves?"

"Somewhat. Rarely, a goblin band will find its way to these parts. When we get to the mud flats we may have to watch for dragons; it's a breeding ground. Still, they'll be small ones. I understand the local wizard considers them his job. Unusual responsibility on the part of a wizard."

Bel digested all of that. "It's a very rich land, and a soft one. A raid wouldn't risk much, and could stand to gain a lot."

Rowan stopped dead in surprise. In her enjoyment of Bel's company she had forgotten what the woman was. She hurried to catch up again. "Of course, the people cooperate against any large dangers. They can be surprisingly well-organized."

"We'll deal with that if it comes up."

"They'll hardly extend their hospitality to you if they think you may be an advance scout for a war band."

"They won't hear of it from me."

Rowan stepped in front of her. "Steerswomen are trusted. I can't let you abuse my goodwill. I can't guide you around the countryside if you'll be using my assistance to find the best way to destroy what you see."

Bel looked up at her with nothing more than mild surprise. "Oh, very well. I won't use what I learn." She stepped around Rowan and continued down the road, leaving the steerswoman behind again.

Confused by the barbarian's nonchalance, Rowan caught up once more. "I don't know if I made myself clear. I'm going to need some kind of assurance from you. I don't know anymore if I should trust what you say."

Bel studied her face for a long time, great dark eyes unreadable. At last she said with careful casualness, "I'm interested in traveling to different lands and seeing things I haven't seen before. I suppose that includes local customs. Now, when I say a thing, I mean it. But that may not hold true for others I meet. I suppose I must . . . make allowances for differences in customs . . . and manners." She smiled benignly up at Rowan. "So I won't kill you for that insult."

As they walked along together, Rowan tried to dispel the feeling that she had tossed stones into the den of a wildcat, and that the cat had greeted her with purrs. She might not be forgiven so easily on another occasion.

Bel settled to the ground by the fire, pulling her piebald cloak around her. "I think," she said without preamble, "that they're part of the moon."

Rowan looked up from her writing, saw that a long conversation was afoot, and carefully put the lid on her ink jar. She had found during the day's march that Bel's times to talk neatly coincided with her own—or possibly the Outskirter was sensitive to Rowan's moods and never started a conversation when she knew Rowan had no interest. "The moon," Rowan countered, "was white."

"Sometimes it was blue."

"Rarely."

"Yes, but think about it; the moon changed sizes. It was bigger sometimes, and smaller at other times."

"That's known." Rowan studied Bel across the fire: a small bundle of various furs, a thatch of dark hair, dark eyes bright with firelight and starlight. The Outskirter was wearing an odd little smile, as though she found the workings of her own mind entertaining. "That's known, as much as anything about the moon can be said to be known," Rowan continued.

"What do you mean?"

Rowan poked the fire with her hiking stick. "Only that no one's ever seen it. We don't know for certain that it ever existed."

Bel was outraged. "Of course it existed! How can you say the moon never existed? I've been hearing of it all my life. The eldest person of my tribe recalled hearing of it. And he told me of when he was young, and the eldest then told him about hearing of it. The tales have existed forever."

"But no tale tells of where it went."

"Ha! That's what I'm speaking about." She leaned back, and her belt caught the firelight, glinting. "Things look larger when they are close, and smaller when they're distant. If the moon changed size, then I think it must have been near sometimes, and far away at others. Perhaps it came too close, and fell down."

The idea surprised Rowan. "It would explain a great deal." She considered. "No. The moon's been gone for a long time, hundreds of years, perhaps thousands. If it had shattered into jewels, many more would have been found by now. And the innkeeper's jewels—if they were imbedded at the time of their fall, they would have been deeper, in a far older tree. No, they're recent."

After more discussion Bel reluctantly agreed. "My father was hardly the first person to visit Dust Ridge, only the first for many years. No one before him found any jewels. He told me they were in plain sight, scattered across the face of a cliff."

"Which direction did the cliff face?" Rowan asked.

"I don't know. Does it matter?"

"Possibly. In every case where the jewels were found on one side of a thing, it's always been the northwest face. It's as if a giant flung them across the land—and the giant faced southeast."

"That may be the answer."

Rowan laughed, amused by the image. "No, it couldn't be, of course. He'd have to be far too tall, and far too strong."

"But why not, if it's just a question of size? There are more strange things in the world than you or I have seen."

Rowan felt a strange chill fall on her. She became aware of the space around and above her: the distance to the road, the edge of the forest close at hand. She sensed the area that the first line of trees defined, heard the wind whistling in the space that curved over their tops. She saw two women huddled by a fire, in a place that lay equally distant from each horizon, in the center of a circle. And she knew, with a mapmaker's eyes, how small that circle was. The world was a very large place, and might well contain such things as giants large enough to scatter objects with a single toss, from the Long North Road to the heart of the Outskirts.

And yet . . .

"Well, let's see." Rowan shifted back a bit from the fire, leaving a wide clear area in front of her. She picked up her pen and, using the blunt end, sketched in the dirt. "We'll simplify. Instead of thinking of a scattering of jewels across a whole range with a single throw, let's consider two points." The piece of ground transformed into a rough chart of the terrain surrounding the jewels. "Assuming that he threw in a southeasterly direction, the shortest limit would be here—" She marked a point with her pen end. "—and the farthest here." She made as if to mark that point also, then saw that her scale was off. She got up and backed farther away from the fire, finally guessing at the position of the Dust Ridge in the Outskirts. "And if we make it as easy for him as possible, we'll have him stand right on top of the first point. All he needs to do is drop his jewel, and we've established the first finding.

"Now to throw, from there, all the way to the Outskirts . . ." She squinted a bit, thinking. "He's throwing well past the horizon. I wonder how he aims, or if he aims? And his jewel has to move very fast, to cover that much ground before it falls." She stepped to one side, and stooped down, quickly drawing a complex of interlocking lines.

Rowan discovered that Bel was beside her; lost in her calculations, she had not noticed when the Outskirter had left her seat across the fire. "What is that?"

"A graph," Rowan began. She prepared to elaborate, but her thoughts ran ahead, leaving her explanation somewhat abbreviated. "It charts the time it takes an object to fall. The horizontal distance traveled isn't a factor. We look at distance traveled here—" And she sketched a second figure beside the first. "Moving objects fall in a curve.

The harder the object is thrown, the faster it moves, and the farther it can travel before falling. And, of course, it helps to start from high up."

She looked up and saw that Bel was not looking at the sketches at all, but was studying Rowan's face. The steerswoman realized she had left her friend behind. Bel could understand maps of a terrain, but she obviously had no means to interpret a map of an event.

"Here." Rowan picked up a white pebble and tossed it into the road. "You saw that it fell in a curve?"

"Of course. How do you think I hit that rabbit?"

Rowan found another, tossed harder.

"Another curve," Bel said.

"A flatter curve," Rowan pointed out.

"Yes . . ."

Rowan turned back to her graph. "Think of this as a chart of the route traveled by the pebble. This line could be the ground, and here's where we start to throw it. This line shows how the pebble travels along, curving back down to the ground . . ."

Bel nodded. "But the ground isn't flat."

"True, but for now we'll pretend there are no hills or valleys—"

"No, I understand that. But your line doesn't show that the ground curves, too. The earth is round."

Rowan stopped short. Bel continued. "You don't need to think about it, normally, but if you're pretending the giant is throwing past the horizon, it seems to me that it would make a difference."

"True." Rowan felt faintly embarrassed for having underestimated the level of Bel's knowledge. She knew aristocrats in Wulfshaven who doubted that the earth was round.

She tried to adjust her explanation to a more sophisticated level, then realized that was a mistake, also. There was simply no way to guess how much knowledge Bel possessed, and of what kind. Instead, Rowan resigned herself to being constantly surprised by the barbarian.

"True, it would make a difference," she repeated. "You have the curve of the earth's surface—" She drew a long arched line. "And the curve of the jewel's path." She drew a second, wildly out of scale, intersecting the first. "And of course, the harder he threw, the more the arc flattens." She drew a flatter path, reaching farther past the curved "horizon."

She looked at the three lines for a long time. "That's odd."

"What?"

She reached out and added one more line to the out-of-scale sketch. Abruptly, she started laughing. Bel watched her in perplexity.

"I'm sorry," Rowan said at last. "Call it a steerswoman's joke. Charts like this can fool you sometimes."

"What do you mean?"

Rowan pointed. "According to this, if he threw something hard enough, it would never come down." Bel looked at the sketches, tilting her head.

"It's ridiculous, of course," Rowan continued. "There's no way to throw that hard, not even with a catapult. But if you could, then the path of the object would curve less than the curve of the earth. When the object fell, it would—" She laughed again. "It would miss the earth."

"And then?" Bel asked easily.

"And then nothing." Using her foot, Rowan rubbed out the drawings. "It doesn't happen that way, of course. It only seems so, because I haven't drawn accurately, I haven't used real distances. Nothing can throw that hard, and nothing thrown can move that fast. It's amusing, but nothing can be learned from it." She sat down again and reached for her map case.

Bel dragged another dead branch toward the fire and began breaking it, standing on the center of the limb and pulling up on the thinner end. It cracked noisily, and she repeated the process. "No giants?"

"Not in this case." Rowan pulled out the smaller map of the jewels' distribution and began measuring with her calipers.

"That's too bad. What about magic?"

"It's beginning to look like that's the answer. Which means no answer at all."

Bel tossed the wood onto the fire. The flames diminished, damped. Picking up Rowan's abandoned hiking stick, she pushed the new pieces into better positions. "Why don't you ask a wizard?"

"A steerswoman ask a wizard? Not likely. Or rather, not very useful. They don't answer."

"I thought everyone had to answer a steerswoman."

"Nobody has to answer anyone; people answer because they want answers in turn. If you deny any steerswoman's questions, no steerswoman will ever answer yours again."

Smiling, Bel sat down next to Rowan. "And wizards don't care."

"Exactly."

Bel's eyes glittered. "There's more than one way to ask a question. And more than one way to find answers." She made a stretching reach and dragged her small pack closer to the fire. "Here's a way I understand." She pulled out a square cloth-wrapped object somewhat larger than her hand. The cloth was silk, Rowan saw, and she wondered briefly how the Outskirter had acquired it. Bel unfolded it, revealing a varnished-paper box, and inside the box—

Rowan laughed. "Cards!"

"Do you know the cards?" Bel began to sift through them, tilting their faded faces to the firelight.

"Well enough, I suppose. But I don't believe in their accuracy."

The barbarian gave her a sad look of reproach but said nothing. She found the Fool and placed it on the ground before her. After a moment's hesitation, Rowan pulled the jewel from its leather pouch and laid it atop the card.

"Shall I shuffle, or will you?" the barbarian asked.

"I don't see that it matters. The jewel can hardly shuffle for itself. You go ahead."

The cards were of the traditional size, large and awkward in anyone's hand, especially unwieldy for Bel. She shuffled them thoroughly, though clumsily, cut them three times with her left hand, re-formed the pack, and pulled the first card.

It was the two of rods, reversed. Bel moved the blue gem to one side and placed the card on top of the Fool. "The situation," Bel began, "is controlled by others, a domination that causes suffering."

"Well, the jewel certainly suffered. See? It's shattered."

Bel glowered. "Are you going to take this seriously?"

"I'm afraid not."

The second card was the Priest, and Bel placed it across the first two. "The way to counter this is by conforming to expected behavior."

"The jewel doesn't do that at all."

"Perhaps if it had, it wouldn't have shattered," Bel retorted. "Now, be quiet, please." She placed the next card in position above the first two. "Fortune, reversed. A bad turn of luck." She threw Rowan a warning glance, and the steerswoman held her peace, reminding herself that it was impolite to mock another's religion, and simply bad tactics to anger an Outskirter.

The next card was the nine of cups, reversed. "At the root of the matter, an imperfection in plans." The Hanged Man. "Suspension. There has been a period of waiting, of suspended decision, but this is now ending." Rowan found herself thinking of an object hurled into the sky and not falling down; suspended, somehow, but that period of suspension over. Suspended like—like what?

Encouraged by Rowan's serious expression, Bel continued. "The queen of swords, reversed. Narrow-mindedness, intolerance . . . these are the influences now coming into effect."

Rowan broke off her chain of thought and leaned closer, interested. "I learned that card differently. Don't you read a face card as representing the influence of a person?"

"Not at all. The person on the card stands for the attributes." Rowan wondered which interpretation was the original, what aspects of life led the more primitive society to take a more symbolic point of view. One would expect the reverse, but it seemed the cultured Inner Lands had either clung to or developed the literal interpretation. It was an interesting observation.

The cards now formed a cross on the ground, and Bel placed the next one to the left of the figure. The five of cups, reversed. Bel squinted at it, thinking. "A new alliance, or a meeting with an old friend, bringing hope."

"But which?"

"Perhaps both. And at this point—" Bel placed the next card above the previous. "Four of swords, that's a period of rest, or recuperation, a withdrawal." Bel looked dissatisfied, then brightened. "Of course! You're going back to the Archives, where you'll rest, see old friends, then gather your forces again."

"Is this reading about the jewel, or is it about me?"

"Your fate is interwoven with its," Bel said confidently. She turned up the next card and put it in position. She looked at it for some moments, puzzled.

"Poor workmanship," Rowan prompted. "Pettiness, mediocrity."

"Yes, but it's in the Spirit position . . . How can the spirit of the jewel be pettiness, or poor workmanship? Poor planning, perhaps? It's very mysterious."

And very vague, Rowan thought. But if the jewel was magical, or part of a magic spell, perhaps it had been poorly made? So that in use, it would fail, resulting in that period of inactivity Bel found in the cards?

Here was the very nature of the cards' appeal, she reminded herself. Presenting symbols, emotionally powerful archetypes open to wide interpretation, they were immensely seductive to any pattern-seeking mind. And above all else, steerswomen were adept in the skill of detecting patterns amid seeming chaos.

In any chaos of symbols, patterns, if none existed, could be easily created. Rowan took a moment to admire the pattern her mind found, to enjoy it in a purely aesthetic fashion—then, with no regret, discarded it. It was fantasy, disguised as information. Nothing could be learned from it.

Much could be learned, however, about Bel and the attitudes of the Outskirters, and Rowan shifted her interest to her new friend and the culture that shaped her. "What's the last card?"

Bel turned it up: the Emperor, reversed. "Dependence," Bel said. "And danger. Either physical danger, or a threat to possessions." Bel thought carefully for a while, obviously casting about for connections, that same search for patterns that Rowan had briefly followed. "I don't see how the jewel itself can be in danger, so it must be that it carries danger. I think we should be very careful."

Rowan picked it up and returned it to its sack. "I'm surprised you don't tell me to simply discard it." That would have been the advice of a true believer in the cards.

"Oh, no," the Outskirter replied, and she smiled as she gathered her cards. "This is more interesting."

Much later, Rowan was still poring over her charts. At last she rose, and not wishing to disturb the sleeping Outskirter, she crossed to the opposite side of the fire. Using her hiking stick, she began again to draw the same graphs, but carefully, accurately. All sense of her surroundings faded. She was like a swimmer, exploring by touch alone the bottom of some rocky pool, trying to create a chart for something that could not be seen, a chart not for the eyes, but for the touch of the mind.

3

"*N*ever just duck," Rowan's old swordmaster had instructed her. "Bad idea! If the enemy comes up behind, how can you tell what his move is? An overhand blow, and you die on the ground instead of standing. Duck and move! Gamble! He's probably right-handed. If he's not striking straight down, he's sweeping from left to right. That's his strongest stroke. Move to the right, fast! Roll! Face him as soon as you can, so you can see what he's doing. Instinct will say roll to the left, keep your own right arm free. Fight it! You'll be rolling into his blow."

The memory brought with it the feeling of sawdust underfoot and the unfamiliar weight of the sword in her right hand. She was aware of the fellow students in line beside her, all of them shifting uneasily at the fervor of the instructor's delivery and his nonchalant acceptance of the existence of enemies who would seek blood. And later, the strain and ache after hours of practicing some single, isolated move under the swordmaster's shouts and curses. Over it all, the sharp tang of sea air that crept over the high walls of the courtyard.

Unbidden, all those things flashed into Rowan's mind in an instant—flashed and were gone in the space of time it took to hear Bel's shout: "Duck!"

Rowan ducked and rolled to the right. The sword came straight down, striking mere inches from her right arm. She kept moving, scrabbling, her left hand searching for some weapon. The man drew back again. Suddenly Bel was on his back. She scratched at his eyes with one hand, one arm around his neck, and he staggered back a step.

Where was her sword? It was by her pack. Rowan sensed the fire behind her head. The pack was beyond it.

The man shrugged Bel off, then whirled. The Outskirter bobbed neatly beneath his blow, eyes aglitter. Rowan's hand touched something: her hiking stick. In an instant she was on her feet. She smashed at the attacker's head with a weak left-handed blow.

He turned back. She shifted her grip, holding the stick like a quarterstaff. Misguided instinct; useless, she realized. The sword shattered the stick in two. She jumped back to keep clear.

Two pieces of stick were in her hands; the one in her right was short and balanced. She flung it like a knife into the man's face. It struck him in the right eye and he shrieked hoarsely.

Rowan turned and dove over the fire toward her sword. She heard the hiss as Bel drew her own sword, then the ring as it met the attacker's.

The guard of Rowan's sword hilt had fouled in one of the thongs on the scabbard. She struggled with the binding and glanced back in time to see Bel's second blow, a two-handed sweep that began over her head and forced the man's point to the ground by sheer momentum.

The upstroke that followed split the man's chest and ended in his throat.

The barbarian stepped aside to avoid the last move of the attacker's sword and watched him fall, his chest a ruin of blood and bone, drained of color by firelight.

Rowan moved to Bel's side, surprised to find her own sword finally in her hand, unused. She looked down at the man. His face worked with strange emotions. His voice wailed and burbled.

"Who are you?" Rowan asked uselessly. But he was silent at last.

They stood together wordlessly; then Bel shifted. "That's a bad place to keep your sword, so far from your hand."

Rowan nodded vaguely, still gazing down. "He was at the inn."

Bel was astonished. "Are you certain?"

"Yes." She turned away from the dead man. Her throat was dry; she felt light and empty. That could have been her, she realized. She could have been the one to end staring blankly at the sky, under blood. She looked at Bel. "Thank you," she said.

The Outskirter eyed her. "Have you never seen a dead person?"

"Yes, I have. But I never so nearly was one. Had you not been here—but I think he was counting on that. He didn't know we were traveling together. He left before we did."

"You're sure he was there?"

She nodded. "He was one of the five soldiers. He was wearing red then."

Bel looked back. "Well, he's wearing red now."

4

*I*t was the sea at last.

They had spent the last two days trudging along the damp road that traced the edge of the mud flats, and when the road turned in and became too undependable they found rides on various rafts and flat barges that wandered among the estuaries. Those waterways widened imperceptibly until it finally became clear that the travelers had reached the shallows of the Inland Sea.

Rowan found herself standing taller, looser, her legs prepared to adjust to changes in footing, even though there were yet no perceptible waves. She was home. She had never been to this port before, knew of it only from her maps. It did not matter; she was home, as the sea was the home of every steerswoman.

The sea had shaped the order, defining the necessary nature of Steersmanship by its own variable nature. The need of precision in knowledge, adaptability in action, clarity in thought, and always the need to know more, to complete one's understanding—all these grew from the dangers of the changing sea, and from the endless sky. They lodged in the hearts of the steerswomen and stayed however long they might travel dusty inland roads. Rowan herself, born on flat dry farmland on the edge of the Red Desert, on the far northern limit of every map drawn—Rowan, who never saw the sea for the first eighteen years of her life—still knew it as her home, the home of her heart and mind.

Bel sat quietly on a bale of wool, carefully erect and unmoving. She watched the wide spaces around the barge as if they might sprout enemies; not nervously, but warily. Rowan could not tell how much of the scene the barbarian was assimilating. Finally they rounded a curve of the shoreline, and the wharves and buildings of Donner came into view.

Donner made a poor port, but it was a necessary one. The Grey-river was a natural road to the sea, allowing easier and cheaper shipment than the caravans provided. But there was no deep harbor there, and the ships anchored far out from the river's mouth. Barges shifted cargo and people from the town to the sailing vessels, providing ample though intermittent local employment, and a certain amount of congestion on the water. The barges competed for greatest speed and capacity, so that as their boat neared the docks, Rowan and Bel found themselves surrounded by great masses hurtling in every direction. The air was full of voices clamoring warnings, curses and demands of right-of-way. The cause of all the turmoil, a mere three ships, stood off in the distance, calm and almost disdainful.

Ashore, Rowan wove through the busy longshoremen. Bel followed in her wake, watching everything with cheerful caution.

They made their way into the thickest part of the crowd and found there a short squat woman directing the action with sharp shouts. She carried a slate that she consulted and marked regularly.

Rowan called to her. "What ships are those?"

"Go away, I'm busy!"

"I'm a steerswoman."

"Damn! Wait, then." Rowan and Bel waited as the woman laboriously simplified a complex set of orders for a blank-faced trio of beefy men, all the while making marks with a black crayon on various boxes and crates carried to and from the place where she stood. The three men wandered off dubiously, and she wrote on her slate.

Without slackening her activity, she spoke to the two women. "That's the *Beria*, out of Southport, for one—and their navigator jumped ship; you'll be welcome there."

"Where bound?"

"Southport again. Then The Crags."

"By way of the Islands?"

"No." She spared an instant to eye the steerswoman. "Sailing west from Southport. Wizard on board; he promises protection. I wouldn't risk it."

For a moment Rowan's heart cried to take that trip; to travel, protected, into that small corner of the sea from which few ships returned.

"Is this wizard Red?" Bel asked.

As she remembered the Red soldiers at the inn, and the attack of the night that followed, Rowan's dreams froze in midflight. "Blue. Our wizard, Jannik, he's Blue. Someone saw him talking to this fellow."

Rowan nodded. The Crags had been Blue for as long as anyone remembered. Still, where wizards were concerned, that was no guarantee of permanence.

She called to the woman again. "We're looking to get to Wulfshaven."

"The *Morgan's Chance*. And calling at no other ports on the way. They'll be heavy laden, and the cabins all booked."

"Who's the captain?"

"Morgan. At the Tea Shop." She pointed without looking up.

They found the establishment overlooking a weedy estuary, the patrons dining and socializing on a broad veranda with dark-stained rails, under the hazy off-white skies. The noise of the distant docks was a faint clamor, and sea gulls swooped above, alert for opportunities for poaching. The clientele was cheerful and chatted quietly over the music of a lap harp played by a tinker who occasionally raked his audience with a gaze of infinite disdain. His opinion went completely unnoticed.

Rowan asked a few quiet questions, and presently she and the Outskirter found themselves standing before a table where two men were poring over a navigational chart. Beside that stood two mugs, a pot of peppermint tea, and a small pottery carafe labeled "Brandy" in fanciful script.

The man seated on the left examined the women dubiously. He was lean, almost gaunt, with glossy black hair and sea-blue eyes. He and his mate were relaxed, comfortable, and dressed in clean clothes. By contrast the two women were travel-worn and somewhat bedraggled, and more than somewhat unscrubbed. They still carried their packs and wore their swords. When Morgan noticed the silver steerswoman's ring Rowan wore on her left hand, he smiled and pulled two wicker chairs from a nearby table. The women seated themselves. "How can I be of assistance?"

Rowan drew a breath. "We need passage to Wulfshaven."

He raised his eyebrows and looked off across the water. "My ship is booked. Possibly I can ask one of my officers to shift in with another." The other man winced; evidently one of those officers would be himself.

Rowan gestured negatively. "I don't want to inconvenience anyone. Perhaps there's room to sling another hammock among the crew members?"

"You wouldn't be offended?"

She laughed. "Not in the least."

"There are some who would be." He rubbed the side of his nose, still gazing into the distance. "We'll do well on this trip, but I have some debts," he said carefully. "I can't afford at this point to lose any money. I'll have to ask you to pay for your food, or bring your own."

Rowan made a rapid calculation involving the prevailing winds, the local weather patterns, and the size of Morgan's ship. She compared the resulting length of voyage to the number of coins in her pocket, with a guess at Donner's market prices. "That's not a problem."

"Good. If you can bring food that doesn't need preparation, all the better. Our cook's shorthanded as it is. We've never had so many passengers."

"Spring," his companion suggested. "Wanderlust."

"Perhaps that's the explanation." Morgan turned his glance on Bel.

"Can this be done for two?" Rowan asked.

"No."

"I can pay full fare," Bel said easily.

"We haven't the room."

"I'll pay full fare for a berth with the crew members."

"We'll be crowded enough with the steerswoman."

Rowan said to Bel, "His cook's shorthanded."

The barbarian smiled beatifically. Morgan made to protest, but Bel spoke up. "And since he can't afford to lose money, I'll generously work for no wages. And I don't suppose he'll need the extra help after the passengers for Wulfshaven leave, so I'll relieve him of myself at that point. How lucky for him that we happened by."

The captain sighed, then raised a finger. "In good weather, you sleep on deck."

"Ha. I prefer to. Why crowd in when it's not necessary?"

"I'll do so myself," Rowan said. She had a sudden vision of nights on deck: warmly wrapped in blankets, cold sweet air on her face, watching the constellations slowly shift behind one or another Guidestar, the comforting creak and shift of the ship beneath her. The prospect made her smile.

Morgan regarded the pair speculatively, then nodded, resigned. "We leave at dawn. You'd best be aboard three hours before, to settle—" He pointed at Bel. "—and get introduced to your duties. Go along." He dismissed them with a wave of the hand and turned back to his charts.

As they wove their way out through the tables, Rowan said, "I know you can cook for two; you'll be called on to do so for a great many."

Bel smiled her small smile. "It's just a question of numbers. You can help with the calculations."

The two women found a public bathhouse down a narrow street, and Bel made acquaintance with the superiority of hot water over cold for bathing, and wooden tubs over pools or brooks. Later, on the justification that she was saving money on her passage, she treated herself and Rowan to an elaborate meal in a well-appointed inn. Bel gave careful attention to the different dishes, seeming to study each with interest, and finding none she did not like.

As they conversed over dinner, Rowan found that the impression she had gained of Bel on the road proved equally true in more civilized surroundings. The Outskirter remained both curious and adaptable, her comments again that intriguing combination of ingenuousness and perspicacity. Rowan found herself ever more comfortable in Bel's company, recognizing in the other not a like mind, but a complementary one.

Their conversation was overheard by a merchant at the table next to theirs, a long, thin man with a beaked nose and a fastidious expression. He was accompanied by a pudgy blond boy, about ten years old. When the merchant discovered that Rowan was a steerswoman, he began to toss her occasional questions: insignificant details about the port of Donner, other points of geography, facts about sailing ships. He asked these as asides in his own conversation with the boy, whenever a convenient point of curiosity arose. He effectively ignored Rowan when not asking a question, and ignored Bel altogether. Although he was elaborately polite, beginning each question with "Tell me, lady," and responding to her answers with an unctuous "Thank you, lady," he seemed to care little when Rowan sometimes did not know an answer. Bel's annoyance increased with each interruption. Finally she said in exasperation, "He's treating you like a servant!" She made no attempt to conceal her comments from the merchant.

Rowan used her fork to push a bit of bread around in a dollop of vegetable paste, keeping her gaze carefully on her plate. "Some people are like that." She knew that she looked meek and subdued, perhaps a bit pale. In fact, the paleness was from fury; the merchant's offhand imperiousness made her seethe with hatred for the man. She discovered herself wishing him dead in a thousand unpleasant ways. The force of her anger and her inability to act fed on each other until she felt dizzy.

"Can't you refuse to answer?"

Rowan looked up at her, attempting to keep her expression neutral. "Under certain extreme circumstances, and this is not one. But I'm familiar with his type. It's usually easier to go along, or simply to leave."

The Outskirter studied the steerswoman's face for a long moment, and Rowan found that she could read in Bel's expression all that Bel could read in hers, through her poor attempts at control. Bel had the look of one seeing a helpless creature victimized. Rowan was surprised; it had not occurred to her that her occupation would ever put her in a position of helplessness, but as soon as she saw it, she realized that it was sometimes true.

But Bel was free to act as she chose. She turned to the merchant. "You. You're bothering me. Shut up or I'll slit your throat." The man dropped his fork.

A serving man was at their side in an instant, carefully polite. "Is there a problem?" Near the entrance to the kitchen, two other servers exchanged words briefly. One hurried off in one direction, one in another; the second soon returned with a calm elderly woman who scanned the room with a proprietary concern. The first came back with a very large young man in tow. The four then stood quietly on the side, watching.

Rowan put her hand on Bel's arm and spoke to the serving man at their side. "We'd like a different table, please."

Presently they were led through the center of the room to a table on the other side. The other diners silenced as they passed through, conversation reviving in their wake, more subdued in volume but livelier in tone.

The new table, in an alcove off the main room, was quieter, flanked by a row of low windows. The shutters were open a crack; Rowan pushed them wider, and the dock noise drifted in faintly. She saw that the haze was clearing as dusk approached. She wished herself on the *Morgan's Chance* and under the stars.

She turned back to find Bel studying her. Rowan smiled thinly. "It has two sides," she admitted.

The proprietress appeared with three mugs of wine and seated herself with them. "My apologies, lady; some people are crass. Reeder always puts on airs." With a tilt of her head she indicated the merchant across the room. "I hope you haven't a poor opinion of our establishment."

Rowan sipped her wine. "Not at all."

"And you, Freewoman?"

Bel made a gesture with her mug, indicating the room and its contents. "I think the establishment is fine; but I find my sense of honor affronted by that what passes for civilized behavior in the Inner Lands. If people had to defend their attitudes, things would be simpler."

"Perhaps. But think of the violence that would result!"

Bel smiled.

The woman continued. "Stay the night, as my guests. Tomorrow, you won't be bothered by Reeder again; he's leaving at dawn."

Rowan sighed; Bel narrowed her eyes. "On the *Morgan's Chance*."

"Why, yes."

The two travelers chose to forgo the entertainment in the common room. A waiter directed them through a door at the end of their alcove, and they were met on the other side by a chambermaid with an oil lamp, who led them down the short corridor.

"How long will our trip last?" Bel asked Rowan.

"It depends on the weather. Perhaps five days."

Bel grimaced. "Five days with that Reeder creature."

The corridor ended at the foot of a short staircase, leading up. Instead of ascending, the chambermaid turned left, leading them along a stone wall with a plastered section in its center. They were in a square open area, rising three stories to the raftered ceiling, each story presenting a narrow balcony along its three inner sides. The doors of the guest-chambers were visible, overlooking the central well.

Out of habit, Rowan oriented herself in an imagined map, the probable floor plan of the inn. They had entered under one end of the first balcony, then crossed the well to the opposite end.

Rowan considered the stone wall. "There was a fireplace here, once?"

"Yes, lady." The girl had opened a closet and was pulling out a collection of bed linens. Bel held the lamp. "This used to be the old common room, I'm told, before business was so good. They added the new dining room, built extra stories here, and sleeping chambers. The other side of the hearth still works."

"The other side being in the kitchen?"

"That's right."

Looking up, Rowan saw a wooden chandelier suspended from the ceiling, unlit and cobwebbed. The arrangement of the building was visually impressive and extremely inefficient. Like much of Donner, Rowan realized.

Closing the door, the chambermaid bundled the linens under one arm and accepted the lamp again. There were no stairs to the first floor on this end, and Bel and Rowan followed her back across the cold open area.

"You shouldn't worry too much about Reeder," Rowan told Bel as they ascended. "Close quarters can be an advantage. He'll come to see me as a person, eventually." But Bel was occupied in peering nervously over the railings as the three women rose higher.

The room was spacious, the beds warm and comfortable after the days on the trail, but Rowan found herself waking over and over, as each doze took the edge off her tiredness. Each time she enjoyed the luxury of sinking into sleep again, but at last she found herself following her thoughts into wakefulness.

They were on the third floor, in a corner chamber. One window faced north, the other east, and the surrounding houses were low-built on the flat land. There was little to obstruct the view. Rowan turned in her bed to watch the Eastern Guidestar, shining in one corner of a window, slightly more than a quarter of the way up from the horizon.

She saw that Bel had pulled the blanket from her own bed and arranged it haphazardly on the floor. She lay on her stomach, in her usual sleeping attitude, with her face away from Rowan. She stirred, then turned, and Rowan saw that she was also awake.

"You're uncomfortable?"

"A little. It's so closed-in." Rowan found the room luxuriously wide. "And high. I keep feeling I might fall."

"You'll have less space on the ship. And it will move, rock."

Bel made a face in the gloom. "I suppose I'll adjust. I'll have to; I can't walk away from a ship."

"There is that."

The Outskirter sat up. "You're not sleeping anymore?"

"No. My mind wants to be busy." A problem was nagging her for attention.

"I can't sit still."

"Let's walk, then."

They rose and dressed, Bel donning, instead of her shaggy vest, a yellow cloth blouse she had purchased in a shop by the bathhouse. If her change of costume was an attempt to fit her surroundings, it was immediately negated when she added her cloak and goatskin boots. Both women buckled on their swords.

Once outside the chamber door, Rowan led Bel to the end of the landing and down the stairs. Along the way they passed rooms silent with sleep, or raucous with snores. One room on the ground floor leaked the mutters of two women in argument, punctuated by an amused masculine rumble.

Seeing no other exit, Rowan found their way through the passage to the dining area. "It's like a maze," Bel remarked, surprised when they reached the large room. "Your sense of direction is better than mine."

"Part of my training."

Outside the night was clear and dusted with stars, the Guidestars nearly balanced opposite each other, the Eastern slightly higher than the Western. Stable points in the sky, they told Rowan her exact position by their angles, and the precise time by the constellations that lay behind them.

Saranna's Inn fronted on a round court where a decorative fountain had been erected with much ornamentation and little skill. Beside it, more prosaic, were a simple well and watering trough, constructed with straightforward efficiency. Around the court the houses were dark and quiet, save one flickering candle in a baker's shop. A breeze replaced the smell of sea wrack with that of fresh bread.

The two women circled around the fountain and paused on the far side by the watering trough. Bel leaned back on the edge, regarding the dwellings. "How can they live so close, for all their lives? They must tread on each other constantly."

"You don't live completely alone in the Outskirts, do you?"

"No, but the tribe, that's different. It's one's own kin, and comrades. When we cross another tribe, then there may be trouble."

"The proximity can be useful. People can barter work, or trade objects . . ."

"We trade, when we have something to trade." Bel jingled the coins in her pouch.

"Where do you get what you trade? Do you sell part of your herd?"

The Outskirter was outraged. "The herd? Never, the herds are life!"

"For a goldsmith, gold is life."

Bel considered this.

Rowan moved to sit beside her. The open court pleased her, its edges crowded with shops, now silent, a pause filled with the imminence of the next day's activity. Events to come; movement.

"What is life for a steerswoman?"

Rowan looked at her in surprise. She had never heard the question posed in that way. Related questions, questions direct and easy to answer, she had often considered, but she saw that those were only pieces of this one. She took a long time to think. Bel ventured, "Is it your books? Those charts you take such care at?"

"No . . . The books and charts are just the means to hold on to what you learn, in a way that makes it easier for others to learn from you. They're a way to—" She thought carefully. "To add up learning, to accumulate it past your own lifetime."

"The learning itself?" The barbarian watched her with wide dark eyes, patient and curious.

"No . . ." Rowan saw that in some way the things she learned were also only pieces. She moved her hands, shaping a space between them, tilting the space as though investigating what lay there. "Facts, ideas fit together. It's the fitting, the paths that connect them, that matters. The pieces can change, but the fitting lies beneath it all. The world is made of such fittings." Then she had the answer, but it seemed too large, and it sat strangely in her mind, like an important childhood memory that explained things that had seemed not to need explanation. "It's the world, I suppose."

Bel accepted that, and a large peaceful silence ended the discussion.

Rowan watched the Western Guidestar shining between two roofs in front of her. As she was watching, it went dark. "It's not long before dawn," she observed.

Bel checked the Guidestar herself and nodded. "Let's go, then." They rose and crossed back to the inn.

5

The ornate double doors of the dining area were locked, and the windows that looked out on the square were shuttered tight. Rowan knocked lightly, hoping to get the attention of the servant who had been sweeping earlier. There was no response.

Bel was amused. "Do we break in?"

Rowan shook her head, then beckoned. "The common room is this way." She led the Outskirter around the building to the left, to its opposite side, where they found a single low door and four shuttered windows facing the small side street. As they approached, the door opened, and a stout woman in an apron leaned out to peer at the sky, with the attitude of a person guessing the time.

"Three o'clock," Rowan supplied.

The woman shook her head aggrievedly. "Late again, and there'll be plenty of early breakfasts, what with that ship leaving this morning." She examined Bel and Rowan. "Up early, or coming in late?"

"A little of both, perhaps," Rowan replied.

They entered the common room and declined the woman's offer of guidance to their chamber. Carrying a single candle, Rowan led Bel to one of the two doors flanking the fireplace, and passing through, they found themselves back in the deserted dining area.

"How did you know this was here?" Bel wondered.

"It stands to reason. If a large fireplace doesn't back on an outside wall, then it's two-sided." She led Bel around the tables, dimly visible in the gloom. "The other side would serve either the kitchen or the common room. The closed-up fireplace in that open area by the stairs backs on the kitchen, so I knew the common room had to connect to the dining room." Bel bumped into a table; they had left the lighted doorway to the common room around a corner. Holding her tiny flame higher, Rowan took Bel's hand and guided her through the alcove and the door to the sleeping chambers.

Bel stopped suddenly at the foot of the stairs. "Listen!"

Rowan heard a faint scrabbling. "Rats."

"So many?" The sound intensified briefly, then ceased.

The two women continued up. "Any large town is bound to have a lot of them. They're attracted by the garbage." The rooms along the second floor were quiet, but dim light showed beneath the doors of two.

As they turned the corner and approached the stairs leading to the third floor, the scrabbling returned, behind them. It was punctuated by a human squeak. "It's only a rat, woman," Bel mumbled derisively.

Rowan looked back across the balcony to the two lighted rooms. Now another room on the left was also lit. "It sounds like they're climbing on the east wall."

The scrabbling turned into a patter of small feet. From the newly lit room the voice sounded again, a faint, weird wailing.

Bel was halfway up the stairs. Rowan grabbed her furskin cloak to stop her. "No. Wait."

"What?"

Rowan looked across the central well, and in that moment all her training, all her skill in perception, observation, integration, and reason, came into play in perfect coordination. She was aware of the space around her, the wall to her left, the staircase behind her, the balcony rail, and the open area beyond. She sensed the chandelier above, the distance from floor to roof. She knew the direction of the sounds, the three lit rooms along the east wall, how they stood in relation to the building as a whole, as clearly as if by some sense of touch. The air around her was alive with meaning.

"We have to get out of here," she said.

"Right now?"

Rowan let loose Bel's cloak. "Yes. Now."

"We'll want our packs." Bel continued up.

"No!" Rowan clattered up the stair after her and, as her head cleared the stairwell, reached out and buried her fingers in Bel's shaggy boot. The Outskirter fell sprawling.

Bel turned over and wrenched her foot away. "Rowan!"

Rowan looked past her to the door of the third floor corner room. White light was spilling out beneath it, growing brighter. "That's our room," she said.

The door burst open, splintering, driven by three gouts of white flame.

"Down!" Rowan shouted over the sudden roar of fire. "Go down!" Then, as loud as she possibly could, she yelled, "Fire! Get out, every-one! Fire!"

Bel stumbled down the stair after Rowan, colliding with her. The now-useless candle fell and rolled off the balcony. "Come on!" Rowan hurried along the landing.

Two doors on the east wall burst outward, flinging with them a woman, a woman in flames. She fell against the railing, clawing at some dark shape that clutched her thigh. The railing broke, and she fell.

Heat, and wreckage; Rowan and Bel paused for an instant. Rowan began to pick her way across the burning rubble.

Around them, doors were opening, voices were shouting, people were running. One man recklessly pushed past Rowan and rushed to-ward the stairs. The wall beside him opened like a flower, gushing smoke. The landing above collapsed. He was buried in burning timber.

The way was blocked.

Rowan turned back toward Bel, seeing half a dozen stunned faces behind her, Reeder and his boy among them. "Windows!" she told them, and ran back the way she had come.

The group followed, and as she opened one of the doors, they pushed past, fighting in panic to reach the window. A half-dressed dark-skinned man reached it first and, with a blow of his fist, smashed out the shutters. He scrambled up the sill, and then a white lance of flame caught the side of his face. His hair was burning.

He fell back, shrieking. "They're loose! They're swarming!" Someone caught him and threw a blanket over his head, smothering the flames.

"What's loose?" Bel shouted, but Rowan knew.

Over the edge of the windowsill, weaving its flat head, came a glittering cat-sized creature. Its hide was shimmering green and silver, its faceted eyes bloodred. Flailing its tail as it sought balance, it emitted a two-toned whistling shriek, an infant version of a dragon's scream.

It froze like a lizard, studying them with one of its side-set eyes.

Rowan stepped forward as it swung to face them, pulled the blanket off the man's head, and flung it at the beast. The blanket burst into flame, and the creature squealed in fury.

Two more small forms appeared in the window. "Out," Rowan said, pushing people before her. A pale woman urged the now-blinded dark man, pulling at his arms.

Bel was already at the railing. "We can't go out the windows, and we can't reach the stairs that lead down."

Rowan looked across the central well and saw that the east and south sides of the top floor were burning wildly. On the second floor, the balcony along the east wall had collapsed to the ground. Directly across, the lower south wall showed spots of fire.

Two people clattered up the stairs to the top floor. How they planned to escape, Rowan had no idea.

"We go over," Rowan said. "Drop down." She swung herself over the balcony, shifted her grip to the bottom of the balusters, hung by her hands, and dropped the last eight feet.

The boy imitated her immediately, followed by Reeder; they hung, dropped, then ran toward the exit to the dining room. The pale woman shouted instructions to the blind man, guiding his hands to the railing.

Bel stood frozen on the landing, staring in shock at the distance down.

The sounds of fire and the crack of weakening timber surrounded Rowan as she looked up. "Skies, no," she cursed in anguish. "Bel! Bel, do it!"

Out of the wreckage along the east wall, small writhing shapes began to emerge from the fire.

The blind man came down in a twisting sprawl. His woman began to follow, and as she hung by her hands Bel suddenly moved. She grit her teeth, grasped the rail, and swung herself over the edge.

The pale woman reached the ground and led her man stumbling to the exit. Under the landing where Bel hung, a door opened, and a burly man and two women in nightshifts emerged. The man wore a sheet. They gazed about in confusion.

Bel looked down once, and Rowan cried, "Don't look, just hang and drop!"

Bel dropped. Behind Rowan, the landing cracked, splintered, and fell.

Bel landed on her feet and made to run. Rowan stopped her.

The exit was buried under the fallen landing.

Rowan turned to the man. "Your window."

One of the women answered. "It's all animals, spitting fire, like. Outside."

Rowan looked around quickly, seeking an option, any option. The east wall looked as though it might collapse inward. Along the south wall, the fire was moving along the rubble of the fallen balcony. The smoke, rising, had completely filled the upper half of the central well; the air Rowan breathed was hot, getting hotter fast, but still clean.

There was a sudden movement in the ceiling of smoke, and Rowan pushed Bel and herself against the wall as the chandelier came down with a screeching crash, shattering on the stone floor. A pair of small forms tumbled out of the wreckage. One landed at Rowan's feet, writhing, trying to right itself. It was the size of a rat. Rowan stepped on its head; it was like standing on a stone. The creature struggled wildly; then suddenly its skull popped, and it lay twitching, emitting a brief shower of sparks.

Bel shouted in fury, and Rowan turned in time to see her swing her sword against the side of a larger beast. The blow injured it not at all, but the force sent it sprawling aside, and it tumbled into the open door of the just-vacated room. The burly man stepped forward and pulled the door shut.

"That won't stop it for long," Rowan said. Instinctively, she began to back along the wall, away from the heat, toward the old fireplace.

Bel came up beside her, looking back at the wall of fire. "We're trapped. We're truly trapped."

"Yes." Rowan looked at the mortared-up hearth and raised her voice to be heard more clearly. "We'll stand up against the fireplace. Perhaps when the wreckage falls, the configuration—" She stopped short, suddenly remembering. "Yes!" She ran to it.

The others followed quickly and found her searching the right-hand edge of the hearth. "It has to be here—"

Bel had not understood. She brought her face closer and shouted, "What?"

Rowan faced her. "A door! There has to be a door!"

One of the other two women had collapsed in terror. The man was trying to pull her to her feet. The second woman pointed at the rubble on the other end of the fireplace. "Door's buried!" she shouted.

"There was another. I saw it!" Rowan turned back, and saw how the wood paneling overlaid the stones. She moved right, and found the door she had seen the chambermaid open. She pulled it wide.

A linen closet. One of the women made a sound of anguish. Bel let out a single, near-inhuman shriek of fury, gripped her sword tighter and swung around to face the inevitable attack of dragons.

Rowan began pulling out linens, throwing them blindly behind her, shouting as she did. "This area was a common room! The fireplace backs on the kitchen; did you ever see a common-room hearth like that, that didn't have doors on *both* ends?" The fronts of the shelves were bare. The left wall of the closet was stone; the right was wood. Rowan could not see to the back.

She smashed the heels of her hands against the underside of a shelf, and the plank lifted and clattered onto the one beneath it. Using both hands, she tugged at the right edge of the second shelf, and it tilted up, then slipped off its supports to the floor.

Rowan stumbled over the shelves, tripping, and fell against the back wall. It was wood.

She regained her feet, pulled out her sword, and put all her strength into a two-handed underhand stab. A half-inch of the point wedged into the wood. She twisted it as she pulled, then checked the result with her fingers: a shallow gouge.

"Bel!" Rowan came out of the closet and gripped Bel's shoulder. "The back wall is wood. We have to break through!" Bel stared at

Rowan blindly, her face that of a warrior's during battle. Then her expression changed, and she understood. She pulled away and scrambled over the scattered linens into the closet. She was stronger than Rowan; her sword was heavier. Shorter, she had room to swing overhand.

The burly man was standing against a wall, one of his women clinging and sobbing, the other standing free and watching Rowan with desperate alertness.

The man was huge. Rowan extended her sword hilt to him. "Take this. Help Bel."

He extricated himself, stepped to the closet, and pulled out the planks of the fallen shelves. Lifting one, he tested its heft. He said to Rowan, "You keep the sword," and pointed past her with his chin.

She turned and saw the shattered chandelier, and on it, three dragons. They crawled over it and over each other, indiscriminately, heads weaving and searching, tails writhing. The largest was as big as a dog.

Behind her, Rowan could hear the thumps as Bel and the man set to work. She stood with her back to the closet, knowing it was only a matter of time before the dragons sighted her. Wondering if, like frogs, they could only see moving objects, she stood as still as she could.

She sensed a presence beside her. Glancing to the side, she half expected to see Bel, but found instead one of the two other women, the self-possessed one. The woman was holding another plank in her hands, dividing her attention between the chandelier and Rowan's face.

One of the dragons sent a random gout of flame splashing against the center of the fireplace.

Rowan searched her knowledge, seeking information about dragons. She found little, next to nothing. She had only her eyes and her reason.

She watched for a few moments, then spoke to the woman beside her. "The larger they are, the slower they move. They'll cover ground quickly, because of the length of their stride, but these don't react as fast as the tiny ones. Those flat heads have no room for much brain; they're not very smart. Their eyes are set on the sides of their heads, but the flame comes from their snouts. So, if they're looking at us, they can't burn us; when they're trying to burn, they can't see us well."

The woman nodded; one of the dragons froze, studying her with its right eye.

Rowan said, "I think they're attracted by motion," and then the dragon swung to face them. Rowan shoved the woman to the left and moved to the right. The flame spouted to where the woman had stood.

Rowan was up against the fireplace. The woman had fallen against one of the pillars supporting the balcony overhead; the closed door of the room behind her began to burn.

Rowan found herself pinned in the gaze of another dragon. She prepared herself to dodge, but a falling piece of timber in its opposite field of vision distracted it. It sent white flame in that direction, then pulled itself off the chandelier to investigate. Rowan hoped it would find enough to occupy itself.

Two remained: the dog-sized dragon on the left, and one slightly smaller on the right. Rowan realized that the woman by the pillar would shortly be trapped between the dragons on the chandelier and dragons that would emerge from the room behind her.

The two beasts were weaving again, searching. The larger shrieked in frustration, tilted back its head, and spat a fountain of fire straight up. Rowan watched the second, and at the instant its weaving brought its face toward her, she ran straight at it.

She brought her sword down on its flat head. The blow drove its head against the stone floor, and it was like striking an iron bar.

The larger creature noticed the movement, took an instant to study Rowan with its left eye, then the edge of a wooden board was driven against its throat. Aim ruined, the flame it spat caught the left side of Rowan's cloak.

The dragon beneath Rowan's sword twisted free, uninjured, and began spitting at random. Rowan dropped to the ground, writhed out of her burning cloak, rolled to the right, and froze. The flames on her cloak snuffed against the stone floor.

The woman's plank had splintered down its length. She flung one half overhead past the dragons, one half to the left. She stood motionless, as the dog-sized dragon cocked its gaze left toward the clattering board.

She was standing some three feet in front of its blind snout. Her face was an agony of terror, but she did not move.

The smaller dragon had sent its flames at waist level, passing over Rowan's head. It subsided and began searching again.

Rowan knew that the tableau could not last. When the dragon on the right was facing her again, she moved forward, in full view of the larger one, and with a sweeping blow, she struck the smaller creature across the neck. Her sword skidded harmlessly up its length, then caught the edge of one garnet eye. The eye shattered with a weird merry sound, like breaking china. The dragon did not cry out but twisted, trying to find her with its remaining eye.

In the moment the larger beast turned its snout toward Rowan, the woman in front of it took three steps back, then broke and ran. The dragon turned back and swept her with fire. Her nightshift flared like a lamp wick.

Rowan scuttled back, grabbed her cloak, dashed to the left and threw the cloak around the burning woman. Then she moved right again, distracting the dragons as the woman rolled on the ground.

Her feint was not sufficient. The dog-sized dragon heaved itself off the chandelier toward the cloaked figure.

"Damn you!" Rowan rushed it, struck at one eye, and shattered it.

The east wall collapsed inward from ceiling to floor, settling like a dropped curtain. Heated air struck Rowan like a blow, and she was thrown back against the wall and to the ground.

Someone was tugging on her arm. She could not breathe. She felt herself pulled to her feet, opened her eyes, then closed them against searing smoke. "This way!" a voice shouted. It was Bel. The Outskirter pulled her along.

Rowan fought. "No, wait!" She stumbled and fell. Bel pulled her up again. "That woman," Rowan cried. "Is she all right?"

Bel pushed her forward. "There's no one."

In blurred vision, Rowan saw the closet door and found the presence of mind to make her way into it. Out of the back wall, two huge hands grabbed her under the arms and pulled. Wood splinters scored her scalp and her back; then she was through and into a pitch-dark room. The man released her and turned back to help Bel.

Rowan groped and found shelves of crockery. Plates crashed to the floor. Bel was behind her again. "Out. Straight ahead."

They were in the kitchen. Rowan regained her bearings and hurried through into the dining room. There, orange light from the court-yard led them to the open double doors.

Two lines of people were passing buckets to and from the well. The water was being poured not on the inn but on the walls and roofs of adjacent houses. Rowan and Bel were pushed aside by the man who had helped them. He broke through the bucket line and ran to the edge of the crowd surrounding the courtyard, and into the arms of his surviving woman.

As Rowan and Bel reached the crowd, there was a shout, and a milling motion off to the left. A word was being passed from person to person. "Jannik!" "Look, there's Jannik!"

"About time," Rowan muttered, wiping soot from her face. She and Bel moved deeper into the crowd.

On the left, the mass of people parted, and a small man emerged and walked across the courtyard. He was no taller than Bel and somewhat round, dressed in silver and green. His hair was white and short, his beard a trim white point. He had the face of a habitually cheerful man.

Halfway across, he paused and looked up at the disaster with an expression of vast annoyance. He raised his hands, and the crowd hushed.

Rowan slipped farther back among the people, urging Bel with a hand on her arm.

Bel resisted. "Don't you want to see this?"

"I want to get out of here."

They left the crowd behind and found their way out and down a twisting street that ended by the lamp-lit docks. Rowan heard a voice exhorting, "Move, man, or Morgan'll skin us." She followed the sound.

They came to a heavily loaded barge where a narrow blond man was cursing at a pair of dockhands, who were viewing the glow above the buildings with interest.

"You're going to *Morgan's Chance?*" Rowan asked.

He eyed her. "Passengers? Come later, there's a barge at dawn."

Rowan indicated Bel with a tilt of her head. "She's crew."

"What, her?" The crewman examined Bel. "Don't know her."

Bel spoke up. "I'm the cook's new assistant. And she's a steerswoman."

He conceded a bit grudgingly. "All right then, get in. But don't rock, mind. We're riding low."

6

*I*t took the better part of an hour to cross the shallows from the loading docks to the *Morgan's Chance*. Their boatmates were all members of the ship's crew, returning before the onslaught of passengers due at sunrise. Most were silent, watching the subsiding glow above the buildings that lined the shore. One tipsy fellow, oblivious to the chaos they were leaving behind, was singing a crude song, most of the words of which seemed to have escaped him. He improvised.

The barge was crowded with crates. Additionally, there were three goats and two wooden cages of ducks. The ducks showed great interest in the proceedings, extending their necks out through the slats as far as possible. The cages, abristle with yellow beaks, emitted a constant natter of avian complaint.

The barge rode low on the water. Where Rowan and Bel sat in the gunwales, Rowan brooding, Bel looking at the surroundings, the calm surface of the water was a handsbreadth away from swamping aboard. Bel leaned over and trailed one hand into the cold, starlit darkness. Then she pulled it out and tasted. "I heard it was salt," she said to Rowan. Then she affected Reeder's condescending tone. "Tell me, lady, why is the sea salt?"

The Outskirter seemed remarkably resilient; for her own part, Rowan found it impossible to take her mind off the disaster they were leaving behind. "No one knows," she answered, half-indifferently.

"Ha!" Bel returned to her own voice. "I can tell you. A wizard had a magical box that delivered him salt whenever he called for it. But while he was out, his apprentice tried to impress some friends by demonstrating its magic. The apprentice forgot the words that halted the spell, and the box kept spewing out salt, until the whole house was filled. In desperation, the friends dragged the box to a cliff and tossed it into the sea. And there it lies, to this day."

Rowan looked at her friend and smiled despite herself. "A possible explanation."

Eventually the barge sidled up to the ship. Cables were tossed down for the cargo. Meanwhile, the returning sailors dragged themselves wearily up rope ladders.

Rowan noticed Bel watching the technique with a grim studiousness and realized that the barbarian had no intention of letting unfamiliarity slow her down again. When her turn came, Bel pulled herself up carefully, clearly considering every step. Rowan followed close behind, with complete ease, keeping an eye on her friend. At one point, a small swell caused the ship to tilt; for a moment, the ladder swung away to one side, hanging unsupported save at the top. Bel looked up in startlement, then down at Rowan and the dark water, then at the ladder itself. Recognizing her safety, she laughed in delight, then ascended faster.

Morgan was at the railing, shouting questions to the arriving crew. "What's the problem ashore?"

Reaching the top, Rowan answered him herself. "Dragonfire."

"What!"

"Saranna's Inn was attacked by nestlings. It's destroyed."

He leaned farther past the rail's edge, gazing out at the shore. A reddish orange glow marked the former location of the inn. "Gods below," he muttered. He turned away, then came storming back. "It's ridiculous, the dragons haven't got out of hand for years. And the breeding grounds aren't even near there. Where was Jannik, fast asleep? Are those fools ashore afraid to wake a wizard?" He cursed again, viciously.

"He came," a crew member answered. "A bit too late, but he came."

A voice spoke from behind Rowan. "You look as though you were in it yourselves." She turned and found the officer they had seen at the Tea Shop with Morgan. "Tyson, ship's navigator," he introduced himself. "We'll talk later." It was customary for any sea-traveling steerswoman to consult with the navigator, to update the ship's charts. "But, you're not injured?"

"No." She brushed her hair away from her forehead. The hand came back sooty. "Singed, perhaps."

Bel spoke up. "But we lost our possessions in the fire. Our traveling packs. We have our clothes and my sword, that's all."

"I'll have the provisions I brought for the voyage," Rowan pointed out. "I arranged yesterday for a crate that I left at the cargo docks."

Tyson looked distressed. "But your notes and your charts?"

"All gone."

His brow furrowed. "I have some chart paper you can have. I'll buy some new at Wulfshaven. And some old pens I don't use. Some ink powder . . ."

"You're very kind."

"And look at you, you haven't even got a cloak. Can't have you catching a chill; I've a spare you can use."

Rowan was taken aback. "You're too generous."

"Nonsense, you're one of us, and we take care of our own." Tyson was referring to the solidarity of spirit that sailors shared with the steerswomen. He stopped a passing crewman and directed him to bring the items from the navigator's cabin, then excused himself to oversee some of the preparations at hand.

"A pleasant fellow," Bel commented. "Perhaps I'll become a steers-woman, so that everyone will be nice to me."

"Then you'd have to deal with the Reeders of the world."

Bel made a face. "True. It's hardly worth it."

When the crewman returned with Tyson's donations, Bel asked for directions to the galley. Unable to explain clearly enough for the Out-skirter, he finally led her personally. Rowan remained on deck and presently noticed her crate of provisions being hauled aboard. A few questions to the purser determined the best place to stow it; Rowan made sure she knew how to find it again. Then she wandered forward, keeping out of the way of the work being done.

A handful of crewwomen jogged past her to clamber up the rigging. They tugged at the mainsail halyards, readying them for the command to set the sails. The women waited at their ease, chatting softly to themselves, calling up to a pair of men working the main sky-sail, all of them visible to Rowan only as distant forms blocking starlight, shifting against the sky as the ship rocked slowly.

Rowan went back amidships, where the passenger barge was expected.

The ship's activities slowly came to a standstill, and crew members became idle. Morgan regained his composure and sauntered about the deck, exuding a carefully assumed nonchalance. Tyson watched him with something like amusement. Eventually the east brightened.

The light revealed a vertical line of smoke onshore where the glow had been. Rowan was standing at the starboard railing, facing shore. Looking around her, she saw that most of the people on deck were on or near the starboard side: deckhands, a few officers, and three early-boarded passengers.

Presently a barge separated itself from the general harbor traffic and poled along toward the *Morgan's Chance*. The sun had cleared the horizon by the time it came alongside.

The passengers took their time negotiating the rope ladders. Morgan approached when a purser's mate clambered aboard; Rowan moved nearer and joined them.

"A whole bloody swarm of them dragons, they say," the purser's mate was complaining. "About fifty, tall as your waist, and smaller. Spitting and hissing, sending fire all over. Never heard of anything like it."

"The passengers," Morgan prompted.

"Oh. Yes, sir. None lost, sir, just all of them upset, especially the ones who'd been staying at the inn."

The witnesses were easy to identify; they were quiet, and the purser and purser's mates had trouble getting their attention. They tended to gaze around them as if a sailing ship were the strangest wonder in existence, and death by dragonfire were the usual human fate, escaped from only by luck. They were filled with what they had seen. Rowan decided to wait to ask them for the details she wanted—perhaps several days, until they were past their shock.

She stopped the chief purser as he hurried by. "You'd do best to tend to the people from Saranna's Inn first. Get them into their cabins and comfortable, and most of all, away from each other. They're standing in a clot together here, do you see? They're just feeding each other's distress. People can become hysterical in situations like this."

He paused, annoyed. Morgan forestalled his protest. "She's a steerswoman, and she's making sense. Do as she says." The purser hurried off.

Rowan eyed the mate who had been ashore. The man threw up his hands. "Not me, lady, I'm fine. Of course, I didn't watch anyone die, either."

Morgan dismissed the man, who went back to the still-boarding passengers. The captain and the steerswoman watched the activity for a while. Then Morgan regarded her a moment, looked off to shore, out to sea, and gazed up at the rigging. He said reluctantly, "If you have any more suggestions, lady, I'll be glad to hear them."

Rowan had many questions, but only one suggestion. "I suggest," she said, "that we leave."

It was some time after noon that Bel shambled on deck. The ship was well under way, finally past the shallows of Donner and into blue water. Bel lurched a bit on the shifting deck, from unfamiliarity or her obvious weariness. Blinking in the bright light, she found Rowan and dropped herself down to sit on the deck. She leaned back against the rail and closed her eyes, giving herself to the sunlight. She had shed the boots and was still wearing the loose yellow blouse she had purchased in Donner. Barefoot, in shirt and trousers, she could have been any sailor, but for the silver-and-blue belt. She was small and wiry and tan. She looked able, nimble, and not at all dangerous.

Rowan had spent the morning arranging her matters as best she could. She had taken the large chart papers Tyson had given her, folded them to smaller size, and cut the folds with a knife. After a visit to the sail locker, and the loan of a needle, a sail-maker's palm, and some cord, she had a pamphlet-sized coverless book of thirty-two pages. Some canvas scraps were transformed into a small shoulder-slung pouch to contain the new book and pens.

While testing her hastily hung hammock in the women's crew quarters, she had noticed that the gum soles of her steerswoman's boots had worn down to the leather. The gum was the same type used by sailors everywhere, to aid in gripping the deck when not working barefoot. She had found the quartermaster, laid down a new surface on the soles, and brought the boots on deck to dry.

Then she had stopped to talk to a pair of crew members new to the trade, to show them the best way to coil a rope so that it stowed in the least amount of space but payed out easily. She hoped to find several such odd jobs to ease the duties of the officers and make herself useful. Done with her lesson, Rowan sent the two men off and sat next to Bel.

"How are you taking to your work?"

The Outskirter opened her eyes, squinting against the sunlight. "Well enough. The food is strange, but interesting. The cook knows his job, but he lacks any sense of adventure. He won't let me experiment."

"His loss. You seem to have an instinct for such things."

Bel made a sound of disinterest and closed her eyes again. "Do dragons carry disease?"

"No. Why do you ask?" Rowan was briefly concerned, then quickly realized Bel's problem. "Here. Stand up."

"No, please . . ."

Rowan pulled her up, against little resistance. "Trust me, it's better this way. Here." Rowan positioned her by the railing and demonstrated. "Stand with your side to the rail and hold with one hand, so." The ship was crossing the swell of the waves obliquely. "No, open your eyes; you need to balance."

"I can balance with my eyes closed," Bel said through her teeth, "when the ground doesn't move beneath me."

"Well, it's moving now." Rowan stood facing Bel, with her back to the bow. "Look past me, to the horizon. Unlock your knees . . . there. Bend them a little. Have you ever ridden a horse?"

"How will a horse help me on a ship?"

"It might be a little easier to explain . . . never mind. You have to get rid of the idea that the ship's deck is the ground; you mustn't try to align yourself to it. You need to find your own center of balance. Don't make the mistake of just trying to keep your head level—"

"I have to keep my head level!"

"Yes, but don't bend your neck to do it. Don't put your head at odds with your body. Use your legs. Bend your knees to compensate for the change in the deck's position . . ." She demonstrated as the approaching swells altered the deck's angle, exaggeratedly bending her left knee as the ship rose on the wave, then straightening and shifting the flex to her right as they rode over the crest.

Bel imitated Rowan's movements stiffly. "That's better," Rowan told her. "Keep your body relaxed; keep your head centered over your torso. Look past me at the waves as they approach."

Bel kept her eyes grimly on Rowan's face. "Must I really?"

"That's how you can tell what changes to expect." Bel shifted her gaze, her tan complexion graying. But as Rowan continued her coaching, the Outskirter eventually began to look more comfortable; whether from gained skill or from the distraction of learning the technique, Rowan could not determine. "Weren't you seasick when you were belowdecks?"

"I was too busy with the cook. I had too much on my mind to notice."

Rowan stopped exaggerating her leg movements and shifted back to her own more natural sea stance. "Then here's something to occupy your mind: At Saranna's Inn, what section did the dragon nestlings attack first?"

Bel attempted to make her own physical adjustments match the subtlety of Rowan's. "Do you mean, north or south? I lost all my direction, inside the building."

"Think about it."

"Well . . ." Bel loosened her death-grip on the railing and tested her ability to balance without support. "As we entered the guest-room section, the corner they attacked was across from us, diagonally. On the opposite side of the open area."

A trio of crew members jogged past aft to where a mate stood, exhorting them to some minor adjustment in the sheets. Rowan prompted Bel, "And?"

"And up. Toward the roof. The corner where our room was."

Rowan said nothing.

Bel considered for a long time. "Did we do something to attract them? What sort of thing attracts dragons?"

"I have no idea. Very little is known about dragons. I don't know what they like; I don't even know what they eat." She looked off to the side, thinking. "But I know that in Donner, the dragons are kept in check by Jannik's powers."

"But sometimes they get loose."

"Sometimes. They chose an interesting moment to do so." Around the two women, the ship's activity rapidly increased. Without thinking, Rowan noted that the wind had shifted, and a major readjustment of the sails was imminent. More passengers had come on deck, either to enjoy the brilliant sunlight, or to observe the crew's movements. Rowan stepped closer to Bel and, with a hand on her arm, directed her closer to the rail, away from the action. "And here's something else to think about: The first night out of Five Corners, we were attacked by a soldier who turned out to be in the service of a wizard."

"So you said. But he wasn't wearing a surplice or a sigil. How could you be sure he belonged to a wizard?"

"I saw him at the inn at Five Corners, remember, and he wore a Red surcoat then."

"Perhaps he just resembled one of the Red soldiers at the inn."

"I don't forget a face." Rowan saw Bel's dubious expression. "I don't," she stressed. "It's part of my training. I could sketch his portrait, right now."

Morgan himself had come on deck and was sending out a steady stream of shouted directions, relayed by mates to all quarters of the ship and up the rigging. Bel had to raise her voice to be heard. "Can you really think that a wizard is responsible?"

"It's a possibility."

"But why would a wizard care about us?"

"I've never attracted one's attention before. And there's been only one change in my activities, one new thing that I'm doing."

Bel looked at her. "You mean that jewel. Of course, it's magic—"

"We don't know that—"

"But I've had my jewels for years, and no one's cared. And that innkeeper at Five Corners, he's never been bothered."

"There's a difference." Oblivious to the noise around her, Rowan reviewed her speculations in her mind. "Several people have the jewels," she said, "but I'm the first person trying to find out about them."

Bel took a few pacing steps and found she had to grab the railing when the ship hit a sudden uneven swell. She moved cautiously away from the rail and leaned her weight against a vent cowling farther amidships. "Are you certain about this? Is this something . . . something your training tells you?"

Rowan came out of her reverie. "No, my training tells me not to be certain, not yet." She smiled. "The steerswomen have a saying: 'It takes three to know.' "

"Three of what?"

"In this case, three instances. In the first instance, it's possible that the soldier was performing a little independent banditry, for his own profit. In the second instance, the dragon's attack may have been pure coincidence. But if anything else of the sort occurs . . ."

"Then you'll be sure."

"Exactly."

Bel made a derisive sound. "Much good it'll do, if the third instance kills you."

"Being unconvinced is not the same as being foolhardy. The possibility alone is strong enough to make me cautious."

Bel's gaze narrowed as she considered the situation. "I don't like this. It feels like we're running away from our enemies. If we stayed in Donner, we could have found out more about that dragon attack. It would have been much simpler."

Rowan found herself agreeing. "But I want to get to the Archives, and this is the only ship to Wulfshaven at the moment."

"So we sail."

"Yes."

There was a small burst of activity, a thumping of leather-soled shoes—no sailor hurrying, but Reeder's boy, dashing to the starboard railing, followed more sedately by a crewwoman. "There!" he cried excitedly. "It was out there!" He pointed. "But I don't see it anymore."

Rowan moved aft, Bel following carefully, unsure of her new sea legs. The crew member, a strong, brown, middle-aged woman, peered out to sea. "Don't see it."

"It was dark-colored, and small. It went up and down, on top of the water."

"Hm. Piece of driftwood, maybe."

"I think it was a mermaid."

The woman suddenly dropped to the boy's height, grabbed his shoulder with her left hand, and covered his mouth with her right, roughly. "Don't say that! That's bad luck on a ship! They're evil creatures, murderous. Do you want to call one?"

"The boy spoke in ignorance," Rowan said gently.

The sailor looked up at her. "Aye. But you know the saying, lady: 'What you don't know, can kill you.'" She released the boy but shook her finger in his face, once, admonishing.

Rowan looked out to sea, seeing nothing. "Perhaps it was a dolphin."

The sailor brightened. "Aye, perhaps." She scanned the waves again.

"Dolphins aren't real," the boy said. "They're . . . they're just heraldic beasts. Like lions."

"Dolphins certainly are real," Rowan told him.

"Lots of sailor's tales of dolphins," the crewwoman added.

"And the steerswomen have verified it, as well." Rowan saw that Bel had come closer, listening to the conversation with interest.

Rowan continued. "More than two centuries ago, a steerswoman went swimming off the bow of a becalmed ship. Dolphins came up to her, pushing her like children at play. They danced on top of the sea, standing on their tails."

"It sounds like a wondrous sight," Bel said. She had found a seat on the roof of the pilothouse. "Lady, what's a dolphin?"

Rowan gathered her information. "A fish, large, nearly as long as a man is tall. They leap in the air as they swim along, and have a hole in the top of their heads. They sing through that hole, as you would through your mouth, but their song is like all the different birds of the air. Their tails are flat, opposite to other fish—" She demonstrated the configuration with her hands. "—and they are so strong that they can balance on top of the sea's surface by moving only that tail in the water. They possess great curiosity, and have never been known to injure a human."

"Are they good to eat?"

The sailor threw her hands in the air. "More bad luck!" she cried.

Bel spoke quickly. "Sea woman, I beg your pardon. I come from a far land and know nothing of the sea. If there is any ritual or obeisance I should make, please tell me now, so I can fend off the evil of my words. And, please, I ask you to teach me what I should know, so that I will never offend the sea god again."

Rowan looked at the Outskirter in admiration. A barbarian in birth but not in attitude—or, again, there seemed to be more to the Outskirters than rumor credited.

The sailor nodded, mollified. "That was well spoken. Aye, I'll teach you, if you need it. Between me and the steerswoman, we'll see you safe."

The boy sniffed disdainfully. Rowan looked down at him and recognized trouble on the way. He said, "Tell me, lady, what's a mermaid?"

The sailor made a grab for him, but Rowan stopped her with a hand on her chest. The woman wavered, agitated, trapped between two customs of equal force.

Rowan dropped to her knees in front of the boy and spoke eye-to-eye. "Child, I will be glad to answer your question, but first I will give you information for which you did not ask. Sailors live on their ships, care for their ships; a ship is a sailor's home. The beliefs of the sailors are like a religion. Now, when you're in a person's home, it is bad manners, it is inexcusably rude, to scoff at his or her religion, whatever your own beliefs. The person has offered you kindness and protection, and you cannot offer insult in return. It is outrageous, uncivilized—" She thought of Bel and amended her comments. "It is crude. It would be kinder, and inoffensive, to wait until we reach Wulfshaven, when we are in no sailor's home, to ask that question. So tell me again, boy, do you have a question for me, at this time?"

The child stared at her, wide-eyed, and the sailor leaned close to his ear. "Say that word again, and I'll throw you overboard."

A voice came from behind them. "What's this?" Reeder's boy broke and ran, clattering down a companionway into the ship.

The crewwoman straightened, startled. "Ah. Sir. You shouldn't sneak up on one like that."

It was Tyson, the navigator. "Now, Marta, I can't help if my boots are silent. You know I would never sneak up on you."

"Aye, sir. Right, sir. Officers never sneak up on the crew."

Bel spoke up. "The boy might have seen a dolphin."

Tyson laughed and clapped his hands together. "Then that's good luck!" He took a few moments to make a methodical examination of the sea off to starboard. Rowan did the same, but neither found any encouraging signs. The sailor, Marta, peered out dubiously; then, with a noncommittal grunt, she returned to her labors.

"Ah, well." Tyson turned back, leaving one arm resting along the railing. As he tilted his head back to view the new set of the ship's sails, Rowan discovered that she rather liked the way his auburn hair looked against the pale sky, how his light eyes contrasted with his broad brown face. She found herself watching herself watching him, a little amused.

Bel roused out of deep thought. "I like what you said," she told Rowan. "About respecting other people's religions. That's very sensible."

Distracted from her distraction, Rowan considered her answer. "I'm sorry, Bel, don't misunderstand me. I don't necessarily respect other people's religions, or any religion. But the people—I respect them, and I give them the honor they deserve, whatever they believe."

"And that boy—would you have answered his question?" Bel turned to Tyson. "He was asking about ill-omened creatures," she explained.

Rowan leaned back against the railing and studied Tyson's and Bel's expressions. "Yes. I would have, had he asked again."

Tyson nodded, with the understanding of long association with steerswomen, but Bel shook her head ruefully. "You. I don't understand you at all, sometimes. Just when you finish saying a hundred things that are incredibly wise, you turn around and act like a plain fool."

Rowan felt a flare of anger. In all the Inner Lands, no one spoke to a steerswoman so insultingly. She was about to retort in kind when, by reflex, her training stepped in. Everything she knew about Bel, in all her short experience with the Outskirter, came to her mind in ordered array: the patterns of Bel's behavior, what Rowan surmised about Bel's context of knowledge and habit, the occasional sudden swordlike thrusts of Bel's quick mind . . .

To everyone's surprise, including her own, Rowan replied with a laugh. "And you," she said to Bel. "Just when I'm convinced you're nothing but a plain fool, you turn around and say something incredibly wise."

Bel wavered, uncertain of how to interpret this. At last she said reluctantly, "Then perhaps between the two of us, we make one very clever person."

"Perhaps that's the case."

Tyson had watched the exchange with some perplexity. "You're an odd pair of friends," he said. "You are friends, aren't you? Traveling together?"

"Yes." Rowan clapped Bel's shoulder in a consciously overacted gesture of hearty camaraderie. "And very advantageous it's been, for both of us."

Bel caught her mood. She said to Tyson, aside, "She covers for my ignorance, and I cover for her flaws of personality."

Tyson smiled. "Flaws of personality?"

"She's difficult to convince."

"True," Rowan admitted.

"She has no gods."

"Also true."

"She's too serious."

"A matter of opinion."

"There's not enough magic in her soul."

"Well, I'm not at all certain about magic," Rowan admitted.

Bel dropped her bantering attitude and stopped short. "What can you possibly mean?"

Rowan regretted the change in mood; nevertheless, she considered carefully before speaking. "The few times I've been faced with something called magical, it seemed . . . well, simply mysterious. As if there were merely something about it that I didn't know. Understand, I'm not giving you a steerswoman's conclusions, here. As a steerswoman, I have to withhold my decision, out of ignorance. But the fact that I can be this unsure . . . that seems to indicate something, to me." She shrugged roughly, uncomfortable with her uncertainty. "Sometimes I feel people call it magic, because they want magic."

"Perhaps Rowan feels that way because steerswomen are immune to some kinds of spells," Tyson said to Bel.

She looked at him in astonishment. "Immune? Can that be true?"

Rowan made a deprecating gesture. "So it's said. It's supposed to be true of sailors, as well."

"Sailors and steerswomen." Tyson nodded. "We're much alike. The sea in our blood, you see."

"That's hard to believe," Bel said. "I know there's real magic in the world, but would it be so . . . selective?"

"I don't know. I haven't enough information," Rowan replied. "But it seems unlikely."

Tyson clapped his hands together and laughed. "Simple way to prove it. There's a chest in the hold; belongs to a wizard. We're shipping it through Wulfshaven."

Bel was suspicious. "So?"

"It's guarded, by a simple spell. Nothing major, so I'm told. But we had to take precautions loading it. Come and take a look." He looked at Rowan, eyes crinkling in humor. "Come, lady, let's look at a wizard's magic; and perhaps we can show your friend something surprising of our own."

After pausing for Rowan to don her now-dry boots, the two women followed him. He led them down a forward hatch to a series of narrow companionways that carried them deep into the hold, far below the waterline.

The air acquired a contained feel, and the slap of waves came from somewhere overhead. They went back along a cramped passage created by the crates and bales that crowded the hold. Following last, Rowan found herself distracted by the variety of shapes, and the odors hinting at what each contained. There were dusty kegs of wine, oth-

ers sending out a tang of brine, chests of some sharp spice; one bale of
wool exuded a cloud of fine powder when Rowan's hand touched it.
She sneezed.

She heard another sneeze and, looking up, spotted Reeder's boy
perched on top of the bale. His eyes were wide with distress at being
caught, his jaw slack. Rowan only smiled and waved, and he watched
dumbly as she followed Tyson and Bel.

Tyson brought them to a corner where several chests were stacked
less precisely. He leaned back against a column of crates made of some
rough pale wood. With a sweep of his hand he indicated rather
vaguely the general area of the chests. Rowan and Bel looked at them.

"Which one?" Rowan asked.

"Perhaps Bel can tell."

"What, me?" Bel gave him a cautious, dubious look.

He spread his hands. "It's a minor spell, I know. Won't harm you,
it'll just . . . warn you. Rowan pointed out, when people expect magic,
they sometimes find it when it's not there. I'd like to see if you can
find it if you don't know where it should be."

Bel raised her eyebrows and rocked a moment, intrigued. She
scanned the area, then cocked her eye at one chest of dark wood, or-
nately carved and inlaid with a pattern of lighter wood. She approached it and, standing at the farthest distance possible, stretched
out her left hand to touch it with index finger extended.

Rowan glanced at Tyson and found him watching Bel with controlled amusement. He so carefully kept his gaze steady that it was obvious that he was avoiding looking at the correct box. Rowan guessed
from the stance of his body that it was one of a pair off to the right.

Bel's finger contacted the chest in question. She held the pose a
moment, then slapped the box disdainfully with her palm. She turned
to the others.

One in the center was unadorned, but bound about with iron
chains and padlocks. It was perched rather sloppily across two others.
Bel stepped up more confidently and rapped it with her knuckles.
"Ha!" Nothing remarkable happened, but the action caused the chest
to rock back slightly, then forward. Bel took a step back, caught her
bare heel on an uneven plank, and threw out her right arm for balance. The back of her hand brushed one of the chests on the right.

With a very unwarriorlike squeak she yanked the hand back vio-lently. The sudden change of motion caused her stance to unbalance completely, and she landed on the deck, narrowly missing a small pud-dle. She pressed the hand against her body with her left arm. "It *bit* me!"

Tyson laughed without mockery and strode over to the chest. He stepped into a space behind it and, keeping his eyes on Bel and Rowan, laid his hand flat upon its lid, fingers spread.

The women watched a moment. He showed no sign of discomfort. Rowan gave Bel a hand up, and they approached.

The chest was about half as long as Rowan was tall and would have come to her knee if stood on the deck; it was standing on a wooden framework that raised it as high as Tyson's waist. It was covered with intricately tooled leather decorated with a swirling meshlike pattern of worked-in copper. Some of the copper lines came together to con-solidate into clearly marked but unreadable runes and symbols. The whole chest was strapped about loosely by plain leather bands with loops on the side, and the wooden stand was padded with leather.

Bel studied Tyson, then touched the surface with one cautious fin-ger. She snapped it back instantly, shaking it as if from a bee sting. Rowan thought that at the moment of contact there had been a brief, faint noise, like an insect buzz, and a thin odor that disappeared im-mediately.

Rowan stepped up, seeing amusement and challenge in Tyson's eyes. She carefully laid her own hand next to his. The leather felt rich, the copper discernibly cool. Automatically she ran her hand across the lid, part of her appreciating the workmanship. She turned to Bel, speechless.

Tyson tilted his head. "Try to touch Rowan."

Both threw him glances of surprise and suspicion. Unable to resist the opportunity to learn, Rowan reached out with her left hand. With vast reluctance, then forced bravery, Bel put her hand in Rowan's.

Quickly they pulled away from each other, Bel cursing. This time Rowan had felt it, but not from the box. It had passed between Bel's hand and hers, not painful, but strong and unpleasant—an eerie sting-ing vibration.

Rowan was suddenly reminded of the feeling one got from gripping a mainsail sheet under a stiff wind: how the wrist-thick rope would be rigid as iron, yet pass into one's hand the massive tension of the fight between wind and canvas, between sea and wood. The ship was a live thing, and holding that rope was like holding a tensed muscle.

The magic of the chest's guard-spell was sharper, violent but somehow similar. Something living had seemed to pass between the hands. Rowan had been like that rigid rope: whatever it was had passed into and through her to reach Bel. Appalled, she stepped back from the box.

There was no apparent reason for the sensations. The power was near-silent and invisible. For a moment her thoughts swirled, automatically sifting, searching for any information that might connect to give hints or theories about the effect. But when her mind came to rest, the only possibilities that remained involved spirits and spells.

Bel was delighted. "How did you load it on the ship?"

Tyson indicated the leather straps and loops. "We had to slip wooden poles into these, then carry it by the poles."

"It's not a bad spell. But even though I didn't know which chest had the spell, I knew that one of them must. For a real test, we ought to try someone totally in ignorance."

Rowan doubted that would make any difference. Although she was immune, after a fashion, she had felt something real. She was certain she would have felt nothing, if it had been at all possible to do so.

And what was her attitude now? She introspected and found that she still possessed no solid opinion. That surprised her, until she realized that she still had not enough facts to come to a conclusion. But, with the facts and new experience she did have—all the tentative ideas and half-formed theories had re-formed on the opposite side of the issue, pointing to exactly opposite possibilities. She felt a mild internal vertigo.

Tyson stroked his beard thoughtfully. "Wait, now." He stepped into the main passage and looked down it both ways. Something caught his attention. He called down the passage. "You! Yes, you, come here a moment, you'll do. Come on!" Reeder's boy rounded the corner hesitantly, his face full of apprehension.

Tyson went back to the chest and beckoned to the boy. He patted the lid. "Put your hand on this, boy."

The lad froze. His gaze flickered among them, from Rowan to Bel, to the chest, to Tyson. His eyes widened. He glanced at the exit, then back to the chest. He clearly had no idea what was planned and just as clearly knew that it meant nothing pleasant for him. He seemed un-sure whether to attempt an escape, or to obey the order of the navi-gator, who was, after all, a very large man. His turmoil immobilized him. He paled. He began to pant.

The three watched his performance; then Rowan laughed despite herself. The others joined in, and Bel clapped him on the back. "Go on, boy." He fled.

Bel turned to Rowan. "What do you think, now?"

"I think . . ." Rowan reviewed her thoughts again. "I think that there is a great deal that wizards know, that I don't."

When they reached the open air again, night had fallen. A jumble of clouds in the west were still faintly underlit by the departed sun, and were crowding toward the zenith. No land was visible, but with a glance toward the Eastern Guidestar, Rowan offhandedly located her-self in her world with perfect precision. She automatically noted the westward progress they had made since morning.

When she looked at Tyson, he was doing the same, although she sus-pected that his accuracy would be less than hers. Then he scanned the horizons. "Wind'll come up before dawn. Rain, as well." She nodded.

Bel sighed. "The crew will be crowded tonight. Well, we'll be warm and dry, at least."

"Overhead leak somewhere down there," Tyson commented. "I hope you're not under it."

"Damn."

He spoke to Rowan. "Lady, does this upset your theories?"

"I had no theories. Only the possibilities of some theories. There are still possibilities, just somewhat different ones."

The three stood by the rail for an hour, watching the progress of the clouds and enjoying inconsequential conversation. Presently the first mate scurried down into the aft cabin and emerged with Morgan in tow. The captain viewed the scene, then issued orders to adjust the sail positions, watching with affected disinterest as he slowly paced the poop deck.

Eventually Bel decided it was time to turn in and made a few good-natured insults about the cook's particularity for early hours and promptness in assistants.

Rowan and Tyson remained, talking idly and companionably. Presently Tyson put forth an invitation, which Rowan considered carefully, then declined. Uninsulted, Tyson stayed with her for another hour; then he wished her good night and retired.

Rowan wandered the deck alone for a while, enjoying the feeling of the deck as it shifted beneath her feet, the subtle changes of wind strength and direction. Eventually her mood shifted a bit, and she found herself regretting her refusal of Tyson's suggestion. This she remedied by knocking softly at his cabin door at midnight.

In the morning Reeder's boy was found dead, lying blue-faced in a puddle of water next to the wizard's chest.

7

"Stupid," Morgan pronounced, shifting through the papers on his worktable. "Foolish. Stupid. He was looking for trouble, or he was too stupid to know when he'd found it. Damn!" He slammed down a fistful of notes and receipts. "Why bother a wizard's chest? There was a warning spell on it; he must have noticed it."

Rowan sat in a low chair across the cabin, legs stretched out in front of her. "It wasn't particularly unpleasant. It can't have killed him."

"No, of course not." He pointed a finger at her. "He tried to open it. He ignored the guard-spell and met the protecting spell. I can't be held responsible for the idiocy of a boy."

Her face was impassive. "He was curious. Intrigued." To herself she added, Challenged.

Morgan grunted noncommittally. Shifting his papers into apparently arbitrary piles, he calmed visibly. "Have you gone over the charts with Tyson?"

"Yes." The hiss of rain overhead grew louder. Someone walked on the deck above, steps slow and heavy.

"Were there many corrections?"

She shook her head. The steps above paused, apparently at the taffrail. "There was nothing incorrect on them, but you'll find quite a few additions. Some areas where not much was known before."

There was a creak as the person above shifted. Morgan nodded. "Good. I'd like to review them with you. Where's Tyson, do you know?"

"On deck."

"In this? Have someone find him. And bring the charts." He caught himself. "Pardon me, lady. I'll get them."

Rowan rose. "No, Captain, I'll go. Excuse me, please." She exited, closing the door on his surprised expression. Wrapping her cloak around her, she climbed the short companionway to the deck.

The wind was strong but not storming. Rain fell in a solid pour, weighing down like a hand on Rowan's head and shoulders. The deck was near-deserted. Through the shifting gray she could faintly make out the back of the helmsman, not far from her, placidly manning the wheel. She turned and went up the steps to the raised poop.

As she came to the top, the wind caught her borrowed cloak and whipped it about like a loose sail. She grabbed at the folds and pulled it close. Its protection closed about her like the walls of a room, water running off her hood in streams before her face. She had to move her whole body to direct the hood opening. She saw a lone gray-cloaked figure motionless at the taffrail, looking off astern, and she moved toward it.

She spoke, but the noise of water covered her voice. She touched his shoulder; he seemed not to notice. Using both hands, she turned him to face her.

It was Reeder. His face was pale with cold, slick with rain. Sparse hair lay wet against his forehead, like lines drawn in ink. He looked at her expressionlessly, eyes blank and bright. His eyes were a beautiful pale green color; she had never noticed that before.

Startled, she stepped back. She made to speak, but he turned away.

Rowan left him and searched every part of the deck for Tyson. The downpour limited her vision to the length of her reach, so that her scope was small, her search detailed. She began from the poop deck, where she left Reeder, and worked forward, and so at last found him up by the bowsprit.

He stood far forward at the angle in the railing. Where the rest of the ship was only dreary, there the violence of the elements showed itself. The seas were not very high, but the ship moved heavily, and the bow smashed each crest, with a noise like the absent thunder.

Tyson faced the seas. Each time the bow met a wave, the impact sent a stinging sheet of spray over the rail; he did not flinch, but only blinked against the water. His cloak was soaked through, and he wore his hood down. He was as wet as if he had been underwater. Rowan guessed he had been there since dawn.

She called out to him, but the hiss of rain, the whistle and rattle of rigging, and the jarring crash of waves covered her voice. She moved closer and shouted.

Some sound, if not words, reached him. He turned and she saw him recognize her—recognize and withdraw, his face a closed door.

A dash of spray slapped across his back and into Rowan's face. She winced and wiped her eyes with her fingers. When she could see, his expression had changed, and he seemed surprised, as though he had thought himself alone despite her presence. It was the cold water on her own face, his realization of her pain and discomfort, that brought him back.

He grabbed her arm, put his face close, and shouted. The words came faintly. "Get out of the weather!" Beads of water hung in his beard like crystals. The cold he had absorbed drew the heat away from her face, out through her hood.

She tried to explain. "The Captain," she began, but she could not make her voice loud enough. At last she put her hands on his arms and looked him full in the face, letting him see her utter refusal to leave him there.

Thoughts moved behind his eyes. He let her lead him away.

They went below, down to the galley. Bel was there, dealing with an immense kettle hung over the brick stove. She looked up in astonishment. "What happened to him?"

Rowan brought him into the warmth. Tyson muttered protests. "Don't fuss, I'm all right."

"You are soaked." Rowan took his cloak. The shirt beneath was as wet as his face. "And frozen." His face was white; he shivered. Bel ladled soup from the kettle into a mug and passed it to him. He wrapped his hands around it but did not drink. His eyes found the fire and rested there.

Bel watched him silently, then turned to Rowan for answers. Rowan told her about Reeder's boy, and Bel listened, eyes wide.

"People should be careful with magic," the Outskirter said. "He ignored the warning. It was a stupid thing for him to do."

"Boys are stupid," Tyson said bitterly. "It's in them to be stupid, and to do stupid things. That's how they learn. Adults should know better."

"It's not your fault." Rowan put a hand on his shoulder and studied his face. "He was down there already. He was looking for mischief. It's horrible, but he found it himself."

He turned to her. "He would have left it alone, after the guard-spell warned him. But he saw us. And I—I dared him."

She had no answer. It was true.

"Perhaps he thought he'd be immune," Bel said. "Perhaps he fancied himself a sailor." The idea set off in Tyson some chain of thought that forced his eyes closed in pain.

The room was thick with dampness and cooking scents. The air was dark and close. The fire painted their faces with warm light.

Rowan remembered such a light, such air, such faces.

She had been a very young girl, perhaps five years old. The harvest was in, and it was very late at night. There was still much to do, and the family had brought their work by the firelight.

Her mother and father were husking fist-sized ears of maize. A morning rain had soaked the ears, and they gave off a visible steam in the heat. Her aunt, a narrow, fragile-looking woman, was sorting beans, and her uncle sat close to the firelight, squinting as he carefully repaired a wicker basket.

Young Rowan was shelling peas, very bored. She absently counted the number of peas in each pod, wondering if they would go past ten. Ten was all she knew.

The adults' conversation seemed not to pertain to her, and she accepted it as a dull background to a dull job. Presently there was a lull, and her aunt began to sing a little song in a high thin voice. Rowan became more interested and stopped counting to listen.

The song was about a bird. Rowan liked that, as she was fond of birds, and there were so few around. The bird, a swallow, flew alone in an empty sky. In the morning it came close to earth and flew very fast, skimming the fields. Later it began to rain, and the swallow passed a barn. Looking inside, it saw that all the animals were in their stalls, warm and safe. At night, it flew high above an empty castle and looked down on the towers, circling around. At last it found a nest and slept, while the mysterious moon crossed the skies. Rowan thought it was a fine song.

But when it was finished she happened to look over at her uncle and saw that he was silently crying. He had stopped his work and closed his eyes. Tears ran down his weathered cheeks.

Rowan was surprised. There was nothing to cry about. The only thing that had happened was that her aunt had sung a song. The other adults ignored her uncle. That upset Rowan; someone was unhappy, no one was paying attention, and it was not right.

Then it came to her that somehow the song was not about a bird but about sorrow. She was confused. There was nothing in the song except the bird, and what it had done. Still, she knew it was so.

Later, after she had been put to bed, she crept outside and stood alone in the back yard. With her back to the house, she could see out to the edge of the cultivated land, past the funeral groves, where the desert began. The sky above was wide and empty; she thought of a tiny bird high up in that sky, looking down on her. She tried to remember the song and sang it to herself. As she sang it, her own eyes filled with tears, although she could not see why they should.

It came to her that there were reasons behind events, reasons she did not know, and that the world contained many things that were other than what they seemed. She thought that perhaps if she could fly very high, she might see a great deal.

Rowan still knew the song and sometimes sang it to herself.

She took off the cloak she was wearing and wrapped it around Tyson's shivering shoulders. He did not look at her, but he leaned back slightly, accepting its warmth.

With a glance toward Bel, Rowan stepped out of the galley into the passageway. She wound her way among the passages, back to Tyson's cabin. Inside, she went into his sea chest and found a warm shirt of white wool. With that, and her arms full of his charts, she emerged to encounter a very surprised purser's mate, his hand raised to knock. Offering no explanation, she told the man about Reeder, doubtless still at the taffrail in the rain. He hurried off, and she went back to join her friends.

8

The first sign of the approach to Wulfshaven was not a view of the mainland itself, but of one and then a series of small islands that swept south from the still-distant mouth of the great river Wulf. The islands were mostly unclaimed, bare earth and rock, but as the *Morgan's Chance* neared the port itself, there were more signs of human hands. Occasionally an island would actually be inhabited, usually by a lone fisherman feeding the land by the offal of his or her trade. More often one of the regularly planned dumps of garbage or a deposit of other fertilizing substances had brought to life some still-deserted island, creating isolated spots of green, lonely but promising.

Rowan and Bel found a place on the poop, out of the way of the increasing activity. Bel sat comfortably on the deck with her back against the aft railing. She had donned her shaggy boots and cloak, to ward off the chill sweeping down from the windy gray sky.

The previous day Rowan had made her farewells with Tyson. After the death of Reeder's boy, he had become ever more distant and solitary, shunning Rowan and conversing with the captain and crew only at need. Rowan could find no comfortable way to approach him, no way to learn why the child's death had affected him so personally. They parted as strangers.

Now Rowan stood near Bel, watching the maneuvers with interest. Although Morgan strode about the deck with an air of nonchalance, his glance was sharp, and his orders quick and precise. The heavy ship wallowed with all the grace he could muster and, in one lovely, astonishing move, sidled up to the wharf, its sails luffing the instant it barely nudged the dock. Morgan allowed himself a small smile, then turned away as if the matter concerned him not at all.

Wulfshaven was a deep harbor, and unloading and disembarking was a far simpler affair than at Donner. A railed gangplank bridged the shifting gap between the wharf and the ship's starboard side. With no luggage to unload, Rowan and Bel simply walked across the plank, and so arrived at last in Wulfshaven.

The steerswoman led the way, skirting a small crowd consisting of a well-dressed portly man leading a nattering group of less elegant fellows: a merchant, with clerks in tow. A number of smaller vessels were docked along the length of the wharf, some of them sailboats in such bad repair that their status had clearly been shifted from transportation to permanent abode. Children hooted and chattered and clattered past to investigate the *Morgan's Chance*.

The wind picked up briefly as they reached the end of the wharf. Rowan had returned Tyson's cloak; she shivered.

"Do you want my cloak?" Bel offered.

"And leave you with just that blouse? No, I'll get another soon enough." She led Bel left, along a broad, weather-beaten esplanade.

"How soon? Are we going somewhere in particular?"

"I have friends here. We'll spend the night with one of them—Maranne, a healer. I lodged with her during my training. I think you'll like her." Shops lined the shore side of the esplanade. They passed a chandlery, a sail loft, and a ropewalk.

"I thought the Archives were north of here."

"They are. One doesn't train at the Archives." Rowan stopped suddenly beside a filigreed iron pole. "What's this?" The pole stood twice as tall as a man and was surmounted by a translucent white sphere. Bel paused while the steerswoman circled, studying it.

Rowan pulled aside a passerby, a fisherman by his dress, and put a question to him. He replied with surprise. "You're new here? That's a lamp. They're all along the harbor."

Rowan looked down the street and saw another at the next corner, and the next; they lined the business street along the harbor, clustering around the open square that fronted the Trap and Net tavern farther down. "But there's no opening," she said. "How can they light the wicks?"

The fisherman beamed with an air of civic pride. "No wicks. They're magic. A gift from Corvus." He hurried on his way. "Come see them at night!" he called back. "There's nothing like it!" The women watched as he continued down to the Trap and Net, where he noisily greeted a crowd of cronies outside.

"Corvus?" Bel asked.

"The local wizard," Rowan said, turning back to the lamp. "Blue.

Though he was Red when I was here last." Abandoning her inspection, she led the Outskirter down the street, brooding. "Why would Corvus give Wulfshaven such a gift?"

"Out of friendship?" Bel's gait had naturally acquired a bit of a roll during their voyage, and she weaved slightly as she tried to compensate for nonexistent waves. "I know the steerswomen don't like wizards, but surely the wizards do a great deal of good? This Corvus, doesn't he help the town at all?"

Rain sprinkled the street briefly, then stopped. A woman pushing a pastry cart paused and viewed the shifting sky with annoyance. "Yes," Rowan admitted, angling around the cart. "He'll predict the weather, sometimes, and always if there's a heavy gale. And if the fishing is poor, he'll give advice that's always true. Still—" Spotting something ahead, she walked faster to the next corner.

A small man was working at the next lamppost, stooping down to deal with something at its base. On the ground beside him lay a leather shoulder satchel, and he periodically removed and replaced items in it with an air of confidence and satisfaction.

Rowan spoke as she approached him, but he cut her off cheerfully. "Hold on a bit, now, this won't take a moment," he said, and continued with his work. Rowan could see that he had opened a small panel, disguised by the filigree, and was involved with something inside.

"There." He shut the panel and locked it with a tiny key dangling by a cord from his wrist. Looking up, he appraised the two women. "Now, how can I help you?"

"I'm wondering about these new lamps," Rowan began.

"Lovely, aren't they?" He slapped the pole familiarly. "You must be strangers." He gave Bel's clothing a second, squint-eyed inspection.

"We just arrived by ship," Bel explained. "From Donner."

"Donner, is it?" His face lit up. He stood and dusted his hands on his trouser legs. "Well, I have family in Donner. My little niece, of course she's not so little now, she married a fellow who—"

Rowan interrupted. "I'm sorry, I'll be glad to give you any news I have from Donner, but first I'd like to ask you about these lamps."

"Well, Corvus, that's our wizard, he gave them—"

"Specifically," Rowan continued, "I'd like to know how they work."

"Oh, no." He clicked his tongue. "I can't help you there. Guild rules, you see."

"Guild? What guild is that?"

"Why, the new Lamplighters Guild. See, when Corvus gave them, he had to teach us the spells to make them work. All very secret, sworn to secrecy, every one of us—" His eyes caught the glint of her gold chain, and his speech ended with a trailing "Er . . ." He sent a confirming glance toward the silver ring on her left hand, then winced. "I'm sorry, lady, truly I am. But I can't tell you."

Rowan gazed at him for a long moment. At last she said, "As I don't have much time to spare, you needn't go into detail. The general idea will suffice." And she waited, suddenly quite still.

The man agonized. "I just *can't.*"

Rowan simply stood, silent. Bel looked from her face to the lamplighter's in perplexity. Finally Rowan turned without a word and began to walk away.

"Lady, please, wait a moment—"

She stopped, then slowly turned around, but did not approach.

"I need to know something—" he began.

"No."

Understanding dawned on Bel's face, and she watched the man with interest.

"Not for myself," he continued, "but for the Guild. I, that is, they ought to know, is your ban now just on me, or will it hold for the whole Guild?"

Rowan took her time replying. "The ban holds for any individual who refuses questions." She made to turn away again, but Bel called to her.

The Outskirter was viewing the lamplighter with concern. "Rowan, this man has family in Donner." Rowan said nothing, and Bel went on. "They might have been in the fire at the inn—"

"A fire?" He said in shock, "My niece, she works in an inn. And her son, too—"

"Do you know the name?" Bel asked.

"No, no I don't." His face showed agony. "But I know the street, Tilemaker's Street." He looked helplessly at the steerswoman, who waited patiently for Bel, saying nothing.

At last Bel said, "Rowan, do you know if Saranna's Inn was on Tilemaker's Street?"

"Yes, I do know," Rowan replied. "I'll wait for you at the next corner."

Down the street she found a street vendor's stall and interested herself in a display of bone flutes and pipes. They were of remarkable workmanship. Rowan tested a flute but lacked the skill to produce any sound at all. She had better luck with the pipes, managing to elicit a mellow hoot from the low register.

Eventually Bel joined her, and Rowan led them along a cobbled street that climbed and twisted up one of the hills above the harbor. They walked in silence, and when Rowan glanced at her, she saw that the Outskirter was deep in angry thought. Finally Bel said only, "Family is important. Rowan, that was cruel!"

They turned up a side street so narrow that the overhanging second stories sometimes had planks laid from one window to the opposite neighbor's. Some were decorated with bright flower boxes. "Bel," Rowan said carefully. "Suppose you discovered that another tribe had stolen half your herd and refused to give you what was yours?"

Bel stopped in outrage. "We'd kill them!"

Rowan turned back to her. "Kill them? How cruel." And she continued on her way, leaving Bel to catch up.

The street doubled back on itself, and when they rounded one last corner, suddenly the area before them opened up. The sea was visible, patched with light and dark by the heavy clouds that moved above. Before them, the roofs of Wulfshaven were a confusion of green-tiled shapes sweeping down to the harbor below.

Rowan stopped before a house on the corner, a haphazard construction of whitewashed brick. Suddenly all the previous unpleasantness was swept away in a river of bright memories. The handful of years in the life of a taciturn farm girl from the northlands, years of struggle and confusion lanced with sudden comprehension and delight, years that ended with the arrival at the Archives of a young woman of confidence, depth, and inner strength—those years were contained in this town, these streets, and one little attic room in this very house.

"Are we going in?"

Rowan smiled. "Give me a moment," she said. "It's been a long time."

Inside, the ceiling was festooned with tied bundles of dried herbs sending out dozens of evocative odors. The room was dark, the shutters pulled to against the coming rain, and a small fire flickered in the hearth. A heavyset blond woman approached them. "How may I help you?"

Rowan quelled her disappointment. "Is Maranne about? I'm an old friend."

"No, she's off in the east quarter. Pulling a tooth and delivering some coltsfoot tea. I'm afraid she'll be quite late."

"Do you mind if we wait and sit by the fire? There's rain on the way."

The blond woman looked at the pair uncertainly: one slightly damp woman, not dressed for the weather, and another in outlandish garb.

"Rowan used to live here," Bel said.

The woman brightened. "Rowan? Maranne speaks of you often— you're that steerswoman. Come, I'll make us some tea." She closed the door against the distant clatter of hooves on the cobbles and led them to the fire. Chairs were drawn and a kettle hung. The blond woman scanned the ceiling for likely candidates. "I don't remember you, but I remember when the Academy was here. Oh, that was a time! People from all over, all those teachers, and experts in this and that. It takes the strangest mix to make a batch of steerswomen." She found some peppermint hanging by the window, then added a tiny sprig of comfrey.

"I remember you," Rowan said. "You're Joslyn. Your father was the cooper."

Joslyn was pleased. "There's an example of steerswoman's memory." The sound of hooves outside became audible again, and with it a shouting voice. "Now, what's that?" She opened the window.

The sound stopped, and an instant later the door slammed open and a large form filled the doorway. "Rowan! I knew it!"

The man crossed the room, and suddenly Rowan found herself engulfed in strong arms and the sweep of his cloak. Joslyn said faintly, "My word, it's the duke!"

Rowan tried to extract herself. His hug was no comradely embrace, as he had often given her, nor even a lover's embrace, but something full of desperate relief. "I knew it couldn't be true!" he railed. "Damn Corvus and his scrying!"

"Artos!" She managed to pull away. "What is this?"

Bel eyed them from her chair. "You know this duke, then?"

He spun aside and pounded a nearby table violently. "That low-born bastard! How could he tell me such a thing?"

"Tell you what? Artos, calm down," Rowan pleaded, knowing well that the duke was one man who could never be calm.

But he did stop, all his native energy held still for a moment while he looked at her and said in a smaller voice, "He said you were dead."

She was astonished. "Corvus?"

"Yes!" He spun away and paced, more quickly than a man his size ought to in so small a room. "He said that he was scrying and saw that you'd been killed. In Donner, by dragons! He said, 'I'm sorry to tell you, but your pet steerswoman is dead.'" Artos stopped and held up his hands to ward off a reaction. "I know, I understand, you're no-body's pet. Those were his words, not mine. But it looks like his scry-stone was mistaken." He paused, then smiled. "Did I mention how glad I am to see you?"

Rowan laughed happily. "Yes, I'm glad to see you, too."

Bel spoke from her place by the fire. "The scry-stone was not far off, at that. We very nearly were killed by dragons."

Artos turned to her, seeing her for the first time. He took in her clothing, her sword, and the piebald cloak draped on the chair behind her, with a speculating gaze. "This is Bel, my friend, an Outskirter," Rowan explained. She turned to Bel. "You should stand when the duke enters."

"He's no duke of mine, and he's already entered." Bel did stand, but it was to swing the bubbling kettle out of the fire. "Perhaps this duke would like some tea?"

Joslyn recovered some of her composure and nervously sidled over to deal with it.

Bel approached. "Well, I'd like to know how to address a duke, and also, how he knew where to find us, and when." She looked up at him.

"I came as soon as I heard there was a ship arrived from Donner, with a steerswoman. If it was Rowan, I knew she would come here; she couldn't be in Wulfshaven and not visit Maranne." He paused. "And the proper address is 'my lord.'"

Bel considered, then shook her head. "That won't do."

"Bel—" Rowan began.

"Outskirter," the duke mused. He had finally placed the term. "That's a warrior, a barbarian."

"True."

"You're small for a warrior."

Bel acknowledged it. "I'm closer to the ground, and harder to knock over."

"That's a large sword for so small a woman."

"I swing it two-handed."

He nodded, his wariness tempered by interest. He leaned back against the table. "That's good. But then you can't carry a shield."

"Ha. My sword is my shield."

"Bel has been traveling with me," Rowan said. "She's an honorable person and has given her word not to lay waste to the Inner Lands while she's in my company."

The duke laughed. He had a huge laugh, as big as his person, honest and uninhibited. "Then you'd best not separate. I believe this woman could do more damage than her size might suggest. Let's sit by the fire and wait for Maranne, and you can tell me the story." He looked around and found Joslyn standing uncertainly by the fire. He dropped into graciousness easily. "I hope this is no inconvenience to you. Pour some tea, and please sit with us."

Joslyn complied, hesitantly, and pulled up a stool, but Rowan noted that the herbalist kept a bit of distance between herself and the visitors. Joslyn found the situation uncomfortable, and Rowan realized with regret that at some point in the past Artos had ceased to be a frequent casual visitor to Maranne's house.

But Bel was completely at ease and settled into a chair, tucking up both legs as if she were seated on the ground. "I've heard something about these dukes and barons and squires you have in the Inner Lands," she said. "How is it that a steerswoman knows one so well? Are you all of the same class?"

Artos gave a half smile. "They say that the steerswomen are the only aristocracy open to the common folk."

"That's not true at all, and it's a bad saying," Rowan put in with some vehemence. "We come from all classes before we join, and belong to no class when we're accepted."

"You're certainly well treated by the people," the duke pointed out. "And they defer to you, grant you certain privileges. . . ."

"The people treat us well of their own accord. There's no law that compels them."

"Custom can have the force of a law."

"Not at all. There's no punishment, no soldiery involved—"

He held up a hand. "Now, let's not get into one of our discussions. We'll be at it all night."

Remembering, Rowan laughed. "Talking until dawn . . ."

"Often, right by this very fire . . ."

Joslyn looked about the room in wonderment. Rowan said to Bel, "The Academy's not a place, it's an event, and the year I trained it was held here in Wulfshaven. Artos was forever haunting our classes."

"So many strange people," he said, and his gaze turned inward at pleasant memories. "From all the Inner Lands. Candidates from far-off towns, teachers, experts in the most peculiar things. So much to see and hear about. I never knew the world held so many things, such strange thoughts . . ."

"He looked so fascinated, and so lonely, that I took pity on him at last and started a conversation. It was easy to become friends. He has a quick mind, as it turned out, and I practically recited my daily lessons to him, most evenings . . ."

"A steerswoman can take pity on a duke?" Bel was amused.

"I wasn't a steerswoman, yet . . ."

"And I wasn't a duke," Artos said. "But my uncle died near the end of the training, and I"—he made a deprecating gesture—"ascended to my position." Then he looked a bit regretful. "I'd like to have seen it all, you know. I learned a lot in my haunting, as Rowan calls it. I know I'm better for it.

"Well." He slapped one knee and leaned forward. "Now you must tell me how our Corvus can be so far off the mark. What happened to you?"

At the duke's insistence, Rowan began with the fire at the inn. As it was not the true beginning of the tale, she found she had to keep backtracking and filling in, responding to peripheral questions as they occurred. The story wound its way through events almost haphazardly, but at last Artos had the whole tale of her jewel, and of her suspicion about the interest of a wizard. She showed him the glittering fragment.

He fingered it, musing. "I've seen this before. That witch-woman, at the edge of town."

"Yes, you were with me. That was the first one I'd seen."

He nodded vaguely, his eyes on the fire. From the depth of his concentration, Rowan suddenly realized that he was thinking in his areas of greatest expertise: violence and defense. Her thoughts ran ahead of his. "You can't be serious," she said.

He looked up. "You could always read my mind."

"The wizard could hardly harm me at this distance."

"How can we know? Corvus saw you all the way off in Donner. And those dragons—that must have been done at a distance. Unless your Red wizard followed you." He returned the jewel.

"Or," Bel put in, leaning forward, "unless it was done by Jannik."

"Help a Red? Not likely. The Blues and Reds hate each other, only the gods know why." And with that, the duke grew silent.

Rowan watched his face, suddenly disturbed. "Something has happened?"

He nodded. "A nasty little war, last year." Avoiding Rowan's face, he addressed his explanation to Bel. "Corvus turned from Red to Blue, and six months later someone's trying to establish a new Red holding just northeast of us. And our helpful Corvus requested—" He spat the word, and abruptly his composure vanished. He slammed the arm of his chair and was on his feet, pacing like a beast. " 'Requested!' "

"Requested how many soldiers?" Rowan asked.

He flung his arms wide. "All of them! All of my regulars, all of my reserves, and—" His mouth twisted. "—as many impressed from the citizenry."

Rowan made a calculation against her estimate of the area's population. "And how many came back?"

"I lost twenty of my regulars. Of the rest—" He paused for effect. "Half returned." He watched the steerswoman's reaction, then continued in a flat tone. "Wizards. Sometimes I think they're all insane." He brought himself back to his chair but did not sit; he gripped the back with his large hands. "Did you know, one of them even brought a basilisk onto the battlefield? Can you imagine it? The damned thing killed as many on their side as ours."

Bel looked at Rowan. "What's a basilisk?"

"A magical creature, usually disguised in some fashion."

"That's the thing of it," Artos said to the Outskirter. "If it looks at you, you die, sooner or later, and how can you tell if it's looking at you when you can't recognize it? It wiped out a squadron on their side, and one on ours. And the ones that lingered, they had it worst. We brought some of them here, no one else wanted to help them. That Red captain, what was his name?" he asked Joslyn.

"Penn," she supplied quietly.

"You should have heard him curse his masters. The poor bastard scarcely looked human at the end."

Joslyn was sitting silent on her stool by the fire, her cup in her lap, her head bowed.

"Your father?" Rowan asked.

The woman looked up slowly. "Tell me," she said carefully. "Have you seen the magic lamps by the harbor?"

Artos spoke through his teeth. "A gesture of thanks."

Bel sipped her tea. "It's trouble if you cross a wizard, trouble if you help a wizard, and trouble if you don't have a wizard, for things like dragons and hurricanes." She put down the cup. "That's altogether too much trouble."

The duke sat down again abruptly. "Rowan, who else knows you're in Wulfshaven?"

"I've made no secret of it."

"Of course not. But Corvus thinks you're dead, and probably Jannik, too. With any luck, your Red wizard does, as well."

"So there's no reason for him to look this way, to scry or try to divine my fate."

"Word may reach him. There may be spies—I'll let it be known that the steerswoman on the ship from Donner turned out not to be you."

Rowan was offended. "Artos, I won't have you lying on my behalf."

There was a shift in his demeanor. Suddenly he was not only a friend, but a duke, a man who gave orders and who chose his own behavior. "I'm no steerswoman. I'll lie if it suits me, to protect whomever I damn well please." He thought briefly. "You're going to the Archives?"

"In the morning."

Artos stood. "Leave now."

"We'll have to wait. It's a full day's journey, and this rain—"

"Take my horse. You'll be there by midnight."

"Artos—"

"No, he's right," Bel said. "The sooner we get to where we're going, the better."

He looked around, and found Joslyn. "Pack them a meal for the journey. And does Maranne have an extra cloak for Rowan?"

"No. Take mine." She went to make the preparations.

"I hardly think this is necessary—" Rowan protested.

"Rowan," Bel said. "Shut up and let your friends help you. The duke knows more about such things than you do, and so do I."

It was true. Rowan was familiar with violence; it was part of the world. But the violence she had met had been random, small-scale—the occasional road bandit, a fleeing criminal. She had defended herself and even killed in defense.

But this—If in fact there was a pattern to the recent events, if there was a single will behind them, then it pointed to the existence of an enemy. She stopped to absorb the idea: *I have an enemy.*

Bel and Artos understood enemies.

9

*R*owan awoke to find a wood gnome regarding her from the foot of the bed. He was perched on the footboard, peering down with droll interest, munching some bit of fruit. When he saw she was awake, he stretched out one long arm to offer her a taste. She accepted politely but only gave the piece a token nibble, as it seemed to have been dragged through several different kinds of dirt. It proved to be a slice of winter apple, identifiable only by flavor. Wood gnomes had no more than a vague recognition of cleanliness.

She looked around the room. The other four beds were empty, but Bel's fur cloak lay on the floor next to one. Bel herself was nowhere in sight.

They had ridden through the long night, with storms gathering around them, gathering, then breaking. They ran Artos's fine war-horse through rain along the north-going river road, a smooth clear track, until the rising hills forced them to walk. Bel rode behind

Rowan, clutching her waist. Though the Outskirter never complained, Rowan felt the tension in her arms at each jolting misstep. But when the sky cracked lightning, the horse remembered battle and cried out challenge to the sound, and Bel, in kindred spirit, sat straighter, balanced, and echoed with a warrior's laugh. Later they wearily dismounted and guided the horse in booming thunder and dancing wind up the rocky, wooded path to the stables nestled under the overhang of the Archives' stone walls.

The wind snatched the stable door from Bel's hand as Rowan brought the horse in, and the slam summoned Josef, the groom, from sleep to amazed discovery of the exhausted women. He led them upstairs to the transients' dormitory, lit a fire, then left them to collapse into the chilly beds.

Now spots of sunlight climbed the far end of the room. Rowan turned back to the wood gnome and addressed him in the language of hand signals that his people shared with humans. "Where woman?" she gestured.

"Woman in bed," he replied, obviously meaning Rowan.

"No. Other woman." She pointed to the bed with Bel's clothing.

"Fur-woman. Noisy woman, gone. Throw rock at me." With an expression of vast melancholy he indicated a spot on his shoulder. Rowan made sympathetic noises. She could easily imagine the Outskirter's reaction on waking to find a strange creature on her bed.

She rose and rummaged through a wardrobe until she found a clean shirt that fit her, then added her trousers. The wood gnome watched, rocking on his perch, long toes gripping the bedstead as easily as if they were fingers. He munched his apple. "Time for breakfast, hurry," he advised.

"I go to find fur-woman first."

He eyed her sadly. "Watch out for rocks."

At the door, Rowan paused. Slanting beams of light from the high, small windows fragmented the corridor into shapes and angles of alternating light and dark. If Bel was wandering out of curiosity, in which direction would she go? Right led to more residences—another transients' dormitory and the permanent quarters. Rowan guessed that if Bel found that those were private rooms, she would double back. The steerswoman went to the left, retracing the path they had taken the previous night; around a corner, then up again to the gallery. Bel might sensibly have done the same, to impress a known route on her memory in a strange place.

The gallery led her back to the entrance hall. A quick check of the stables downstairs showed them to be deserted. Rowan climbed the narrow stairs again up to a lookout room above the entrance: empty, the dusty close air cool and motionless, windows still shuttered against the previous night's rain.

She descended and entered the informal hall on the left. A series of great double doors filled the wall on the right. When open, they communicated on a cool stone courtyard. They were closed now, and the high-ceilinged room stood in darkness but for the far end, where a door stood open to the next chamber; a rectangle of light, where faint voices could be heard.

Crossing to it, she entered the map room. The room was tall and long, slanting at an angle away from the entrance where she stood. Cool, clean air circulated freely through the tall open windows. Morning sunlight fell on the three ranks of long tables, whose surfaces tilted up to take advantage of the illumination.

On two walls, between the windows, the stones had been plastered, then papered and transformed into huge maps. One was a rough working chart, drawn as accurately as current information permitted, but hastily, with much amendment and many hand-scrawled notes. The opposite wall was currently blank, freshly papered; it served as an alternate when the first needed to be redrawn more concisely. Usage switched between the two with predictable regularity.

But it was the great master chart at the far end of the room that drew Rowan. Her eyes went to it as she approached, passing between the worktables.

The map ran from floor to ceiling. The wall there was curved concave, so that a person standing at a certain point could see all the map's expanse without the distortion of visual foreshortening. The point of best vantage was outlined on the stone floor in a brass rectangle.

The floor was slightly raised in the area before the master chart. Rowan climbed the three steps and moved to the rectangle.

In a single glance, she saw the areas of change: positions corrected, details where none had been before. For a moment she felt an internal shift, as if she were on a deck that tilted to a wave too small to change her direction but large enough to alter her perspective.

"What do you see?"

She turned. Below her was a woman twice her age, dark-haired, dark-skinned, blue-eyed. Keridwen, the chartmistress.

Rowan laughed happily. "I see lakes in the mountains. A stream runs from one—that contributes to the Wulf. Another fjord south of The Crags."

"And three new towns on the Shore Road." Keridwen climbed the steps. "You're not due back until next year, Rowan. Is there trouble?"

"Perhaps," she replied. "But I've found something. I need to talk to the Prime."

"She heard you were in. Someone was sent to wake you."

"I woke before she arrived. Or perhaps I missed her in the corridors. Unless it was a wood gnome that was sent?"

Keridwen laughed. "They returned early this year. A very mild winter."

"Not where I was traveling." Her mind returned to Bel. "But I'm looking for a friend of mine, who woke before me."

"I've seen no strangers today. Perhaps she found the kitchen, and breakfast?"

"Or upstairs?" There was a high, bright chamber above the map room, used in fair weather to copy charts for storage.

"I came from there."

"I'd better continue, then. She may find this place . . . strange."

Rowan left by the door opposite to the one she entered. It gave onto a short passage whose right wall held tall doors. She swung them open and looked out; the courtyard revealed was empty.

Rowan found herself pausing, struck by a feeling that had been growing, unnoticed, in her. She stepped into the courtyard and then realized: it was familiarity. She felt like a person returning to a place of her childhood, finding it familiar yet strangely altered. But the place was the same, and some subtle change was in herself.

It had been well over three years since last she had been at the Archives. She had traveled long and mostly alone, over lands unknown to her when she met them, then well known to her through scrupulous observation. Her logbooks had returned to the Archives by other hands, and news of the place had reached her through the words of others. And yet, across that distance, she knew where every room lay, knew the names of all who dwelt there. She could walk into the Greater Library and place her hand immediately on the shelf where her own writings were stored.

This small courtyard had been a particular favorite of hers. It was cool even in high summer, and always sheltered on windy days. She remembered bringing old logbooks there to study, and reading them with fascination; then, sensing a presence behind her, turning to see the smiling wrinkled face of the very steerswoman who wrote them. She remembered an evening celebration not long after the arrival of herself and her fellow trainees from Wulfshaven; nine of them gathered in the courtyard, Janus playing flute, herself talentlessly struggling with a mandolin, Ingrud plying her squeeze-box with gusto; others laughing and conversing, sound echoing off the ancient walls . . .

On an adjacent side another door opened, then another, and the passage on that wall was transformed into a veranda on the courtyard. A woman peered at her, then approached: Berry, tall and dark-haired, recognizing her nearsightedly. "Rowan, is it? The Prime is looking for you."

Rowan smiled at her. "Fine greeting. You're looking well. Yes, I want to see her too, but first, have you noticed an Outskirter going by, or perhaps in the libraries?"

"An Outskirter? What, a shaggy barbarian here?"

"Not too shaggy; she's a woman. Well, shaggy perhaps, if you consider her clothes. But you haven't noticed her, then."

"Hardly! Is she dangerous?"

Rowan considered. "Under certain circumstances."

She left by the doors Berry had opened and looked down the passages. The one on the right led to the Prime's study and residence. After a moment's consideration, Rowan went left.

She passed a study and paused to check inside. Two women and a stocky man of middle age were gathered around a worktable. Graphs, some of startling configuration, were pinned up haphazardly around the walls of the room.

Rowan made to leave, but the man caught sight of her. "Rowan! You're back before your time. Come, take a look at this."

"I'm sorry, Arian, I'm looking for a friend who may be lost in the passages." But she found herself intrigued and stepped inside. "Are you making progress?"

"None to speak of. Still, surprises keep coming up." One of the steerswomen with him looked up suddenly, as if remembering something. "Henra is looking for you," she told Rowan.

"Yes, I've been told." But she suddenly recalled the calculations she had made on the road to Donner. "Wait, I have something." She came to the table and found a blank sheet of parchment. "Look at this." Sketching quickly, she briefly explained the problem of the dispersal of the jewels.

Arian tapped the rough chart. "With an area that wide, your imaginary giant would have to stand very far back."

"And be very tall indeed," one of the steerswomen noted.

Rowan laid a straightedge across the scales, indicated a number.

"That's too tall," Arian said.

The other steerswomen spoke up. "The ground would never support him, do you see? He'd sink in. He couldn't eat enough to live."

Rowan was annoyed at the digression. "It needn't be a giant, a tower will do. It's a giant for the purposes of the problem." She turned back to the chart. "So. He stands this far away, he's this tall, and throws parallel to the ground. The area his throw covers, assuming, shall we say, twenty objects in his hand . . ." She read off two numbers from the right-hand scale and made a simple calculation.

Arian looked at the result. "Straightforward enough."

Rowan held up an index finger. "But." Turning over the sheet, she redrew the chart with greater precision—and with its elements at slightly different aspect to each other. "He throws again, this time—" She paused significantly. "Angling upward." She handed the straightedge to the steersman.

He laid it on the chart. "The area covered . . ." He looked up. "But the path doesn't intersect with the ground."

"Look at the time it takes to fall."

The straightedge swept across the scales. "Infinite?"

"Look again."

A shift. "Zero?"

"The objects never come down."

He leaned back. "That's impossible. They have to come down."

"Of course it's impossible," Rowan said. "Of course they have to come down. Do you see? I've found a situation where our usual methods fail."

Squinting in thought, Arian studied. "No," he said at last. "It's not the method that's at fault. It's the problem. You've set up an impossible situation."

"We don't know that."

"Impossible giants—"

"Or very possible towers!"

The second steerswoman spoke again. "Be hard to build a tower that high."

Rowan threw up her hands. "But we're not concerned with the difficulty here—"

"You can't ignore crucial elements," Arian put in.

"That's hardly crucial—"

"There is obviously," he stated carefully, "something wrong with the problem. We know that the techniques work, but we're getting an impossible answer. It can't be our method that's at fault, so it must be the problem itself."

Rowan drew back. "Arian, that is backward reasoning, and you know it well. You mustn't deny information simply because it differs from what you expect. You're not thinking like a steersman—"

He interrupted, his voice stony. "Rowan, I do not need your instruction in how to think like a steersman."

She stopped short, curbed her temper, then began again. "We know that the approaches handed down to us always seem to work, but we can't always see why—"

"Exactly what I've been working on these years, with my 'backward reasoning'—"

"But there may be different ways to look at it. You've been working from the inside out; but if we can—" She sought an analogy. "If we can map the edges we may be better able to see the whole. We may be able to work from the outside in."

The other steerswomen exchanged glances. One shook her head minutely, but the other tilted her head in Rowan's direction. She obviously agreed but was unwilling to enter the argument.

Rowan prepared to speak again but was interrupted by an arrival at the door. "Rowan? Do you know the Prime is waiting for you?"

She grit her teeth, unwilling to leave battle. "Arian, you must excuse me," she said. She exited with exaggerated dignity.

As she turned toward the Prime's offices, the messenger tapped her shoulder, then pointed in the opposite direction. "The garden," the woman corrected, then disappeared on further errands.

When Rowan arrived at the herb garden, the fact of the season's change asserted itself, the blooms of late spring already giving way to those of early summer. A tall patch of knapweed raised shaggy purple heads by the door; the rosemary beside it was past flowering.

In the distance Rowan heard not conversation but music. Surprised, she threaded her way on the flagstone paths to the garden's center.

There stood, among the plots of herbs and flowers, four pear trees, set each in a corner of a patch of marigold. The path between was widened there and curved. At the intersection of the crossing paths stood two low stone benches.

Henra, the Prime, sat on one. Beside her sat Bel the barbarian. They were singing together.

Rowan approached slowly, fascinated.

They were singing an ancient song about a knight lost in a magic forest. Both sang the melody, though Bel added an occasional ornate turn that pleasantly countered Henra's steady note. They reached a point where their words and melody diverged. The Prime interrupted, saying, "I learned that part differently. Teach me how you know it." Bel sang on alone. Her voice was strong and mobile, not deep, but with a husky dark edge to the tone.

Henra then sang her version in a voice clear and pure as fresh water. When she reached a familiar section, Bel joined her again, eyes closed, head tilted back.

As Rowan reached the benches, the song ended. Bel opened her eyes and spotted something among the branches of the pear tree. "Ha! There's one of them!" She leaped up, then scrabbled among the loose stones by the walk. Above her, a wood gnome began flinging down poorly aimed bits of twig, hooting and jeering.

Rowan restrained her. "There's no need to worry. They're harmless."

"Harmless, ha! Look at those teeth!" These the gnome bared yel-lowly.

Henra was signaling up to him. "Stop, stop. Woman not hurt you. You come down now."

"No. Bad woman, dirty." He spoke in broad emphatic gestures, then hugged himself to a branch, rocking.

"This woman my friend," the Prime told him, but he shrieked fury. The sound attracted the attention of another gnome, who abandoned his inspection of the rain gutter to investigate.

"The gnomes are friendly," Rowan told Bel, but the Outskirter shouted "Ha!" and struggled to aim her stone. A steerswoman on the other side of the garden noticed the ruckus and began to approach.

Henra caught one of the gnome's hands and shook her index fin-ger in his face admonishingly. Rowan clutched at Bel's throwing arm and stepped in front of her, blocking her aim. Outskirter and wood gnome uttered near-identical sounds of frustration.

Abruptly, Rowan and the Prime stopped and looked at each other. Henra began laughing, then Rowan joined her. "I think we're doing similar jobs," Rowan noted. They released their respective charges and helplessly dropped to the bench.

Bel glowered down at them. The gnome leaped to the ground and escaped.

Wiping tears from her eyes, Henra leaned back at last and exam-ined Rowan. The Prime was a small woman, shorter than Bel, and fine-boned and delicate. She had a grace and presence beyond her size, and Rowan, at average height, had always felt huge and clumsy beside her. She seemed half-magical, like an elf out of song, with an-gular features and long green eyes. Her face was a lined map of wis-dom, but age had neither grayed nor grizzled her waist-length hair. Instead, it was laced with silver; no longer plain brown, it was the exact color of smooth sunlit water pouring over dark earth.

"Your friend has mentioned that you've had some trouble," Henra said.

Rowan's mirth faded. "That's right. It's going to take some ex-plaining."

The Prime considered, assessing Rowan's demeanor. She turned to Bel. "If you cross the garden to those doors," she said, indicating them, "you'll find yourself in the dining hall. There are some at breakfast already, and others will be along soon enough." She smiled. "I think you'll find the company enjoyable."

Rowan followed the Prime back into the cool corridors to her office. Inside Henra seated herself in a massive armchair by the cold hearth. From a stool beside her she picked up a blue knitted lap robe; so deep in the Archives, in the central room, the stone walls were an effective barrier against the warmth of day. Wrapping the robe around her legs, she gestured for Rowan to take the chair on the opposite side of the low wooden table before her.

Rowan went to the chair but did not sit. She felt as if she needed to move. She wanted to pace; she wanted to stride to some open window and view the forested land rolling to the horizon. She wanted her charts, her book, her pen and calipers in her hand—but they were gone.

She saw that the Prime had noticed their absence and was waiting for her to speak. Rowan shifted her weight back and forth. "I was attacked on the road to Donner," she said at last.

Henra tilted her head. "One of the hazards of traveling." She still waited; an unlucky encounter on the road was not, in itself, enough to send a steerswoman back to the Archives.

"It was a wizard's man," Rowan said. Suddenly she felt she could sit, and she did.

Henra leaned back slowly. Her emerald gaze flickered as she sifted possibilities and implications, then fell on Rowan. "The one thing we do not need is the active enmity of a wizard. We take pains not to cross them." Rowan knew that well. It had been stressed in her training, passed on to her, along with an unexpressed, slow-burning anger against the wizards' secretiveness, their refusal to impart information.

Rowan shook her head. "I had no idea I was working on anything to interest a wizard." She pulled out the little leather sack, opened it, and removed the glittering fragment. "I was investigating this." She passed it to the Prime.

Henra studied it, turning it over in her hand, and Rowan began to speak. She described its history, detailed her findings, and gave her justifications for straying from her assigned route. Maps were brought out, and with them spread out on the low table, Rowan sketched the pattern of dispersal, that narrow oval that stretched from the eastern curve of the Long North Road into the heart of the Outskirts. She reconstructed the graph she had made during her conversation with Bel on the road to Donner, and described Arian's indignation at her speculations.

The Prime considered the information, questioning her carefully. At some point a tray of tea was brought in, along with rolls and honey. At some other point, the remains were removed. Lost in the exchange of information, Rowan did not notice the intrusion until Henra graciously thanked the woman, who smiled and exited wordlessly.

At last Henra leaned back in her chair. "And at no point did you encounter any wizard? Or any person known to work with a wizard?"

Rowan examined her memory again, wishing she had her logbook. "Not to my knowledge, not until Five Corners. And those men never spoke to me. Nor asked about me, as far as I know. I think someone would have mentioned it if they did."

"Which means," Henra said carefully, "that they already knew all they needed."

"Exactly."

"Then they know more than we do."

"That's not all." Rowan recounted the dragon attack on the inn in Donner, and Corvus's surprising knowledge of the event. She added Artos's conviction that she was in danger even in Wulfshaven. Artos, and his skill in warfare, were known to the Prime.

Finally Henra sighed. "The obvious solution is to abandon this investigation," she began.

"No!"

The Prime glanced at Rowan, then smiled. "That doesn't suit you."

"We've never been a threat to any wizard. I can't believe this jewel can be that important. It doesn't do anything, not that I've seen."

"Perhaps you haven't seen all there is to see."

"We can't let them limit us!" Rowan was on her feet, pacing. "Isn't it enough that they won't share their knowledge with us?"

"Their secrecy is their strength," Henra reminded her. "If everyone had access to their knowledge, the folk and the wizards would be equal. And if we had that knowledge, it would be free for the asking."

Rowan stopped short. "Then this must have something to do with their power."

"Possibly." Henra turned the jewel over in her hands; it caught the light from a high-set window and flashed, once. "Or, they may see that the course of investigating the jewels will lead you to other avenues, that may in turn lead you to their secrets." She handed the blue shard back to Rowan, carefully folded her lap robe, and rose. "This is a large decision. Let's join the others."

Rowan watched her cross to the door. "Do you know what we're going to do?"

Henra turned back to her. "I know what we have to do. I don't know that we will do it."

Rowan and the Prime found most of the Archives' inhabitants lingering over bits of breakfast in a hall whose tall windows looked out to the garden on the one side, to a sweep of woody hills on the other. Bel was seated near the head of the table, and eager questioners on all sides were taking the opportunity to ply her with queries about her exotic background and the customs of the distant Outskirts. The steerswoman at the head shifted her seat in favor of the Prime, and Rowan found a chair on her right, across from Bel.

"There's our wayward child," an elderly woman beside Rowan greeted her affectionately. "It's good to see a young face again."

Bel took in the comment, then looked around the table. "Are there no other steerswomen Rowan's age?"

"Steerswomen begin by traveling," Rowan replied. "The largest part of our work is done on the road and the sea, observing and learning. Most steerswomen travel all their lives."

"Until they get too old," Keridwen put in, from the end of the table.

"Or," Arian added, "until they find some particular area of study which no longer depends on constant fact-gathering."

Bel's glance went to his ring. "You're a steerswoman?"

"Steersman," he corrected. "Yes, there are a few."

"It's not forbidden?"

Several laughed, and Arian snorted derisively. "Most men seem to be satisfied to live by their muscles. Well," he admitted, "to be fair, most men learn to live by their strength early on, and never lose the habit."

"Very few men apply when the Academy is held," Rowan added. "And few of those complete the training. Those who do, manage quite as well as the women. In fact," she said with a nod to Arian, "at present we have more steersmen than ever in our history. Three."

Someone shifted uncomfortably. Rowan looked around the table. "What is it?"

The steerswoman beside her placed a hand on her arm. "Possibly only two, dear. We've lost track of Janus."

"Last year we heard of a ship lost at sea," Henra added, "sailing from Donner to Southport." Southport, Rowan knew, had been on Janus's planned route.

"Was he on it?" Rowan asked.

"We don't know."

Rowan digested the information, then found Bel watching her. "It happens," Rowan explained.

Bel turned to Josef, seated two spaces to her left. "Are you the third steersman?"

He put up his hands in protest. "No, not me! A simple groom, beast-tender. Wouldn't be here at all but for the love of my life." He made a nimble snatch at Berry as she passed with a pitcher of water.

Berry made an equally nimble dodge. "As you can tell, my husband learns his manners from the beasts, as well." But she smiled.

"But you're Rowan's age. Shouldn't you be traveling?"

Berry placed a pitcher of water carefully on the table and took her seat next to Josef. "I'm going blind," she explained matter-of-factly.

Bel was appalled. "How awful! But can you still be a steerswoman, blind?"

"If there's a way, we'll discover it," Henra said.

"Work of the mind, that's what you want," Arian advised. "Some huge, rare, imaginative problem."

Berry nodded at him with suppressed amusement. "That's a good idea. Perhaps I'll join you in your math . . ."

"Skies, no, girl, you're not good enough—*oof!*" The elderly steerswoman next to Arian had elbowed him mightily in the ribs. "But it's true."

"Of course it's true," the woman said. "But you needn't beat her with it. She has other strengths."

Henra looked around the table, then spoke to Keridwen. "Where's Hugo?"

"Still in his room, I believe. On chill mornings, he's likely to stay there until noon."

"Tell him to come here, please."

Keridwen hurried off, and the Prime helped herself to another biscuit.

"Hugo has made a study of the wizards," Rowan explained to Bel.

Keridwen returned presently with a frail elderly man, who leaned both on her shoulder and on a walking stick as he approached. He viewed the assemblage. "What's this? A meal at this hour?" He squinted his watery blue eyes at the sky. "Don't tell me it's morning!"

Henra's smile was affectionate. "Come sit by me. I need your advice."

Rowan vacated her chair and pulled another close beside Bel. Hugo lowered himself down carefully. "Ah, now, lady, you don't fool me for a moment. It's my manly companionship you're after, admit it. And more than mere companionship, isn't it true?"

The Prime laughed lightheartedly and spoke as if reciting the lines of a familiar jest. "Now, Hugo, what can you mean? You know you're far too old for me."

"Oh, so you say now! But the gap shrinks, they tell me, as you grow older. A few years from now you'll join me by the fireside, and we'll toast our toes together, and dream of things we might have done. And do a few of them, as well."

Rowan took in Bel's astonished expression, recognizing her surprise as the same that she herself had felt when first seeing the steerswomen behave so informally with each other. She leaned toward the Outskirter. "We're not an aristocracy," Rowan explained quietly, "and we're not an army, or a religion, either. Whatever doesn't affect our work, doesn't matter."

As if to illustrate the point, Henra made one small gesture, and the table fell instantly to attentive silence. Hugo sat the slightest bit taller, and the wry humor slipped from his face, replaced by the intelligent, waiting expression of the perfect steersman.

Henra spoke to the group. "Rowan was attacked by a wizard's man."

Every face turned to Rowan. In a visible rapid wave, their shock turned to seriousness, and they waited, silently, for more information. Only Josef made a sign; his fist slammed on the table, once. No one looked at him.

Henra continued. "It was one day's travel south of Five Corners."

The elderly woman next to Arian spoke. "You're certain he was a wizard's man?"

"At the inn I saw five Red soldiers. I recognized him as one of that five," Rowan replied. The woman nodded. No one questioned Rowan's ability to recognize the face of a man seen once, in passing, as part of a crowd.

Henra turned to Hugo. "Which wizard controls that area?"

He sat quietly a moment, rheumy blue eyes flicking at the action of his thoughts. "That's difficult to say, lady. Olin, north and east of Five Corners, he's Red these days. Or was, as of winter. Five Corners, that's at the limit of his area, as clear as these things can be made out."

Rowan spoke up. "No one seemed surprised to see wizard's men in the tavern."

"With the recent clash, there must be a lot, traveling to their homes. Five Corners is a likely stop for any of Olin's men, returning."

"I didn't know he kept soldiers."

"Ah, yes, well, neither did I, until he sent troops against Corvus and Abremio. It means he must have a keep somewhere, and we've been assuming he didn't."

"Don't all wizards have keeps?" Bel asked.

"No, not at all. Jannik, for instance. All he has is his house in Donner. Mind you, no one's ever been inside." He rubbed his nose thoughtfully. "Now, Olin, he's always been especially confusing. Seen rarely, never in the same place twice, always alone. Often the only way to know he's there is by the sudden appearance of some magical event."

Henra leaned forward, intent. "Might Five Corners be his, these days?"

"Hard to tell. His boundaries have always been especially vague. It's not Jannik's; it might be no one's, or Shammer and Dhree's."

Rowan remembered Artos's complaints. "The new Red holding?"

"Right. They're two, working together as one; I don't understand the arrangement. They're Red." He turned to Henra. "They're the culprits, I believe, or somehow wrapped up in this. I don't know that Five Corners is theirs, but it's possible, and they're the only new variable in the equation." Hugo addressed himself to Bel. "Understand, the wizards and the Steerswomen don't like each other, but there hasn't been violence between us for centuries. We can't get rid of each other, so we tolerate each other. But now a steerswoman has been attacked by a wizard's man—Rowan, could he have been acting on his own?"

Rowan thought briefly, checking over her conclusions. "No. There were five wizard's men at the inn; there are five roads away from the inn. They left before Bel and I did; whatever road we took, we would have met one. This was planned."

Berry looked around, as if searching the faces she could not clearly see. "There are other steerswomen traveling in Shammer and Dhree's holding. Why was Rowan attacked, and no one else?"

Henra nodded to Rowan. With all eyes on her, Rowan pulled out the little leather sack, lifted its string over her head, and opened it. "Here's the other new variable in the equation," Henra said.

Hugo took the jewel and scrutinized it while the Prime recounted Rowan's story with perfect accuracy.

"Wizard's make, for certain," he said when she finished. He turned it over in his hands again. "I can't think of any jeweler's process that could do this. Sarah—" He passed the jewel down across the table to the elderly steerswoman on Arian's left.

She peered at it closely. "It's built in layers—the silver-colored backing, then the gem. The lines are etched, so that the metal lies both on the surface and into it." She scraped the edge of the fragment with one fingernail. "The last surface is like very thin glass, but no glass can be made that thin. Strange texture . . ." She passed it diagonally.

The next woman was pale and delicately beautiful, the only sign of her age the silver glittering in her ebony hair. She looked at the jewel carefully, then closed her eyes, rubbing her thumb across the smooth surface. "Oily . . ." She looked at it again. "It's made of oil, somehow, or has oil in it. If fine olive oil were perfectly clear, and somehow made solid, it might be like this."

Sarah took the jewel again, cleared a space in the center of the table, and placed it there, standing to get a better vantage. The other steerswomen shifted and leaned closer. "That's a good point. You can't polish anything to this smoothness. I believe that top surface was poured on as a liquid, then solidified, somehow."

"Magically," Bel put in confidently.

"Perhaps," Sarah admitted.

The Prime spoke to Bel. "May we see your belt?"

The Outskirter stood to remove it, and it was passed around.

"They were all found in the same place, far in the Outskirts," Rowan explained. "It's the largest concentration I've heard about; I think something could be learned by going there, to see."

"With a wizard on your trail," Berry observed. Josef winced.

"One or more." Every face turned to Hugo. "Think for a moment about Jannik. His control over the dragons isn't complete, but it's almost so. Could another wizard send a spell to break it? Sometimes one or two nestlings can escape and cause trouble, especially the tiniest ones. But Saranna's Inn was—where, the center of town?"

"Not far from the harbor," Rowan said. "Tilemaker's Street."

"And the mud flats are at the edge of town. That's seven miles they had to travel, through the streets—no, isn't there a shallow gully that runs near Tilemaker's Street?"

"That's right."

"And how many dragons were there?"

Rowan counted. "Seven, that I saw myself. More outside, which I didn't see. Someone reported fifty, but the layman's eyes can fool him, in emergencies. At a guess, at least twenty-five, total."

Hugo shook his head fractionally. "I don't believe that can happen."

Bel looked around the now-silent table. "Then Jannik was in on it, Rowan guessed."

"I saw it was a possibility," Rowan said.

Hugo was deep in thought. "Two wizards, cooperating across a line of mutual hatred . . ."

"We need to decide what to do," Henra said.

Arian was surprised. "Decide? One decides when one has options. Where are there options here?"

"Are there none?" She concentrated on Arian. "Very well, what do you see happening next?"

"Rowan continues her investigations. She'll have to be very alert, if she's attracted the wizards' attentions . . ." He trailed off. "But if they're determined, they'll get her eventually."

"Then we must make this move more quickly," Sarah put in. "If we all work on it, and if we send out word to those on the road—"

Berry interrupted. "Then we each become the same threat that Rowan is. And, collectively, the entire order of Steerswomen becomes a threat."

"But if we work fast enough—"

"How fast is fast enough?" Keridwen challenged. "It can't be done instantaneously."

Watching the Prime, Rowan realized that Henra saw an answer, but was patiently waiting for the rest of the steerswomen to duplicate her reasoning; she wanted the chain of thought to be clear in their minds, wanted it to be each person's own possession.

"What is the most basic statement of the problem?" Rowan asked, half to herself, musing.

That was an often-repeated phrase in the early education of a steerswoman-in-training, and conversation stopped in surprise at Rowan's presenting it to steerswomen of such advanced experience. But Berry, not many years from her own traineeship, caught the mood. "Investigating the jewels is dangerous."

Henra encouraged them. "Two options, on this level."

"Work in danger," Rowan said, "or abandon the investigation."

Response was immediate, from several corners. "We mustn't abandon it." "We have to learn all we can." "We can't let the wizards rule us." "No one controls us."

The Prime nodded. "That choice is rejected. We work in danger. The options are two . . ."

Keridwen considered. "Accept danger, or change the situation . . ."

"Accepting the danger is accepting death—and incidentally, an end to any investigating," someone noted.

"The first choice is rejected. How can we change the situation?" Henra prompted.

"Find the source of the danger and counter it," another steerswoman offered.

"The source of the danger is the wizards," Hugo noted. "We can't counter them."

"No," Rowan realized. "The source is their knowledge of our actions."

There was a silence. Bel looked around the table in perplexity. Annoyed, she said, "It's obvious. You have to work in secret. Why is that so hard to see?"

"Because it is so hard to accept," Henra replied.

"It is absolutely opposite to everything we do and believe in," Hugo expanded.

She would have to deny information, Rowan realized. She would have to refuse questions, or—worse yet—give false answers.

Henra surveyed every face around the table, then spoke carefully. "Rowan would have to travel to the Outskirts under an assumed identity. No one must know who she is, what she seeks, or that she's a steerswoman."

No one spoke, and Bel looked at them in confusion. "But what's the problem?"

Abruptly, Rowan said, "I won't do it." Faces turned to her. "Lady, I understand, truly I do," she continued, half pleading, "but I can't agree. There must be some other way. To lie, to walk the earth *lying* . . . Humankind needs truth. We all know that; we need it like air and water and food, to survive, to function in the world . . . I'd be like a poison, twisting things everywhere I went, *hurting* people." She laid her hands against her cheeks and shook her head. "No."

Henra took it all in, considering. "Arian? Would you do it?"

"Me?" He looked up, surprised. "Well, I don't like the whole idea, but I do think it's the best solution. And someone has to do it." Then he smiled. "Oh, you're clever, Henra. Most of the folk don't even know there are steersmen among the steerswomen. I'd never be suspected. But when it comes down to the actual doing of the thing . . ." He thought. "I feel much as Rowan does. I think it would . . . pain me. And my work here . . ." He sighed. "Try to find someone else. Please, exhaust every possibility, and if you find no one, then yes."

Henra nodded, then looked to her left. "Berry?"

She was startled. "What?"

"Would you do it?"

She stared around in stunned disbelief. "Me?" Then, slowly, she said, "Yes . . . yes, send me." She spoke to Henra, her voice urgent. "I'll do it. I'll do anything. I'll lie a thousand times. I'll steal if you ask it. Anything! Please, send me . . ." She gazed up into the sky, her dim eyes bright with tears. "On the road, one last time . . ."

"She's blind," Sarah protested.

Berry turned on her. "I'm not blind, not yet! I can see shapes and colors. I won't walk into a tree; I won't fall off the edge of the road." She addressed them all. "And I know those roads, and I can read a map, held close."

"But she can't observe," Arian said. "And she couldn't spot, say, a jewel imbedded in a cliff. In new territory she could get lost."

The Prime said nothing; she was looking at Josef.

He nodded slowly, then turned to his wife, taking both her hands. "When the time comes for eyes, you'll have mine."

"You'd go with me?"

"No." He laughed a little. "I'd *stay* with you, wherever in the world you may be. You and me, we'll walk under the stars together."

She touched his face and moved close to study his expression. Then she leaned her bowed head against his shoulder.

Josef's eyes met Henra's, and his face was full of calm entreaty.

Henra spoke. "Josef is not a steersman, but with Berry to interpret what he saw, something could be learned. Perhaps not enough, but something. And no one would guess that she was a steerswoman."

"Rowan."

Rowan turned to the Prime.

"You're still the best choice," Henra said. "You're familiar with the jewels, you're highly observant, flexible and imaginative in thought. We would learn the most, if you were the one to go." She held up her hand. "I understand your disagreement. But I want you to consider this: It will be done. Won't you help us do it the best way we can?"

The Prime stood. "Don't answer. Please think. We'll all speak again this evening." The chairs shuffled, and the steerswomen dispersed one by one, until there was only Bel, watching Rowan, and Rowan, silently watching Josef whispering gentle words to Berry.

At last Rowan rose and walked away.

10

"*I* don't see what the problem is."

They were walking down the winding dirt path that led from the Archives to the riverside below. Oak trees surrounded them, gnarled roots invading the edges of the path.

"Don't you want to find out about these jewels?" Bel continued.

"Yes. But I'm just not willing to lie."

Bel snapped a twig she was carrying and tossed the pieces into the underbrush. "I don't understand you. You were willing to learn about them, even if it put you in danger. But you won't do a simple thing like lying."

Rowan felt a return of the sudden, sharp need that had sent her out of the stone walls of the Archives, a need for a sweep of air that knew no obstructions, for the unbounded sky above her. She walked a little faster, to escape the net of tree branches overhead. "It's not such a simple thing." Of its own accord, a part of her began trying to formulate an explanation, a calm steerswoman's explanation; but the part of her that held the information for that answer was churning with confused emotion.

"Ever since I became a steerswoman—no," she stopped, surprised. "Ever since I was a child . . ." Her voice trailed off, her mind sifting through memories like hands sifting through chaff, seeking a single grain of wheat.

When had it happened, when had she learned to care what was true and what was not? Children lied, they all did, and ranks of casual lies crowded into her thoughts. No, I didn't drop the eggs. No, I didn't tell Father. Yes, I finished all my work.

One single lie stood in high relief, not a great lie, but one that had lasted long into her adolescence. Periodically, she would leave the house and fields, taking some small bit of food, and make the long trek to the farthest of the funeral groves, the last bit of green before the desert took true possession of the land. She would explain that she was going to visit her uncle's tree, and the family would say quietly to each other, "Poor Rowan, his death affected her so badly." But it was not true. She went from a need to see something other than the house, the yard, that dusty path leading to the town of Umber. She knew everything in her world, knew it too well, and there was nothing more that her mind or heart could do with it.

But north . . . Past the groves, there was land no hands had touched. Raw earth, lacking only water, fertilization, and seed. It waited there, waited out the centuries for the slow spread of humankind. It was emptiness to the limits of the sky. At last that view, too, became familiar, but she still returned, without clearly knowing why.

She needed to see different things, change in the land and in the faces of people. But there was a stronger need, one she discovered the day that Keridwen had come to Umber in her own travels. Rowan discovered that the steerswoman *knew* things, and speaking to her, she realized that there was another landscape, one to be traveled endlessly, the limits of which she could never exhaust.

So Rowan and Keridwen had sat together late into the night, Rowan asking first about places, then about people, then about the ideas of people, then about the idea of ideas . . . And Keridwen's an-

swers had grown richer and deeper, as her expression changed from indulgence, to surprise, to interest.

Sometime near midnight Rowan had realized that the aspect of the
discussion had changed to that of a conversation between equals; not
equals of knowledge or of experience, but of method of thought. They
shared a perspective, a deeply rooted way of approaching life. The
night ended with Keridwen telling her of the Academy to take place
in Wulfshaven some four years from that time. Rowan spent those
four years learning to read and write, to do sums, and scrupulously attempting to chart the land she knew, in the hopes of gaining some
skill for her training to come.

She had spent her life alone in her strangeness, and had met only
one other person like herself. When she joined the Academy, she was
like an exile who had returned home.

Looking around, Rowan discovered that she and Bel had arrived at
the riverbank and were seated on a rotting log near its edge. The Wulf
spread out before them, flat and serene. A thin haze of clouds was
moving in from the west, and high above, a mere dark speck, a hawk
hung motionless.

"Truth," Rowan said to herself, then turned to Bel. The Outskirter
was watching her with concern. She had not intruded on Rowan's
thoughts, but was carefully waiting, with true warrior's patience. She
knew that Rowan had to follow her own path to her own answers, and
that the answers, once found, would be shared.

"If you're traveling down a road, and you ask for directions, and
someone lies about them, what happens?" Rowan asked.

"You get lost."

"If you want to know when to plant your fields, and someone lies,
what happens?"

"You go hungry."

"If there's a troop of bandits coming, and no one tells you?"

"You die."

"People *need* truth! They need it to be happy, to know what to do,
to *live*!" Rowan rose. A single step took her to the water, and she stood
with her gray boots mere inches away from the tiny lapping waves as
she gazed out at the line of trees on the opposite shore.

"What you say is too simple," Bel said. "Some things are less important than others."

Rowan looked up at the clouding sky, where the motionless hawk still hung. She saw with the whole of her vision equally, and her hearing brought her what her eyes could not see, the shape of space behind her. Lightly moving wind brushed her arms, and damp air floated up from the river before her, against her face and body. She sensed the crushed weeds that lay under the soles of her boots, and the solid earth beneath. She felt the weight of her own body, muscle and bone, connecting her to that earth, the limits of her skin defining the space she occupied. Simultaneous, interlocking, all senses added up in her being to a single perception, a single clear instant. The whole of her surroundings came to her in one perfect moment, all of it real, and all of it true.

"They're going to take it all away," she said.

Bel said nothing.

Some wizard was changing the nature of Rowan's existence. She could either accept an arbitrary limit to her mind's reach, and so be less than a steerswoman, or deceive, and so be no steerswoman at all.

She loved it too much. Less was better than none.

Abruptly, inconsistency caught at her mind: the hawk—it had not moved.

Rowan began to analyze what her senses had brought her. The breeze was from the southwest. Would it be different higher up? There should be a downdraft of cooler air over the river; a hawk would have to beat and circle to maintain the same perspective. The forest was alive with small game; a hawk would have found prey by then.

"Get back," she told Bel, and quickly moved away from the river's edge.

They stopped among the trees, Rowan trying to see the speck through the new green leaves above. Bel had no sword, but a wicked knife had appeared in her hand. "What is it?"

Rowan spotted it. "We're being watched. Or the Archives are."

"By a wizard?"

"Who else can fly?"

Bel peered up. "Will he attack?"

"I don't know. It hasn't moved. Perhaps we weren't seen, or weren't recognized."

Bel nodded. "Then it's watching the Archives. We should tell them."

"Yes. Let's keep off the path." Rowan led the way through the forest, accurately cutting around the twists of the dirt track, first walking, then running.

They entered by way of the stables, breathless from the climb. Inside, Josef was currying Artos's horse, Berry seated on a barrel nearby.

Rowan stopped, trying to calm her breathing. "Berry," she said. "Berry, I'm sorry, I'm going to do it."

Berry and Josef exchanged a glance; then he silently went back to his work. Berry rose. "What made you change your mind?"

"The Archives are being watched. By something that flies."

"It's not just me, anymore," Rowan told the resident steerswomen. They were assembled in the chart room, eight women and two men, some in chairs, some seated casually on the edges of the sturdy copying tables, one standing by the window, occasionally scanning the sky. To one side of the room, Josef and Bel stood watching the proceedings.

"I was thinking about my own life," Rowan continued. "I love the steerswoman's life, and I wasn't willing to change it. But first this restriction, and now this . . . spying . . ." She was standing before the three steps that led to the master chart. She spread her hands in a broad gesture. "How long before we become so changed that none of us are steerswomen anymore? The whole way of life is threatened, for every one of us. I . . ." She paused, shaping her thoughts. "I can't stand for it. I have to try to stop it, whatever it may take. Or at the very least, I have to know why."

Sarah smiled with a teacher's pride. "Spoken like a steerswoman: she has to know why."

There were quiet comments around the room as they consulted each other briefly. Suddenly weary, Rowan sat down on the lowest step and watched them, waiting.

Henra stood and addressed the gathering. "This is no small thing. We all will have a hand in this, I'm afraid, and if someone asks, it would be best if we could refrain from revealing Rowan's mission . . ." She trailed off, uncharacteristically hesitant. Rowan recognized on the Prime's face the same confused pain Rowan felt at the prospect of living with deceit. As Arian had said, when it came to the doing of the thing . . .

Abruptly, Rowan remembered a simple bit of medical knowledge learned from Maranne in Wulfshaven: a poisoned limb is amputated.

"No." Faces turned toward her. "Steerswomen mustn't lie. I have to resign the order."

Shock filled the room, followed by protests. Amid the babble of voices, Rowan felt suddenly empty, a hollow shape of flesh with no center and no identity.

Bel and Josef turned perplexed gazes at each other. Speaking above the noise, Bel asked, "But can't she join again, when her mission is finished?"

"It's never been done," Arian said.

"Not true," Hugo put in, and the people quieted to hear him. "When I was training, there was a steerswoman, named Silva—"

Henra nodded. "Yes."

"She mapped the nearer western mountains," Keridwen supplied.

"That's right. But that was later." Hugo continued. "While on the road in the east, she fell in love with a farmer there. She left us to marry and live with him."

"And he died," the Prime said.

"Pneumonia. But his love was all that kept her there, and she became unhappy. She fostered her children to his sister and came back to us."

"And did very good work," Keridwen added, her eyes on the master chart, where the near edge of the western mountains showed clear and accurate.

The Prime turned back to Rowan, and she was like a woman released from some great pain. "Will that suit you?"

Rowan nodded mutely. She felt distant, as if she had already departed and was on some long unknown road with no guidance.

She looked down at her left hand and saw the silver ring on her middle finger, the band with that odd half twist that made it a thing both mysterious and logical: an object of three dimensions, yet possessing only one face, one edge, folded back into reality by the simple laws of geometry. Without thinking, she removed it and held it in the palm of her hand. It seemed weightless.

More quickly, as if by hesitating she would lose her commitment, she slipped the thin gold chain over her head and let it dangle from her fingers. She looked at Henra.

"Hold on to them," the Prime said, "and wear them again when you can."

Rowan placed them both in the leather sack on its thong, nestling beside the uncanny jewel. Tucked under her blouse, the sack felt faintly heavier, a promise set aside.

Henra sighed, then reorganized herself, efficient. "You'll have to choose another name—and remember to answer to it."

Looking faintly puzzled, Keridwen added, "She should wear a different cloak, as well. We're not the only people who use gray felt cloaks, but each one of us does."

"That green cloak she arrived in," Hugo suggested.

"That will do," Henra agreed. Passing Rowan as she climbed the stairs, she walked to the master chart. "Now, as to her route: she'll have to avoid both Five Corners and Donner—"

"But that's not enough." Heads turned to the side of the room, where Bel stepped forward from her place by the wall. Behind her, Josef crossed his arms and nodded grimly. The Outskirter continued. "She can't just go, and dress differently, and not use her own name. She needs a reason for going, something that no one would think twice about. She needs something else to *be*." She scanned the faces in amazement. "Don't you people know how to protect yourselves at all?"

The accusation pushed past Rowan's weariness of spirit; she discovered herself angry. "Yes, we do," she said vehemently, then with awkwardness corrected her choice of words. "Yes, they do. Steerswomen can protect themselves from bandits and cutpurses on the road. They can protect themselves from wild beasts. They can protect themselves from those who would abuse their good natures. We've never had to, never wanted to deceive."

Bel stood before her, solid and sensible: "Time to learn."

Suddenly, without derision, Josef laughed. "Look at you, a bunch of steerswomen," he said. "You know so much, but the one thing you don't know about is lying." He held up his index finger, like an instructor. "Well, I can tell Rowan how to fool people. The best way to lie is to tell the truth."

The steerswomen looked at each other in perplexity. Bel expanded on Josef's statement. "That's right, you say true things—except, you leave some things out. That way, the person takes what you've said and makes his own conclusions—the wrong ones, because of what's missing."

Josef gave her an affirming nod. "And that's your lie. And the second best way is to tell the truth—something obvious, something the other person knows down to his bones—and add your lie onto it, so long as it fits in."

"The person knows that the part he can check is true, and if the rest makes sense, he'll believe it," Bel said.

"And the last good way to lie is to say nothing. Let the other person guess as much as he likes, and when he's dead wrong," he said with a smile, "you tell him how clever he is."

The group relaxed. The alien concept of deception had been reduced to principles. One thing every steerswoman understood was the application of principles.

More confident, Henra said, "Very well. Without compromising ourselves, we can help Rowan by seeing for her what's unsaid." She gestured. "Rowan, stand up please." Rowan rose and stood before them, the great master chart looming at her back. "Now, everyone, imagine you've never seen her. Try to remove that information from your mind. What can you tell, just by looking at her? What is this woman?"

Rowan waited under their discerning gazes. What was she? Ignoring her present pain, she thought back to her childhood, before she had met Keridwen, when no one around her shared that most basic part of her nature. What had she been then?

Nothing. She felt a return of that emptiness, that blank solitude and unnamed yearning that had characterized her life before. She felt, again, like the child who saw too much, thought too quickly, and had no one who could understand her.

"She travels, constantly, outdoors," Sarah noted. "See how dark her skin is, how streaked her hair. And she travels on foot; look at her stance, and the development of her legs."

"The upper part of her body is not developed," Arian said. "She's not a laborer; she doesn't live by the use of her muscles."

"Her fingers are ink-stained," Henra said. "It's the sort of staining that lives in the cracks of one's hands and can't be removed. She uses a pen, every single day."

"She might be a scribe," Keridwen suggested.

"A scribe who travels?" Arian said. "Not likely."

"Notice how composed she is," Hugo put in, tilting his head in study. "This is a woman who knows she can handle whatever she gets into. And see how she watches us? She's thinking, and she's used to thinking. She's used to figuring out for herself what to do."

"That spells steerswoman to me," the dark-haired woman noted.

"Try to put that out of your mind," Henra said.

Rowan listened to the information, considering the clues as if they applied to some stranger, grateful for a problem to occupy her loneliness. A scribe would not travel, not often. Would a clerk? A student?

Berry addressed Rowan. "Say something."

"Say something?"

"Anything, just speak. Describe the weather."

Rowan looked out the window. "It's a beautiful, cloudless day. It's comfortably cool, but the sunlight coming in heats the stone floor. I can feel a draft from the warm air rising." She realized that she had noticed more than the average person would, and had supplied the information casually. She would have to stop that.

Hugo made a wry face. "Well, by that voice, she's educated."

"No," Berry said. "Or, not necessarily. In the north, they have that careful manner of speech, even among the uneducated. And the crispness of her consonants, and the rhythm, that confirms it. She's from the north, past the western curve of the Long North Road. Far north, I'd say, from the sound of her vowels. I think she's from one of the farthest settlements, by the Red Desert. I'd place the town nearest as Umber."

Bel looked at Rowan in amazement. "Is that all true?"

Rowan winced. "Exactly."

Henra was disturbed. "That's far too precise. She advertises her origins."

"But Berry's using a steerswoman's ear," Arian said. "Would the average person notice this?"

Everyone turned to Josef. "Average person, eh?" he said wryly. "All right, well, she sounds a little . . . foreign, but not so much. I wouldn't think twice. Say it again?" Rowan repeated the sentences. Josef nodded. "Maybe educated. Sort of . . . stiff."

"Bel?"

"You all sound foreign."

Henra nodded. "Perhaps that will do, then. As she'll be traveling in the south, it may be sufficient to simply admit she's from somewhere in the north. Bel, take Rowan's place for a moment."

They exchanged places, Bel eyeing the group with suspicion. Then she stood before them, a solid, wide-legged stance, strong arms relaxed, hands comfortably by her sides. Her chin was tilted up in unvoiced challenge.

Rowan looked away briefly, filling her eyes with the gray of stone walls, clearing her mind of preconceptions. Then she looked back, with a fresh point of view.

She saw it immediately, and her voice and three others spoke together. "A warrior."

"Undeniably," Henra admitted.

"A solitary warrior," Hugo amended. "One not used to regimentation."

"And she'll be on the road," Berry pointed out. "A traveling warrior; that means a mercenary."

Rowan took that information and tried to integrate it with what had been said about her own appearance, feeling a touch of surprise, as if she had expected all her steerswoman's abilities to vanish with her ring and chain. She speculated. What would bring two such people together? Why would they travel? What would be their relationship?

It fell together with the perfection of a discovered truth. So perfect, and yet so untrue; it was like an immense joke, and she laughed, bitterly. The steerswomen looked at her in amazement.

Rowan spread her hands and addressed the group. "I've got it."

11

*H*e had killed a man, his first week on the road.

He was a little surprised at how calmly he had done it. He had killed him as simply as he would kill a wolf, and it was a wolf, really, a bandit. The gods only knew what the man expected to gain

from a boy like Willam; just an easy victim, perhaps. Still, Willam had
heard the sound, strung his bow with a mindless speed, and let fly as
soon as he saw the knife. He actually had not felt afraid at all.

He was smart enough not to trust to a speed and cold-bloodedness
he had only felt the once. But he began to worry about the wisdom of
keeping to the deserted back trails. Close to his home village, he had
thought it best. He knew he was conspicuous: a big lad with red-blond
hair, brown eyes light enough to be called copper by most, and at fourteen years well on his way to acquiring a blacksmith's burly arms and
shoulders. One sentence was enough to identify him to anyone he
knew, and he surely did not want word to get back to his father. Not
that he thought his father might follow. Plenty of young people left
home; Will had just left a bit sooner than most.

He had been sorry to leave, and frightened, as well. Strange, how
one could be frightened of something big and vague, like leaving
home alone, and be calm face-to-face with a real bandit. Maybe that
was how it was in life. Willam didn't know.

Those last few weeks at home had been too strange, too busy to
allow much time or space for worry: trying to go about his days as normal, doing his work, then spending every spare moment in his shack in
the yard, even slipping out at night, to make his preparations. No one
bothered him in his shack. There had been enough accidents over the
years that people had the sense to stay away. If they wanted him, they
always stood at a good distance and called out. They were cautious.

He was cautious, too. He had not been, when he was very young,
but experience had taught him harshly—taught him to think carefully, move slowly, control as much as possible. One had to take risks
to learn, but he discovered that if he was careful about everything else,
then the one risk he took would not hurt him. He could do almost the
same thing, over and over, taking just one different risk each time, and
in the end he learned what he wanted to know. And he knew it all the
way down to its bones.

Other people didn't think like that, he knew; they acted, for the
most part, on impulse and emotion. Perhaps that was why what he did
was so incomprehensible to them, and sometimes frightening. Still,
when they needed something special, it was to him that they came.

But magic did not help him on the road. His bow helped him. And
caution.

Caution told him to stay to the back trails as long as he could, then caution told him when it was better to take a main road. Unfortunately, by that time, he was lost.

Leaving his village, he had struck northeast, taking his bearings from the Eastern Guidestar at night, doing the best he could by guesswork during the day. Eventually he met the river Wulf. Actually, he thought he had met it a dozen times; any river he crossed was the Wulf to him, until he reached the next one. When he finally did come to its banks and stood gaping in astonishment at its wild speed and impossible width, he felt more than a little like an ignorant village boy. Bitterly, he reminded himself that that was exactly what he was. However fantastic his mission, however high and mighty his plans, it was best to keep that fact in mind.

A riverman took one of Willam's small supply of coppers in return for a trip across, and Will spent the passage carefully protecting his pack from the spray slapped up from the windy water. On the other side, a careful check proved that the contents were safe and dry.

From there he began to travel due east, and within the hour he was hopelessly adrift in the trackless woody uplands. He beat his way cross-country for a full day until he found a path. It went south, but he took it.

But soon he was no longer traveling alone. He met a merchant on the path, and she had a very good idea: travel south to the main road and try to connect with an east-going caravan. Will did not have the fare, but no one would stop him if he wanted to tag along. Naturally, he would not be under their protection, but it would take quite an attack to really threaten a caravan. Will was glad of the suggestion; perhaps a bit less glad at the company.

As they walked along, the little donkey kicked up a bit, and Willam danced to the left, out of the way of the hooves. Astride it, the merchant struggled with the reins and cursed in quiet aggrieved tones. Will smiled. He liked the donkey, and he didn't like the merchant.

"Attise, can't you control that beast?" the merchant's bodyguard complained. Attise sent back one of her flat glances and said nothing, still maintaining her precious dignity. Willam hoped the donkey would throw her.

"I can't see why he should complain," the bodyguard continued to Will. "Her master used to ride him, and from what I hear, Attise is a feather by comparison."

Willam spoke from the side of his mouth. "Give her time. She'll catch up."

The bodyguard looked at Will in surprise, then threw back her head and laughed. "Ho, Attise!" she called. "Why aren't you fat, like the other merchants?"

"I'm not a merchant," Attise replied in a carefully indifferent voice. "Technically."

"She's a clerk," the bodyguard confided to Willam. "Technically."

It was the bodyguard, Sala, who made the traveling enjoyable. She was cheerful and absolutely straightforward. She said exactly what she thought. Perhaps it was her skill at arms that gave her confidence, but it seemed to be more than that; she was a woman who looked the world straight in the eye.

She reminded Will of a cat who lived in a gristmill in his hometown. The cat, small and solid, all efficient muscle, greeted visitors with benign good nature and loved to be petted and entertained. But its greatest delight was battle; it killed rats and thieving birds with heart-stopping speed and precision, and it was always on watch for more opportunities for murder. Sala was like that, Willam thought: cold-bloodedly amiable. He wondered with a trace of boyish excitement if he would ever have the opportunity to see her in action.

But remembering the cat made him remember his little sister. She had loved that cat, and she would squeal with glee whenever she saw it, toddling toward it on her chunky legs. The cat, perhaps wisely, stayed just out of her reach, friendliness struggling against natural caution at the girl's awkwardness, and the pair would weave their way endlessly about the room, to the amusement of onlookers. She was the only girl in the family, and so bright, so mischievous, a constant amazement. Will's love for the child was total, unconditional.

He had often asked his father if they might find a kitten for her, and he really believed his father was about to, just before that day when two of Abremio's men appeared. Then the girl was gone, kittens were forgotten, and Will was left with only his ever more silent father, a brother too old to feel close to—and a dark, obsessive hatred for the wizard who had stolen the only person he truly loved, confiscating her as if she were some object.

It occurred to Willam that if the people in The Crags and the surrounding villages were more like cats, more like Sala, Abremio could
not simply do whatever he pleased.

The people in The Crags were like Attise, and perhaps that was why
he disliked her so immediately: he had the villager's disdain for the folk
of the city proper. They never said anything directly but always danced
around the subject with flowery phrases, looking down their noses at a
country person as if he smelled bad but they were too polite to tell him.
They were more concerned with how they dressed and how they
seemed, than with what they really were, or what they could do.

Attise spoke plainly enough, when she spoke, but she had that
same way of seeming to watch and judge a person, and watch and
judge herself, as if matching her behavior with some rigid internal
standard. It made him uncomfortable. And she was never sponta-
neous; everything she did seemed planned. Will had the feeling that
it was all for show.

For instance, Attise had a map, and a good one. But whenever they
came to any crossroads absolutely nothing else would do but that they
all stop while she carefully dismounted, drew the map from its place
in her baggage, and laboriously consulted it. Why she did not keep it
more convenient, or why she did not try to memorize part of the route,
Will had no idea. She would study it at length, no trace of confusion
or uncertainty tainting her expression, pack it away, remount, and say,
"This way," in a voice of absolute authority. The exercise soon became
tedious, and Will became more and more certain that she did it only
to appear important.

"You shouldn't be so hard on her."

Will came back from his thoughts and found that Sala was walking close beside him, Attise and the donkey some dozen feet ahead.
"What?" He had been watching the merchant, and his distaste must
have been showing on his face.

"Attise. She's really not so terrible. She's just in a bad situation."

Will glowered at the merchant's back again. "More like she carries
a bad situation around with her."

Sala considered. "The problem," she said carefully, "is that she
doesn't know how to act."

"You'd never guess it."

She nodded. "That's the idea. She's really just a clerk, as I said. She's used to traveling around in her master's wake, doing his figuring, keeping his accounts. She knows about his business, but she's never had to deal with people, or decide anything. But when her master broke his leg, just when he was about to expand his business—" She paused, looking confused at the complexities of finance. "I don't really understand how it works. Somehow, they have the money now, and they won't have it later . . . I don't see how that can be . . ." She gave it up and shrugged. "Well, Attise knew the right things, and no one else did. So he sent her."

"And you went along?"

Sala shifted her pack to a more comfortable position and tested the convenience of her sword hilt. "I'm for hire. And a merchant doesn't travel alone. Not if she likes living."

Up ahead, Attise was affectedly scanning the landscape, her face carefully impassive. "Well, she doesn't act as if she does," Will said. "I mean, she doesn't seem to enjoy anything."

"She doesn't," Sala conceded. "She's too worried. If the new customers thought she was inexperienced, they'd try to take advantage of her. So she has to look as if she knows what she's doing, and act like a merchant, but she's never had to consider that before. She doesn't know how. And she doesn't like it, not at all. She likes numbers."

Will thought about it. Sala's explanation made sense, a little. If the merchant acted as she naturally did, she would give herself away.

For a moment, the whole thing looked different, as if he had a bird's-eye view. Attise actually was watching herself and putting on a fake manner. It showed, really, when he thought about it.

But did she have to make everyone else unhappy? "She'd probably do better business if she let people like her," Will grumbled.

The bodyguard tilted her head and gave him a lopsided grin. "She has money. She doesn't need friends."

But Willam still did not like the way Attise looked at him. At first, Will had tried to engage her in conversation, but finally gave it up; not that she would not reply, but she didn't seem to encourage it, answering in the shortest phrases possible, with no proper opening for reply. And sometimes she would give him a strange look, a slow calculating stare, as if she were adding things up, then turn away silently. It was Sala with whom Willam conversed.

When they first met, she had asked him where he was traveling from, and he had replied in what he hoped was an offhand manner with the name of one of the towns he had passed through. Over her shoulder Attise gave him that look and then went back to blandly viewing the scenery, and the conversation lagged, then limped in the wake of her brief attention. It was nothing more than one look, but it acted on Willam like a bucket of water over his head. Sala was amused.

Somewhat later the merchant spoke up casually. "I've been through your town, with my master. Late last year. Do you know Corey, the blacksmith there?"

Will had prepared for that sort of thing. "No, I didn't often get into the town proper. There was a lot of work on the farm, and not much time for what my dad calls 'foolishness.' But when I was little, my mother sometimes sent me in to the weaver's there. Perhaps you met him? He's a tall thin man, with dust-colored hair. Michael." Will had carefully studied the town as he passed through, thinking it would be a good place to claim as his home, once he was far enough from it.

She looked at him. "No." Then she turned away, and Will was briefly disturbed. He could not tell if she had made up that business about the blacksmith just to test him, or if she believed him about the weaver. It gave him a turn; his own father was a blacksmith.

At one of the crossroads they came across a party of tinkers, with racks of wares on display. Attise halted the party and made a great show of examining everything the tinkers had, though her utter disinterest was deadeningly obvious. The tinkers saw that immediately and matched her for bland disdain. Willam found the whole thing tiresome.

But at one point she was studying a beautiful embroidered blouse, and she turned to him almost casually. "What do you think of this?"

The weight of the fabric in his hands, the stiff, intricate embroidery, brought a rush of familiarity to Willam, and a touch of homesickness. It was the work of the Kundekin, the kind of lovely handwork with which those mysterious craftspeople filled their idle hours. But for all its beauty, it was common in their opinion, mere exercise to sharpen the eye and hand. Near their enclave in The Crags it could be got cheaply. It was practically given away, else their closets would be full of the stuff. The tinker was charging twenty times its worth.

Willam felt brief pleasure at seeing such a familiar item, then a small shock when he realized that Attise had chosen to ask *him* about it.

He saw that she was giving him that look again. He said nothing, but she returned the blouse to the tinker. "I believe," she said, "that I'll do better by going directly to the source." Her mouth made a smile, but her eyes did not, and she turned away.

As they continued down the road, Willam's mind was spinning. Attise suspected he was lying, that he was not what he claimed, even knew he was from The Crags. But she was doing nothing, saying nothing. Why? Was he truly so obvious? Was she sneering at him, inside? At that thought Will flushed, first in embarrassment, then in anger. Sala threw him one speculative glance, threw Attise the identical glance, then became lost in her own thoughts.

They made a camp that night in a stand of oak off the west side of the road. Sala efficiently scouted the area, pronounced it safe, and set to making a small fire to dispel the cool of night. Attise settled down to study her damnable map and let her bodyguard arrange their sleeping rolls.

Willam hung back from the fire. It wouldn't do to bring the charms in his pack close to the flames. He was not certain how much distance was actually required, but if he erred, it would best be on the side of caution.

He carried his pack some twelve feet away past a small crowd of ferns and began to pull out its contents. Finding his sleeping roll near the bottom, he spread it out on the ground.

Sala watched in puzzlement. "Here, boy, what are you doing?"

Will looked up sheepishly. "Well . . . I thought two ladies might not like a man to spend the night so close . . ."

Sala laughed in good-natured derision at his manly conceit. "I think our virtue is safe with you. Come here, you'll be glad of the fire later tonight." Will grinned with seeming embarrassment, gathered his gear untidily in his arms, and set it up close to Sala's roll. The charms he left behind, masked by the ferns. He could retrieve them in the morning.

But when he looked up from his arrangements, he saw that Attise had abandoned her study and was giving him that look. "Willam," she said slowly. "Obviously we don't feel any threat from you. But you don't return that regard."

"What?"

She pointed with her chin toward the ferns. "Whatever you left back there will certainly be safer close to hand."

Will was speechless, wavering between denial and disbelief.

Attise tilted her head. "Why don't you let me see it? If it's so valuable, perhaps I'll want to buy it." Her face was blank, but her eyes watched him.

Suddenly he hated this woman, hated her silences, her disdain, her air of superiority. She was toying with him! She believed him not at all, and she had spent the day teasing his lies out of him. It was all a game, to make him squirm for her amusement.

And for that one moment, his fury made him rash. He drew himself up slowly and stood, and let her look at him for a long moment, matching her gaze unwaveringly with his own. "Very well," he said at last. "I'll be glad to show you. Perhaps you will want to *buy* one." He sneered that word, with a sudden release of his helpless anger. "But you'll have to step away from the fire to see them. It isn't safe, otherwise. They're magic, and fire releases the spell."

He knew how events should run. They would be impressed, like the people at home. They might even be frightened; they would try to make peace with him.

But it did not happen that way. Instead Willam suddenly realized, quite clearly, that he was in terrible danger.

12

*B*el's sword was in her hand. She spoke carefully. "Don't move, boy. Not a single move."

Rowan sat, her map abandoned in her lap. Her sword was by her right hand, but she did not take it. She stayed completely still, her eyes never leaving the boy's, her body alert and ready for any change in the tableau.

Willam had traveled from The Crags, by his accent, his manners, his recognition of the distinctive work of the Kundekin. She knew which wizard held that city, and he was the most infamous. Appalled, she breathed, "Abremio."

The boy jerked at the sound of that name. His young face was pale, and he trembled, but his beautiful copper-coin eyes did not waver from Rowan's face. At last, through clenched teeth, he said to them, "Do it, if you're going to."

Bel was in sudden motion, and Willam made half a step back toward the ferns, and then she was on him. One hand gripped his shirt-front and swung him off balance; the other brought her sword around. Then he was sprawled, half-suspended from her clenched fist, the point of her sword at his throat.

"I say we don't bother to question him first," Bel said mildly.

Rowan was beside them, her own sword in hand. She stood between the stand of ferns and the locked pair, blocking the way. "Wait."

"He's a wizard!"

Rowan gripped Bel's arm, delaying the thrust that would have followed the words. She said to Willam, "Boy, were you boasting? Tell us, and on your life, you'd better believe I'll know if you lie."

He gasped, astonished, "I'm not a wizard!"

"Then he serves one," Bel said.

"What did you leave in the ferns?" Rowan said; she saw him glance in that direction and hesitate. "You haven't the time to think of a lie. Answer!"

"It—it is magic, but—"

"I knew it!" Bel snarled.

"But it's nothing! It's—it's just—" His face worked, then, as if it pained him to admit the truth. "A real wizard would call them just toys. . . ." He looked up at Rowan, astonished—pleading, and he seemed to be a person unused to pleading. "Please, let me go. I'm not worth his notice."

"His notice . . ." Rowan paused in puzzlement, then began to piece together the evidence of the boy's words and reactions. How must all this look to him?

Bel was equally confused. "Whose notice?"

Then, nodding slowly, Rowan lowered her sword. "Abremio's. Let him go, Bel. He doesn't serve Abremio." She smiled a little. "But he thinks that we do."

Bel released Willam in astonishment. "Us?"

He lay on the ground, rubbing his chest. "I thought, when you named him . . ."

"I thought I was naming you," Rowan said wryly.

"Me?" It came out a childish squeak.

"Who knows what guise a wizard might travel in?"

Bel watched Willam with suspicion. "It still might be him." She stepped around, so that he had a woman with a sword on either side.

Rowan studied him. His panic had eased a bit once he knew they were no minions of that wizard; he was waiting with a combination of confusion and wariness.

She considered the clues. "You're afraid of Abremio's attention. Is he likely to be looking for you? Did you steal something from him, perhaps?"

He sat up, cautiously. "No. He stole something from me."

"What was that?"

"My sister."

"This Abremio steals women?" Bel asked. She directed her query not to Willam but to Rowan, and the steerswoman saw that the boy took careful note of that. Abruptly she realized that she and Bel had ceased to be innocent travelers in his eyes. In acting to protect themselves, they had compromised the only protection they had. There was no longer an easy explanation for their movements. She cursed herself silently.

But what explanation was there for Willam? He had threatened the use of magic and was frightened at the thought of attracting Abremio's attention. "Why does Abremio care about you?"

He thought carefully before replying. "Why does he care about you?" he asked.

He was as cautious as they. Bel smiled despite herself. "We don't know that he does," she replied.

He looked from one to the other. "I don't know for sure, either. But if he doesn't care, it's because he doesn't know I exist."

"You're a danger to him?" Rowan asked.

"No. Not yet." His composure was returning as they spoke. Then an idea occurred to him, and he looked suddenly intrigued. "But you are, aren't you?"

Bel's sword was across his throat again, the guard close under his left ear. "Boy," she said in a perfectly reasonable tone, "I want you dead. My friend"—she nodded up at Rowan—"doesn't agree. But she's a sensible person, actually. She won't risk our lives on a kindhearted whim."

"The odds are against you," Rowan pointed out, "unless you can convince us that you're harmless to us."

His fear had returned. "I am!"

"The more we know about you, the better we'll be able to judge that. The less you know about us, the less risk you are."

"Don't ask questions," Bel clarified. "Answer them."

He took a deep shaky breath and looked up at Rowan. "I won't betray you. Because I think we're all on the same side. I'll tell you anything you want."

She considered. It was difficult to believe that this big clumsy-looking boy, so obvious in his deceptions, could represent any direct threat. He looked more than a little foolish, sitting awkwardly on the ground, his possessions scattered about him; the warrior beside him could dispatch him as simply and negligently as she might snap the neck of a snared quail.

And yet—

"The package you left in the ferns contains something magical?" she asked.

"That's right. Charms. They're useful, in a small way. But they can be dangerous, if you're not careful." He held up his right hand for them to see. As Rowan had noticed before, the hand lacked its last two fingers. The underside of the arm was also scarred, as from an old burn, and his right eyebrow was faintly ragged. Abruptly the pattern made sense, and she realized that at some point in the past he had flung that arm across his face to protect his eyes from sudden fire.

"Why were they given to you?" Bel asked.

"They weren't." He looked stubborn, as if he had often had to defend that statement. "I made them."

"You said that you're not a wizard," Rowan pointed out.

"No. Not yet."

"Are you an apprentice?"

"No." He looked earnest. "But I'd better become one, don't you think?"

"Easily said, less easily accomplished," Rowan observed. Wizards sometimes acquired apprentices; but where those young people came from, no one knew. They were never of the folk in the wizard's own holding. They appeared, apparently from nowhere, and more often than not vanished abruptly, never to be seen again. Only very rarely was it possible to make a clear connection between the disappearance of a known apprentice in one part of the Inner Lands and the sudden appearance of a new wizard in some other region. Even in those cases, the apprentice's antecedents were either untraced, or untraceable.

The boy went on. "I have to find a Red wizard. Abremio's Blue; so is Corvus, nowadays. I don't want anything to do with the Blues."

"What makes you think that any wizard would accept you?" she asked.

"Well . . ." Willam spoke grimly. "I suppose he'd have to. It wouldn't do to have one of the folk walking around doing magic, would it? He'd either have to take me in, or kill me."

Bel leaned closer. "Then he'll kill you."

From his position he could not comfortably look her in the eye, but his expression was defiant. "Maybe not."

But Rowan had reached her conclusions. She gestured to Bel to relax her guard, but the Outskirter was wary and did not comply. Will watched the silent argument in confusion.

Rowan casually sat down on the ground next to them, placing her sword across her lap. "You're going to become a wizard so that you can kill Abremio, for taking your sister."

It was an obvious conclusion, but Willam startled a bit when she stated it. Bel gave one delighted "Ha!" and released him again, stepping back to sheathe her own sword. She sat down herself, pulling her cloak under her, and viewed Willam with approval. "Can your magic do this?" she asked.

The sudden change in their mood made him no less uncomfortable. "No," he admitted, studying each of them in turn. Something in Rowan's watching and waiting expression made him amend his statement. "That is, perhaps. If I caught him by surprise. But I can't count on that. And I'd never get him alone. I don't want to hurt anyone else." He spoke with intensity. "That's his way, not mine. I've never used it to hurt anyone."

"Except yourself," Bel pointed out.

He was embarrassed. "I don't think that counts."

"It's not a game, and no one's counting," Rowan said. "Abremio can do as he pleases." If Willam did join the ranks of the wizards, Rowan suspected that he would soon learn to do as they did.

"But—they're not all like him!"

Rowan gestured vaguely; it seemed to her that it was only a matter of degree. But she admitted, "He's the worst of them."

"Stealing women?" Bel asked. "What does he do with them?"

"Children," Rowan corrected. "Of both genders. And no one knows." Before leaving the Archives, she had spent two intense hours with Hugo, as he briefed her on the known details of the six major wizards. Hugo had learned in his own travels that Abremio occasionally sent a pair of soldiers to confiscate an infant or a young child from its family. It occurred rarely enough to seem a unique event to the folk involved, yet often enough to form a habit recognizable to someone who observed widely. "Was there something different about your sister?" Rowan asked Will. Often, though not exclusively, that was the case.

He was puzzled. "No . . . small for her age, perhaps. She spoke early and walked late, that's all. Why do you ask?"

But to answer would be to admit a larger scope of knowledge than she was supposed to possess. As had often happened on this journey, she found nothing she could safely say, and so said nothing. It was the worst sensation, to close the lid on her knowledge, a wrenching unpleasantness. She set her mouth in a grim line to keep from speaking and looked away, trying to control her instincts.

"I wish you wouldn't do that!"

She turned back and found Willam glaring at her in fury.

"You—you treat me like I'm stupid, or like I'm nothing. But I can figure things out for myself. I know that you're both spies, from a Red wizard."

Bel and Rowan exchanged a startled glance, then Rowan seized the idea and turned it over and over in her mind.

It was the perfect answer. It explained all their actions: their original deception, their reaction to Will's claims of magic, their attack on him, their unwillingness to explain themselves. Will had assumed that they served a Red wizard because of their fear of Blue Abremio.

They did not have to lie at all; it was deception by silence. Without a word passing between them, Rowan and Bel agreed on their new identities.

As spies, they would hardly admit to being spies. They both sat simply looking at Willam, waiting for him to realize that. Eventually he did, and grudgingly let his temper cool.

"We're not enemies," he pointed out. "I hate Abremio, I don't want anything to do with any Blue wizard. I'm looking for a Red. So, we're on the same side."

"It would be a good idea if you forgot that we're anything but a merchant and a mercenary," Bel said. Rowan could not help but smile; the statement was perfectly true on every level, yet served only to reinforce the credibility of their new deception. Even her smile, she realized, added to the effect.

"I won't give you away," Will assured Bel, and included Rowan in his glance. "But, well . . . maybe we can help each other."

Bel looked at Rowan. "It might be a good idea. . . ."

Rowan's humor vanished. "I don't like it."

"But if his magic is any good—"

"We don't know that it is." Rowan was reluctant to have anything at all to do with magic, but as the supposed servant of a wizard, she could not admit to that. She hoped Bel could follow her reasoning without prompting.

But Bel turned back to Willam. "Show us this magic, then," she suggested.

The boy hesitated. "But you don't want people to notice us . . ."

"And it would attract attention?" Rowan asked.

He nodded. "It's rather loud, most of the time."

"You can't do it quietly? Put a spell of silence on it?" Bel wondered.

"There's still a lot about it that I can't control." He rubbed his damaged right hand, an unconscious, musing gesture.

"What does it do?" she asked. "What do you use it for?"

He looked a little sheepish. "I can dig wells. And help clear boulders and stumps from new farmland."

"The boulders vanish?"

"No . . ." He searched for words. "Sometimes they break apart. Sometimes they just . . . leave. Very fast."

"How is that dangerous?"

He looked at her darkly. "It's not good to get in the way."

"I believe that's true of every sort of magic," Rowan said.

But Bel was delighted. "It sounds very useful," she said, ignoring Rowan's interjection. "I think this is a good meeting. I'm sure we can help each other."

"No!"

Bel and William looked at Rowan, startled.

"I don't think it's a good idea at all." She wanted to say: If the wizards are ignoring their own lines to cooperate against us, if every wizard is our enemy, then we do not want one of their fledglings at our side. We don't know enough about them; we don't know why they act as they do. This boy wants to learn their ways, and their ways are all against us. We would never know when he might turn.

She could say none of that. All she could say to Bel, in Willam's presence, was: "Think about it."

Bel shook her head, a broad emphatic gesture. "If you find a perfectly good sword by the side of the road, you don't throw it away."

"What if you suspect it's cursed?"

Bel replied, stressing each word, "You use what comes to hand." Will nodded, watching Rowan for a response.

Rowan took a breath, trying to calm herself. She turned to Willam. "And how would we help you?"

"You take me with you," he said. "And when we return to your master, you tell him about me."

"A recommendation?"

He nodded.

"And what makes you think we carry any influence?"

"Perhaps you don't. But it's better than me just showing up on his doorstep. And if I really do prove myself . . ."

"Where's the harm?" Bel asked. Rowan saw that Bel was trying to suppress amusement. "*If* we have the chance, we let it be known that Willam helped us, and that he'd make a good apprentice."

Willam was waiting for Rowan's answer, his face open, sincere, eager, guileless . . . and for a moment, she cared about him and what might happen to him. "Will," she said honestly. "You shouldn't become an apprentice. I hate to think what it will do to you. No good will come of it."

Something in her expression reached him, and he was taken aback, suddenly uncertain. Then she understood; it was her sincerity. Never before had he seen sincerity in her face, and it broke her heart to realize that. "Trust me," she said to him, knowing she had never given him reason or evidence to trust her.

"My sister . . ." he began.

"Do you realize you're not the only one?" Rowan asked. "He didn't single you out; it's simply something that he does, periodically. Does that make any difference to you?"

"No . . ." he said at last. Then he became more certain. "Maybe it makes it worse. And it's not the only evil he does. I've seen how he works, a bit. I lived near his city, The Crags—but you knew that."

Rowan called into her mind a detailed map of that area. Willam's village had to be on the near side of the drawbridge, far enough from the city proper that he had not acquired its involuted manner of speech, but near enough that pronunciation of individual words was the same. He had lived close enough to the city to be familiar with Kundekin handiwork, and that eliminated the farther-flung villages under the city's direct influence. Also, he had been near enough to enter the city on occasion and see Abremio's daily manner of rule at first hand.

She hazarded a guess. "Oak Grove."

He stopped short, disturbed. "That's very close. Langtry." He went on. "Anyway . . . I guess I have to stop it, if I can."

She nodded, comprehending. "You've been working on this for a long time."

"A long time . . . working so hard . . ."

"Attise." It took Rowan a moment to remember that that was her name. "Maybe we *can* help each other." Bel said it simply, watching Rowan's expression, and it occurred to Rowan that the statement might carry more than one meaning.

"You're from the new holding, aren't you?" Willam asked. "The one they fought the war for, with those two wizards together?"

"Shammer and Dhree," Rowan supplied without thinking, then realized that her reply would be taken as an admission that he had guessed right.

"Do they have an apprentice?"

"No." She sighed and spoke to Bel. "If either of us has the opportunity, we'll put in a good word. That's the only promise we can give." It was a true statement, as true as she could make it, and still it carried in its heart a hundred unspoken lies.

But it satisfied Will, and he laughed with happy relief.

13

"*I* would very much like to see what he can do," the steerswoman said.

Bel looked back at Willam, who was chatting with one of the caravan's mounted guards. The man was riding a rather bedraggled horse, and extolling the romance of his lifestyle, with expansive gestures and more than a little condescension.

The boy ambled along beside him, with his odd, distinctive gait. His strides were slightly longer than his height would suggest, and he walked smoothly and jarlessly, as if he were carrying a load of eggs in his pack. It seemed easy and natural.

The donkey trotted along beside them in cheerful high spirits, due simply to the fact that it was no longer carrying Rowan. It had protested being ridden from the first, and now that it carried only her baggage and Bel's pack, it seemed to feel that its little universe had been restored to rightful order. Its bad temper had completely vanished.

Bel added to Rowan's statement. "Without attracting attention."

"He did say it was loud."

"I wonder what sort of noise it makes?"

"I can't imagine." Like the donkey, Rowan had been restored to a more natural mode—she was walking. Her clothes were not the best for such exertion—the wide split skirt hissed around her legs annoyingly, and the boots were too new to be comfortable—but she walked and felt easier in her mind for the swinging familiarity of it.

There were two main roads running east and west in the Inner
Lands. One, the Shore Road, stretched east from Wulfshaven and
eventually ended in Donner; but it was an ill-kept route and wasted
many miles by laboriously tracing the northern shoreline of the sea. It
served mainly to connect the little villages each with its neighbor.
Only by happenstance did it form a continuous road with both ends
terminating in major towns.

But the Upland Route, which they had chosen to take, was centuries old, a good and dependable route east. It crossed the Wulf some
miles north of Wulfshaven, dipped south to the city itself, skirted the
hilly country that ranged down from the north, and traveled northeast
and then due east to Five Corners. It was part of the major caravan
route, and from Five Corners transported goods could continue in several directions.

But that town was too likely to recognize Rowan and Bel from
their earlier visit. They planned to leave the caravan long before that
point and wend their way across country and along less direct roads to
the Outskirts.

The day had turned warm early on, and both women had added
their heavier outer clothing to the donkey's burden. They walked in
the midst of a faint haze of road dust raised by the travelers ahead
of them. Rowan breathed it in as if it were sea air.

She was using her resurrected sense of freedom to engage in her
normal activity: she was finding things out. Denied the direct approach of questioning the travelers closely, she was utilizing a combination of close observation and the normal degree of idle curiosity she
might be expected to display as Attise. Her restrictions took on the aspect of a game, and she ranged up and down the caravan's length.

A pair of point riders headed the line, on hard-worked, scruffy
ponies. A horse-mounted scout periodically came into view in the distance, signaled them, then disappeared again.

A charabanc drawn by a team of donkeys came next, carrying the
well-to-do who did not wish to exert themselves unnecessarily. A
party atmosphere suffused the group of strangers, but Rowan found
them disinclined to indulge in idle conversation with a walker. She
recognized their origins by their accents, and rightly identified one
narrow gentleman from the upper Wulf valley as escort to the six ox-
carts of tin ingots that followed a few spaces behind. Tin was mined in

the hills of the upper Wulf, by one of the two known enclaves of the mysterious Kundekin, and the man's sentence structure showed the influence of long conversation with those normally reclusive people. Rowan speculated to herself on the effects of so large an import of tin on the metal-poor economy to the east.

The carts were followed by a handful of young horse-mounted travelers, all of a group, jesting with one another. They chatted freely but superficially and seemed more interested in a series of pranks played by one of their number. The most frequent victim was a lone Christer pilgrim, an attractive target due to his air of blind self-confidence and his unvarying reaction of dull puzzlement.

In all, some twenty wagons and carts made up the main body of the line, interspersed with riders and walkers. Some, like the tin importer, were planning to travel all the way to the junction at Five Corners. Others took advantage of the caravan's protection for local trips, the fee for such participation being minimal. Still others traveled with the caravan for some significant segment of their journey, separating again when necessary; Rowan and Bel belonged to that category.

Rowan watched Will for a moment. "I wonder how one comes to be able to work magic."

The Outskirter was surprised. "Everyone knows. You're born with the talent."

"Young Willam doesn't seem particularly remarkable."

"Ha. You can't tell just by looking."

"Making it easy for anyone to claim magical talent."

Bel shook her head in mock aggrievedness. "There you go again, doubting. You doubt that the moon ever existed, you doubt the gods, you doubt the cards, and you doubt magic. Is there anything you don't doubt?"

"Quite a lot," Rowan told her, laughing despite herself. "I don't doubt that some things people believe are true, and some are false. And I don't doubt that there's some means to tell the difference." Then she admitted, "But I sometimes doubt that I possess the means." They pulled abreast of an oxcart loaded with beer kegs, and the conversation was forced to end, lest the drivers overhear.

The guard turned away to patrol, and Willam caught up with the women. "He says that last year at this time, the caravan was set on by bandits right here." Under his concern, Rowan detected a buried trace of wild boyish curiosity.

"Then it won't be, this year," she decided, knowing that bandits who worked in groups tended to keep distinct territories and so had to vary their tactics. Will managed to look both relieved and disappointed. "Not at this location, that is," she added, and his expression became too mixed to interpret.

He was distracted by the group of walkers just ahead of the beer cart. Four men and a young woman had been trading turns pulling a two-wheeled luggage cart. Three of the men now positioned themselves between the poles and jogged in time, moving the cart closer to the front of the line, their exertions aided by the cheerful "Hup, hup" and handclapping of the woman. Their remaining companion strolled along at his ease, in parody of haughty condescension.

"What's in the cart?" Will wondered.

"Instruments. They're musicians."

Will watched them depart, then wandered back to study a farm wagon carrying a load of provisions and a silent, sad-eyed family of four.

Bel scanned the line ahead and behind, then shook her head in amazement. "Things go differently in the Outskirts."

"I imagine so."

"Everything here is so easy—and comfortable."

Rowan was taken aback. "Not at all. If these people traveled each alone, they'd certainly be robbed."

"What about steerswomen? Aren't they robbed?"

Rowan paused to form a reply that would not betray her connection with the Steerswomen if overheard. "They carry little. And what they have of value—that is, information—is free for the asking."

"So they're not molested?"

"Yes, but rarely. So I hear."

Bel considered. "So these travelers band together and they're safe."

"Safer," Rowan corrected.

"The Outskirts are never safe."

Rowan wanted to ask her for more details, but decided it would seem too odd. Instead she satisfied herself with reviewing the information she had gleaned from Bel in previous conversations, trying to organize it in her mind. Bel noted her preoccupation and turned to amusing herself by trying to keep track of Willam's wanderings. Presently a pony cart doubled back from the head of the line, and a lunch of dried meat and bread was passed out to those whose payment had included the service. The day wore on, pleasantly enough.

"So." Damaine, the caravan-master, pulled up beside Rowan. "Only as far as Taller Ford, hey?" He was a slim, energetic man, dressed in bright red linen trousers, a square-cut sleeveless shirt, and a broad-brimmed hat. His dust-brown hair was tied behind the nape of his neck.

Rowan raised her voice to be heard over the creak of the beer wagon. "I'll be heading south, and then east. To Alemeth."

"Alemeth!" He blew air through pursed lips. Then his eyes glittered. "Silk!"

"That's right."

"Then you'll need transport for your goods." He began to calculate.

"We'll probably go by sea, once the deal's established."

"It's off the regular lines." He had a good knowledge of his competition's habits.

"We may hire our own."

He threw up his hands in mock distress. "Think of the expense!"

"Think of the convenience!" Rowan laughed.

"No, now, where are you based?"

They entered into a cheerful discussion of the relative merits and costs of the competing modes of bulk transportation. Rowan found her mathematical ability coming into play naturally, and was able to calculate rates and mileages with offhand ease that startled Damaine and gave him occasional pause. The conversational give-and-take was both lighthearted and cutthroat. Soon Rowan realized, with some surprise, that this occupation was one she could be good at, and even enjoy. She and the caravan-master ended up laughing in admiration of each other's expertise.

One of the guards up ahead hallooed, waving his hat at his master. Damaine acknowledged with his own signals, then cupped his hat behind one ear to catch the explanation. Walking down among the cart noise, Rowan could not make out what was said.

"Hmph." Damaine turned to her. "Did I see you writing letters last night?"

She nodded. "Yes, keeping my master posted." In fact, the letters served to report her movements and any new information to the Prime. Arian had provided Rowan with a deviously clever mathematical cipher that permitted her to conceal her information economically within very few paragraphs. There was no particular reason at this point to suspect her letters might be intercepted; she had detected no sign of scrutiny since she had left the Archives. Still, it was a reasonable precaution.

The address to which she sent them was a nonexistent one far in the upper Wulf valley, ostensibly her point of origin. But to reach that area, her letter would have to pass through Wulfshaven itself, and a notation on the address suggested it be routed through the offices of a small herring fleet. Such interim destinations were common with letters traveling long distances, trusted to the hands of a succession of strangers. However, one of the clerks in the offices was a failed steerswoman who had maintained friendly relations with the residents of the Archives. The plan called for her to reroute the messages.

Rowan had managed to send one communication from a small village the travelers had passed through on the road south to the caravan route. It consisted merely of assurances that she had met with no problems yet. How long it would take to reach its destination, Rowan had no idea.

She had spent the last few evenings enciphering the news of her and Bel's encounter with Willam. She said to Damaine, "When we reach the next town, I'll see if I can find someone going west who might be willing to carry a letter."

"Well, you won't have to wait," he replied, gesturing up the length of the caravan. "There's a steerswoman up ahead, coming this way. You can pass the letters through her."

Rowan's thoughts froze, then went into a flurry, trying to guess who it might be. Who was on this road; who was traveling west at this time?

And how could Rowan avoid meeting her?

She thought of Janus, assumed lost, and she hoped desperately that it was him. But Damaine had not said "steersman." She resisted the temptation to ask Damaine if it was a man or a woman approaching. Steersmen were so rare and notable that it was unlikely the guard ahead would simply use the general term. Also, she reminded herself, as Attise she should not care which it was.

She tried to let none of her thoughts reach her face. "Good," she said to Damaine. Steerswomen were frequent and reliable letter carriers. To refuse would have been too conspicuous.

Somewhat later, she crossed the line in front of the beer cart and joined Bel and Willam, who were idly chatting with the Christer pilgrim. Will glanced in annoyance as she gestured Bel aside. Since he had decided they were allies, he took mute exception to their excluding him from any consultations, but he never protested, for fear of losing their indulgence. Bel handed him the donkey's lead and stepped back behind the wagon with Rowan.

"There's a steerswoman up ahead."

Bel tilted her head. "And she'll recognize you?"

"Almost certainly. There aren't that many of us, and the older ones, the ones I haven't met, are working the limits of the Inner Lands far from here. Very likely, it's someone I trained with."

"And she won't know anything of your doings."

"It will take some explaining. And, there's the chance she'll give me away before I can explain at all."

Bel nodded. "Then you'll have to avoid her."

"Exactly."

Bel scanned the length of the caravan. "There are enough people for you to lose yourself, if you know when she's passing by. I'll scout ahead and warn you."

"And you'll give her a letter." Rowan explained the custom to Bel. "I'll have to step aside to add a note and to address it. Then you can run it up to her."

Bel smiled at a happy thought. "Let's have Willam do it. It will make the poor fellow feel useful."

Rowan could not help laughing. "That's a good idea."

They rejoined Will and the pilgrim. Rowan pulled from her baggage the folio of letter paper that she carried in place of her steerswoman's logbook. Bel picked up her conversation with the Christer and gestured for Will to stay with her as Rowan stepped to the side of the road.

There was no time to melt sealing wax. Rowan made do by folding the paper several times over and tying it with a bit of ribbon. She spit onto her ink stone, mixing a bit of powder, and addressed it, propping the folio against her knee.

She had to hurry back up the line to reach Bel and Willam, waving the paper a bit to dry the ink. She wondered briefly if she looked too undignified at the moment to be a proper merchant.

"Will."

He turned to her.

"Here, be careful of the ink. I need you to run up ahead and pass this on to a steerswoman who's coming this way."

He opened his mouth to speak, very probably to ask why she did not simply wait until the steerswoman reached her. Rowan gave him a warning look, and he closed his mouth again. In the presence of the Christer, he could not ask for her justifications. Resigning himself to his mysterious mission, he shifted his pack to a more snug position, tightened one of the ropes that served as a strap, took the letter, and headed off.

He did not exactly run, Rowan noticed, but extended his stride to a smooth ground-devouring lope. Piecing the clues together, she decided that fire was not the only thing that might threaten the safety of the charms in his pack.

The pilgrim noticed. "Is there something wrong with his legs?"

"I don't know," Rowan replied.

The Christer looked after the boy, then began to hold forth with a long, boring, and largely spurious list of medical recommendations.

It was half an hour later when Will rejoined them, by the simple expedient of standing still as they caught up to his position. "She's going to be camping with the caravan tonight. I thought you might like to know."

Rowan was taken aback. "What?"

The pilgrim had left their company, and the boy felt free to speak. "She fell in with the musicians up ahead. I think she's a musician herself."

The name spoke itself before Rowan could stop it. "Ingrud."

He was surprised. "You know her?"

She managed to prevent herself from explaining further and lapsed into one of her silences. Bel took over. "Let's say we know of her. And that we have to avoid her, or at least Attise does."

He glowered. "I wish you'd told me."

Rowan turned on him. "What did you do?"

"Well . . ." he began defensively. Ahead, a few heads turned in their direction at the loudness of his protest. He continued, quieter but vehement. "Steerswomen are good sources of information. You can ask them anything, and they have to answer, no matter what. I thought—" He stepped closer and spoke still more quietly. "I thought, with what you're doing, you'd want to know something about what the land is like farther up this road. And a merchant would want to know, anyway."

"She's going to come looking for me?"

"I told her you had some questions . . ."

Rowan threw up her hands in exasperation, furiously turned away to calm herself, turned back before she could, and pointed one finger a bare inch from his face. "Don't do that," she said in a low, vicious voice. "Don't go off making plans for us on your own initiative—"

Angry, he spoke louder. "Well, if I knew a little more about what you're—"

Bel slapped his shoulder once, very hard. Caught off-stride, half-turned, he stumbled, and Rowan stepped out of his way—

—then abruptly countered her instincts in panic and stepped back in to grab him—

—and countered instinct again to change her sudden clutch into a smooth interception, a catch with some give in it. Like catching a tossed egg—

She ended with both knees on the ground, one arm across Willam's chest, the other gripping his left shoulder from behind. His right arm was flung around her neck, a fistful of cloth on her back clutched in his half-hand. His left arm was thrown forward, to ward off the ground or to cushion his fall.

They froze. Willam held his breath. Rowan waited.

Eventually she said, carefully, "Is anything going to happen?"

He looked at her, eyes wide. "No," he replied. He sounded not at all certain.

Bel stood to one side, puzzled, but the look on their faces had stopped her from offering help. Instead she intercepted two little girls, locked in deep converse, who were about to trip over the pair.

Rowan cautiously helped Will up. Speaking close to his ear, she said urgently, "Can't you do something to make those things safer?"

He gazed about with a stunned expression, like someone amazed to be alive. "No," he said. "I mean, I don't know. I was never able to find out."

She urged him into a slow walk. They began to drop back as their fellow travelers continued at a steadier pace. Bel tugged the donkey back into motion and fell in with them.

"If the charms are this dangerous, perhaps you should get rid of them," Rowan said.

He shook his head, partly in dissent, partly to clear it. "I don't know that the spells would have escaped. *Sometimes* they do, if you drop them. Not always. It's just hard to be sure. I've never carried so many at once. If one releases, they all will, this close to each other."

Bel had caught the substance of the conversation. "What would have happened?"

Shock and guilt on his face, Willam looked up the line of travelers and wagons, then down it, then at the surrounding landscape. It came to Rowan that it all would have been affected in some terrible way. "Nothing good" was all he said.

Bel looked pleased. "Then you ought to be more careful. A good weapon should be treated with respect."

He nodded vaguely, then came back to himself. "The steerswoman," he said.

It took Rowan a moment to remember that he was not referring to her. "Ingrud," she amplified. "I'll try to keep out of the way tonight. When you or Sala see her, tell her that I've changed my mind. She'll be too occupied to think much of it."

Rowan sat in darkness on the edge of the camp, on the far side of the charabanc, her back against one tall wheel. The team of donkeys that had pulled it during the day were contentedly grazing around her and tugging at their staked tethers, her own beast among them. Behind her, travelers and drivers were gathered into cheery groups. Some were dancing.

Listening, Rowan identified the instruments: a pair of three-stringed viols, a bass flute, a bodhran, and a banjo, all led in a mad swirl by Ingrud's squeeze-box. The music was an ancient dance tune, "Harrycoe Fair." Nearby, someone was trying to dredge the nonsense lyrics from memory and making a bad job of it.

Rowan sullenly tossed a pebble at one of the donkeys. It fell short, and the animal ambled over to investigate, on the chance that it might be edible.

The music stopped, to scattered applause and appreciative comments. It did not start again, and the voices picked up their conversations. Apparently the musicians were taking a rest.

Someone approached. Rowan looked around the wheel to see Bel wandering in her direction, the very image of nonchalance. Beyond, in a circle of chattering people, Rowan caught sight of one energetic figure topped by a wild cloud of smoky-brown hair.

Rowan turned back and waited. Her donkey, appetite satisfied, came over to her and lowered itself to the ground. Shifting to one side, it found that the length of its tether was just sufficient to allow it to lean its head against her knee. It did so, and heaved a little happy sigh.

Bel sat down beside her, eyes reflecting the light leaking under the charabanc. "I like her. She's an interesting person."

"I wish I could talk to her." Rowan and Ingrud had their differences and were perhaps not the best of traveling companions; yet somehow, despite their talent for annoying each other, they had forged a friendship during their training. It was an odd friendship, one that seemed to require equal doses of distance and proximity.

But now Rowan felt a need as compelling as hunger. She needed to see Ingrud again, to find out how the road had treated her. She wanted to compare notes with her, to read each other's logbooks, to reminisce about their training and share dreams of further roads ahead.

Instead Rowan was sitting in darkness, listening to Ingrud's music in the distance.

"I think you'll need to talk to her," Bel said. "She's carrying one of the jewels."

Stunned, Rowan turned to her. "You're sure it's the same? Did she show it to you?"

"She's using it as a brooch for her cloak."

Rowan felt a sudden chill. Ingrud was carrying a jewel in plain sight. And whoever had tried to strike at Rowan was looking for a steerswoman with a blue jewel—

"She's in danger, and she doesn't know it." She shoved the donkey aside and rose to peer past the charabanc toward the firelight. Ingrud was no longer in sight. "Can you get her over here, alone, on some pretext?"

Bel considered. "She's too popular at the moment. I'll wake her from sleep later tonight and tell her there's something she should see."

"She won't trust you," Rowan said. "Not even a steerswoman would go off into the dark with a total stranger. Not on this road, not in this season."

Bel thought a moment, then smiled. "I'll bring Willam. She likes him. He's been plying her with questions all night."

"Questions?"

"Yes." Bel laughed. "He seems to have a lot of them. He acts as if he wants to know everything about everything."

As Bel made her way back to the firelight, Rowan felt an odd stab of jealousy. She thought: He should be asking those questions of me.

14

"*T*he merchant Attise, isn't it? You're having no problem, I hope."
Rowan looked up at the mounted guard, trying to affect an air of dignified distraction. "No, there's no problem, thank you. I needed to think, and I thought a bit of a walk might help matters."

He shook his head indulgently. "Oh, that's not a good idea, merchant. Wandering off in the dark by yourself. With all the noise we made tonight, every thief and cutthroat for miles around is surely headed this way. And possibly arrived. We're one of the first caravans this year, and they've had a hard winter, I think."

Rowan knew that to be true. "I trust your excellent patrolling."

He laughed. "Best of the lot, that's me. Still, it's good to be safe. You'd be wise to take yourself off to sleep."

Only a solitary thief could manage to slip into the camp. Rowan carried a sword, and believed it unlikely she could be caught by surprise in these circumstances. "My bodyguard will be joining me shortly."

His face brightened. "Sala! Now, she's certainly impressive. And knows her business well. A fine soldier, and a fine woman, too, I think. She could probably teach me a thing or two. I wouldn't mind wrestling her, any number of ways, if you catch my meaning."

Rowan suppressed a grin. "I'll tell her of your high opinion."

He considered. "You do that." He turned his horse and moved off, a musing, contemplative expression on his face. Rowan turned back to her own thoughts.

The first thing she'll do, Rowan thought, is shout my name. Then she'll ask why I've left my route. Then she'll wonder why I'm dressed so oddly . . .

Rowan would have to speak first, she realized. She needed to find some way to prevent Ingrud's quicksilver emotions from giving Rowan away to whoever might still be awake to listen. But she could not think of what to say or do, and then she heard people approaching and knew she had run out of time.

They were speaking, Ingrud's tone dubious, Bel's reassuring, as they came around the side of the charabanc. Will followed in their wake, suspicious of Bel's behavior and Rowan's change of plans. Rowan moved back to prevent the light from catching her face too soon. She waited until the trio reached the point where the wagon completely blocked them from the rest of the camp, then stepped forward. "Ingrud . . ."

She had been wrong about her friend's reaction. Ingrud's narrow, foxy face quickly showed first surprise, then delight; but when she took in the strange clothing, she stopped short suddenly. One glance showed her that Rowan's steerswoman's ring was absent.

To Rowan's amazement, Ingrud burst out in dismay, "No! Not you, too!" She turned to one side in helpless outrage and pounded her own right leg with a fist. "This can't happen again!" Angry, she stepped forward and shook her index finger in Rowan's face. "I will *not* be put off this time! I'm *going* to get an explanation!"

Rowan pulled the hand down, tried to calm the steerswoman. "Ingrud please, not so loud . . ."

"You and Janus have a lot to answer for—"

"Janus?" Rowan shook her head, then dismissed the non sequitur. "I'll tell you anything you like, but please, we mustn't attract attention."

Puzzled, Will said to Bel, "They do know each other. I asked the steerswoman, and she said they didn't."

Bel was distracted by an approaching guard. She stepped forward to reassure him. "They're old friends," she explained when he pulled up. "I'm sorry about the noise, but you know how it can be when old friends meet . . ."

"You are going to explain this!" Ingrud asserted, oblivious to everything except Rowan. "Janus can do what he likes and be damned for it, but you're my friend . . ."

Rowan realized with astonishment that Ingrud was close to tears. Abruptly ashamed for she knew not what sin, she held out her arms to her friend. Ingrud went silent, and then Rowan found herself embracing a helplessly weeping woman. "It's all right," she tried to reassure her in the midst of her own confusion. "I can explain everything. It's all right . . ." She looked up over Ingrud's shoulder at the guard. "I— I'm afraid my little joke went badly," she extemporized. "I shouldn't have tried to surprise her."

The guard relaxed a bit and looked to Bel for confirmation. "Really, there's no problem here," Bel said. "We're sorry we bothered you." He nodded, said something to her that Rowan could not catch, and wheeled off.

Ingrud calmed at last, and Rowan managed to get her to sit on the grass beside the charabanc. The steerswoman insisted through her tears, "You had better tell me what's going on."

"I was about to ask the same of you," Rowan replied. "What's the matter? And what's this about Janus?" She found a handkerchief in a sleeve pocket and gave it to Ingrud.

Ingrud pressed it across her eyes, as if she wished to blot out the world as well as her tears. "He's left."

"What do you mean? I'd heard he was missing . . ."

"No, he's left, he's quit!" Ingrud looked up. Light from under the charabanc played across her face. Her agitated hands worked at the handkerchief. "I met him in Deaver's Well last autumn. He was traveling with a band of tinkers. He's not a steersman any longer!"

Rowan rocked back as if from a blow. "He's resigned? But why?"

Ingrud shook her head widely, smoky curls moving across her shoulders. "He wouldn't say. I asked him, and he wouldn't tell me. He wouldn't tell me where he'd been, what he'd been doing . . ." She closed her eyes again. "He refused to answer any of my questions. So he's under our ban. I told him so. He said he didn't care."

"Incredible . . ." Rowan groped mentally, searching for some approach by which to understand what she was hearing. Steerswomen had left the order before, for many reasons, internal or external. But to resign without explanation, without that simple courtesy to one's fellows; and worse, to place oneself under the Steerswomen's ban by refusing information . . . Small wonder Ingrud had been so upset on seeing Rowan without her ring and chain. It must have seemed that the impossible had happened twice, and this time to a better-loved friend . . .

But while one part of Rowan's mind was filled with concern for Janus and confusion about his motives, another was casting about, seeking connections and finding none. She said, half to Bel and half to herself, "It probably doesn't have anything to do with us."

Bel nodded, satisfied, but Ingrud looked up.

"I don't know what Janus was doing, Ingrud," Rowan continued. "I had heard that he was missing, that's all."

"And what about you?" Ingrud's face showed a mixture of anger and concern.

Rowan hesitated. "Will." He was startled by her sudden attention, then squinted suspiciously. "I think the steerswoman will need her cloak in a moment."

"You're trying to get rid of me," he accused.

Bel nudged him. "Of course she is. Now do as you're told."

With ill humor, he complied.

Rowan gestured for the Outskirter to sit beside her. "This is Bel," she told Ingrud, and then proceeded to deliver a rapid, concise explanation of the jewels, the evidence of wizards' interventions, the Prime's decision, and her own mission.

Ingrud interrupted her then. She looked carefully into Rowan's face, studying her expression. Ingrud's tilted eyes were a lovely mixture of brown and green. Rowan remembered them as always filled with merriment, but now her gaze made Rowan shy back. "Are you still a steerswoman?" Ingrud asked quietly.

Rowan drew a breath and expelled it slowly, calming herself. She found that it was difficult to say. "Technically, *temporarily* . . . no."

Ingrud looked dazed, incredulous. "I hope all this is worth it."

"I think we're in a great deal of danger. All of us, the whole way of life."

"It seems impossible."

Rowan leaned forward to stress her point. "The wizards are putting restrictions on us. They've never done that before. We can't permit it; who knows how far they'd take it, if they had that power over us?"

"And what's so special about these jewels? What magic can they hold?"

"None that's visible. They seem to do nothing at all. I've carried one for over a year, and it's had no effect on anything, that I could tell. Bel's carried hers for over ten years. And you carry one yourself, so Bel tells me." Rowan pulled the little sack from around her neck. Her ring and chain jingled faintly against each other as she pulled the jewel out and handed it across. "Is this the same as the jewel on your brooch?"

Ingrud studied it, then looked up in amazement. "This is the source of all the problems? Of all these ridiculous schemes?"

"Ridiculous schemes? Ingrud, that's a poor phrase—"

"This is nothing!" She held it up to Rowan and Bel, and it flashed dimly in the starlight. "It's a decoration, a trinket!"

Bel was studying Rowan, waiting for her response. Rowan found herself growing angry at Ingrud's behavior. "Then," she said, "it's a decoration that can't exist, and a trinket that comes from nowhere."

"Don't be ridiculous. They're perfectly normal." Ingrud handed the blue shard back to Rowan. "And I know where they come from. I've been there."

15

*W*illam sat on the edge of a stonewalled well in the little town square, seething in fury. A promise is a promise, he thought, even for a spy. Attise was not going to lose him so easily.

For the hundredth time Willam wished that Sala had been working alone, or with someone other than Attise. Sala would have stood by her word, Will was certain. Although, he realized, Attise had not actually promised to let Will stay with them—she had promised to help him if she had a chance. What she thought of as "a chance" she had left undefined. That was exactly the problem when dealing with her; her words, her meanings, kept slipping around, twisting and wriggling like tadpoles.

Of course, that was an asset for a spy, and it explained why Attise was in charge. Sala was likely too honest and straightforward to do well without someone like Attise directing their work. After all, spying was a nasty business, even for a good cause.

But it had been a cruel trick. Willam had walked a full morning with the caravan before he realized that Sala and Attise were missing. Attise had calmly sent him to the head of the line after breakfast, supposedly to distract Damaine while she and Sala spoke to one of the guards on some important subject. He had not noticed that they were gone until noon, and the thing was, they *had* been talking to the guard, and the important subject was that they were leaving the group early. Attise had not exactly lied to him, not this time.

"Likely you're looking for lodging?"

Will, watching the meager traffic in the village square, had been so lost in internal complaint that he had not noticed the villager coming up from behind. His road-sharpened suspicion was alerted. He didn't like people who approached in ways designed to go unnoticed.

But it was unlikely that he would be robbed in full daylight in the center of town. "Maybe. But there's no inn here?"

The man made a sound of derision and made a gesture with one hand; the other held a cloth-wrapped object, open at the top. "Town like this? Not enough business. But I've got room, if you want it. Reasonable." He lifted his package, which was revealed to be an open jar of some sort of liquor; he took a long draught from it.

Will was extremely reluctant to associate himself with the man. He looked around the village square. Immediately visible along the high street were a tannery, a bakery, a smithy—he felt a warm familiarity at that—an unidentifiable shop whose sign was at the wrong angle to see clearly, and a row of small dwellings. The street wound off north through what looked like pastureland. The only cross street seemed to dead-end in both directions.

Very likely he could find someone to give him sleeping space in return for work, or he could doss down in one of the pastures, if no one minded. But the man before him was the only person to approach him in the hour or so that he had been sitting on the edge of the stonewalled well.

It struck him as a little odd. Perhaps the village had had more than its share of bandits, or perhaps the war had passed over them, and the people were wary; but if that was so, why was this one fellow so interested? It felt wrong.

But he had to talk to someone. He turned back to the villager. "Do you have room for three?"

"Three?" The man's face acquired a calculating look.

"Three people. And one donkey. I'm supposed to meet some friends, or rather, I'm trying to. We got separated on the way. They haven't arrived, have they? Two women, one of them a mercenary?"

The man blinked. "Mercenary? I'd have heard." His avaricious expression was replaced by a thoughtful one. "There was a steerswoman came through two weeks ago."

That was Ingrud, Will realized. "No, that's too long ago. My friends might be three days ahead of me, no more."

"No, there's been no one."

They had to have passed through the town, unless they had cut across country. Perhaps they had attempted to do that, gotten lost, and had to double back; Attise was so obviously hopeless with directions. They could easily be behind him. "Well," Will began to figure. "I don't have any money myself. One of my friends was carrying all we had." That should keep the man on the lookout for Attise and Sala. "I guess I'll have to sleep in a field. Though I wouldn't mind spending the night indoors, for a change." He allowed himself to look disgruntled. "If my friends arrive tonight, we'll be able all three to stay with you. If you're willing to come find me . . ." The opportunity to charge lodging for three instead of two insured that Will would be told when the two women arrived.

The villager considered. "Rain tonight," he observed.

Will peered at the sky as if this was news to him.

The man wavered, then said grudgingly, "Miller. Talk to the miller. Might be there's a shed to shelter in."

Will beamed. "Well, thank you, friend. That's kind of you."

There was a shed, but there was no miller; gone for the evening, Willam assumed. He let himself in and found a collection of empty sacks and a pile of lumber. The sacks made good bedding, and he found himself more comfortable than he had been for a long time.

Lying in the gathering dark, he took the opportunity to review his plans. If he could not find Attise and Sala here or farther up the road, he would just have to take himself to Shammer and Dhree alone. He knew from the steerswoman that their keep was somewhere north of here. Once he got near that lake Ingrud had mentioned, someone would know where the wizards were, or at least in what direction to look. He wondered briefly how two wizards could share one holding, then dismissed it as their own problem.

But that Attise. He shifted in annoyance. He kept trying to do well by her, but she was so secretive, so deceptive, so close-mouthed. How could you deal with someone like that? How did Sala manage it?

Likely Sala was no spy at all, but just what she seemed: a mercenary, a hireling. But she actually seemed to like Attise, though he could not see why. Perhaps because she, at least, knew what Attise was up to, was in the spy's confidence. He seethed. If he knew as much as Sala, maybe he could get along with Attise better, but she would not give him the chance.

He hated being kept in the dark, being pushed around. It was an easy, cheap thing, to push people around. All one needed was to be stronger, or to be smarter, or to know something that could be used on people. But it did not give one the right.

He knew how easy it was. He had pushed the other children around, when he was a child. He was always bigger, always stronger than the children his age, and some who were older. He was the leader by right of strength, and he was never afraid of anything or anyone. He soon learned that he could make the others do exactly as he pleased; and he had enjoyed it, he remembered, with more than a little guilt.

But he had stopped doing that sort of thing, stopped it when someone else bigger and stronger than him, stronger even than his own father, had taken from him the one thing he loved the best: an innocent, helpless, beautiful little girl. He could still hear her shrieking, still see her struggling against the soldier as he held her before him on the great horse. And the other soldier's sword against his father's chest . . .

And the memory of that day had driven him, with cold hatred, past what he had thought was possible: nurturing a tiny chance discovery, cautiously, thoughtfully, through reason and experimentation, into an unsuspected power.

No one had the right to use strength against the innocent. When he was a wizard himself, he would make sure no one ever victimized anyone again. He had to, *because* he was strong. Because he could work magic.

He reached one hand to the reassuring bulk of his pack, then turned over and slept.

Something in the small of his back gave him a sudden shove. He rolled, tried to get loose from the sacks, and ended up half standing, knife in hand, back against the wall.

In the dim light from the cracks in the wall, a figure was squatting beside his pack. "I can't figure if you're abysmally stupid or abominably clever." It was Attise, her voice heavy with weariness.

Will did not relax. It was dark in the shed, they were alone, and for all their traveling together, he still did not know this woman. "You tried to lose me."

"Yes, I did, and made a poor job of it, I can see." She sighed in exasperation and rose. "Come on."

He managed to stand. "Where are we going?"

"To Carroll's house."

" 'Carroll'?"

"Our host. Let's see what—what Sala can make of you."

She strode off, leaving him to scramble his possessions together.

She led him to a small cottage that seemed more a small hill of ivy than a dwelling. The leaves pattered and trembled in the drizzling rain.

As they entered, a rotund woman looked up from setting the table in the front room. Her black hair was pulled back severely from her face and bound in a single greasy braid, and her shapeless clothes had seen too much use and too few washings. "That him?"

"Our wandering lad," Attise confirmed. Her carefully affected voice covered her annoyance.

Sala entered from an adjoining room, carrying a kettle for tea. "Willam!" She was delighted and put down the kettle to clap him on the shoulder.

"I'm sorry I got lost," he told her, trying to look sheepish.

"No harm done; we're all together again." She beamed up at him.

The housewife seemed satisfied. She gestured at the table. "Well, have some breakfast, then, or maybe it's lunch—who can tell the hour in this weather?" she grumbled.

The travelers seated themselves and made an attempt at casual conversation with the woman. This proved futile in the face of her continuing diatribe against her husband, delivered in monotonic segments as she moved to and from the kitchen. "I know he's at Miller's again, deny it as much as he likes, drinking that brew old Grandfather Miller makes, coming back at all hours. Useless he is, or next to it. No skill, no money—" She raised her voice a bit. "And no children here either, if you haven't noticed." She grunted disparagingly. "Useless."

Attise attempted to redirect her conversation. "Well, we're certainly grateful for the lodging . . ."

"Hmph. No skin off his bum; I do all the work, not that we can't use a few coppers. I tell you . . ." She wandered off, still muttering, and a long pause followed until it was clear that she intended to remain there.

Sala went to the window and peered outside. Attise passed Willam a bowl of cold stew, yesterday's by the look of it. Will set to with a wooden spoon and a chunk of black bread, and found that his hunger made its flavor incidental.

"How did you find us?" Attise asked him.

He spoke between mouthfuls. "I knew where you were going. Ingrud told me."

"Ingrud?"

"That's right. You kept me away from her after you talked, I guess because you thought I'd ask about what you said to her. But before that, earlier that evening, I talked with her a lot."

Oddly, Attise looked a little regretful. "Yes, I remember."

"Well, I asked her where Shammer and Dhree kept residence. She didn't really know, because all that's new since last she was in these parts. But from what she'd heard from the people coming back from the fighting, most of the action was taking place near someplace called Lake Cerlew. I asked her how to get there. It's north, and this was the first northbound road I found when I doubled back."

"And you assumed we were going to Shammer and Dhree?"

He nodded, tearing off a piece of bread to soak up the last bit of stew. "Where else would you go? But I didn't think I'd actually catch you up."

Sala turned from the window, pulling the shutters against the rain. She wiped mist from her face with one hand. "You didn't catch up with us," she told him, shaking water from her fingers. "We doubled back." She sat down next to Attise.

"We left the road, circled the town, and entered from the north," Attise told him. "We wanted to prevent anyone from connecting us with the caravan. We're claiming to be traveling through from Morriston, between here and Lake Cerlew." She turned to Sala. "And now he arrives in town, coming from the south, telling everyone he was with us."

Willam stopped eating. With a strange thrill, half fear, half excitement, he realized that this was no mere stop along the way. Attise and Sala had intended to come here; there was some job, some mission they had in this town; and if he could help them, somehow, their recommendation would carry more weight with their master.

"People haven't been very curious," the mercenary pointed out to Attise. "Perhaps those who spoke to him won't be the same as those to whom we gave our story."

"It could be awkward." Attise considered carefully. Watching her face, Willam could sense her sifting through possible explanations, alternative deceits.

"This wouldn't happen, you know, if you didn't keep me in the dark," he said.

Attise looked at him as if he were speaking in tongues. "What?"

Rain hissed in the dirt of the street outside. "You're always deciding for me. You never let me know what's going on. If I knew, I wouldn't make these mistakes. I could *help* you."

She seemed unable to find a reply. After a moment with nothing forthcoming, Sala took over. "The less you know, the less danger you're in. And we abandoned you because we like you, and we don't particularly want you to die. If you stayed with us, one day you'd follow us into a trap."

Attise found her voice. "Perhaps today."

Will was shocked, then thrilled, then wary. "Here?"

Sala disagreed. "If anyone wanted to harm us, they would have tried already," she said to Attise.

"Assuming they know I'm the right person. They certainly don't—yet."

"Perhaps the whole thing is innocent. Perhaps Ingrud was right. She's not a fool, you know." Already, Willam realized, it had happened again; he was once more mere spectator to some incomprehensible exchange between the two mysterious women.

"She's a steerswoman," Attise conceded.

"There you are."

"No. The conclusions one reaches depend on the information one has. She may have been fed deceits." Attise drummed ink-stained fingertips on the table, considering.

"Then let's assume that she was, and that you're right, and there's nothing in this town for us. Let's go on our way."

Attise said nothing, but sat thinking.

"What you're going to do will identify you, just as if you shouted your name," Sala noted.

To establish his presence in the conversation, Will said, "Your right name."

Attise's blue-gray gaze flicked in his direction. "True." She tilted her head to the sound of someone dashing across the street at a staggering run, escaping the drizzle, and turned her attention back to her bowl an instant before the door clattered open. Their host entered, and proved to be the same fellow Willam had met by the well. Faintly weaving, the man discovered the trio in his front room and regarded them with a certain amount of foggy confusion.

"No, one shouldn't make assumptions of that sort," Attise spoke up, fabricating a conversation to continue. "One region's common-place is another's rarity." She gestured with her spoon at Willam, marking him the recipient of her opinions. "Even a dreary little spot like this one; I have every intention to visit the shops and manufac-tories before we leave. The possibility always exists, and nothing's so satisfying as cornering the market on some lovely item that your com-petitors will never be able to obtain."

Will glanced at Carroll, then tried to play along. "As long as peo-ple want to buy it."

"Exactly." She nodded. "To be desirable, any product should be ei-ther beautiful, or rare, or uniquely useful. Better, some combination of the three."

He made a wild guess. "And there's shipping cost."

Her smile seemed genuine. "Of course. The smaller, the better."

Will began to enjoy the game, until he saw Sala's expression. She had her back to Carroll and so was free to let her face show her thoughts. She disapproved. She glowered at Attise. It came to Will that when a mercenary disapproved of something, it was something dangerous.

There was a noise: "Ah!" It was a nasal sound of discovery and confirmation, and it came from the kitchen. Carroll's wife swept in with a display of self-righteous dignity, a shrewish expression, and a wooden ladle, which she brandished at Carroll. "Look at you, this early in the day, *and* in front of guests!"

Immediately, with perfect grace, the man corrected his posture, composed his expression, and stood regarding her coolly. Will, who had seen many persons drunk, marveled at his control. "Woman," Carroll intoned in a dignified voice. "You do carry on."

His wife gathered herself for a reply, then wavered. His act was per-fect. She began to doubt.

He crossed his arms, perhaps a trifle slowly but without difficulty. "Tend more to your work, and less to your—" He paused to choose the exact word. "Intrigues," he finished.

She squinted up at him, then turned the squint on the others in the room, as though suspecting them of collusion. Attise watched with bland disinterest. Sala studied the pair as if she anticipated a sporting event. Will contrived to appear stupidly puzzled.

The woman made a throaty sound of disappointment and left the room. Carroll sniffed wetly.

Turning to his guests, he greeted them gravely and inquired after their comfort. Attise looked aside, as if wishing to find a polite way to express her opinion, then gave it up. She pushed out a chair. "Why don't you join us for some tea?"

The man looked toward where his wife had gone, then glanced back at the door. He stepped to it, pulled a little cloth-wrapped jug from a hiding place behind the brick doorstop, and brought himself to the table. "Well, thank you, I don't mind at all." Seated, he laid one finger aside his nose conspiratorially and added a bit from the jug to each cup, hesitating only momentarily before Willam's.

Will found that the stuff evaporated on its way from the front of his mouth to the back, and he coughed. Carroll nodded gravely at him as if he had expressed some deep insight.

Attise tried to draw the man into conversation, but he seemed far more interested in replenishing his cup, and he replied vaguely to questions about the types of local handicrafts. Yes, there was a tanner, a weaver, a potter, a silversmith. Yes, they did fair enough work. Eventually Will, who had politely drunk three cups of the fiery tea, discovered an urgent need to visit the outhouse and excused himself from the stilted conversation.

The back yard was as shabby as its inhabitants, unkempt, with a large trash heap tucked in one corner. Will thought it was a shame; the house itself was lovely, old stone and ivy. But as he looked about, he noticed that the adjacent yards all had their own piles of odd discards, items not useful for compost or fertilizer.

As he emerged from the bushes that discreetly screened the outhouse, he heard a crash of pottery. Carroll was standing by the trash heap; he looked up suspiciously as Will approached, then relaxed as he recognized the boy, taking rather long to do so. Will glanced down and noticed the liquor jug on the pile, smashed, and several more of its mates, some new, some of them very old indeed. He laughed to himself and leaned toward Carroll confidentially. "Your secret is safe with us." The man regained his careful dignity and wandered off on his own mission.

When Willam reached the front room, Attise and Sala were in deep conversation, listing the different types of shops Carroll had mentioned. Will found his chair and picked over the remains of their meal.

Pulling her purse from inside her blouse, Attise inspected the contents. She passed some coins to Sala. "Get a few supplies, from as many different shops as possible, and see how much gossip you can collect in the process."

"Are you going to try our hostess?"

Attise looked toward the kitchen and winced. "I'm not certain I can coax her away from her favorite subject. I'll check a few of the other shopkeepers, in my role as a merchant. The weaver, perhaps, or the tannery."

"To begin with," Sala noted.

"Of course." She looked in her purse again, seemed to calculate, and was displeased with the result. She returned it to its hiding place.

"What about me?" Willam asked.

"Stay out from underfoot."

"That's stupid," Sala said vehemently.

Attise looked at her in surprise.

The mercenary continued. "If you must go about advertising your presence, at least try to confuse them. If this is a trap, then they're expecting a woman traveling alone. They may not have caught up with the fact that Willam and I are with you. If you keep him by your side, you might throw off some suspicion, and they may be slower to realize what's afoot."

"I'd rather work with you," Willam said to Sala.

"I don't need help. I'll be doing the easy part. She's the one who's jumping into the fire."

"If there is one," Attise commented. "And that's what we need to discover."

They passed the tannery by, but tucked between two houses Attise found a potter's, little more than a ramshackle shed. The front was constructed of ill-sorted planks of varying ages and colors. No door was visible, but a merry whirring was heard from inside, and Will and Attise made their way around the side to an opening that had been created by the simple expedient of removing several planks from one wall.

Outside the rain had stopped, but the single room inside was dark and dank, save for a shaft of weak sunlight that descended from the ceiling, where a section of the roof had been levered up and propped with a pole.

In his patch of sun, the potter was happily at work, humming a little tune, a lean, fair man with wild curly hair. He spared the visitors a friendly glance; then a second, speculative; then, surprisingly, a third, amused. "Give me a moment," he called, and braked his wheel.

"Well, strangers." He turned on his stool and leaned, elbows on his knees, to examine them with twinkling blue eyes. "Are you lost? Looking for directions? You can't have come in here on purpose!" Will noticed that the lower half of one leg was missing, replaced by a long wooden peg.

Attise laughed a bit. "Actually, I did." She introduced herself and Willam. "I'm a merchant, passing through on business to the south. I thought it might be useful to examine the local wares. Occasionally one can find something worth transporting, something unusual, perhaps, or fine work."

"Fine work?" He leaned back and laughed out loud. "Well you certainly won't find any of that here." He made a sweeping gesture to indicate his workshop.

Attise eyed the rickety shelves and their contents with an expression almost apologetic. "I'm afraid not." She was acting more natural, Will noticed, easy and friendly, without her usual, close-watched stiffness.

"No, cheap and sturdy, that's my stock-in-trade. The things I make are easy to replace, and people break them without a second thought. Sometimes they do it just for fun. In fact, around winter solstice I make a hundred plates, just for the folk to smash at midnight. You could never eat off those plates, but they do make a lovely sound."

Watching Attise's reactions, Will noticed that she and the potter seemed to have some natural affinity for each other. He wondered if she planned to seduce him. Spies often did, he understood, for information.

But Attise inclined her head politely, with a cheerful smile. "Well, I won't take any more of your time." She glanced up at the little skylight, checking the hour, then stopped, curious. "That can't be very efficient."

"It isn't," he admitted ruefully. "But then, neither am I, and it suits me well enough. When the sun moves, I move too. It's a good excuse to take myself off for a bit of friendly conversation and a pot of brew."

"But there's no tavern in this town."

"No, but we manage well enough. Old Grandfather Miller supplies the brew, and the best conversations are always found in your neighbor's kitchen."

"There is that," she said. "But it makes it harder on the stranger. After days traveling, a brew and a conversation are things to cherish."

He made a wry sound. "It's all local gossip, local intrigues; you'd find it boring, I'm afraid."

"Not at all. If you travel long enough, everything feels local."

"There is that," he said, and at that phrase, he and Attise suddenly looked at each other in mutual astonishment and spoke simultaneously. "Where are you from?"

They laughed together, and she went on. "You're not from here?"

"No, not at all. My town was Denham Notch, on the West Road. It's far north, off the western curve of the Long North Road."

"Where the West Road turns from northwest to southwest."

He clapped his hands. "You know it! I thought you might. Skies above, you're like a fresh wind off the desert. I knew I liked you as soon as you spoke. Where's your town?"

"Terminus, at the other end of the road."

They were going to reminisce, Will realized; bored with the conversation, he took himself off to one side to examine the potter's ware. Attise and the potter kept chatting like old friends.

"Terminus! I've been there a dozen times when I was a point rider on a caravan. That was before this." There was a thump as he slapped his peg.

Behind one of the shelves, the wall was stone, not wood; the outside of the adjacent building, Will realized. He reached behind a row of pots and touched the wall. Pulling back his hand, he found it coated with a damp powder. He smelled it, then tasted it.

"But I never saw you there," the potter said to Attise.

"I'm hardly memorable."

Will turned back. Attise had found a seat on a workbench and was swinging her legs cheerfully. "You know," Will began, and the potter turned back, a little annoyed. "This stuff that's growing on your walls, it'll get on your pots."

The potter eyed him. "It does, sometimes."

"Well, I could scrape it off for you. You should do that, once in a while."

Speaking to Attise, the man said, "Your lad's getting bored. Why don't you send him off wandering for a bit?"

Attise was watching Willam with that sharp, too-intelligent gaze. "No," she said. "He tends to get into trouble if he's left to his own devices."

Will tried to look sheepish. "Really, I don't mind doing it for you. It'll keep me busy."

They exchanged glances, and the potter shrugged. "Suit yourself." He turned back to Attise. "No, I would have remembered you." Willam could hear the smile in the man's voice.

Will found a potsherd and another stool and, moving the items from a high shelf, began scraping the stones, using a broken jug to catch the powder. The conversation behind him wandered haphazardly. Willam soon finished his first section, replaced the pots, and began on the next.

"Did you find it to be true?" the potter asked Attise at one point. "Aren't the people friendlier in the south?"

Attise made an affirmative sound. "I think it's the desert that does it to us. Life is so fragile in the north, you have to work so hard, live so carefully. It makes us cautious."

"Well, I never regretted settling down here. There I was, stumping my way north off the Upland Route with my mind full of misery, and these people took me in. They didn't know a thing about me, but they made me feel like pure gold. You won't find a finer town than Kiruwan."

"Have other strangers settled here and found the same thing?"

There was a pause. "Well." Willam heard him shift. "No other strangers have moved in. No, everyone else is native."

Willam abandoned his stool for the third shelf.

"Perhaps you can advise me. Is there anything in this town that I might find worth buying?"

The potter took his time in answering. "There's Lena, the weaver. She does some interesting things. And you might try the jeweler."

"A small town like this can support a jeweler?"

"Well." There was a rustle and thump as he stretched his legs. "He makes most of his money as a silversmith. But we do have enough people coming through in winter to make his other work pay. I suppose you might find something you can use." He did not sound very enthusiastic; possibly he had a grudge against the man.

Will heard Attise jump to the floor. "Then I'll look in on those two. Thank you for your help, and the conversation."

"I enjoyed it." He sounded a little regretful.

"Willam." Will turned to see Attise beckon. "Let's go."

"But I'm not finished."

"He's a hard worker," the potter observed. He was looking at Will a little differently; Will could not identify the change.

"Can't I stay for a while?"

"I don't mind," the man began, but Attise interrupted.

"No." She was studying Willam, and it suddenly occurred to him that nothing he had been doing had missed her notice. "I think I need him with me."

Outside, Will detoured to carry the broken jug out back to the trash. Once out of sight, he dug out his grubby handkerchief, poured the powder into it, knotted the ends, and discarded the jug.

They found Lena, the weaver, plying her shuttle in a little room completely filled by the bulk of her loom. She listened to Attise's requests grudgingly, then conducted them into a second room, where bolts of cloth were stacked haphazardly. Attise duly inspected the work, but Will could tell she was not really interested; and try as she might, she could not draw Lena into casual conversation.

It came to Will that visiting the weaver's was mere distraction. Attise was marking her time, waiting for something to happen. There were too many things Willam did not know, too many events outside of his control. And the caution he had learned so dearly from his spells began to prick at him. If there was danger somewhere in this town, he—and perhaps even Attise herself—was walking into it blindly.

16

"Are you learning anything?"

Attise looked up at him. "Nothing to speak of." They strolled down the street together in silence for a while.

Will slipped to Attise's opposite side, to avoid the muddy gutter. "Well, what are you looking *for?*" But he expected no real answer.

She stopped before a tall-windowed shop. "Perhaps this." Stepping across the gutter, she entered, pausing at the door to motion Willam to follow.

Inside, tall shutters had been pushed wide open, and the broad room was surprisingly bright. The walls were covered with shelves displaying plates and cups of silver and pewter. Toward the back, the room opened further into a workshop with benches and a small unlit stove.

Standing near the windows were a number of dark wood cases, lined with velvet of different colors to offset the varied contents to best advantage. A hasp on the front of each case suggested that they could be locked, although lids and locks were not in evidence. The velvet was dusty in some cases, worn in others, new in a few.

Attise scanned the shop, then strolled idly to the first case and examined the contents. A collection of red and pale-green stones set in silver was displayed on yellow velvet. Will reluctantly found himself fancying an openwork ring of subdued elegance.

"Well, here we are, then, here we are!" A little man bustled in from the rear of the shop. He was of Attise's height, with a high forehead, dark hair, and a beard of more gray than black. "Lovely work, that, lovely work. Some of my best." He approached and indicated an item. "There, you see? Delicacy, that's my specialty. You won't find many who can manage work like that." He seemed delighted by his own expertise.

"It is lovely," Attise admitted.

"Oh, yes, and—" He held up one finger. "—if silver's too dear for your purse, I can do much the same in pewter." He bustled over to a second case, sifted through its contents casually, and came back with a dusky twin of Will's ring, with a paler stone.

Attise took the ring and studied it. By now Will knew her conceits from her genuine reactions, and he realized with some surprise that she was keenly interested. "Where do you get the stones?" she asked the shopkeeper.

"Ah. Well." He drummed his fingers and pursed his lips. "Garnets from the schist in the local hills, lots of that, as you can see; but people always underestimate its versatility, don't you agree? Peridots, they're from the north, and someone came in last year with a lovely chunk of tourmaline—never saw anything like it, and I think you'll agree I've put it to good use . . ." He wandered to another case.

Attise turned to Will. "Isn't your mother's best dress blue? Or was it violet?"

"Ha, ha." The jeweler shook a finger at her. "Now, you can't fool me, not in a town like this, tongues wagging all the time. You're not idly passing the time. You're a merchant, and you're inspecting my goods to see what you can use. Well, I'm more than glad to help you, and I'll even give you a hint: Volume discount is a distinct possibility, yes. Especially with these garnets. Really, I can't seem to get rid of them."

Attise replied with careful casualness. "But garnets are so . . . common, in so many places."

"Oh ho." His brown eyes crinkled, and he bounced on the balls of his feet. "The unusual," he said expressively, then paused for effect like a showman.

He stepped back to a cupboard against the wall, unlatched it, and pulled out two small trays covered with black velvet, which he carefully placed on top of a display of garnets. Then he stepped aside to view the reaction.

Will's response was an involuntary "Oh . . ."

"Incredible," Attise breathed.

The works displayed were all constructed of larger and smaller panels of a rich gem. Shifting light fragmented the color into every shade of blue, in shapes that reminded Will of frost flowers on the surface of frozen water.

Each panel, large and small, was embellished with silver inlay: intricate geometric patterns, emblems, and in some cases even landscapes. One necklace of startling beauty showed scenes from a hunt: in the center panel, a stag, wild-eyed, leaped a rushing brook, hounds in pursuit, all perfectly depicted in tiny silver lines.

"What's the stone?" Attise asked. "And how do you manage to cut it so thin?"

"Oh, now . . ." The jeweler pursed his lips. "I'm not about to let that little secret out, am I?" He indicated the trays emphatically. "There's no one else who can do that work, no one but me. And of course, the more rare something is . . ."

"Of course." Attise's mouth twisted, and she examined the hunt necklace again. "But these silver lines . . . are they filigree? It doesn't seem possible."

"Well . . ." He surrendered to a need to boast. "No, they're not constructed at all. You see— " He leaned close and pointed at the stag. "I etch the patterns, with a tool of my own devising—very fine as you can see. Then I set the gem in a wash . . ." Attise shifted her attention to the man's face, listening intently as he explained. "The wash is an adhesive, and when it dries, well, I polish the surface of the gem, just a bit, and the adhesive comes off the surface and stays in the etches."

Attise thought a moment, then blinked. "Then you pass it through a wash of molten silver?"

The jeweler clapped his hands and laughed. "Well, there you are! That's exactly what I do! And the silver stays in the lines."

Attise nodded distractedly and ran her index finger across the face of one panel. "And you seal it with . . . is this a varnish?"

"Something like," he conceded. "More of a gum, really . . . now wait, wait a bit." He came to himself and shook a finger at her. "Here, now. I can't go telling you everything, can I? That's not good business."

She laughed. "No. Not at all. Forgive me, I have some interest in the craft." She turned back to the display. "I might find some customers for such work. Do you manage to sell many?"

"The process is tricky," he admitted reluctantly. "I find I have to charge more than people hereabouts and coming through are willing to pay. Except for the smaller pieces; actually, some of those move quite nicely." He indicated a group of brooches and a trio of tiny

pendants. Too small for scenes, they were decorated with simple geometric designs.

Something about the brooches jogged Willam's memory. Abruptly,
he remembered that Ingrud had worn one as a clasp on her cloak. He
was about to comment, but stopped himself when he could not recall
how Ingrud's known movements would intersect with Attise's pretended ones.

"What about these rings?" Attise asked the jeweler.

The little man winced. "Not at all popular, I have to admit. A bit
of an error on my part. People don't seem to like to wear them where
the gem touches their skin." Willam touched one experimentally and
found the oily surface eerie and unpleasant.

Attise sifted through the rings and found one with a simple but
striking design. She began to slip it on her middle finger, then stopped
and shifted it to the third. "I see what you mean," she told the jeweler.
"But they do serve as a good example of your technique." She turned
to him. "I'd like to give this some thought."

"Of course, of course! Mustn't rush into things, but I don't have any
doubts, my work is unique! Still, think, and come back later. Take that
ring to keep, if you like," he waved his hand. "No charge, call it a sample. Just as well to be rid of it, actually." He tapped his cheek thoughtfully. "Now, if you come back, make it the evening, if you don't mind.
I have a little something to do; in fact, I ought to leave now."

"Business?" Attise asked nonchalantly.

"Ho ho!" He bounced again. "Business of a personal sort. A lovely
little lady, housemaid down at the first farm up the main road. It's her
afternoon free, but she never goes far, her mistress is an invalid, very
devoted, she is. Now, if you want to talk sooner, you come there, ask
for my Ammalee. Don't worry about interrupting, business before
pleasure . . ." He bustled off, closing and locking cases, then pulling
the tall shutters in. Attise looked long at her ring, eyes narrowed in
thought, oblivious to all else, until the jeweler hurried them out and
locked the door.

They returned to their lodgings, Attise in a black, silent mood, impervious to questions. Back at the ivy-covered house, they found Sala
sitting on a bench in the sunlight with a group of small packages and
a disgruntled expression. "I never met such a closed-mouthed lot.

You'd think I was a criminal, the way they brushed me off. I could hardly get them to do business."

Attise tested the grass, found it too wet, and settled down beside Sala. "What did you get?"

"Some cheese, dried meat, and hardbread." Sala, catching Attise's amused look, gave a wry half smile, and continued. "No gossip, no details. The war hardly bothered them. They've had no contact with wizard's troops. The potter moved here ten years ago. Everyone else has been here forever."

"We did a little better. Here." Attise slipped off the ring and passed it to Sala. The mercenary studied it with suspicion.

"It's the same."

Attise nodded.

"Ingrud was right?"

"No." Attise thumped one knee in frustration. "No, it seems—" She moved her hands as if there were something between them. "It seems as if it ought to fit, but it's all too facile." She dropped her hands. "I talked awhile with the potter. As it happens, he grew up near the place I did, and he was quite open with me, for a while." Sala was interested, and Attise made to continue, paused, then looked significantly at Willam.

He bristled. "I'm not going anywhere."

"Will—"

"I do whatever you want, but you never tell me anything. You're just using me—"

Sala interrupted. "Of course we are. And you're using us. It seems fair to me. Now go away."

"But I could help you better. And maybe you could help me better, too, and easier, if I knew what was going on." He turned from one to the other, Sala's face stubborn, Attise's full of weary exasperation. "Maybe you think I'm not much, but I'm not stupid, I can see things too. Why did the people stop being friendly?"

"What?" Sala was taken aback, but Attise watched him closely.

"The potter said that people here were friendly to strangers, but they weren't friendly to you, or to me. The jeweler was friendly to Attise, but the weaver wasn't." Calmer, he sat on the wet grass and looked at Attise intently. "It's something to do with that jeweler. Something important is going on here, isn't it?"

Attise hesitated, then said, "I hope so."

"You don't know for sure?"

"Not yet."

"What will you do if you find out there is?"

Her mouth twisted. "Run away."

"And report this to Shammer and Dhree?"

The women exchanged glances; then Attise took a moment to think. She leaned forward. "What did you take from the potter's shop?" Sala looked surprised at the change of subject, then watched Willam with renewed interest.

Will was not surprised at all. "There's some stuff that grows on stone walls, and in caves. In Langtry, we had a lot of it. People had to scrape down their walls regularly, especially in cellars."

"And?"

He knew what she wanted and shrugged uncomfortably. "And I use it in my charms."

"What does it do?"

With great reluctance, he said, "It works with the other things in a spell, one of the spells I know."

Attise said nothing else, but sat watching him, waiting.

"I don't think I should tell you anything else," Will said at last.

Willam noticed with some surprise that Sala was looking at Attise as if concerned for her. She touched the merchant's arm to get her attention. "Don't press the boy. I think it's a good thing. The more magic the common folk know, the better matters will go for everyone."

Surprisingly, Attise made no protest against the comment, but only stirred uncomfortably. "I don't have enough information."

Suddenly Willam noticed that Attise was tired—no, exhausted. She seemed weak and worn, and her expression bleak. She turned away. "Willam," she began, not looking at him. "I'm sorry that you think I'm being unfair. It's not my doing, it's the situation."

"You mean that because of your mission, you get to push me around."

Her voice was flat. "I don't mean to push you. I simply do what I need to do. It's because I don't do what *you* want me to that you have a problem. Now, please leave for a while, so that Sala and I can discuss this."

Watching her, Willam slowly recognized again what Sala had pointed out to him once: that this woman was doing something against her own will, acting in a way that she hated. Sala had meant it differently, but now he realized it was true in a deeper sense. Somehow, in some important way, Attise was helpless.

His anger evaporated, and what was left, surprisingly, was pity. "If you don't like working for Shammer and Dhree," he said, "why don't you quit?"

She closed her eyes and shook her head, and Willam could not tell if that meant that she could not quit, or that she could not tell him why, or that she did not want to talk about it. He began to wonder if it was possible to quit the service of a wizard, if it was permitted at all. Perhaps Shammer and Dhree would do something terrible to her if she tried. Perhaps they were no better than Abremio—maybe there was no difference between the behaviors of Blue and Red. But that could not be; there had to be some difference.

Suddenly he wished, truly and sincerely, that he could do something to help Attise. Without preamble, he said, "When I'm a wizard, I won't do this to people."

She understood. But she turned back, and amazingly, he saw pity for him on her own face. "When you're a wizard," she told him sadly, "you'll do what wizards do."

The front door thumped open, and a thin voice demanded, "Have you seen him?" Carroll's slatternly wife stormed out, fists on her hips, glaring up and down the damp sunlit street.

Startled, Attise looked at her once, blankly, then rose and turned aside to deal with her own dark thoughts.

Sala exchanged a glance with Willam. "Meaning your husband?"

"Who else? Slippery devil, saying he's off visiting, saying he doesn't know where the money went." She whirled on them, shaking her fist vehemently. "All the good coin you gave me, gone! Never drinks, doesn't touch a drop, he says! Well, I'll catch him at it, one of these days, and when I do he'll be as gone as the moon. I tell you . . ." She wandered back into the house, muttering, leaving a large silence behind her.

Will tried to find something to say, to recover from the unresolved, interrupted discussion. Something comradely. "I'd drink if she was my wife."

Sala glanced at Attise's back and played along. "Never marry. Or marry someone more entertaining."

"Or smarter; you'd think she'd have it figured out by now. I guess she doesn't look at the trash heap much."

"Trash heap?"

Attise had turned back and was looking at him as if he had said something astounding.

He paused, puzzled. "That's right," he told her, confused. "Out back. There's a dozen broken jugs in the trash. And some not very old, either. She doesn't have to try to catch him at anything—those jugs tell the story themselves."

Attise looked at the house, then the other houses, with a faintly stunned expression. "This town doesn't have a communal trash area."

He could not tell if she was asking him or telling him. "No," he confirmed. "From the yard, you can look along the whole row of houses—"

But she had swept into the house, through the front room, past the still-grumbling wife, and toward the hall to the back door. Will hurried after. "Where's Bel?" she asked when she saw he was still with her.

That was Sala's real name, he knew; but Attise only slipped and used it when she was excited or upset. The mercenary caught up. "Here."

As they emerged from the rear door, Attise turned left, ignoring the trash heap Will had mentioned, and hurried on, intent.

"What's the matter?" Will asked. They had crossed the back garden and were passing through the next yard. An elderly woman emerged from a chicken coop and stared in bleary confusion as they swept past.

Attise made an offhand apology to her and continued on to the next yard. "Either nothing, or everything," she said to no one in particular.

"What do you mean?"

But she was absorbed in her urgency and did not reply until Sala repeated the question. "Contradictions. That's what's wrong with this town." Attise stopped and scanned the area. "We have a saying," she continued distractedly. " 'There are no contradictions.' " She spotted her goal and hurried on.

"Who's 'we'?" Will asked Sala, but she waved him silent and followed Attise, fascinated.

To Will's amazement, they stopped by a pile of trash behind one of the shops. Sala peered at it while Attise stooped and began rummaging through, heedless of the dust and dirt.

"What are you looking for?" Sala asked.

"Nothing specific." Attise pulled out a pair of wood laths connected by an odd rusty hinge and examined them closely. "But I shall be very interested in what I do find." She dropped the laths and was briefly absorbed in the study of a tangle of string. The mercenary dropped down beside her and watched as she extracted from the tangle a short white splinter.

"Contradictions," Sala hazarded, "between what you know and what Ingrud said."

Attise kept the splinter and moved to another side of the heap. "And," she said, poking at some potsherds, "between the way the people of this town act, and what they tell us." She found a boat-shaped piece of dark wood as long as her hand, cracked down its length. She stopped and gazed at it, lost in thought, then looked up at Sala and Willam as if surprised to find them there. Hefting the wood, she studied the shuttered windows at the back of the shop. Will realized that the shop was the jeweler's, and as he watched Attise, he found himself reminded of the careful, thoughtful expression Ingrud had worn when he had asked her questions.

"What sort of trash does a jeweler leave?" Attise asked.

Sala paused in surprise. Then, inexplicably, she laughed. "Not the sort you have there?"

Puzzled, Will recognized one item. "That's a shuttle, a shuttle from a loom."

Attise had returned from her thoughts strangely lighthearted. She grinned up at him, and he found the expression incongruous on her face. "That's right," she said. "And this—" She held up another item. "—is half of a bone needle, broken." She pointed at parts of the heap. "Rather many bits of string and thread, too short to be of use." She reached in, pulled out a potsherd, and indicated it. "Stained on the inside; that's from dye." She dropped the items and stood, dusting her hands. "Until very recently, the jeweler's shop was held by the weaver."

"He moved his shop?"

"I think that if we ask, we'll be told that he didn't. He's a recent arrival. And here's the proof." She pointed with her chin at the heap.

"But," Will said, "the potter said he's always been here. Was he lying?"

Attise nodded.

"What happened to the weaver?" Sala wondered.

Attise pointed down the row of shops. "She moved onto the cross street, to that new house on the end. It's not a proper shop at all; it's not set up correctly. It's just a dwelling, pressed into use." She turned back to the jeweler's. "He took this one because it's one of the oldest buildings in town, supporting the claim that he's always lived here."

"But why would the people lie?" Willam asked.

"Why does anyone do anything?" Attise replied. "To make their lives better, or to prevent them from getting worse."

Sala nodded. "Rewards or punishments."

"In this case."

"The jeweler is a wizard's man."

Attise held up a cautioning finger. "And we mustn't let on that we know."

"And this was all designed—"

"To convince me that I'd been mistaken. That I'd been . . . chasing the moon."

Sala laughed a little. "We have that saying, too."

"That surprises me not at all."

Will looked from one woman to the other. They ignored him completely.

"And here we stand in full daylight, in sight of the back windows of the jeweler's shop," the mercenary said.

Attise was amused. "He's visiting Ammalee, who is a housemaid for an invalid living at the first farm up the main road." Will remembered the conversation.

"So his shop stands empty."

The merchant made an airy gesture. "Convenient for us to break into and discover all sorts of fascinating items pertaining to the making of jewelry."

"Which you'd recognize?"

"Some. Not all, because of his 'secret process'—"

"But they'd be the sorts of things that make sense."

"Exactly. It would be the *sorts* that were important. Items unidentifiable in specific, but recognizable as to type."

"To someone used to thinking that way . . ."

"Such as myself."

The jeweler might be a wizard's man, Attise had said. "Are you going to kill him?" Will asked.

They turned on him in surprise. "No," Attise told him. "We're going to act naturally, and leave here."

"And report to your masters?"

A quick glance at each other, another glance toward the shuttered shop, apprehension on their faces, and suddenly it was as if a toy house of twigs collapsed inside Willam, revealing something hidden within, something startling. Everything was changed.

He said in slow amazement, "That jeweler was sent here by Shammer and Dhree themselves. You don't serve them at all."

They faced him. Attise was wearing her watching-and-waiting look, but, strangely, Sala was standing as if ready for sudden action, dark eyes full of danger. A memory came to him unbidden: When he had first met these two, it had been Attise who had saved his life.

She spoke. "Willam, if you want to find Shammer and Dhree, follow the main road north to Lake Cerlew. Make your way along the shore to the east; someone there will know where to send you. I don't recommend you approach the jeweler. It's best you're not connected with us."

Sala listened in growing astonishment, then turned on her. "You can't mean that. We mustn't let him go!"

"It will take him some time to reach the wizards. We can vanish into the woods."

"It's too risky."

This was impossible. Attise, whom he hated, was trying to save him from Sala, his friend.

"I won't have the boy hurt, Bel. He's innocent. And you said it yourself: The more magic the common folk know, the better things will be for everyone."

By that statement, Willam identified another change, but it only added to his confusion. "You don't serve a Blue, either. You—you don't serve any wizard at all."

Sala narrowed her eyes and shifted, but with a gesture Attise asked her to wait. Attise turned to the boy, spreading her hands in a wide gesture of honesty. "Willam, I'm not a spy. I'm a steerswoman."

"No," he said immediately. "Steerswomen never lie."

She nodded, and her mouth twisted a bit. "True. Say, then, that I'm a lapsed steerswoman. I was one, until the time came that I needed to lie, to save my life. I'll be one again, when that time is past." She shifted uncomfortably, but her gaze remained steady on Willam. "The wizards want me, Willam, all of them. They're hunting me. Don't betray me."

And then he finally realized that it had to be true. Ingrud had recognized her, had been distressed, had talked about that steersman who had quit the order. Attise had needed privacy to explain something to her. And Attise sometimes knew things she should not, recognized connections invisible to others, and pieced things together in a way unlike other people. Nothing was as it had seemed.

To a steerswoman, lying must be like torture. Attise must have been dreading every day, suffering through every conversation with a stranger. It would make her quiet, so that she would not lie unless she had to. It would make her angry, to go against her training so. And she would be bad at it, as bad and as transparent in deceit as Attise was.

And it had to do with wizards. Attise was in danger from the wizards; she was somehow a victim of theirs.

The steerswomen never used their knowledge or their intelligence to hurt people. They knew more than anyone except the wizards, and they never used it to control, never tried to have power over others. They were not like most people.

They only cared about learning and discovering, and they shared their knowledge joyfully. In that they were as innocent and direct as children. Willam knew well the evil of using power against the innocent. He had been helpless that time; this time, things stood differently.

Attise was watching him intently, without annoyance, without anger, without fear or discomfort, without deceit. She was watching him like a steerswoman, but her eyes held a question, and a steerswoman's questions had to be answered.

"I won't tell anyone about you," he said. "I won't betray you. I'll help you, if I can." And he could, he realized, perhaps better than anyone else. He lifted his head a bit higher. "But, tell me, lady . . . tell me all about wizards."

17

*I*t was as easy as laughter, as natural as breathing, as joyful as the swing in her step on the road. Attise the reluctant merchant fell from her mind like a muddied cloak, and Rowan felt right in her heart for the first time in what seemed like a lifetime. It did not matter to her that she walked in danger; it only mattered that she could speak and act freely again, and that the power given to her by her training and nature need not be hidden like some secret sin. The one true concern she had was that she might die before the puzzle was solved, and that would be tragedy indeed.

To protect the hope of an answer: that was the goal, the duty and the pleasure. She felt it with more urgency than even the need of preserving her own life. To stay alive served the goal.

And in the meantime, as she and her comrades clambered alone, up and down the hilly countryside, she was doing what her spirit had designed itself to do. She was answering questions.

"Since as far back as the Steerswomen's records reach, there has always been a wizard resident in the city of The Crags. This probably accounts for the heavy-handed control Abremio holds; The Crags has never been without a wizard. It depends on its wizard to a degree not found in any other holding. Its politics depend on his decisions, and its workings depend on his magic. How long this situation existed before our records, we don't know.

"We do know that sometimes thereafter, a wizard became established in Wulfshaven, on a far less formal basis. The log-books of the first steerswoman, Sharon, make some oblique references to the event. In fact, it was clear that she approved of it."

"More fool she," Bel muttered. The Outskirter fussed a moment with the frogs on her cloak as the wind picked up and whirled it around her legs. She had never resigned herself to the loss of her own piebald cloak, left at the Archives because of its conspicuousness.

Willam looked at her, then checked Rowan's reaction to the seemingly heretical statement. But Rowan merely nodded.

"Yes. Sharon herself said that, over and over, at a later date. A lot of her logbooks are filled with complaints about her own misjudgments. But humans aren't infallible, and conclusions depend on the knowledge at hand."

She gathered her information and continued. "So, those two holdings are the oldest. For many years there were only two wizards, and believe it or not, there was no animosity between them."

Willam was puzzled. "But they fight all the time, now."

Rowan held up a finger. "That's not quite true. They fight periodically."

"Same thing."

"Not at all." Rowan was annoyed at that twisting of facts. "Get your information right. They clash, regularly. In a large way, once a generation. In a small way, several times, and you can count on two shifts of alliance each generation." Rowan found that the information that Hugo had given her at the Archives was falling more clearly into place in the retelling, and she reminded herself that such was often the case.

"So. That's how matters remained, for nearly two hundred years. Around that time, the lands around the Greyriver began to increase in population. As the town at the river's mouth became an important port, dragons appeared, first in small numbers, then greater." She noticed Bel's sidelong glance and continued. "At the same time, two new wizards established themselves. One took residence in the port and immediately took the dragon problem in hand. No one contested his holding, least of all the townspeople, and the town even took its name from its first wizard."

"So there was a wizard Donner who did what Jannik does now?" Bel asked.

"Who's Jannik?" Will queried.

"The wizard in Donner," Bel supplied. "He controls the dragons there. Or doesn't, depending on his mood."

The boy turned his wide copper gaze back to the steerswoman. Despite herself Rowan felt a shift in her breath. Those eyes, so strange in color, were so beautiful. He was a beautiful boy, and would be a handsome man one day soon.

"But which wizard is after you?" Willam pressed.

Rowan had explained her mission to him. "We don't know for certain. But there's good reason to suspect that it's Shammer and Dhree."

"And that's where we are now, in their territory." He seemed to give the fact careful consideration.

"Possibly."

He nodded grimly. "Good."

"There's no reason to be pleased about it."

"I agree with him." Bel was a few steps ahead, and Rowan, perturbed, moved up to where she could watch her friend's expression.

The Outskirter continued. "I'm tired of this. I don't mind danger, but I don't like it forever waiting just out of sight. I want to see it face-to-face, or I want it to go away."

"It will go away," Rowan assured her, "when we reach the Outskirts." She smiled a little. "Then you'll only have your old familiar dangers."

"I'll be glad to see them," Bel admitted. She looked at the sky and at the track ahead. "And it's time we found a place to spend the night." The Outskirter lengthened her stride and pulled ahead on the trail.

The steerswoman watched a moment, then returned to her explications to Willam. "Now, the second wizard, a woman, claimed the upper Wulf valley. The area was largely uninhabited at that time, and she lived, for the most part, the life of a recluse—"

Will interrupted. "But what do they *do?*"

"Do?"

"What kind of magic? Is it different for each wizard?"

Rowan considered. "Not really. Any specialties they favor seem to be based on their situation. Jannik in Donner has control of the dragons, but there's no indication that another wizard couldn't do the same. Corvus, in Wulfshaven, has knowledge of the movements of sea creatures and the weather, but he's based in a major seaport, where those things are of vital interest to everyone."

He brooded a moment. "Abremio seems to be able to do anything."

"So I hear. I'll ask you about him at length, in a bit," Rowan said. "You have firsthand knowledge."

"But I've never seen him do what I do."

"And what exactly do you do?"

He hesitated. "Well, I've told you . . ."

"Yes. Rocks and tree stumps. Digging wells." She spotted Bel, who had wandered off the path ahead looking for a discreet campsite. They exchanged waves, and Rowan led Will toward the Outskirter. "You've told me what it's for, or at least the use you put it to. But how exactly do you do it?"

"Well, I place the charms around the object, or under it, or in a hole . . . Then I have to put fire to them. That has to be done from a distance—"

"How? Magically?"

"No," he admitted, embarrassed. "I tried that, but I can't make it happen. I use a burning arrow. Or sometimes, a sort of path made out of straw, or crumbled bits of another charm."

"And then?"

He shrugged uncomfortably. "When the fire reaches the charms, the spell releases."

"And it's not good to get in the way," Rowan added, remembering his earlier description.

"That's right."

Rowan nodded. "How do you make the charms?"

He did not answer. Rowan stopped and turned to face him, one hand on his arm. He avoided her glance, looking pained and unhappy; it was an expression she had seen before, on a few other faces.

"Will," she said, "I'm glad you're traveling with us. I like you. And I think that on this journey, I can use all the help that I can get." She paused. "I'm not a real steerswoman at the moment, but the time will come when I shall be again. You can refuse to answer me now, but you can't forever."

He stuttered a bit. "I know that. It's just—maybe I won't be able tell you anything, not ever."

"How so?" Ahead, Bel hailed them again, but Rowan ignored her.

"Well . . ." His face worked with thought. "There are some things the wizards don't ever tell the folk. About how their magic works."

"There are many things the wizards don't explain," Rowan conceded cautiously. "The reasons behind their actions, their shifting allegiances, and the workings of their power."

"And we don't know why."

"Correct."

"But that's just it!" He swallowed. "We don't know why they hide those things. Maybe there's a *reason*; maybe it's the right thing to do. Maybe it's something people shouldn't know."

Rowan said nothing, but let him work through the problem alone. On the horizon, the westering sun cut below the heavy bank of clouds that hung above like a flat ceiling. For a moment the world turned gold and dove-gray, and a fine drizzle fell briefly, then ceased. One part of her mind noted that there must be a rainbow somewhere over her right shoulder.

"This magic I can do, it's just something I figured out for myself," Willam went on. "There was nobody—" He struggled for a moment. "There was nobody wiser than myself to tell me what it means, or what to do about it. I just don't know enough. Maybe it would be terrible if anyone else knew how it worked. Maybe it's terrible that I know."

"And how am I to judge, without information?" Rowan said.

He shifted the pack on his back and used both his hands in a wide, pleading gesture. "Lady—Rowan, I'm going to be a wizard someday. When I am, if I find that they're keeping their secrets for some mean reason, I promise you that I'll tell you everything, anything. But until I really know it's safe, please, don't ask me to do something that might be bad." He dropped his hands, looked stricken. "I can't do anything that hurts people."

He stood before her, a tall boy, bigger than his years, strong for his age, more intelligent than his peers, possessing some secret power— and begging her, humbly, to not make him hurt anyone.

"You'll be a poor wizard," Rowan said. "Or, you'll be the best of them." She turned away and walked toward Bel's waiting figure.

He caught up with her in two long strides. "You won't ask me again?"

"I'm going to think on this awhile."

Bel had found a clearing a few paces off the south side of the trail. A damp circle of ashes showed where some previous traveler had camped, months earlier. A tangle of low birches surrounded it, and Bel was using the branches to create a rain fly from the merchant Attise's cloak. She had refused to abandon it when Rowan returned to using her own gray felt cloak, declaring it to be too useful.

"We'll need a fire tonight, with this damp."

Rowan scanned the sky and decided that the mist would continue to midnight without converting to a proper downpour. "If we can get one going at all, we might be able to keep it all night."

Bel was digging in her pack for the trail provisions purchased in Kiruwan. "If we can find dry wood after all that rain."

Rowan and Willam foraged through the underbrush and managed to acquire a pair of stout damp branches, which Willam cracked methodically and effortlessly across his knee. A handful of dry twigs and needles from the lee of a lone fir tree was the best that could be found for kindling, and Rowan plied her flints doggedly, creating a series of merry little blazes that guttered dismally against the logs. As she tried with one last pile of needles, Willam spoke up reluctantly. "Let me try."

Rowan eyed him a moment, then rose, slapping the damp from her trousers.

Willam went to his sack, opened it, inserted one hand, and felt inside carefully. What came out was one package, the size of his fist, wrapped in oilcloth. Rowan moved closer to observe, and Bel watched him cautiously from across the clearing. He spared the Outskirter a single glance, then studied Rowan, his face unreadable. Perhaps it was a surrender of sorts, or a bargain: he could not tell her, but it seemed that he was going to show her.

The package unrolled to reveal a layer of wool, and nestled in it, separated from each other, were three objects wrapped in paper. Willam removed one, carefully rolled the others back into the oilskin, and replaced it in his pack, which he carried to the edge of the clearing and secreted behind a weedy tussock.

Returning to the fire site, he seated himself on the ground. Rowan dropped to the ground beside him.

The paper was secured by twists, which he casually undid. Inside was a quantity of black gravel that faintly glittered. Taking a pinch of the gravel between his fingers, he crumbled it to powder onto the logs, creating a thin line along the surface of each. Rowan noted that the lines continued from each log to the next, creating a continuous network, then recognized that the lines formed a hexagram. The final arm continued outward from the heap, ending a foot outside the first circle. There Willam arranged Rowan's little pile of needles, adding one more tiny pinch of the black gravel. He paused a moment, studying what remained in the paper; he had used less than a third of the quantity.

Finally he twisted the paper closed again and methodically returned it to its place in his pack behind the tussock. When he returned, Rowan wordlessly handed him her flints, and he gestured her back, doing it twice before he was satisfied with her distance.

With his back to her, she could not clearly see what he was doing, but from the sound it seemed nothing more than striking sparks into the pile of kindling. He tried three times; then there was a sudden hiss, and he stepped back quickly.

A line of sparking fire fled from the kindling, sped to the logs, and raced along their lengths, spitting madly. There was a group of sudden quiet noises from the wood, like gasps, and one log abruptly split down its length with a loud *crack*. Rowan was aware of a sharp, acrid odor.

Flame flared, faded, leaped again, and then the fire settled down to blaze in earnest. Bel fearlessly strode over, kneeled by the fire, and peered at the still-sparking wood. "Can you make anything burn?"

The boy watched her broodingly. "No. I can't burn stone. But I can break it. It's easy."

"Is that when it becomes noisy?"

"Yes. Very. And dangerous."

Rowan moved to Bel's side. Each log, she saw, was burning individually, along the line the gravel had traced. Using the toe of her boot, she rearranged the wood so that the flames better fed each other.

Bel looked up at her. "Are you going to ask how he did it?"

She shook her head. "No." But she sat up long that night in thought, watching the fire.

They spent the next day following the narrow trail down one ridge and up the next. The land began to open, and deep in one valley the travelers came across an abandoned farm, with a burnt-out, ruined cabin. There was no sign of the previous inhabitants, but when they crossed a fallow field they found a low hill of violent green, such as grew where corpses were buried. Rowan considered the extent of the mound and calculated. "More than those who lived in that house. I suspect this was a battle site."

"That definitely puts us in Shammer and Dhree's holding?" Bel asked.

Rowan shrugged. "That depends on which side won this particular battle."

The past winter and now the spring had claimed the land for wilderness, all the shouts and the clash of arms lost in the past as though a hundred years had gone. Only the mound remained, its shape unnatural, its green too bright, feverish. The travelers stood silent for some time, each lost in thought. A fresh light wind rose, and the grass shivered, then rippled like the shining surface of a rising wave. The valley was a bowl of clean sunlight, quiet, and when Bel shifted the creak of her gear was a sudden, strange, human sound: an intrusion.

Willam studied the scene grimly. Bel looked about, faintly puzzled. With a gesture, Rowan led her friends around the edge of the mound, and they continued east.

They soon left the farm behind, and their spirits lifted again. Rowan could ignore, briefly, the sensation that danger hovered somewhere, like a high hawk, too far to see.

She studied the land about her, comparing it with the few maps she had. As Attise, she had allowed herself only the sort that the common folk usually carried: copied from those of the Steerswomen, but by a less exacting eye, with less detail, excluding information not of interest to the average traveler. Rowan made corrections and additions, and found satisfaction in the routine.

With deception and manipulation abandoned, the three travelers had learned to be at ease with each other, and the going was enjoyable for itself. Rowan amused herself watching Bel's reactions. "Everything keeps changing," the Outskirter commented. They were moving along a rocky ridge, among stands of young pine.

"How so?"

"The Outskirts are much the same everywhere. The only differences come when you get closer to the Inner Lands, like the approach to Five Corners. But here, you'll have one kind of tree for a while, then pastures, then flat land, like the mud flats in Donner. Every place is different, with different kinds of life."

Rowan nodded. "Certain terrains encourage certain types of vegetation and certain types of animals."

"There aren't many different animals in the Outskirts. It's the goats and us, for the most part."

"And the goblins."

"Yes. And the demons. And insects."

They continued in silence for a while. Halfway up the ridge, the view was clear to the north, and the two women paused. Half a mile away, pines gave way to maple, which carpeted the hills to the horizon. Far off, a line of silver indicated a distant lake.

Bel looked up at the sky, as if expecting it, too, to be different from the Outskirts. "The Inner Lands seem to go on forever."

"They don't," Rowan told her. "They end to the north, just past the land where I was raised. It's red earth there, and no one's been beyond it yet. There are a few mountains visible to the west. I often wondered about them. They're probably an extension of the same range that runs north from The Crags."

Bel puzzled that over, trying to piece together Rowan's picture of the world. "And what lies west of those?"

Rowan looked dissatisfied. "No one's been there to report. Or perhaps some of Abremio's minions have gone, but they haven't given out any word." She mused for a moment, then continued. "The southern shore of the Inland Sea is inhabited, too, but not to any great distance. The vegetation gets odd farther south, and it's hard to introduce anything useful. It might be a worse version of what you have in the Outskirts."

Bel nodded. "Goats." She adjusted her pack and began to continue the ascent, tugging the reluctant donkey's lead. "You need goats about if you're going to spread the greengrass. They'll eat anything."

Rowan followed, sidestepping on the steep ground. "They can't eat redgrass or blackgrass."

The Outskirter looked back. "Of course they can. Our herds do it all the time. We couldn't survive if they didn't."

"It must be a different type of goat." With dust from their scrambling rising around her, Rowan's mind filled with speculations and calculations. "That might explain a great deal. It might even be one of the reasons the Outskirts keep moving."

Bel was puzzled. "Moving? How can they move?"

Pausing to brace herself against a splintered tree trunk, Rowan gestured out at the far horizon. "East. The Outskirts have been shifting for hundreds of years, and the Inner Lands spreading behind them. You can trace the shift by comparing the maps at the Archives. Some thousand years ago, this was the Outskirts." Bel took a moment to peer about in plain disbelief. Rowan laughed. "It's true." She continued. "Your goats might do well in the south. What a difference that could make to the people there . . ." They continued on silently for some time, the steerswoman lost in thought.

Bel watched her with amusement. "You're going to be writing a lot tonight again, aren't you?"

"What?" Rowan came back from her preoccupation with difficulty. "Yes, I suppose I am." Since Willam was in their confidence, she openly treated her folio like a proper steerswoman's logbook, crowding the pages with her close, eccentric handwriting.

"Don't you sleep anymore?"

"Too often, and too long," she replied distractedly.

Will came back up the trail to meet them. Like a ranging puppy, he had the habit of "following from in front," as folk called it; he would lope ahead, just out of sight, double back to check their position, receive some unspoken confirmation recognized only by himself, then wander off again when his curiosity got the better of him. Generally Rowan simply swung along at her own efficient pace, with the ease of the long-distance walker, and Bel ambled beside her tirelessly, taking a step and a half to Rowan's one.

"I flushed some turkeys up ahead," Willam informed them breathlessly when they reached the ridgetop. "They didn't go far. I'm sure I can get one for our dinner."

Rowan grinned. "That's a good idea. You give it a try."

Since she had dropped her disguise, the change in her relationship with the boy had altered astonishingly. She often wondered how she had ever found him difficult. It had seemed before that he was always in the way, always had to be considered and planned around—a mere nuisance. She had never understood what Bel saw in him.

But now she saw what Bel had seen: a big healthy lad, strong and intelligent, always trying to please. He was by nature cheerful, yet when Rowan answered questions he was all attention, wide copper eyes focused on her face in utter concentration. She began to learn the style of his intellect. Less quick, less flashy than the sharp minds she knew among the steerswomen, Willam tracked down her ideas doggedly, winning his understanding more by single-minded persistence than native talent. Once understood, the information the steerswoman imparted became like rain on dry ground; it soaked in deep, and made something grow—something he could use, either to nourish himself, or to turn into a weapon in his private war.

The change, she knew, was only in herself; she was relieved of deception, and her mind was free to work on its familiar paths. She recognized for the first time that lies worked damage in two directions.

Willam had strung his bow and was giving more of his attention to the tops of the trees than to the path he was walking. He stubbed the toes of his oversized sandals.

"Shall I take your pack?" Rowan volunteered. "I wouldn't want you to fall with it again." She laughed. "I don't think my nerves could take it." The donkey was carrying hers and Bel's.

"If you walk carefully," Willam replied reluctantly. "You can't stomp down on each step the way you do."

His demonstration of the previous day had impressed her. "I've seen how you carry them."

He surrendered the surprisingly heavy pack and jogged ahead. Rowan, in odd high spirits, amused herself by imitating his walk. There, she thought, now I'm carrying magic. But it was mere words; she felt no different.

All that remained, she reminded herself, was to get to the Outskirts. No wizard intruded there, and in the anonymity of the ranging tribes, she and Bel could make their way to Dust Ridge and see what might be found. There lay the greatest concentration of the jewels; so beautiful, so mysterious—and so seemingly useless.

The detour to Kiruwan had taken them off their projected path. They were north of the Upland Route, and Rowan was leading the trio due east. They would cross the Long North Road well north of Five Corners, which suited her well, as it was the area she had covered immediately following her training, and so was intimately familiar with it.

Willam planned to part with them when they crossed the Long North Road. He would follow it, either south to Jannik, or north to Olin's holding. Rowan had suggested Jannik, despite Will's dislike of Blue wizards; Jannik had a known home, while the location of Red Olin's keep was still a mystery. Additionally, Olin was the most capricious and peculiar of all the wizards.

Up ahead, Willam had left the trail and was moving cautiously and quietly among the trees. Rowan and Bel dropped farther back and finally stopped, not wishing to alert the game.

The boy was out of sight when Rowan heard the soft sound of the bow's release. High to the left, the branches of one tree shivered, and amid the drumming of wings, four birds burst from the greenery, leaving one behind, thrashing in the leaves.

Willam was standing at the foot of the tree when Rowan and Bel reached him. "It's stuck," he said disgustedly. "Can someone give me a boost?"

Rowan looked up and spotted the bird, impaled flapping on the long arrow, lodged among the close branches. "You're a good shot."

She carefully set his pack on the ground, and by climbing on her shoulders, Willam was able to reach the lowest branches. He clutched one and swung himself onto it, then continued up nimbly.

Bel watched dubiously.

"There aren't any tall trees in the Outskirts," Rowan said, remembering.

"No. There are a lot nearby, where the Inner Lands meet the Outskirts." Bel tilted her head for a better angle. "But I've never seen anyone go up one. He looks like one of those wood gnomes."

Far above, invisible among the leaves, the boy gave a cheerful whoop. "I can see past the next ridge from here! Wait . . ." Twigs rustled, and a few moments later the turkey fell to the ground at Bel's feet, quiescent. She inspected it, very pleased, then found a leather thong to tie its feet to her belt. It was a good-sized bird, and Rowan found herself speculating about nothing more esoteric than the nearness of dinnertime.

But shortly she looked up at the treetop again. There was no sound or sign from Willam. Disturbed, she called up to him.

His voice came down. "Wait . . ."

Beside Rowan, Bel was instantly alert.

"Someone's coming," Will said, and his next words were masked by the sound of his rapid descent.

"How many?" Rowan called as he came nearer. "What sort of people?"

"It's soldiers." He hung from his hands and dropped to the ground. He was disheveled and panting, with bits of twig and leaves caught on his clothing.

Bel had dropped her pack. She stood with one hand resting as if casually on the sword hilt by her right shoulder. Rowan unconsciously did the same. "How many were they?"

"Six, lady," Willam replied between gasps. "I counted six. And horses."

"The soldiers were mounted?"

"No, only two horses, with packs."

Bel was grim. "There's a blessing. We'd have no chance at all against six mounted soldiers." The Outskirter took it for granted that the strangers represented some threat.

"Have we a chance against six walking soldiers?" Rowan felt momentarily disoriented. Was it mere coincidence? Or would their peace be lost, so soon . . . "How were they dressed?" she asked Willam. "What were their weapons?"

"Swords, all. No spears. And cuirasses."

"Did they wear sigils?" Bel asked.

"Too far to tell. But their surplices were red."

Rowan calculated. "Shammer and Dhree, or possibly Olin; it might be either."

Bel's dark eyes glittered. "They're coming for us."

"We can't know until we see how they react." But internally, she was certain.

"That may be too late."

Rowan scanned the area: rocky land, gnarled underbrush, and the overhanging oaks. "How far away were they?"

"Half a mile, I make it," the boy told her.

Bel nodded with satisfaction. "What's our plan? It'll be a job to fight them. We might do well to avoid them, this time, and act when we're better prepared. We're fewer, we're forewarned, and we're more mobile." She caught Willam's astonished look. "Sometimes," she told him, "it's wiser to run."

"I'll follow whatever's decided." He turned to Rowan. "Lady? Are we going to run?"

Abruptly Rowan discovered a strange fury in herself, and an undeniable call, something that had built unnoticed during those short days of peace. She inspected the anger as if it were a phenomenon of nature, amazed—and then not amazed but comprehending, and finally agreeing with it in both logic and emotion. She reached her decision.

"No," she said, then looked down the path, eyes narrowed. "Not this time. Not anymore."

18

*I*n the failing light, the smoky fire gave more heat than illumination, and a single thin black line stretched straight up from it, absolutely still in the unmoving air. The chart and papers spread before the gray-cloaked, hooded shape were barely visible in the shadows of the trees, the figure unmoving, as if lost in thought. Nearby, a little donkey was tethered; the curious swiveling of its ears was the only motion in the camp.

Not a leaf rustled, not a sound was heard until a high voice shouted, "*Now!*"

Three men ran forward past the camp, turned, and stood with swords drawn, blocking the way back up the path. More soldiers, two women and a man, jogged up to the fireside and ranged themselves behind the seated figure.

There was a pause; no one moved or spoke. Eyes narrowed in suspicion, the squad sergeant stepped forward and prodded the figure gently with the point of her sword.

Rowan pushed back her hood and turned to look up, backlit by the fire, face shadowed. "Yes?"

The sergeant struck an arrogant pose, her sword point on the ground, both hands braced on its hilt. "No good to resist us, lady. We've come to get you."

Rowan calmly glanced at the squad arranged around the clearing, then nodded. "I see." Adjusting her cloak about her, she rose and faced them.

"I think she has a weapon under there," one soldier said.

The sergeant gestured her squad members closer, one of them pausing to untie the donkey. "Pass it over, then, lady. You've got to come with us."

There was no fear in Rowan's face, only the calm alertness of a steerswoman. She paused, then said carefully, "I'm sorry to hear you say that."

To the right, a tiny blaze flared, and the sergeant turned. Suddenly bright flame ran hissing along the ground, ran like a wild living thing, sped across the path, and twisted back behind Rowan. It shaped some image that burned in the eyes, a mystic diagram, a work of magic. They were surrounded by glowing, burning lines.

The sergeant's throat sprouted a bright wet shaft. She staggered, fell.

The donkey brayed and twisted, and the soldier grasping its lead was tugged off-balance onto his knees. A second arrow appeared in the ground, inches from his foot. Regaining his feet, he drew his sword, turning just in time to see Rowan's blade an instant before it struck across his eyes and drove into his brain.

Bel ran from cover across the lines of fire, and her sword met another with a sharp ring. Her opponent was confused by the eerie fire, but at that familiar sound regained his reflexes and returned the attack with terrified fury. The Outskirter laughed.

Rowan dodged an overhand blow and dashed to the far side of the hexagram. A female soldier, eyes bright with reflected flame, turned on her. Rowan parried once, then moved left to avoid a thrust coming from behind.

Bel's man took two steps back, and Will's arrow caught him high inside the thigh. Bel moved forward and swung, striking at the same point. Her blade reached bone, then she twisted it out. He fell, wailing, trying to block the severed artery with one fist. She abandoned him.

And suddenly the numbers were even.

Rowan parried with all her strength, studying the woman's style, searching for some weakness, some opening. She sensed the movement behind her again; the man was maneuvering, trying to keep her pinned between two opponents. She dove, then pulled to the right. She knew Willam was behind her in the shadows, and she heard him shifting to get clear of her. He tried for the soldier beyond Rowan's pair and missed.

That man was occupied with Bel. The Outskirter worked deftly, almost nonchalantly.

Rowan scrambled back; heard Willam retreat. She feared that her male opponent would turn and attack Bel from behind, but the Outskirter found one spare instant and used the strategy herself. Her blade struck Rowan's man across the back. He was shielded by leather, so no blood was drawn, but some bone broke and his right arm was disabled. He switched hands deftly and turned on his attacker.

Rowan was alone again with the female soldier. She angled right, and Willam ignored her and ran to the left around the now-guttering hexagram.

The woman was huge, muscular, adept—and far too good. Rowan, overmatched, constantly retreated before her, trying to angle her motion to bring her foe around to Bel's side.

Will was staying out of the action, as instructed. But he watched desperately, looking for an opening.

As the hexagram faded, there was a fizzing flare beyond Bel; the boy was providing more illumination. In the new light Bel shot a glance at Rowan, and they exchanged one mote of information: the steerswoman shook her head; the Outskirter nodded.

Under the distraction of the flare, each turned, moved across five feet of open ground, and exchanged opponents.

Willam wavered, confused. He had been told to spare the soldier Rowan fought, but now she was fighting two.

The swordswoman towered over Bel like a giantess, and Bel had to double-step back to stay out of that long reach. She did not try to match force for force, but dodged and twisted, using her own heavy sword against her opponent's as a fulcrum for her movement.

Rowan tried to concentrate her attentions on the injured soldier, but found herself driven back by his partner. She had to prevent them from separating to attack from two sides, and so kept stepping back and to the left. When the injured man broke away to circle her, she recognized the moment and shouted, "Willam!" She did not hear or see the arrow's flight; she heard the impact and a man's cries, and saw him stagger back into her field of vision. He had been struck but did not fall, the shaft protruding from his chest. He clawed at it.

Bel's adversary was undone by her own advantage. An overhand blow at the length of her reach was met by Bel's sword and left her the slightest bit off-balance for a mere instant. Bel pivoted forward, dropped down under the woman's long arms and, with her back on the ground, drove her blade up beneath the edge of the cuirass and into the soldier's stomach. The giantess writhed once, then toppled like a tree.

Will's victim had stumbled, dazed, to the edge of the clearing. He had three more shafts in him but stubbornly refused to die.

Rowan fought a simple holding action on her man. The rhythms of movement came to her like a drill, and she doggedly followed it, while he followed his own, in a dance of reflex and training.

But in a moment when she had circled right, he saw the whole of the clearing before him, and there was panic in his eyes as he realized that every one of his companions had fallen. He made half a dozen errors in his fear. Rowan took advantage of none of them.

Willam finished his stubborn victim by simply stepping up and slashing his throat with a hunting knife.

Bel pulled herself from beneath the body of the female soldier. She wiped the blood from her eyes with her fingers. "What a mess," she commented in a mildly aggrieved tone.

Will moved closer to Rowan and her opponent, not interfering but watching with interest. In the midst of parries, the soldier spared the boy a glance of terrified incomprehension. Rowan continued the drill.

Bel retrieved her sword. Seeing her approach, the man turned to break and run, but Rowan dropped and clutched his right leg, then scrambled away from the wild sweep of his sword as he spun back.

Bel swung at him without aggression, and he reflexively met the blow. Behind him, Rowan regained her feet, took careful aim, and struck the side of his head with the flat of her sword. He sank to the ground.

She dropped her sword and leaned her hands against her knees, breathing heavily.

A crashing and stumbling in the undergrowth told her where the donkey had fled. In the distance could be heard the frightened cry of one of the soldiers' horses. Rowan gestured to Will, and he set off after the animals.

Bel inspected the soldier. Between gulps of air Rowan called, "He's not dead?" The plan had called for Rowan to identify and single out one member of the attacking squad, the one possibly most tractable. Rowan had frankly assumed that it would be a woman; fighting women tended to be smaller than men, and so relied more on intelligence. The steerswoman had hoped for someone more intelligent, more reasonable than the average soldier. But that huge swordswoman had been beyond Rowan's ability to hold.

"He's alive." The Outskirter rolled him over. "We'll need some rope."

Rowan's racing pulse recovered. "Yes. I believe we'll find that one of those horses is carrying some."

When the soldier awoke he found himself bound, arms to his sides, ankles together. He was propped up against a boulder by the rising edge of the clearing.

The scene of the ambush lay before him, his comrades lying in their blood—at Bel's suggestion, they had not been moved, to create a stronger effect upon the mind of the captive. Black lines showed where the strange fire had run, and there was a thin acrid odor piercing the smell of blood and dust and sweat.

Two women stood before him. One was small and sturdy, a brilliant swordswoman who had felled the best fighter in the squad, a woman twice her size. The second was unimpressive, mild-looking but for eyes that watched too closely, saw too clearly, and seemed to understand too much.

The steerswoman squatted down beside him. "The first thing we need to know," she said, "is who sent you."

He mustered a brave front. "You're getting nothing from me."

"Don't be a fool!" She rose and gestured to the carnage in the clearing. "None of this was our choice. We have no quarrel with you personally. Answer our questions and you can go on your way." At that Bel glowered, but held her peace.

"I'm not stupid, so I'm not talking."

"You're stupid if you'd rather be dead than alive."

"Going to kill me if I don't talk? Lot of good it'll do you."

Rowan paused to consider the statement. "An interesting point."

Bel could contain herself no longer. "You can't mean to let him go!"

"No. Not after all this. He'd run straight for his master, and we'd have the whole situation repeating. We can't hope to ambush the next lot."

"If we can get him to talk," the Outskirter pointed out, "he won't dare go back to his master." She turned to the man. "Do you understand? You can live if you choose to."

He was a long time answering. "You don't know wizards."

"You'll have a chance."

He seemed about to reply, then stopped and shook his head.

Rowan tried again. "If you won't tell us who, will you tell us why?"

He glanced at their faces, looked away, and said nothing.

Willam arrived, leading two restive, wild-eyed horses. He took in the scene with his wide coppery gaze but did not interrupt.

"And now we have a problem," Rowan said dispiritedly.

Bel crossed her arms and tilted her head at the man. "I think it's obvious. If he won't answer, we'll have to make him answer."

It took Rowan a moment to get Bel's meaning. "You mean we should force him to talk?" She felt her stomach twist. But the Outskirter was right; it was, in fact, obvious.

Defending oneself against attack, attacking those who planned harm—those were easy to justify, as direct and clear as killing an animal for food, or protecting oneself from rain and cold.

But, interrogation enforced by pain . . .

"I wouldn't know where to begin," Rowan said; but as soon as it was spoken, she realized it was not true. A smattering of knowledge; a few facts about anatomy arranged themselves of their own accord, and presented to her a framework for action. It would be very easy, she realized, to cause the man pain and damage, without endangering his life. She could do it. As a steerswoman, she felt a moment's incongruous pleasure in recognizing a field of information she had already possessed, unknowing. But it was not information that she was happy to discover.

Bel shrugged. "I know what to do."

The facts of the situation again ordered themselves before Rowan, doggedly presenting the same conclusion. "No. I can do it." However much her friend might be involved, Rowan was the source and reason for the fight. It was her responsibility. This dirty job was her own.

It slowly dawned on the soldier how serious was their intent. He looked from one woman to the other in growing astonishment and finally fixed on Rowan in disbelief. She leaned forward, speaking reluctantly. "Your last chance, friend. Who sent you, and why?"

He was pale. "What're you going to do?"

They altered his bonds, first freeing his left hand, bracing it against the top of Bel's pack, then securing it in place, palm up. He struggled desperately and quieted only under the influence of a choking hold from Bel, held long enough to bring him to the edge of fainting.

Rowan took a moment to regather her determination. She pulled out her knife and examined it reluctantly, testing its edge, wondering if she would ever be able to use it to eat again. It came to her that, quite sensibly, she would.

Shaking his head to clear it, breathing in heavy gasps, the soldier spoke to her. "You, you're a steerswoman."

"That's right."

"It's a bluff, right?" His voice quavered in desperation. "I mean, you lot, you're not that sort, are you? You steerswomen, you're supposed to be, supposed to be . . ." He ran down.

"Supposed to be?" Rowan prompted.

He swallowed. "Well . . . good."

She digested his words. "Last chance," she said again, and felt on her own face a mirror of the panicked pleading that she saw in her victim's. Bel watched her sidelong.

Rowan looked at the knife, looked at the soldier, looked up at the sky. She drew one shaky breath and stepped forward.

Bel's hand was on her shoulder. "Wait."

"No." A mote of anger sparked in her. She dared not interrupt herself, but knew she must act in the momentum of her decision.

Bel grabbed one shoulder and pulled her around to face the other way. She spoke quietly. "Get out of sight."

"What? Why?"

"Because you're no good!" Bel hissed. Then she continued more calmly. "A torture victim's mood is just as important as the pain. You're sorry for him, and he knows it. You don't want to hurt him."

Rowan turned to her blankly. "I don't."

"Well, I do!" Her eyes blazed. "I *hate* him. I'll be glad to see him suffer. And he's going to suffer, not because of you or because of me, but because he made an evil choice, to serve a wizard who means us harm."

Rowan attempted to formulate a reply, but Bel pressed on. "When you start cutting him, you'll want to stop, and he'll want you to, and you'll know it, and he'll know it. It'll be back and forth between the two of you. You'll look for any excuse to stop. He'll use that against you." She stopped and glanced once at the man. "Let me do it. I'll take him apart and enjoy it."

"It's my job."

"The job belongs to the one who can do it best." The Outskirter's gaze challenged her, but as Rowan watched, her friend's expression changed to reluctant sympathy. "Rowan, cold blood's not for everyone." She jerked her head. "Get out of sight."

The horses had quieted, and Rowan had no desire to upset them again. She led them down the path, until it curved and the clearing was out of sight, tethered them to a stout fallen tree, and turned away to where the path's edge sloped down to the ravine below.

An outcropping of rock stood a few feet down the slope. Rowan climbed down and found a seat, looking north across the darkening landscape. Northwest, a lake caught the failing sunlight, a single silver line in the distance, like a sword.

From up the path there came an odd sound, like the cry of an unidentifiable small animal. The horses shifted nervously.

The evening was clear, and to her right the Eastern Guidestar hung like a beacon, twenty-five degrees up from the eastern horizon, forty degrees south of due east. Unseen over her left shoulder, the Western Guidestar stood, higher than its partner and dimmer at present.

The sounds in the distance became more continuous.

She felt a strange combination of relief and shame. The responsibility was hers, and she had abdicated it, and deep inside she was glad to do so. It made her feel somehow unfit; it rankled.

The noises became appalling, inhuman.

Bel was right; the job was best done by one best suited for it. And yet—

She tried to distract herself. She realized that it would take a problem to lose herself in solving, something useful, confirming her own skills. She sifted, searching, the soldier's voice a weird music behind her thoughts.

The jewels—irritating, frustrating, apparently *useless*, yet still the fulcrum on which all these events pivoted. But the information was too slight and too familiar. More was needed for further thought to be effective.

She wanted something more technical and involving, something with information and principles to grasp and work with. That incidental paradox that she had argued with Arian about . . .

An object flung with great force from a high tower, at a certain upward angle: by using straightforward techniques known to any steerswoman, by taking them further than anyone had before, Rowan had seemed to demonstrate that it was possible for the object never to strike the ground.

It was quite obviously false. Things simply did not happen that way. And yet, why would the techniques work in other circumstances but fail in this one? She reconstructed the details of the problem in her mind, and the events in the distance, the strange sounds, and her own shame faded from her awareness.

She recognized that there was an interrelationship between the height of the tower and the force of the impetus. The higher the tower, the less force was necessary. At a great enough height, one needed merely to let go of the object, and it would fall away, never quite reaching the ground; slightly lower, and it would reach ground eventually.

The shorter the tower, the more force was needed, until eventually the object could be flung by someone standing at ground level. But the force required was impossible, immeasurable—and she reminded herself that "impossible" and "immeasurable" were not the same idea. It was patently impossible to construct a tower high enough—she knew too well the restrictions on the variables involved—but the force of the impetus was merely immeasurable.

She had a feel for the quantity, however; she could *imagine* it, in principle, but not with precision. She disliked that. It was too vague.

And it left her with the same glaring contradiction that had so outraged Arian at the Archives: No matter what the numbers said, objects did fall to the earth.

But did they? Every single time?

Approach it from another direction. What does not fall?

Birds flew, by some technique known to themselves. Wizards were said to fly and could make things fly, possibly by the same means. Clouds floated, but they were vapors, like steam, mere fogs risen above ground level. When she had been a child, she had dreamed of tying a rope to a cloud and being lifted into the sky. She imagined herself a child without knowledge, looking at the world as a child did. Would a child be surprised to hear of objects that did not fall?

Not at all. The sun did not fall, nor the constellations, nor the Guide-stars. Children, and for that matter, most adults, took that as a given.

But the sun did not fall because it was no object moving across the sky. In fact it was the stable center of the universe, and the world moved about it in a great circle, spinning improbably on its axis. Rowan remembered how amazed she was when she had first learned that. But once known, it was easily confirmed, by any number of methods.

The stars were far suns, or so tradition said. But this was unprov-able. In any event, they were immeasurably distant.

The Guidestars hovered forever in the sky. They did not fall, but neither did they move. They hung immobile on the celestial equator and seemed to shift only as the traveler below changed position on the world's surface.

They were neither far suns, nor immeasurably distant. Their height was easily calculable from their apparent displacement when viewed from different locations on the world. Though they were very high in-deed, if they had been suns the world would have been aflame from the heat of their proximity.

But they did not move.

She noticed vaguely that there was silence from up the path, had been for some time, and that Willam was seated beside her. The boy was shaking, rank with sweat. Rowan ignored him and returned to the seduction of the problem.

Reason and reasonableness were at odds. Something was wrong, ei-ther in the calculations, or in the formulation of the problem, or in the principles by which she understood the world.

And that was the possibility that Arian had overlooked. The error was not necessarily in the calculations, nor in the construction of the problem.

She checked the numbers over and over, trying to quantify the vaguenesses, to identify and limit the areas of missing knowledge. She kept reaching the same results: It might be true. It might be possible for a falling object never to reach the ground. And more: Under cer-tain conditions, it might actually be *impossible* for it to do so.

At some point she realized that Willam was gone, and in retrospect remembered that he had risen, stepped to one side, vomited, and returned up the path.

The sounds in the distance began again.

She was briefly taken by nausea at imagining the nature of those proceedings, and in her single-mindedness she found herself annoyed at the interruption. Of their own accord, her thoughts slipped back into the fascination of reason.

What would actually happen, taking the calculations as valid? Precisely, how would an object flung to that height behave?

It would move away into the distance, past the horizon. And then?

If it never reached the ground, it would simply continue, completely around the world. Eventually, it would come back into view from the opposite horizon, crossing the point where it had started.

No, not quite—because the world would have turned a bit in the interval.

This made the computations more complicated. Annoyed, she altered the orientation of the object's path, from north-south to west-east, on the equator, to minimize the effect of the world's rotation. It helped.

Abruptly, in a leap of reason, she flung it higher, far above the minimum height necessary for an unfalling object—

She came to her feet and spun to seek the Western Guidestar hanging motionless above her—

And was face-to-face with Bel. The Outskirter had spoken.

Rowan shook her head in momentary confusion. "What?"

Bel repeated, her face showing vast dissatisfaction. "It's no use," she said. "I think he's under a spell."

"He won't say anything?" She vaguely recalled a wild, weeping voice in the distance, and that it had spoken at length.

"It isn't that. He talks. He's even eager to. But he just doesn't make any sense. You'd better hear it yourself."

As Rowan approached, she looked once at the state of the man's hand and arm, then kept her eyes to his face. Unfortunately, her observation and memory were too good. The sight stayed with her, against her will; and then she chose to remember it, and recognize and accept the results of her actions.

Bel dropped one hand on the trembling man's right shoulder, in a gesture that seemed almost friendly. His head snapped up, and he looked at her, wild-eyed. "No! That's all there is, I swear it, I don't know any more!" His skin was white, slick with sweat.

"Of course," Bel reassured him. "But just repeat it for the steerswoman, there's a good fellow."

He looked at Rowan and began to speak, urgently, desperately. As she listened, Rowan felt her scalp prickle.

What she heard was not the incoherent gibberings a man might make in delirium. The sounds were organized, inflected like speech, and the look on the soldier's face reflected the meaning he believed them to carry. The pattern of inflection teased the ear, mimicking reason—but not one of the utterances matched any single true word. The effect was uncanny.

At the end, his communication slipped into comprehensibility with a plaintive "That's all, please, I'd tell more, but that's all they told me."

Rowan stood helpless, sick with horror. Somehow, this was the most appalling result of magic she had yet witnessed—worse than the casual death of Reeder's boy, crueler than the orchestrated slaughter of innocent people by a swarm of dragons, stranger than Willam's eerie traveling fire. This man's very will and sacred reason had been twisted by some wizard, twisted for a purpose incidental to his own life.

Rowan crouched down beside him, studying his face. He avoided her gaze, his breath hissing behind clenched teeth.

"Listen," she said carefully, trying to sound kind and reasonable. "I'm sorry, but there's a problem here. We believe you're under some kind of spell." He screwed his eyes shut, ignoring her. "I know you think you've told us something," she went on, "but you haven't really. It's an illusion."

He looked up at her, and a small sound escaped from the back of his throat. Realization grew on his face, and with it the terror that the evening's events were not finished, that there was more to come.

"Perhaps there's some way you can get around it?" Rowan said. "Can you approach it from some other direction?"

A strangled cry escaped him, and then he was speaking again, in a high pleading voice—all sounds with no sense.

"No, wait," Rowan told him. "It's no good. Try to calm down . . . start with something simple."

Beyond hearing her, he cried his desperate monologue.

"Try to tell us your name," she suggested, and touched his shoulder, attempting, irrationally, to comfort him.

He tried to writhe away from her hand, twisting at the ropes. His left arm slipped slickly in its bonds, raw flesh and bone tangling against rope. He uttered a gurgling cry and fainted.

Bel let out a gust of air. "Well."

Rowan sat back on her heels and was silent for a long time. Finally, she nodded.

"What happens now?" Willam asked. He was as pale as the soldier.

Bel made to answer, but Rowan stopped her with a gesture. She spoke to Willam. "Get me some cloth. The spare linen shirt from my pack should do." He hurried to do it.

Bel came closer, suspicious. "What are you going to do?"

Rowan found Bel's knife. "To start, I'm going to bandage this arm." She cut the ropes that held it, carefully disentangling them from the muscle and tendon.

"You're not going to let him go?"

"That is exactly what I am going to do." She took the shirt that Willam handed her and began tearing strips.

The Outskirter rounded on her. "Are you insane? Don't you know what will happen?"

"I think I have a good idea." She gestured Will to bring a waterskin.

"But he didn't betray his wizard, and now he knows it. There's no reason for him not to return to whoever sent him and say that we hadn't been stopped."

"Very probably that's what he'll do." Seeing that the soldier was regaining his senses, Rowan instructed Will, "Give him some water. No, don't untie him. I'm sorry, friend. I'm helping you, but it will still hurt."

"They'll know where we are!" Bel leaned close to Rowan's face. "They'll know where we were, they'll know where we're going, and they'll find us in an instant!"

"They'll have the information to do so." Rowan took the skin from Willam and poured water over the hand and arm. The man shrieked and fainted again.

"Rowan." The Outskirter spoke seriously. "You've always seemed a sensible person, if inexperienced—"

"Thank you." She did not have needle and thread to stitch back muscle and skin, but she noticed that Bel's work had been very clean and efficient. The hand would be useless, but the man's life was in no immediate danger.

"But this is pure madness. It's nothing less than suicide." The soldier groggily came to again and startled at seeing Bel's face so close. She stepped back, annoyed. "Rowan," she repeated, and waited until the steerswoman looked up. "I don't care to die."

"Good. Neither do I." Rowan turned back and continued the work, noticing that she was learning more about the anatomy of the human arm than she had previously known.

Bel said nothing more.

Rowan finished the bandaging, untied the man, helped him to his feet, gave him a bit of food and water to take, and led him to the head of the trail. He stood, swaying and trembling, looking about in disbelief. Rowan gestured with her chin. "Go on."

Behind her, Bel made a wordless sound of rage, and the soldier stumbled, turned, and left down the trail at a staggering run.

Bel set loose a flurry of curses. She stormed back to her pack, flung off the ropes, and dragged it aside as Will watched in amazement. "It's impossible, it's insane, and I'm having no part of it." Her movements were jerky with agitation. She pointed back up the rising path. "I am going *that* way. I'll probably get lost, and I don't care, because I'd have a better chance of survival. I'm *not* following you to suicide."

Rowan stepped over to one of the bodies of the slaughtered soldiers and examined its trappings. Without looking up she asked Will, "What do you think?"

He glanced from one to the other, confused. "I—I don't know. I'm glad we didn't kill that man; it's not his fault he's under a spell, but . . . Lady, I think we *should* have. It would have been safer . . ."

"I didn't think you could be so stupid!"

Ignoring Bel, Rowan pulled the helmet from the corpse's head and studied it, thinking.

"I can still catch him," the Outskirter said through her teeth.

"No."

"Rowan—"

"Here." She tossed the helmet to Bel, who reflexively caught it. "Does it fit?"

"Fit?"

Rowan turned to the boy. "Will, are you any good at tracking? I know how to do it, but it's mostly theory with me. I expect you've tracked game before . . ."

"Yes."

Bel turned the helmet over in her hands, watching Rowan with suspicion.

The steerswoman stood. "I'm sick of running, and I don't care to dodge any more attacks. I want to find out who's responsible." Her mouth twisted. "And since our poor friend couldn't tell where he came from, he will kindly lead us there."

Bel stood, stunned. Then slowly, she began to laugh. She tossed the helmet into the air, caught it, and pulled it down on her head. It fit.

19

"How do we get in?" Bel wondered.

"The same way every guard gets in."

The cliffs were a riot of raw stone and wild levels. It disturbed Rowan; her maps showed the lake as smaller, the cliffs smoother and slightly farther north. This area had been *made* this way, made recently, and by magic.

One arm of stone reached out into the lake; its far edge probably marked the limit of the original cliffs. Now, rock rose sheer from the waters to cradle the pale gray walls of the fortress. The perimeter seemed to be constructed of massive single blocks, one for each of the six faces. Rowan could think of no source for such stone, no way to quarry it, and no way to transport it. In the dawn light it seemed more like ceramic than rock.

Without a doubt, the fortress belonged to Shammer and Dhree.

Rowan and her companions had tracked the wounded soldier for two days, until a heavy storm had battered the forest. When it had cleared, they found that all traces of his trail had been eradicated. By continuing in his last known direction, they came across indications of the original squad's outward-bound passage, but no sign that the survivor had returned that way. The three agreed that the man had likely died in his attempt to return home, victim of hunger, weather, and his weak condition; but the trail left by the horses and people of the outgoing squad was still readable. By following it backward, the travelers eventually found a northbound road that finally led them to the lakeshore.

"Will, we need you to stay here." His face darkened, but Rowan forestalled his protest. "I'm not trying to exclude you. You're our last line. If we don't come out in three days, you have to head back to the Archives. It's important that the Prime know what's happened. Will you do it?"

He nodded reluctantly. "I guess it makes sense. But you had better tell me all about any magic you saw, when you come out. I'll wait here and keep the horses ready."

"Good lad. Do you still have the map?"

"Yes." He pulled it from his shirt. "What's the route to the Archives?"

She did not look at the map, but kept her eyes on the fortress. "Follow the cliffs along the west shore of the lake until it turns north . . ." Rattling the parchment, Willam puzzled over the chart as Rowan continued, reciting the complicated directions precisely, with offhand ease and only half her attention. ". . . and when you reach the Wulf you should be able to get passage to the Archives. There's a landing; most of the rivermen know where to find it." She turned to him. "Is that clear?"

He looked a bit bemused. "Yes."

She took in his expression, then laughed. "Attise the merchant wasn't very good with maps, was she?"

"No." He made a wry face. "I used to wonder if she wasn't a bit thick."

"I was afraid that if I showed any skill at all, I'd show all of it. I was truly bad at pretending."

"And here we go," Bel said, "into the middle of it, pretending all the way."

The two women were dressed in attire removed from the corpses of the soldiers they had slain. The outfits were not truly uniform, save for the leather helmets, cuirasses, and the red surplices. The individuality of the remaining equipment allowed Rowan to risk retaining her gum-soled steerswoman's boots. To the casual glance they were not remarkable, but they provided better traction than leather soles, and they were silent.

"I've had practice since then," Rowan said.

They had been watching the fortress since the previous day, observing the visible movements of guards on the perimeters, and the entry and exit of supplies and personnel.

From the front entrance, a railed causeway led along the rocky arm to the road at the base of the cliffs. The end of the causeway was closed off by a barred iron gate set in a stone arch. Each party entering was in the company of a soldier. At the gate, the group would pause; the soldier would step up to the right side of the arch and do something unseen from Rowan's angle, and the iron bars would swing slowly open to admit the party. The bars moved with no visible human intervention.

Rowan took a moment to review what she knew about the recent war: the cursory tale Artos had given her, and the incidental information gained from Hugo as he outlined the present status and attitudes of the known wizards. With her knowledge of the lands involved, and logic to fill in the blanks, it would have to suffice. She gestured to Bel and began to clamber down the tumbled rocks to the road below.

The arch of the gate was mortared stone, the iron bars as thick as Rowan's wrist and completely clear of rust. It was new, as new as the changed landscape.

Rowan walked to the right of the arch as if familiar with procedure. Temporarily shielded from the sight of the guards at the other end of the causeway, she took a moment to examine the stones.

At eye level, one block had been replaced by a small square brass door. A turn of the little handle opened it easily. Inside, the back surface was faced with ceramic, with a recessed circle in the center, decorated with a complex pattern of copper lines.

Rowan sighed, relieved. "Simple enough." Bel ignored her, occupied with keeping the reactions of the guards at the keep's entrance under observation, while simultaneously trying to project an air of nonchalance.

The women had carefully searched the possessions of the soldiers they had slain. Each had carried a small wood-and-copper disk, like a talisman or amulet, embellished with unreadable runes. The steerswoman removed hers from a pocket built into her confiscated sword belt and fit it into the recessed circle.

There was a quiet sustained tone, a single deep musical note, heard but faintly. Of its own accord, the heavy crossbolt slid aside slowly, and the gate swung inward. Bel froze and stood watching it as a cat might have watched a dog, her lips peeled back from her teeth.

Rowan came to her side, looking down the causeway. "Expect magic, Bel."

A cool updraft from the lake below countered the heat beating down from above. The women walked along the smooth-surfaced road through an atmosphere that seemed to have no temperature, no real presence.

Four guards manned the entrance to the fortress proper. Three stood in proper soldierly stance, watched by the fourth, who stood at his ease, viewing everything with an overseer's disgruntled disdain.

The guards could not be expected to know every single soldier in the wizards' employ; the purpose of the spell at the magic gate certainly was to prevent entry by unauthorized persons. Rowan gave the men a casual acknowledging nod as she and Bel passed by and turned to the left. "Easy enough," Bel said under her breath.

"You there! You two!" They froze.

The senior guardsman stamped after them in outrage. "Look, you, if you've *both* got the amulets, you're *both* supposed to use them. You know that—it throws off the tally."

Rowan thought quickly. "She doesn't have one." If the amulets were used to get into the fortress, then only people originating from the fortress would have them. "She isn't from these parts. We pressed her in Logan Falls."

"What? Who's 'we'?"

"My squadron. We're returning from the war."

"You two, alone?"

"We were with Penn's squadron."

"Showing up now?" He stood with fists on hips. "Took your damn time, didn't you?"

"I was sick."

He grunted disgust, then looked alarmed. "No, Penn's squadron, that's the one got in the way of that basilisk, wasn't it?"

"That's right."

He took a half step back. "It's all right," Rowan assured him. "It just turned out to be dysentery. Then we got snowed in and had to wait until spring to travel. And then, well . . ."

Bel spoke up. "We got lost."

He barked a laugh. "Infantry—don't know its ass from its earhole. But look, you been mostly mustered out since then, didn't you hear?"

"Not a word." She tried to catch the style of his speech, to mimic it. "No way to."

"Mph. Should've headed home instead."

"Home where? Mine's pretty well flattened."

"We decided we liked the life," Bel put in.

"Liked it?" He found the idea immensely amusing.

Rowan remembered a comment Artos's regulars often made. "Could be worse. We could be working for a living."

He recognized a standard soldier's sally. "Well . . ." His manner shifted to grudging familiarity. "We've gone and lost a few of the standing, lately. Wouldn't be surprised if you found a place. You look likely, anyhow," he said to Bel. "Go talk to Druin; he's took over for Clara." Rowan nodded as if the statement made sense to her. "Go on." He made a vague gesture to the left and plodded back to his station, muttering to himself.

The two women walked away purposefully and presently found themselves in a small interior courtyard with passages in three directions. Pausing, Rowan carefully placed its size, shape, and orientation within the blank hexagon that was her mental floor plan for the fortress.

"Now where?" Bel wondered.

"I don't know." Rowan's mouth twitched with amusement. "Do you think we should try to report to Druin for assignment?"

"He'd just put us to work."

"True." Rowan examined the courtyard, trying to relate the angles of the exits to the shape of the rooftops she had viewed from the cliffs. "That man's shift has four hours to go." She knew that from her earlier observations. "He'll probably go for his dinner after that, and he may or may not meet Druin in the mess and mention us. We have about four hours before we're suspected."

"That's not a lot of time." Bel tilted her head. "If we did report to Druin, and he took us in, then we'd have as much time as we want, and good excuses to be wherever we are."

Rowan turned back to her friend, amazed and delighted. She laughed, quietly. "Bel, that's—that's *audacious*!"

The Outskirter acknowledged Rowan's reaction with a little self-satisfied smile.

"I would be expected to have some familiarity with the fortress."

"We'll scout around a bit before we show up," Bel supplied.

"That's the answer." Rowan scanned the three passages, then chose one that seemed likely to keep close to the outer wall. "This way." It was large and wide and showed signs of the previous passage of horses. They followed it cautiously through a series of interlinked courtyards, each with side doors; it was likely a delivery route for supplies.

The critical question was: How did the fortress guards normally behave when off-duty? Were their movements circumscribed, and to what degree? Certainly they could not have the free run of the entire keep, but just as certainly they were not simply confined to barracks. Such an existence would be too grim and limited, and the life of the resident guards would be too unpleasant to attract a sizable loyal corps.

There had to be compensations for the work. The only analogy Rowan had was Artos's regulars and the house guards at his mansion. The house guards had an easy job with a certain amount of prestige and were an affable lot, as a rule. The regulars were natural soldiers and enjoyed their alternately ordered and chaotic existence. Gratitude from the townspeople, a romantic image, steady employment, and in many cases a general improvement over their previous existence attracted people to the ranks. The pay was not great, but Artos had more volunteers than he could use.

The house guards were on a wry, friendly basis with the servants and workers, and from that relationship Rowan took her cue.

In one courtyard they came across a wagon laden with small odd-sized wooden crates, where a burly, disheveled man and a slim, pock-marked woman of middle age were occupied with tediously bringing the cargo into a side door. Rowan paused and turned back. "Need some help?"

Possibilities were three: servants were considered of superior rank and would refuse to associate with guardswomen; servants were of inferior rank and would be amazed, possibly frightened, at Rowan's offer; or, questions of rank were inapplicable between the two groups, and the response would be based purely on the freedom of action normal to off-duty guards.

The man ignored Rowan, but the woman looked up with mild surprise, then smiled. "Thanks." She tapped her assistant on the shoulder as he made to unload another crate. Pausing in his work, he watched intently as she indicated Bel and Rowan and pointed from the boxes to the door; then he nodded pleasantly at the pair. He was deaf.

Rowan pulled down one of the crates and hoisted it to her shoulder. It proved to be lighter than it looked. "Where do these go?" she asked. Bel followed her example with an obviously heavier box, behaving as if she considered the work nothing unusual.

The woman indicated. "Through that door, through the room, up the stairs." She paused and winced. "No further, I guess. Wouldn't look good." Attracting the disheveled man's attention again, she attempted to give him a more difficult, complicated instruction. Eventually comprehending, he led the way.

The room was large and long, lined with cupboards and shelves, apparently to store certain nonperishable items, but the crates they were carrying had a different destination. Rowan and Bel were led through a door in the back and up a set of narrow stairs with a landing halfway up, where the direction reversed. At the top was a second landing, and there the man put down his crate, indicated those carried by the women, then indicated the floor. When they complied, he pointed at Rowan and Bel, back down the stairs, pointed at himself, and made a motion toward a short corridor behind him.

Without thinking, Rowan replied in the wood-gnome language of gestures. "I understand. We go down now."

Those particular phrases were simple and obvious, easily comprehensible to an intelligent person; but the formality of the gestures, and the fluid naturalness of their use, surprised him. It was more than pantomime, it was language, and he seemed to recognize something of this.

With a look of surprise and concentration, he repeated a phrase, pointing at himself, then extending his index finger near his right temple. "I understand." He said it twice, testing the moves.

When they reached the lower room again Rowan and Bel found that the pockmarked woman had not been idle. She had carried a number of crates from the wagon to the side door; a simple division of labor was implied that would prevent the workers from jostling each other and speed up the task.

"I'll take the stairs," Rowan volunteered. Bel set herself to shifting crates from the front door and passing them to Rowan at the stairs' foot.

When the steerswoman delivered each crate to the top landing, sometimes the deaf man was there, studying her with shy friendliness. Sometimes he was absent, and she began to catch the rhythm of his work and understand how much time had to pass while he brought each crate down the corridor.

After transferring one crate to his care and pausing until he was out of sight, she dashed down the stairs as quickly as possible. Meeting Bel in the middle of the storeroom, she took the burden from her there. "Try to work a little faster. I need you to be three boxes ahead of me. And see if you can make them light ones."

With Rowan and the man working at one pace, and Bel and the woman outside working at another, it did not take many trips before three boxes sat waiting at the bottom of the stairs. Rowan chose the smallest, hurried up to the first landing, and placed the crate in a spot invisible from above. Returning below, she took a second and managed to reach the top with it in time to hand it to the man above.

Back at the lower landing, she used her knife to pry up the lid of the first crate. The thin wood was held by tacks and offered little resistance. She was able to detach it easily, but temporarily abandoned it to run down for the third box.

Just as the deaf man came into sight, she placed the third crate on the top landing, waved at him, and turned back down.

The box she had opened contained a dozen wooden spools, similar in type to those used for thread, but much larger. Wound around each was a strand of some substance as thick as heavy yarn, in bizarre colors, garishly brilliant. Loosening the end of one strand, she found it strangely stiff. She pulled out a foot-long length and tried to cut it. She was briefly shocked when the knife failed to cut completely through; if she rewound it, the mark would be visible, and suspicious. But a second panicked attempt detached the segment, and she wound it into a tight coil and slipped it into the pocket with her amulet.

Pounding the lid closed caused a din that prompted Bel to peer up the stairs in surprise. Rowan ignored her, finished the job, and brought the box to the top landing to find the deaf man waiting.

Back at the bottom, Bel passed along a somewhat heavier crate. "This is the last." When Rowan delivered it, she could not help speaking to the man again. "Work finished." Those signals were more abstract, and she amplified them with gestures including the stairs, the box, herself, and the man, and a negative shake of her head.

He watched in fascination. Then, with the crate precariously tucked under one arm, he replied. "I understand." He paused, thinking, then hesitantly added, "You go down now."

She grinned at him, charmed by his intelligence, and waved a farewell.

As they left the storeroom behind, Bel asked, "What did you do?" "I made a friend and acquired a souvenir."

Reassured by their casual acceptance by the woman and her assistant, Bel and Rowan continued their explorations. They encountered storerooms, stables, a smithy, and a woodshop, but no residences. The people they met, though sometimes surprised, never raised protest.

For this first reconnaissance, the steerswoman selected routes that kept them close to the outside wall, in order to gain a sense of the overall shape and limits of the keep, and seek future options for discreet departure. Of those, they found two.

The first was nothing more than a low window in the wall itself, but by leaning over the edge, one could see that the cliffs below were a trifle less sheer than elsewhere, with rocky projections down to the surface of the lake. Conceivably, a person with a rope could lower herself down the face of the wall and scramble laboriously to the water. Unfortunately, the window was in a busy area, and an observer standing nearby would have a clear view of the entire descent; further, the escapee would have to swim to the shore. Rowan was not surprised to learn that Bel lacked that skill.

The second exit was a small gate on the north side, facing the body of the lake. Stone stairs led down the cliffs to a wharf, where a jolly gaff-rigged sailing dinghy bobbed, a pleasure boat. The gate was closed by an iron grille, locked, and equipped with the same brass box found at the end of the front causeway. Possibly their amulets would open it, but she dared not try, remembering what the guard had said about a "tally."

The women peered through the grille.

"That's our best chance, if we need to leave quickly," Rowan said. "Can you handle that boat?"

"A simple matter."

They retraced their steps to the first courtyard they had found and took a different exit. By asking a passing washwoman, they found the barracks and training area of the resident guard and presented themselves to Druin.

Rowan repeated their story to him, filling it with many details of the action during the war, altered from the point of view of the observers who had reported it to Hugo, to the point of view of a soldier in its midst. She included a certain number of likely soldierly complaints, including invective at the insanity of using a basilisk in close combat. Long before she had finished, she saw Druin's gaze wandering in boredom and knew that she had convinced him of their authenticity.

It took him a moment to realize that she had stopped speaking. "Yes. Well." He regathered himself, attempting to look official, and succeeding in looking harried. "Of course we can use you. Mustering people out, everybody coming and going—confuses things. And this new business; just makes it all worse."

Rowan remembered that he was new at his job. "What happened to Clara?" The guard at the gate had mentioned her as someone Rowan might be expected to know, and so it was desperately necessary to avoid her.

Wincing, Druin looked off to one side and scratched his beard vigorously. Rowan decided that he had fleas. "Not a good story. Had a little run-in with Themselves." He gave the word a capitalizing stress. "Lay low when they're around, that's all. Don't attract attention."

"Can't you be more specific? So we won't do the same thing Clara did?"

Glancing around as if his comments might be overheard, he said,

"Could, but I won't. No good chewing it over. Best forgotten." He eyed Bel, with evident approval. "Where'd you get her again?"

"Logan Falls. She did well in the fighting."

"I expect so—you're both here. Shame about Penn. How'd you escape that basilisk?"

Rowan shrugged. "Can't imagine. I expect it didn't notice us, personally, in the confusion. Just lucky."

"Mph. Well . . ." He scratched his left thigh absently, musing, then called out across the yard. "Ellen! These two are yours."

The woman came over, leaving behind a trio of men whom she had been berating for sloppy behavior. At her departure they slinked away unobtrusively. "Good. I'm trying to get another squad together to go after that steerswoman."

Hiding a thrill of fear, Rowan knit her brows as if puzzled. Bel managed to appear innocently delighted at the prospect of a hunt.

Druin was outraged. "What, more? We're too shorthanded already."

"What's this?" Rowan interjected. "We're after a steerswoman? Is she some kind of criminal?"

"Don't know," Ellen said indifferently. "We're supposed to stay clear of them, generally. Always liked them myself. But there's something about this one that's got Themselves all in a bother, and touchy, as well."

"Now, how can we keep proper security," Druin complained in exasperation, "with three quarters of our people off chasing the moon, I ask you?"

"Don't know. Why don't you ask Themselves?"

"Not me." He made a sound of dry irony, then returned to business. "Well, you show these two around, give them something temporary. We'll see about more search parties later."

Ellen was a big square woman, broad of stomach and blunt of features. Her arms bulked with muscle. Leading the pair through the passages, she studied Bel briefly. "You, what's your name?"

The Outskirter provided her alias.

"Fine. You look competent. Small, maybe, but size isn't skill. You've got something about you, an air, confidence. Bet you could show some of us a thing or two."

Bel acknowledged that with a tilt of her head.

"And you—"

When Rowan responded with her own assumed name, Ellen gave her longer, more careful consideration. "You're smart, aren't you? That's it. You don't look like much of a fighter, not at first glance, but I can tell you're thinking all the time. I'll bet you're good, and I'll bet it's because you can think fast on your feet. I'll assign you together— you're a good combination."

Behind her back, Rowan and Bel exchanged cautionary looks. Ellen was perceptive and a good judge of people; they would need to stay out of her sight as much as possible.

The women's barracks were wide and airy and surprisingly clean. A ten-year-old girl was industriously scrubbing the wooden floor, and she paused to look up with wide-eyed hero worship as the women entered. "Take any free bunk you like; there's plenty," Ellen said to her charges. "Down the hall that way are a few double rooms, for when you need company and privacy at the same time, so to speak. If you consort with the house servants, use their quarters, but tell me ahead of time! Absent from barracks during your sleeping time without me knowing, and that's bad trouble for you."

The Outskirter and the steerswoman selected bunks and stowed their kits, and Ellen continued their orientation. They paid a visit to the armorer, who declared their equipment in remarkably good condition but issued them both ceremonial spears and traded the sword Rowan had taken from her would-be captors for one somewhat lighter. He also gave Bel one of the admitting amulets. He tucked it directly into her sword-belt pocket, causing Rowan a moment's nervousness, but apparently Bel had already discarded the one she had originally carried.

In a practice session under the eyes of Ellen and the resident armsmaster, Bel defeated Rowan three times in such quick succession that the steerswoman was dazed by the Outskirter's skill. Tested against the master himself, Rowan held her own, to his surprise. In a bout against Bel, he declared himself the victim of unorthodox techniques.

Back in Ellen's cramped quarters, the officer scanned a list. "Something simple to start with. Night duty on the northeast wall.

You pace the limits, exchange recognition with the guards on the north and east at each end of your walk. If you see someone acting furtive or rowdy, one of you bring him to Druin, the other keep your post. Keep an eye on the lake for any approaching boats. And don't let the servants walk the walls; they try to use them as shortcuts, but they're not allowed." She looked up. "Get some rest; report to the night officer here at dusk. That's all."

"Yes, ma'am," Rowan replied. Then she cautiously ventured, "But I doubt we'd be able to get any sleep the first afternoon we try."

Bel picked it up. "All this is new to me. Perhaps my friend can show me around a bit? We'll stay away from any restricted areas you tell us about."

"No. I want you rested. If you can't sleep, talk or daydream if you like, just do it in your bunks."

In their absence, the barracks had acquired another inhabitant; a guardswoman was fast asleep on one of the bunks, the little scrub-girl seated on the floor beside her, industriously cleaning the woman's cuirass with an oily rag. When Bel and Rowan removed their gear, the girl dashed over to show them the best way to arrange it at the foot of the bed. Bel spared her a grin and a tousle of the hair, which elicited a shy smile but no words.

When the girl left, Rowan moved to the bed-foot and retrieved the coiled strand from her sword belt. Bel came closer to watch.

The strand unwound and rewound easily, retaining whatever shape Rowan bent it in. It was colored fiery orange and dull brown in alternating segments. Scratching it with one fingernail, Rowan found that the orange was its inherent hue, the brown painted on. At both ends its cross section showed a gleaming central core. She could not identify the outer substance, but its feel reminded her faintly of the gum used to coat the boot soles of steerswomen and sailors, though it seemed more rigid. It had no taste.

"Should you put your tongue on that thing?" Bel whispered. "It might be poisonous."

"Whatever its use, it's intended to be handled by humans. If it's poisonous, it's not very, and one lick shouldn't hurt me." Nevertheless, she paused to check for any internal reactions. There were none.

Using her knife, she found that she could easily strip the outer layer, peeling off thin curling slivers. She exposed one end of the core, recognized the color, and again tasted. "Copper," she confirmed.

"But what's it for?"

"It might have any number of uses. It's thin, it's very tough, it holds a shape, and it's probably impervious to weather." She glanced at the soldier across the room, who was breathing heavily in sleep, and continued. "It would be excellent for tying things. Sailors would love it."

"Nonsense. You know it's magical."

Rowan sighed. "Yes. But it's not *doing* anything magical."

"Just like that jewel of yours."

"True." And there was nothing more to be learned.

20

Despite Rowan's comment to Ellen, they did sleep. The scrub-girl woke them at dusk with an offer of hard rolls and fruit juice.

They found their night's duty uneventful, its tedium relieved by the ribald comments of their counterparts on the north face, as each pair's pacing brought them together. The women managed to respond like true soldiers, with earthy insults. Bel also amused herself by singing quietly as she walked, which Rowan enjoyed. The steerswoman rarely sang when others could hear; her own voice, though true in pitch, was plain and colorless.

To one side, the surface of the lake and the overcast sky merged in a black, featureless void. To the other, the fortress presented observers with an array of cupolas, balconies, and courtyards, and windows lit with gentle lights, most of which were extinguished, one by one, as the night proceeded. Rowan studied the configuration of rooftops as she paced.

At midnight their relief arrived, and the two women made their way to the staircase in a corner tower and descended. Sometime during the shift the wall sconces had been lit, and soft, unflickering light streamed from behind opaque shields. Pausing to examine one, Rowan found that she could not remove the shield. Cautiously she thrust one finger behind and encountered something hard and hot. She pulled back quickly. "These might function like the lamps in Wulfshaven Harbor."

"If Corvus can do it, I suppose Themselves can."

At the first level, Rowan unexpectedly turned aside, went down a short passage, and turned left, the opposite direction from their route back to the barracks and mess.

Caught unawares, Bel hurried to catch up and fell in beside her. "Where are we going?"

Rowan made a gesture. "So far, we've come a bit more than halfway around the keep. I want to complete the circuit, and on a different floor. I noticed something about the layout while we were on guard."

"And what's that?"

They were moving down a wide corridor, with doors on the left and a display of muted tapestries on the right, between light sconces, more decorative than those in the stairway. They passed two servants in whispered conversation, who silenced as they approached and resumed when they had gone by.

"From the walls, it looks like the keep is organized in three concentric hexagons. The outer wall and adjacent buildings, such as we saw on our first reconnaissance—that's the first hexagon." On the left, space opened into a gallery with arched windows. Noticing that the servants were out of sight, Rowan slipped into it, Bel following.

The windows showed an alley below and a rank of buildings across. Past them, the tower joining the northeastern wall to the eastern could be seen. Rowan turned back. "And now we're in the second hexagon."

Bel puzzled over this. "Like rings, inside each other?"

"That's right."

"And where are we?"

They continued down the hall. "The front gate and causeway are on the south. We're now on the east side; counting our movements yesterday, we've gone three quarters of the way around."

"I see. But I'll never know how you keep direction indoors. What are you doing now?"

Rowan had stopped to look behind the tapestries and found bare stone wall. "There are no doors on this side."

"And no windows. We can't even look at the inner ring." Bel viewed her friend sidelong. "And now that's what you want to do most."

"More than that; now I want to go there."

The corridor angled, following the native geometry of the fortress as a whole. Just past the corner, they finally found a narrow door, tucked between two tapestries.

The door was propped open with a wooden block and led to a cramped staircase winding down. Following it, they found another open door; the room beyond was in blackness. Rowan listened for a moment but heard nothing. She slipped in and stood motionless, waiting for the atmosphere and the sound of her breathing to bring her some sense of the room's shape.

Bel paused briefly, tucked behind the door's edge to cover any sudden retreat Rowan might need to make. Nothing happened, and the steerswoman beckoned her in. "No magic lamps here?" Bel complained in a whisper.

"Apparently not."

Light flared suddenly, pottery crashed, and a girlish voice cried, "Oh!" Then she said angrily, "You startled me!" A foot stamped petulantly. "How dare you?"

Rowan fought an urge to run, knowing it would only cause worse suspicion. Bel had dropped the point of her spear to fighting position, squinting in the light, and Rowan laid a restraining hand on her arm.

The room was brilliantly lit, and a slim girl stood by an opposite doorway, one hand flung back, the other steadying her against a cupboard from which some crockery had fallen. She was of Rowan's height but fragile-seeming, and young, no older than Willam. A cloud of dark ringlets framed a face with a small, up-tilted nose, pointed chin, and long dark eyes under straight brows. It was a beautiful face, of that characterless perfection that Rowan always equated with having no face at all.

The girl wore a light silk gown, possibly her nightshift, over which was thrown a hooded cloak of startling beauty. Blue satin folds bright as sparkling water fell from her shoulders to sweep the ground, white satin showing at the lining. The cloak needed no ornament other than its elegant construction and the flare of its movement as the girl

stepped closer. She viewed Bel with haughtiness and spoke with sarcasm. "My, isn't she fierce?"

Bel relaxed her posture, and Rowan apologized. "Sorry, child. Instinct and training."

The girl turned her dark gaze on Rowan. "And what might you two
be doing here?"

The room was a kitchen. Rowan managed a wry comradely smile.
"Possibly the same thing you're doing."

The girl stamped her foot again. "You must speak to me with more
respect!"

Taken aback by her outburst, Rowan made to reply, but the girl
continued, pacing in anger.

"You guards are all the same, none of you want to treat me correctly. I'm not a servant, remember that, and I'm not one of your
cronies." She stepped close and shook her finger under Bel's nose.
Rowan caught a faint scent of musk and dried sweat. "You should
come to attention when I pass in the halls, and—oh!" She threw up
her hands. "Those comments! There'll be no more of that, I tell you.
Remember what happened to Clara."

"Miss," Rowan managed to interject, "I'm sorry. Nothing of the
sort entered our minds. You caught us by surprise, that's all. No disre-
spect was intended."

Catching Rowan's tone, Bel spoke up. "And, miss, pardon me, but
I'm new here, and I don't know much of anything yet. Please, so I
won't make the same mistake again—who are you?"

The girl regained her control and eyed the Outskirter archly. "I'm
Liane." She tilted her head, gauging reaction, then turned away and
wandered, as if idly, down along the preparing tables. "If you're all that
hungry, you may as well help yourselves." A condescending smile was
turned in their direction. "Don't worry. I won't tell on you."

They leaned their spears near the door and came farther into the
room. Liane graciously indicated the cupboards, and Rowan found a
cold leg of mutton inside one.

"And, please, what is it that you do?" Bel continued. Liane's only
reply was an expression of self-satisfaction.

The steerswoman had already solved the girl's puzzle, but was at a
loss to express it politely. "She . . . holds a delicate and influential position."

Liane laughed and clapped her hands. "I like that! Delicate and influential, that's very true."

Finding a pewter plate, Rowan arranged careful slices of meat, added some bread, and passed it to Liane. Then she cut more casual chunks for herself and Bel. "I must admit, miss," she began cautiously, "that I've always wanted to meet you."

Liane stopped with a slice halfway to her mouth. "Why is that?" A pattern of little bruises showed along one arm.

"It seemed to me that you must be a remarkable person, else—" She spread her hands to include the keep at large. "Else how would you be here?"

The girl looked surprised and gratified, and her expression softened. Here, Rowan thought, was possibly the best source of information they could hope for. Liane was young, naive, and in a privileged situation. The high opinion she had of herself was at odds with the attitudes of those around her; she was certainly lonely, and possibly easily flattered.

"Understand," Rowan said to Bel, "a wizard could have any companion he chooses. Willing or unwilling, I suppose. The field of possibilities is large."

"Large indeed, and more willing than not. Really, the way some of those people behaved!" Liane fluttered her fingers fastidiously. "Beneath me. I didn't try to attract attention at all."

She was altering her speech patterns, Rowan realized, and trying to adopt a form she considered superior. Likely her normal style was more like that of most of the guards. A local girl.

"And despite that, you were chosen, from everyone." Rowan tried to sound impressed.

"Oh, yes." Liane sighed ostentatiously. "It was love at first sight, I suppose."

Bel was more dubious. "With which one?"

The girl feigned surprise. "Why, both of them." She gave an arch, self-satisfied look. "They're *very* close."

The Outskirter frowned in thought as she tried to work out the logistics.

Rowan manufactured an envious expression. "Some people are born for good fortune."

"Not all love and fun, I tell you," the girl stressed seriously, slipping into natural speech, then slipping out again. "Mine is an important responsibility! When they're distressed, or out of sorts, when their spells go bad and their plans don't work, who do they turn to?"

There was a large pause before anyone recognized that she expected an answer to so rhetorical a question. Bel surrendered. "You?"

"Yes, indeed! And if I can't soothe them and cheer them up—" She made a wide gesture. "Everyone suffers."

"Are they out of sorts now?"

Her expansive mood faltered. She rubbed her nose with the back of one hand: an unconscious gesture, natural and poignant. "They're very demanding," she eventually replied.

"Is it this business with the steerswoman?" Rowan queried nonchalantly, remembering Ellen's comments.

Liane showed disgruntlement and picked up another slice of meat. "Nothing else. I hate her. Everything's in an uproar, just when we had gotten decently settled."

"We might get sent out in a search squad," Bel volunteered.

"I hope you kill her. No," the girl amended, "that would only make matters worse."

"It's not really fair," Rowan said, trying to voice Liane's own thoughts. "Shammer and Dhree have just fought a dreadful war. I imagine they'd like to rest and enjoy themselves, rather than worry about some fugitive."

Bel discovered her role in the conversation and began to play it. "Not at all," she said to Rowan. "They have a responsibility. If this woman is some criminal, then she ought to be punished."

"I'm sure they have other matters to attend to. How important can one woman be?"

Brooding on her hatred for the mysterious steerswoman, Liane commented distractedly, "It doesn't matter if she's important or not. They still have to catch her. But they don't have to like it."

Rowan stopped short. Implications crowded her mind, each demanding attention. Misunderstanding her silence, Bel tried to carry on the investigation. "If they don't like it, why don't they stop?"

The girl's gaze refocused, and she slipped back into her superior manner. "That's hardly the sort of thing soldiers should worry about. You just do as you're told, and leave the decisions to your betters. Well." She pushed away her plate. "Let's leave the mess for the scullions. It will be a great mystery. Don't you have to report to someone or go and guard something?"

If they reported to the night officer immediately, the lost time would not be difficult to explain away. Nevertheless, Rowan said, "Perhaps, miss, you'd let us escort you back to your chambers?" She thought it likely that Liane's rooms were within the central keep.

The girl smiled charmingly, tilting her head. She had apparently decided that she liked this understanding guardswoman. "Well. That's well spoken, but explaining you would take more trouble than it's worth. However—" She tapped one cheek thoughtfully, amused with her own idea. "I think that tomorrow I'll ask if I might be allowed to have a small contingent of my own, a sort of honor guard? Would you two enjoy a job like that?"

Rowan was astonished. "Very much, miss," she said quite honestly. Bel's grin possibly seemed feral only to Rowan.

"That's good. I'd like it, too." Liane turned away, allowing the cloak to swirl dramatically about her, very conscious of the effect. Pausing at the door, she made a gesture back toward the stairs. "Go on. You're dismissed."

Ascending the stairs, Rowan's steps began to slow of their own accord. Halfway up, she discovered that she had stopped climbing.

Bel paused, looking back down at her. "What's the matter?"

"Nothing. But wait a bit, I need to think. Something Liane said." The conversation had yielded possibly important information, and Rowan stood silently as she organized the implications of three off-hand comments.

It doesn't matter if she's important or not. Possibilities were two: the steerswoman was unimportant; or there was no way to determine her degree of importance.

They still have to catch her. There was an impetus to do so that was outside of Shammer and Dhree's control. Possibilities were two: a natural impetus consisting of the real threat she represented; or an artificial impetus.

They don't have to like it. Shammer and Dhree resented the situation. Possibilities were two, and not mutually exclusive: they resented

the waste of their resources; or they resented the existence of the outside impetus.

That resentment itself presented two possibilities: it was justified;
or it was unjustified.

If their resentment was unjustified, it implied unrealistic attitudes.
At least in the two wizards' minds, it was justified.

If it was justified, then they believed she was unimportant, and
they disliked acting against their own judgment against a threat
they did not see as real. The impetus, then, was irresistible—and
artificial.

The steerswoman turned to Bel. "Shammer and Dhree are acting
under orders."

She half expected Bel to doubt her and require lengthy justification, but the Outskirter digested the statement, then nodded
minutely. "You're certain."

"Yes."

"Who gives orders to wizards?"

Possibilities were two. "Either the decision was made by the wizards in concert, with Shammer and Dhree dissenting but forced to follow the majority . . . or there's some single authority set over all
wizards."

"If there were, why would they ever war against each other?"

Possibilities were two. "If the authority exists, either it doesn't care
or it approves."

They continued up and then along the second-floor corridor, planning to return to their barracks by completing their circuit of the
fortress. As they turned the final corner, they saw in the distance the
last member of the squad they had ambushed, the man they had tortured. He was alive.

21

They flattened themselves against the wall.

He was descending an open staircase, moving like a recently risen invalid. His bandages were fresh, his clothes and person clean. A solicitous comrade walked beside him, speaking in low tones.

"If he turns this way he's bound to recognize us," the Outskirter muttered.

"I doubt he'll ever forget your face." There was a door by Rowan's right hand. She slid closer and tested the latch. It was unlocked. A tap on the shoulder got Bel's attention, and the two slipped through. Rowan eased the latch silently closed.

The dim corridor they found was warmer than outside, with a faintly muffled feel. Trying to orient herself, Rowan felt a moment's confusion, and then amazed gratification. Briefly, the danger outside vanished from her thoughts. Rowan called her map to mind. "This is it. We're in the center." The ceiling there was lower than elsewhere. Rowan ran her hand along one wall. It was paneled in rich dark wood, kept gleaming by much attention.

"Yes." Bel looked around. "The inner fortress, nestled within the outer one. Do you think he'll come in here?"

Rowan shook her head, thinking. "Possibly not." She made a gesture back toward the door. "That's the part that most people deal with. Official rooms, residences—everything connected with the outside is conducted there."

"Then this is important." They were speaking in whispers.

"But the door isn't guarded, and it stands in plain sight. This area isn't really secret or protected. Perhaps it's just meant to be secluded."

"Or perhaps there's something in here that takes care of intruders by itself."

Fear and excitement fought each other in Rowan. "And that might signify something very important indeed."

"This hall seems normal enough. In fact, it's more pleasant here than in the rest of the keep."

"Perhaps that's its only purpose. The wizards may keep their private chambers here."

"And everyone would avoid them." Bel looked back at the door. "Well, we can't go back out without being seen. And someone else might come in soon."

"Yes." The corridor ran straight for some twenty feet and came to a cross juncture. A single, heavily carved door faced them from the intersection. Rowan approached it cautiously, Bel trailing ten feet behind, watching their back.

Reaching the door, Rowan paused and leaned close. Voices leaked faintly from within. She shook her head once in frustration, then glanced both ways down the crossing corridor. Deserted, with more doors. She added their orientation to her mental map, chose the direction that seemed to have the most options, and indicated that Bel should wait at the intersection.

She took five slow steps, her gum-soled boots dead silent on the carpet, and a door on the right opened. A slight, dark man emerged, his arms full of bundled clothing. Rowan slipped into a more normal pace and made to continue by nonchalantly. Bel stepped back out of sight.

He dropped the bundle. "Say! You can't be in here!"

Rowan stopped and looked about in puzzlement. "Sorry. Made a wrong turn." She turned back.

"You, there!" he called after her. "Stop!"

Rowan ignored him. He called again, then set up a cry for guards. A bustle and clatter grew ahead, and abruptly Rowan's alternatives had vanished.

She was trapped three ways, with the servant behind, the guards ahead, and the door by which she and Bel had entered, with people possibly outside—

She made the only choice she could, and Bel was ahead of her, already at the door. The Outskirter reached for the latch.

There was a faint snap, and Bel spun back as if struck, slamming up against the wall.

A guard-spell!

Rowan felt a hand on her shoulder, turned, and fisted the servant across the face. Then the guards were there, three men, and she was gripped by too many—and too strong—hands.

Bel had recovered her balance and stood weaving slightly, watching dazedly. Rowan wanted to tell her to flee, but it came to her that her friend would do no such thing. One of the guards spotted the Outskirter. "Here, who's that one?"

They must not both be caught. Rowan's mind went into a flurry, then clutched at an inspiration.

She struggled wildly, aiming a kick at the man's crotch. "*She's* the only reason you lowlives caught me. You're all too stupid except her."

One man laughed harshly. "Not too stupid to know there's no women in the inner guard." He called over to Bel. "You! How did you get through that door?"

Rowan spoke before Bel could. "She was *chasing* me! Slipped in behind me. She's too damn fast and too damn smart."

"Is that right?"

Bel wavered on her feet. She seemed hesitant, her reactions oddly slowed. The spell, an aftereffect, Rowan thought. Bel, keep up with me!

Bel, beginning to catch on, approached. "That's right."

One of the guards shook Rowan. "So how did *you* get in?"

She ceased struggling abruptly and leaned her face mere inches from his. She made her voice brittle with spite and disdain. "I got in because your pitiful little guard-spells have no effect on *me*."

Someone's grip faltered. "Gods below, she's a wizard."

"No." Understanding grew on the servant's face. "I know who she is. She's that steerswoman."

"What, the one all them squads were sent for? She's here?"

"Yes, I'm here." Her fear lent credence to the sneering anger she feigned. "I've been in the midst of you for days. You wouldn't have caught me at all but for *her*." She jerked her head in Bel's direction.

Her ploy was not working. Bel should have been participating, playing up, filling in the story. Instead, she stood to one side, still dazed, watching with the desperate attention of someone trying to follow a situation suddenly too complex.

Rowan needed a reaction from her, a convincing one, and quickly. Taking advantage of the guard's weakened grip, she pulled half-free, took one step toward the Outskirter, and spit in her face.

Bel went blank in shock and stood for a moment, stunned. A sound grew inside her; then she released a single furious shriek and went for Rowan's throat with her bare hands.

Rowan dodged back into the arms of the guards, and one of them stepped forward to fend off Bel's onslaught. "Ho, hold it there!" He laughed. "They want this one alive, I think."

"Keep her away from me!" Rowan pressed herself deeper into her captor's grips.

"We'll handle the steerswoman, girlie. Calm down!" Bel subsided, looking at the man with a wild eye. "You done good," he assured her. "Probably a promotion in this for you."

"So, we take her to Druin?" The man spoke close beside Rowan's ear. Her heart stumbled. Druin would remember that the women had come in together; the ploy would fail.

"Not this one." The servant approached and viewed Rowan with a self-satisfied, superior air. "She goes straight to Themselves, and no delay." He nodded to Bel. "You come, too."

But when the servant emerged from the room to which they had been led, Bel was instructed to return later to make her report. Rowan exchanged one glance with her before passing through the door the servant held wide. The Outskirter's expression was stony, with what emotion Rowan could not guess. Accompanied by two of the guards, the steerswoman stepped in to meet the wizards.

When she saw them, her first reaction was: Gods below, they're children!

22

hey were not quite children, but they were very nearly so. They might have been twins in their pale, dark-haired similarity. Both were tall and slim, the young man slightly wider across the shoulders; both moved with self-conscious grace, the young woman somewhat more quickly; both looked out from behind identical smooth faces through the same wide-set brown eyes.

The young woman stood by a round oak table, as if she had just risen from one of the two chairs. She wore a blue shift, simple but of beautiful workmanship, as fine as Kundekin-make but without their usual ornamentation. Her thick black hair fell in a braid to her waist. Behind her, a narrow window showed the walls of an interior court, dimly visible in the predawn glow. A lamp—not magical, but oil-burning—stood on the table, soft light falling on a sheaf of papers before her, and on a vase of daffodils. With affected disinterest she watched Rowan and the guards approach.

Her brother, who had just entered through a far door, studied the scene with an air of vast amusement. His hair, the identical color and the identical length, was caught at the nape by a plain silver circle. He crossed to a low chair with its back to the cold hearth and slouched, comfortable as a cat, stretching his long, loose-trousered legs in front of him and steepling his fingers.

Rowan stood between the guards, watching and thinking. She waited for the wizards to speak.

The young man spoke first. "What a lot of fuss she's caused."

"She certainly doesn't look like much," his sister observed.

Rowan could not remain passive. "Neither do you, I must say."

"Speak when you're spoken to!" the young woman spat.

"Yes, do," her brother amplified. Then he smiled slyly. "But tell us what you mean."

"You're very young."

"Are we?" The sister raised her brows affectedly. "How can you tell? We're wizards." She threw out one hand in an airy gesture. "We might be a hundred years old, a thousand!"

It was impossible. Even if a wizard's power could maintain the semblance of youth, voice and movement gave the two away. They were self-conscious, uncertain. They were feigning behavior designed to cover their inexperience. They overcompensated. Life was new to them. They were young.

"You're seventeen, about," Rowan said. "And your brother, not more than a year younger."

"So you think," the girl said archly, but her brother's amusement confirmed Rowan's guess.

"Try and hide something from a steerswoman," he said. "But it's an odd steerswoman, isn't it, who sneaks around in disguise, claiming to be something she's not, infiltrating a wizards' fortress."

"Strange events create strange results."

He raised an eyebrow. "Is that a Steerswomen's adage?"

"No. An observation."

"Ah, yes. Very observant, the Steerswomen." He sank a bit deeper into the chair, his body more relaxed, his eyes more alert. "I wonder what else you've observed, what else you might know. You weren't very kind to our minion, you know." His smile vanished. "I can't imagine why we should be any kinder to you."

Rowan felt a chill, but her gaze did not waver from his. "I'm sorry about your man; but I think that you'll find that sort of thing isn't necessary in my case."

The sister came around the table and leaned back against it, in a semblance of nonchalance. "Meaning what?"

Rowan spared one glance for each of her guards. "Meaning," she replied, "that I won't try to keep anything from you. Meaning that I'll give you any information you desire."

The rhythm of the exchange came to a halt. Her response had been unexpected. Brother and sister exchanged puzzled looks. Finally the young woman said in a light voice, "She's afraid of what we'll do to her. She's a coward."

"I don't think so," Rowan said. "But I'm not stupid. I don't wish to die, or even to suffer, particularly." She smiled thinly at their confusion. "Here." The guards shifted nervously when she reached into the neck of her cuirass; she turned a flat gaze on them, then continued, pulling out the leather pouch where her ring and chain nestled beside the mysterious jewel. As the wizards watched, she placed the ring on the middle finger of her left hand and slipped the chain over her head, its gold glittering against dull leather. "There. Now I'm a true steerswoman again."

She found, with surprise, that her emotions had relaxed, her body stood at ease. In the clutches of the wizards, she was suddenly like a prisoner freed. She was at home again, the home she carried with her. Her mind was clear, and she knew exactly what to do. Facing the pair, she said calmly, "Ask, and I'll answer."

The young man shot his sister a glance. She said stubbornly, "It's a trick," and he turned back, watching with narrowed gaze.

"It's no trick. Steerswomen do not trick people."

"And you expect us to believe it's as simple as that? You don your symbols, and you're suddenly trustworthy?"

"It's not at all simple," she told them. "It only seems so from the outside. And you're free to believe anything you like."

"Impossible," the young woman muttered.

"Wizards are under the Steerswomen's ban," her brother pointed out.

"Not at all. A person is put under ban once he or she refuses to answer a steerswoman's questions, or lies to her." She turned from one young face to the other. "I don't believe either of you have ever spoken to a steerswoman at all, and you haven't lied to me yet. The ban can't apply to you. The only reason I used deceit was my desire to survive. You tried to kill me."

He snorted. "Not us."

"You be quiet!" the girl told him. He raised his brows at her speculatively, but said nothing. Rowan made mental note of the exchange.

"Once you knew the soldiers were ours, you came here," the female wizard continued.

Rowan shrugged.

"Why? Once you defeated them, why not run?"

Rowan thought. "Curiosity."

The brother was astonished. He threw his head back and laughed.

"It's true," she went on. "I know too little; it makes me vulnerable."

He made a vague gesture. "You know *something*."

"I don't even know which of you is which."

He smiled up at the ceiling. "I'm Shammer." His sister made no comment.

Rowan nodded.

"Very well." Dhree recovered her composure and ostentatiously turned her back, giving her attention to the vase of daffodils. "Then answer our questions, steerswoman." She toyed with one of the golden blooms. "To begin with, why are you being hunted?"

Rowan stopped, stunned. "You don't know." Not a question, a statement.

Dhree carefully showed no reaction. Shammer watched from his chair, head tilted insolently.

If they had sent their soldiers against her, and they did not know why, then her conclusion had been right: they had been ordered to do so. Who could give commands to wizards?

"You seem to be held in low esteem," Rowan hazarded.

"What do you mean?" Dhree asked, controlling anger, and her brother smiled at her discomfort.

"You're being treated like servants," Rowan said.

"If we were held in low esteem, we wouldn't be here at all," Shammer drawled.

Meaning that they were there by permission, that leave had been granted to them, the right to claim and defend their holding. Granted by whom?

"Possibly true." Rowan opened the sack again. "Then perhaps you can make something of this." She passed Dhree the enigmatic chip of blue.

"What is it?"

"It's the reason you were told to capture me."

The wizard took it in her hand, glanced at it once, twice; then, astonishingly, she flung it down on the table. She whirled on Rowan in outrage. "Don't be stupid, steerswoman, and don't play games." She stepped close and glared down at her. Rowan noticed how fine the wizard's skin was, and how clean her hair. She smelled faintly of rosemary. Her voice hissing spite, she said, "Do you really think you can fool wizards?"

The steerswoman was not intimidated. "If you're going to tell me it's a decorative object, I won't believe you. I've been told that already, by someone who was clearly trying to deceive me. I know it's magic."

"Of course it's magic! But it's common, we use them every day, in any number of spells. I could show you a hundred like it—"

"No. Not quite." Her brother had risen and moved to the table; he was turning the jewel over and over in his hand.

"What do you mean?" Dhree hesitated, then reluctantly came to his side.

He indicated. "Look at the coating. It's constructed differently."

"That's your area."

"Of course it is. You're theory, and I'm execution. Well, dear sister," he said, his tone heavy with sarcasm, "theorize."

She studied it, touching it with one forefinger. "Is that coating inactive?"

"Yes, indeed."

"Then it's protective." Her aspect had altered. Gone was the bravado, the venom. She showed the clear concentration of an intelligent mind involved in solving a problem. Other considerations had vanished. Rowan felt an odd, sad touch of kinship with her.

"Protective from what, I wonder," her brother said.

The young woman stared at the jewel, but her attention was turned inward. "Environment," she said at last.

"Ours don't need this protection. And they survive any sort of weather."

"Then a different environment entirely. Desert, perhaps." She looked at him. "You've worked with the Grid."

He shook his head. "They're nothing like this."

Rowan fought to keep her excitement from her face. Information, she thought.

Dhree turned her attention back to the steerswoman. "Where did you get this?"

"That one, from an irrigation ditch in farmland by the eastern curve of the Long North Road. And there are many more, scattered across the countryside in a broad line that runs southeast from there clear into the heart of the Outskirts. If you have a map, I'll show you exactly."

Brother and sister, side by side, gazed at her suspiciously. Then Dhree gestured to one of Rowan's guards, who hesitated, then stepped back to the door to call the servant.

"Maps, Jaimie," Dhree instructed when he arrived. "Covering the lands north of the Inland Sea. The librarian will know which." She paused. "And bring another chair for this table."

It was a strange collaboration.

At times Rowan forgot where she was and with whom she was dealing. She presented her information as completely as if she were speaking to steerswomen, and as long as she was the person speaking, she could become lost in the work itself.

It was only when she felt a question about to escape her that she stopped short and remembered: If she asked a question, they might refuse to answer. On their refusal, she could no longer reply to their questions, and all progress would cease.

And her first question was about the maps.

Shammer took one from the group presented by the servant and unrolled it on the tabletop. At first Rowan could not orient herself to it; it seemed to be a work of art, executed in a style delicate and beautiful, like a watercolor painting. Then abruptly, with a small internal shock, she recognized along the right edge the course of the river Wulf. Southwest she found the city of the Crags, with the fjords depicted in maddening detail. The center of the map was dominated by an immense sweep of mountains, the same that lay on the western limit of all the large-scale maps in the Archives.

And, west of the mountains, *past* the mountains, on the other side of those mountains which no living person had been known to cross: A string of lakes like jewels on a necklace. A range of weird, twisted hills. A river broader than the Wulf, longer than the Greyriver, writhing northeast to southwest and vanishing at the map's edge.

She stood silent. Her hands hung limp at her sides. She forgot to breathe. She suddenly remembered a long conversation she had once had with a Christer, as he tried to describe to her the sensation of holy epiphany.

And she said to herself: Don't ask them. Don't ask.

Where had the information come from? Who had been there? Who had seen it? How had they traveled?

Who had drawn that map, with so steady a hand, such elegant colors? How precise were the measurements? Were there communities beyond the mountains? Were there wizards?

Shammer released the edges, and the map rolled closed again. "Wrong one." He swept it to the floor impatiently.

Rowan wanted to rescue it and cherish it as if it were a living thing.

The wizard pulled out another chart, read the legend on its outer edge, and spread it on the table. "This one, I think." Dhree tilted her head at it and nodded.

From where Rowan stood, across from the wizards, the map was upside down. That should not have mattered, but the style was so different from that used by the Steerswomen that she was momentarily confused again.

It seemed that the mapmaker considered roads to be no more important than the natural features of the land. Rowan located a brown-and-green shape that she finally understood to be the salt bog, and managed to locate the eastern curve of the Long North Road nearby, dimly marked by a faint gray line. Again she felt that internal shift as the chart became comprehensible.

"Here." She indicated. "There are a number of farms between the Eastern Curve and the salt bog. They're irrigated from this brook—" Astonishingly, one of the irrigation ditches, probably the largest, was marked. "That's where my jewel was found. I began to ask, and then search for more . . ." Dhree handed her a stick of charcoal. Rowan overcame her reluctance to deface the map and drew, from memory, the location of each finding. "And finally, I heard that there are a large number deep in the Outskirts." She drew a narrow oval, encircling the northern findings, sweeping southeast, and terminating in the middle of a huge area colored dull brown. Leaning closer, she found a jagged line crossing the oval at its far end. It was labeled "Tournier's Fault." "That must be what the Outskirters call Dust Ridge."

Shammer made a face. "What a bother, walking all that way, just to see more of something you've already seen."

"It might be important." Dhree knitted her brows in a frown of thought.

"Perhaps you should go there, Sister."

"Perhaps I will, if we can't get any answers from Slado."

Her face impassive, Rowan grasped at the name.

"And how soon did you realize you were being hunted?" Dhree asked.

"It was after I left Five Corners to return to the Archives." She described the soldiers at the inn. "One of them accosted me on the road later. I don't know who controls that area, but the soldiers were Red."

"That's Olin," Shammer told his sister. "Such a stupid man. He always does too much, or too little. Or nothing, when the mood takes him."

"He's insane," Dhree said, half to herself. "Really, that basilisk . . ."

"Still, as she was crossing his holding with her questions, I suppose he's the one who's started all this."

"Maybe not. I can't imagine he'd place any more importance on this jewel than we did."

"The only importance the jewel seems to have," Rowan pointed out, "is the degree of attention it provokes." She took a risk. "I expect Olin was also acting under orders."

Shammer's only response was a twitch of his lips, and the muttered word "Orders."

Rowan tread carefully. "It's interesting. I always assumed that wizards are ones who give orders, not take them."

"Don't become too interested." But both their faces showed the hate they held for the one who gave them orders. They would disobey if they could. And that meant that they could not.

Discussion continued. They dined—a late dinner, or early supper, Rowan could not tell which. The day had dawned overcast, and the shift of Rowan's sleeping time had skewed her usually reliable time sense. The courtyard outside showed no shadows.

Rowan explained that the jewels were a recent phenomenon. "The earliest date I can pinpoint for their appearance is about thirty-five years ago. I have that date for only two of the findings; the others are indeterminate but don't contradict it. And it's interesting that the farms between the Eastern Curve and the salt bog are relatively new. None existed before thirty years ago."

Dhree drummed her fingers on the tabletop. "And why was that, do you know?"

"Demons in the salt bog was the rumor. But only rumor. No one living there had ever seen one."

"That's odd. Demons are never found in the Inner Lands."

Shammer thought briefly. "It's possible. They need salt water."

Rowan puzzled. "But there are none on the shores of the Inland Sea."

A wry smile. "It's the wrong sort of salt."

Rowan put that aside for later consideration.

Eventually exhaustion overtook her, and the wizards decided to consider her information and continue in the morning.

They wondered what to do with her. "We certainly can't keep her in the dungeon. Considering, that is, all the help she's giving us." Shammer spoke as if amused, but behind his air Rowan could still read suspicion and wariness. He was off-balance.

Dhree, musing on the jewel, did not look up. "One of the inner guest rooms. We need bars on the windows, a strong bolt, and an opening in the door for the guard to watch her."

"So we do. That's a day's work on the window for a mason." He pursed his lips, fidgeting with the end of his queue. "I'll do it myself. An hour or so." He departed, humming, possibly relieved to be leaving the theoretical discussion for work more direct and practical. Rowan was left with Dhree.

"What happened to your entourage?"

Rowan was puzzled. " 'Entourage'?"

The wizard pushed aside the charts and jewel. "Yes, those mercenaries who fought for you during your attack. Our man reported that his squad was badly outnumbered."

Rowan's mouth hung open for a moment; then she laughed long and without restraint. Dhree frowned.

"Your man," Rowan said when she had recovered, "assumed I would never show up here to give the lie to his story. I had two assistants, no more."

A muscle in Dhree's cheek twitched. "And the three of you overcame our trained soldiers?"

"That's the case."

"Where are your hirelings now?"

Rowan neglected to correct the term and answered only the question. "Not here," she said regretfully, internally limiting "here" to its most circumscribed definition.

"How unfortunate for you."

Her prison was a small, comfortable room, luxurious in its appointments. The bed was goose down, with silk sheets and satin coverlet, curtained with lace. A comfortable chair stood by the hearth, where a small blaze had been kindled. Bare spaces on the wall and the off-center arrangement of furniture betrayed the removal of certain items, possibly objects useful to visiting fellow wizards, dangerous or forbidden to common folk. An empty bookcase occupied one corner. Her guard politely instructed her in the use of the magical lamps that illuminated the room; a small brass wheel on the wall by the door, when turned, caused the light to dim and go out according to her wish.

When he left, Rowan settled before the fire, fighting sleep to give herself the time she needed to think. She was a steerswoman again.

She had used that fact as both tactic and technique.

It was a tactic of delay. Cooperating with her captors was buying her time, the time she needed to devise an escape.

And it was a technique of manipulation, far more effective than any web of lies; with every true sentence she spoke, the wizards gifted her, by their reaction and response, with information they would never betray to direct questioning.

Each new fact was like a card, and she sat late into the night, mentally shuffling and spreading them, watching the interlocking patterns appear and dissolve. The branching of possibilities began to narrow, and the patterns started repeating, but she played them, over and over, fighting not only to recognize, but to understand.

When at last she turned down the lamps and took herself to bed, she had managed to reduce all her still-incomplete knowledge down to one fact, true and inescapable: Something was wrong, and her whole world was at that moment in the very act of altering. It was changing from something she now recognized as badly misunderstood into something whose new nature she could not even guess.

She slept without dreaming.

23

*E*xcept for the fact of being a prisoner, Rowan could find no complaint for the treatment she received. Breakfast was excellent, and the servant who brought it inquired after her comfort during the night. Despite her assurances, he offered extra bolsters, a softer quilt, a finer bed robe; when his list of suggestions eventually worked its way down to musicians to divert her, she stonily called it to a halt and requested his personal absence.

She chose from the selection she found in the wardrobe, grateful at least for the fresh clothing. Presently her door was unlocked, and she was conducted back into the presence of the wizards, and the business was picked up from the previous day.

As their discussions continued, Rowan began to see the inefficiency in the wizards' division of labor. Dhree was quick to follow dense theoretical matters, but when Rowan pointed out practical considerations, she had difficulty altering her ideas to accommodate them. Shammer was able to recognize detail and devise immediate solutions to practical problems; but in questions of theory he first waited for Dhree to reach her own conclusions, then laboriously explain them to him.

It was a flawed arrangement, not a true collaboration at all. In every situation, one or the other had to be dominant, and the necessity of communicating across the gaps in their understanding slowed the pace of learning. As the discussion moved from mere fact to speculation, Rowan found the pair more and more isolated in their intellectual corners.

They considered the question of the jewels' distribution.

"As you can see," Rowan began, indicating the narrow oval drawn on the map, "there's a definite direction to the findings, with the largest concentration, I believe, here." Dust Ridge. "This is one of the findings with a date that I'm certain of. Since the opposite end of the trail seems to have the same date"—the farms by the salt bog—

"I'm considering the likelihood of a single event or agent being responsible for the entire dispersal."

Dhree frowned in thought. "Such as a man, walking along, throwing the jewels as he went?"

"The path begins on one side of the salt bog. There was another finding not far from the other side, and in line with the first, and with Dust Ridge." Rowan indicated again. "No man could walk through the bog."

"He flew," Shammer said easily. "Only a wizard would possess the jewels to begin with, and flying's no difficult matter for one of us."

"You say the jewels are common. If the wizard in question was using them while he flew, or carrying them, perhaps there was a flaw in his spell, and he fell."

The young man pursed his lips. "He wouldn't use them in a flying spell. They're not strong enough."

Dhree paused briefly, then objected. "It ought to be possible."

"He'd fly ten feet off the ground, at walking speed, with little real protection. Small children could pick him off with stones. But he might have been flying by other means, and carrying the jewels."

Rowan considered. "If he dropped them as he flew, he must have been flying very fast; at Dust Ridge, the jewels hang halfway up a cliff."

Both wizards had difficulty visualizing that. The steerswoman elaborated. "If a man is riding on a fast horse, and he drops a coin, it doesn't hit the ground directly under the point where he dropped it."

Dhree caught on. "He and the coin share the same velocity, until the influence of the motivating force is removed from the coin. It falls, losing horizontal speed, gaining vertical speed." She took a sheet of paper and a pen. "How high up were the jewels found?"

"Halfway up the cliff. I'm afraid I can't be more specific than that." In sudden inspiration, Rowan turned back to the map and found Tournier's Fault. There, along the line marking the cliffs, she found dimly marked measurements. There were no units assigned to the number; were they feet? Miles? But she indicated them to Dhree, and the wizard tilted her head to read, closed her eyes briefly in thought— and then, astonishingly, drew a rough version of the very graph Rowan had used in her argument with Arian, a chart showing the range and interrelationship between possible height, speed, and falling time for falling objects.

Dhree showed the chart to her brother, who used an affected disdain to cover his incomprehension. Dhree was wise to his behavior. She tapped the chart. "Here. The normal falling path was interrupted by the cliff—"

Twisting his mouth, he said, "Tell me what I *need* to know."

In exasperation, she indicated a point along one of the scales. "Here's your range of speed."

He glanced at it once, then shook his head. "Impossible."

"Nonsense! It's just a question of finding a strong enough force—"

"It may be lovely in theory, but it simply can't be done. Forces like that can't be controlled."

"It ought to be possible. If you can find a usable spell, scale up its strength—"

"You can't simply scale things up without considering the effect on the materials and spells involved. In extremes the results become unpredictable."

"If the theory exists, there must be a way to implement it. You're approaching this backward—"

He tilted his chin up. "One of us is."

The course of this argument was very familiar, Rowan noted with amusement, remembering Arian. Seeking a way out of the impasse, she tried the opposite approach. "Shammer." When he turned to her, she continued. "Forget all this for a moment. Suppose you wanted to lodge a cluster of objects halfway up a cliff; try to think of the sort of spell you would use."

Response was immediate. "I wouldn't need a spell at all. Close up, a very good catapult would do the job."

"Imagine that you weren't close up."

He blinked. "Any number of means."

"And I assume that they're all magical."

"You assume correctly." His fingers drummed on the tabletop, and his face acquired the introspective, concentrated look of a person involved in work of the imagination. "I could use a spell that would fling the objects hard enough to leave the ground and strike the cliff. But it's tricky—and dangerous. I'd have to arrange the spell so that it would activate in my absence." He smiled wryly. "In other words, I'd set it up, then run like the devil. With that sort of thing, it's not a good idea to get in the way."

The phrase jogged at Rowan's memory. Where had she heard it? Then it came to her: Willam.

Dhree spread her hands. "Then that's the answer."

"No." He frowned, dissatisfied. "The spell isn't directional—it works in a sphere. The objects would go in every direction: up, down, all around." Reaching across the table, he pulled the chart closer and studied the narrow oval. He tapped it with one long finger. "You wouldn't get anything like this."

An idea occurred to Rowan, and she approached it carefully. "You said that some objects would go up. With a large enough force, I suppose they might never come down again."

The concept amused Shammer immensely, and he laughed offensively. "Silly woman. Everything that goes up, comes down."

But Dhree knit her brows. "It ought to be possible—"

Shammer glowered at his sister, stressing each word. "It can't be done."

Over lunch, they accused her of murder.

"Don't play innocent, steerswoman. You've killed at least two of the regular guard."

"Are they dead or just vanished? Perhaps they took the opportunity to flee your employ."

Shammer's gaze narrowed, and he did not reply. Vanished, then, Rowan concluded, and not due to her.

Dhree picked up the tale. "One man and one woman. They disappeared about the time you were captured, or just before."

Shammer, legs crossed with ankle on knee, flicked a speck of dirt from one soft leather slipper. "I don't like loose ends. It's untidy."

Rowan was about to truthfully assert her innocence, when she stopped short. About the time she was captured? Before? Or could it have been just after?

The missing man, she realized, was the fellow she and Bel had spotted, the survivor of their ambush. Bel would have eliminated him immediately, to prevent his identifying her and connecting her with the captured steerswoman.

And who was the vanished woman? Bel herself, fled? If so, why bother to kill the man? With him dead, Bel could possibly remain a member of the guard, needing only to explain Rowan's absence . . .

Then the answer came to her. The vanished guardswoman was herself, reported missing by Bel, the deed laid at the door of the notorious steerswoman.

"I believe I know who you're referring to," Rowan said to the wizards. She cast about for a true statement. "Violence is unfortunate. I . . . apologize for its necessity."

That seemed to satisfy them. "Violence is a rather simple means to some ends," Dhree remarked.

Shammer indicated to the servant to pour more wine. "One always does what's necessary."

The day passed, but the purpose of the jewels remained a puzzle.

"You said," Rowan prompted, "that you use their like regularly." That was the closest she could come to a direct question.

Dhree caught on. "And that's all we'll say about them."

"It's difficult for me to speculate without more information," Rowan pointed out. "I believe that, together, we may be able to solve this. Since it's as much a mystery to you as to me, it's to both our benefit."

"More to ours than to yours," Shammer commented, "as you'll never have the opportunity to use what you learn." He was seated on the windowsill, enjoying the afternoon sun.

"Steerswomen never use their information," Dhree said with derision. "If they did, they'd be more powerful than they are."

The steerswoman surprised herself by replying heatedly. "We do use our information," she said. "We're not interested in anything as petty as power over others, and if you're planning to kill me or keep me your coddled prisoner forever, then it's pointless and stupid to keep me in the dark."

"A little more respect, please," Dhree said without anger.

Shammer pulled a droll face at Rowan. "I'm afraid you'll get nothing there. My sister is too cautious. Very wise of her, don't you think? But that does remind me—" Stepping away from the window, he came to the table, eyes twinkling. "I think you might find this amusing." He pushed aside the charts and papers, reached into a pouch on his belt, and pulled out a small gleaming object, which he placed before the steerswoman.

It was a tiny silver statuette, as tall as her thumb. The figure was strangely stylized, and it took her a moment to make sense of it. It seemed to be a dancer, poised on one foot, one arm arched high above its head. Its other arm trailed to one side, as if it had been captured in the moment of executing a graceful turn. The figure was otherwise featureless, its gender indeterminate, the oversimplification of form lending it an eerie beauty. The dancer was standing on a flat silver base, from which a silver bar rose, arcing up in a half circle to where the raised hand touched it.

And attached to one side of the bar, destroying the weird grace of the sculpture, was Rowan's blue jewel.

Shammer held up one hand. "Watch." Carrying the figure to the window, he placed it on the sunny ledge, and with a dramatic flourish, stepped aside.

The figure began to dance.

It knew only one move, the completion of that swirl promised by the curve of its back and the sweep of its hands. It spun, slowly, then faster, sunlight glittering off its body.

Rowan watched, appalled and entranced. "Is it alive?"

He laughed with delight and, for once, completely without affectation. "No, not at all! It's magic, dear lady."

Dhree made a noise of exasperation, but her eyes showed admiration and affection. "You're showing off."

"Yes, indeed, and I love it."

He gave Rowan the dancer to keep, so amused was he by her astonishment. Later, back in her comfortable prison, she studied it, speculating and generalizing.

The jewel did finally seem to have a use; in some fashion it imparted life to the silver figure. Perhaps that was the overall purpose of such jewels: to animate the inanimate. What might be accomplished by such animation, what purpose the power might be put to, remained open, indefinite. The jewels might be useful in any number of spells.

The figure stood on her windowsill, innocently graceful, weirdly evocative, dancing in the light of the falling sun.

Through the window, across and below, Rowan could see the guards on the west wall in conversation with another pair, probably their evening replacements. Shortly, the first two left, and the new guards watched with odd interest until they were out of sight. Then the shorter guard shifted her weight, tilted her head up at her partner, and by those two characteristic moves, Rowan recognized Bel.

This section of the perimeter had not previously been Bel's assignment; Rowan wondered if the new arrangement represented the promised promotion. The woman who accompanied the Outskirter was of the tall, broad-shouldered type that seemed to dominate the female contingent of the wizards' resident guard. The two stood casually scanning the area, then consulted briefly. The tall woman stooped to deal with something buried in the shadow of the edge, and Bel strolled to the near edge, to look left and right, then down.

She was facing Rowan's window; the tall woman's back was turned. Rowan tried to signal, using broad gestures, but failed to attract the Outskirter's attention. Turning around, Rowan scanned the room for something more eye-catching.

Shammer's dancer was on the sill. She thought of using the jewel to catch the sun's light, but realized it was too small, and its natural color too dark. On a low table by the hearth were the plate and glass from her dinner, brought in on a silver tray. She quietly moved the crockery and took the tray to her window.

Bel had walked to the corner tower and was returning, carrying what looked like a wooden bucket filled with straw. She gave it to the guardswoman, who acknowledged her with a glance, and returned to her work.

Using the tray, Rowan mirrored the sunlight onto Bel's face. Bel's head jerked up, and she looked to the window, then stepped closer to the edge of the wall.

Had Bel been a steerswoman, Rowan could have conversed with her using the wood-gnome language of hand gestures, exaggerated for distance. As it was, the sum total of Rowan's communication consisted merely of "I am here." What use Bel might make of the information, she had no idea.

Bel did not acknowledge but, appallingly, stepped back and tapped her companion on the shoulder. The woman looked up, and with one hand Bel indicated the steerswoman.

In shocked instinct, Rowan ducked back out of sight. What was Bel doing? Could she gain something by pointing out the prisoner to her new partner?

When she had calmed herself, Rowan looked out again. Both women were gone. She immediately regretted her reflex; whatever Bel's purpose, Rowan could trust her. The important fact was that Bel was still at large, and still in the confidence of the resident guard.

If Rowan could manage to get out of her room, she could find Bel, and both could escape, possibly by water. Willam would have begun on his way to the Archives, if he was following her instructions. She hoped that he was.

Rowan could not count on Shammer and Dhree's continued indulgence. As soon as nothing more could be learned from her, she would be useless to them.

She had only one man guarding her. If he was eliminated, she had a slim chance of making her way out of the inner ring of the fortress—

And then what?

She did not know the usual movements of the inner guards. The only place she could be certain of finding Bel was the women's barracks at the proper sleeping time for those on Bel's new shift. As it was a day shift, Bel would sleep at night. The barracks could easily be full of guards.

Rowan might do better to try to slip away by herself. She disliked the idea, but Bel was in no immediate danger. If Rowan could get out, she might contrive to send a message.

The first step was to get past her guard. Once out, she could make her decisions based on what she encountered.

She needed to get the man inside her room, and alone. And some way to deal with him, once he was inside. She scanned the room, questioning each object: Is this a weapon?

Nothing was, so she set a trap.

She lay fully clothed on her bed past nightfall, leaving her lamps dark, letting her fire die, permitting the guard to assume that she already slept. Just before his evening replacement was due to arrive, she rose silently in the dark.

The armchair was heavier than she had guessed, but she could not let it drag as she moved it. Tilting it back, she found its center of gravity and managed to lever it off the ground and lift it, its lower edge propped against her thighs. Walking carefully and awkwardly, she brought it to the side of the door and lowered it painfully to the floor.

A tall coatrack was moved nearby, three feet behind the door's edge. The guard's grilled opening was too small for the rack to be seen through it.

The low rectangular table by the hearth was easy to move, but presented more of a problem; she would need to hoist it over her head and hold it there, adjusting it silently. The chair gave one soft creak as she climbed it, and she froze, fearing that the guard would enter to discover her standing on it, the table clutched in her arms, a pose more than suspicious. She heard the man shift slightly, but he said nothing and did not investigate, apparently dismissing the sound.

The light from the grille did not fall on herself or any of her arrangements. Trying to keep her breathing quiet, she turned the table with its feet in the air and, using her own head as a balance point, slipped the edge onto the door's heavy upper sill. Her calculation had been perfect, and the opposite end of the table came down and rested easily, propped on the top of the coatrack. It would be stable, she hoped, until the swing of the opening door or a blow of her hand struck the rack. Descending, she moved the chair clear of the events she hoped would follow.

Presently the evening guard arrived, and the two men exchanged a few words. Nothing was said about suspicious noises.

Rowan returned to her bed and sat, composing herself. All that remained was to get her guard to enter. There seemed to be only one way to make certain that if he entered, he would enter alone. She balked at the thought, trying to find an option that did not require behavior so—embarrassing.

There was none. Resigning herself to necessity, she rose, stepped to the grille, and stood casually, her own trap looming above her head.

"Excuse me."

The new guard turned, not surprised; he had heard her approach.

She smiled. "I'm sorry, I just can't sleep. I hope you don't mind if we talk?"

He wavered, confused, caught between duty and traditional respect for steerswomen. "Talk, lady? What about?"

"Oh, nothing in particular, just to pass the time. It's a long lonely night ahead." She permitted him to see how carefully she studied his face. "What's your name?"

He peered in at her, and she saw wide dark eyes and heavy curls of black hair. He was a handsome man, possibly vain, and Rowan blessed that, hoping it might make her job easier. "Geller, lady."

"Then, good evening, Geller." She inclined her head with facetious formality. "I'm Rowan."

"I know."

She groped for something else to say to keep the conversation moving. "Do you enjoy your work for the wizards?"

He hesitated, then answered truthfully. "Not much, lady. But the war ran over my town. It's work." He was watching her intently.

"Well." She stepped a bit closer. "I wonder, if you would be so kind, could you show me how to work the lamps in here?"

"There's a wheel, by the door," he said, indicating with a little jerk of his head.

"I'm afraid I can't see it." She did not bother to look, and he saw that. She kept her eyes on his and forced another smile, cringing inwardly.

There was a very long pause. "I shouldn't come in there."

"No one needs to know." Suddenly her embarrassment overcame her, and she dropped her eyes, unable to face him, knowing that the gesture would be misread. "Do I have to be more . . . obvious?" She raised her eyes again. "I can be, if you wish."

But she saw that Geller's beautiful face was screwed up as if in pain. "Lady . . ."

Rowan stopped short. "Yes?"

"Please, don't do this, lady. It's not . . ." He groped for the word. "It's not fitting."

They viewed each other through the grate, he with pity, she with astonishment, then shame.

At last she nodded slowly. "Thank you, Geller," she said with dignity. "You're right. It's not fitting." And she walked alone back to her bed.

When the shift changed at midnight, she attempted the same ruse with the new guard, to identical effect.

The next morning the servant politely brought her breakfast again. She ignored the food, pacing the limits of her chamber. The knowledge she had gained from the wizards nestled like a seed in her brain; the need to pass it on to someone was agony.

The servant watched speculatively, then withdrew.

She could formulate no plans; she could take no action. No decisions were open to her, and there were no means by which to alter her situation. Although they might not yet realize it, she was of no further use to Shammer and Dhree, and they were unable to reveal anything more to her about the jewels. She would have to spend the day with them seeking to learn one last thing: a means to make her escape.

Eventually she noticed that the guards had not arrived to conduct her to the wizards. The morning wore on, and her breakfast dishes were not removed. She questioned the man at her door, but he knew nothing.

It was past noon when her escort finally arrived and brought her along the now-familiar route. Surprisingly, when they entered the wizards' study, the room was empty. The guards did not leave her, and when she spoke they did not reply. When she attempted to make herself comfortable at the table, they indicated that she was required to stand between them.

All her progress in gaining the wizards' grudging confidence had been somehow lost, she realized, and with rising apprehension she prepared herself to face the new situation.

When they entered, Shammer and Dhree remained standing on the opposite side of the room, as if she were dangerous or diseased, watching her with flat gazes of pure hatred. Some moments passed.

At last Dhree spoke. "We'll be rid of you tomorrow."

"That's rather soon." Rowan wanted to start them talking, any sort of conversation, anything to give her some hint as to what might have happened and what she might now expect.

The wizards regarded her as if she had not spoken, but Dhree amplified, seemingly more for her own satisfaction than from any desire to assist Rowan. "Someone's coming to"—she sneered the word—"*collect* you."

Rowan nodded slowly. "Someone sent by Slado, or Slado himself?"

There was no reply. Shammer shifted uneasily, as if there was something he wished very much to do with his hands.

Rowan tried again. "If we only have one day left, perhaps we should get down to work. With luck, by the time Slado arrives, you might know as much as he does."

They ignored the comment. As if against his will, Shammer said in a toneless voice, "We've found more evidence of your handiwork."

Her handiwork? What was she supposed to have done? Two disappearances had been blamed on Rowan, both Bel's doing. The one had been mere fabrication to cover Rowan's own absence from the resident guard she had joined; the other was Bel's elimination of the last member of the ambushed squad, to prevent his identifying the Outskirter.

Might Bel have eliminated someone else? To be blamed on Rowan, the deed would have to have been done at the same time as the earlier disappearance. Who else presented such immediate danger?

Someone who had seen Rowan and Bel together, certainly. But the inner guard were a separate corps, and the members of the outer guard whom Rowan and Bel had met were not likely to be introduced to the captive steerswoman and would not connect her with the Outskirter.

Who might have had the opportunity to make that connection? Someone who had seen them together, who might have been likely to see Rowan in the wizards' company—and whose absence might have gone unnoticed for two busy days.

Rowan attempted to dismiss the matter. "Disappearances didn't seem to distress you earlier. As you said, one does what's necessary."

Shammer took four long steps forward and backhanded her across the face.

She fell against the closed door, stunned, dazed. The guard on her left dragged her to her feet with a bruising grip. She staggered against him, regained her balance, and passed one hand across her face to find a split lip.

Abruptly, she understood. "Liane."

Shammer struck with his other hand. The guard on the right prevented her falling, and the two men supported her emotionlessly.

When she recovered, she said, "If Slado is coming for me, I think he'll expect me alive." Some of the words were slurred.

Cold confirmation came from across the room. "Unfortunately."

Shammer, his eyes full of murder, took two careful steps back, then turned away.

Regaining her balance, Rowan composed herself slowly. All advantage had been lost. She tilted up her chin. "So I'll meet Slado. How interesting."

With his back to her, Shammer said, "You'll meet him and die." He gestured. "Get her out of here."

"One moment." Dhree came a bit closer. "I understand that your little game of last night was quite the joke among our inner guard. Pitiful."

"It was the best I could manage."

"I think you'll find that your new guards are, shall we say, above temptation? Still . . ." Her expression turned speculative, interested. "Perhaps you've been a little lonely? Perhaps tonight you could use some . . . company?" She studied Rowan's reaction, eyes glittering cold amusement. "What do you think, Brother?"

"No." He half turned, his eyes blank. "She might enjoy it."

The guard at her door was female, a tall angular woman who watched her with the pitiless eye of a bird of prey. Above temptation, as Dhree had said; the rule against women in the inner guard had been altered.

She tried to clean the blood from her face and clothes, but found there was no water in her ewer. The woman at the door ignored her request, and Rowan did the best she could with spit and a silk handkerchief.

In the evening the guard changed shift, but no food was brought, and the remains of her breakfast had vanished. She sat long at the window, silent, watching the light fade, then the starlight glitter on the roofs and cupolas. And slowly her mind became as still as her body, for there were no plans she could make, no routes to investigate. Options had vanished. Possibilities were zero. She sat in the darkness, unsleeping.

When the shift changed at midnight, her guard was Bel.

24

The Outskirter grinned up through the grille. "I've been promoted."

Rowan stared down at her, astonished, then urgent. "Bel, let's get out. Now."

Bel glanced in both directions, then walked a few feet to peer down the intersection in the corridor. She returned. "Not yet."

"Someone's coming?"

"No."

"Unlock the door."

Bel did so, but when Rowan pulled it open and made to leave, the Outskirter stopped her with a gesture. "We have to wait."

"Why?" Rowan spoke urgently. "Bel, I know the layout here now, and you know the internal guard movements. If we can get to one of those exits we found, we might have a chance." Rowan did not know how early Slado or his minion would arrive, or how long she and Bel would need to slip out of the fortress; they had to move, now.

"No, we've got something better. We've got a plan." Bel peered closer. "What happened to your face?"

"Shammer. Who do you mean by 'we'?"

"Willam and me."

Rowan drew a breath. "He didn't leave? He was supposed to leave."

"I needed him here. We've set up a diversion."

Rowan thought rapidly, then shook her head. "There are too many guards here. They won't all run to it, and those who don't will know to head straight for me. I'm too important a prisoner."

Bel smiled rather uncertainly. "You'll be the last thing on their minds. And it doesn't matter if they run to it or run from it, so long as they run. But here—" She reached behind and pulled something from under her cuirass. She passed it to Rowan inside, and closed the door.

It was a bundle of cloth. Rowan shook it out, and a breathtaking swirl of silvery blue spilled from her hands, sweeping the floor. Liane's cloak.

"It'll be a good enough disguise in the confusion," Bel continued.

Yellow light from the grille played on the garment. "It won't work. They know she's dead."

"The wizards?"

"That's right."

"Then they're keeping it to themselves. As far as the outer keep is concerned, she's off visiting. I thought it was odd."

Rowan crushed one handful of satin folds, feeling the weight and beauty of the cloak, thinking of the vain, lonely girl who had worn it. "What is Will going to do? Do we signal him, or he us?"

"Neither. We wait. You have to stand by the window and watch the Western Guidestar. When it goes dark, count one hundred. Then we move."

"And what happens?"

"Something." The Outskirter winced. "I'm not certain what—he didn't explain it well. People will panic, so we'll have to keep our wits about us."

Magic. Aside from lighting fires in wet wood, creating patterns and pretty sparkles in the process, what exactly was Willam capable of doing?

Rowan stepped to the window and studied the stars quickly. The Hunter's shoulder had slipped behind the Western Guidestar. The Hound's nose would have to approach within five degrees before the Guidestar would wink out. That would be near half past one o'clock. They had more than an hour.

Rowan returned to the door and looked down through the grate. Bel had resumed her position as guard. "I only know the one exit from the inner chambers," Rowan told her. "But from there, there are any number of routes to a few ways out of the fortress. If the confusion's going to be general, we might do well to head for that staircase leading to the dock on the northeast side. We could escape by water."

Her back to the door, Bel shook her head. "That won't do. It's the wrong direction. We go out the main gate, over the causeway."

Rowan's heart froze. "Bel, that's the worst possible choice. We'd be visible for too long. We'd have to deal with the guards inside the gate, and stop to work the spell at the end of the causeway. We couldn't possibly move fast enough."

"It's the only way. It's all arranged. We'll deal with the guards as best we can, and Willam will take care of the spell."

"Can he do that?" Rowan was dubious.

"He says so." Bel spared a sidelong glance over her shoulder. "Shouldn't you stand by the window?"

"In a bit. I saw you, on the wall yesterday. Why did you point me out?"

"I wanted Willam to have some idea of your location."

Rowan stopped short, then laughed. The face of a boy, she realized, was little different from the face of a woman somewhat older than he. With a woman's shaped leather cuirass, the disguise would be impenetrable. "What was he doing?"

"Placing his charms. They have to be a certain distance from each other. He's been working like a madman, making more of them during the last two days."

"Do you think it will work?"

Bel shrugged. "I'm no wizard." She paused. "Rowan?"

"Yes?"

"When those guards cornered us . . ." The Outskirter hesitated again. "You spat in my face."

Rowan was ashamed. "I thought we weren't very convincing," she explained. "I wanted to make you angry."

Another pause. "It worked."

"Do you hold it against me?"

"No." Bel shifted slightly. "But never do it again."

Rowan returned to the window and stood the rest of her watch with the best patience she could muster.

Outside, the day's overcast had long passed, and the stars hung crystalline in a black midnight sky. Between rooftop and turret, Rowan sighted a section of the lake, where small waves scattered the starlight, sending white sparkles dancing on the invisible water. The world seemed to exist in black and white and shades of pale gray, clear and without distractions. On the wall in the distance, seen but faintly, a pacing guardsman paused and gazed out at the same quiet scene Rowan was viewing, untroubled, peaceful. Eventually his head tilted up, and he and she saw in the same instant the nightly vanishing of the Western Guidestar.

Rowan began counting, swung the blue cloak about her body, and stepped to the door. "Twenty," she said to Bel.

The Outskirter jogged to the left intersection of the corridor, looked both ways again, and came back.

"Forty," Rowan said.

Bel took a deep breath, released it, and shook her arms to relax the muscles. She seemed calm and cheerful.

It was otherwise for Rowan, and she felt a stepwise increase in tension with every number her mind shaped. "Fifty," she said. "Do we really have to wait this long?"

"One hundred was what Willam told me. I hope you're both counting at the same pace. Is it sixty yet?"

Rowan paused for five counts. "It's seventy." Under the rhythm of the counting, she discovered herself reviewing alternative routes to the front gate; she had information to use, she realized, and that knowledge served to steady her. "Eighty."

Bel pulled the door open, and Rowan slipped through. "Lock it again. It might throw them off. Ninety."

The Outskirter looked up at her, eyes aglitter. "I have a sword for you. I left it behind a tapestry outside the door with the guard-spell."

"Good. I'll need it. One hundred."

They followed the corridor, Rowan three steps ahead, wrapped and hooded in Liane's cloak, Bel following behind like an escort. They went left, then right, seeing no one. At the top of a broad stair, Bel stopped Rowan with a touch on the arm, then indicated. Listening, they could hear measured steps and muttered voices below. Two people; one walked away, and the other remained at the bottom, out of sight.

Close to Rowan's ear, Bel whispered, "There's always one guard at that post."

"What's keeping Willam?"

"There's no way to know. That man is inner guard; he probably knows about Liane. I'll have to catch him off-guard. You stay here." Bel paused a moment, thinking, then began running noisily down the stairs, footsteps startlingly loud. "You! Come here, lend a hand—"

"What? What are you doing here?"

Standing silently, waiting for Bel to do her job, Rowan was half distracted by a short, faint vibration beneath her feet. She looked down at the carpet.

"I'm guarding that steerswoman—something's wrong!"

"Wait here, I'll get help."

"There's no time, you'll have to do—"

There was another vibration, stronger; Rowan looked up, and an instant later she heard distant thunder.

"What was that?" And the man made one more sound, a wet choking cough.

Rowan knew what it was. She flew down the stairs to find Bel pulling the point of her spear from the prone man's throat. "Was that noise from the north?" Bel asked. Far off, someone shouted, a long muffled sentence.

"Yes," Rowan replied. Their way to the gate led south.

"About time." Bel abandoned her spear for the dead man's. "Let's go."

Rowan resumed her place in the lead, struggling to maintain a relaxed, casual pace. Halfway to the door with the guard-spell, they were surprised by a bleary-eyed servant who peered from a room in perplexity. "Themselves are up to something," Bel explained, offhand, as they passed. "Go back to sleep." The man gaped at her, then vanished with a look of fear.

Again the thunder rolled, louder. Wordless shouts came from behind, and the two women understood simultaneously that the time had come to run.

As Rowan reached the door to the outer keep, the floor suddenly bucked once, then shuddered, like a ship hit by heavy seas. The air was full of a roaring rumble. Nearby, someone screamed. Pulling the door open, Rowan pushed Bel through, and in an instant the Outskirter handed her the hidden sword.

There was thunder to the north, and the floor writhed unbelievably beneath their feet. Bel was thrown to the ground, but Rowan stood balancing wildly. About her, half-dressed people had appeared, clinging to the walls, crying to their gods and their families.

Abruptly and simultaneously, all the lamps went out. In the darkness Rowan found Bel and dragged her to her feet. Fading thunder left the air filled with shouts; then a crowd of organized footsteps approached, stumbled against the fallen, and reorganized with curses: soldiers. The squad swept noisily past Rowan and Bel, hurrying north.

Bel made an anguished sound. "We have no light."

Throwing one hand against the door, Rowan oriented herself, her internal map twisting in her mind. She exulted. "We don't need it. This is better." She guided Bel's hand to her shoulder. "Slowly."

"We can't see where to go."

"I know the route." She led the way, keeping measured stride, desperately matching her movement with the vivid image in her mind. One of the terrified residents stumbled against her, and she shoved him away roughly.

Pausing, she shuffled sideways, groping with her left foot to find the edge of the stairway she knew would be there. "Down."

A handful of people pushed past them, their voices a chaos of panic. Some took the stairs, stumbling, crying, and they broke around Rowan and Bel like a swirl of water. Rowan clutched the banister and stepped carefully, Bel still gripping her shoulder.

Reaching the bottom, Rowan saw a moving light in the distance, bouncing weirdly, approaching amidst the sounds of many feet. It was another squad of soldiers, their leader carrying a brilliant glowing object: a magic lamp like the wall sconces, but mobile. The beam played across the small crowd, swept once across Rowan, then returned to her. Thinking quickly, she turned her back to them and clung to Bel as if afraid, hiding her sword with her body, letting the light catch Liane's silver-blue cloak.

"The wizards' dolly," Bel shouted above the noise of panic-stricken civilians. She waved them on. "I'll take care of her."

The light swung away. Someone shouted to the growing crowd in an authoritative voice, "Stay where you are. Stay out of the way. It's being dealt with. Stay where you are." Protests and begging questions were ignored as the squad hurried on.

In a sea of babbling voices, Rowan thought furiously. Her dead reckoning had brought them but a few turns from the front gate, but that gate was guarded at the inside. How could they get past?

She could hear the now-buried nervousness in the people's voices, the panic lying just below the surface. None of them knew what was happening, and all were afraid. She briefly felt pity for them, and then an idea came to her.

Drawing a deep breath, she let out a long wailing shriek, feeling Bel startle beside her. "We have to get out!" Rowan screamed. She stepped into the crowd, clutching, and found someone. She shook him wildly, shouting into his face, "It's magic, something's happening! We'll all be trapped!" He tried to twist away in panic, and Rowan heard those nearby begin to echo her words, voices rising.

She shoved her unwilling assistant forward brutally. "That way! The front gate is that way!" Her hands found more people, and she pushed them, shouting, emitting the most bloodcurdling screams she could manufacture.

Panic spread. Rowan quieted herself and pulled back against the wall, out of the way. Someone took up the shout "This way!" and ran staggering, calling others after him. With a goal for their fear, the people fell into loose organization, helping each other as they stumbled toward escape.

Rowan felt sudden fear. "Bel?"

"Here." The Outskirter's voice came from nearby, to Rowan's left.

Relief. "We stay at the back." She found Bel's hand and reoriented herself. "Come on."

The group found its own stumbling way to the gate, and Rowan and Bel followed, more by tracking the sounds than by the steerswoman's skill. A burst of starlight ahead, and a babble of voices, and the crowd met the four startled guards at the gate.

The sergeant had a torch of real fire and grim presence of mind. "Calm down. No one's leaving."

There was a chorus of protests, and Bel shouted wildly, "It's magic, something magic's got loose! It's killed the wizards!"

Rowan took it up. "It's out of control!" She thought that might even be true.

"It isn't," the man replied against the cries of the people, but his face showed that he doubted. His men tried to herd the crowd back, but a woman broke through suddenly and ran down the causeway, one of the guards following, cursing. She threw herself against the spell-locked iron bars at the end, and he gripped her brutally and dragged her away.

A streak of fire flew toward the magic gate and lodged there, spitting sparks. There was a burst of light, a loud *crack*, and the stone and iron flew apart in a hundred pieces. The woman collapsed in a bizarre cloud of cloth and blood, and the soldier clutched at his face and fell, screaming. A shadowed shape ran to the gate from the road.

"Now!" Bel shouted, pushing through the stunned crowd. Following, Rowan broke through in time the see the sergeant's head fall from his body, and Bel's swing, out of control, ending in a bystander's chest. Rowan stabbed her blade in a disbelieving guard's face, wrenched it free, then turned to see the last guard stepping back, stiff-legged, briefly unmanned by surprise. The crowd fell back.

Rowan and Bel ran along the causeway. Halfway across, they were met by Willam; he carried his bow and three arrows, their heads aflame. Stopping, he gave two arrows to Bel. "Hold these."

Rowan pulled at him. "Are you mad? They won't be distracted forever—they may be coming now."

Bel wrenched her away from him with furious strength. "Shut up." Abruptly, Rowan's mind reorganized itself, and she turned to look back at the fortress.

She saw Will's first arrow end in the last guard's chest, and the man clutched at it, shrieking.

The dark towers were outlined by a glow of fire in the north quarter. Ordered shouts and chaotic cries came to her ears. With a look of desperate concentration, Willam set his feet carefully and lifted his head toward the overhang of the main entrance. His burning arrow flew high, slowed, arched, and fell. By its light, Rowan had seen its goal: the window of an observation post, now unmanned. He'll never make that shot, she thought, then knew with certainty that he would.

The last arrow lofted, painfully slow at the top of its flight, then clattered against the sill and rolled in. There was a pause, then flickering light as something inside caught fire.

"Now run!" the boy screamed, and the three ran madly, staggering past the pile of bones and raw meat, clambering over the remains of the ruined gate. Just as they reached the road, Rowan felt something like a huge invisible hand smash against her back, pick her up, fling her forward in a crowd of flying rock, and flail her body once against a wall of stone.

She came to with a dark shape crouched over her: the Outskirter. Bel looked over her shoulder. "She's alive." There was no response from Willam.

Rowan sat up and found that parts of her body were numb: her left arm and hand, the left side of her chest, the inside of her right forearm. Her right knee throbbed; her back stung as if scored. As she pulled herself to her feet with the Outskirter's help, the grip of her left hand failed, seemingly because some of the fingers bent backward.

She limped over to where Willam stood silent, at the end of a road that now stopped abruptly at the edge of a cliff. Rowan looked out at the fortress.

The causeway was gone, along with the front entrance and the entire front face. Beyond stood a maze of half-ruined walls, and then standing walls, open rooms clinging to their sides like barnacles, all seen by the glow of fire in the ruins of the west quarter, where horses screamed.

As she watched, two of the distant suspended rooms collapsed to the ground like silent sighs.

An immeasurable force, set loose by a boy. A giant fist that smashed, a giant hand that flung stone through the air . . .

"Did you know it would do this?"

He stood silent, expressionless, looking at his work; then he nodded minutely.

Bel came up behind them. "It's a good job, don't you think?" She grinned whitely in a face blackened with dirt and soot.

Rowan touched the silent boy's shoulder and for a moment was amazed that he was mere flesh and blood, merely human. There was no magic to be seen in him. He was only a boy of the common folk, but he had done what seemed impossible. "Willam . . . will you stay with us?"

He turned to her, copper eyes blankly reflecting distant fire. "For a while. Where are we going?"

In this flickering quiet, in the silence after the shock, the world seemed vague, and her mind slowed. She groped for an answer.

"To the Outskirts?" Bel asked.

Of its own accord, information ordered itself in the steerswoman's mind and gave her replies without conscious effort. "I told Shammer and Dhree I was going there. They may have passed it on."

"To the Archives?" Willam suggested.

"I need to get my information to them, but I won't do it in person. If the wizards think I've gone there, they might harm it." Cling-

ing to the framework of her ordered knowledge, her thoughts took
shape again, and she knew what to do. "We need a defended position. Arms, and someone to direct them, someone who won't fail to
stand by me."

"Where do we find that?"

"Wulfshaven. Artos."

25

*T*he city of Wulfshaven held its breath.

One week earlier, Artos had unexpectedly ordered his soldiers
to battle-readiness. Word was sent to those on leave, and they came
into town from their furloughs, faces wary and perplexed. The citizens
they passed questioned them, but they had no answers to give.

Two days later, Artos called his reserves to active duty, and those
men and women kissed their spouses, children, and parents, and set up
their encampments on the lawns of his mansion and in open fields
around the city limits. The sentries on the perimeter were not concentrated in any one direction.

The day after that, a troop of cavalry was sent north, followed by
another of foot soldiers. Their destination was not known, but
message-runners sent to their position returned only a day later.

And the next day, word came that Artos was no longer in his mansion but kept residence in the small fort that barracked his regulars.

Daily business proceeded, but with many glances over the shoulder
and much speculation in taverns and in private.

In the Trap and Net, as everywhere, speculation was very active
and very quiet. Wary glances were directed at the door as each new
customer arrived, and when at last it was a steerswoman who entered,
one of the drinkers hailed her with a gesture, saying to his companions, "Now we'll learn something, I reckon."

But Rowan ignored the summons and stepped quietly to a corner
table overlooking the harbor, where two men with tankards before

them sat alone in friendly conversation. She stood without speaking until one of them looked up at her. "I've been waiting," she said then.

The wizard Corvus examined her with a mild gaze. "I rather thought you might be," he admitted. "It must be very boring."

There was a long pause. "Hardly."

He laughed. "Then you are easily amused. Why don't you join me?" He spoke to his companion, whom Rowan recognized as a local fisherman. "Selras, would you excuse us? I believe I have some business with the steerswoman."

The fisherman absented himself politely, but with a perplexed expression. He would have a tale to tell that night, Rowan thought, of a wizard and a steerswoman who against all custom and expectation had business with each other. She wondered to whom he would tell it, and what the ending might be.

She seated herself, sitting carefully on the edge of the chair, one hand before her on the table. The other hand was in a sling, its fingers stiffly splinted, and her face showed the marks of old bruises. She said nothing, but watched Corvus patiently, and he returned her gaze with an identical expression.

The wizard was a man of striking appearance, all darkness, dressed in black and silver. He was tall, lean, and broad of shoulder. His hair was a cap of gleaming black curls, his short black beard silvered to either side. His skin was dark, as dark as was ever seen in people, nearly true black.

Among the folk of the Inner Lands, any shade of skin was likely to be seen, any color of hair, seemingly without rhyme or reason; but that pure combination of darkness was rare enough to be noticed—and to be prized. Women of such appearance tended to cultivate an air of depth and mystery. Such men, being conspicuous, found that high courage and intelligence were expected of them, and so often actually acquired those traits.

Corvus's manner contradicted none of those expectations, and the only lightness in his appearance was the pale sky-blue of his eyes.

The two sat for some time. At last Corvus gave a slight smile. "You're forbidden to answer my questions. I'm forbidden to answer the very questions you are most likely to ask. I find myself wondering how this problem can be circumvented."

"I volunteer information, without the necessity of your asking for it," Rowan said quickly. "I ask only questions I believe you're free to answer." Then she waited for his reaction; the entire conversation depended on his acceptance of the conditions. And the conversation had to take place.

He made a small sound of amusement, but his eyes were speculative. "It's an odd technique."

"I've used something similar in the past."

"With Shammer and Dhree, I assume."

She was startled, but managed a grim smile. "You've heard. No one else here seems to have. I thought perhaps I might have outrun my own news."

"My means of acquiring news is, shall we say, less bound by time and distance." He leaned back, and the veneer of casual friendliness he habitually affected seemed to falter somewhat. "Very well. Since the privilege of asking questions is yours, you should begin."

"Are Artos's military preparations necessary?" She was in Corvus's home city, and if the wizards planned to attack her, he would certainly have been told, and possibly would serve as the agent.

"I'd answer if I could, but I don't know what he's expecting."

Despite her tension, Rowan appreciated his ability to adapt to the limitations of the conversation. "The duke expects attack. From what direction, he doesn't know. The source is likely to be one or more wizards."

Corvus seemed to consider. "I know of no wizard who might hold a grudge against Artos."

He was being willfully obtuse, and Rowan frowned, anger and frustration battling within her. "The grudge, as you call it, is not against him, but a dear friend of his. That is to say, myself."

"You seem to have many friends. Powerful friends, I should say." And again he was amused.

Rowan sensed a clue in his words, but could not identify it. She believed she was missing something. Suspecting that a direct question would be refused, she tried an oblique approach. "Power is usually seen as the power that commands others. Of my friends, only Artos has such power."

"Wizards also have that power, and in addition, the power to command nature itself."

She was definitely missing something, something important. "Are any wizards likely to use this against me?"

"We have more immediate concerns."

Her confusion became complete. In the midst of this business directed at herself, was it possible that they would be distracted by other matters? Could she be so wildly fortunate? "If I asked what those concerns were, would you be able to answer me?"

He smiled at the careful logic of her question. "It would depend on the depth of the answer required."

It was a dead end; there was no way to sidle around that response, no way to guess what question he might not refuse. She needed his answers, had to discover whether or not a steerswoman's curiosity would call down battle on an innocent town, cause her friends to die for her, and end her own life by the hand of magic.

She changed direction with one desperate risk. "Has Slado lost interest in me?"

His smile vanished. In the midst of the homely, familiar tavern, he seemed a living shadow of gleaming metal and blackness, and she was sharply aware that the power she feared was present in his person. "No one should know that name."

"Shammer and Dhree were indiscreet."

"Stupid children," he said spitefully. "I was against them from the first."

"Then you're wiser than Slado."

He watched her, all friendliness vanished from his demeanor. "They died, you know." He tilted up his chin and waited for her reaction.

Maintaining her calm, she replied, "Yes, I thought they might have. I'm sorry. They were pitiful, in their way."

"And everyone is wondering who's responsible. We know you didn't do it."

"No, I didn't kill them. But I am responsible."

"Only a wizard could have destroyed that fortress. Whoever it was will give himself away soon enough."

His meaning came to her at last. "You believe that one of your number is a traitor."

"We know it. You'd save us a lot of trouble if you revealed his name."

Rowan was stunned.

Corvus continued. "We now know that all your dangerous cleverness was an illusion, and everything you know about those jewels was fed to you. You were told to look for them." He tapped the tabletop to stress his point, then spoke tightly. "You're serving someone, steerswoman, and it's only a matter of time before we discover who, and deal with him in our own way."

She could not believe her luck. To confirm it, she observed, "So you're watching each other, and I'm simply beneath your notice."

Wrapping his hand around his tankard, he relaxed. She was no danger to him; the threat came from her wizardly master. He regained a measure of his former manner, watching her a bit wryly.

She needed more. "You know about the jewels. Shammer and Dhree didn't. Are you in Slado's confidence?"

He seemed indifferent. "I have my own sources."

"Do you know what the jewels are? Why they're so important?"

His expression grew dissatisfied.

"I doubt your sources will help you there, if Slado chooses to keep the information to himself."

"It's a matter of time," he said again, patiently.

She was dizzy with relief. She looked at the ceiling and looked around the room, unbelieving, her mind a flurry of thought with no outlet. It seemed she was safe, for the moment, and she almost surrendered to it, almost rose and walked out, leaving the wizards to lose themselves in their misguided internal disputes.

But the safety, she knew, was an illusion and would shatter in the end, perhaps under worse circumstances. Better that it shatter now, by her own hand. She turned back to Corvus. "I'll save you time, effort, and strain on your sources. No wizard helped me. No one fed me information. There is no traitor, and I'm even more dangerous than you think."

He gave a short laugh. "That's ridiculous. You didn't destroy that fortress. There's no reason you should care about the jewels, no reason you should take such trouble."

"There were reasons enough. At first, curiosity. Later, because my investigation so interested the wizards."

He shook his head, disbelieving.

"Steerswomen never lie, Corvus. And no wizard could have fed me my information, because I know more about this one thing than any of you do, except Slado." She slapped her own chest, an abrupt, tense gesture. "I know what the jewels are."

His brows knit, and he studied her with a narrowing gaze. "Then enlighten me."

"A good choice of word." She drew a breath and began. "Corvus, how many Guidestars are there?"

He did not hesitate. "Two."

"Really? Interesting, if true. I'll rephrase: How many Guidestars were there, originally?" Catching his puzzled expression, she brushed away his reply. "Don't tell me, I'll tell you. Four."

She went on, speaking rapidly. "Two is all that we can see, all that we know about. On the celestial equator, immobile, as all can see; but not really, Corvus, not in truth. They do fall, but too high, too fast. They can never reach the ground. They fall in the direction the earth turns, and at the same speed, and so only seem each to hang forever above its one spot on the earth. It's so obvious, isn't it, once it's pointed out?

"But why are there only two? Humankind has never pressed far enough east or west for one of the pair to sink out of sight below the horizon. What would happen if someone did travel so far? I think I know. As one Guidestar disappeared, another would rise on the opposite side. And it would be that way, all around the sphere of the earth; a traveler would always see two.

"That is, until some thirty-five years ago. It's different now. These jewels are part of a fallen Guidestar."

His expression answered her next question without her asking.

"You didn't know," she said.

A hundred speculations crossed his dark face; he shared none of them. At last he said, reluctantly, "Someone told you this."

"No. I only used reason, evidence—" Her mouth twisted. "And a small ability with mathematics."

He made to speak, stopped himself, shook his handsome head in disbelief, and began again. "How—" He corrected the phrasing. "I can't think of any way to bring down a Guidestar."

"Why not the same means by which they were lofted?"

"That was long ago."

She leaned back a bit in pleasure. He had admitted that the wizards themselves had set the Guidestars in place. "You think you don't have that ability any longer? The ability exists, but perhaps you don't recognize it. The force that destroyed Shammer and Dhree, for instance. Shammer himself said it; such things are tricky, and dangerous. And Dhree: she said it was just a question of multiplying the force used. If their two abilities were combined in one person, perhaps that person would find the problem laughably simple." She leaned forward and said quietly, "I wonder if Slado is laughing."

His eyes were on the window and the harbor outside; his mind was miles away. Then he looked at her sidelong. "One can't help but wonder at his reasons."

It had happened, the change she was looking for, the shift in his demeanor. Clutching at the hope, she spoke to him with simple directness. "I'd tell you, if I knew. And I'll tell you, when I do know. It's only a matter of time."

He nodded minutely, and for that space of time, at that one place in the world, regarding that one matter, they had ceased to be opponents. "Slado is playing some game of his own."

"Yes," she said urgently. "And it's a big one, possibly the biggest ever. The Guidestars were originally set there for a reason, and it's not merely to aid navigation." She stopped in mild surprise, then continued in wonderment. "The steerswomen are always taught to be able to navigate with and without the Guidestars. I thought it was for the exercise, but it's something held over from earlier days, isn't it?"

"Very likely." His mouth twitched; then he spoke a bit reluctantly. "The existence of the Guidestars makes one particular category of spells easier to effect."

"Do you need all four? No, I'll retract the question, I doubt if you can answer."

But he did. "Some of the spells in question are simple, and common; for those, one Guidestar would suffice. But there are a few—complicated, and very important . . ." He became silent.

"You don't use those spells yourself," Rowan said, "or you would have noticed the missing Guidestar."

"That's true."

Rowan did not ask who did use them; she believed that she knew. "Would there be problems if those spells were lost forever?"

He squinted in thought, and the squint became a wince. "The effects wouldn't be noticed for some time. Eventually . . . I don't know enough. There could be some very bad results."

"Bad for whom?"

He gave her a piercing look. "Bad for everyone, lady. We wizards do have our uses."

She reached across and tapped his arm like a conspirator. "Then Slado has some purpose more important to him than the welfare of the folk and the wizards. He's your enemy, Corvus."

"All wizards are each other's enemy, in some way," he admitted.

Rowan noticed that the tavern was completely silent. Someone had noticed a steerswoman in conversation with a wizard; now many stood watching, and more had left. Corvus sent a long mild gaze around the room, taking in every face, then made a small gesture—and the rest of the crowd departed quietly. Only the barman remained, standing beyond hearing with nervously shifting eyes. Corvus ignored him.

"That's a useful skill," Rowan commented in amusement.

"Sheer force of personality." He turned back, studying her speculatively. "When I thought that you'd been helped by a wizard, you could have left it at that," he pointed out. "We assumed that you yourself presented no threat to us, and we probably would have left you alone."

"Am I a threat, Corvus?"

"You know that you are."

"Then I'll introduce you to someone even more dangerous. A fourteen-year-old boy, the son of a blacksmith, uneducated, untrained, unable even to read. But able, if he so desires, to shatter a wizard's fortress."

His face went blank with amazement. "A boy killed Shammer and Dhree?"

He had forgotten the rules, and Rowan's only reply was her smile of satisfaction. "It's impossible," he said carefully. "I'd like to meet this boy, but frankly, I don't believe that you know what you say."

"It's the truth. And he wants to meet you; in fact, I promised to recommend him to a wizard, if ever I had an opportunity. I recommend him to you now. He'd like to be your apprentice."

He shook his head. "We choose from among our own."

"A separate people? That's something else we didn't know before. But it's not working very well, is it, if you have to use two wizards for one job. I must assume no one better was available."

"That was Slado's doing." His expression grew grim at the thought. "It was too soon."

"Not by his lights. Part of his game, Corvus; he wanted that holding established right now, immediately. It must be important to him." Rowan watched the wizard's face change as he internally assembled facts known only to him, to some result that he found deeply disturbing. "I won't ask you what you're thinking," Rowan said. "But perhaps you'll tell me, one day, of your own accord." She rose. "Come. Young Willam has something he'd like to show you. I think you'll find it interesting indeed."

Some ten years earlier, a clever sailing captain had thought to avoid docking fees by bringing his ship past the public wharves, to a private landing up a narrow corner of the harbor. The ship moved slowly, and sounding leads were thrown every five feet of the way; but on a short starboard tack, between one sounding and the next, the hull met a narrow jagged rock, was breached, and the holds filled with water. The ship remained, half-submerged, more decrepit every year, to become the hated enemy of every riverman, confusing the currents and releasing unexpected debris.

Willam removed it.

During his hectic preparations of the previous week, Rowan had been his shadow. She asked no questions, but by some unspoken agreement he abided her presence. She understood little of the proceedings and was annoyed by what she did recognize. They seemed simple processes: distillations and precipitations such as an herbalist might make, but using no plants. At one point she thought he was making tea from some powder, but during the process, when he discovered one hand damp from the brew, he flicked his fingers dry, and the droplets fizzed into sparking flame as they flew.

Now he stood, his bow in his hand, Corvus at his side, on the west bank of the river. The wizard had seen none of Will's preparations but had watched with interest from the bank as the boy scuttled about the wreck, one of Artos's regulars his dazed-looking, cautious assistant.

The day was hot and thick with damp, the sky a white dome of haze. Downriver, the harbor docks were crowded with spectators.

"Is there any danger for those people?" Artos asked.

Will shook his head distractedly. "Not at this distance. I didn't use that much."

The duke was suspicious and uncertain, but did not protest. Behind him, Bel was tending a merry little blaze, three rag-tipped arrows on the ground beside her.

Rowan stood, a wide-legged, stable stance, waiting for the ground to become the rolling sea she remembered from the fortress. She had not seen Will's magic at the last violent moment, had had her back to it as she ran. This time she intended to watch.

Willam made a gesture to Bel, and the Outskirter lit one arrow, turned it to even the flame, and handed it to the boy. He stepped up to the water, waded into it up to his knees, and nocked the arrow. With the smooth ease of a true archer, he aimed and let fly in the same movement.

The bolt ended in a pile of straw braced against an afterhouse on the tilted deck, and the straw flared. Will ran back to shore. Bel stiffened, bracing herself, but Rowan stood looser, preparing her body to absorb the motion.

Nothing happened. There was a long pause, and people began to look at each other in perplexity.

"I, I'm sure I did it right—" Willam stuttered. He reached to Bel for another arrow.

Corvus put a hand on his shoulder. "The charm in that straw was the first you set?"

"Yes . . ."

"They absorb water."

"I didn't let it get wet—"

"The air is damp, and you set it hours ago. And even before that, if it wasn't properly protected, it might have drawn water from the air. Are all the charms the same?"

"No. I use two kinds. One releases easiest by fire, and the other by, by a blow, or if another charm nearby is released."

"You use the one kind to activate the other?"

"That's best." They were oblivious to all else, lost in discussion of magic.

Corvus gave a small, almost kindly smile. "But enough heat will release the other sort, too, won't it?"

Willam looked in amazed realization from the wizard's face to the ship, where the afterhouse was rapidly catching fire. He said in a vague voice, "You'd better get down."

Corvus dropped prone with no hesitation, Willam beside him. Artos and Bel exchanged glances and more slowly made to imitate them. The little band of Artos's regulars looked about in confusion, some laughing nervously.

And the spell released.

It was like thunder from the sky, like standing next to a lightning-strike. Time seemed to slow as Rowan's thoughts sped more quickly, and she saw the rapid action with perfect clarity.

Water sped away from the wreck, moving out in a circular wave so violent that it broke in an instant, the stable surface around it like stone by comparison. Spray dashed straight up in a fountain impossibly high.

The ship separated into a hundred pieces, and each piece seemed to flee in its own direction: the bowsprit hurried across the river, the deck shattered and flew up into the air, the sides of the hull seemed to seek earth, pushing the water flat, then down, and Rowan briefly saw the shallow river bottom.

The poop deck became a cloud of splinters that rushed toward her. She turned and dropped to the ground, bits of wood pattering against her back like hail.

There was a long, echoing quiet, and a second wave of water dashed against the shore like a breaker.

Bel let out a delighted hoot and went to pull Willam to his feet. "That was wonderful!"

Artos and Corvus rose more cautiously, and something seemed to pass between them as they viewed each other. Rowan stood up, splinters falling off her to the ground.

Bel was thumping Willam's back, and he took her congratulations quietly, wearing the same expression he wore when he had viewed the destroyed fortress. He looked like a man who had been told some shocking news, secretly knowing that he was to blame.

Corvus took in the group with a long, slow gaze. His eyes ended on Artos. "I suppose, if I tried to kill these two, you and your men would do your best to prevent me."

"You'd have to use some powerful magic," Artos said evenly.

The wizard nodded, and he looked a bit sad. "I don't want to hurt them. Rowan." He turned to her. "Steerswomen are very good at discovering reasons. If there's a reason I shouldn't eliminate you and this boy, it's one that I ought to know."

She did not hesitate. "You won't do it," she said, "because it would do you no good."

He raised his brows in surprise, and she continued.

"Willam and I are nothing special, nothing unique. Killing us would solve nothing." She approached him, her boots pushing splinters into the ground. "That's why I told you that no wizard was helping me; that's why I didn't hide behind your misconceptions. I'm just a steerswoman, Corvus, and a common one at that. Four years past my training, wandering about the world with no better mind than my sisters."

She stood before him, studying his face, urging him to understand. "As long as you wizards thought I was unique, you hunted me. I've managed to avoid you, or escape from you so far; perhaps I can do so for many years. It doesn't really matter; in the end, I think, you'd kill me if you really wanted to.

"But what then? Do you think the Steerswomen themselves are remarkable? Will you destroy the Archives? I don't doubt that you can do so, easily enough.

"But the Archives don't make us what we are. Will you hunt every steerswoman? We're scattered throughout the known world, and we'd go into hiding. It would take a long time, but perhaps you'd destroy us all, yes, and the new ones we'd train in secret."

Looking up into his dark face, his pale eyes, she saw that he was disturbed. "But there's one more thing, Corvus," she told him. "There's Willam."

Bel shifted, eyed Willam, then led him by the elbow to Rowan's side. The three stood together facing the wizard: warrior, thinker, and child.

"He's just a boy," Rowan said. "Of the common folk. All he has is his eyes, his hands, his reason, and his courage. You can't destroy that, and you can't command it. He's not unique, and he's not trained. He's no steersman, he's the son of a blacksmith—but he knows, and I know, secrets you claim for your own. And if it weren't we two, if it weren't now, it would be someone else, sometime soon . . .

"How will you stop us, all of us? Will you break us down to bar-barism? Will you kill every son of a blacksmith? Every merchant who uses a simple formula to calculate profits? Every farmer who can add? Every chambermaid who dares to look at the stars and wonder?

"Will you? Then, wizard, who will you rule?"

Corvus spoke, his voice was very quiet. "I don't want to do any such terrible things. I want the world to be as it's always been. It's not a bad world, really, as a whole."

She gave no ground. "The world is changing. You know it and I know it, but neither of us knows why. Watch what happens, Corvus, and when the time comes, choose your side. But remember us, that's all. Remember."

Corvus accepted Willam as apprentice.

It was against tradition, against common and wizardly wisdom. Corvus gave no reason, and Rowan's mind filled with a hundred specu-lations, each more dreadful than the last. But she satisfied herself at last with the recognition of one simple fact: It was what the boy wanted.

As they turned to leave, Willam stopped, suddenly recognizing his departure for what it was. He paused in realization, then rushed to em-brace Bel, his head bending down against hers, and she held him qui-etly for a while.

When he came to Rowan, he took her undamaged hand in both of his. His eyes were full of amazement and gratitude. "Will I see you again?"

"It might be years. It's a long way to the Outskirts. And no means to guess what may happen between here and there. Or after."

"You're still going?"

Her mouth twisted. "There's something I'd like to see."

He looked displeased, and it came to her that he disliked the idea of her traveling about without his protection. She laughed despite herself, and he became a bit sheepish.

"Well," he said, "I won't forget you, or what you said to Corvus. Don't you forget me, either. I made a promise to you."

It took her a while to remember. "That if the wizards kept their se-crets for some mean reason, you'd defy them and answer what I asked."

"That's right." He nodded shakily. "I'll stand by it. You have my word."

The pair walked away, up the riverbank in the hazy air, to the road that led back to Wulfshaven Harbor. Rowan, Bel, and Artos watched in silence.

"Artos," the steerswoman said at last, her eyes still on the boy. "Stay by him. Be his friend. Don't let him forget what he is."

"A common man. So he'll become a wizard with the true common touch?"

"If we must have wizards, that's the kind we need."

They turned away, but for Bel, still watching, her face uncertain.

"You're not pleased with this?" Rowan asked.

"I ought to be. I'm not. I'm worried for him. But I do think it's a good thing. A wizard with one of the common folk as apprentice; I wonder how that will affect Corvus?"

"I wonder how Corvus will affect Willam," Rowan countered.

Bel released a pent-up breath and looked up at her. "Well, he said he'd help us, one day, and I believe him. We have his promise."

But the steerswoman took a long time in replying. "Wizard's words," she said. "A wizard's promise."

BOOK TWO

THE OUTSKIRTER'S SECRET

1

*H*is hand shook, and the mark he made with the bit of charcoal wavered as he drew it: a small, lopsided cross, one arm trailing off unevenly. The frail, dark-haired boy looked up at the faces around him. "More than twenty," he said. His voice cracked.

At the center of the table, one stolid gray man studied the chart with tightened eyes, then shook his head and spoke quietly. "Twenty-four, that'll be. Two war bands." A silence filled the room as the implications of the information were grimly considered.

The little farmhouse kitchen was crowded, with some thirty people, men and women, standing and sitting around the battered wooden table. It was only the stillness of the occupants that rendered the room bearable. There was no jostling: Each person present was deeply engaged in thought.

The chart was crude, drawn hurriedly and with much amendment directly on the surface of the broad table. Its scale was large, its compass very small indeed, but to the people in the room it contained everything in the wide world most important.

A small idea floated to the surface of one slow mind. "Now, Dalen," a voice spoke up, "you've got some Outskirter blood in you."

The crowd murmured approval, and the man addressed replied calmly, "Some and more."

"Well, then, how will these ones think?"

The steerswoman said, "Blood won't tell you how people think." As one, all turned their attention to the person seated at the end of the table.

She was a mild-looking, unremarkable woman of some twenty-four years, with sun-streaked hair and sun-browned skin. She carried no air of command, and had neither the physique nor the manner of a seasoned warrior. But at that moment, every person in the room waited for her to speak, waited to risk his or her individual fate and the fate of their village on whatever she might be able to tell them. She was a steerswoman. A steerswoman might not know everything, but everything that a steerswoman did know was true.

This one, Rowan by name, had come to know a bit about the Outskirters.

She leaned forward and studied the chart, one hand ruffling her hair musingly, repetitively, as she thought; a man seated beside her watched the action with a degree of disapproving puzzlement, as if it were not quite proper for a steerswoman to possess such a thing as an idiosyncrasy of behavior. She ignored him, and sat considering the lay of the land as depicted, testing distance, timing, movement in her thoughts. "With only two war bands," she began abstractedly, "chances are they're both from the same tribe. That's a disadvantage for you, because they're accustomed to working together. If you manage to kill one leader, his or her replacement will be well known to the other band, and their cooperation won't falter." She laid one finger thoughtfully on the cross the boy had made, marking the war bands' position. "They probably won't expect resistance, certainly not organized resistance. It's good that you're forewarned." She spared a glance for the nervous boy, whose wit and speed might prove to have saved his town. He blinked at the steerswoman's approval, and a hint of pride crept past the fear to his wide eyes.

She spoke to him, indicating the area between the town and the Outskirters' position. "What sort of land is this? Hilly?"

"Some," the boy said. "Hilly this side the brook, flatter t'other."

She gestured for the charcoal. He relinquished it, and she notated his descriptions. "Forested?"

"Yes."

"How old a forest? Is there much undergrowth?"

Other voices began to supplement the boy's, at first hesitantly, then more quickly, words overlapping as the steerswoman amended the crude chart: Yes, they told her, undergrowth here, thinning out there, a particularly tall bare hill to the east . . . Rowan expertly placed her mind's eye atop that hill, looking back at the town, transferring facts from map to imagination, inferring what useful knowledge an Outskirter scout might gain from such a vantage point.

The map grew in detail, and within the overdrawn lines—lines rubbed and shifted, lines that altered the significance of other lines—

focus and precision began to emerge. The options for quick and secret movement of twenty-four warriors began to narrow. Soon there were only two possibilities.

"If they attack at dawn," Rowan said, and in her mind she saw them doing so, as clearly as if she witnessed it, "they'll have to move into position in darkness. In that case, they must follow the brook." By starlight, in forest and brush, no strangers could be sure of their path; but the brook led directly into the town itself, a clear unguarded road through the forest.

A young farmer hazarded disagreement. "But look, land's flat behind these hills, easy way to town from there." He pointed.

"That's the other possible route. But if they do come around the back of the hills, they can't attack at dawn. They'd have to be moving into position now, at night, and it's too dark for them to find their path."

"Torches. We'd not see them, from this side . . ."

She shook her head. "Outskirters won't travel by torchlight."

An elderly, bent-backed woman seated across from Rowan squinted in thought, her tiny eyes nearly level with the tabletop. "Split," she grunted.

"Pardon me?"

The old woman reached out to indicate the brook, the hills. "Split. Come at us f'm two sides." And she nodded with dour satisfaction.

Rowan took her meaning. "They might do that. Or they might all come down the brook. Or all around the hills." But which possibility would the barbarian raiders prefer, which would be most appealing, what habits of tactic might guide an Outskirter's choice?

Rowan looked to the side of the room, where her friend and traveling companion stood alone, apart from the townspeople—looked once and just as quickly looked away.

Bel was leaning back against the end of the stone hearth, a bowl of stew in one hand and a biscuit in the other, watching the deliberations with cheerful interest. Dark-haired, dark-eyed, she was small in height, solid in structure, and stood, even in her present lounging pose, with the easy, dynamic balance of a fighter. Anonymously dressed in sandals, felt trousers, and a linen blouse, she might have passed notice but for an eye-catching belt she wore, of flat blue gems set in linked disks of silver, stunning in its rough beauty.

Unseen in her bulky pack were a pair of shaggy goatskin boots and a patchwork fur cloak. No outward clue identified her as an Out-skirter.

Rowan did not ask for Bel's advice.

As a steerswoman, Rowan could ask a question of any person, and that person must answer truthfully. It was the other side of tradition's contract: anyone might request information from a steerswoman, and it would be provided, truthfully, to the best of the steerswoman's knowledge. The only enforcement against one side's breaking of the contract was the canceling of the other: lie or refuse information to a steerswoman, and never again would any steerswoman answer even your most casual question.

Rowan could ask Bel what the attackers might do. And Bel might answer truthfully, to the detriment of her fellow Outskirters, her own kin; or she might refuse to answer at all. On her refusal, Bel would be placed under the steerswoman's ban—and worse, in this case: her friendship with Rowan would be severed forever.

Rowan declined to place herself or her dearest friend in any such position.

She tapped a location on the table-chart. "This is my best guess—here, where the banks of the brook are steep on one side, and brushy on the other. We can set up an ambush, come down on them from the banks and trap them against the undergrowth. We'd have them com-pletely by surprise. We ought to get into position soon, and we mustn't travel down the brook itself; we would have to wade sometimes, and we might be heard by a scout already in position. Is there someone here who knows a forest path well enough to lead us there through darkness?" At this, the dark-haired boy's eyes widened still further, and he nodded mutely.

Rowan heard Bel shift uncomfortably and guessed the reason, but said nothing to her.

The old woman spoke up again. "An' if that's wrong? If they're not there?"

Rowan spoke regretfully. "If we try to ambush them at the brook, and they've all taken the hill route, then the town is lost. We can come back and try to fight them in town, but they'll be here before us. They are excellent fighters, all, and our numbers aren't superior enough to make up the difference."

She straightened and addressed the villagers, scanning the room to meet each gaze individually. "Three options, then, and you can weigh them for yourselves." She named them, choosing a face for each possibility. To Dalen: "Ambush at the brook, with a very good chance of success if that's their route, disaster if it isn't." To the old woman: "Split into two groups, one in ambush, and one waiting near the hill, with a fair chance for one group and a poor one for the other." To the young farmer: "Or all go to the hills, with less than an even chance if that's their route, and no chance at all if it isn't."

Bel spoke. "There's another way."

Some turned toward her, but Rowan did not, not wishing to direct too much attention toward the Outskirter. She said only, "And what's that?"

"Abandon the town." Now all heads turned, including Rowan's.

The Outskirter remained leaning at her ease, sopping stew with her biscuit as she spoke. "They don't want your lives, they want your property. They'll take your livestock, all the stored food they can carry, anything pretty and portable, and anything with workable metal. Then they'll leave."

"Burning houses as they go?" someone asked.

"That's right."

"And our fields?"

At this Bel shrugged.

Rowan brought attention back to herself. "If any fires are started, they'll be hard to control. You'll certainly lose some of your fields."

"But you'll keep your lives," Bel pointed out. "You can build again."

"There is that," Rowan conceded reluctantly. It was a legitimate option.

The idea was attractive to some, and tentative, murmured discussion began. But when his opinion was requested, Dalen drew himself up carefully, dark eyes growing darker. His reply to the quiet question was delivered in a tone chosen to carry: in effect, an announcement. "That's the coward's way."

"That's true," Bel admitted, matter-of-fact.

For an instant, something in her manner attracted him, and he gave her a quick, puzzled glance, a half smile of half-recognized kinship, then turned back to the assemblage. His voice was neither mocking nor scornful, but permitted the saying of the thing to com-municate his opinion. "Scattering at the first threat," he said. "Ants have more honor."

Rowan felt constrained to point out, "Scattering at mere threat is honorless, true; but scattering in the face of undefeatable force is sensible."

"And these Outskirters," he asked her, pointing with his chin to the chart, "they're undefeatable?"

She sighed. "No. But it will be difficult."

And on that question, the gathering divided.

One voice raised an opinion; another interrupted and was interrupted by a third. The old woman set to tapping one gnarled finger on the chart, muttering explanations to a girl behind her, who shook a headful of wild red curls, disagreeing in rising tone. Two burly men from the back of the room sidled forward to argue over some feature on the map, someone in a far corner began to complain in a baritone whine—and the crowd deteriorated into clots and pockets of discussion.

Rowan discovered Bel hunkered down beside her chair, and leaned closer to hear her speaking under the noise. "You're talking as if you plan to fight alongside these people."

"I do."

The Outskirter shook her head broadly. "That's not sensible. If we want to reach your fallen Guidestar, that deep in the Outskirts, we're going to need to travel with a group." She glanced about and came closer, speaking into Rowan's ear. "We could try to join these war bands' tribe and travel with them for a part of the way. But they won't accept us if the raiders recognize you as someone who fought against them."

"I assume that's the case."

"Why don't we just leave, and join the tribe when the fighting's over? It's not our battle."

"It is my battle," Rowan said, then turned to look her friend directly in the face. "Bel, for the last week these people have fed and sheltered us while we rested, befriended us, and let us replenish our supplies free of charge. They've been kind and generous."

"They'd do those things for any steerswoman."

"True. And in this case, the steerswoman is myself. I cannot simply abandon them to disaster."

"It would make our way easier." Bel jerked her head at the squabbling crowd. "Our mission is more important than these people."

"No. My mission is for these people, and for others." Rowan studied the Outskirter's stubborn expression, then saw it slowly alter, as Bel read on Rowan's face, as clearly as if it were spoken, the request that the steerswoman was unwilling to make. Rowan had forgotten, again, how easily her own expressions betrayed her thoughts.

She was abruptly ashamed, as if she had undertaken a planned manipulative tactic. The idea was abhorrent. She looked away.

"Bel," she began, consoling herself with simple statement of fact, "at this moment the village's situation is precarious. As long as that's so, as long as I feel that the addition of even one extra fighter might make a difference," and she turned back, "I will fight."

Bel glowered at her for a long moment. "Precarious," she repeated, and with an expression of vast distaste gave herself to thought.

The noise in the room began to lessen. Through some internal process, the villagers were slowly coalescing into a unified group. Their leader was not Dalen, as Rowan had half-expected, but a pale, jittery woman of middle age with smoldering eyes, who spoke fervently, passionately, using short, quick gestures.

"Rowan?"

Rowan turned back to the Outskirter. "Yes!"

"The war bands will come down the brook."

Rowan sighed in relief. "I rather thought they might."

"It leads right into town, and they don't know they're expected. The idea of attacking at dawn is too attractive."

"Thank you."

"Don't thank me; I want to reach the Guidestar, and I don't care to watch you die," Bel said vehemently. "You tell your villagers to use bows, as many as they have. The Outskirters won't have archers. An ambush with bows, and the village will win easily, and one fighter more or less won't matter." She looked up at Rowan and enunciated each word fiercely. "Now will you leave?"

"As soon as I pass this on."

Bel rose, and brushed her trouser legs as if they were filthy. "You're lucky that I like you so well."

"Yes," Rowan admitted. "Yes, I am."

Bel stalked back to her position, and Rowan rapped the table to gain the room's attention. A hush fell instantly, and the villagers turned to her, now a unified force with a commander and a single, all-important purpose. They lacked only strategy. The steerswoman gave it to them.

2

*O*n the evening before Rowan's departure from the Steerswomen's Archives, the air had been sweetly cool outside, warm and faintly dusty in the northeast corner of the Greater Library. Three cushioned chairs stood close beside the snapping fireplace. Rowan sat in one—uneasily, on the edge, bending forward again and again to study one or another of the many charts that lay on a low table before her. In the second chair, Henra, the Prime of the Steerswomen, nestled comfortably: a small, elderly woman of graceful gestures and quiet self-assurance. Silver-brown hair fell in a loose braid down her breast, and she wore a heavy robe over her nightshift, looking much like a grandmother prepared to remain all night by the bedside of a feverish child—an appearance contradicted by the cool, steady gaze of her long green eyes.

The third chair was empty. Bel sat on the stones of the hearth, cheerfully feeding the fire to a constant, unnecessarily high blaze. "Enjoy it while you can," she said. In the Outskirts, open flame attracted dangerous creatures by night.

The charts loosely stacked on the table had been drawn by dozens of hands, and their ages spanned centuries. Each map showed a sweep of mountains to the left, a pair of rivers bracketing the center, and a huge body of water below all, labeled INLAND SEA. From chart to chart, across the years, scope and precision of depiction grew: the edge of the mountain range became delimited, the river Wulf slowly sprouted tributaries, Greyriver later did the same, and the Inland Sea began to fulfill its promise of a far shore by acquiring a north-pointing peninsula.

Each map also noted an area labeled THE OUTSKIRTS; each showed it as a vague empty sweep; and each showed it in a different location. Set in order, the maps revealed the slow eastward shifting of the barbarian wildlands.

Bel regarded the charts with extreme skepticism. "I don't doubt that the women who drew the maps believed that that was where the Outskirts were. But did they actually go there? And were my people there? And a word like 'outskirts' might mean many things. Perhaps they just intended to say, 'This is the edge of what we know.' That would explain why it keeps moving."

"I don't think so. Look at this." Rowan had pulled one map from the bottom of the stack: a recent copy of an older copy of a now-lost chart from nearly a thousand years earlier, purported to have been drawn by Sharon, the founder of the Steerswomen. On it, the Outskirts were improbably shown to begin halfway between the tiny fishing village of Wulfshaven and the mouth of Greyriver, where the city of Donner later grew.

Rowan indicated. "Greyriver, deep in what was then the Outskirts; Sharon knew that it was there. The term 'outskirts' did not represent the limit of what she knew."

Bel puzzled. "How did she know it was there?"

"No one knows."

"Is it shown accurately?"

"Yes."

"She must have gone there."

"Perhaps. Most of her notes have been lost. Nevertheless, to Sharon, Greyriver was part of the Outskirts."

The Prime spoke. " 'Where the greengrass ends,' " she quoted, " 'the Outskirts begin.' Those were Sharon's words."

Bel made a deprecating sound. "Hyperbole," she said.

"What?" Henra was taken aback; Rowan was not, and she smiled over her chart. She had learned not to be surprised when the barbarian made use of sophisticated ideas.

"Hyperbole," Bel repeated. "Exaggeration. The greengrass doesn't just end. It runs out, eventually. Either your Sharon didn't know, or she wasn't talking like a steerswoman, because it's not an accurate description. Perhaps she was trying to be poetic."

Henra recovered her balance. "I see."

"Well." Rowan sighed and returned to her work, sifting through the charts before her, uselessly, helplessly. There was no more to be done; all was prepared, as well as could be, all packed and ready for the first leg of her journey. Nevertheless, she reviewed, and reviewed again.

Rowan was to leave first, and travel eastward cross-country to a small village on the far side of the distant Greyriver; Bel would go south to the nearby port city of Wulfshaven, there to attempt to maintain the illusion that Rowan was still at the Archives, and later to leave ostentatiously alone, by sea. The plan was designed to deflect from Rowan the passing attention of any wizards.

The wizards and the Steerswomen had coexisted for long centuries; but the wizards, by blithely refusing to answer certain questions, had consistently incurred the Steerswomen's ban. Their refusal had engendered in the Steerswomen a deep-seated, slow-burning resentment that had grown over the years, eventually becoming as pervasive as it was ineffectual. The feeling was largely one-sided: for their part, the wizards tended simply to ignore the order entirely.

But the previous spring Rowan herself had managed to attract their notice, and merely by doing what every steerswoman did: asking questions.

She had not known that her investigation into the source and nature of certain pretty blue gems, decorative but otherwise useless, would be of any interest to the wizards. But when she and Bel were first attacked on the road by night, then trapped in a burning building, then waylaid by a ruse clearly designed to divert the investigation, it became obvious that the wizards were indeed interested, and more than interested—they were concerned enough to take action, for the first time in nearly eight hundred years, against so seemingly harmless a person as a steerswoman.

In the course of what had followed, many of Rowan's questions about the jewels had been answered, although none completely. And the course of her investigations had gifted her with answers to questions unasked and unimagined.

The jewels were in fact magical, and were used by the wizards in certain spells involving the animation of inanimate objects; but what the spells were, and how they were activated, Rowan had never learned.

The jewels' pattern of distribution across the Inner Lands, which had at first so puzzled her, was explained by a fact both simple and stunning: They had fallen from the sky. They were part of a Guidestar—not one of that pair that hung visible in the night sky, motionless points of light, familiar to every Inner Lander, but one of another pair, previously unknown, which hung over distant, possibly uninhabited lands, somewhere on the far side of the world. Why one had fallen remained a mystery.

That the wizards, jealous and mutually hostile, should abandon their differences to cooperate in the hunt for Rowan, seemed a fact as impossible as the falling of a Guidestar, until Rowan learned yet another secret: there was one single authority set over all wizards, one man.

She knew that his authority was absolute; the wizards had sought to capture or kill her without themselves knowing the justifications for the hunt.

She knew that they resented his control of them but were unable to deny his wishes.

She knew his name: Slado.

She knew nothing else about him—not his plans, nor his powers, nor his location, nor the color of his eyes.

The belt that Bel wore was made of nine blue shards from the secret, fallen Guidestar. Her father had found the jewels deep in the Outskirts, at Dust Ridge, which the wizards called Tournier's Fault. It was the largest concentration of such jewels that Rowan had ever heard of. The description of the finding, and Rowan's own calculations on the mathematics of falling objects, led her to believe that at Dust Ridge she might find what remained of the body of the Guidestar. Knowing this, she had to go there.

A current chart in her hands, Rowan retraced the long lonely route across the breadth of the Inner Lands, to that little village past Greyriver, where she and Bel would meet again to enter the Outskirts together. It was the one part of the journey of which she could be certain. Beyond that point . . .

Setting the map down, she took up the top chart from the sequenced stack and studied it with vast dissatisfaction. It differed wildly from all the others.

Gone were the western mountains, the two rivers, the wide sea; this map showed a single river at its left edge, running south, then curving southwest to the edge of the paper. Intermittent roads tracked the banks, occasionally branching east to end abruptly in small villages.

A tumble of low hills ambled vaguely across the southern edge of the paper; a second river with a few tributaries began seemingly from nowhere and ended without destination; a short stretch of shore marked INLAND SEA made a brief incursion, then stopped, unfinished. In the low center of the chart, a jagged line trailing northeast to southwest bore the notation DUST RIDGE (TOURNIER'S FAULT).

Despite its size, despite its scale, the rest of the map was empty.

Rowan glowered at it. It was drawn by her own hand.

She had reconstructed it from one she had seen as a prisoner in the fortress of the young wizards Shammer and Dhree. While their captive, Rowan had freely given all information requested, as befitted any steerswoman; since neither wizard had yet lied to or withheld information from a steerswoman, they were not under ban. Rowan herself had carefully avoided courting the ban, by never asking Shammer and Dhree any questions she suspected might be refused, and by this means the conversation had been able to continue for the best part of two days.

But in their eagerness to learn, the wizards had inadvertently revealed more than they suspected. Giving Rowan the opportunity to see a wizard-made chart of this section of the Outskirts had constituted one such slip. Their map of those unknown lands had been astonishingly complete, and to a detail and skill of depiction unequaled by the best of steerswomen. But despite Rowan's sharp eye and well-trained memory, with no chance to copy immediately what she had seen these few unsatisfying details were all she could recall.

She knew her point of entry into the Outskirts; she knew her destination; she knew next to nothing between the two.

She caught Henra watching her. The Prime smiled. "You must add to the chart as you travel. And bring it back to us, or find a way to send it . . ."

"When I return, I'll come out through Alemeth . . ." Alemeth was far enough south to suggest a straight-line route west returning from Dust Ridge.

"Then send it from there. After Alemeth, I think you ought to go to Southport, and do some work in that area."

This was new. "Southport?"

"No one is covering Janus's route." Janus, a steersman, one of the few male members of the order, had inexplicably resigned, refusing to explain or justify his choice; he was now under ban. "And," the Prime continued, "Southport has no resident wizard."

"In other words," Bel said with a grin, "when you're done with this, lay low for a while."

Rowan made a dissatisfied sound. "Keep out of sight. Hope the wizards forget about me."

And, for the moment, they seemed to have. How long that might last, no one knew.

According to Corvus, the wizard resident in Wulfshaven, the wizards had decided that Rowan's investigations must have been directed secretly by one of their own number. They were now involved in mutual spyings, schemings, and accusations, trying to discover the traitor, and had effectively dismissed Rowan as being a mere minion.

Rowan had herself disabused Corvus of the idea. He had neglected to pass the information on to his fellows.

What Slado might do when the truth was discovered was impossible to guess. He had motives of his own behind these events, Rowan was certain. He had some plan.

Rowan shook her head. "We don't know why Corvus is letting his fellows search for a nonexistent traitor." She found a mug of peppermint tea on the floor, where she had abandoned it earlier, and took a sip. It was long cold. She studied green flecks of floating peppermint, then used one finger to push a large leaf aside. "He must gain something by it, some kind of advantage."

"What might that be?" Henra prompted.

Rowan made a face. "That's impossible to guess." Certainly, Corvus was as interested as she to learn that a Guidestar had fallen, as surprised that Slado had not made the fact known among the other wizards. Perhaps Corvus planned an investigation of his own, an investigation that confusion among his fellows would somehow serve to aid. Nevertheless, for whatever reasons, the result was that, for the time being, Rowan was again free to investigate as she pleased—

—because Corvus wished it so.

Rowan found that she was on her feet, her chart, forgotten, sliding with a rustling hiss from her lap to the floor. Shadows from the flickering fire ranged up against the walls, across the long room, shuddering against the stone walls and the motley ranks of bookshelves.

She looked down at Bel, a backlit shape seated on the stones of the hearth, and made her answer to those dark, puzzled eyes. Her voice was tight with anger. "I'm the advantage. Corvus is using me."

The Outskirter took in the information, considering it with tilted head, then nodded. "Good."

"What?"

"If he's using you, then he'll want to help you. He'll want you to finish your mission."

"I don't want a wizard's help!"

"Too late. You've got it."

"If Slado is trying to keep the Guidestar secret from the wizards," Henra put in, "then Corvus can't move, can't investigate it himself without attracting attention. Perhaps he can learn something by seeing how Slado behaves among the wizards, but for outside information, for—" She spread her hands and made careful, delimiting gestures. "—for an understanding of the effects of these events . . ."

"He needs me."

"He needs you. You might be his only source. You might be the only one able to discover why the Guidestar fell."

"And find why Slado wants to keep it secret," Bel added. She leaned forward to retrieve Rowan's fallen map. "Corvus himself didn't know, until you told him." She regarded the chart thoughtfully, her eyes tracing undrawn lines of unknown routes across the blank face of the Outskirts.

But what help could Corvus provide, across those empty miles? And at what price?

"Gods below," Rowan said quietly. "He's made it true. I am a wizard's minion."

The Prime spoke quickly, leaning forward, emerald eyes bright in the gloom. "You're no one's minion, not even mine. What Corvus decides to do is his own choice. Your business is to learn. He's under ban, and you have no obligation to tell him anything."

To be a steerswoman, and to know, but not to tell . . .

As she stood in that wash of firelight, Rowan felt the long room behind her, felt it by knowledge, memory, and sensation of the motionless air. She faced the warmth of the hearth, and the far, unheated corner of the room laid a cool, still hand on her shoulder.

High above, all around, the tall racks and unmatched shelves stood, like uneven measurements, staggered lines across and up the walls. The books they held had no uniformity: fat and narrow, with pages of parchment or pulp or fine translucent paper that would stir in the merest breeze, between covers of leather, cloth, or wood. Each book was the days of a steerswoman's life, each shelf the years, each wall long centuries in the lives of human beings whose simple hope was to understand, and to speak. And Rowan knew, without turning to look, where lay that one shelf in the southeast corner that held her own logbooks: five years of her eyes seeing, of her voice asking, of her mind answering.

Her books stood to the left on the shelf. The right-hand end was empty. And more shelves waited.

"I will tell Corvus," Rowan said slowly. "Without his needing to ask." And she sat.

Her cold cup of tea was still in her hand, and Bel shifted the stack of charts to clear a place for it on the table. Rowan set it down and composed her thoughts.

"Whatever Slado is up to," she began, "it looks to be bad not only for the folk, but for the wizards as well, else he wouldn't need to keep it secret from them. For some reason, he can't let his plans become known—so the thing that we most need to do is to *make* them known, whatever part of them that we can see; known to everyone, even the wizards." She looked at the Outskirter, at the Prime, then spoke definitely. "It will make a difference."

The Prime was motionless but for her gaze, which dropped once to her hands in her lap, then returned to Rowan's face. "So the truth becomes a weapon."

Rowan was taken aback, and paused for a long moment. "That's true." It seemed such an odd idea: innocent truth, a weapon. Then she nodded, slowly. "It's always been true. Truth is the only weapon the Steerswomen have."

"Look." Bel was holding two maps, Rowan's unfinished one and the copy of Sharon's. The Outskirter laid them one atop the other, then turned to raise the pair up with their backs to the fireplace. Yellow light glowed from behind, and the markings showed through, one set superimposed upon the other. The viewpoints suddenly struck Rowan as uncannily similar.

Fascinated, she reached out and took them from Bel's hands.

On both charts: west, a small, known part of the world, shown as clearly as could be managed by the cartographer; in the center, a long vertical sweep labeled OUTSKIRTS; beyond, emptiness.

Sharon's map, and Rowan's: the oldest map in the world, and the newest.

Bel's dark eyes were amused as she watched her friend's face. "You're starting over."

Rowan separated the charts again and, across near a thousand years, looked into the face of her sister.

She smiled. "Yes," she said.

3

"*Y*our friends have headed into an ambush," Bel announced.

The old woman looked up from the campfire and peered at the travelers. She was large-framed, ancient muscles slack within folds of skin, heavy belly slung on her lap, and her features were gnarled around a vicious scar, ages old, driven across her face from right temple to left ear. One eye was blind. "Have they?" She spoke calmly; she watched intently.

"Yes." Bel unslung her pack and nonchalantly strolled into the encampment, Rowan following with more caution.

It was a temporary bivouac, a mere holding place for the packs and equipment of the raiding war bands: a shadowy glade among the firs, cleared and flat, a little rill conveniently nearby. Midmorning sunlight dappled the deep greens and browns, splashing shifting spots of white on the old woman's sunburned skin, her threadbare tunic, her single wary eye. The tiny fire was a snapping orange flag in the gloom.

"A boy spotted your camp at sundown and warned the villagers," Bel continued. She dropped her pack and seated herself uninvited on the ground, idly nudging the earth banked around the fire with one shaggy boot, a pose lazy and ostentatiously comfortable.

The old Outskirter turned her attention to the steerswoman standing at the edge of the camp, half in shadow, ill-at-ease. "That one of them?" The question was addressed to Bel.

Rowan had been warned to expect Outskirters sometimes to dismiss her. She answered for herself. "No," she began, intending to continue.

"Good. Have to kill her, otherwise." The woman returned to her task, breaking branches into kindling, grunting under her breath at each snap. "Well, if you're not going to attack me, what is it you want?"

Bel gestured Rowan over, and the steerswoman approached, her expression held carefully impassive. She lacked Bel's ease of dissemblance; no steerswoman could lie in words, and Rowan's training and own natural inclinations rendered her unskilled at lying by behavior. She had only two choices: to permit her face to be the natural mirror of her thoughts, or permit it to show nothing at all. There was no easy middle ground. Rowan chose the latter extreme.

Joining Bel by the fire, she doffed her pack and sat down on it. There was a loud creak, and the old woman looked up with a sharp glare intended to freeze; she was met by a flat, blank gaze, impassive, impenetrable. Rowan had learned that the effect was often daunting; it did not fail her now, and the woman wavered. "At the moment," Rowan said, in a voice so mild and carefully modulated that it communicated only the content of the words, "we want nothing from you." This was perfectly true. Bel spared Rowan a grin of wolfish pleasure.

Bel's plan to gain acceptance into the raiders' tribe depended on timing and knowledge of tradition and unbreakable custom. The time was not yet. The travelers waited.

During the long pause that followed, Rowan's Inner Lands etiquette began to require that introductions be made. She quashed it.

There was kindling enough, but the old woman continued her job,
unnecessarily: a delaying tactic. Unknown to her, it worked more to
Rowan and Bel's benefit than her own. "It takes more than an ambush
of dirt-diggers to stop warriors," she said derisively. "You should have
joined them. Plenty of booty."

Bel tilted her head, dark eyes amused. "We didn't like the odds."

"You're afraid," the old woman said scornfully.

Bel took no offense. "Of some things. Such as fighting against bad
odds beside strangers whose skills I don't know, who don't know mine,
and who use strange signals to direct the battle."

During the speech, the old woman's interest in Bel began to alter,
and by the end, she had abandoned pretense of work. She squinted
her sighted eye at Bel, and Rowan read there clearly, for the first time,
curiosity. "Where are you from?" she asked slowly. Rowan could not
see what in Bel's words had prompted the question.

"East."

The ancient Outskirter grunted once and sat considering, as if the
single word spoke volumes to her. Eventually she indicated Rowan.
"Her?"

"West," Rowan supplied. Then, because it was against her nature
to give so incomplete an answer, she added, "I'm a steerswoman."

This won her an astonished look. "Ha!" It was a word, not a laugh,
but laughter followed. "One of them. A walker and talker." And to
Rowan's surprise, she dropped into a parody of graciousness. "Tell me,
lady," she said, following the form used by some common folk, "what's
a good village to raid, hereabouts?"

Rowan answered truthfully. "The area is new to me, and I've been
avoiding towns on this journey. The only town I can advise you on is
the one I just left, and about them I can tell you this: Your warriors
have walked into an ambush. Any survivors should be returning very
soon." She heard a rustle far behind her, and voices in the distance. "I
believe that's them now."

"You have sharp ears," Bel commented, pleased. One voice rose
above the others, in an anguished wail; Bel cocked her head, then addressed the woman. "If your tribe is very far from here, you'll need our
help, I think."

"You should have helped before," the woman spat.

"We're here now," Rowan said calmly.

"We don't need you, and we don't want you."

The noise grew closer: several people, traveling quickly and with difficulty, abandoning silence for speed.

"I wonder if the others will agree," Bel said.

The voice that had cried out cried again, inarticulate, and the old woman startled. Someone shouted: an urgent hail. The woman responded "This way!" and lumbered to her feet as quickly as old bones would permit.

The sounds grew rapidly closer, and a male voice called out, "Dena!"

"Here!" The old woman hurried to follow the sound.

Bel was on her feet and beside her in an instant, Rowan close behind. "Quickly," Bel said, "do you want our help or not?"

Dena stopped to stare at her blankly. "No. Go away."

"You there! Lend a hand!"

All turned at the voice, and Bel slapped Rowan's shoulder urgently, once. "Go." The steerswoman hurried ahead into the brush.

There were four of them: one man with a bloody face supporting another staggering with three arrow shafts in his thigh, and behind, a third man half-dragging a woman who was clutching the front of her vest over her abdomen with both fists, sobbing helplessly at each movement.

Rowan rushed to her side and slung one arm across the woman's back to the man's shoulder. "Here." She gestured, urging him to link hands behind the woman's knees to carry her.

He was panting, his face pale with shock, and he looked at Rowan in confusion, seeing her clearly, for the first time, as a stranger. "Who are you?" he gasped.

"My name is Rowan." She gestured again, hurriedly. "Here, like this—"

There was a hand on her arm: Bel, holding her back. Rowan protested, "What—"

Bel spoke to the man. "That's her only name."

Concern for the plan to gain acceptance vanished in Rowan's desire to help. "Skies above, Bel, let me go—" Bel's fingers became like iron bands. Rowan caught the man's expression.

Panic and desperation were struggling in his face with something else, another force, equally compelling. His gaze flicked between Bel's face and Rowan's. His mouth worked twice, as if there were something he needed to say, but did not want to.

Between them, the wounded woman writhed once and emitted a clench-toothed wail as an appalling amount of blood worked its way between her fingers.

The question resolved itself. Custom and tradition combined with need.

He turned to Rowan. "I'm Jermyn, Mirason, Dian." Bel vanished, gone to help the other wounded, and Jermyn locked his right hand on Rowan's shoulder and quickly swung the woman off the ground as they linked hands behind her legs. "Help me get my wife to camp. I think she's dying."

It was the help they rendered that gained the two travelers the right to ask for assistance of their own. But it was the exchange of names that guaranteed it would be granted.

They began the short trip to the tribe's main encampment slowly: three wounded people supported and aided by four whole, carrying as much of the cached equipment as they could manage. Soon, they were moving more quickly, with only two wounded members.

Rowan paused, looking back to where the body of Jermyn's wife lay in the trackless brush, abandoned. "Aren't they going to bury her?"

The others were already far ahead. Bel had dropped back, waiting for Rowan. "Customs differ. Even among the Outskirters." She winced. "My people wouldn't leave her like this. But we wouldn't bury her, either."

At the last, Jermyn had sat long beside his wife, holding her hand, while his comrades shifted impatiently, waiting for her to die so that they might continue. Their only interest seemed to be the length of delay.

The steerswoman turned away and joined her friend, disturbed. She remembered a poem Bel had once recited, that included a death rite. "You'd burn her body?" It made her think much better of Outskirters, to know not all were so callous.

Bel adjusted the load she carried: two packs, her own and one belonging to the man whose leg she had helped steady while the old woman painfully extracted three arrows. "No. That's only for heroes." One pack was on her back; the other she shifted from hand to hand by its straps.

"What, then?" Rowan took the extra pack from her.

"First," Bel informed her as they resumed following the Outskirters, "we'd divide her."

" 'Divide'?" Rowan was puzzled.

Bel gestured. "Cut her up. Into pieces, at the joints."

The spare pack dropped to the ground as the steerswoman stopped short, stunned and sickened. "What?"

"With the torso in two pieces." Bel had paused ahead and was looking back at her, matter-of-factly.

Rowan swallowed her distaste. Customs differed, as Bel had said. "And then?" Her voice sounded thin to her own ears.

"We'd cast her."

"You're using that word in a way I don't know."

The Outskirter gestured with both hands: in front of her, then out and around. "Spread the pieces, as far as possible. Distribute them across the land."

"Whatever for?"

"For the sake of the land's soul."

Religion. Rowan took a breath and released it, then regathered the spare pack. Even in the Inner Lands religion was the one thing most varied, and most inexplicable.

Religion, she thought again, with a touch of amused derision, then remembered: the farm of her childhood, the desert so frighteningly near, grim and red but for the distant holy green of the funeral groves—and the nearer groves, huge and old, one sheltering the farmhouse itself. And more: small phrases spoken to ward off evil, daily beliefs unfounded but cherished by her family, the great solemn Midsummer Festival of joy and sacrifice . . .

In the absence of thought, one fell back on habits of emotion. In the world of her childhood, to cut the body of a dead person was sacrilege.

But she was not a child, she was an adult, and a steerswoman. There was no reason to believe that the disposition of a corpse had any effect on its departed inhabitant.

She tucked the pack awkwardly under one arm and rejoined Bel, and they continued after their guides through the brush. Presently she spoke again, with a nervous half-laugh of relief. "Do you know," she said, pushing aside a low branch to aid their passage, "for a moment, I was afraid you were going to tell me that your people eat their dead."

"No," Bel replied. "You'd have to go much farther east than my tribe, for that."

4

"Three left? Three from two dozen?" The dark, angular man leaned close to the wounded warrior's face. "And how could that happen?"

The single war chief who had survived the raid twisted his leg involuntarily under the ministrations of an elderly healer. "Outnumbered. Outmaneuvered. Ambushed."

"And how many did you take down?"

A wince, either of pain or dismay. "Hard to see. Maybe five."

"Five!"

Seated nearby, Rowan wondered which five of the brave villagers had fallen, and found in herself small sympathy for these Outskirters.

The camp was pitched against the edge of the forest, one side nestled beneath overhanging evergreens, the other open to a green, rolling meadow, where the tent shadows now stretched away from the vanishing sun, long fingers indicating the east. The tents themselves were of varied construction and materials: tall pavilions of billowing cloth, battered with age and usage; long low structures of stitched hide; canvas shelters in military style. Looted, Rowan guessed, from various sources, over a period of years.

The tribe's leader was dark-haired, his face a complexity of sharp angles and weathered lines, and he wore his patchwork cloak with the rakish flair of an actor, over canvas trousers and an Inner Lands cotton shirt. He mused, small eyes glittering. "They must have had warning." Rowan did not volunteer explanation, but despite herself glanced at her companion.

Bel sat across the fire from her, halfway back amid a group of lounging and seated warriors. A thin, bedraggled woman of middle age was moving among the people, passing out slices of venison from a wooden platter. She reached Bel, and Rowan saw but did not hear Bel's "Thank you." The serving woman paused momentarily in surprise, then continued on without reply.

"Well." The leader sat back on his haunches and blew out his cheeks expressively. "Well, it happens." He dismissed the mystery with blunt pragmatism. "Fall almost on us, winter coming," he reflected. "We'll have to move further out, take on one of the goat-tribes." He scanned the encampment, counting heads. "And we'll have to be clever about it." He addressed the assemblage in general. "Think about it. Any ideas, talk to me." He caught Rowan watching him, nodded a greeting, and moved over to join her.

"And you're an odd one, Rowan steerswoman," he said, as someone shifted to make room for him to sit, "wandering out in the wilderness."

"I'm often wandering out in the wilderness," she replied. "In fact, I enjoy it."

"But never through such dangerous lands as these." He tilted his head at her humorously, firelight and fading sunlight combining to highlight high cheekbones. "Hanlys, Denason, Rossan," he introduced himself, then added, "seyoh." Rowan recognized the Outskirter term for a tribe's leader.

"You and your people are the most dangerous things we've yet found on our trip, Hanlys," she commented, knowing this would be taken as a compliment. "And if I understand correctly, you won't harm us."

"True enough. We're obligated. Unless you decide to harm us now, that is."

"It isn't likely. I believe Bel and I are going to need all the friends we can get." The serving woman had reached them, and brusquely handed the seyoh and Rowan their food. "Thank you," Rowan said, offhand, and the woman turned away abruptly, changing her course to distribute in another section of camp. Unfed persons to Rowan's right voiced rude protests, which the server ignored.

Rowan looked after her. "Did I say something wrong?"

Hanlys snorted. "Shocked her, more like. We're not soft on our servants, like some." He tilted his head infinitesimally in Bel's direction. "She's from east?"

"That's right." She could see Bel speaking earnestly to a warrior seated next to her; his reply consisted of a head shake, a scornful twist of the mouth, and a dismissive hand gesture.

"Strange company for a steerswoman."

"She's very good company indeed. And the best I could ask for, if I'm to get to where I'm going, and find what I'm looking for."

"Going and finding?" He made a show of surprise; Rowan began to find annoying his faint air of condescension. "I thought the way of steerswomen was to walk wherever the wind took them, and ask too many questions along the way."

Rowan necessarily conceded the substance of his remark. "Generally, something like that is the case. Although we move less randomly than you might think." She took a moment to miss her past life: roaming through the green wildlands, wandering into welcoming villages, charting, noticing, questioning and answering, making endless discoveries, large and small. Now she sat in a barbarian encampment on the edge of the dangerous Outskirts, on a journey to find the source of magical jewels. It seemed a very unlikely situation.

She shook her head. Her old life now seemed distant, poignant, carefree. "Lately," she told the seyoh, "I seem always to be searching for something in particular."

His smile was indulgent. "And what do you search for, steerswoman?"

Rowan said wryly, aware of how odd it would sound, "A Guidestar."

A warrior seated nearby, who had been following the conversation, interjected a comment. "Ha. Look up."

Involuntarily, she did so. The sky was near fully dark, with only one Guidestar, the Eastern, visible, hanging eternally motionless against the sky over the shadowy meadow. Its twin, the Western Guidestar, was hidden by the overhanging branches of the forest. Stable, immobile, unchanging, these two points of light were the markers by which humankind located itself on the surface of the world, counting the passage of time as each night the slow constellations marched across the sky behind them.

Rowan prepared a reply to the warrior. "I'm not looking for the ones you can see," she began.

"If you can't see them, you can't find them." One of his cohorts gave him a friendly shove in appreciation of the joke.

"I'm looking," Rowan replied patiently, "for one that has never been seen—from here."

This was greeted with silent thought. "They can both be seen, everywhere," another person ventured.

"No." Looking around, she discovered herself to be a center of attention. Despite the unlikely setting, the situation was one she understood, and she easily stepped into her role.

She shifted position back a bit and, leaning forward, drew a circle in the dirt between herself and the seyoh. "Look. Here's the world, as if we're looking down at the pole. And here are the Eastern and Western Guidestars." Two dots. "Can you see? If you travel far enough in either direction, one or the other will be left behind, around the curve of the world." She added two more dots. "And you'll see a new Guidestar, in the opposite direction."

They puzzled over the diagram. One man leaned over to trace the circle with his finger, eyes squinted with the unaccustomed effort of abstraction. "That's the world?" He seemed unconvinced.

Another, more quick, ventured, "We've traveled a fair bit. Why has no one never seen that happen?"

From over Rowan's shoulder, a creaking voice spoke. "It's too far."

Rowan turned and found the old healer leaning above her. Abandoning dignity, he eased himself to his knees, scuffled over to the drawing, and pointed, as pleased as a child. "Look at that. You'd have to go . . ." He thought, his watery eyes flickering. ". . . near a quarter the whole way around the world to see the next Guidestar." He settled himself more comfortably, cradling his pouch of medicines in his lap, and looked up at Rowan with a bright gaze, curious and expectant. Someone tapped him, then rudely gestured him to leave. He stubbornly ignored the request.

"That's close," Rowan replied. The others present appeared skeptical. "But," she added, holding up one finger, "if in fact you traveled that far, you might not see one, after all." She reached down and smoothed the dust over one of the secret Guidestars. "One has fallen."

More faces, pale in firelight, turned toward Rowan, then turned among themselves in puzzlement, and some argument.

"They can't fall," one warrior woman loudly replied to the man beside her. "They can't fall—they're *stars*."

"But if they *did*," he protested, appalled by the idea.

"They're not stars, they're objects." Rowan had to raise her voice. "They're things. Stars move across the sky at night. The Guidestars seem not to move, unless you move yourself beneath them. They are different."

"They are stars." The arguing woman turned toward her. She had a narrow face, sharp as a hatchet. "They're special stars, there's only two, and they haven't fallen. They *can't*."

The healer was watching Rowan in fascination. She was tempted to speak directly to him, to offer her information only to that old, quick mind behind the sunburned wrinkles; but her duties were not just to one person.

She changed her method. Speaking to the woman, she said, "Why only two?"

"Two is all we need."

"Need for what?"

"Direction. To tell where we're going."

"To say that they're for something is to say that they exist for your benefit."

"Why else?"

"And that they were put there."

"Yes . . ."

"By whom?"

"By gods."

Rowan leaned back. "They *were* put there. By wizards, and for their use." A certain category of simple spells, Corvus had told her, required the presence of at least one Guidestar. Certain larger spells, he had speculated, probably required the presence of all of them.

"By wizards? Wizard things, up in the sky?" The idea was beyond credibility. "No. There's no wizards out here."

"Olin's not far," Hanlys pointed out, jerking his head to indicate direction: west. The limits of Olin's holding, always vague, might come as near as the western bank of Greyriver.

"We're Outskirters," the woman stressed. "Wizards leave the Outskirts alone. We're not their goats, like Inner Lands folk."

A part of Rowan resented the metaphor; but as a steerswoman, she conceded its truth. "You're fortunate in that." She considered the diagram in the dirt, then wiped it clean with a sweep of her hand. "And without meaning any insult, it doesn't much matter if you believe me or not. I know where the Guidestar has fallen, and that's where I'm going."

The healer studied the blank space as if the marks were still there. "Long trip, just to look at something," he commented.

She smiled at him. "Long trips are the best kind."

Across the fire, Rowan noticed Bel standing among her own small audience, speaking to a female warrior while four men listened with expressions respectively dubious, bored, scornful, and annoyed. Some comment of Bel's made the young woman look at her in sudden surprise, then laugh and—to Rowan's astonishment—pat Bel's shoulder as if comforting a child. Bel stiffened, eyes cold.

With a gesture, Rowan caught her glance and beckoned. Bel was not a person to take insult casually, and Rowan thought it best to distract her as quickly as possible. Bel turned her glare unaltered on the steerswoman, but approached, edging her way through the seated warriors. The healer departed, with some reluctance, at a gesture from the seyoh.

Bel seated herself beside Hanlys, glumly. "What?"

Rowan addressed both Outskirters. "As I understand it, the assistance we gave the wounded warriors, and the fact that Jermyn willingly asked for my name, give us the right to assistance in turn. This tribe is going east, Bel; I assume you want us to travel with it?"

"Until they choose another direction, yes," Bel said, looking with sidelong dislike at the seyoh.

Her unspoken opinion was wasted on him. He rubbed his sharp nose. "And you're welcome to. If nothing else, you're both amusing."

Bel gathered herself to retort, but Rowan spoke first. "Sometimes I think that half of the Inner Landers' interest in steerswomen is the diversion we supply," she admitted.

Bel quieted herself. "And these people know the lay of the land," she added, reluctantly. "You might ask for information to add to your empty maps, the parts we won't see ourselves."

Hanlys replied to Rowan's questioning glance. "Of course. Can't hurt us any. Let's do it now."

Rowan rose, intending to fetch her pack, but the seyoh waved her to sit, then caught the attention of the serving woman, whose duties were now finished. "Ho, you! The steerswoman's gear!" The woman delivered a flat glare, then wandered off.

Rowan noticed the healer standing to one side near a particularly tattered tent, conversing with a pair of elderly persons of indeterminate gender. All three wore ill-fitting clothing, ancient, barely serviceable, and unclean, save in the healer's case. The steerswoman recollected from Bel's coaching that there existed two categories of Outskirters within a tribe: warriors, who defended the tribe and its flock and conducted raids; and mertutials, who did not fight, but attended to matters of daily maintenance—cooking, cleaning, various kinds of service. These then, with the woman fetching Rowan's gear, and two others tending the sleeping children in their tent, comprised this tribe's mertutials. Bel had not mentioned that the work carried so little prestige.

Hanlys turned back to Rowan. "How far are you going?"

"Dust Ridge."

He shook his shaggy head. "Never heard of it."

"Perhaps four months' travel, eastward," Rowan told him, "assuming we meet with few difficulties."

"A long way. I don't know anyone's been that far."

"I do," Bel put in. "My father. And I've been most of the way myself."

Behind Bel, three warriors adjusted their positions and began gaming with a pair of dice. Jermyn, who had been seated nearby, rose to leave, but they cajoled him and beckoned. He hesitated, then joined the game with a studied gaiety that did not reflect in his eyes.

The seyoh spoke to Bel, expressing his opinion of the ways of her father's land. "A hard life, and hard travels so far out." He shook his head. "Things needn't be so difficult."

Bel leaned forward, brows knit. "A hard life is good. It keeps a warrior strong."

"Ha. It's fighting makes a warrior strong. And good fight deserves good reward." He tapped the ground between them, where the diagram had been obscured, emphasizing his point. "What do you gain when you battle out there, hey? A few more goats, is all, and the right to run them in the direction you want. Till you meet another tribe won't let you by, or wants a few more stinking goats themselves."

Bel's answer was cold. "The herd is life."

He laughed and spread his hands. "Not here."

The mertutial woman reappeared, and Rowan took the pack with an unthinking "Thank you," at which Hanlys grunted amusement. Bel shot him a glance, but said nothing.

They spent an hour bent over the charts, as the seyoh helped the steerswoman amend them. His knowledge, supplemented by occasional comments by other warriors, included eastward areas to the distance of perhaps eighty miles. Rowan had been under the impression that Out-skirter tribes generally covered a wider range than this, but she forbore to mention it, not wishing to prompt a possibly insulting response from Bel. Rowan also marked areas to the north and south that she would not be crossing; the more complete she could make her maps, the better for future travelers. She became engrossed in her work.

Eventually Hanlys noted, "Your friend doesn't seem very happy."

With some difficulty, Rowan pulled her attention from the chart and saw that Bel had walked away from the center of the camp to stand facing out into the darkness, alone. As Rowan watched, Bel began walking slowly to the left, her face invisible. "No," Rowan agreed, puzzled. "I should think she would be. She's going home." She took a moment to wipe the ink from her fingers with a rag from her kit, her eyes still on the lonely figure.

The seyoh made a sound of resignation. "Well, it's no surprise. She's not comfortable with us. She's different." He shrugged, in a vaguely eastward direction. "Probably doesn't understand our ways. Her people are far from civilization." He caught Rowan's eye and winced apology at speaking against her friend. "They're just a bit stiff-necked out there, old-fashioned, see. They can't help it. Try not to hold it against her; I don't. We've accepted you both, and you both have our hospitality. That's Outskirter honor." And he nodded his head with careful dignity.

"I see." Rowan did not believe him; Bel was anything but stiff-necked. Clearly something was bothering her that she did not feel free to articulate.

Rowan considered. She wrapped her pen and inkstone in the rag, rolled her charts, and returned them to their case. "Excuse me," she said to the seyoh, and went to find her friend.

In the dimness at the edge of camp, Bel was a collection of gray, shifting shadows. Rowan found her more by hearing than sight: the crunch of gravel beneath the Outskirter's boots, the creak of leather and the soft hush of her breathing.

She was walking the limits of the camp, slowly, moving quietly. Rowan heard the hiss of grass as the breeze swept in from the meadow, the shivering rattle when it met the forest's edge, and sensed Bel's attention shifting at small inconsistencies of sound: a clattering as a dead twig tumbled from the high branches, the fluttering pass of a trio of bats, the rustle and snap as some tiny predator found tinier prey.

"What are you doing?"

Bel was disgruntled. "What no one else is doing."

Rowan added up the clues of her behavior. "You're standing guard."

"That's right."

"The others don't seem concerned."

"They're fools."

The steerswoman fell in with her friend's careful pacing. "How long will you keep this up?"

"Until they put that fire out."

Goblins were attracted by fire at night, Bel had often told the steerswoman. Rowan looked back at the camp. The flickering light was blocked from sight by two low canvas tents. Its faint glow was visible only high above, where it eerily outlined the branches of the overhanging trees.

Bel had also said that there were no trees in the Outskirts; they were not, then, beyond the admittedly vague limits of the Inner Lands. "I don't think goblins are common in these parts," Rowan said.

"They don't have to be common to be here."

They continued their slow pacing of the perimeter. The sounds shifted from those of wind and open meadow to the night sounds of forest, cool and close. Voices drifted from the camp: a single person, speaking in declamatory style, others laughing. "You don't like this tribe," Rowan observed.

Bel's voice was tight. "No."

They were completely alone in the darkness. "Why not?"

Away from the camp, Bel's answer came immediately. "They're not good Outskirters. And it'll do no good to tell them so."

"You're the only Outskirter I know well," Rowan observed. Underfoot, the gravel changed to soft pine needles. "It's hard for me to look at you and know how much is unique, how much common to all Outskirters. What's wrong with these people?"

"What's wrong with these people is your people. The Inner Lands. This tribe has been weakened by them. Things are too easy here." Bel's posture shifted: a slight drop of one shoulder, then the other, the brief weaving motion Bel often made when thinking. "I wouldn't mind if they decided to live completely like Inner Landers, in farms and towns and such, because that's a useful way, too, even though it's weak. But what they've done is taken some Inner Lands ways, and lost some of the true ways . . ." She turned abruptly and, slapping Rowan's arm once, pointed back to the camp. "Look. Where is their herd, where are their handicrafts? Raiding is fair; if you can't defend your goods, you don't deserve them. But if you only live by preying on the weak, then you're weaker than your prey. These people would die without the Inner Lands nearby. They're not good Outskirters, just bandits."

"I see . . ."

"And Hanlys is a warrior, did you notice?" Her voice was outraged. "Yes . . ."

"Well, that's wrong. You choose a seyoh from the mertutials. If your leader knows only how to fight people, and not how to fight the land, or hunger, or disease . . ." She made a sound: a harsh breath released through her teeth, a sound of disgust. "This is what you get. These people are stealing your goods, while they steal our name. I wish a troop of goblins *would* come down on them."

Rowan sought the right word. "They're . . . degenerated?"

"They're primitive."

Through gaps in the ring of tents, Rowan studied the crowd of warriors around the campfire: men and women clean though unkempt, rough-mannered but friendly and lively. She thought she could see part of Bel in them, but did not mention it.

But then she thought of the raiders' disinterest in the death of Jermyn's wife, of their abandonment of her remains to scavenging animals, and she began to see that these Outskirters did lack something that Bel possessed in full: perhaps a depth of heart, or breadth of understanding.

"Do you want to leave them?" After taking so much trouble to win their assistance, it seemed unlikely.

"No," Bel confirmed. "But don't expect me to tell them that I like them."

"I won't." The very idea distressed Rowan. "The tribe is moving in the morning," she pointed out. "If you stand guard all night you won't travel well."

"That's true." The Outskirter stopped herself abruptly, then let out an amused "Ha!" She looked up at the steerswoman, shadowed eyes glinting starlight. "If we sleep near the center of the camp, then any goblins that come will get at these fools first, and we'll have plenty of warning."

Rowan found herself laughing, despite the possibly grim vision. "There is that," she conceded.

Bel clapped her shoulder. "Let's do it. They can take their chances."

They returned to the center of the camp and found entertainment in progress. A huge red-haired warrior was pacing by the fire, singing a humorous song in a booming voice. Rowan and Bel took seats beside the offending fire.

The song told of an Outskirter scout who seduced a farmer's daughter, inspiring her to steal her father's possessions, one by one, as gifts to her lover; a clever, saucy tale—and one that Rowan had heard a dozen times in the Inner Lands, with a tinker in the role of the Outskirter.

The hatchet-faced woman rose next, to recite a heavy-rhythmed poem which included many lovingly depicted gory battles, whose points or purposes remained obscure. The warriors listened intently, but the steerswoman noted one face not watching the recitation. It was Jermyn. During the previous song, he had showed ostentatious hilarity; now he sat, expression blank, eyes on the ground. One of his dicing companions nudged him to direct his attention. He did not respond.

Bel and Rowan were seated across the fire from him; Bel was following Rowan's gaze. "He should sing a song for his wife. Or tell a story, or a poem; something to mark her passing."

"I don't believe that he wants to," Rowan observed. Jermyn's companions continued to display no sympathy for his loss, and he seemed to wish to pay it no attention himself; finally mastering his emotions, he fabricated an expression of interest and turned up his face toward the performer, to display it.

Had Bel not spoken the next words, Rowan would have: "It's wrong."

"Yes."

The woman's recitation came to a thudding end, and in the space that followed, someone seated far back from the fire underwent a degree of cajoling, as friends called for an amusing story. The person reluctantly began to rise to his feet, a lopsided grin on his face.

Bel stood. "I'll do it." She stepped forward.

Her appearance was a surprise, exciting quiet comments from the warriors, some of dubious tone. Bel ignored them and took up her position by the fire, to the right, where the fewest people sat behind her. Rowan saw her in profile, face flickering pale in firelight, starlit darkness behind.

The tune was slow and gentle, filled with the rich, long notes that Bel's voice carried best. The lyrics followed no standard form that Rowan recognized; they wandered, with no clear rhymes, only suggestions of assonance, falling at unexpected points in the melody, line endings now lagging, now running ahead of the natural symmetry of the tune.

> "Who has seen her, following the wind,
> From end to end, long hills
> Winding, black and midnight when her voice
> Comes shadowing down the sky?
> I know her eyes from ages past, and this
> A year ago, a day,
> Still too wise for the touch . . ."

Melodic cadence and lyric resolution seemed to wrap around each other. Rowan began to catch the sense behind the structure: an endless, forward-moving spiral, as each element strove to complete itself, found itself out of step with its partner, and so was impelled to continue.

> "... Her eyes now light in light on dark,
> Her voice a silent, known and humming
> In my heart only: wider, call and empty.
> Her fingers pulse the edges of the sky ..."

The style of grammar was peculiar, the choice of metaphor hardly comprehensible: the song seemed to use words in a fashion very different from the usual. The steerswoman struggled briefly, then understood that a hundred unheard implications echoed unperceived behind each phrase. She began to listen more with her heart than her ears, grasping at the emotions that trailed behind the words. First they seemed like moving shadows; then like pastel banners of silk; then she understood how to hear the song, and its images opened to her.

It was a love song, but the strangest she had ever heard. The woman who was its subject seemed absent, though bound to return; but from the manner in which the composer attempted to convey her nature, it was clear that she was perceptible only to him, like a spirit, or a ghost, coming to him alone, mysteriously.

> "... I lose my days in days of days,
> I know my time by nights of yes or no,
> In going, stepping into dark,
> And standing, marking yes or no ..."

Although the form was new to her, Rowan sensed that the song was ancient, passed from voice to voice, altered subtly across the years. The composer was as gone as his lover, as mysterious as she, known only to the listener for the space of time that his words and music were lifted into the night air by Bel. Defining his lover, he defined himself; showing what he loved, he showed the most secret part of his soul, showed it easily and willingly.

In all Rowan's short life of only casual love, she found herself for the first time wishing to know someone who would speak of her in words like these.

> "Until my own hands meet once,
> And fleeting, learn her place among
> The empty spaces I will arrange myself
> Among the changes of the dark. I will
> Find myself in waiting, forget I wait,
> And what is known, unknown. When she is gone,
> I am sole and only . . ."

The flickering fire, the harsh, still faces vanished; but Rowan remained aware of the forest, of the cool quiet atmosphere smelling of greenness and water, of the sky where, amid the glittering stars of the Fisherman, the Eastern Guidestar shone, a stark needle-point of light.

> " . . . And she will tell me, when she speaks again: the cry
> Of stars, the sweet of light, the secret tang of numbers.
> When last I sang she smiled, and I will sing again
> While all the world and winter rain complete,
> Until fleeing has no home but her words,
> Last known, last awaited, last spoken, last heard."

The elements of structure approached each other, met: the song ended.

There was a long silence, and Rowan rode on the silence as if it were still song; it seemed endless, holding within it all the time needed for the mind to reach across the wide world, across time and history. She felt empty, but not diminished, as if all that lay in her heart had left her body to become water, sky, the air itself.

She was a hollow reed, and the wind had blown through her, the wind that circled the world, that had been everywhere and touched everything and was still touching it. That wind had blown one pure tone through her soul and departed, and she waited, disbelieving that it could be gone.

A motion brought her mind back to camp, leaving a piece of her heart in the wilderness. Bel shifted from one foot to the other in a fashion characteristic to her at the completion of a performance, smiled her small smile, and crossed over to seat herself by Rowan's knee.

The steerswoman studied her friend: a small, compact shape of bone and muscle, fur and leather, poetry and violence. Beneath a shock of short brown hair, the familiar dark eyes glowed in pleasure. Rowan shook her head, amazed.

There was a scattering of ground-pounding Outskirter applause, and Rowan looked across the fire for Jermyn's reaction. He was gone. "What happened to Jermyn?"

A man beside her replied. "Ran off." And he reached behind her to give Bel's shoulder a friendly shove. "There's a new way to do battle: turn a man to an infant with a song, and send him crying."

The steerswoman looked at him in shock. He had not been listening; or, listening, had not understood. It did not seem possible.

"Better than swords," one woman added with a laugh, lounging back to lean on her elbows. "Easy victory, no blood to either side."

Rowan found it difficult to control her distaste. "I don't believe that was the intention."

Bel's eyes flared. "That was 'The Ghost Lover,'" she informed the woman stiffly. "Someone ought to have sung it, or something like it, so I did."

Hanlys joined the conversation. "It worked on Jermyn. Looked like a ghost himself."

Bel had altered the way she was sitting, becoming more upright, more balanced. "It's one of Einar's songs," she said coldly.

The woman who had spoken earlier indicated deprecating comprehension. "I suppose they still sing those old songs," she said, and made a vague gesture intended to refer to the east, actually indicating south by southwest.

Rowan recognized danger in Bel and tried to redirect the conversation. "Who's Einar?" she asked.

"The first seyoh, from the oldest times we know. He made our laws. And he was a poet, and a singer."

"A legendary figure," Hanlys put in, for the steerswoman's edification.

"Not only legend! He was a real person!"

The woman disagreed. "If he lived, why does no one have his name in their line?"

"Because he loved a ghost! You can't get children on a ghost."

The male warrior spoke under his breath. "Loved a ghost, ha. Goat, more like, out there," he said, and then events moved too quickly for Rowan to forestall.

From her cross-legged position, Bel was on her feet in a single fluid movement. Her sheathed sword had been on the ground beside her; now the naked blade was in her hand. "Enough!" Light flickered on the weapon as it moved: then, abruptly, it was standing alone, vertical, its point buried in the earth by the fire, while its owner pointed an accusing finger that moved slowly around the circle of faces, indicating each and every person singly. "This is a challenge!" Fury filled Bel's voice, a fury Rowan recognized: the fury of battle. Bel's dark eyes glittered, cold stars in a shadowed face. "Come forward!"

Around the circle, puzzled faces stared, pale in the shuddering yellow light.

Rowan sat frozen in disbelief. "Bel, are you insane?"

"No!" Bel whirled back toward her. "No, this is too much!"

Rowan found herself at Bel's side, inside the circle of faces, one hand half reaching out to restrain her friend, held back only by the knowledge that such an attempt would be very unwise. She pleaded. "No, it's a misunderstanding, it's a difference of opinion—Bel, you can't mean to fight all of them!"

"I don't have to. I fight one, that's law." Bel's hand swept the circle again. "Choose your champion, if you have one, if there's one among you can stand on two feet alone!" The warriors had not moved.

"You insult my customs," Bel spat out, "you insult my people, my tribe, my blood, my heroes and forebears. You insult the Outskirts, you insult its air with your fetid carrion breath!" She whirled in the flickering light, confronting the impassive faces, a wild storm awaiting release. "Choose, you vermin, you rodents, you dung-worms!"

From his position among the seated warriors, Hanlys cleared his throat experimentally. "Pardon me, lady?"

Rowan could scarcely believe that she was being addressed. "Yes?"

He gestured. "We don't need this."

"Excuse me?"

He indicated Bel, somewhat apologetically. "Can't you control your friend?"

Rowan discovered that now it was she who was insulted. "She's not my servant," she said, voice flat, "and she's not my dog, either. She's a free woman and a warrior." The steerswoman was suddenly, coldly calm. She stepped back to her place among the warriors and sat. "I won't interfere with your traditions." She said to Bel, "I wish you good luck."

A single "Ha!" expressed Bel's opinion of luck.

Murmurs passed between the faces, and Hanlys looked even more uncomfortable. "Well." He caught Rowan's eye and, with a little shrug, rose. "I'm sorry for this, lady."

"No need. It's between you and her."

He winced. "Not quite." His gaze flicked around the circle, and he made a rapid series of small gestures.

Whether Bel understood the signals or merely recognized their import, Rowan could not tell, but the Outskirter suddenly spun and reached for her weapon. Then all warriors were on their feet, and one pair of hands clutched for her sword arm, another stopped her left hand an instant before it reached the hilt, and someone grabbed her from behind with an arm around her throat, lifting her from her feet. Bel thrashed wildly, kicking out, and connected with one man's chest, another's stomach, and then disappeared in a mass of struggling forms.

None had drawn a weapon.

Rowan found herself standing alone, aghast, as a writhing crowd worked its way away from the fireside, out between the standing tents, off toward the edge of camp. Bel's was the only voice raised, in furious, inarticulate shouts. Then all vanished from sight.

Rowan followed the mob to the limit of the encampment. There it struggled to a halt, reconfigured, and a thrashing thing was expelled into the darkness. It came back instantly, flailing wildly: Bel, striking out with both fists toward any person within reach. She received the same treatment as before, as both arms were captured, by several people, and rendered harmless. She was turned about forcibly, and again ejected. She came back. The process was repeated.

"Lady? Rowan?"

Rowan turned. Jermyn stood before her, one arm looped through the straps of two packs: Rowan's and Bel's. In his other hand was Bel's sword, now sheathed.

He glanced once at the melee and had the grace to look deeply ashamed. "You'd better take these."

"Will they hurt her?" Rowan almost believed it might be better if they tried to.

"No. You both helped us. But they won't let her come back."

Rowan took the equipment, looking up into a face made large, eyes made small, by tears. She suddenly wished not to leave him here, among false comrades who mocked his pain. She wanted to ask him to come away.

But before she could speak, he stepped back. "Thank Bel for the song," he said, and was gone.

Rowan made her way to the edge of camp and circled around the mob. Bel stood, darkness at her back, frustrated for the dozenth time. She shook with fury, eyes full of murder.

"Bel."

The Outskirter turned to her with a choked shriek of hatred. Rowan fell back a step, then recovered, and stood quietly, holding out the pack and sword.

Bel was a moment in recognizing her friend; then she took the gear without a word, spun away, and tracked off into the night, leaving Rowan to follow. Behind, the warriors dispersed, one by one.

5

"How safe is it, traveling in the dark like this?"

Bel was long in answering. "Not at all."

They had walked some time in silence. The raider tribe's camp was already two miles behind, hidden by low brush and a small copse of spruce. Looking back, Rowan saw no light; the fire was either blocked by trees, or had been finally extinguished.

Before them, the landscape was a vague starlit sweep of hilly meadow, with a dark loom of forest to the north, smaller blots of trees scattered to the east. Rowan followed Bel, a half step behind and to the Outskirter's left. The steerswoman realized that they had exactly reversed their usual positions. In the Inner Lands, Rowan had always led, a half step ahead, on the right.

"Do you know this area?"

Bel replied with an expressionless "No."

Rowan's step faltered. "How are you guiding us?"

"By my ears." The Outskirter paused, and both women listened.

A breeze rose, and the meadow grass hissed and visibly undulated, rolling black shadows like fleeing beasts. Behind, the spruce and brush gave out muted rattles, branches cushioned by leaves and green needles. Ahead: a series of harsh high clatterings, like brittle brush bare of leaves. Three sources of this sound: one nearby to the right, one farther away and straight ahead, one distant and slightly to the left. When the wind shifted, Rowan could hear from the forest to the north the sound of water over stones.

Eventually, Rowan asked, "What does a goblin sound like?" Near the raiders' familiar fire, the threat had seemed abstract, unlikely; here, nearly blind, in unknown territory with both Guidestars weirdly shifted west, she found the possibility disturbingly believable.

Bel provided the information reluctantly. "Alone, like a man walking quickly." She led on, angling to the right. "In a group, they call to each other." She stumbled on an unseen tussock, and Rowan managed to catch at her arm and prevent her from falling.

"What sort of call?"

Bel recovered, readjusted her pack, and continued. "A sort of rasping squeal, and a rattle." A pause. "I'd imitate it, but I might draw one."

Rowan drew up short. "Not that rattle we're moving toward?"

"No. That's tanglebrush."

The Outskirter was disinclined to converse. Rowan left her friend to silence, and the two continued together into the quiet night.

Informed that Bel was depending on hearing, Rowan did the same, and at once began feeling more and more at ease. This was not yet the dangerous, unknown Outskirts; it was hill and grass and forest such as she had walked on and through all her adult life. Her night-traveling skills reasserted themselves, and she began listening for movement, not of goblins, but of animals large and small, of the echoless loom of unseen bushes, and of stealthily approaching strangers. She heard the call of a nightjar, the rustling of field mice, and once, in a lull of the breeze, sensed the sudden breathless hush of owl's wings above. The rattling tanglebrush was a tantalizing oddity, and she struggled internally, resisting the impulse to approach one and kindle a small fire by which to examine it.

A chorus of yelps rose in the distance, and Bel startled. "What was that?"

"Foxes." Rowan discovered that without noticing, the women had exchanged positions: Rowan was again leading, comfortably. "They like this sort of land." In Bel's months of traveling the Inner Lands alone, she could easily have missed that particular sound. "They'll stay away. They don't like humans."

Bel made no reply. They walked on, as the land began to slope.

Rowan wished to find something to say, some way to remove from Bel the dishonor of the raider tribe's treatment. It seemed impossible.

She searched and considered—and soon found herself mired in speculations based on incomplete knowledge of Outskirter traditions and codes. She tried to form an analogy by reference to Inner Lands groups who claimed to hold honor highly: certain cadres of soldiers, highly placed aristocrats, priests of some sects. Nothing seemed applicable.

Then she tried again on a simpler level, and realized suddenly that Bel, through no fault of her own, had been made to look a fool in front of a friend. "I don't think much of those raiders' manners," Rowan said, spontaneously. To herself, the comment seemed inane.

But Bel relaxed somewhat. "And that," she said aggrievedly, "is what you Inner Lands think Outskirters are." The matter was closed. She turned to practical concerns. "Do you have enough water, or should we try to find a brook to camp by?"

Rowan began to feel better. She elbowed her shoulder-slung water bag, and it emitted a jolly little gurgle. "I have enough."

"Then let's stop here. I only wanted to put some distance between us and that mob. They might change their minds and turn on us."

It seemed unlikely. "All right." Rowan paused, and tried to scan the area. The ground had flattened again, and was clear enough for their purposes. Only a few low bushes sprouted in the darkness, one of them a tanglebrush clattering with a quiet, brittle noise in the now-light breeze. The women unslung their packs and set to flattening a section of the knee-deep greengrass.

As they arranged their camp, another Inner Lands danger came to mind. "The villagers mentioned occasional wolves," Rowan said.

"And a fire would keep them away. Rowan, I won't have a fire here."

"You'd rather meet a wolf than a goblin?"

"Of course." There was a grin in the Outskirter's voice, and she once again became completely herself. "I've never met a wolf." She settled her gear with a thump of her pack at the head of her bedroll. "But just in case, we'll sleep in shifts. You first."

The Outskirts had no border.

Despite the knowledge, Rowan had more than half expected to be awakened to a wild endless sweep of redgrass rolling to the limits of the horizon, cheerfully spotted with white goats—and likely to suddenly sprout an infestation of bizarre creatures, or a shouting horde of sword-waving barbarians.

But the pale gray light of the cloudy morning showed terrain no different from that of the Inner Lands. The dewless meadow was greenly carpeted with clover and one of the various sorts of greengrass called "panic" by common folk. The land remained flat to the east, grew hillier to the south. North, the forest sent a long arm eastward, and shielding her eyes against the sun as it rose into the clouds, Rowan discerned the woods curving south again in the distance.

But close beside Rowan's resting place stood the intriguing tanglebrush. She pulled herself from her cloak and bedding to examine it.

Rising as high as her waist, its black branches, randomly right-angled, doubled back and forth on themselves, creating a seemingly impenetrable mazy dome. The outermost twigs bore flat, narrow leaves as long as her hand, gray on one side, blue-black on the other. Each leaf stiffly presented its dark face to the rising sun. Beneath the edge of the dome, as if in its shelter, grew a patch of the vermin weed redgrass.

"Do the leaves move as the sun moves?" The leaves of some plants in the Inner Lands did so.

Bel's mood had repaired itself in the night. Now she was occupied with rolling her piebald cloak and securing it to the outside of her pack; the day was already warm. "Yes. Don't put your hand in there. There are thorns, and the sap is poisonous."

Rowan had been about to do exactly that, and drew back sharply. She would have to learn to investigate more cautiously than was her usual habit. They were going into Bel's country, and anything unfamiliar should be checked against Bel's knowledge.

"Are you ready?" Bel had already shouldered her pack.

Rowan was dismayed. "No breakfast?"

"Eat as you walk." She passed the steerswoman some hardbread and cheese. "We'll take a long rest at noon, with a fire for cooking, if you like. And you can write in your book then." Rowan was accustomed to recording her day's observations in her logbook in the evening, by firelight. That would have to change.

"A moment." Rowan retrieved her own felt cloak from her bedroll, shook it, folded it, and stowed it in her pack, using its cushioning to prop her tubular map case more securely. Hesitating, she uncapped the case and pulled one chart from its center, the one she and Hanlys had amended. She unrolled it and held it up to compare with the landscape around her. Bel moved closer.

Rowan mused over the new notations. "If we travel due east, we'll cross through some forest before we reach the veldt." This was the name the Outskirters gave for the wide plains of redgrass. Beyond, where blackgrass predominated, was the prairie. "We can reach it in less than three weeks."

Bel scanned the landscape. "I don't know about that. We can travel quickly if we travel alone and don't meet any trouble. But we ought to try to stay with the next tribe we meet, even though it slows us down. The land isn't very bad here—it's mostly Inner Lands and not much Outskirts, but that will change. It'll be safer, and easier, to travel in a group."

Except for the tanglebrush, Rowan had yet to note any evidence of the depredations commonly attributed to the Outskirts. How soon, she wondered, would it alter? How quickly, and how completely?

She rolled up the map and replaced it. It slid inside its mates and down into the case with a hollow thump, one of the sounds in all the world that Rowan found most satisfying. "Very well, then," she said, "until we do meet a tribe, let's cover as much ground as quickly as we can, alone."

The clouds had moved in sometime after Rowan's second watch the previous night; now they deepened and darkened. The breeze hesitated, backed, and a light sprinkle of rain swept in, then departed. In the east, the sun disappeared as it rose.

Rowan gauged the wind expertly, checked its direction against her memory of the previous night's sighting of the Guidestars. It was blowing from the west, steadily. Weather moved generally from west to east, and despite the gray above, she knew from the wind and sky that there was fairer weather coming. As she recognized this, the rain returned, falling more steadily.

"This could last into the afternoon," she told Bel. "I hate to lose the time, but we might do well to move into that bit of forest ahead, set up a rain fly, and wait it out."

Bel was disappointed, but agreed. "We can use the time to practice swordsmanship. If you fight against Outskirter weapons, you'll need to change your technique."

"I'm sure you'll teach me what I need. And if I find the time, I can try to chart this area more carefully." And they trudged eastward together, through the light drizzle and the shifting air, to the shelter of the woods.

It rained for twelve days.

6

By noon on the first day of rain, a steady downpour had established itself, relenting only occasionally and briefly. The air was hot and heavy, and the weather, slow as treacle, moved up the land from the southeast. Travel was postponed, for that day and for the next. The third day began with a lull and a brief west wind that tried and failed to clear the gloom. Then lightning skirted the eastern horizon, and by noon all was again steamy heat and rain.

The two women coped as best they could, stripping to their underlinen to endure the humidity. Rowan dropped to a seat on her bedroll under the tarp. "Does this sort of weather happen often?"

"Sometimes. But usually in the spring. Never this late in the year, not that I can remember." Bel was seated beside her, crowding close to avoid the water dripping from the edges of the canvas, attempting to dry her hair with one corner of Rowan's felt cloak.

Rowan stepped back out of the shelter and set to cleaning a pair of rabbits that had fallen to her snares overnight. Water intermittently drizzled onto her head as branches above bent and sprang under accumulated weight.

"Well. The weather makes fools of us all, so they say." The rabbits were two bucks, fat and well fed. She wondered if she would be able to start a cooking fire in the damp; they had dined on cold food for the last three days. Rowan began designing a fire shelter, and mentally tallied the number of birch trees she had noticed in the area. Birch bark burned when wet.

"Some people can guess the coming weather, sometimes," Bel said, muffled under the cloak. "You're usually good."

"Perhaps it works differently in the Outskirts." The Steerswomen had no more reliable information about weather than did the folk. There were rules, usually dependable, but rules were not principles, and so could not be trusted.

"Red sky at night, sailor's delight," Rowan mused as she slit one buck with her field knife. The rain had broken briefly at sunset the previous evening, and the sky had gifted them with a wild glory of orange and poppy red. And the rain had returned with darkness.

Bel watched Rowan at work, then rose. "Let me do that."

"No, I'd rather. I'm deathly bored." Study of rabbit anatomy was a small diversion.

"I know." The Outskirter reached among her gear and pulled out a sheathed sword, one of two she carried alongside her pack. "Look at this instead, then tell me what you think of it." Puzzled, Rowan took it from her hand and relinquished her place in the drizzle to Bel.

The sheath was cured hide, similar to that of Bel's other sword; small differences in markings told Rowan that this was not the weapon Bel commonly used, but a new acquisition.

"Where did you get it?"

"At Five Corners, a week before I met up with you."

The hilt was of horn, and the guard. Rowan drew the sword. It was black, edged with dull-colored metal. She felt the flat. "It's wood."

"Except for the edge."

Workable metal was at a premium in the Outskirts. "An Outskirter sword?"

"That's right."

There were no trees in the Outskirts. "Where did the wood come from?" The grain, barely visible black on black, curled wildly in tiny interlocking swirls.

"It's a tanglebrush root." Bell gathered a handful of rabbit entrails and flung them far in a fast sidearm motion. Rowan thought briefly of scavenging raccoons. "Tanglebrush sends down one large root, about so long." Bel demonstrated with bloody hands; something over four feet. "If you burn off the bush, you can dig up the root. Then you cure it with slow heat."

Rowan hefted the weapon. It seemed well balanced, though the width of its cross section made it move through the air more sluggishly than a metal sword of similar length. "You have a steel sword."

Bel nodded broadly. "And you won't find many like it among the tribes. I won it from someone, who won it from someone else—it must have come from the Inner Lands, a long time ago. And that's why you have to learn how to fight against a tangleroot sword. People will try to win your sword from you."

Rowan traced small figures-of-eight in the air; her elbow and the sword's point were splashed with running drops off the edge of the tarp. "They'll try to confiscate it?" She wiped the blade and set to admiring the weapon's design: an interesting solution to problems of scarcity.

"They won't sneak up on you and snatch it. That is, no one in any tribe that we travel with will." Bel severed her rabbit's neck and held up the head and attached skin, taking pleasure in the neatness of her work. "It's a formal tradition. If you covet someone's weapon, you have the right to challenge him to a duel."

Rowan disliked the idea. "Not to the death?"

"No. That's wasteful." Bel balled up the head and pelt and tossed it after its viscera. The skin spread in the air as it lofted, like a flying squirrel. "To disarmament, to a killing blow stopped at the last moment, or to surrender. The winner gets the choice of weapons."

The better fighter acquired the superior weapon. Rowan nodded thoughtfully and turned to careful study of the sword, considering weight, length, resilience, and possible advantages and disadvantages in strategy.

She did not care to lose her sword. Of all those she had used or owned, the sword she now carried was the only one with which she felt something approaching the true unity of fighter and weapon. She had no intention of permitting anyone to take it from her.

The sword was one that Bel had stolen for her during their escape from the fortress of the wizards Shammer and Dhree: a standard-issue guardsman's sword, stolid, unadorned, seemingly unremarkable. But although there was no magic power in Rowan's new sword, she suspected magical processes behind its construction. It was lighter than its length suggested, and a shade stronger than its weight would lead one to assume. It held its edge longer, and under stress it revealed the slightest hint of flex, permitting her to use more aggressive maneuvers, moves that would risk breakage in a common sword, or cause its user to be trapped in a disadvantageous stance.

With her knowledge of these differences, the steerswoman now found during practice that her strategies became incomprehensible to her opponents, while maintaining to herself an elegant interior logic. She began to enjoy using the weapon and became, for the first time in her life and to her great surprise, a superior swordswoman.

"Let's go."

The steerswoman looked up. Bel was cleaning her hands with dirt and leaves. The rabbit carcasses, legs tied together with a strip of skin, were draped over a low-hanging branch.

"What?"

"Let's practice."

"In this weather?"

The Outskirter raised her brows. "You plan never to fight in the rain?"

Rowan laughed. "Very well, then." She stood, tossed the Out-skirter weapon hilt-first to Bel, and found her own sword.

They moved into a larger clearing nearby, and as they faced off, Rowan took a moment wryly to note the oddity of the scene: rain spattering through the trees all around, a murky humid sky lowering above, tendrils of ground mist snaking and vanishing, whirling around the legs of two women who were carefully, intently assuming a battle stance—both damp as otters, and clad only in their underlinen. Then Bel made her move.

They stepped into the drill as if stepping into a dance, patterned and familiar, as Rowan studied the action of the Outskirter weapon, trying to reason out its weaknesses and turn them to her advantage.

Eventually Bel stepped back. "No."

"What?"

"You're trying to use your edge against my flat."

Rowan used the respite to regain her breath. "Your flat is wood. I thought to be able to chip away at it and weaken the sword."

"It'll take you forever." Bel pushed wet hair from her eyes. "And I have more weight, and more strength. You'll exhaust yourself." She beckoned, raised her sword. "Try again, with your usual style. But slowly."

Artificially slow movement was more tiring than swordplay at nor-mal speed, and Rowan's muscles trembled as her weapon met Bel's careful downstroke. Rowan parried, and as ever, the superior resilience of her sword began to absorb some of the power behind Bel's blow, af-fording Rowan an easy escape.

She began to take it: a shift of weight, a half step back, preparing to take advantage of her opponent's longer recovery time—when Bel said, "No. Come in."

Reluctantly, Rowan moved her weight into the stroke, found her strength overmatched, slid her blade up Bel's, instinctively shifting to the strongest section of her own sword—

At Bel's word, they paused: face-to-face, edge-to-edge at guards. "I don't like getting this close," Rowan told Bel.

"I know. Now twist your edge. No, *away* from my guard, and use all the strength you can." Rowan complied, to no visible effect whatsoever. "Good." Bel stepped back and dashed the water from her eyes with one forearm. Rowan vainly attempted to wipe her fingers dry on her singlet, to improve her grip. "Now again," the Out-skirter said when both were finished, "full strength, up to speed. And then halt."

Rowan tried to repeat the moves: downstroke, clash, flex and slide, step forward, guard-to-guard, and vicious twist—

"That's right." They disengaged. "Now look." Bel held up her sword for Rowan's inspection.

Where the blade joined the guard, the metal edging showed the faintest dent. Rowan put her hand over Bel's and turned the sword in the grayish light. On either side of the dent, the metal had lifted slightly from the wood. Bel indicated it. "That's the weakest point on an Outskirter sword," she said, "where the metal comes up to the hilt guard."

Rowan considered the implications. "And it's the strongest part of my sword."

"That's right. You'll never see two Outskirters with wood-and-metal swords using this technique, because it sets weakness against weakness. But for you, it's your strength against their weakness." She took up her position. "Again."

A long drill, and they did not stop this time. Applying the new technique, Rowan found that she shifted stance more often, more completely, and more abruptly than was her former habit. She strug-gled to adapt; then she caught the feverish rhythm, moved with it, felt her effectiveness grow, and a strange wild joy rose in her. She began to love it.

"Halt!" Bel called out, and pulled away. Rowan found she was ex-hausted without having been aware of it. She leaned forward, hands on knees, and drew long deep breaths. Bel came forward and displayed her weapon.

At the guard, one side of the edging had completely lifted from the wooden blade, in a short battered curve. "When you reach this point, try to get your edge under the loose end, and work it up."

Rowan wiped her forehead against her shoulder. "If I pull away, I'll leave myself open."

"Don't pull out—get under the edging, and then slide your blade alongside your opponent's." Bel took both swords and demonstrated the configuration and movement: a scissoring action. Rowan could see that in battle the force would peel away the metal from the wood.

She was impressed. "I can completely destroy the other fighter's weapon."

"That's right."

"That's quite an advantage." Something occurred to her. "When you won your metal sword, were you using a wooden?"

"Yes."

"How did you ever manage to win?"

The Outskirter grinned and stepped back. "Like this."

They set to again, the same drill, and Rowan found her moment: parry, flex and slide, forward, hilt-to-hilt—

Bel shifted, spun, vanished.

Battered metal lay lightly across the back of Rowan's neck. Bel's voice came from behind. "You'll have to watch out for that one."

7

*T*hey resigned themselves to traveling in the rain.

Every second day, they stopped early to dry their clothing by damp, smoky fires, which they extinguished at dark. They practiced swordplay until Rowan had successfully destroyed the tanglewood sword; Rowan updated her logbook, its pages limp with dampness in the shelter of the tarp; and Bel found occupation for idle hours in trying to learn to read and write, clumsily scratching letters in the muddy earth with a stick.

They counted miles.

"This can't continue," Rowan stated. The older forest was slowly being left behind, tall spruce and birches grudgingly abdicating to scrub pine, briar, blackberry.

Bel made no reply, disentangling herself from a net of brambles.

"It's going to take forever." They were making less than fifteen miles a day.

"Isn't Hanlys's information of any use?" Bel asked.

Rowan made a wordless comment of disgruntlement. The raider tribe's seyoh had proved to have a very vague understanding of mileage. "The brushland should break—at some point," Rowan said. "Then some wide greengrass meadowlands with occasional young copses. It's going to take longer than we thought."

Bel did not reply; Rowan knew that the Outskirter's thoughts, like Rowan's own, were on their food supply.

From the start, Bel had maintained that the Outskirts had no game, and that only association with a tribe, with its attendant herd, could insure survival. Rowan, accustomed to occasionally living off small game and wild plants during the more isolated segments of her routes, had accepted the statement only half-seriously.

But when she noted the appearance of the stiff, rough-edged red-grass, which the deer never touched, and its slow intermingling with the green of panic grass and timothy, she also began to note the disappearance of smaller animals. The rabbits, the mice, and even certain birds, were gone.

"Grouse," she enumerated to herself, as she struggled through the briar. "Quail, titmice. Finches."

"What?"

Rowan had not realized that she had spoken aloud. "Where are the birds?" To give the lie to her observation, an egret lifted in the distance, rising above unseen water, white wavering wingstrokes dim against the mist-laden gray of the sky.

"You won't see many, deeper in the Outskirts," Bel replied. "If a tribe moves close to the Inner Lands, flocks of birds will follow it, but only for a while."

Rowan paused to wipe sweat and condensation from her face. "Perhaps we should head for that water. There may be ducks."

"Can you catch a duck?"

Rowan made a vague gesture. "Probably. I know the theory, but I've never tried it."

The water was an east-running brook, slow and shallow, and there were no ducks; two more egrets fled to the sky at the travelers' approach, and three smaller birds, possibly herons. In autumn, with no nestlings, they had no reason to return. Rowan caught frogs, and one snake, while Bel watched from the banks with immense amusement.

They built a fire shelter out of brush, and Rowan eventually started a damp, smoky fire with some of the birch bark she had wisely saved from the forest, now far behind. The flame needed constant attending, due to the smallness of the bramble branches with which they fed it.

They cooked; they ate; they calculated.

"We have enough food," Bel said, "to get back to the Inner Lands from here. We should think about it."

Rowan had already been doing so. She sighed. "How long do you think we can extend what we have?" She had traveled on short rations before, and knew her own limits. She did not know Bel's.

"Let's check your maps."

They abandoned their meal to stand head-to-head; Bel held the sides of their cloaks together to provide shelter for the chart. Rowan traced with one finger the intermittent tracks to the east of Grey-river. "There's something here . . . a few houses, not really a village. Farms."

"Is your Steerswomen's privilege always dependable?"

Rowan winced. "No. But nearly always, yes. And it's harvest by now; most people will be more generous. Can you tell if there's likely to be a tribe nearby?"

"There's *likely* to be one, anywhere east of here. But I haven't seen the signs yet."

"What signs do you look for?"

"Goat muck, cessfields, and redgrass eaten to the roots. Bits of corpses, if there's been trouble."

Rowan replaced her map and they returned to their dinner. "How likely are we to end up in bits ourselves?"

"If we approach them right, they'll wait to talk first. We'll only end up in bits if they don't like our answers." Bel took another bite of food, appreciatively. "The smoke doesn't help the frogs," she observed, "but it's good for the snake."

It was late afternoon, and the travelers considered themselves in place for the night. Rowan wiped the grease from her fingers and rose to set up the rain fly, musing on Bel's several plans for gaining the acceptance of a tribe. "How is it that I never knew that you had three names?" she wondered as she worked.

"I never told you any of my names at all," Bel pointed out, and Rowan recollected with surprise that this was true. When first they

met, Rowan had overheard Bel's first name being used by an Outskirter tribe that was peacefully patronizing the inn at Five Corners;
the steerswoman had simply addressed the Outskirter by the name she
had heard, as a matter of course.

"Bel, Margasdotter, Chanly," Rowan repeated to herself, reminding
herself of the elements: given name, matronym, line name. "Perhaps,"
she mused aloud, "I should choose two more names for myself. Anya
was my mother, which makes me Anyasdotter; and for a line name—"
She stopped, catching Bel's expression.

The Outskirter sat stiffly, her face all glower. "That's not a good
idea."

Rowan recovered. "I'm sorry." Then: "But why isn't it?"

Bel wavered, then returned to eating. "If you name yourself as an
Outskirter," she said, her words barely comprehensible around a
mouthful of snake, "you're saying that you are an Outskirter. People
will expect you to act like one, and they won't forgive you any mistakes you make in proper behavior." She paused, then continued reluctantly, and more clearly. "And making up a line name out of the air
would be saying that our lines mean nothing. It's an insult."

The steerswoman was contrite. "I didn't intend it that way."

"I know. But they won't. Don't try it."

The greengrass vanished.

It was as subtle a process as Bel had first described to the Prime:
first one noticed occasional patches of redgrass, then more, and eventually one realized that for some indeterminate length of time no
greengrass had been seen at all. Certain other green plants remained,
however: thistle, with autumn-brown stems, and purple blossoms
faded to white; milkweed, sending up drifting silk into the air on
mornings of less rain; and dandelion, heads ghostly gray, rain-beaten
to damp drab blots. All of them, Rowan noted, plants with airborne
seeds.

The redgrass surprised her by growing taller than ever it had in the
Inner Lands, where it was routinely pulled as soon as it appeared.
Here, it became knee-high, then waist-high, stiff tall reeds with abrasive blades growing in a three-ranked pattern, and fat beardless seed
heads. At first Rowan thought it a different plant altogether; rain
seemed to dull its colors, soaking and darkening the bright red faces of

the blades to dull brownish brick. They waded through it, its blades clutching and tugging at their clothing.

They came to a place where a patch of grass had strangely faded to gray. Bel passed it by, but Rowan lingered, curious. She touched one pale blade, and it disintegrated, leaving sooty smears on her fingers; she touched a shaft, and it split, oozing clear fluid that stank with a foul, greasy odor.

Bel paused and looked back at her. "Don't bother with that," she advised.

"What is it?" Rowan parted the grass to peer into the center of the patch, despite the stench. There was a clearing within.

"It's probably a corpse," Bel said, approaching. "Or part of one. It looks like someone's been cast there."

Rowan drew up short. "Oh," she said, now disinclined to investigate. But she had already reached the center, and it held no human remains. "It's a fox."

It was long dead, desiccated skin over delicate bones, fine fur faded, sprawled under a tangle of rotted reeds. No scavengers had dined on it; natural corruption had had its way, and the only breaks in the crusted pelt were the result of the more unpleasant internal stages of decay, long past, when the body had swelled and burst.

"One of those animals we heard by the raider camp?" Bel moved closer to study it, tilt-headed. "It's a strange-looking creature."

They left the gray patch behind, Rowan brushing her fingers across the wet grass tops as she walked, to clear off the scent and the fluid. "The fox is a small predator," she said, falling into a steerswoman's explanation. "It's shaped like a dog, and graceful as a cat. It's beautiful when alive, and its pelt is highly prized. I wonder how it died?" Then she answered herself, body continuing to walk as her mind stopped short, surprised. "It starved to death. It must have wandered too far from the Inner Lands, and found nothing to eat . . ."

"What does a fox eat?"

"Everything we'd like to, but can't find."

Three days later, they found signs of a tribe.

They had crested a rise and stood looking down into a shallow, rolling field half-obscured by shifting mist. The ground was stubbled, redgrass cropped to the roots and dying in a patchwork mottle of yellow and brown; occasional smears of pale gray emitted their particular, distinctive stench. Fog and curtains of rain hid the far horizons while intimating replication into the distance, suggesting to shocked eyes that the desolation continued past the limits of sight, forever.

Rowan stood stunned. "What happened here?"

The scene seemed to please Bel, who regarded her with mild surprise. "Goats."

"Goats did all of this?" Rowan reached down to pull at a bit of longer grass by her feet. It did show the marks of grazing: fibrous blades stripped and abraded to strings, stiff reeds chewed through at varied heights.

Farther from Rowan's position, the grass had been cropped shorter, and farther, shorter still. The field below appeared entirely lifeless.

Bel had begun to amble down the slope; Rowan hurried to catch up.

"Watch your step," Bel said, the instant that Rowan's left foot slid violently out from under her. A quick clutch at Bel's shoulder saved the steerswoman from landing prone in a puddle of unidentifiable ooze.

Bel helped her to a steady stance. "You have to step solidly," she instructed. "You can walk around it now, but later you won't always be able to."

They continued down into the field. "What was that?" Rowan asked.

"Goat droppings."

Rowan stopped and turned back to it. "Then the goat was ill."

"No. It's always like that." Bel found herself walking alone. She stopped, annoyed. "Rowan, you're not going to study goat muck, are you?"

Rowan intended to do exactly that. "This was not a healthy goat." She found a twig and prodded at the translucent puddle. It was infiltrated with short wet fibers. "I wonder what it was eating?"

Bel made a gesture that included the entire visible landscape.

As they descended, Rowan noted that not every plant had been consumed. Tanglebrush bushes, ranging in a loose, staggered line, seemed denuded, but closer examination revealed that they had merely rolled their leaves tightly closed against the rain. She spotted movement among the bushes, and cautiously called Bel to a halt. "What's that?" A bobbing object, splotched black, brown, and white.

Bel looked, then smiled. "That's dinner."

The goat seemed pleased to find human company in the barren wilderness. It greeted them with happy relief—and met its death too quickly to recognize betrayal. As the travelers cleaned the carcass, Rowan considered the differences between it and its Inner Lands cousins. There were many.

Its hair was not white and short, but long, as much as eight inches in length, splotched randomly. Farm goats had short black horns; their counterparts of the Outskirts veldt carried heavy weaponry, two inches thick at the base, growing almost straight back, and only curving outward at the tips. Rowan recognized the source of the wooden sword's hilt.

She became distracted from her study by a glance at Bel's expression. The Outskirter seemed worried. "What's wrong?"

"This is a good goat. It shouldn't have been lost."

"We're fortunate that it was." Of itself, Rowan's mind entered into a series of calculations that brought a very pleasing revision in the number of miles the two women could safely travel before food would again become a concern.

Bel shook her head as she severed one of the legs at the knee. "We look after our herd very carefully. If the flockmaster finds even one goat missing, scouts are sent out."

Rowan paused. "Should we be expecting scouts?"

The Outskirter rose and gave the misty, drizzling meadow careful consideration. "I don't know," she said at last. "I think these people left very quickly."

Rowan imitated her, gaining no additional information whatsoever. "How can you tell?"

Bel shrugged and returned to their work. "Only by the goat."

There was no brush for a fire shelter, no wood to burn; Bel declared that it was time to use Outskirter methods. In future days Rowan came to designate, somewhat arbitrarily, the frogs and snake as the journey's last meal in the Inner Lands, the goat as the first meal in the Outskirts.

Bel instructed Rowan to dig a pit, then occupied herself with cutting squares in the cropped turf with her knife. She lifted the small blocks, brushed off the dirt in the dead roots of the upper layer, and demonstrated them to be a type of peat. The women built their fire in the pit and covered it with the tarp, one end propped up with the now-useless wood sword, and so prepared their first fresh meal in four days.

"I should warn you," Bel said as they settled to dinner, "that you're going to be sick."

Rowan stopped with the first bite partway to her mouth. "You told me that the goat wasn't ill."

"It wasn't." Bel continued slicing cooked segments from the carcass, wrapping them in oiled cloth for packing. "It's nothing to do with that. If someone from the Inner Lands eats Outskirter food, she'll be ill, for a while. It always happens."

In most cases, Rowan knew, it was water that carried diseases, in the crowded sections of cities, or in villages where unsanitary conditions prevailed. She and Bel had been drinking local water throughout their journey thus far, to no ill effect; certainly, Rowan reasoned, the problem Bel referred to must result only from food prepared in a tribal camp, under possibly primitive standards of cleanliness. She considered that it might not be polite to point this out to Bel.

She shrugged, and began to eat. "How ill, and for how long?"

"Perhaps a day. Then you'll be fine, and you won't have any problems with the food again. It will affect me, too. Outskirters who leave the Outskirts for any length of time have the same problem." She considered the chunk of fresh roasted meat in her left hand with open longing, then shook her head. "I should wait a day. Then we won't be sick at the same time, and can take care of each other." She left her work and brought some dried beef strips and hardbread from her pack.

"What's it like, this disease?" Rowan asked.

The Outskirter gave a short laugh. "Many trips to the cessfield."

It was unlikely that Rowan would be able single-handedly to alter the established cooking habits of an entire Outskirter tribe; at some point it would be necessary for her to pass through what seemed from Bel's description to be a transient adaptive malady. She sighed. "Charming. I shall look forward to it." She continued to eat. "How long after eating Outskirter food does one begin to feel ill?"

Bel was tearing with her teeth at the tough strip. "About two days," she said, chewing stolidly. "Although that's usual for returning Outskirters. Perhaps you'll take less time."

"Perhaps it won't affect me at all."

The reply was muffled. "Ha."

8

"How do we do this?"

It was two days later; two days of trudging through gloom and showers across the endlessness of dead and rotting redgrass stubble that marked the tribe's trail. Bel scanned the barren land and the scattered tanglebrush, then looked up at the lone figure on the hill. "We walk directly to him, always choosing an open path. He mustn't think we have friends waiting in ambush."

The warrior began to move, angling away to the left. "When he sees how we approach, he'll know we want to meet. If he keeps moving away from us, we must stop, and make it clear that we won't follow, or he'll think we're hostile." She led the way down the slope, and the figure paused again, watching.

After long days traveling alone with Bel, the addition of another human being was oddly disturbing. The sudden presence of the distant figure seemed inexplicable, its upright stance incongruous, its motion peculiar, and its possession of an intelligent mind unlikely. Rowan found herself regarding it as a strange animal, unpredictable and possibly dangerous. But when they came within fifteen yards, it proved to be only a man in Outskirter garb, shaggy-haired, bearded, watching them with shadowed eyes.

As they approached, Bel spoke quietly to Rowan. "Something's wrong."

Rowan studied the figure. She could see nothing that might have prompted Bel's comment, but took the fact as given. "He's from the tribe that lost the goat?"

"Yes."

"Perhaps he thinks we stole it."

"We did steal it. Until we strike a trade for it, it's considered stolen. But that's not it."

They continued to approach the man. "You said the tribe left quickly."

"Yes." Bel's gait became more easy and natural, a danger signal to Rowan.

The steerswoman considered. "The tribe encountered some trouble. He thinks we might be involved."

"Yes."

Possibly the trouble had taken the form of an attack by a hostile tribe; perhaps the man was overcautious after a lost battle. "How can we reassure him?"

"We can't. And it's too late for us to back off. We'll just have to be exactly what we are, and hope he sees it soon enough."

"And if he doesn't?"

"Fight. Or run. Whichever we can manage."

At a distance of fifteen feet, Bel stopped, Rowan pausing beside her, and they stood facing the man quietly for some moments. There was no gesture from him, no word and no signal. He held himself completely still, and Rowan was abruptly certain that there were other warriors near, whose existence and location this man was trying not to betray by unconscious behavior.

She glanced about: no one else was visible.

At the moment Rowan decided that he was never going to move at all, he did, slowly. Reaching over his shoulder, he pulled a black, metal-edged sword from its sheath and stood with its hilt in his right hand, the flat of its blade resting across a bare left forearm. A motion of his shoulders threw back the damp patchwork cloak, leaving both arms clear and in sight, showing a black, shaggy vest thong-tied over a wide expanse of chest.

Bel drew her own sword, and the man's eyes widened at the gleam of bright metal. She laid it on the ground before her, hilt to the right, then stepped back a pace. Rowan made to imitate her, but was quietly told, "No. Keep your sword in hand, and stand with your back to me. I'm unarmed; you watch behind. Don't look over your shoulder at him, he'll take it as a threat."

Rowan complied; and, not knowing what to look for, she looked at nothing, carefully, intently: the wide, empty land, the bare undulating hills, the textureless gray skies. She listened in a widening circle, hearing Bel's gear creak behind her, a crunch in the wet stubble as the man adjusted his stance.

As Bel was about to speak, Rowan noticed something. "There's movement in front of me, at an angle to my left, just past the second rise." The motion stopped, then began again, crested the low hill, and revealed itself. Rowan relaxed. "Goats, two of them."

Bel spoke up to the man. "Two goats, at ten by you," she announced. Rowan wondered at the turn of phrase.

She heard the stranger reply. "And a warrior, at five by you." In the far, windless distance something moved, colorless against the dead ground, visible only by its motion. It traced a slow arc to Rowan's right, then paused, as if watching.

Rowan stared at it, deeply disturbed. It was a person, she knew, but had she not been alerted to its presence, she would never have seen it, could barely see it even now. It came to her that the world around her was alive with information, none of it recognizable or comprehensible to her. Her trusted senses, her dependable intellect were inadequate here, and the fact made her feel more helplessly unarmed than if she were naked and without a sword.

"We took a goat yesterday," Bel told her man. "If it's yours, trade is due you."

There was a long silence. The distant, half-seen object apallingly sprouted recognizable human arms, made broad gestures: signals, certainly, to the man behind Rowan, possibly replies to similar silent signals from him. Rowan wished she could face the nearer stranger. He was close by, he was undisguised, but she could not read his face, she could not interpret his reactions, she could not *see* what he was doing.

Bel was facing the closer enemy; it was fitting. Bel was the better fighter, Bel was the native. Rowan's job was to guard their backs, and she set to her job with a grimmer, more intense concentration.

The far warrior was signaling again, and reinterpreting the distortion of distance, the steerswoman saw that he had turned around and was gesturing to someone past him, someone beyond sight. Rowan suddenly surmised a relay formation, and understood that there might be dozens of warriors nearby, spread invisibly across the landscape, moving to surround the travelers. Her stance had shifted, of itself, in unconscious preparation for sudden action. She now reviewed the path that she and Bel had used to approach this area, tried to guess if it was still clear, and began planning a retreat.

Bel and the near warrior had been conversing; in retrospect Rowan understood that he had asked to see what she was offering. Bel said to the steerswoman, "Stand as you are, I'm shifting." Rowan felt her friend step forward; she heard her slip off her pack, and the slap of thongs as it was opened.

Rowan saw a motion to her left and was about to speak when Bel's warrior said, "Warrior at three."

"I see him," the steerswoman confirmed to Bel; to her eyes, it was merely a spot of variegated brown, difficult to focus on, moving with suspicious purpose.

Bel was fussing with the pack's contents. "Check nine," she said quietly.

"What?"

"Is there anyone to your right?"

Rowan scanned the area. "I don't think so."

She heard Bel step forward again, heard the warrior come to meet her, and realized that Bel had walked past her own sword and was now face-to-face with the warrior, completely unarmed. Rowan found that she hated the idea, and strained to keep herself from turning around.

There was silence behind; then the man spoke. "How many goats did you take?"

"One."

"This is too much."

"I know. It's what we have. It's yours."

The man in front of Rowan was signaling again, this time to Rowan's right.

"Someone's coming," Rowan said. "They're going to close us off."

Bel said to the warrior, "We'd like to meet your seyoh."

"Where's your tribe?"

"We have no tribe. We're traveling. Perhaps we can travel with you."

He made a negative sound, then amended, reluctantly, "It's not for me to decide. Let's have a look at your friend."

Bel called to her. "Rowan, set down your sword and come here."

"Put it down?" She could hardly believe the order.

"Yes. Do it."

With the greatest reluctance, Rowan set her weapon down onto the rotted stubble, finding she had to clench her empty hands into fists to keep them from clutching for it again.

Bel and the stranger were five feet apart, Bel standing with the blatant ease that told Rowan she was ready for instant action; the man studied Rowan with a mild-mannered calm that she recognized as his version of the same preparedness.

"This is Rowan," Bel said. "She only has one name. And I'm Bel, Margasdotter, Chanly."

The names were volunteered, and the warrior was under no obligation to offer his own. His bright black gaze puzzled over the steerswoman. "You have no family?" He was holding the handleless knife blade that Bel had offered him, one of eight that Bel and Rowan carried as trade items.

The steerswoman found herself reluctant to speak more than was necessary. "I have family."

"She's from the Inner Lands," Bel supplied.

"You're a long way from your farm." He turned the blade over in his hands, enjoying its gleam, its balance.

"I'm not a farmer, I'm a steerswoman."

He shook his head; the word was meaningless to him. "Warrior, at nine by you," he said then.

Rowan spun left and saw an Outskirter, clearly visible, perfectly recognizable in a bold piebald cloak. The person was signaling. Bel put a reassuring hand on Rowan's shoulder. Rowan turned back. "We're surrounded."

"Yes." Bel spoke to the man. "What's your answer?"

He studied the women. His hair was shaggy black to his shoulders, his beard unevenly trimmed, his face a sunburned brown with black chips of eyes. Rowan saw that his sword was now sheathed.

He slipped the knife blade into his waistband, then abruptly stepped back and gestured widely to his comrades. Rowan startled at the suddenness, wondered what he was saying. A finger of sunlight broke through the clouds, and indicated a gully past the warrior, as if it had tried to find the trio, and missed. It vanished, and a light rain began.

"Get your weapons. It's a long walk to camp."

Bel slapped Rowan's shoulder with a delighted "Ha!" They retrieved the swords, and when she held her weapon again the steerswoman felt a shade more proper, more fit. They were still surrounded.

"Are we accepted?" Rowan asked. She wiped the blade on her sleeve, made to sheathe it, but discovered that her hand and arm did not want her to do so.

"Not yet. But we have a chance to explain our case. If we can convince them we're not enemies, they might take us in."

"We don't know that they're going in our direction."

"Yes, we do." Bel shouldered her pack. "There isn't any grass left to the west. They've been there. They have to go east, or at least easterly." She turned to the man, who had approached again and was waiting for them. "Can we make camp by nightfall?"

He scanned the flat, sprinkling sky, calculating. Sudden as buckets, the downpour recommenced, and the distances closed in and vanished into rattling, roaring gray. Rowan hastily sheathed her sword and drew up her hood.

The warrior had been caught with cloak open and his face up, and was drenched in an instant. He laughed and shook his hair like a dog, then turned his face up again as if being battered by the fat, cold drops was the most pleasant sensation in the world.

"Who knows?" he shouted over the noise. He dashed water from his eyes with his fingers, wiped his face with the heels of his hands, then cocked a bright black eye at the women, amused. When he nodded past Rowan, she turned and discovered two more warriors, one standing not four feet from her side, the other posted beside Bel. Their approach had been completely unnoticed. Raised hoods and closed cloaks rendered them eerily neutral: genderless, and without personality. They did not speak.

The first man pulled up his own hood and leaned closer to the travelers, to be heard above the rain. "We'll just keep walking until we get there, shall we?"

9

Rowan awoke to heavy, musty air, the sour odor of wet fur, and the sound of rain. Shifting on her bedroll, she found that someone had replaced her sodden cloak, which she had been using as a blanket, with a heavy felt cover, thick enough to be a rug. She had been unaware of the exchange.

"Bel?" Nothing was visible in the sealed air of the tent; the grayness was just one shade above black, and the dark seemed less an absence of light than an intrinsic feature of the smell.

Rowan shoved the cover aside and cast about with one hand, searching for her pack. Someone, probably Bel, had laid her sword alongside her bedding. The steerswoman considered, then stood to strap it on, rising carefully, uncertain of the available headroom.

She paused and listened. There was no sound but hers in the tent, no breathing but her own. Outside, amid the pattering hiss, she heard movement, muffled voices. She groped her way along the tent wall and suddenly found a flap and threw it back.

Brilliant sunlight struck her with an almost physical force, and she drew back, one arm thrown up against the glare. She had been fooled by the sound: there was no rain, and every vestige of cloud and mist had vanished. The brightness was too much for her sleep-bleared eyes. Above and below the shield of her arm, she caught only glimpses of wild red ground and painful blue sky.

Someone brushed by, then turned back and abruptly fingered the loose edge of Rowan's blouse. "This is filthy. I'll get you another," a female voice said, and then the woman was gone.

"Thank you," Rowan replied in her general direction. She wiped at her tearing eyes with her sleeve and tried to see the world.

Redgrass.

Down the hills and up them, over ridges and out to the edge of sight, was a single sweeping carpet of redgrass, rippling in the steady south wind. The grass had already been dried by the morning sun, and its natural brilliance had returned; colors trembled across the land as each individual blade twisted and bent, now showing a brown side, now a bright red. It was difficult to focus clearly on the shifting and flashing; the earth looked feverish, as if Rowan were delirious but unable to decide on the particular hue of her hallucination. Driven by the wind, the hollow reeds tapped against each other, rough blades rustling, setting up a rattling hiss that Rowan had mistaken for the sound of rain.

In front and beyond, hills ranged, broken by two staggered ridges, then falling faintly lower as they reached out toward the horizon. A far lake sparkled silver in the distance, edged with looming dark shapes—trees, Rowan assumed, blinking with the effort of seeing past the grass. Then she corrected herself. There were no trees in the Outskirts, and this, finally and surely, was true and pure Outskirts.

The air held a scent, like cinnamon and sour milk, over the freshness of departed rain. The tent beside Rowan wafted up a miasma of must and goat. Somewhere someone was roasting meat.

Rowan could see no green plant life at all. Clumps and thickets of tanglebrush, gray and black, were recognizable nearby. A few rocky outcrops showed on one of the ridges, and far off the land displayed jagged black lines, caused by what, Rowan had no idea.

And the sky above was empty and blue: blue as a lake of pure, fresh water.

Someone shifted behind her, and she turned to face a large male Outskirter, in full gear. He regarded her silently and warily.

"Hello," Rowan said, hoping he found her as innocuous as she knew herself to be. "Have you seen my friend around here?"

"I might have. How would I know him?"

They had come in at night, in rain, and had gone directly to sleep. Possibly news of their arrival had not been passed on to all the tribe members. "A woman," Rowan told him, "smaller than I am." She held out a hand to demonstrate the height. "Dark brown hair, brown eyes. Her cloak is not as fine as yours." The man's cloak was not Bel's random patchwork, but a striking gray and black diagonal design. "An Outskirter, like yourself."

"Ha. There's only one like me."

"Well, yes." He was nearly twice Bel's size, and blond. "And there's only one like her, as well, more's the pity. We were brought in last

night, by a warrior, one of the men guarding the flock to the west. I
don't know his name."

The warrior nodded, as if this confirmed information he already
possessed, and it came to Rowan that if she had presented any tale but
the truth, matters would have turned to the worse. This man was assigned as her guard.

As they stood regarding each other, Rowan's Inner Lands habits
began to demand that an introduction be made. She tried to remember the rules Bel had laid out, but found nothing that covered interaction with a person assigned to watch her. She followed her instinct.
"I'm Rowan, a steerswoman, from the Inner Lands. I only have the
one name." Replying with his own full name would imply an acceptance he had no authority to render, but she hazarded to ask, "And
you are . . . ," knowing that mere first names were sometimes bestowed
more freely, and wishing to have some means of addressing him.

The Outskirter delivered a narrow glare and rubbed the back of his
neck uncomfortably, his sword strap creaking. "Hm. That fellow who
brought you in has gone back to his band." His dislike seemed more
formal than personal. "Well, I don't suppose you've killed anyone yet.
Have you?"

She was not sure this was a joke. "Not so far."

"Here."

Rowan turned at the new voice and caught a tossed wool shirt.
"Wash at the creek, or no one will want to associate with you." The
woman vanished again, leaving Rowan only with impressions of
height, long dark hair, and a bundle balanced on one shoulder.

Rowan looked at the shirt in her hand, then held it up for the man
to see. She waved it slightly. "How do I find the creek?"

He made a satisfied sound, then motioned with a nod. "On the far
side of the camp." He paused. "You can't go through. I'll lead you
around."

"Thank you."

His reply was a grunt.

The tent she had slept in was one of a cluster of four crowded together, back-to-back. Some of skin, some of felt, all in shades of gray
and brown, they might have been cloud shadows against the wild
color of the surrounding redgrass.

As she followed the Outskirter around the body of the camp, Rowan saw that all the tents were in groups of four, back-to-back like cornered soldiers. Between the groups she caught intriguing glimpses of the life within. Spaces between the clusters seemed to define avenues, annexes, even courtyards; it was like passing by a village of cloth and leather houses. People walked along those paths she could see, most of them moving quickly, as if on some errand; they glanced at her once, then studiously ignored her.

As they rounded the south side of the camp, they passed a group of five children, playing at battle—using real weapons, Rowan realized. One made boldly to challenge her presence, but her guard stopped him with a hand on his shoulder and an admonishing finger in his face, and with gestures directed the children's attention away from the steerswoman. But he paused among them long enough to correct one fierce young girl's sword grip; the others watched the instruction intently, then picked up their adventure where it had been interrupted.

The groupings of the tents fell into some larger pattern: a star, it seemed, though Rowan could not from her vantage count the points. The wind brought the smell of cooking again, and she surmised a central open area, with a fire pit.

When they passed another of the tent city's points, Rowan found herself at the crest of a little dale, looking east. Below, the creek reflected the blue of the sky, stable and peculiar amid the noisy, shimmering red and brown. The motion of the colors rendered the scene freakish, unreal, the sloping perspective seemed about to shift without ever quite doing so, and the tapping of the reeds never ceased, but rose and fell like rain on the ocean. Rowan gazed down dizzily and felt as if her ears were tired inside, from the noise.

Over the sound, half-audible voices came up from the creek: cheerful, comradely shouts, playful squeals. Her guard nodded down at the creek. "There you go, Rowan," he said, and she wondered if the use of her name signified anything. "Don't be too long, or you'll miss breakfast." And he sat, apparently with every intention of watching her as she bathed.

As she descended, slightly unsteady, Rowan fought an urge to turn back, to lose herself among the tents and people. Her eyes, and her mind, remained uncomfortable with the sweep of shuddering colors, the cruel, immobile black, and her body was uneasy, unable to find its proper balance as she moved down the slope to the waterside.

But at the creek, to her surprise, she found green life: a crowd of scrub pines, and an incongruous patch of gray-headed thistle. Her eyes rested there as if they were the only real things in the world.

The bathers were all women, standing hip-deep or sitting neck-deep in the cool water. One of them was annoying the others by skimming her palm across the surface to send up sheets of spray. Her cohorts soon dealt with the prank by mobbing her and forcing her head below the surface until she indicated surrender.

On the fringes of the group, all alone, was Bel.

"Ha," Rowan's companion said. "You took your time."

"I didn't know the hour," Rowan replied. She slipped her sword strap over her head and kicked out of her boots. Each person's clothing, whether neatly or haphazardly arranged, had its owner's weapon lying on top, hilt carefully pointing to the water—handy for quick recovery in case of danger. Rowan followed their example, wondering to herself if the precaution was necessary.

She waded into the cool water, feeling small stones beneath her feet. "I think I insulted my guard, by asking his name," she told Bel, then dipped beneath the surface to rinse the first layer of dirt from her body. Below, sound closed in with a familiar closeness, and her sight was limited to shafts of sweet white light, brown creek bed, and a number of blurred naked human bodies. She had an odd desire to remain there.

She resurfaced to the incessant hiss and tap of the redgrass, the rattle of nearby tanglebrush, the shifting red and brown. On the far side of the creek, some Outskirts plant had put out a patch of magenta blossoms. The effect was faintly nauseating.

"No one will tell you their names, not until we've been accepted," Bel reminded her, studying a raw spot on her own stomach, an abrasion from wearing wet clothing for days. Bel scooped water onto it, then rubbed off a patch of dead skin.

"Should I tell them mine?"

"Yes. Every chance you get." Bel raised her voice to the bathing women. "This is the friend I mentioned, the steerswoman, Rowan. She only has one name."

"Ha," someone said, and the women went back to their business.

"Will that knife blade buy our way in?"

"Nothing will buy our way in, and you shouldn't say it like that. The knife blade was for the goat we took. And the fact that we bothered to trade for it instead of stealing it shows them that we mean well."

Rowan became confused. "Wouldn't they respect us more if we did steal it?"

"In a way. But if we want this tribe to become our tribe, even temporarily, we can't do anything that's against its interests." Bel moved to the shallower bank and sat down in the water, leaning back a bit, water slapping against her breasts. Her short, muscular legs extended before her, half floating.

"When do we meet the seyoh?"

Bel kicked up a few splashes with childlike pleasure. "I expect they're discussing us right now, and they'll plan to hear our story sometime this afternoon."

"That's good. I'd like to get things settled. I feel a bit odd being half ignored." Rowan imitated her friend and found the contrast between the cool water and the oddly scented air refreshing. Because it was natural for her to do so, she gazed at the longest perspective, out to the horizon. The scene stubbornly refused to integrate; it became weirder, wavering, and the magenta flowers jabbed at her vision like a nail in her eye.

She focused on the creek bank and concentrated on the conversation. "The people act as if I'm supposed to be invisible, but don't have the manners to be so correctly."

Bel laughed. "That's well said. And it's true. But the fact is, you are doing it correctly. You're supposed to act as if you don't have the manners to be invisible. You should force people to notice you." Bel raised her voice again. "Who has soap?" There was no reply from the bathers. "Well, I'm used to my own smell. But it will be a hard time on anyone who has to stand near me . . ." Something landed with a splash between the two women. "Ha." Bel retrieved the grayish lump and began vigorously scrubbing her hair with it, to little visible effect.

"I'm not accustomed to blatantly drawing attention to myself." But Rowan found herself liking the Outskirter approach. It seemed like a game of skill, a small competition of self-esteem.

Bel passed the soap to Rowan. "You don't have to. It's not required. But they'll think better of you, if you do."

"I see." The virtue of the soap, Rowan discovered, lay largely in its abrasive quality. There was much to abrade. She set to work. "Will it affect our being accepted?"

"I don't think so." Bel leaned forward and submerged her head, massaging trail dirt out of her scalp, rose, and wrung out fistfuls of short hair.

Four of the bathers upstream had gathered in a knot, waist-deep in water, to discuss something in low tones, punctuated by girlish laughter, subdued and decidedly unwarriorlike. Rowan eyed the group, then suddenly tossed the gritty soap in their direction, a high lob calculated to land in their center. "Thank you for the soap," she called out as it fell.

One woman instinctively caught it, her comrades just as instinctively turning and diving away, to leave her standing alone, surprised, with the lump in her hand. She looked Rowan full in the eyes, suppressing laughter that seemed not derisive but friendly. She thought a moment. "No, thank *you*," she said, then passed the soap to another and waded out to dry.

Rowan considered the tone of the words. "Was that an insult?"

"Yes," Bel said, eyes amused. "But a weak one. Yours was better."

The steerswoman tried to recall under what conditions a simple "thank you" might constitute an Outskirter insult. The rules of behavior were not yet fully organized in her mind, and she shook her head. "This is going to take some time."

"You're doing well so far."

Rowan laughed. "Purely accidental, I assure you." She closed her eyes to enjoy the strange scents and the sunlight.

Her ears immediately told her that it was raining, hard. She winced involuntarily, blinked her eyes open again, and found that for an instant, the world consisted of fragmented blots that only settled into coherence reluctantly. She forced herself to look around carefully: the brook, the women, the veldt, the hills, her guard—"Do you have a guard?"

Bel tilted her head at the opposite bank of the brook. "She's being clever. Either for the practice, or just to show off."

Rowan looked in the direction indicated, but saw no one. "Where?" She rose and waded toward the far bank, curious, then stopped, finding the combination of unsteady vision and water motion too difficult to manage.

"Think 'goat,' " Bel called.

Rowan found three goats, all difficult to discern among the redgrass motion. The farthest, she decided, was the warrior: it seemed to move less often, and less naturally. She considered that if she decided to climb the bank, the warrior would reveal herself. An effective configuration: one guard on each side of the brook.

She returned to Bel's side. "I hope the seyoh sees us soon. I don't like not clearly knowing what's to happen next."

Bel had climbed from the water, stepped to her clothing, carefully reversed the direction of her sword hilt to face her new position, and sat on the bank. She tilted her face back, letting the sun and wind dry her. "In a way, I don't like it either. But it might be best. The longer the wait, the better for us."

"Why is that?" Rowan rearranged her own sword and lay down in the sand beside her clothing. She shut her eyes again and tried to ignore the sound of the redgrass.

Bel changed the subject. "How do you feel?"

"Fine." Rowan laughed a bit. "But my eyes don't like the Outskirts. I suppose I'm just not used to it, the way the colors move. It seems unreal." Her reaction seemed foolish, and it embarrassed her to reveal it.

Bel made a dubious sound.

Rowan recalled Bel's warning about Outskirter food and understood her friend's concern. She sat up to speak reassuringly. "Bel, it's been more than two days—"

The grassy hill, rising to her right, seemed to lean over like a wave, ready to topple on her. To her left, the open land jittered and writhed. She froze and screwed her eyes closed. "Should it affect my vision?"

"No. It should affect your digestion."

"My digestion is fine." It was true. With eyes closed, she once again felt completely normal: healthy and fit, with the water cooling delightfully on her skin in the sweet breeze and the sunlight. She loved the sour spicy scent of the air; it intrigued her with promises of strangeness, newness. She knew next to nothing about this land, and beneath the distracting noise of the redgrass, found a part of herself that was happy as a child at the prospect of discovery.

She opened her eyes cautiously, concentrating on Bel's familiar face. The hill remained a hill, and this time the land to the left seemed solid of itself, though vaguely threatening, with horizon foreshortened. But now, by contrast, the water of the creek looked strange: solid, like a gleaming band of metal. The remaining bathers seemed only to exist from the waist up: macabre half persons moving normally, casually, unaware of their horrible condition.

"It's that everything is so very different," Rowan asserted, forcing herself to continue looking. "I'll adjust. If Outskirters can get used to it, I can, as well."

"We're born to it."

"I suppose that's the case." Stubbornly, she continued to study her own reactions.

Bel rose to recover her clothes, and Rowan followed, directing her own actions cautiously. "But at one time," the steerswoman continued, "your people must have needed to adjust, like me, when they first came to the Outskirts." She began to dress.

Bel pulled on her own blouse. "No," she said when her head emerged. "We've always been in the Outskirts."

The tribe members were beginning to gather by the fire pit at the center of the camp for the morning meal. It was a casual process: people congregated in disorganized groups, or sat alone, or appeared and took their food to other parts of the camp. Those who sat and stayed, conversing or musing, were handed rough pottery cups of broth and round biscuits by three elderly mertutials, assisted by a pair of children.

Bel and Rowan were cautiously conducted by their guards to one side of the area and instructed by gesture to go in no farther. Bel took the limitation with evident good humor, and ostentatiously joined a group of six warriors seated on a light woven rug outside a nearby tent. She introduced herself and her companion politely; the group fell silent, then shifted their seating to define a circle that definitely excluded the two strangers and their watchers. They returned to their interrupted conversation, which concerned an epidemic of lameness in that part of the flock pasturing in a location referred to as "nine-side."

Bel explained the system used. "You think of a circle, and put numbers around it. Twelve is always straight ahead, in the direction the tribe is moving, or has been moving, or intends to move, if that's decided yet. Then you count around the circle to the right, starting with one."

"Why isn't one straight ahead? It makes more sense."

"I don't know. That's how we do it." Bel beckoned a passing mertutial, who was inclined to ignore them. "Twelve is straight ahead," she continued, "six is straight behind, three to the right and nine to the left."

Perhaps perplexed by the necessity of the instruction, Rowan's guard attempted to exchange a curious glance with his partner. She ignored him, maintaining a studied air of disinterest in their charges, fooling no one.

"It's an odd system; it'll need getting used to," Rowan said, then immediately realized that it need not; as a mapmaker, she was accustomed to 360 degrees in a circle. Twelve divided into it neatly, giving exactly thirty degrees to each Outskirter point, a felicity she found peculiar. "Why twelve?" she wondered aloud, then answered herself: to divide neatly into 360. "Why three hundred and sixty?" To divide easily by twelve. Her half-voiced musing prompted Bel to require explanation.

They were finally provided breakfast—the mertutial, an elderly man, bald but possessing a waist-length beard that was pridefully well groomed, handed them steaming cups; he moved with a dignity markedly different from the mertutials of the raider tribe. He was clean and healthy. His hands, though aged, were steady, and his back was straight.

Looking up at him, Rowan recalled some of Bel's instruction on proper Outskirter society: Mertutials were persons whom age or injury had rendered unable to serve as warriors. Nearly all mertutials had once been warriors. This man had survived hard life in the wilderness to serve the tribe in a second role, and possessed the same degree of honor as he had had in the first—quite a different situation from the way of the degenerated raider tribe.

"Thank you," Rowan said to him, taking her cup; and looking up at him, she paused, wondering suddenly what strange dangers, what solitudes, what wild and furious battles he had passed through in his long years to live to this day, when sustenance itself rested in his hands, passing from his to the outstretched hands of younger comrades.

"You're welcome," he replied, and she saw in his eyes that despite her strange clothing, he took her to be a warrior: that to him, hers was now the defense, the strength, and the violence, all for the sake of her tribe.

A warrior never thanked a warrior, nor a mertutial a mertutial; but across the line that demarcated their roles, gratitude was always recognized, and rendered.

Then the old man was gone, leaving Rowan with a cup in one hand and a meat-filled biscuit in the other. She spoke to her companion. "Bel," she said, "I like your people very much."

On further consideration, Rowan declined to partake of the breakfast; she had yet to experience the illness Bel had predicted, and she still hypothesized that she might delay its onset by delaying the ingestion of tribe-cooked food.

Seeing the steerswoman place cup and biscuit on the carpet, Bel asked for explanation, and was annoyed when she received it. "It won't work. You ate that goat we took. You've been eating it for two days."

"Nevertheless."

Bel shook her head at Rowan's stubbornness, then ate the steerswoman's breakfast as well as her own.

It was dysentery, Rowan discovered one hour later; and it did not last one day, but three.

By evening she was unable to reach the cessfield unassisted, to the discomfiture of her guard. Other provisions were made, which duty Bel handled, until she was struck with the illness herself the following morning. Rowan recalled very little of that day, except the constant presence of a silent child, of indeterminate gender, who urged her by gesture to drink as much water as she could hold.

On the third morning, Rowan found herself alone, vaguely aware that she had slept uninterrupted through the night. She shakily dressed and made her way out of the hot, goat-smelling tent, compelled by a bleary desire to sit out in the breeze. The view briefly confounded her: incomprehensible colors, sky too bright, earth shuddering and roiling in waves of red and brown. She dealt with the problem instinctively by taking four staggering steps away from the tent's entrance and dropping to a seat on the ground, facing the tents instead of the open veldt.

Bel approached, in the company of a mertutial, an old woman whose hair, a complexity of tiny plaits interwoven into a single fat braid, reached nearly to her knees. Her face, with its squat, broken nose and tiny blue eyes, was weirdly compelling; Rowan vaguely felt that she should know it.

They settled beside her, the woman displaying a distinctly proprietary air. "You're right," she said to Bel. "She's up at last."

Rowan attempted to concentrate. She seemed to recognize the woman without actually remembering her. It was an interesting phenomenon.

The woman reached for Rowan's wrist, and Rowan found that she accepted this action without question; it was familiar.

"How do you feel?" Bel asked. Rowan had forgotten that she was there.

The steerswoman considered long, during which period she briefly lost the question, then recovered it. "Tired," she replied at last. "And very stupid."

The old woman laid a hand on Rowan's face, directing her gaze into her own. "Well. Not surprising." She peered at Rowan's eyes.

And Rowan remembered: the woman had visited her before. She was the tribal healer. Rowan recalled the intelligent, concerned gaze, and with sudden embarrassment recalled her own behavior. She had become possessed of the idea that the woman harbored secrets, and had responded to her constant inability to answer questions with the patient argument "I'm a steerswoman, you know."

"I'm sorry," Rowan said.

The healer understood perfectly. "No need," she replied, patting Rowan's cheek in a motherly fashion. Rowan wondered how many people this woman had killed when she was a warrior.

The healer turned to Bel. "She'll be fine. I've never seen it strike anyone this hard before, but she's past it now. Make sure she keeps getting plenty of water."

Bel nodded. "Good. We're sorry to be so much trouble. I know people have been waiting to speak to us."

The healer gestured another mertutial over and instructed him to bring a light meal. "You'll feel better tomorrow," she told Rowan. Then to Bel: "You'll need to travel carefully for a few days, not too hard, but I think you'll manage."

"Is the tribe going to be moving?" Rowan managed to ask. The woman refused the question with an apologetic glance, and Rowan suppressed an urge to add, "I'm a steerswoman, you know."

The healer had learned something of the ways of steerswomen during Rowan's illness. "Your ban won't serve you here. If you know I can't answer, don't ask the question. You'll speak to the seyoh tomorrow afternoon."

Rowan found that the scene around her was rapidly becoming more precise, though maintaining a translucent, airy quality. Without changing, the breeze was suddenly very cool and refreshing.

"That's good," Rowan said. "We have a lot to say." Somewhere at the back of her mind, a part of herself was independently reviewing the information she planned to present. She watched it at work, with a detached pride.

The healer departed, and the food arrived: broth and bread. It was delicious.

As she drank and ate, she began to notice the sounds of the camp. The hiss and rattle of the veldt was unending, but from the center of the camp wafted voices, music, and intriguing clatters that she finally recognized as two fighters training with metal-edged tanglewood swords.

She heard Bel sigh, and turned to her, finding she had to move her entire body to effectively redirect her gaze. "Is there a problem?" She was aware of a brief flurry of thought, just below full awareness, as dozens of possibilities for potential problems shuffled and sorted themselves.

Bel looked disgruntled. "We've been refused."

Rowan sat very still as the shuffling proceeded, caught the answer as it flickered by. "The seyoh. Not the seyoh and the council."

"Yes. It takes the entire council to decide to accept us. The seyoh can reject us alone."

10

*T*he tent was open on two sides; Rowan and Bel sat in cool sunlight, the seyoh half in shadow, her loose, white hair like a streamer of cloud hanging down her body.

"It is a fine knife," she said, turning it over in her narrow hands, testing its edge expertly with one thin thumb. "And worth more than the goat." She set it down on the patterned fabric carpeting the floor and turned dark, calm eyes to the travelers. "We will give you food for your journey, to even the score. You may leave now."

Rowan sighed. She was still tired, and had to remind herself to sit straight. "We had hoped," she told the seyoh, "that we might remain with your tribe and travel in your company for some time, if your route goes east."

The old woman shook her head; a broad, sweeping motion, very similar to Bel's own characteristic negative. "We don't want you. I see that you are no danger to us, and your passing through our pastures has not cost us. But we don't need you, especially one like you who is so unfamiliar with our ways."

"I learn very quickly," Rowan began.

Bel spoke up. "The steerswoman has things to say that you need to hear. Even if you still decide to have us go. It's important."

Rowan doubted that the Guidestar and the actions of distant wizards might be considered important to Outskirters; she wished that Bel would not overstate their case, however it might aid them. Nevertheless, she organized her thoughts. "It has to do with the Guidestars," she said, "and the fact that one of them has fallen. There are more Guidestars than the two of you can see in the sky. We are trying to cross deep into the Outskirts, to a place where one of the other Guidestars has fallen—"

"I don't care where you are going. You may not do so with my people."

"But we hope," Rowan continued, and tried to compact her tale, to tell it quickly and compellingly, "we hope to find out why it fell. If one Guidestar can fall—"

"And I hope you discover your reason. I wish you well. We have cared for you while you were ill because you did us no harm, and approached us honestly, and did not steal from our flocks. But now we are done with you."

Rowan made to continue, but Bel gestured the steerswoman to let her take over. She leaned forward. "This means more than you think," she told the seyoh seriously, and Rowan wondered at the trace of urgency in her voice. "It doesn't seem so to you, because everything you know has stayed the same—"

Holding Bel's gaze, the seyoh lifted her chin fractionally. The movement held some meaning for Bel; instantly, without protest, she ceased to speak, relaxed her posture, and waited.

The seyoh nodded an acknowledgment. "Take what supplies you need. The knife is a good tool and weapon, and will serve us well." She settled back, gestured. "Now leave."

Bel made to rise, but Rowan wavered, disbelieving they were being dismissed without a full hearing. She wanted to try again; somewhere, she was certain, were the right words to convince this woman to take in the travelers.

Bel read her intent, forestalled it with a hand on Rowan's arm. She spoke to the seyoh. "Thank you. The help you gave us is worth more than the food we gained, and the knife we traded." What followed seemed a formal statement. "My birth-tribe is far east of here. Its seyoh is Serrann, Marsheson, Liev." It was a gift. Should this tribe encounter Bel's, possession of the names would constitute an introduction, and might prevent hostilities.

The seyoh's eyes warmed with a smile that worked its way past her dignity to reach her mouth. "Thank you," she said. "Good luck, and travel carefully."

11

*R*owan waded waist-deep through dry grass that clutched at her clothing and scratched at her boots. The world was a swirl of red and brown, shifting and shuddering, and the air was awash with sound: an endless hissing and a patternless pattering chatter that filled her ears completely and overflowed, taking up residence in her buzzing skull. The blue overhead seemed unlikely, not to be trusted; she half expected it to curl down and twist in among the reeds, to open chasms of sky beneath her feet—

"Rowan, wait!"

She came to a stop like a ship at sea and turned into the wind, sails luffing. She rocked against nonexistent swells. Instinct made her plant her feet wide and shift her weight against a wave that was a tussock that refused to move to her expectations. Unbalanced, she fell to a seat among the grass.

Bel appeared, and hunched down beside her. "Are you all right?"

The tall reeds defined a little room around the two of them, and the grass sounds were intimate and comprehensible. "Yes," Rowan said, perplexed.

"Why did you go ahead like that?"

"I'm not sure." She recalled a vague impression that it was possible to outpace the scenery.

The Outskirter studied her, and Rowan studied herself, both with equal suspicion. "Can you stand?" Bel asked.

"Yes." She did not much want to. Instead, she reached out and plucked a shaft of redgrass, turned it over in her hands. The stem was resonantly hollow, the diameter of her smallest finger; the nodes were wide, the sheaths loosely wrapped, and the blades emerged in a three-ranked pattern, instead of the two-ranked that greengrass followed.

Bel became impatient. "You've seen that already."

"A moment." A weed, nothing more; uncommon in the Inner Lands, but not unknown. Leaves brown on one side, red on the other. "All right." She accepted a hand up, keeping the stalk in her other hand.

Shuddering colors all around her. Motion, to the limit of the horizon in the north, motion breaking around a solid line of black to the south, motion rising and falling in a series of slopes ahead to the east. The breeze was in her face, speeding wild lines of brown and red directly toward her; it was sinister, threatening. The colors seemed to hover, sourceless, ineffable.

She looked at the reed in her hand. Leaves brown on one side, red on the other. It was just the wind. "Let's go."

Bel said dubiously, "Stay close, and stay behind."

The grass growth hid the shape of the land beneath, and some of Rowan's steps jarred against sudden rises, or dropped sickeningly into dips. Bel was having no such problem. "How can you tell how to step?"

"Watch the grass tops."

The idea was not attractive. Rowan recalled a similar situation, when she had been trying to teach Bel to overcome seasickness.

"Watch the waves," she had told Bel, advising her to act exactly opposite to instinct's inclination.

Rowan wished it would rain; wished the colors to gray, the grass to dampen and silence. She watched the grass tops dizzily and stumbled along behind the Outskirter.

They had been traveling for one day and the greater part of a second. The tribe was out of sight; the tents, people, goats—familiar visual anchors—were gone. There was only the rolling veldt: unpredictable color shimmering across her eyes, fragmenting her vision. Rowan had walked that day as though blind, had slept that night as though still walking, dreaming incomprehensible patterns of flailing light and dark, and roaring voices. She awoke exhausted.

There was little conversation, and most was provided by Bel, commenting on those aspects of Outskirts wildlife that presented themselves: "This is a slugsnake. It likes to climb things, so don't stand still." "Those tall shapes in the distance are lichen-towers. They only grow by water." "That's a hawkbug, up there. It won't bother you,

you're too big." "If this bug lights on you let it bite. It's harmless, and it will tell its hive that you don't taste good. You won't be bothered again." "If this one bites you, kill it as fast as you can. It will burrow into your flesh and die there, and you'll have to cut it out with a knife." Disturbingly, the two insects seemed indistinguishable. But Rowan listened, accepting the information, accumulating facts for later and, it was hoped, more coherent consideration.

The next morning, as she was drawing water from a steep-banked creek, Rowan attempted to steady herself against a crusty boulder that bulked from the water's edge over the bank. As she leaned her hand against it, the object's surface gave away, and her left arm sank in, to the elbow. She felt sharp lines of scratches against her arm.

Overbalanced, she fell, instinctively clenching her fist, grasping for some purchase. Her fingers squelched in damp pulp, finding thin stiff things inside, like wires—sharp. They cut; she let go, but her fingers tangled among them. She stumbled, splashing into the shallows on her knees; her hand twisted, found more wire, cutting her palm and fingers—

Her cries brought Bel, who appeared behind her, steadying Rowan's body with her own, one hand bracing the trapped arm. "Don't move, you'll make it worse."

Rowan hissed between clenched teeth, "I think I've hurt myself." Where she had squashed it, the pulp was fluid, drenching her cuts, stinging wildly. She made an involuntary sound and squeezed her eyes shut. "What do I do?"

"For now, stay still. Do you have your balance?"

Rowan adjusted her knees minutely; the shift in position caused her hand to move in its trap, and more pain. She hissed again, then managed to say, "I'm steady."

"Stay put." Bel moved away. Wet sounds, crunches, tiny snaps. A sweet, greasy odor puffed into Rowan's face, again and again. At last she felt air on her forearm, and Bel's hands closed around her wrist. "Now stand up, but try not to move your hand."

Using her foot, Bel had flattened the gray surface around Rowan's hand down to the dirt of the creek bank. Clear blue fluid puddled and ran into the water, oozing from white pulp pierced by broken black spines. Around Rowan's hand, the substance was untouched; a soggy mass, white above her hand, pink below, looped throughout with glittering black.

Rowan stood, left elbow awkwardly bent as Bel braced her hand against movement. Despite this, there was a small shift; the steerswoman made a choked sound and beat her thigh with her right fist, twice, then froze and gasped, "Now what?"

Bel eyed her. "Relax your hand, but don't move."

She released Rowan, pulled out a knife, reversed it, and used the handle to carefully push the reddened pulp away from the coil. With thumbs and forefingers protected by two pieces of leather cut from her leggings, she snapped the sharp loops, one by one. Rowan watched, body tense and poorly balanced, breathing shallowly.

She fell to her knees when her hand came free, then cursed viciously and at length when Bel submerged it in the creek. The water cleaned but did not soothe. Eventually Rowan said, "Let go."

Both women were in the shallows, Bel on one knee, Rowan half-sprawled. There was more red in the water than the steerswoman cared to see. Her hand was an undifferentiated mass of pain, and when she pulled it from the creek, blood and water trailed down along her arm, dripping off her elbow. She breathed carefully, slowly. "Was that thing poisonous?"

"Not much." Bel was watching her. "Just enough to make it hurt worse."

Rowan uncurled her fingers carefully and studied the damage. "Do you still have one of those bits of leather?" Her voice was tight.

Bel did; and before Rowan could react, Bel used it herself, reaching over and swiftly extracting one three-inch spine that had entered Rowan's hand from the side and extruded from the base of her palm.

The steerswoman had run out of curses. "Thank you," she said weakly.

"Are you going to faint?"

Rowan looked around. The light was too bright, the creek surface too distant. "I don't think so." She blinked. "I've a needle and thread in my pack."

Rowan discovered, in the most unpleasant way possible, that Bel was not adept at small work. The Outskirter's hands were trained for strength, not nimbleness. Strength was what she used, pinning Rowan's arm against a rock as she worked, forcing it abruptly under water to clear the blood. And Rowan used her own: spending all her energy in clutching one arm around her drawn-up knees, trying to direct all tension away from her brutalized left hand.

Bel substituted patience for skill, and repair was a long process. "Yell if you like," she said cheerfully. "It won't bother me."

"I don't care to," Rowan replied, or tried to reply; the sounds emerged from behind her clenched teeth as a rasping hiss, oddly intonated.

Bel found it perfectly comprehensible. "Suit yourself." But Rowan did yell, at another unexpected dousing, when the icy water found a way to wash in directly against one finger bone. It was like being struck by a hammer.

The sound left her too exhausted to struggle, and she sat limp, unable to raise her head. Her face ached where she had pressed it against her leg. "What was that thing?" Her own voice sounded distant.

Bel spared a glance from her work—and to Rowan's utter astonishment, she replied with an outrageous imitation of the steerswoman's own style of speech, complete with the throaty vowels and crisp consonants of Rowan's northern accent. "An Outskirts plant, called a lichen-tower. It grows along watercourses, and possesses—" She paused to find a suitably pedantic phrase. "—a stiff spiraled internal structure, permitting it to grow to extreme heights—"

She did not finish her explication, as Rowan became weakly hilarious. Bel paused to watch her. When the gasping laughter ran down she gave, for the first time, what Rowan considered fair warning. "Again." She pulled Rowan's hand into the water, pulled it out, treating the limb as if it were not a part of Rowan's body, but only attached to it. She resumed her repairs, this time on the palm side.

Rowan eventually found her voice again. "It should be tall," she said, of the lichen-tower; Bel had mentioned such plants before.

"It was a young one."

They did not travel the rest of that day, and in the afternoon, as Rowan watched blearily, Bel systematically destroyed eight immature lichen-towers growing on the creek's bank, all of which Rowan had assumed to be boulders. Whether the destruction represented revenge, custom, or had some useful purpose, the steerswoman was too tired to ask.

*   *   *

Rowan learned to fear the Outskirts, and remembered that she ought to have done so from the outset.

She was accustomed to fearing specific dangers in the Inner Lands: wolves, bandits, lightning, storms at sea, and, eventually, the enmity of wizards. But the world was background to those things, and they inhabited it. Bel had told her of specific Outskirts' dangers, and Rowan now knew many by name and habit; but they seemed discrete, separate, existing within no comprehensible framework, so that the next day, when Bel stopped her with a gesture and the merest touch on her arm, Rowan froze instantly, scanning for danger. "What is it?"

Bel replied only by pointing. Rowan followed her finger to the horizon, but saw only the chaos of moving colors. There was no way to discern anything unexpected against such a view.

She looked at her friend. Bel's expression was not one of caution, but amusement. "You don't see it?"

Rowan relaxed somewhat, spreading her hands. "Where?"

Bel continued to point, but walked forward, circling to the left. When she came around to face Rowan again, her finger indicated the space between them.

Rowan squinted. "Insects?" She realized that there was a cloud of insects at just head height, some circling, some hovering. Bel gestured Rowan forward, and the steerswoman circled as Bel had, keeping her eyes on the insects, puzzled. They seemed unable to move beyond some defined boundary; some of those hovering appeared to hover with motionless wings—

When she reached Bel's side, the angle of sunlight caught slim silver traces around the insect cloud. "Is that a spiderweb?" The cloud was in midair; there was nothing nearby from which to hang a web. Bel's finger moved carefully, outlining a shape.

The flying and suspended insects were contained within a canted oval dome of gossamer, its long axis pointed downward. Below the axis Rowan saw a bit of redgrass blade, less than an inch long, apparently floating at knee height, then saw the line that attached it . . .

Bel's finger traced again, along a ghostly line that slanted down from the open side of the dome. The line came to ground, upwind, and the configuration came together in Rowan's eyes—but she shook her head in disbelief. "A kite?"

She followed the tether to its root, and met the kite-flier: a skinny four-limbed bug, some six inches tall, standing knock-kneed among the redgrass. One sticky arm clutched a redgrass reed of extremely dubious stability; the other held a ball of spittle from which the fine line extruded, ascending to the aerial web.

Moving quietly, Rowan lowered herself to the ground beside it, cradling her injured hand in her lap. "What is it?" She grinned at the bug, enchanted.

Bel tilted her head. "I thought you'd like it. It's a trawler."

" 'Trawler,' as in a fishing boat?" Rowan laughed out loud. "It's trawling the air!"

"I don't know about fishing boats, but 'trawler' is its name. When it's caught enough flying bugs, it will pull its shoot to the ground and have lunch."

"The shoot is its net?" Rowan leaned closer to the bug and sighted up along the tether. The bit of redgrass hanging from the shoot provided stabilizing weight. The trawler, outraged by the steerswoman's proximity, voiced two sharp clicks. Rowan startled, and the creature took the opportunity to transfer the spittle-ball onto a grass stem, then clambered quickly away through the redgrass, all knees and elbows.

"That's right. If a hawkbug catches a trawler, sometimes it will save the shoot, and drag it through the air itself. The shoot can last for days."

That afternoon, as they rested before dinner, Rowan drew out her logbook, clumsily, with one hand and one elbow, and settled down to update the entries. She had had no inclination to write since leaving the last tribe, and no mental effort to spare; but it occurred to her that an attempt to notate her observations might aid in her comprehending them more completely, and provide a distraction from the pain of her hand.

Bel had her own occupation: smoothing a patch of ground near her bedroll, she painstakingly began drawing letters in the dirt with a stiff redgrass reed, practicing writing. Rowan had found that the Outskirter had a sharp memory for the shapes and sounds, but unused as she was to small work, her letters tended to look very peculiar, starting large and growing larger as she tired.

As she worked, Rowan became aware of a faint humming sound, like the passing phantom noises one's own ears might manufacture. In retrospect, she realized that it had been continuing for some time. Experimentally, she blocked her ears, and the noise vanished. Bel looked up from her laborious writing. "What's the matter?"

"An odd sound," Rowan replied, trying to pinpoint its direction. It was impossible; the dim sound lay at the threshold of hearing and was intermittently masked by the sound of redgrass.

Dropping her reed, Bel stood and scanned the land, then closed her eyes, listening. "I don't hear it."

"It's very faint."

"What does it sound like?" But at that moment the breeze died, the grass quietened, and Bel caught the noise. She froze, then smoothly and soundlessly dropped into a sitting position on the ground. She said nothing, but held Rowan's gaze with an expression of warning.

"What—" Rowan began, but a minute motion of Bel's hand silenced her, and she froze. The noise became somewhat louder.

Minutes passed, and eventually Rowan attempted to move one leg to a more comfortable position; she received a look, a widening of Bel's eyes more communicative than words.

The Outskirter was afraid. It took Rowan a long, stunned moment to believe it.

Bel was her guide, Bel was the native, Bel was the warrior, wise in the ways of her land. Never before in the Outskirts had Rowan ever seen her truly afraid. It came to Rowan shockingly that if Bel was frightened, then her own survival depended upon following instructions instantly, completely.

Bel wanted silence and stillness. Heart pounding, muscles yearning for action, Rowan complied.

More time passed. Rowan listened to the inhuman humming, watching Bel for more unspoken signs. Their two shadows slowly lengthened.

The noise grew again, and Rowan found that she could locate its direction: south by southeast, behind her, to Bel's left, distance unknown. Bel visually gauged the distance between her own hand and her sword hilt, a mere foot away within easy reach. Rowan carefully did the same.

The sound faded slightly, stopped, then abruptly returned, much quieter. Rowan thought of the low hills that lay behind her; the source of the humming had passed behind one and emerged again, farther away.

At long last it diminished to near-inaudibility, regaining a directionless quality. Bel relaxed, then caught Rowan's eye with a questioning expression, pointing to one ear. Realizing that her hearing was sharper than the Outskirter's, Rowan moved only her fingers in a cautioning gesture.

. At last the noise disappeared, and she spread her hands to communicate the fact, not presuming to decide for herself whether the danger was over.

Bel drew and expelled a deep breath. "Close, but not too close." She rose, somewhat stiffly, her eyes still wide, her gaze flicking about the landscape.

"What was it?" Rowan found that her jaw ached. She had been sitting with teeth clenched for over two hours.

"A demon," Bel said. She turned slowly in a complete circle, making a careful study of the surroundings, listening and looking. Rowan attempted to rise, stumbled as a cramp took her left leg. "They're rare," Bel continued. "They make that noise, constantly. We're lucky that your hearing is so sharp. I might not have noticed in time."

Rowan massaged her left calf awkwardly with her right hand and followed Bel's example in searching the horizon for she knew not what. The land was empty, the grass near-silent in the stillness. "What would have happened?" There were legends of demons in one part of the Inner Lands, but legends only.

"It would have come for us, and killed us." Bel looked at the direction where the sound had vanished, and began to relax. "They're attracted by sound."

"All sound? Do they chase goblins, tumblebugs? Tanglebrush?"

"I don't know. But if one hears you, it comes. They've destroyed entire tribes." She began gathering their equipment, urgently. "Let's leave. Now."

Rowan packed her pens, her ink stone, her book, her bedroll. "Is there no way to defend against them?"

"If you stand in front of one and wave your sword, it sprays you with a fluid that melts your flesh from the bones."

Rowan grimaced. "And if you don't wave your sword?"

"It does the same."

"What do they look like?"

"No one I know has seen one." Bel rolled her cloak, tied it to her pack. "I know some tales, and one song where a demon appears. They're said to stand as tall as a man, colored silver or gray, and have arms like slugsnakes. They have no head, and no face."

Rowan attempted to envision it. "How do they see?"

"No one knows."

Their camp dismantled, the women moved off quickly, in a direction opposite from the demon's last known position. The new route headed more to the north than had been planned. Rowan made no complaint. She walked behind her silent friend, listening to the Outskirts.

12

*T*hey did not hear the demon again, but began to sleep in shifts, for fear of missing its approach. With less rest, they traveled harder in the mornings, when they were freshest, paused more briefly for noon meal, and stopped earlier in the evening. Soon, Bel was again searching for tribe signs; Rowan dizzied herself by trying to do the same, scanning horizons that daily became more obscured as the travelers approached and entered an area with many small, high hills.

Bel paused on one crest, again signaling Rowan to a stop beside her. The morning was windy, the grass raucous, roaring, and the contrasts of color across its surface flaring, bright and alive, like fire. The sky above was blue and white, motionless, frozen. Rowan felt trapped between the land and sky, had a wild impression that she might suddenly fall up, away from the jittering, burning hills into the icy heights. The Outskirter gazed eastward, and Rowan waited; with the slackening of her wearied concentration, the landscape collapsed into visual chaos.

Eventually she realized that Bel was not examining the land to the east, but only facing in that direction; her attention was elsewhere. Rowan studied her: a clear and familiar shape against the writhing background. Bel stood with a lazy nonchalance that to Rowan's eyes communicated total alertness. Rowan spoke, quietly and cautiously. "What?" Her thoughts immediately went to the demon; above the grass noise, she could not hear any hum.

Bel gestured at the landscape: a motion so elaborately communicative that the steerswoman instantly recognized it as false, designed to deceive. "We're being followed. Look confused."

Rowan gazed at the distance, slowing, forcing the view into some semblance of true land, hills, rocks. She shook her head as if perplexed. "Is it a person?" she asked.

"I don't know. If it is a person, he's very good. It might be a wounded goblin, going along the ground, or a small goat."

"Can you tell where it is?"

"Not exactly. Behind us. West."

Rowan startled at a noise. "What was that?" A brief rattle, not behind, but ahead.

"Slugsnake in a tanglebrush," Bel said indifferently. Slugsnakes were harmless.

Bel threw up her arms as if the lay of the terrain had defeated her, and slipped out of her pack. "Pull out your maps, and settle down as if you're checking our route. I'll go ahead, like I'm scouting, and try to double back and catch him."

Rowan began to comply, vainly trying to sense the follower without looking in his direction, attempting to use a combination of hearing, peripheral vision, even smell. Her skin tingled, as if, with her other senses useless, she might manage to locate him by some extension of touch.

She understood Bel's strategy. "I'm bait," she muttered, uncapping her map case.

"You have to be. It's too late to hide, and you can't move without being seen. I can. If he tries to come near you, I may spot his motion. Keep your sword handy."

Bel wandered off to the east, and Rowan seated herself on the Outskirter's pack, holding the map before her. The slugsnake rattled its tanglebrush.

The wind faltered, faded to silence, then rose again, slowly. At first quietly, then more loudly, the grass began again its tapping, hissing, until it became a sound so constant as to hold no meaning whatsoever.

A person who followed in hiding could mean no good; there was danger, and Rowan was alone.

And suddenly, under the impetus of that danger, Rowan accepted the sound of the Outskirts, without conscious thought; she accepted it and dismissed it. It was expected, it was background. It held no information; with her eyes on her charts, she waited for other sounds, for something unexpected.

Unexpectedly, the tanglebrush had not rattled in the wind.

Under the guise of comparing chart to landscape, Rowan rose and looked in that direction. Bel was there, crouched to the ground, her body blocking the tanglebrush from view. Rowan looked away.

But Bel's body could not have blocked the sound.

Rowan looked again. Bel was not there, but her cloak was—draped over the brush in perfect semblance of a cloaked Outskirter crouched among the redgrass.

As if absently, the steerswoman moved closer to her pack and sword. Turning in a slow circle, she alternated outward glances with longer gazes at her map. The chart covered territory left far behind, days ago; she did not truly see it, but tried to study the images she gained from each outward glance, tried to absorb them, to hold them clearly in her mind.

To the east: hills, slowly ranging lower in the twisting distance, and the decoy cloak in the foreground. South: small hills of writhing redgrass, then longer hills, rising to a false horizon.

West, where the follower was hidden: lower land, flatter, with occasional stands of tanglebrush, merging eventually into hazy distance. In the wild sweeps of motion, no recognizable sign of a person, nor of an animal. North: a peppering of single conical hills that rose above the grass and at the limit of sight, where red and brown merged to a dull brick red, a gray meandering line of what she guessed to be lichen-towers.

East, and she had finished her circle: the decoy, and no sign of Bel. Rowan was alone.

Her heart beating hard, she stared blindly at the chart in her hands; and suddenly, of itself, her mind added the quartered images together, completing the circle of her sight. The world came to her, entire and whole, all senses simultaneous, shockingly clear:

She stood on the rocky crest of a conical hill, part of a series that swept from the north, joining into wild ridges in the south, with flatland to one side, hills and dales to the other; grass covered the earth, a deep carpet, waist-high everywhere but the stony hilltops. The sky was a blue dome, arcing, perfect, clouds crowding in from the south; she felt the shape of those clouds as surely as if she were touching them.

To the eyes, sky and horizon met, but she knew that sky and land continued beyond sight: skies she had seen, land she had crossed herself, and farther lands beyond those. All touched each other: a continuum sweeping from the mountains west of Wulfshaven, across two great rivers, through green forest to red veldt to the place where she stood, and past her to the east, and the north, and the south.

She stood with stone beneath one foot, bare earth beneath the other; redgrass began below her position.

—Alone, on top of a bare hill. She made a perfect target.

She sat. Outskirters carried no bows. (Why not? No wood but tangleroot—too stiff? Too short?) A knife could be thrown. A tangleroot knife would be too thick to fly well, too dull to do damage at distance. She noted the distance of a thrown metal knife, mentally marking a safe circle around herself.

Wind shifted from east to north, and the tone of the chattering grass altered. To her mind, the sound was no sound, it was identical to silence; she ignored it. True sound in this world was patterned sound: a man walking, an insect hunting. She heard nothing.

Colored waves of turning and twisting redgrass—movement caused by wind, by its force and direction. The motion had a source and a reason; she did not try to hold the colors, or to watch them, but let them sweep unimpeded across her sight. And it came to her that she could use that motion, that what she sought was motion at odds with that patterned sweep, and that, if it were there, it would show clearly.

And then it came, suddenly and quickly, in the corner of her eye, a flicker of contrast so sharp that it seemed to burn: color out of pattern, diagonal movement against parallel—and sound: three crunches, as feet abandoned stealth. She found her sword and spun.

A thump, a wild rattle. Bel's cloak was on the ground. Grass hissing, leaves twisting, bright color showing the departing motion, as clear as a shout, as clear as a finger indicating: *There!*

The attacker was fleeing, crouched beneath the grass tops, the disturbance of his motion drawing a contrasting line within the sweeping colors. He had discovered Bel's ruse, had seen Rowan spin, sword in her hand, had lost his advantage.

Rowan heard Bel approach from behind, recognizing her steps as easily as if she walked among silence. "He fooled me. He went for me instead of you."

The angle of the motion changed abruptly and vanished; the person was moving south, artfully using the grass's motion as cover for his own. But he could only move at the same pace as the windy patterns; if he tried to move faster, then—

Brown where there should have been red, red instead of brown. "There!" She found that she had shouted it.

"He's very good," Bel commented.

The statement made no sense—Rowan could *see* him! "Can we catch him?" She wanted to, desperately, furiously.

"Too late."

He vanished again; he was far enough away that the wind's pace was safe. Rowan did not know his position.

No, she did: she knew his speed and his direction. She calculated, her eyes tracing the only possible invisible path. "Which way around that hill, do you think?" He could not climb it without being seen.

"It depends. He might be running to someplace in particular."

The hill would make eddies of the patterns, like water around a rock, hard to predict. If he passed on the near side, he would give himself away. "The far side," Rowan said.

"If he hasn't lost his head."

A brief splash of brown against red, an instant before it disappeared behind the hill. "There." And he was gone. The women were alone under the windy sky, above the chattering grass.

"He might have been a scout," Bel ventured.

"Would a scout attack as a matter of course?" Rowan asked, turning to Bel—

—and clarity of perception vanished as suddenly as a snapped twig. Its loss broke the steerswoman's heart. "Oh, no . . ."

"What?" Bel stood before her, solid and familiar—under a sky too wide, too blue, above a roiling meaningless mass of brown and red . . . The Outskirter turned to see if something behind her had prompted Rowan's reaction.

The steerswoman looked around: rising and falling slopes of color, spots of black, the horizon too near, nearer than she knew it to be. She sank to a seat on Bel's pack, hand limp around her sword hilt, and cursed, weakly and repetitively.

"What's the matter?"

I'm on a hill, Rowan told herself, and the rocky hilltop did become real; but it seemed to exist alone, as if floating unmoored on an ocean of red-and-brown waves. "I could see . . ."

"See what?"

See as a steerswoman saw: completely. No frantic, piecemeal stitching-together of sight and sound and scent; see entirely, feel herself in the world, reason what she could not perceive, and know it all as true.

"See everything," she said.

Closing her eyes, she sensed the hill below her as suddenly as if it had just risen up from the ground. She matched its shape with her memory, pictured the pattern of terrain it had inhabited so sensibly, considered the wise redgrass that had told her so much, so easily, and tried to add all those ideas to her inner vision of the world.

Experimentally, she opened her eyes again. Bel was crouched close in front of her, brows knit. Behind her were the hills that Rowan expected: but too flat, like ranked landscape cutouts in a traveling pantomime theater.

It did not matter. She told Bel, and she told herself, "I can do it. I did it, and I can do it again."

Bel said nothing.

Rowan spoke bitterly, a fury directed only at herself. "I *knew* what the grass was saying to me. If that man had come at me, I would have seen him, I could have taken him!"

Another realization struck her abruptly, and her anger vanished, replaced by shame. "Bel," she said, "you can't forever fight for two, guard two, feed two." She gave a weak laugh. "I can hardly believe it; that you've done this much, this long, for me . . ."

"I'm doing it for myself."

"Perhaps. But . . ." Briefly, patterns and pieces fell together in her mind, then fragmented. There was reason and sense behind the Outskirts; it was a place, as surely as was the Inner Lands, with elements interlocking: wind, grass, water, life . . .

"I don't care to be a burden to you," she told her friend. "Starting now, I will . . . I will cease to be some *package*, that you have to deliver."

Bel considered, studying Rowan's face; and then she nodded satisfaction. "Good. It's about time."

13

*R*owan dreamed of the sea.

The water was gray and sunlit silver, alive with small waves moving clean and regular as mathematics. Above, the sky was a perfect clear dome of blue, where stars were faintly visible, although it was full daylight. High overhead the Harp stood, Vega gentled to dim comradeship with the coolly brilliant sun.

She stood on a deck, the wind two points aft of starboard, her ship running fast on a close reach. The vessel was shaped like a cargo ship, but small, no more than fifteen feet abeam. Perfectly fitted, it was of simple design, without ornamentation, but constructed of the richest of woods, dark-stained and gleaming, showing everywhere the handiwork of master craftsmen.

Facing aft, she saw that the poop was deserted. Without looking elsewhere, she knew that there was no one else aboard.

She controlled her ship by thought alone.

She was in no way surprised by this. It seemed to her that it was proper, but it was immensely difficult. Mere wishing was not sufficient;

every detail of control must be held consciously, simultaneously. The angle of the rudder, the set of the sails, the particular tension on each sheet—she was aware of each, as aware as if by touch, and each must be maintained, or moved, in perfect respect to the currents of wind and water, by force of will and wisdom.

Constant, interlocking, interdependent, the details filled her mind completely, but other than these, her thoughts were few. Within this work, there was no room for such things as personality, identity. In command of all, she was herself diminished. Time passed in her dream, and as slow as stones, a feeling began to grow in her that she had another task at hand. Eventually she understood that it was that she must also chart her course. Taking navigational sightings, the subtle interplay of numbers—all seemed beyond her now. Yet it must be done.

Turning her body and making the few steps to the plotting table were actions identical in kind to her control of the ship itself, and had to occur without lessening her other awareness. Standing still at the plotting table freed her to see what was lying on it, and she found that she possessed no calipers or rulers, no pens, no charts. Alone on the table lay only a huge leather-bound book.

A single ribbon marked a place. She eased slack into the jib sheet, adjusted the rudder more tightly against the current, and caused her hands to open the book.

Words: line after line, for page on page. Straining to encompass their meaning, she began to see that the words comprised specific, detailed instructions. Her course was here, described not by maps and headings, but by single words, one after another. Each individual action that would take her to her destination was laid out, precisely, step by step, moment by moment. She need make no choices, but only enact.

She was satisfied. The handwriting was her own.

And in her dream, it now seemed that she had been running in this fashion for a very long time. In her dream, it seemed fitting.

For an unmeasured length of time she traveled so, the sun never moving, the sea and stars never changing. Her mind was completely inhabited by the innumerable small and large details of control—constant, blending, endless—following her route without the need of thought, trusting the book and her previous self for the truth of her course and destination.

A moment came when she again added awareness of her hands and eyes to the sum of her task, and again a measure of her self faded briefly, then returned, as she turned another page.

Her eyes rested on the new words as she waited for comprehension to occur. She became aware that it was taking long to do so. Something had changed.

She struggled dully to stretch her attention to include more of the page, to piece together the lines of ink into comprehensibility. For an instant she succeeded, and the marks resolved—

Into broken lines, skewed letters. Huge, clumsy words trailing wildly down the page. Fragments of sentences, in a hand as blunt and awkward as a child's.

She was incapable of dismay. She turned herself back to her task. The ship hesitated, shied, settled. Her journey continued.

And beneath her endless work, behind her unwavering concentration, deep within her slow, cool thoughts, Rowan recalled from that book only three facts:

That the broken words had held no meaning to her; that they filled the rest of the book, to the very end; and that the handwriting was Bel's.

Very quietly, someone spoke her name.

14

"What?" She was on her feet, her question was spoken, and her sword was in her hand, before she realized that she was awake.

Bel was a silent shadow beside her, watching the darkness. She pointed with her chin, a motion only dimly sensed.

There was a flickering smear of light in the distance, yellow in the blackness and the blue-tinged starlight. "Brushfire?"

Bel did not reply, concentrating on the glow. She seemed to be listening, but not to the steerswoman.

Rowan studied the light. It was broadening. With no referents, there was no way to guess its size or distance. No breeze brought its scent; the air was still, humid, dead.

Something flared at its edge—a patch of tanglebrush, catching all at once, with a sudden, distant roar. Something moved across the light, then something else, then many things . . .

"Come on!" Bel was gone, running to the fire. Rowan followed, redgrass snagging at her trouser legs. She saw Bel pause, sweep once with her sword, and then continue. When Rowan reached the place she tripped over something in the grass, something in two pieces, that thrashed.

Over the rising roar of the flames, Rowan heard sounds: rusted hinges, a rhythmical clatter. There was a wordless cry from Bel, the sound she made in battle, but no clash of metal.

Rowan hurried on. Figures were visible in the firelight, flailing, converging on two points.

Something snagged at her left arm from behind, and Rowan spun to the right, momentum freeing her and adding force to the stroke of her sword as she came around again.

She had aimed at the height of a man's neck; the stroke swept harmlessly over the goblin's head. She let her sword spin her again, aiming for the creature's waist as she came around again.

It was gone. Then something raked at her scalp and tore her tunic down the back. She stumbled forward, turned left, struck out blindly in an upswing.

The blow caught the goblin under one arm, which separated from its body with appalling ease to fall twitching to the ground. The creature did not seem to notice. It clutched out with its remaining hand, and Rowan made a quick stab into its chest. It did not stop or fall or pull away, but pushed toward her, driving her point deeper. Its hand jerked forward at her; she ducked her head out of reach, and the hand clutched at the sword itself, trying stupidly to shove it aside. The edge bit deep into the finger joints.

Rowan thrust harder, tried to bring her blade down to slash the torso open. Too much resistance; she twisted instead and felt the point make a small slicing arc within the goblin's body. She gasped at the effort. "Gods below, don't you know when you're dead?"

It squealed and rattled, seemingly in frustration only, then freed its hand and reached again for her face. She kicked at its stomach, then pulled out her sword as it fell back.

A sound behind her. She turned and swung down at the next creature's shoulder. Her blade hit shallowly, then skittered off. The thing had hide like horn.

She dodged, struck at the arm joint from beneath, dodged, struck again. The creature closed on her as if it still had limbs to clutch her with.

For a frozen instant its face was inches from hers. By firelight she saw its features: hard brown flattened skull, six black knobs trailing down in a double row—eyes. Its mouth thrust forward at the end of a pointed chin, opening and closing, horizontally and vertically, four curved rasps as long as fingers at each corner.

She brought her sword up close to her body, caught the goblin under the chin, thrust back into its neck. The head fell back, the body forward.

An arm came across her from behind, serrated down its length, points angled inward. She pushed herself into the elbow, levering the wrist out with her hilt. Something snapped, and she was free. She turned back to face the fire.

The one-armed creature was flailing its remaining arm from the shoulder, its elbow and hand flapping uselessly. Rowan kicked it again, sending it into one of its fellows, and another came at her from the right. She knocked its arms aside, sliced off its head with an angled upstroke, did the same with the crippled one as it rose, did the same with the third, turned when a rattle told her there were more behind her again—

And she stopped counting.

She was moving constantly, too fast to think or plan, trusting the only strategy she knew would work. She dodged, took off their hands at the elbows, their arms at the shoulders when they reached for her, used the moment that followed to strike off their heads. The difficulty was in the numbers; in the time that she dealt with one, another was coming from behind, a third stepping over the first . . .

None of the creatures learned from the deaths of its fellows. They were stupid, like insects. They tried to grab at her slashing sword as if it were a club, lost their hands, their taloned fingers, and their lives by their own stupidity.

And the legs of the headless fallen continued to move. She tripped twice, once to end tangled among the thrashing dead limbs, and one of the living creatures fell on her, its mouth rasps closing on her sword arm . . .

Then its head tilted freakishly forward and rolled off over her shoulder. For an instant she saw a man above her, his wide dark eyes full of battle fury. He spun away.

Before she could rise, another goblin tried to fall on her and impaled itself on her sword. Rowan cursed. Using both hands, she swung sword and goblin over her, to smash the creature against the ground to her right.

For an instant, nothing attacked. She freed her weapon and set on another goblin, striking at its neck from behind.

It did not work; tough plates shielded the back of its neck. The goblin turned, and she struck again, up under the chin, and this time it did work. She seemed to have time, so she relieved it of its arms as well, as it staggered and fell.

She went for another, slipping her blade around it to reach the front of its neck . . .

After the third time doing this, she realized that she was now attacking them from behind, that their attention was on someone else.

There came a moment when the one she reached for fell before she struck it, and through the open space she saw the man again. In the three-second lull he looked at her in amazement, then shouted "Ha!" as if in greeting. He turned right, kicked a goblin that was almost on him, dispatched it with an efficient version of Rowan's technique, and turned again to deal with another on his left.

Rowan eliminated three more, from behind. The fourth was facing her but seemed undecided, as if it had forgotten something. It lost its head while it was waiting, and she met the man's eyes again across the creature's fallen body.

The onslaught was diminishing. Rowan had time to see that the fire was to her left; it had become a long undulating line trailing ahead of her. Behind, it had spread out into a fan. The flames seemed reluctant to move into the redgrass in her direction, and she realized that they were following an easier path along a growth of resinous blackgrass.

A goblin between herself and the fire line turned, surprised to see her. She felled it, and saw that others were moving between her and the flames, all their attention on the blaze. They seemed to be trying to touch it, but were driven back again and again by the heat. Their weirdly jointed arms snapped forward toward the flames; their heads rocked dizzily. They jittered on trembling legs.

She thought to go after them, had an instant to wonder if she ought, then turned to try and assist the stranger in his work.

"Get back!" It was Bel's voice. Rowan could see a knot of action beyond the man, realized that Bel was working her way toward him, saw that the man was working his way toward Rowan, and understood that her own job was to secure their escape route.

She turned and found that a handful of the creatures were coming in from the darkness, squealing and clattering as they scrambled toward her. She sidestepped one, heard a grunt from the stranger as he dealt with it, eliminated the next herself, and stepped back when a third stumbled over a tangle of quivering corpses. She trod on its neck, which snapped with a sound she found deeply satisfying.

She brought another down, and saw that nothing more stood between her and the darkness of the veldt. She looked back.

Only Bel was still in action, backing constantly toward the man, who walked slowly, matching her pace, watching all sides as he approached. His left arm was pressed close against his body; there was blood. Then Bel shouted once, and they both broke into a run.

Rowan led. Once she came upon one of the creatures, and paused to kill it. Later, in deeper darkness, another rose suddenly from the grass to clutch her around her arms, pinioning her. She cursed when its rasps grazed her cheek, then felt its left arm give way to the stranger's blade, sensed its head fall back from a two-handed twist by Bel.

She stumbled over its body, took a few steps, then stumbled again when something tried to pull her down. She almost struck out, then realized that it was Bel.

"Sit." Bel guided her into position and sat at an angle beside her, one shoulder against Rowan's. The stranger dropped to the ground and completed the triangle, and the three of them sat facing out, gasping for breath, watching the darkness. Rowan could feel Bel's heartbeat, and the man's, against her back.

They were on a slight incline, Rowan facing up, away from the distant fire. She tried to speak and found she had not enough breath. She listened instead, for a sound like a man walking alone, for a rasp and a rattle.

When their breaths began to quieten, Bel spoke. "How badly are you hurt?"

Rowan almost replied, then realized that the question was addressed to the stranger.

"Averryl, Leahson, Chanly." He paused for more air. "My left arm is bad. I may cross the line on that one." Cross the line, Rowan remembered: become a mertutial.

"Ha. Not with a right arm like yours. Bel, Margasdotter, Chanly."

There was a long pause before Rowan understood that it was her turn. "Rowan. That's my only name. Will those creatures come after us?"

"No. We're too far away now. With the fire going, they'll be more interested in it than in us."

"So it's helping us now?"

"That's right."

Rowan paused for more air. She could hear the distant roar and snap of the flames. The cries of the creatures were all squeals now, freakishly ecstatic. Other than that, the night was quiet.

She found her pulse slowing. "That's good." Behind her, Averryl was shaking. He swayed once. "We should see to your wounds, if we can in this dark," she said. "Does 'Chanly' mean you're related to Bel?"

She felt Averryl half turn in surprise at the question, felt him stiffen in pain at the movement. Bel supplied, "Yes, but likely far back, at the beginning of the line. There are a lot of Chanlys."

Averryl's breathing had slowed, but Rowan was disturbed by the way his heart was stumbling. He said to Bel, "Why doesn't she know that? She's not a child. Though she fights like one."

Rowan wondered how to react to the insult. "I'm from the Inner Lands," she told him, "and I know next to nothing about the Outskirts. I've never fought a goblin before in my life."

There was a moment's silence. "Rowan, I beg your pardon." He spoke with sincerity. "Knowing that, I change my opinion." His breaths came more quickly, shallower. "You are very brave, and very clever."

Rowan turned in time to catch him as he crumpled forward.

15

The steerswoman said, "His name is Averryl, Leahson, Chanly. He's one of yours, and he needs your help."

She stood in the lee of a small hill among many small hills, on shreds of redgrass, which were cropped to the roots and dying. A heavy wind drove across the sky, not touching her, but sweeping and snapping the patchwork cloak of the warrior who stood on the crest above. Rowan's sword lay on the ground at her own feet, hilt to the right, as she waited for a reply.

It was long in coming. The warrior shifted stance, paused as if in great thought, shifted again, then studied Rowan with eyes narrowed. "Averryl was lost four days ago," she said. Rowan noticed her gaze flick to Rowan's right, and guessed the next words before they were spoken. "Warrior, at three by you."

It was a lie. From Averryl's description of his war band's deployment, and its likely rearrangement after his disappearance, the nearest warrior should arrive from the opposite side. Rowan quashed a brief rise of anger; this woman knew nothing of the Steerswomen's traditions, nor could she recognize Rowan as a member of the order. Lies told under such circumstances carried no ban. Instead, Rowan took the ruse as confirmation of her own understanding of the war band's configuration.

"He was sheltering in a stone field not far from the stream southwest of here." Rowan wanted to turn to point, but decided that it would not be wise. "He awoke to find a troop of goblin jills settled nearby, between his position and the next point. He decided to work away from them, back to the previous point, and spent the day trying to slip through the approaching jacks without being noticed. By nightfall he found another troop of jills, and realized he was in the middle of a forming mating mob. He set a fire, hoping to distract them, and to focus their numbers, so that he might escape."

"That's a dangerous move." And extremely unlikely, the warrior's attitude implied.

"So it seems. It almost didn't work; the fire caught too quickly, and the goblins converged too rapidly. He was trapped. My companion and I were nearby and saw the light. We came to help."

The woman considered the information with a show of suspicion so extreme that it was obviously fabricated for effect. "It's too late in the year for mating mobs." She had straight black brows, large eyes, and a wide mouth. On such a face, emotions showed easily and were easily feigned.

"Perhaps that's true; I wouldn't know." Rowan grew annoyed again; providing Averryl's names ought to have constituted her own credentials. "But I have been told that the weather is much warmer this season than has been the case in previous years."

The suspicion grew further, into a parody of itself. "You're no Outskirter."

"No." The fact was obvious; but admitting to being an Inner Lander might amount to requesting to be victimized. "But my companion is. She's traveling more slowly, with Averryl, perhaps a day or so behind me."

"Because of his wounds." Disbelief dripped from her voice.

"Yes. As I told you." Averryl's guide might be called upon to fight for two people; Bel had decided that Rowan was the better choice to send alone for help. The steerswoman dropped her attempt to control her emotions. "And he told me that you yourself would be working this position. You're Jann, Linsdotter, Alace, and the man probably now sneaking up on my left should be Merryk, Karinson, Gena. Unless he's switched with the man at the inner point, who, I believe, is your own son Jaffry." She stood looking up at the woman, her feet broadly planted and her chin uptilted. She realized that, unarmed as she was, her pose made a proper Outskirterly show of defiance.

Jann broke her act with a lopsided grin. "Ha! Sneaking up on your left, is he? Ho, Merryk!" She called across the distance. "Stop sneaking up, there's a good fellow! We've found Averryl!" She added wide-gestured signals to clarify the information.

"About time," came the shouted reply. An Outskirter seemed to emerge from the ground and began working his way toward the pair.

Although he was not tall, he was the broadest person Rowan had ever seen, and seemed to carry more weapons than he might reasonably be expected to use in one lifetime. As he approached he added, "He was probably sleeping. I've tried to break him of the habit, but it's just no good. He backslides. Generally at night." Arriving, he studied Rowan a moment. "Good disguise."

Jann thumped him on the stomach. "That's his rescuer. And he fell asleep, true enough, in the middle of a mating mob." She recounted Rowan's story for his benefit, as all irony dropped from his attitude.

At the end, he nodded decisively. "Good. Jann, you work your way inward, and pass the word for a reinforcement for my point. And have them double the middle line in this quarter. There might be a good number of loose goblins wandering around that never reached the fire."

"That's an excellent plan, except for the personnel," Jann told him. "*You* work inward and have Orranyn send a replacement for my position, and—" She turned back to Rowan. "In what direction did you leave them?"

"Southwest."

"And for Jaffry's point as well," Jann said to Merryk, "and double word out to him to intercept us."

"Now, Jann, a sortie dragging train is bull work. I'd do better—"

"That's wrong. If we're going out to meet the odd goblin with a wounded man in tow, we need people who are fast, and that's me and Jaffry. And if any of the beasts try to break to center, we need someone solid working this point, and that's you. Nothing gets past you."

Merryk rocked on his heels musingly. "That's true."

"And it's four for one if we should need to drag train. Do we?" This to Rowan.

Rowan was following the conversation with a great deal of difficulty. "I'm sorry, but you're using words I don't understand. Or using them differently than I do."

"Can Averryl walk?"

"Yes, but not easily, nor for long. He's lost a good deal of blood, and I believe he's in more pain than he admits to."

"We'll manage." Jann sheathed her sword and, with a jerk of her chin, directed Rowan to recover her own weapon. Merryk set off at a flat run to the northwest and vanished instantly among the little dells.

"Lead on," Jann instructed. Rowan complied, the warrior falling in on her left, one half step behind, Bel's position in the Inner Lands. It made Rowan feel a bit odd, as if the days had unrolled back to the time when she had been the leader, and the answerer of questions, in the Inner Lands. Her boot slogged into a puddle of goat muck, and the illusion vanished.

They traveled some time in silence. The whistling wind across the denuded hilltops was a sound so constant that it vanished from her awareness, even as it covered the sounds of their footsteps. Rowan found that she missed the sound and sight of standing redgrass; she had learned to depend on the information it communicated. But a tribe had passed through here, and tribes laid behind them a trail of desolation.

For the sake of conversation, Rowan tried to frame a question for Jann, one that might not be taken as a threat to her tribe's security. She was about to ask when a male voice spoke.

"Fletcher," it said in a venomous tone, and Rowan could not tell if the word was a name or a curse.

She just prevented herself from stopping short and turning to face the newcomer, suspecting that it would merely advertise her inexperience. This was Jaffry, she realized, Jann's son, come to join them as planned. How long he had been walking in their company, she had no idea.

Jann replied. "If Averryl dies, we'll make it a blood duel." She was answered by a surly grunt, and Rowan took a moment to glance back.

Jaffry was a subdued young man just past boyhood, with his mother's dark features and a long, angular body. He had fastened his cloak down the front, transforming himself into a loping piebald pillar with a human head. Taking the opposite approach from Merryk, his only visible weapon was an Outskirter sword, its hilt above his right shoulder, and he carried no pack or supplies that Rowan could see. He had assumed a complementary position to Jann's: on Rowan's right, two paces behind. The three of them made a lopsided flying wedge, defending against no seen enemy.

"Shall I make the challenge, or do you want it?" Jann continued.

Her son was slow in replying. "Me. He's beneath you. There'd be no contest."

"Ha." Jann grinned broadly. "A boy should be proud of his mother. And you could use that sword of his. Now this one," she said, indicating the steerswoman, "she's got a good sword, too. I'll tell you now"—this to Rowan—"if you stay around very long, I'll win it from you. Just to give you fair warning."

Rowan silently thanked Bel for the practice sessions. "I think," she said with a degree of pride and confidence, "that I'll keep it." A black pit marked a burnt-out stand of tanglebrush, one of Rowan's chosen landmarks, and she adjusted her course. They trudged on across the rolling landscape.

Somewhat later, Jann spoke again. "Perhaps," she said to her son cheerfully, "the goblins got to Fletcher, as well."

Jaffry's reply was inarticulate, but seemed to contain a hopeful note.

16

"And where was Fletcher in all this?"

Averryl was sitting propped against Bel's pack, scooping handfuls of gruel to his mouth from a wooden bowl with his good hand, Bel holding the bowl off the ground before him. She eyed Jann at the question, then with a glance warned Rowan to keep her curiosity to herself.

Rowan was annoyed. Bel had managed to impress upon her that a stranger asking too many questions about details of a tribe's defense might be taken as a raid scout, and Rowan had successfully controlled her instincts while traveling with Jann and Jaffry. But as much as she disliked not asking questions, she liked less being constantly reminded of the necessity.

"I don't know. We relayed at sunset. The goblins were between us, so I tried to work toward Garvin's position when I found myself surrounded." He studied the bowl as if it required all of his concentration to do so. "What is this?"

"I don't know," Bel said.

"Maize," Rowan provided. "It grows in the Inner Lands. A tall greengrass with edible seeds. You grind the seeds and boil them in water for this kind of gruel."

He followed the explanation with pain-bleared difficulty. "It's good," he said.

Jann seemed about to make peevish protest to his changing the subject, then stopped herself and began again, patiently. "You didn't find Garvin."

"There was no sign of him. Here's something." He indicated Rowan. "That one." He was slightly feverish, rambling. "Bel told me. If you ask her a question, she has to answer. *Has* to. It's a rule."

Jann spared Rowan a glance of perplexity. "That's stupid," she said, and with no more consideration dismissed the steerswoman. "Fletcher," she began again. "Fletcher and Garvin both should have seen your fire from their positions. They should have come to help you."

"Then they're dead. Fletcher's in heaven and Garvin's in hell. Can't help me from there." Rowan had never heard Outskirters use Christer religious terms; it struck her as odd. Apparently it had the same effect on Averryl. "Funny way to think of it," he said. He closed his eyes and leaned back against Bel's pack, abandoning the rest of the gruel. "I'm going to rest now," he declared.

Jann made an exasperated sound, but laid one hand on his good shoulder sympathetically. "You do that." She checked the sun's position. "We'll stay here for another two hours," she told the others, and rose. "We can try to move after that. The tribe may move to meet us, but we can't count on it. We could be on our own for a week." She took in Rowan, Bel, and Jaffry in a sweeping glance of confident leadership. "How are our supplies?"

"Rowan and I have some dry food from the Inner Lands, like that maize flour, and powdered beef. About twenty sticks of bread from the last tribe we met . . ."

"Some goat strips and a bit of rabbit that's rancid by now," Rowan added.

Jann jerked her chin questioningly at Jaffry, who paused, grinned a shy grin, and then from somewhere about his person extracted half a smoked goat leg.

Jann showed mock admonishment. "Where did you get that?"

"Had it for days."

She beamed. "What a clever boy."

They settled in, Bel feeding the fire with lopsided squares of peat. The remainder of the gruel was passed to Jann and Jaffry. The youth's eyes widened at the unfamiliar taste, and showed regret when the last of it was gone.

When the meal was finished, Jann bundled her cloak into a cushion for her back and settled against her pack to doze. Bel caught Rowan's eye, then leaned over and tapped the sole of Jann's boot to get her attention. "When we reach your tribe, we're going to claim shelter."

Jann sat up quickly, her dark brows knit. "I don't know about that."

"It's not for you to decide. Unless your tribe has taken to sending its seyoh to work the outer circle."

Jaffry was seated facing away from the group, watching the horizon. He turned to give his mother a sidelong look of amusement, then turned away. Jann said to Bel, "I can't promise anything . . ."

"We don't need promises from you. We saved your man. And we were wounded, as well. Show her your back, Rowan."

The deep scratches itched madly. Rowan made to comply, with some embarrassment, but Jann waved dismissal.

"I believe you," she said to Bel. "Well, you know your code, I suppose. I didn't think so, from her." She jerked her head in Rowan's direction. "She looks a bit out of place. It's odd to see someone like you travel with her."

Rowan disliked being referred to in the third person. "We work well together," she said. "And I've learned a few things in the last month. Enough, for example, to eliminate more goblins than I could count at the time."

Jann studied Rowan with a gaze that doubted her every statement. "Well," the warrior said reluctantly, "it's a sure thing you'll be given shelter, so as far as I'm concerned, you're part of us. So I'll ask you—" She became intent. "Didn't you see any sign of other warriors when you found Averryl?"

Bel shook her head. "Averryl and the goblins, that was all."

"According to Averryl," Rowan put in, "the nearest man was due east of him, with another south by southwest. From the course your tribe was following, if the goblins were as spread as Averryl described, the man to the east must have met them first."

"It seems like Averryl told you a lot."

"Does it matter? If we're to be given shelter, as you say?"

Bel was drawing concentric circles among the torn grass roots. "He told me more after Rowan left." She pointed to her sketch. "Garvin at three, Averryl at four-thirty, and Fletcher trailing at six."

Jaffry grumbled near-inaudibly. "Best place for him." The trailing position was considered safest for warriors of below-standard skill.

Jann ignored him, studying the circles on the ground. "Garvin could have been driven north and outward. That doesn't explain Fletcher."

"He might have seen the fire," Bel hazarded, "tried to approach, and was felled himself before he could get close enough to Averryl."

"Maybe," Jann allowed with great reluctance.

"Or been driven back," Rowan suggested.

"Or run," muttered Jaffry.

"Enough," Jann told him without heat. "We're not trying to prove cowardice."

Rowan considered. "What are you trying to prove?" she wondered.

It was Bel who answered, head tilted and eyes narrowed speculatively at Jann. "Incompetence."

"Perhaps." Jann leaned back again, arms crossed on her breast. She seemed to be following some inner thought, and her face lost its animation in the motionless pursuit, her dark brows a straight black line across her face, black eyes turning dull as chips of cold coal. The contrast disturbed Rowan; something alive in this woman had drifted to icy stillness. Jann looked, in her quietude, more remarkably like her son.

Bel watched in puzzlement, but did not interrupt, and Rowan followed her example.

The silence seemed to settle and spread, and the hot east wind faded, leaving the air cooler, but dull and heavy as iron. The cook-fire snapped as bits of blackgrass in the peat flared minutely, and a tiny rustling betrayed the presence of a ground bug, scavenging nearby. Far above, a hawkbug dipped, rose, and hovered, its wings a blur of pale translucent pink against massing clouds to the east.

The land to the east sloped and settled to a broad flat plain, brown with redgrass cropped too close to survive. In the distance, lichen-towers marked the banks of an unseen brook, and beyond them the piled clouds grew grayer to the horizon. There, lightning flashed. Rowan counted the seconds for the sound to reach her.

Eventually Jann remembered the travelers' presence and roused herself, with some difficulty. "No offense meant to you two," she began, then roused further, becoming herself, sounding cheerfully nonchalant. "But let's not talk of it. It wouldn't help, and it might affect your opinions . . ."

"Our opinions will matter," Bel told Rowan, "if the tribe accepts us for more than a short time."

"Matter how?"

"If this Fletcher person is alive," Bel said, "it sounds as if you and I might help decide that he should die."

17

"You kill incompetents?"

"If enough people die from their incompetence."

They were making their way slowly across the land, moving northeast to intersect with the tribe's presumed course. Bel continued. "You can't keep an incompetent person in the tribe. And if he's too stupid to see that he's incompetent as a warrior and chooses to cross the line by himself, then he's a danger."

"Fletcher's not incompetent." Averryl spoke between steps; his left arm was strapped close against his body, and a stiffness seemed to have spread down his entire left side. He limped heavily, moved slowly. "He's different." Another step. "Not a crime." Step. "If he could help . . . he would have . . . so he couldn't."

"You shouldn't talk," Rowan advised. "You need your breath for walking."

"Distracts me."

Jaffry signaled back, and Jann and Averryl stopped in response, Rowan and Bel following suit. The young man continued forward, then stopped and made broad gestures with his arms to the distance. Far off, Rowan could discern a tiny, gesturing figure. "Can you tell what he's saying?" she asked Bel.

The Outskirter shook her head. "It's different for each tribe."

"It's a scout," Averryl said. "Maud. Sent back to us." A pause as more signals were exchanged. "She has supplies, if we need them." More gestures. "Jaffry's saying that we don't." The communications ended, and the figure angled away. Jaffry beckoned, and the travel resumed.

Night fell none too soon, and dinner consisted of breadsticks and slices of smoked meat. They soaked Averryl's bread in water to soften it, and he consumed only a little meat, lying down to eat.

He watched the darkening skies with eyes too bright. "Rain," he said. "The weather's been strange, but I'm learning it. Heat lightning in the east, that means rain."

This was against Rowan's native logic, but contradicted nothing she had seen since entering the Outskirts. Jann was dubious, but to reassure Averryl she permitted Rowan and Bel to pull their canvas rain fly from Bel's pack. Averryl was bedded down beneath the slanting fly, the others on bedrolls nearby.

When the rain came at midnight, they gathered around the open sides of the shelter. There was no room for all of them inside; instead they sat on their folded bedrolls, facing inward. Cloaks were arranged so that the hoods lay across the top of the canvas to seal out the rain, the rest of the material draping to the ground down their backs. Averryl slept on, heavily; neither the rain nor the maneuvering woke him.

Soon it was discovered that Rowan's cloak repelled water best, and was sufficiently wide to close the entire tall end of the shelter. They used it for that purpose, and Rowan, cloakless, bedded down in the cramped space next to Averryl's sprawled form.

Bel and Jann sat in the two remaining open sides. Jaffry found the remnants of a nearby tussock outside and, seating himself on it, transformed himself into a one-man vertical tent by swaddling his cloak about him and pulling the hood down across his chest.

Outside, chill rain came down in fine, hissing drops. Inside, the air was warm with the heat of four bodies, one fevered. Rowan curled on her bedroll and felt a bit guilty of her comfort. "I suppose," she said,

"you Outskirters can sleep sitting up." The sound of her voice seemed
not to disturb the injured man.

The darkness was absolute, and when Jann indicated the invisible
Jaffry with a jerk of her head, Rowan understood it only by its sound
and her knowledge of Jann's habits of movement. "On nights like this,
away from the tribe, we all sleep sitting up." She provided the information grudgingly, as if she felt any person ought to know this.

Bel sounded half-asleep already. "If I didn't know better," she murmured, "I'd say it was Rendezvous weather."

Jann was annoyed. "We had Rendezvous eight years ago."

"Mmn. But the weather . . ." Bel sighed a sleepy sigh.

Rowan couldn't resist. "What's Rendezvous?"

Bel stirred, then forced herself to wakefulness. "Rowan, must you
ask me now? I don't mind your being a steerswoman, but must you
make me one, too?"

"What's this?" Jann asked.

"She asked a question. By Inner Lands custom, you have to answer
a steerswoman's questions. Otherwise, they won't answer you when
you ask, and you might need to know."

Rowan laughed quietly. "I'm sorry, Bel. Yes, I want an answer, but
no, it doesn't have to be right now."

Jann was quiet a moment, then answered, puzzlement in her voice.
"Rendezvous is when we meet," she suppled hesitantly. Bel made a
sound of extreme disgruntlement, then noisily adjusted herself into a
more comfortable position.

Having found another source of information, Rowan decided to
bother Bel no more, and shifted closer to Jann, talking quietly so that
her friend might sleep. "By 'we,' you mean Outskirters? More than one
tribe?"

"Yes." Jann paused again. "Was Averryl right, do you actually have
to answer every question?"

"Yes."

"From anyone at all?"

"Yes. Unless they refuse my questions, or lie to me."

"Then," Jann said, "what are you doing here?"

Rowan smiled in the dark. "We're chasing a fallen star." The full
explanation could well occupy her until daybreak. "But information is

best passed by finishing one subject before moving to another. I'll tell all you want, but if you don't mind, can you tell me about the Rendezvous first?"

Jann considered, possibly gauging the importance of the information against a theoretical betrayal of her tribe's interests. Then she shrugged. "Every twenty years, all the tribes that can find each other gather together. Nobody fights, and nobody steals. We meet, share food and stories, dance . . ."

"A celebration?"

"Yes. Sometimes people will change their tribe at that time, usually because they fall in love; Rendezvous is a good time to do that. Or a person with an unusual skill might join a new tribe, if he thinks he'll do better there."

"Why every twenty years?"

"It's always been done that way."

"What did Bel mean about the weather?"

Jann was dubious. "In songs and stories about the events of different Rendezvous, the weather is strange. Whenever it's mentioned at all."

"Strange in what way?"

From the sound, Rowan assumed that Jann had made a descriptive gesture. "It changes, suddenly. Rain, and then a clear sky. Lightning when you don't expect it, tempests . . . But you can't take that as a fact, it's just an artistic consideration."

Rowan's reaction was delayed by her being taken aback by the phrase. "Artistic consideration," she repeated.

"That's right. It's symbolic, or a dramatic effect, or a contrast to the events. It serves the meaning of the story, the truth *inside* it. You can't assume it really happened."

Rowan was accustomed to Bel's conversation revealing unexpected flashes of intellectual complexity. But it was against common Inner Lands appraisal of the barbaric tribes to the east, and without being aware of it, Rowan had come to believe that Bel's more sophisticated traits were unique to herself, and not held by Outskirters in general.

The steerswoman had fallen back on the easier explanation. She was very surprised to discover, first, that she had made such an assumption, and second, that it was wrong.

Bel heaved an ostentatious sigh and resigned herself to joining the conversation. "It's not symbolic, it's true. My grandmother told me that in her time, you could tell when to Rendezvous just by the weather."

"But you only need to count. Twenty years."

"That works, too."

"But the weather doesn't work at all. I've been to two Rendezvous, and the weather was dry."

"It used to work. Now it doesn't."

Rowan spoke up. "Bel, weather can't be that regular. If Rendezvous happens every twenty years, one couldn't possibly count on bad weather each time. Unless bad weather is normal for the time of year, every year."

"No," Jann said. "Rendezvous comes at the vernal equinox." Rowan was again surprised by her choice of words: this time, a technical term used most often by sailors. "We have rain then, but not like this, and not hail and snow, as it says in the songs."

"It's in *all* the songs," Bel emphasized. "The weather used to be peculiar during Rendezvous, and then it changed."

"Suddenly, or slowly?" Rowan asked. A suspicion began to form in her mind.

Bel thought. "I don't know. But no one minded. It's much nicer to Rendezvous in fair weather. And the Face People stopped coming, too, which nobody regrets."

Jann asked, "Who are the Face People?"

Rowan knew the answer from earlier conversations with Bel. "The Face People are the last Outskirters, living far in the east. To the best of anyone's knowledge, beyond the Face People there are no more human beings at all."

"Why are they called the Face People?"

"The Face is their name for the part of the Outskirts they live in," Bel told Jann. "You're too far west for them to Rendezvous with you, but my tribe was farther out, and the Face People used to come. They're primitive. And nasty. And they eat their dead." Bel adjusted her cloak across her back again, letting in a brief gust of cold air. She pulled her bedroll around her legs. "I'm going to sleep now, so if you must talk, do it quietly."

But Rowan had one more question. "Why did they stop coming?"

"Perhaps they can't count to twenty."

Bel slept, and while she slept, in whispers, Rowan told Jann the tale of the fallen Guidestar.

18

*R*ain concealed the dawn.

Rowan was awakened by Averryl. He was attempting to rise, and had managed to push himself up to knees and one hand, then remained so, muttering unintelligibly, weaving as he shifted weight onto and off of his left leg, which seemed to pain him. Bel and Jann were no longer at their posts, and light from the open edges of the shelter was dim and tinged with brown.

Averryl was barely visible in the gloom. "Lie down." Rowan wrapped one arm beneath his chest and laid one hand against the small of his back, urging him down. "Come on, rest. It's too early." Against his skin, her hand and arm were immediately hot and wet.

He seemed not to hear her, but understood her hands. He collapsed, with something like relief, spoke in a loud, slurred voice that Rowan could not understand, and abruptly became completely still. Shocked, Rowan checked his pulse. It seemed too slow, and too forceful.

Through the open shelter sides, Bel and the others were nowhere in sight. Rowan took her sword and clambered outside—to be startled by a strange man, who was striding up quickly.

"He's in there?" he asked, then hurried forward and was under the shelter before Rowan could challenge him.

She stood bemused. Another scout, she hypothesized, then found her pack and soaked her spare blouse from the waterskin while rain drizzled down her neck.

The stranger was sitting on his haunches, studying Averryl silently. Rowan gave him one cautious glance, then set to bathing Averryl's back with the wet cloth. The man watched a moment, then without a word took the shirt from her and continued the job.

She sat back. "I'm Rowan," she said, then added, as she had learned to, "Only the one name."

"Garvin, Edenson, Mourah." He gestured. "Help me turn him."

The sick man, who had revived under the cool water, protested peevishly, but when the newcomer reassured him, he recognized the voice and struggled to become alert. "Garvin?"

"None other."

"Where were you?"

Rowan handed Garvin the waterskin, and he resoaked the cloth. "I never saw your fire. Met a troop and ran like a tumblebug. I know when I'm in over my head." He wiped the cloth down Averryl's chest. "Looks like you don't."

"I was surrounded."

"Mm. Well." Garvin examined, but did not touch, the injured arm. The wound itself was wrapped in linen torn from Bel's spare blouse, secured with thongs. Below this, the forearm showed a single raised ridge along the inside to the wrist, and the middle two fingers of the hand were visibly swollen. The other fingers and the thumb seemed normal, which followed no logic Rowan could discern.

Averryl relaxed under his comrade's ministrations, and presently Garvin caught Rowan's eye and jerked his head in suggestion that they speak outside.

The drizzle had stopped, and the air had begun to move, a light west wind. Garvin peered at the sky, then shook his head in incomprehension of the weather's pattern. "Do you think he'll lose the arm?" Rowan asked.

The warrior was surprised. "No. No . . ." His eyes were deep-sea blue in his tanned face, and an old scar arced from his left temple to the side of his nose. He studied the steerswoman speculatively from under bristling yellow brows, then, by way of explanation, held out his own thick forearm and with one finger traced a line that followed the ridge on Averryl's arm. "Goblin spit. Runs down the nerve, here." The finger ran down to his palm, which he tapped thoughtfully. "He'll lose the use of those fingers, for certain. He'll be able to use the arm itself, but he might not want to. It'll pain him forever."

Rowan nodded. She knew that damage to a nerve often resulted in paralysis of a part of the body farther from the backbone. "What about the fever?"

"Well, that's the thing. If he gets past that, he'll do well enough." With that he descended into internal musing, eyes automatically scanning the horizon as his expression faintly mirrored his thoughts.

Abruptly, the wind swept from west to north, and the clouds above began to roil. Garvin stared up, slack-jawed. "Look at that."

With uncanny speed, the cloud cover churned and seemed to tumble gray masses down toward them, which bled into streamers of mist that trailed off to the southeast before they reached ground. Breaks showed in the layers above, revealing a blue first faint, then brighter. Around the little camp, spots of yellow sunlight illuminated the decimated redgrass. To the north, a clearly demarcated line of clear weather appeared, sped toward them, swept in, arced overhead, and flew south, bringing a coldness that descended so suddenly that Rowan's ears popped.

She and Garvin traded looks of amazement. "Rendezvous weather?" the steerswoman hazarded. Garvin gave no reply.

A voice hailed, and, squinting against the brightness in the distance, Rowan recognized Bel, waving. The Outskirter paused to stoop to the ground, then approached at a jog trot, dragging something behind.

Leaving Garvin to tend Averryl, Rowan went forward and met her friend. "What do you have there?"

"A tent for Averryl. Did Garvin arrive?"

"Yes. But I meant, what are you carrying the tent on?"

"This is a train. No, don't examine it; pull it. I have to go back and help. The tribe is moving."

Rowan positioned herself between two poles whose grips were worn shiny from countless hands. "Where is the tribe going?" She took a moment to wonder where such lengths of wood had come from, in the treeless Outskirts.

"It's not going, it's coming. They're pulling everything up and moving here." She gave Rowan a dray-beast's slap. "Go."

By the time she reached the little camp, Rowan had acquired companions: six goats had come up from behind, passed, then doubled back to pace alongside her. They jittered, shaking flop-eared heads in disapproval of the barren ground.

Their voices drew Garvin from the shelter, and when Rowan dropped the train grips, he immediately fell to dismantling the conveyance, standing on one side and directing Rowan to imitate his actions on the other.

The frame of the train was made from two poles, some twelve feet long, and a four-foot spreader. Behind the grips, the gap narrowed away from the puller, as in a travois, but with a single small black wheel at the point. Between the grips and the wheel stretched a hide platform, apparently part of the tent itself. Garvin released the wheel on his side and twisted his pole, and it slid back, collapsing the structure. Rowan did the same on her side.

Hot damp breath blew down her neck, and something nibbled at her hair. Garvin reached across and shoved the goat away from Rowan; it protested, then clambered forward, over the train and past the rain fly. Two more goats joined it, appearing from the right, and when Rowan paused to look about, she counted a full dozen nervously wandering animals.

"Hey-oh, Rowan!" someone called from behind. Rowan turned, and the person waved at her from a distant rise, then angled away to the south. It was no one she knew.

Garvin was taking the poles themselves apart: they were constructed of four-foot lengths of tangleroot wood, the mated ends revealing curious twisting joints, reinforced by wood strips and leather straps. Rowan imitated Garvin's actions.

She spotted another warrior far off, moving from her right to her left, and understood that this was the direction the approaching tribe followed. More goats appeared, reluctantly trailing after the figure.

The steerswoman made to continue disassembling, but Garvin stopped her. "No. We want one long pole, one short each." That was what they had. He chased away a kid goat that was perched atop the folded mass of the tent, and began to untie lashings. The kid complained, skipped aside, and made a dash to regain its position.

It was swept from its feet by a tall woman, and draped across her shoulders as she strode into the camp and strode out again without pausing. There was another person beyond her, and yet another beyond, pacing her at measured distance, all warriors in gear, but without packs.

"Who chose this spot? It's terrible!" Two train-draggers had appeared, and dropped their loads. One fell to work, and the other fell to complaining, pointing here and there at inadequacies of the terrain. Three walkers with outsized packs came up to the cold remains of yesterday's fire, and examined it, shaking their heads, then scuffed dirt to cover it. They found a better location ten feet away, dropped their packs, withdrew implements, and set to digging a shallow hole. More goats straggled through.

Rowan and Garvin did not bother to take down the rain fly where Averryl sheltered; they drove stakes, looped thongs, and prepared to draw the stitched hide up and directly over the tarp itself. Four more draggers appeared, found positions, and began to disassemble their trains.

"There, there, *there!*" a high voice squealed, admonished by a quieter deep voice. A flock of children flurried forward, parting around Garvin and Rowan like a burbling tide around rocks as they passed. One little girl froze and stared at Rowan, giggling in hysterical shyness at seeing a stranger, and was drawn off by a bent-backed old man. "Hush and stay away, now, Averryl's sick." A serious-faced blond boy paused and stooped to peer in at Averryl, then stationed himself protectively nearby as a crowd of over a hundred goats of every size, age, and combination of colors swept in, through, and out again, exactly as the children had done. An elderly woman dropped her train by the new fire pit and began unloading blocks of peat.

Bel appeared, pulling a train, locked in conversation with a gray-haired man who spoke with much gesticulation and walked with a limp. She spared Rowan a wave. The man took an item from the train's platform, stumped over to Rowan, and handed it to her: a foot-square box of stiffened wool fabric, patterned in maroon and violet. Not knowing what else to do with it, she tucked it under the rising tent as she and Garvin lifted the lower end of its short uprights. The guardian boy left his post to help, pulling the tent's side into shape.

A shadow fell over Rowan's shoulder; she looked up and found three other tents, erected back-to-back in a square with her own. As she secured the last guy lines, a woman nearby said, "Like this, Rowan," and showed her the best way to cross the lines of the adjacent tent.

"Thank you."

A man approached, wearing two shoulder-slung pouches, straps crossing on his chest. He was of warrior age, but he carried no sword; the steerswoman noticed that he lacked a left arm. "Rowan!" he greeted her, and then said, "Which one?" indicating the tents with his only hand. Before she could reply, Garvin, now inside the tent, held open the entrance flap and waved the man inside. The flap closed, to be reopened an instant later as the rain fly and its two gnarled poles were thrust into Rowan's arms. Atop the tent, an overlap slapped open from below and was tied into place by hands that vanished a moment later.

"Rowan?"

She turned to see an Outskirter standing behind her; he slid a pack from his shoulders and brushed a strand of white hair from his face. A thick white braid trailed down his broad chest, and his eyes were black in nests of weather-beaten wrinkles.

"Kammeryn, Murson, Gena," he introduced himself, and added with a gentle smile, "Seyoh. Welcome to our camp."

The steerswoman stood bemused, arms full of canvas and tangleroot, and looked around. She was in the middle of a town.

Her newly erected tent faced the central square, where the fire pit was already being put to use by two squabbling mertutials. Other tents circled the areas, entrance flaps and occasionally entire sides rolled open and secured above, to show inner chambers carpeted with patterned cloth. Outskirters—warriors and mertutials both—strode, wandered, or bustled according to their individual duties. Half a dozen warriors arranged a carpet before one of the open tents, dropped packs, and settled to relax and converse.

"Thank you," Rowan said to Kammeryn, "but I feel a bit odd being welcomed to a place when I haven't moved ten feet from where I originally stood. Perhaps I should say to you, 'Welcome to my former bivouac.' "

19

"We have been told that you are a steerswoman. Now you must tell us what that means."

The adjoining walls of four adjacent tents had been rolled up to the ceiling and tied in place, creating a single large chamber, its remaining walls rippling like water from the chill wind gusting outside. Above, vent flaps were turned up, affording sixteen identical views of crystalline blue sky. Their configuration against the flow of wind occasionally set them humming faintly, disharmoniously.

Rowan and Bel sat in the center of a thin carpet angularly patterned in blue and white, surrounded by a circle of eighteen seated Outskirters. Kammeryn sat directly before his guests, an armed cushion of the same design behind him. Rowan took a moment to scan the faces. There was no clear demarcation between warrior and mertutial; but she noted that the woman on Kammeryn's right was of his own age, and certainly a mertutial, and that the man to his left was younger than Rowan, and surely a warrior. There seemed to be a general trend toward maturity, progressing around the circle to end at the seyoh's seat. Rowan wondered if, should Kammeryn die, the circle would simply shift, adding one young face at the beginning.

"I said a great deal to Jann, about myself and my purposes. She didn't pass the information on to you?"

"Jann spoke to me only, briefly, and returned to her position on the outer circle. What you have to say, we need to hear from you."

Rowan nodded, and gathered her information into a coherent explanation. "That I am a steerswoman means that I am a constant student. I try to understand everything I encounter. I study what I see, and if there are people who can inform me, I ask questions of them.

"The simplest thing I study, and most constantly, is the land itself. I chart the country I cross, as accurately as possible. That skill of steerswomen is the one of the greatest uses to people in the Inner

Lands, and it's what we are best known for. But we are also interested in the people of the lands we chart, their ideas, actions, and traditions. And many more things: why plants grow where they do, the nature of objects, of natural events, how to use mathematics to navigate and to measure and describe . . ." She paused, discovering a more concise and inclusive statement, and its simplicity surprised her. "The Steerswomen are actually trying to answer only three questions: what, how, and why."

"To the Steerswomen," Bel put in, "knowledge is life."

"That's a very simple statement," the seyoh told Bel, "and true in every way."

Someone behind Rowan caught Kammeryn's eye, and he made a gesture of formal recognition. The person addressed Rowan, who turned to face the speaker. "But not everything is significant, to every person. One learns what one needs to know, to survive." It was a woman, just past middle age, her hair two sweeps of dusty crow's wing down her breast.

"There's more to life than survival," Rowan told her. "Bel sings, for example, and she doesn't do it to survive."

"I've never heard Bel sing," Kammeryn said, with a dignified nod in Bel's direction, "but I can tell you this: She does sing to survive. It keeps her spirit alive."

Rowan smiled. "I learn to keep my spirit alive. And I give what I know to whomever should need it, and that keeps my spirit alive, too."

The council considered the statement; then a young man at Kammeryn's left was granted the floor. "And have you finished with the Inner Lands," he said, in a challenging tone, "that now you come to study the Outskirts? Perhaps we don't want to be studied."

"I don't wish to interfere with your people in any way. And no, we haven't finished with the Inner Lands; I don't believe we ever shall."

"But you've come here."

"Yes. For a particular reason," she told him, then spoke to the assembly at large. "For the most part, the steerswomen travel along their assigned routes, studying whatever they encounter. Later, when they're too old to travel well, or if they so decide at a younger age, they may choose one subject and try to understand it in depth." She nodded to Bel, who unfastened the belt she wore and passed it to Kammeryn. "This is what I'm studying now."

Nine silver disks, with silver links between. Each disk held an odd, flat jewel of opalescent shades that fragmented and shifted in the light from the vent flaps: sky blue, midnight blue, pale water blue, and one jewel showing shades of rich amethyst. The gems all had thin silver lines crossing their surface, as if inlaid: some parallel, some branching geometrically from a central vein.

Kammeryn fastened the catch and held the belt up, looped around two spread hands. "Beautiful. And a waste of good metal." He passed the belt to his right. It began to make its way around the circle. "And I approve," he continued. "Beauty is its own end."

"Have any of you seen that sort of jewel before?" Rowan asked.

The grizzled man who now held it shook his head. "Stolen from the Inner Lands, I would guess. We don't have jewel-cutters."

"My father made it," Bel told him, "of jewels found in the Outskirts."

The information inspired puzzlement, and the belt continued its journey smoothly, each person studying it and indicating unfamiliarity as it passed through his or her hands. But Kammeryn's gaze held both Rowan and Bel, and he shook his head, not at the jewels but at the two women.

"A treasure hunt," he said. His voice held deep disappointment.

"No," Rowan replied. She leaned forward. "I want to go to the place where the jewels were found, and see how they lie, and what might be there with them." She took a breath before revealing the most startling fact imaginable. "These are the shattered pieces of a fallen Guidestar."

The jewels' progress stopped, abruptly. They were now directly behind Rowan, and she could not see who was holding them; but she saw all around her faces turning toward that invisible person, bodies leaning, one hand reaching.

The old woman on Kammeryn's right was the only person to show no surprise. "Something so beautiful could only come from the sky," she said when the seyoh recognized her, and then she nodded, slowly, almost sleepily. Her expression was blank and serene, representing possibly calm wisdom, possibly age-raddled stupidity.

"No Guidestar has fallen," the youngest member said, then realized he had spoken without being recognized, and silenced, flushing in youthful embarrassment. Kammeryn reassured him with a glance, then made a small gesture that indicated general discussion was permitted. The young man continued, hotly, "You Inner Landers think anyone who can't build an outhouse is a fool. But we have eyes. The Guidestars are still there."

"Unless—unless there are others we've never seen." Rowan had to turn to see the speaker: a woman, somewhat older than Rowan, red hair cropped short, face broad of cheekbones, pointed of chin. It was she who now held the belt, looped over one hand. Small blue eyes, pale and bright as diamond chips, flickered as she thought, blinking as if their owner's mind were moving too quickly for her to follow.

Rowan was pleased to find herself understood. "Yes. There ought to be four, as far as I can calculate, with the other two hanging above the opposite side of the world. The way the fragments found are distributed, all in a line from the Inner Lands to the Outskirts, the speed that would be necessary to send them so far so quickly, the fact that the Outskirts jewels lie imbedded in the face of a cliff—all these things tell me that they must have fallen from the sky. And the only things that stand in the sky are the Guidestars."

"And the true stars," the eldest woman said.

"True stars are distant suns," someone put in. "They'll never fall."

"And what does this have to do with us?" another asked.

"We have to help them, if they need help," the young man told the speaker with awkward dignity; he was new to his position in the circle. "They risked themselves to save Averryl." And he traded a careful glance with the red-haired woman, who nodded as if in confirmation—the matter of Averryl, it seemed, concerned her particularly.

Kammeryn assumed the floor again. "And what help do you want from my tribe?" he asked Rowan and Bel.

"Bel has told me, and I've learned that it's true, that traveling alone in the Outskirts is dangerous and difficult," Rowan said. "If your movements are going to take you east, then all that we ask is to travel in your company, for as long as our route lies near your own."

"For as long as that's so," Bel stressed, then added, "Even if it will be more than seven days."

Rowan turned to her, surprised. "Seven days?"

Bel did not explain, or look at her; her gaze held Kammeryn's.

The seyoh studied Bel with narrowed gaze, then spoke to Rowan. "We must help you, that's true," he informed her. "But there is a limit to our obligation. A seyoh can extend the tribe's hospitality for seven days, but no duty can force us to keep strangers among us beyond that time."

Rowan was taken aback. "I didn't know that." She looked to her companion again, for explanation of the omission of this information.

Bel ignored her. "It will have to be for more than seven days," she reasserted to Kammeryn. "It will have to be for as long as you're going in our direction."

The seyoh's eyes narrowed. "You cannot demand this of us."

"You'll want to do it."

"How so?"

Bel turned to the steerswoman. "You didn't tell him the rest."

"The rest?"

"Tell him about Slado," Bel instructed.

Kammeryn was as perplexed as the steerswoman. "Slado?"

"The master wizard of the Inner Lands," Bel told him. "He works in secret, and the other wizards follow his orders, even when they don't know his motives."

"Why should we care what wizards do? They're far away from us."

Bel paused to scan the circle, meeting each gaze individually. She pointed up. "Because their *things* are hanging in our sky." Abruptly, she turned to Rowan, and addressed her in the Inner Lands form. "Tell me, lady, what's a Guidestar?" In the past, Bel had used the form only in half jest.

Rowan was taken aback; but the answer spoke itself. "A magical object, created and lofted into the sky by wizards, long ago. It moves, from west to east, and the rate of its motion is the same as the speed of the world's turning. For this reason it seems to hang forever motionless above the land." Rowan became fascinated by Bel's face: the Outskirter's expression was identical to that she had worn while in wild battle, slaughtering goblins.

"What is it for?" Bel prompted.

"The wizards use them in certain spells, to effect purposes beyond my knowledge."

"Why did one fall?"

Possibilities were three. "Either it was made to fall, or it was permitted to fall, or its fall could not be prevented."

"Why did Slado know it had fallen, when no one else did?"

Possibilities were two. "Either he has sources of information his fellows lack, or he caused it to fall himself."

"Why would he want it to fall?"

"I don't know." But possibilities were two; the same two that lay behind every human action. "To make his life better, or to prevent his life from becoming worse."

"Why would he hide the facts from the other wizards?"

Two. "Either he does not trust them to understand the benefits, or they would not benefit, but suffer."

"Thank you, lady." Bel turned back to Kammeryn, dismissing Rowan so completely that the steerswoman felt she had vanished. There was only the wide, rippling chamber; the bold, primitive pattern of the carpet; the ring of faces, warriors and past-warriors; and the empty squares of sky above, humming in the wind.

"Don't you wonder what a wizard likes?" Bel asked Kammeryn. "What he feels makes his life good? I do. And I keep thinking: power. And what does he think will make his life better? More power. If Slado wants more power, when will he stop? When a harmless steerswoman did nothing more than ask questions about pretty gems, he sent his underlings to hunt her and kill her. I know, I was there, and we barely escaped with our lives. And Slado is spreading his power: he's been making new holdings in the Inner Lands, and if he keeps on doing it, so that his puppet wizards are everywhere in that country, what do you think comes next, Kammeryn?"

Kammeryn spoke without hesitation. "No wizard can reach us here. They are far away."

Bel held his gaze; she did not speak; she pointed to the sky.

A man to the left of the circle indicated a desire to speak. Kammeryn was long in recognizing him; his eyes were still on Bel's, but they were shuttered, shielding the thoughts moving behind them.

"Perhaps," the old man began after receiving permission, "perhaps, as the steerswoman said, this wizard couldn't stop the Guidestar from falling. Perhaps he's growing weaker, not stronger."

Bel turned to him. "Then, what does a person do when he's losing his strength and doesn't want anyone to know?"

And it was the seyoh who answered, thoughtfully. "He uses what strength he has more often. More forcefully. And more visibly."

"Whether he's growing or fading, for us, it's the same result," Bel said. "He'll come here; or he'll send his minions; or he'll send his magic. We have to be ready." She drew a breath. "This is what the steerswoman needs from you: to travel with this tribe, as long as it moves her nearer to the fallen Guidestar, and to be free to leave when it doesn't. And this is what I need from you: to come and go, leave and return freely, anytime I choose."

There was a stir. Several persons wished to speak, requesting permission by glance or gesture.

Bel spoke louder, as if the flurry were audible as well as visible. "If we come near another tribe," she told the council, "I need to speak to them, and tell them everything we've just told you. It'll do no good for only one tribe to be prepared. I have to tell them all."

Kammeryn waited as the requests slowly subsided, until only one member persisted.

It was a dark-haired man past middle age, his face and neck crossed by scars. "That's too dangerous. We don't know if we can trust you. You might betray us to another tribe, and bring them down on our herds."

"I won't."

"They might follow you back to us."

"I won't let that happen."

"How could you stop it?"

"I'm very good."

"If you stay among us, then your duty is to this tribe, and no other. You follow our laws, abide by the words of our seyoh, and do nothing that risks our safety."

"There's a higher duty than duty to the tribe."

"No." The man showed no emotion. "It is the only duty. If this tribe suffers, if our people die, then what does it matter what happens to strangers?" He turned to Kammeryn. "Let them stay for seven days, then send them away. For anything else, you need a consensus. If you call for a consensus, I will not agree."

Bel slapped her hand down forcefully on the carpet. "My people are in danger, or they will be, all tribes, all Outskirters. If not soon, then one day, and who can say when?" She faced Kammeryn. "If you don't help them, you're hurting them. Your tribe. Yourself."

"Can Outskirters fight wizards?" Rowan was surprised to hear herself asking.

Bel looked at her: the first acknowledgment of Rowan's presence since Bel had finished asking questions and cuing answers from a steerswoman. "It doesn't matter if we can. We will." Then she seemed to speak to herself, but clearly, definitely. "Everything I know about Slado and his wizards, I hate. Everything I know about my people, I love. And this is what I love best about them: They fight."

20

D ismissed, Rowan and Bel left the council to continue its deliberations. Rowan felt dazed by the turn of events; distractedly, she gazed around the camp.

A spit was turning over the fire in the center, tended by an old woman who spoke to a child as she worked, the child squealing laughter. The two mertutials who had dug the fire pit were standing to one side of their creation, prodding the ashes with a stick and shaking their heads in vague dissatisfaction. A group of warriors lounging outside their tent were engaged in a discussion that alternated quiet words with bursts of hilarity. Garvin sat on the bare ground by Averryl's tent, deep in conversation with the small blond boy who had guarded the rain fly during the invasion of goats. In the distance, someone was blowing a series of breathy notes on a flute, with much experimentation, very little skill, and a few frustrated curses.

The Outskirters were dressed much as Bel was and spoke in accents little different from hers. To Rowan, they seemed each to carry a similar air: a combination of confidence, straightforwardness, humor, interest, and hidden, surprising subtlety.

Like Bel herself. They were her people.

Rowan turned to study her friend. "It seems," the steerswoman said, "that you have a mission of your own."

Bel nodded broadly, but did not meet Rowan's eyes. "I'll travel with you to the Guidestar, to see what's there; and I'll see that you get back to a place you can reach your country from, or help you find a tribe to take you. But after that, I'll leave you, and go north, and try to talk to the tribes there."

"I'll be sorry when you go." She was sorry already. "I didn't think, Bel; I didn't consider what all this might mean to the Outskirters."

Bel gave an easy shrug. "They're not your people."

"No, but they're yours, and you're my friend. Now I'm worried about them."

The Outskirter looked up at her. "Rowan, you can't worry about everyone. I'll take care of telling my people; you find your Guidestar and figure out what Slado's up to, so I'll have more to tell."

Rowan laughed, shook her head, and clapped Bel's shoulder. "I consider that an excellent division of labor." They went out into the camp together.

Garvin waved them over to Averryl's tent. "He's livelier, but confused," the warrior said of the injured man. "He says he doesn't remember walking to the camp. I can't convince him that he's stayed put." The women joined Garvin on the ground, and Rowan found herself being calmly scrutinized by the boy. She introduced herself; he responded with "Harramyn."

"Only one name?"

"I'm too young to name myself like an adult. But my line is Mourah, and my mother is Kree." He spoke her name as if expecting an appreciative reaction.

"So you'll become Harramyn, Kreeson, Mourah."

Harramyn nodded, and Garvin made a deprecating sound. "Hari."

The boy corrected him patiently. "No, I'm too old for 'Hari.' "

"Are you a friend of Averryl's, or perhaps a relative? You seem very worried about him."

"I'm not related. My mother likes him, but he's not my father. She wouldn't want anything to happen to him. I'm going to help Mander."

"Who's Mander?"

"*You* know." He tucked one arm behind his back, and wiggled the other enthusiastically.

Garvin gave him a thump. "Don't make fun of Mander. He can do plenty of things that you can't. And never will."

"Ha. I'll never have to. I'll never cross the line; I'm going to die with my sword in my hand."

Another voice spoke. "Yes, and sooner rather than later." The boy was hefted up by strong hands, then settled down again into the lap of the red-haired woman from the council meeting. Harramyn frowned and wriggled in her arms, as he tried to decide whether her comment was a clever jibe or a dire prediction.

She introduced herself. "Kree, Edensdotter, Mourah." She resembled her brother Garvin very little; he was broad-shouldered, pale-haired, she compact and fiery. His eyes were a wide, deep blue, hers small and close-set, of a sharp blue so pale as to be almost colorless.

Rowan was disturbed. "Has the council decided so quickly?" It did not bode well.

"No," Kree reassured her. "I stepped out, to get you settled. You'll be sleeping in with my band, for tonight, at least. With Averryl here, and Fletcher who knows where, there's room."

Bel nodded, satisfied. "Good; that's better than having a tent to ourselves. The more people, the warmer, and it's turning cold all of a sudden." She made a suggestion: "If we're accepted, you could use me in Fletcher's place. Or Averryl's, if he can't fight."

Kree considered, then poked her son in the ribs. "Will Averryl be able to fight?" she asked him.

"Mander doesn't know."

Displeased, Kree sat considering implications; from her demeanor, Rowan understood that Kree was chief of her war band. Kree spoke to Bel. "Are you any good?" Bel's reply was a small smile, which seemed to satisfy Kree. "And you?" she asked Rowan.

The steerswoman winced. "I don't yet know what my status should be, if I'll be permitted to serve as a warrior. But I think I can hold my own: Bel and I traveled alone from the Inner Lands, and we've made it here safely."

"The Inner Lands . . . how far is that from here?"

"About five hundred miles."

"Eight hundred kilometers," Bel added, translating to Outskirter terminology.

Kree permitted herself to be impressed. She gave Hari another poke. "Show them where to sleep. And where's their gear?"

The boy scrambled to his feet and disappeared into the tent, returning with packs and Rowan's cloak, which he seemed to consider a very peculiar object.

Bel took it from him and passed it to Rowan. "Lead on, Hari."

"Harramyn," he corrected.

The afternoon passed, and very differently from Rowan's first experience among an Outskirter tribe. There, people had avoided acknowledging her and spoke to her only when necessary, or when tricked into it. Here, every passing person seemed to seek an excuse to come by her tent, to address her, and especially to call her by name. It was: "Rowan, how is Averryl?" "Are you really from the Inner Lands, Rowan?" "Here, Rowan, come lend a hand," and "Hello, Rowan, what are you doing?"

"I'm writing," she answered for the dozenth time, on this occasion to a mertutial who had paused before her as she sat outside Kree's tent. "I'm trying to record the things I'm learning in the Outskirts, and what I see that I don't understand yet."

"Writing . . ." The old man thought long, then shook his bald head disapprovingly. "We used to do that. We gave it up." And he hurried off on his duties, arms full of dirty laundry, leaving Rowan bewildered, with a hundred questions trapped between her mind and voice.

"Ho, Rowan!" But it was Bel this time, returning from a stroll between the encampment and the inner circle of guards.

Rowan greeted her with relief. "I should have gone with you. This is getting tiring."

"I thought you liked answering questions." Bel settled down on the rug, stretching her short legs before her and leaning back on her elbows.

"I do. But not the same ones, over and over."

"Say you'll tell them later, all together. It can be like a story. That's what I've been doing. Everyone wanted to hear about Averryl's rescue; I'm going to make a poem of it."

"Please don't embroider. If someone asks me, I'll have to tell the true version."

"Ha. The true version is what I'll tell. It was a good fight."

"Yes. And I sincerely hope I'm never in another like it." She closed her logbook and rubbed fingers that were stiffening in the chill air over eyes that were blurring from close work. She had been trying to conserve her paper, writing as small as possible, forcing herself to be concise. Even with these tactics, there was too much for her to effectively notate: hundreds of observations, large and small, a sea of detail.

Bel looked at her sidelong. "You've been sitting there since I left you?"

"Yes. Trying to catch up." She had had no opportunity for the last few days, and little before that, to make her entries. Looking around, she realized with surprise that the deepening of the chill in the air was due to the approach of evening. "I had no idea," she said.

"A steerswoman never gets lost, except in her own thoughts," Bel observed wryly. She thumped Rowan on the back. "Take a walk. Everyone's busy getting ready for evening meal and bed. They won't bother you."

Rowan left her book and pens in Bel's care, and was only greeted twice on her way to the camp's edge. There, looking out, she could find no sign of the inner circle, only some twenty goats in two unequal flocks, nuzzling the barren ground, shaking their flop-eared heads in annoyance.

It was quiet out on the veldt, despite the icy breeze: no redgrass stood to chatter in the wind, no tanglebrush, no rattle and rasp and squeal of goblins. Behind her, the camp noises defined an audible delimited shape, like a safe room with invisible walls. Following an inner impulse, she skirted the camp, circling around to where she could look out to the east—for all the past month, east had been her direction, eastward lay her unmarked road and her final destination, and she found herself seeking it, trailing toward it as surely as a banner driven by western winds.

As she came around a cluster of tents, she noticed that someone was sharing with her the quiet fall of evening on the veldt.

Kammeryn stood some forty feet out from the camp, facing the horizon. Rowan was reluctant to interrupt his solitude, but she was certain that he had heard her approach. She did not know if it was more polite to greet him, or to ignore him, or to turn away and walk elsewhere. She made her choice by making no choice, and stood quietly a few paces to the side and behind him, waiting for him to take note of her. But he did not acknowledge her, did not turn to her or speak, and minutes passed.

He seemed not to be musing idly, but studying something. She tried to find what was holding his attention. The land around the camp was used and barren, up the near hills, across them, up the farther hills. The tribe had already passed this way, had only doubled back for Averryl's sake. They could not remain here long; perhaps this was Kammeryn's concern.

Beyond the hills the land was lower, and not so visible. Scouts would have told Kammeryn what lay there; perhaps he was making his future plans.

In the farthest distance, at the limit of sight: an irregular line, lit glowing pink from the light of the falling sun behind the camp. It was too low to be mountains, too high to be part of these low hills, and too nearby to be the distant Dust Ridge. No such feature was marked on Rowan's poor maps. She stepped forward unconsciously, fascinated, gaining no better perspective.

When she reached Kammeryn's side, she saw that he was not looking out, but up. "The Eastern Guidestar," she said.

He nodded, slowly, accepting her presence without surprise. "If it fell, would it fall here?"

"On the camp? I don't know, but it's not very likely."

He stood silent again, and the world grew darker as the sun disappeared. More stars began to show: the Eye of the Bull, the Hound's Nose, and at the horizon, the Lion's Heart.

The seyoh's voice was very quiet. "If they both fell, how would we know where we are, how would we know where to go?"

"By the true stars, and by the sun." If the Guidestars fell, she suspected that there would be greater and more urgent concerns than the one he voiced. And yet she sympathized with him; loss of direction was important to his life, and was the one result most easily comprehended. "Navigation by the stars is complicated, and less accurate," she told him, "but it can be done. If you like, I can teach you, or one of your people. If you feel the need."

"Unseen Guidestars," he said quietly, "and a Guidestar falling, wizards coming to the Outskirts . . . How can what you say be true?" His face was no longer distinguishable in the gloom.

Rowan could find no further thing to say to lend greater force to her knowledge. "It is true," she told him. "And the things Bel said—I hadn't considered them before, but yes, I believe her. Sometime, I don't know when, but soon or later, these things will affect your people."

"The council cannot reach consensus," he said. "My word will only permit you seven days."

Her heart sank. "I'm sorry. I've come to like your people. I almost feel at home here."

He was a dim gray shape, his white braid falling across his heart like a shaft of light. He spoke, not like a seyoh, but as a man, with reluctant, disbelieving wonder. "How can Guidestars fall? They've been there forever."

"They haven't been there forever. Nothing has been anywhere forever." It seemed too large a statement; she doubted it herself, even as her heart and mind both recognized its truth. "You yourself haven't been here forever," she told him, "nor your people. Long ago, their lands lay west of here; longer ago, farther west. And before? Who can say? But they must once have had a home."

Out of the gloom he answered, and it was in an altered voice, soft, but with a slow subtle rhythm: the voice of a storyteller:

" 'They came at last upon a river, cool and deep, wide in silver sunlight. Here to the banks, and north and south, ran redgrass, deep, and high as the waist of a man, and the air was sweet and warm. The people said each to the other: "Our wandering is ended, and now we will stay. This place is our home."

" 'But Einar said to them: "This is not your home." And in forty days, when the land was made barren, he led them across the river; and they traveled for twenty days.

" 'The people climbed long into a high land, where the sun shone around them on every side. In endless winds the grasses danced and spoke, and there were glittering stones upon the ground. The people looked up into light, around into light, and down into shadows below, where they saw the peaks and hills that rose from mist like stars from night. Every eye saw only beauty, and the people said to each other: "We will not leave here, but remain in this land. This is now our home."

" 'But Einar said: "This is not your home." And in thirty days the redgrass was silent in its death, and Einar led his people down into the valleys; and they traveled for twenty days.

" 'Around the valleys stood high hills like hands to shelter the herds and the people. Small brooks fell far from above, to cross and cross again the lands below. The goats climbed among the falls, finding rich redgrass between, and shelter from the winds. Below were roots for the people, and blossoms, and level ground for the camp.

" 'The people then said: "We will stay here. This will be our home." And every eye turned to Einar.

" 'Einar took up his weapon and flung it down onto the ground. Spreading his arms wide, he cried out to his people in a voice of anger: "This is not your home, and this is not your home, and this is not your home!"

" 'And the people understood that he answered them for the future; that they were never to have a home; and that, being answered, they must never ask again.' "

The steerswoman heard him turn to her, invisible in darkness, and she could not tell if he still spoke from the tale, or was now using his own words: "We are the wanderers on the edge of the world. We are the warriors of the land. We are the destroyers, and the seed." He turned away. "You may stay with us, both of you, for seven days, by my word. In seven days I will give that word again, for another seven days, and again after that; and I will continue for as long as I choose. If ever I tell you to go, you will go immediately. If you ever betray my tribe, you will die."

Rowan held her breath, then nodded at the dark, and the stars, and the wind from the veldt. "Thank you," she said.

21

*I*n the morning, there was rain again. A velvet mist hovered close to the ground, ghosting up the sides of the tents in the gray light, and the soft pattering reminded Rowan of redgrass.

As she emerged from the tent, Rowan discovered a curious object lying on the ground before the tent flap, half-buried in the dirt, as if a passing foot had crushed it, casually or maliciously: a tangle of bright yarn, blue, green, and white, looped about a pair of broken tangle-brush twigs. She nudged it with the scarred toe of one boot and reconstructed it in her imagination. It resembled the sort of hanging decoration called a "god's eye" in the Inner Lands, favored in poorer households. What its Outskirts significance might be, Rowan had no clue; it might have been a child's lost toy, a lucky fetish, or, more disturbingly, a curse-object. Choosing the route of caution, she left it undisturbed and went about her day.

As she was returning from the cessfield, a little girl came dashing by. She stopped short at seeing Rowan, ran up to her, all thrill and urgency, stopped again at the prospect of addressing a stranger, and finally lingered in shy indecision, studying her toes.

"Yes?" Rowan prompted her.

The child replied with her chin tucked tight to her chest. "Kree," she began.

"What about her?"

"Looking for Kree" was the muffled reply.

"I haven't seen her," Rowan answered. And the girl was gone.

At the edge of camp, Rowan found a little crowd of some dozen people: warriors, mertutials, and children, all chattering excitedly. Among them, Rowan spotted a pair of long arms gesturing, heard a voice exclaiming cheerfully, "Come on, back off, wait, I have to report to Kree first."

Rowan joined the small crowd and asked a male warrior, "What's happening?"

He was more interested in the focus of the crowd's attention. "We figured you dead," he called out.

The warrior addressed caught the man's eye with a gaze of deep disappointment. Then, with a preliminary outfling of arms, he assumed a broad, theatrical, clasp-handed pose of gratitude, a pained expression of piety, and directed both at the sky above, as if this constituted reply. The man beside Rowan snorted in derision, but more others laughed, and some clapped the newcomer on the back. He pretended to stagger from the force of the blows. "So, do I have to wade through you to get to my chief, or is someone going to fetch her?"

"I sent Sith with a message," a mertutial told him.

"Ah. Wonderful. And by now Sithy's at the cessfield, torturing a tumblebug." He was a long man, with long bones in a long body, less muscular than the average warrior; his piebald cloak flapped to the action of angular elbows, an effect faintly ridiculous. His dank hair was decidedly yellow, his beard woefully sparse, and his long face showed his emotions clearly, emphatically, so that as he winced in indecision the expression was so extreme as to become the very archetype of indecisiveness. He visibly rocked, as if brains and gawky body were at odds with each other. This was Fletcher, Rowan realized. The missing warrior.

"Well," he said, "well . . ." He kicked a knotted bundle that lay at his feet. "Take a look at this." He dropped to the ground, folding his legs beneath him like a nesting crane, opened the bundle, and spread it and its contents for display:

A number of crusted, uncured goatskins; a tangle of knotted strips of the same material; an oddly chipped stone the size and approximate shape of a flattened hand; and two lengths of tanglebrush root, apparently split from one piece, showing a number of gouges along their lengths . . .

Rowan came closer, maneuvering around others who were now stooping or sitting beside the items. One woman held up the collection of skins, revealing them to be attached to each other clumsily with thongs, to form an object like an irregular gappy blanket, singed and blackened down one edge. The steerswoman reached between two observers and came back with one of the root segments. It was nicked and chipped along one side only, and the splintered end began at a particularly deep cut.

"It makes a poor weapon," she remarked.

Fletcher nodded appreciatively to the crowd at large. "And that"—he pointed—"makes a poor party suit." The woman had slipped the skins over her head, and the whole arrangement flopped ludicrously about her body as she undertook a series of poses, as if displaying finery.

"Someone wore that?" Rowan asked.

"Wore it to his own funeral," Fletcher replied, catching Rowan's eye; and abruptly, he stopped short, his mobile features stilled in amazement.

To Rowan's own surprise, his gaze quickly tracked a route familiar to her in the Inner Lands, never seen yet in the Outskirts: from her face to the gold chain at her throat, to the silver ring on the middle finger of her left hand, and back to her face. "A steerswoman."

Rowan was bemused. "That's right."

Sky-blue eyes stared at her dumbly; then suddenly he snatched the chipped stone from the hand of a man who was examining it and thrust it at Rowan, all excitement. "What do you make of this?"

She took it; and seemingly of itself, it shifted in her grip into a comfortable, balanced position. "A hand-axe."

He watched her face, fascinated, then made a wide, questioning gesture that included all of the accoutrements.

Rowan added them together in her mind. "One of the Face People."

" 'Face People'?"

"Primitive people, living on the eastern edge of the inhabited Outskirts," she provided. "They're not normally seen this far in."

He nodded, slowly, and seemed to lose himself to thought for a long moment. Then he broke his trance and threw up his arms. "A steerswoman said it, it must be true," he declared, then addressed the crowd. "Did you catch that? Primitive people. Not normally seen this far in." He turned back to Rowan. "And you can add to your information that they're nasty little fighters, slick as a snake, quick as a weasel. I'd rather face a troop of goblins."

"You nearly did." It was Kree, approaching with the girl Sithy in tow.

Fletcher rose to his feet to meet his chief. "How's that?" he asked. "Averryl was caught by a mating mob."

And all the wild energy vanished from his body, all the life faded from his face, until only blank shock remained. He stood, head tipped back as if from a blow, wry mouth slack, long hands dropped, his stance so limp that Rowan feared he might fall.

He drew a shallow breath as if to speak, but then did not. Kree watched him, saying nothing more, permitting him to suffer. He waited, helplessly silent, acknowledging her right to do so.

At last she answered the unspoken question, and the jerk of her chin gave both direction and dismissal. "He's alive. Mander has him." And Fletcher sped away, damp cloak flapping wildly about him.

Rowan watched him depart. "So that's the missing Fletcher," she commented.

"Yes," Kree said, looking after him. "And he'd better have a good reason for having been out of his assigned position."

Rowan looked down. The chipped stone was still in one hand, the broken club in the other. "I think he does," she said, and passed them to Kree.

Later, as she was dragging a trainful of waterskins up from the creek, Rowan encountered Bel, returning from a stroll among the flocks. The Outskirter fell in beside her, amused. "Have you decided to be a mertutial?"

"I must do something," Rowan said. "I can't simply lounge about like a guest." She had received her assignment from the cook, wanting some simple physical activity, something that would occupy her body while leaving her mind free. But she had overestimated her strength and made the train too heavy; furthermore, the wheel tended to stick unexpectedly, and her absorbing analysis of Inner Lands regional accents was constantly interrupted.

Bel, rather pointedly, did not offer to help, but ambled along companionably. "I wanted to ask Kree if she'd decided to use me, but she's busy with debriefing."

"With what?" The wheel froze again, and Rowan dragged the dead train fully five feet before it loosened.

"It needs grease," Bel commented. "Debriefing. Someone is reporting to her, formally. A scout will debrief, or a war band back from sortie. Or anyone who's had something happen to him that's particularly important."

"That would be Fletcher," Rowan told her. "He killed a Face Person."

Bell was taken aback. "This far west?"

"Apparently. And it occurs to me: If a Face Person had come this far west, perhaps he'd been even farther west, and was just now returning. We almost met a solitary traveler ourselves."

"You think it was the Face Person following us?"

"What do you think?"

Bel considered. "Whoever it was, he moved well, very crafty. If it was a Face Person, and the rumors about them are true, he could easily have been following us for days before I noticed him."

"Could he have been following us again later, at enough distance that he crossed Fletcher's position and was caught unawares?"

"Perhaps," Bel said. "Yes."

The train wheel emitted an evil squeal. Bel stepped back and gave it a shove with her boot.

Rowan changed the subject. "What have you heard about Fletcher?"

"Next to nothing; I haven't bothered to ask. Jann and Jaffry have some grudge against him, but Kree must like him, or she wouldn't keep him in her band. And Averryl defended him to Jann, if you remember."

"Fletcher and Averryl are close friends." Rowan pulled, and Bel walked, for a few quiet minutes. "Fletcher is an Inner Lander."

Bel's surprise was extreme. "Out here? And in a war band? Impossible. Who told you that?"

"No one, at first. I heard him speak. He doesn't have an Outskirter's accent. And he knew me as a steerswoman without being told. Later I asked Chess, the head cook, and she confirmed it. She said he's been here over a year."

Bel considered. "Good," she said. She was following the same reasoning that Rowan had. An Inner Lander among Outskirters was a circumstance strange enough to inspire suspicion; but if Fletcher had been in the Outskirts for over a year, he could not be connected to the wizards' recent hunt for Rowan.

"But it's odd. I'd like to talk to him."

"Ha. You're just tired of the Outskirts, and want to hear some Inner Lands gossip."

Rowan laughed. "Perhaps that's the case."

They arrived at the camp, where Chess clearly wished to berate Rowan for slowness but wavered, still uncertain of the steerswoman's proper status. She finally relieved her ire with a generalized grumbling tirade, largely unintelligible, delivered at the threshold of hearing.

Bel waited in the lee of the cook tent as the two women unloaded the train, after which Chess hesitated, unable to decide whether she ought to find Rowan another assignment or free her to converse with the warrior. Bel ostentatiously gave no clue as to preference, loitering nearby, humming a little tune as she watched the fire tenders at work. Rowan played along, waiting by the cook's elbow, wearing a smile so patient that it could not help but irritate.

The cook's discomfort was ended by the arrival of Eden, a mertutial whose chief work seemed to consist of relaying Kammeryn's requests. "He wants to see you, both. And Rowan should bring her maps." Rowan and Bel followed her, leaving Chess to her muttering.

The sky flaps of Kammeryn's tent were closed against the intermittent rain, but one wall had been raised to admit light. The open wall faced away from the camp's center, indicating a desire for privacy.

Kree was present, and Fletcher, with the Face Person's possessions gathered tidily beside him. Dignified, Kammeryn performed introductions. Line names were handed down through the female side; Rowan noted without surprise that the transplanted Inner Lander possessed only two names, and that his matronymic was an un-Outskirterly "Susannason."

"Fletcher tells me that you recognized these objects as belonging to folk called the Face People," the seyoh said to Rowan. "I would like to know more about them."

"I didn't recognize the equipment," Rowan replied, "I reasoned its origins. What I know about the Face People I learned from Bel."

Bel regarded the objects with her head tilted, then leaned slightly left, then right, as she often did when organizing her thoughts. "The Face People," she began, "live far to the east. The Face is their name for that part of the Outskirts. I've never seen them myself, but I've heard of them from older members of my home tribe. They're primitive. They don't have very many handicrafts, and not very good ones; they don't make metal, and will steal any metal they can find. At Rendezvous, if they're called on to sing, or tell a tale, they never do.

"They're said to be smaller than usual. Their men stand about my height. No one has ever seen their women."

Rowan interrupted. "There must be women."

"I only know what I was told." Bel continued: "They're vicious fighters, and they're very crafty at keeping hidden. They talk little, and they take offense easily. Once one of their tribes broke truce at Rendezvous."

The other Outskirters present were appalled. "What was the reason?" Kree asked, clearly unable to conceive of such a thing.

"I wasn't told. And," Bel finished, "they eat their dead."

Kree let out a breath through her teeth, disgusted. She turned to Fletcher. "Does that match the man you killed?"

He twisted his mouth and made a wide gesture of assent. "Looks like. He was small, sort of scrawny." Fletcher, when speaking, could not be immobile; of themselves, his quick hands sketched a shape in the air, an invisible Face Person. "You could see how his muscles lay on his bones"—he indicated the imaginary figure thoughtfully—"with nothing between them and the skin. I'd have said he looked sickly, but he moved like a flash, and one time he got hold of my arm"—his own arm and hand demonstrated—"and I thought his fingers would squeeze straight through. He fought like a madman, like he didn't care if he lived or died."

Rowan indicated the equipment. "That looks about the level of handicraft that Bel mentioned." She turned to Kammeryn. "Some days ago, Bel and I discovered that we were being trailed by someone. He fled before we saw him. We think it was the same man."

"Then he's no longer a danger. No other scouts have sighted strangers; he was alone."

Fletcher apologetically corrected his seyoh. "I didn't see this fellow coming until he was on me. And Bel did say they're good at hiding."

"I'll send word for the scouts to be more wary. But—and meaning no insult, Fletcher—you are a young warrior. You still have much to learn. Someone more experienced might have sighted him sooner."

Fletcher blew out his cheeks. "Well. I might not have seen him at first, but I saw him in time."

"You seem to be good at that," Kree reassured him. Rowan noted that the reassurance seemed necessary; Fletcher sent Kree a small, wry glance of gratitude.

Kammeryn leaned back, then nodded at Kree. "Please step outside and speak to Eden; tell her to have the warning relayed to the outer circle."

As Kree rose to leave, Fletcher followed; but Kammeryn stopped him with a gesture. "Bel and the steerswoman are undertaking a journey to the east. I believe that part of their route will cross the same area you traveled in your walkabout. I'd like you to tell them about the land they'll be going into."

Fletcher had paused half-risen; he stared at Kammeryn, mutely, then glanced once after the departing Kree. He looked very much as if he wished to escape.

Rowan was puzzled. "Anything you tell us might help a great deal," she said.

He gazed at her, motionless in his awkward position. Then, with slow unwillingness, he settled down again and waited. Rowan drew out her charts, Bel shifting nearer to see.

Fletcher was oddly tentative as he leaned forward to study the map. He tilted his head to view the notations, as no Outskirter had: he could read. His gaze and his finger went to one particular feature. "Tournier's Fault," he read aloud. "Dust Ridge. What is it?"

"It's a cliff, if Bel's information is correct. And it's where we're going."

"Why do you have it marked so clear?" His finger swept back across the blank expanse of the map. "How do you only know about that one place?"

Rowan briefly explained about having seen a wizard's map. "I couldn't recall all the details, since it was some weeks after seeing their map that I had any chance to try to make a copy. But since I was particularly interested in Dust Ridge, I managed to impress that section in my mind. I'm sure the distance is correct, and its length, and its configuration. I need to know what lies between there and here."

Fletcher looked away and sat silent for a long moment, then reluctantly brought his attention back to the map. He drew a breath.

"More rivers," he said, and indicated; a small, inexpressive movement, very different from the wild, wide gestures Rowan had come to expect of him. "Scores of rivers here." He did not elaborate, neither by words nor gestures, but paused again, waiting.

Rowan exchanged a glance with Bel. "Try to re-create the route you took," Bel suggested. "That would be easiest."

He nodded, then proceeded to trace a route across the unmarked chart, describing the terrain he had encountered, using the fewest possible words. Rowan notated every landmark he had passed and, using her knowledge of geological patterns, sketched in likely approximations of surrounding areas.

Kree rejoined them, entering quietly to sit beside Kammeryn. Fletcher seemed not to notice her.

At one point, the width of the observed area widened. Rowan asked why. "Went further north on the way back" was his terse reply.

As the trail continued east, Fletcher became even less communicative, using ever shorter phrases and sometimes single words: "Hills." Rowan had to prompt him for expansions and explanations. Bel and the other Outskirters watched in silence, then patiently, Bel with growing puzzlement.

At last Fletcher ran out of words completely, his finger resting at a place where Rowan had assumed several small rivers converging. Fletcher sat as quietly as if he were alone.

"What's there?" Rowan asked at last, cautiously.

"Swamp."

"How far does it extend?"

"Fifty kilometers." His route began to arc north, leaving the swamp.

"No, hold a moment." Rowan recalled the demon she and Bel had heard. "This swamp, was the water fresh?"

He did not wish to reply. "Sour . . ."

"Was it like seawater? Have you ever tasted seawater?" As an Inner Lander, he might have done.

"Different." His finger wanted to leave the swamp behind. Rowan surmised some dreadful event having occurred in that location.

But his statement could be considered to correspond with the wizard Shammer's description of a demon's needs, and Rowan was very interested. "Did you encounter any dangerous creatures in this swamp?"

He did not reply, and only by looking up from the chart did Rowan realize that he had been reduced to gesture: he nodded.

Kammeryn spoke. "If the steerswoman is going to pass near there, she will need to know what she might meet." There was no admonishment in his words.

After a moment's hesitation, Fletcher neutrally delivered straightforward descriptions of a number of unpleasant creatures: round-backed beetles some three feet high, equipped with pincers, fore and aft; wasplike swarmers whose sting induced dizziness and temporary blindness, but which ignored persons unless disturbed; a man-sized soft lizard that dwelt in a lair beneath the mud in shallow water, springing on its prey by means of a trapdoor, and possessing huge jaws with a triple row of needle-sharp teeth.

Rowan's original planned route crossed directly through the swamp. She amended it.

Fletcher had used more words in his descriptions than he had spoken during the entire previous hour; the act seemed to release some internal pressure, and his manner became easier as he traced the rest of his route, which had swung north past the swamp to end in an arid area. "And then I turned around," he finished.

Bel's perplexity had grown during his descriptions, and now reached the point of suspicion. "Where were you going, that you traveled so far from your tribe?"

His answer was again terse. "Walkabout."

"That's a long walkabout." Bel was frankly dubious.

He paused, and Rowan expected him to revert to silence again; instead, he slipped back into his old manner: an eloquent wince, an apologetic half smile, a wide gesture made by hands more natural in motion than in stillness. "Well, I wasn't all that certain I wanted to come back."

Kree spoke. "We're glad you did." Again, the reassurance.

The steerswoman could resist no longer. "What is 'walkabout'?"

It took a moment for the Outskirters to decide who was to reply. "It's a rite, a tradition," Bel said. "It's one of the things you do to become an adult and a warrior. The candidates go out into the wilderness for six weeks. You choose a direction, walk in as straight a line as you can, and deal with whatever you meet."

"Alone in the Outskirts?" She looked at Fletcher's route drawn across the chart; it was far more than six weeks' travel. Assuming that the tribe had been located farther west at the time of Fletcher's journey, the walkabout might have taken months. "It sounds impossible to survive."

"Not completely alone," Bel continued. "Candidates go out in pairs, but they keep a distance between each other. They're not allowed to associate, or communicate."

"Or assist?"

"If your partner rescues you, it means you fail the test."

Rowan began to ask what it meant if one failed to rescue one's partner; she stopped herself. Beside her, once again immobile, sat Fletcher: an energetic, expressive man reduced to quiet and stillness. His walkabout partner had not been summoned to add his or her information to Fletcher's. Fletcher's partner had not survived.

Rowan forced herself back to her map. "This helps us a great deal. We can follow most of Fletcher's route, swinging north here"—avoiding the deadly swamp—"and turning southeast here, where you went north. It's not the most direct line, but at the least we'll know what to expect. After that, we'll simply strike out across the land," and she unconsciously quoted Bel, "and deal with whatever we meet."

Bel leaned forward to study the result, then nodded with satisfaction. The chart had begun to resemble a true traveler's map, and the gap between known route and goal was suddenly, miraculously, manageable. Success seemed less a hope, and more a likelihood.

"Good." Kammeryn made a gesture, and Rowan passed him the map. When the seyoh took it, he turned it around, but not to read the notations—he was illiterate. Rowan saw that he had adjusted its directions to correspond with reality: Kammeryn was seated facing south, and held the map with south on top.

His gnarled finger moved, indicated. "The tribe," he said, "will stay with you to this point, and continue, so." The tribe's route continued due east as the travelers' wended southeast. "We'll try to pause here . . . and later here; all depending, of course, on whether the grass is good. We'll move further north here"—far above the swamp—

"there will be too much blackgrass and not enough red. You should be able to rejoin us near," and he traced a circle, "this area."

Mastering her surprise, Rowan hurried to mark the tribe's projected positions.

Fletcher was astonished. "We're changing our route for the steerswoman?"

Kammeryn's glance denied him the right to question his seyoh; Fletcher managed to suppress what should have been a splay-armed gesture of acquiescence into a mere flutter of fingers on his knees.

Bel was delighted. "That's good! We can travel lighter, and harder, if we know we have people to return to."

Amazed, Rowan shook her head. "I hardly know how to thank you," she told Kammeryn.

His eyes were thoughtful. "Don't," he said. "When you return, our tribe will see you first, and hear first what you found."

"But—" It was Fletcher, his confusion overcoming his etiquette. With a nod, Kammeryn gave permission for his question, and Fletcher fairly burst out, "But why are they going? What's there?"

Kammeryn leaned back, considering, and Kree's sidelong expression told Rowan that Fletcher would receive no answer. But the seyoh surprised her. "We are finished here," he said. "Ask that question of the steerswoman when you leave."

Rowan gathered her materials, and Bel and Fletcher rose to go; but Kree stopped them and turned back to Kammeryn, small bright eyes intent. "That's not a good idea."

He made a show of surprise. "How so?"

She was hesitant to explain in front of the strangers; but the seyoh waited. "You've circumvented the council's choice," Kree finally said, "and they won't like it if you throw your own decision in their faces. It's better the tribe doesn't know. They don't need to be told why you choose to send us where you do."

"I don't see how we can prevent it. The steerswoman is sworn to tell the truth, if she's asked."

Kree knit her brows. "She should do as you tell her."

Rowan remained half-risen, one knee on the ground, pen and ink stone in one hand, charts in the other. "I can't. If he tells me to be silent, or to lie, I can't do it."

Kree addressed the steerswoman. "Understand, I'm in favor of your being here. Mine was one of the voices that spoke for you in the council. But it's important that the council show unity to the tribe. If you go about telling everything, it will come out that some of the council did not want to accept you."

"I can't help that. And if it's true, how can it hurt for it to be known?"

"The tribe doesn't want to see its leaders divided."

"It's better to see what is, rather than what one wishes were so." Rowan became very aware that one side of the tent was completely open, that any passing person could overhear everything that Kree wished to keep secret. She was also aware that no person had passed by since the meeting began. Apparently, custom or law prevented eavesdropping. Fletcher himself seemed both appalled to be privy to such dissension, and avidly interested.

Kammeryn raised one hand. "I cannot force the steerswoman to be silent; and I will not try to. The tribe has one leader: the seyoh. *I* am not divided. You may leave."

22

*F*letcher and Rowan were seated on a rug before Kree's tent. Bel had decided to walk the area between the camp and the inner circle of defenders; she was composing a poem, she explained, and walking helped her to think.

The morning had passed, and the noon meal. Rowan and Fletcher's food, however, still sat before them: Rowan's because she could not speak and eat at the same time, Fletcher's because partway through the tale he had forgotten that it was there.

He shook his head slowly, blinking as he gazed about, as if Rowan's story had transported him to the far lands where the events had occurred, then abruptly dropped him back into the Outskirts. "Falling Guidestars, and intrigue, murder, and wizards . . ."

"Yes. It's hard to believe." Told in words, the events seemed hardly credible.

But Fletcher was deeply disturbed. He turned to her. "Do you really think this wizard, this Slado, has some interest in the Outskirts?"

"I don't know." She picked up the bowl of stew that sat before her; it was long cold. "Perhaps he hasn't, yet. But everything Bel said makes a great deal of sense to me. If he keeps expanding his power in the Inner Lands, then yes, he'll turn this way someday."

"I don't know . . . The wizards, they don't only do bad things, do they? They help, too. I've heard that the people in The Crags live very high, thanks to their wizard. And that woman wizard, does something with the crops . . ."

"Isara, in the upper Wulf valley. And Jannik in Donner keeps the dragons under control. Or doesn't, if he takes a disliking to you." She used a piece of sour flatbread to scoop the thick stew. "And they have their little wars; not so little if you find yourself conscripted into one. I think you'd find all this likelier if you knew wizards as I do." She studied him a moment. "There's no wizard in Alemeth," she observed.

"Alemeth?" Fletcher came back to his surroundings quickly and shot her a bright, amused glance. "Now, what made you say Alemeth?"

She smiled. "Your accent."

"You've been there?"

"Never. And I've never heard an accent quite like yours, either." Fletcher's consonants were slurred and soft, his intonation light and mobile, far different from the clearer rhythms and flatter tones of the Outskirters. "I tried to place it, and I couldn't. I thought it might be The Crags, because of the lilt; but the pattern is too different. That left only accents I've never heard at all, and that left the western mountains, or southeast, around Alemeth; Alemeth seemed likelier. And now," she said, settling back with her bowl and bread, "now I want your story. What's a silk-weaver doing in the Outskirts?" Alemeth was famous across the Inner Lands for the quality of its fabrics.

"Weaver? Ha! as we Outskirters say. Never touched a bobbin in my life." He adopted a haughty demeanor and held it just long enough to impress it upon her. "We were bakers. My family, that is."

She coughed stew. "Bakers?" She could hardly imagine a more unlikely profession for a man become a wild barbarian.

He shook a finger at her. "I can make a custard tart you wouldn't believe."

She laughed, long and freely. "Do you know, I could use a custard tart just now." After long traveling through strange, grim lands, she found Fletcher's foolishness refreshing.

"Ah, well, there you are, you see. No likely chance of that out here." And he glanced about disparagingly; but the glance turned into a long gaze of pleasure, at the tents, the veldt, the windy white sky. He seemed to forget her and sat looking at his world with deep satisfaction.

"You like it," Rowan observed.

"No place I'd rather be." Fletcher took a deep breath, blew it out, then gave an embarrassed wince. "I guess you'd have to blame youth," he said, "or adventurousness, or a sense of romance . . . I don't know. But my grandfather was an Outskirter, and from the time I had enough words to ask him to tell me, he'd tell me. The most astonishing tales—do you know, half the town thought he was a born liar, made it up as he went along. But I knew, because I listened all the time, put it all together, until I felt like I could pick out of a crowd all those people I'd never seen"—he indicated spaces in the empty air—"his family, his war band, tribemates, all those fierce women he loved . . .

"It was so much bigger than the way I lived. Nobody's life depended on what my family did. If we didn't bake, well, someone else would—not so well, perhaps, but no one would starve. But you see, everything he did mattered. Life and death. I wanted—" He looked sheepish. "I wanted to do something big."

"Why did your grandfather leave here?"

He shrugged. "Hard times drove his tribe inward, they raided a village and lost, he lost a leg, a village girl nursed him, one thing led to another."

Rowan noted again the object he wore on a thong around his neck: a cross, some four inches tall, made of Inner Lands wood. "Are Christers so forgiving that they'll help a man who attacked their town?"

He gave her a mock-pious look. "It's true. My grandmother was a Christer, and once my grandfather was hurt, he was helpless. We don't kill a helpless man."

Rowan was both interested and dubious. "Can you be a Christer and an Outskirter at the same time? Isn't there some conflict?"

"Not so far." He pursed his lips. "We've nothing against defending ourselves; I can manage to do my duty to the tribe. All I ask is privacy to say my prayers, and a chance to render a little kindness now and again." He laughed. "You watch, I'll have all these barbarians converted, eventually." He assumed a sudden expression of panic, glanced about as if expecting attack, and showed relief at finding none. "Well, perhaps not," he conceded.

"Anyway," he went on, gesturing with one hand, to paint the picture, "so there I am, young weed of a boy, head full of tales. I try the family business, and it's, let's say, less than fascinating. And the little boy grows into a very bored man, head still full of dreams.

"So eventually I figure out that I can damn well do as I please, and what I please is to become an Outskirter. Told the parents and the uncles and the aunts, and you can believe I didn't hear the end of it until I'd walked off out of earshot, and over the horizon." His hand made an arrow to that direction.

"And what did your grandfather think?"

"Well, he was gone by then. But he'd helped me before, learning swordplay and such. I guess I must've had the idea before I knew I had it. It was already somewhere in my head that I'd see the Outskirts someday.

"And, do you know, it's exactly like I thought it would be—and not."

"How so?"

He thought long, several varieties of puzzlement crossing his face. "Well . . . I expected it to be exciting, and it is. And I expected there to be monsters, and enemies, and comrades, and there are. And I expected to love all that, and I do . . ." He struggled to find an explanation, his brows knit so tightly that his entire face became a single squint of concentration.

Then the answer came to him. Abruptly, he grabbed a fistful of the patterned carpet and held it up to show her. "I didn't expect to love *this*."

She was bemused. "You love the rug?"

"Yes! Look at it, someone made it; *Deely* made it! And that!" He pointed to the neighboring tent. "See that patch, on the left? Last winter, it was so cold, and the coals were left too high under the tent floor; that whole corner got singed. That's Orranyn's tent. And that." A train. "The wheel sticks on that one, you have to give it a solid kick before you pull first time, then it's fine all day. And look at this." He picked up the rough pottery bowl that held the remains of his stew. "The clay; I found that, in the banks of a stream we passed six months ago. I had to tear out the lichen-towers over it. Now it's a bowl." He put it down slowly, puzzling over it, puzzling over himself. "It's strange. I do love these things: little things, daily life . . ." He looked up and pointed. "See how the sun comes over the tent?" They were sitting in its dim, peaked shadow. "And there's a hawkbug." Above. "And Chess!" The mertutial was stumping along between the tents, gathering empty bowls. Fletcher flung himself to his feet, throwing his arms out dramatically. "Chess," he declared, "I love you!"

The old woman grunted. "Ha. It's all talk. Come to my tent at sundown. Bring a present." Taking the remains of their meal, she wandered off.

Fletcher watched her, with a smile of affection and something like pride. He looked down at Rowan from his gangling height. "Am I a lunatic?"

"No . . ." She gazed around, at the world he had come to see and had learned to care for more than he expected. "I feel that way sometimes, as well. It's the large things in life that drive us, that we measure ourselves by; but it's the small things, the daily things that—that become precious to us."

"That's it." He dropped to sit beside her, quieter now. "That's the very word; they're precious." He cupped his hands, a tiny, cherishing gesture. "I want to hold on to them, somehow. I want them safe. I want them to be this way forever." He shook his head, amazed at himself, and opened his hands to free their contents. "And it wasn't for the small things that I came to the Outskirts."

"Was it the small things that brought you back to this tribe?" Rowan asked him. He turned to her, suddenly blank. "In Kammeryn's tent," Rowan went on, "you said that you weren't sure you wanted to come back from walkabout."

The expression remained, identical to the one he had worn while helping with her charts; a wordless emptiness lying immediately behind his eyes.

She instantly, deeply regretted broaching the subject. She found it hurt her to see Fletcher so, to see someone so alive and lively driven to sudden stillness. Fletcher did not speak, but nodded infinitesimally.

"I'm sorry," Rowan said sincerely, "I can see that's a bad memory. If it's nothing I need to know, I won't ask of it again."

He sat motionless, expressionless. Eventually words found their way back to him. "Thank you," he said.

After evening meal, as the falling sun faded the western sky to pale pink, faint green, clear blue, Bel recited her poem to the tribe.

It was a tale of wizards and magic in the distant Inner Lands, of small people standing against mighty ones; of a woman who held to truth against the lies of the powerful; of another who set cunning and violent skill against cruel force; of a boy with a secret talent and a need for justice—all three brought together by glittering chips of blue that had fallen from the sky . . .

Rowan listened, fascinated, hardly recognizing herself in the tale. Bel depicted the steerswoman as different than she felt herself to be: more innocent, more intransigent, purer, perhaps, and certainly wiser. Young Willam seemed darker than he had been, suffused with fate, choosing danger for the sake of honor. And Bel, as the speaker of the tale, was never described, and so only seen by her actions: she became an elemental force, a wind from the wildlands driving its way to its goal.

There was nothing in the story that was not true. Rowan could match each event to memory. But Rowan had not seen herself like this at the time; had not, she realized, seen herself at all. She had seen only the things she needed to do, and how to do them; the things she needed to know, and what kept them hidden; and, in the end, a small piece of the truth.

When Bel spoke of the Guidestars, the tribe looked up, although the sky was too light to see them. When she spoke of the steerswoman, faces turned toward Rowan, speculative, then nodding. Through the art of her words, Bel caused Outskirters to understand a steerswoman.

And when Bel told of the deceit and cruelty of the wizards, some brows were knit in thought, and some eyes were wide in astonishment;

but by the end of the poem, Rowan found in the faces of many of the warriors a mirror of her own anger and resolve.

"I was wrong."

Rowan turned around. Kree was sitting behind her, with young Hari asleep across her lap, his arms and legs sprawled with a child's disregard of comfort.

"If those evil people are going to come here," Kree told Rowan, "everyone needs to know. We'll need to act together."

"Can different tribes learn to act together?"

Kree was definite. "Yes. They'll follow their seyohs, and stupid people don't become seyohs. They know a threat when they see it. When something threatens a tribe, the warriors fight. If something came to threaten all tribes, we'd all fight. We attack. We protect." She ran one callused hand down her son's back, and he stirred in his dreams, shifting into a position even less likely. "Kammeryn is very wise," Kree said.

There was another sleeping face among the people: Averryl's. He had emerged, shakily, from Mander's tent just after the meal. Sometime during Bel's poem, exhaustion had overtaken him, and he had leaned back briefly to support himself against Fletcher, there to fall asleep against Fletcher's chest. Fletcher had moved only once, locking his long arms in front of his friend's body, to prevent him from falling, and had remained in that uncomfortable, protective position for the rest of the long evening.

When darkness approached, the fire tenders hurried to bury the flames. People began to disperse, several pausing at the far side of the fire pit to exchange a few words with Bel, whose every reply seemed to include a definite, affirming nod. Yes, Rowan imagined her saying, everything I said was true.

Rowan pulled Bel aside as they were entering Kree's tent for the night. "What is it?" Bel asked.

Rowan waited a moment, permitting the members of the war band to finish entering, before she spoke. "I have a question."

Bel glanced once at the disappearing warriors. "Yes?" They stepped farther from the entrance.

"If you're on walkabout and your partner gets in trouble, it's your duty to rescue him, correct?"

"That's right."

Stars were appearing above. The breeze whispered. "If you fail, are you held responsible for his death?"

Bel raised her brows, an action barely visible in the gloom. "It happens fairly often. If people suspect you failed through incompetence, yes. You might face a blood duel when you return. Or if you refuse to help through cowardice, then that's the same as murder, and you can be executed. But those things are hard to prove; it's just the two of you, out there alone. Usually, no one's held to blame." Bel shifted uncomfortably, and Rowan suspected that she would not like what she heard next. "Remember, the candidates are children."

"Children?"

"Around thirteen years of age is usual. Some go earlier, some later."

Rowan found the idea appalling. "But Fletcher went last year, and he wasn't a child."

"No, he was." Bel shook her head broadly. "It's a passage: if you're an Outskirter, then you're a child until you go walkabout, and a warrior after. Formally, as far as the tribe was concerned, Fletcher was a child."

"And his partner was some thirteen years old."

"Yes. It's sad."

Rowan was thinking of Fletcher's expression when, against his will, his thoughts were forced to dwell upon his journey. And she remembered another face that carried a look that was as quiet, as dark, as deep. "Is Jaffry the only child Jann has?"

Bel looked up at her with interest. "I don't know."

In the morning, Rowan was again the last in Kree's tent to rise. As she stepped into the cool sunlight, something crackled under her foot. She looked, and then stooped down to examine it.

It was a statue, some eight inches tall, cleverly constructed of split and woven redgrass reeds and blades, depicting a goat rearing on its hind legs. The artist had used the variations in grass color to good effect, creating the shadows of musculature, suggesting the sweep and swirl of long hair in the wind, outlining wild eyes.

But it had been destroyed: torn, crushed, ground into the dirt.

Rowan looked about for someone to question, then hesitated. The condition of the statue was ominous, suggesting a malicious ritual. If this was the case, she suspected that any question asked of a casual passerby might be refused. She had been careful to avoid testing the Outskirters' acceptance of her steerswoman's privilege. Should she now be required to place one or another tribe member under her ban, the tribe as a whole would be less comfortable with her presence among them.

Rowan rankled at the necessity of limiting her natural scope of questions; but she needed to travel among these Outskirters. Until she was certain of the tribe's indulgence, she must bend to any suspected requirements.

Bel, Rowan decided, was the safest source of either explanation or explication of limits to investigation. Rowan decided that the next time she could find a quiet moment alone with her companion, she would ask, at the very least, whether asking was permitted.

23

*J*t was a long time before any such quiet moment was found; the following morning, the tribe moved again.

In the space of an hour, the cloth-and-leather city vanished. Tents became trains, possessions became packs. Excited children and complaining goats were ushered into flocks. The unseen outer circle of defenders drew invisibly closer. Scouts scattered beyond, and the inner circle was doubled, its nearer members close enough to hail with a shout.

There were no shouts. Wide-armed signals were passed back and forth, inward and out. Rowan wanted to ask their meaning, but restrained herself, and set to the task of deciphering them by context.

Kammeryn's arm swept an arc in the air, crossed it, then arrowed to the horizon. The signal echoed its way through the herders, to the inner circle, to the outer, to the distant scouts: a visible, silent reverberation. The tribe moved: walkers, train-draggers, herders, and goats, all tracking across the barren land toward new pastures to the east.

Rowan and Bel traveled among a contingent of pack-carrying warriors: Orranyn's band, which included Jann, Jaffry, Merryk, and Garvin. Bel was instantly at ease, trudging along companionably, chatting to Merryk about the usefulness of his assorted weaponry.

Rowan, by contrast, felt very peculiar indeed. She was accustomed to solitude; but here were no less than one hundred and fifty people moving together through the wilderness.

Kammeryn led: a tall and dignified old man, striding at an easy pace, his aide two steps behind him. Flung far to the seyoh's left and right were two persons assigned to the signal relay, one a mertutial, the other a warrior—the job was appropriate for either category. Behind Kammeryn were warriors with heavy packs, followed by warriors and mertutials dragging train.

Rowan and Bel traveled behind this group, within a second contingent of pack-carrying warriors. Behind them walked persons carrying much lighter packs, including two war bands, whose chiefs occasionally checked over their shoulders for signals from the rear relay, posted alone far behind.

The morning was clear and windy, cold air cutting down from the sky, so that the surrounding walkers provided no shield for persons traveling in the heart of the tribe. Rowan bundled herself into her cloak, listening with curiosity to the conversations around her: family discussions, wry observations, and a few flirtatious comments tossed back and forth from various positions within the tribe. This was no army, Rowan told herself; despite its defensive configuration, it remained in motion, as it had been in stillness, a community.

At noon, Chess and her assistants distributed meat and bread, and the tribe ate as it walked. Children began to tire, and some of the smallest were loaded onto trains, there to doze, oblivious. After the meal, conversation lagged, and Jann, Garvin, and Orranyn began to amuse themselves by singing as they walked.

When the tribe stopped for the night, arrangements were casual. The evening was fair, though chilly, and only three tents were erected: the seyoh's, the healer's, which also served as a dormitory for the least hardy elders, and a group tent for the fourteen children. Some children, Hari among them, complained at being consigned to the tent, and two of them, Hari and a gangly girl near walkabout age, were permitted to remain with the adults.

To Rowan's surprise, Hari did not choose to sleep with his mother's war band. He arranged his bedroll among Orranyn's people, next to Garvin, who accepted the boy's presence without complaint.

"Garvin is his mentor," Kree replied to Rowan's question.

"What does that mean?"

"It means," Bel put in as she approached, carrying two bowls of food, "that Garvin is the person in charge of Hari's education. Every child gets a mentor, at about Hari's age." She handed one bowl to Rowan and settled down beside her.

Rowan looked at the contents: a thin slice of goat meat, tightly rolled and crusted with an unidentifiable substance, arranged on top of toasted cubes of what proved to be crunchy bread. All were cold. "No hot food?"

"Not tonight."

Fletcher arrived, with his dinner and Kree's. He sat down with such a wild splaying of joints that Rowan expected nearby persons to be scattered like twigs. Miraculously, he avoided bumping anyone; the effect was incongruously graceful, after the fact.

Rowan continued to Kree: "You're not teaching Hari yourself?" She noticed Fletcher watching her closely.

"No," Kree replied. "Mothers don't mentor their children. We tend to be biased. It's easy to become slack."

"My mother was my mentor," Bel said, taking a bite of meat.

"Well, that's rare."

Rowan crunched some of the bread cubes. They had a sweet, smoky flavor. "Who decides who is whose mentor?" She tried the meat.

She did not hear Kree's reply, as all her concentration was suddenly occupied with preventing herself from gagging. It was the flavor of decay, dried decay, that coated her tongue with cloying dust. She sat very still and slowly exhaled through her nose. The odor of her own breath was like rotted, oozing redgrass.

She saw Fletcher watching her with a wide, close-lipped smile of pure enjoyment. She forced herself to swallow. "You were waiting for that," she accused him. Her teeth felt dry.

"Oh, yes."

Kree and Bel exchanged puzzled glances.

"What is it?" Rowan asked.

He set to his own dinner with apparent pleasure. "You take red-grass stalks, and toast them over a fire. Then you grind them and roll the meat in it. I don't think there's any real food to it—people can't digest redgrass, it just goes through the same. It's done purely for the flavor."

Rowan looked at her dinner and grimaced. "I wonder why they bother?"

"Variety," he said. "It's goat meat for breakfast, goat meat for lunch, and goat meat for dinner. You get your variety however you can."

After the meal, as the darkness began to gather, Fletcher and Kree took themselves to Mander's tent, to check on the exhausted Averryl. Around the encampment, mertutials cleared away crockery, and people began to bed down for the night.

A pair of children wove their way from their tent through the sitting and lying Outskirters, to arrive at Rowan's side: Sithy, and a little boy so young as to still be unsteady on his feet. "Chess says," Sithy began; she paused as if regretting her bravery, then continued, "Chess says give this to you." It was the longest speech Rowan had ever heard her make.

"What is it?" Rowan took the tattered object. It felt faintly greasy in her fingers, without leaving residue, rather like the gum soles of her own boots. She peered at it in the deepening twilight.

"Chess says—" And Sithy paused so long that Rowan wondered if she forgot the question. "Says you like . . . things," the girl finished. The little boy beside her watched both faces in turn, with wide blue eyes too fascinated to blink.

"I do like things," the steerswoman reassured them. "I like to find out about them. Do you know what it is?"

"No . . ." The girl's voice was barely audible.

"Where did you find it?"

"Bodo found it." Sithy gave her companion a shove, which sent him reeling. He recovered, and tottered back to her side.

The object, colored a pale brown, was shaped like an empty sack, about the size of Bodo's head. The inner surface was slick; the outer had a rough texture. Rowan took a closer look and tested the material with the edge of a fingernail. Particles came off, too small to see in the gloom. She rolled them between her fingers: sand, or something very like it.

"Bodo," Rowan said, "where did you find this?" The child looked at her with the same silent astonishment he might have afforded a talking dog.

"In the grass . . ." Sithy supplied.

"I found it in the grass!" Bodo suddenly announced, with perfect articulation and much volume. Either the memory or the act of declaration itself amused him beyond control. He emitted a series of gleeful squeals interspersed with precise ho-ho-hos.

Rowan placed her left hand in the sack and attempted to restore it to its original shape: oval. "Bel," she called.

Bel excused herself from a discussion with Merryk and Jann and approached. "What?"

"Is this a goblin egg?"

Sithy's jaw dropped at the concept, and she shook Bodo silent.

Bel took the sack and immediately shook her head. "No. Goblin eggs are white. And thinner." She attempted to examine it, but the light had diminished past usefulness. She handed it back to Rowan. "You'd better wait until morning to study it."

"I suppose you're right." Rowan considered, then brought the object close to her face. A faint scent wafted out of its interior—musty, cloying, like the gland scent of some unidentifiable animal; but over this, a sharp tang she recognized immediately: the sea.

She addressed the children. "Thank you. I do like things, and I'm very glad to have this." She waited until the pair had departed, then said to Bel, "I think it's a demon egg."

Bel thought for a moment, then nodded. "Let's tell Kammeryn."

24

ammeryn sent warnings to the scouts, then informed the chiefs, who carefully instructed their war bands: Watch, listen, report any signs of demons instantly. But the night passed with no news.

In the morning, Mander, the healer, searched Rowan out and found her reexamining the tattered object by daylight. The steerswoman gained no new information, other than confirmation of the object's color.

Mander spoke without preamble. "How do your hands feel?"

Rowan looked up. "My hands?" She flexed the fingers and found them slightly stiff from dryness, which she had attributed to exposure to the cold wind the previous day.

Mander took her left wrist and studied the hand with a proprietary air. "Bodo's hands are itching, fingers and palms. I think it's from that thing he found."

Recalling Bel's description of a demon spraying corrosive fluid, Rowan became concerned. "How bad is he?" Her own palms began to itch—a purely emotional reaction.

"Not bad." The healer subjected Rowan's right hand to the same scrutiny. "Have you washed them yet? Wash them again. I'll give you some strong soap. Don't let anyone use the same water after. If it gets worse, I have some salve. And you'd better throw that thing away."

Rowan followed Mander's directions carefully, carrying a water sack to the cessfield and pouring the water over her hands instead of immersing them in the carrier; it would be used again, and she did not want any possible contamination to occur. She emptied the remaining water, slung the loose sack over her shoulder, and turned back to camp; but as she was crossing the border of dying grass at the edge of the cessfield, she stopped abruptly, then looked around.

She had noticed at the old encampment that redgrass suffered from the presence of human waste: grass nearby bleached, then rotted, exactly as it had done in the place where, so many weeks earlier, Rowan and Bel had found the dead fox. Ghost-grass, it was called, and it had ringed the tribe's cessfield in an area some eight feet wide.

But here, after only one night of camping, the ring of decay was already three feet wide, affecting not only the redgrass, but tanglebrush, blackgrass, and a low, bulbous blue plant she had learned to call moss-wort. Rowan attempted to imagine the extent of destruction that would be caused by a tribe remaining stationary for two weeks or more, as was usual in good pastures—and became disturbed.

As she walked back to camp, she considered that it must be more efficient to dig a pit for waste and confine its ill effect, rather than set aside a flat area—and so wide a one, at that. The Outskirters could not have caused more destruction with their waste if they had actually planned to do so. And she immediately began to wonder if that was the case.

A question to Chess provided the answer. "The land is our enemy," the mertutial told her as she stowed the water carrier onto a nearly loaded train.

"But you can't mean to harm it!"

"Why not?" Chess secured the straps on the load. "It means to harm us. It tries to kill us every day. We harm it back."

"But that doesn't make sense."

Chess's only reply was to deliver a sidelong look of derision. The steerswoman continued, "If you destroy the grass, how will you feed your herd?"

"By moving on."

Rowan took further questions to Bel, who was occupied with organizing her own equipment and Rowan's. Bel paused to consider, head tilted, then nodded. "It's true. The land is our enemy. Most things in the Outskirts are our enemies. We kill the goblins, we tear down the lichen-towers, we burn out tanglebrush."

"When you need to, or simply as a matter of course?"

"As a matter of course." She passed Rowan her pack. "We kill a goblin whether it's attacked us or not. If we find their eggs, we destroy them. If we camp near lichen-towers, we'll pull them down. It's the right thing to do."

"But you're also harming the redgrass; the goats need the redgrass!" Then Rowan stopped in realization. "And they destroy it, themselves," she added, surprised. The goats grazed the reeds close to the roots; the stubs then died. She found another question. "How long does it take the redgrass to recover?"

Bel shrugged into her pack. "Who can say? We never stay long enough to find out."

Nearby, Kree was counting heads. She came up short. "Where's Fletcher?"

"Went off to do his prayers," someone replied, disgruntled, then pointed. "Coming back just now."

Rowan looked, and saw Fletcher approaching at a cheerful lope, clearly visible across the open landscape.

Kree watched a moment, then made an indulgent gesture. "Well, if his god protects him, more power to it, and to him, too."

Another voice spoke, in a barely audible grumble. "Fletcher finds enough trouble to need a god all to himself."

Kree's response was a single glance that rendered the speaker silent. "It's true Fletcher finds trouble." She pitched her voice for all her warriors to hear. "And I'm glad of it. Fletcher has a talent for finding trouble before it finds someone else, and for dealing with it. Whether it's his prayers that protect him, or his wits, I don't care. The result is the same. He's one of the strengths of this band."

Fletcher had approached near enough to hear the comments. "And if you want an example of the usefulness of prayer," he called out, "here's one."

Rowan saw what he had. "Be careful how you handle it," she called, and drew nearer. "It irritates the skin."

Fletcher eyed the object with wild suspicion. "Mine, or its?" Unlike Bodo's find, Fletcher's was unbroken. It bulked round and full, wobbling faintly between Fletcher's bony hands, from the motion of internal fluid.

"Where did you find it?"

"About a kilometer from the edge of camp, toward position seven." Fletcher gingerly placed the object on the ground, where its shape flattened somewhat. "There I was," he said, "settling down for a friendly chat with the Almighty Lord, and I practically put my knee down on this thing. Wouldn't have noticed it otherwise. I like to think I was guided." He acquired a piously smug expression, then dropped it with a laugh. "Well, maybe not. At the best, I was prevented from landing square on top of it."

Rowan suppressed the urge to cut the object open immediately; the contents might be corrosive. This was Kammeryn's tribe, and any possibly dangerous action ought first to be cleared with him. Bel went to fetch the seyoh. "Did you hear anything?" Rowan asked Fletcher as she stooped down to peer at the presumed demon egg.

He raised his brows. "Such as?"

"Humming. A single tone, sustained. It's the sound demons make."

"Nothing. I hummed myself, a bit. But nothing else."

Bel arrived, with Kammeryn in tow. The seyoh examined the demon egg without touching it, conversed briefly with Rowan and Bel, then made the suggestion that Rowan had hoped for.

She took over. "We should clear this area," she said. "If the surface irritates, the contents might do so as well, and to a greater extent. There's liquid inside; it'll spread."

Clearing the area consisted simply of continuing preparations for the day's travel, then directing people to step back from the object. Bel acquired a wool rag from a mertutial, then covered the egg and steadied it with her hands, leaving an opening in the covering on the far side. Reaching across, the steerswoman sliced into the exposed surface with her field knife, turning away her face to avoid any splashes.

The opening tore; the object collapsed. Inside: only a clear fluid that spilled and sank into the ground immediately, exactly as would water.

Rowan was disappointed. "Nothing more?" She had hoped to find a demon embryo. But Bel removed the cloth, and it was true: there were no other contents. Rowan leaned forward cautiously and sniffed the ground. The scent was of seawater, with an additional sour tang that she had smelled only once before; but the overlying musky trace was entirely unfamiliar.

Rowan sat up. "Fletcher?" He approached.

She did not like to upset him; but she needed to know. "Does this smell like your swamp?"

He tested it. "Yes."

*   *   *

Rowan and Bel walked that morning with Kammeryn.

"According to the wizards Shammer and Dhree," Rowan said, "demons need salt water, and a salt water different from that found in the Inland Sea. North in the Inner Lands, there is an area called the salt bog; I've been there, and the water smelled a bit like that egg. There are legends that demons once existed in the salt bog, but no one in living memory has ever seen one."

"If they need special water," Bel added, "that would explain why they're so rare. And why we see signs of them now that we're moving closer to Fletcher's swamp."

"Perhaps the Face People have some experience of them."

Kammeryn mused. "Face People, demons, wizards. You bring strange things, steerswoman."

Rowan was taken aback. "I bring nothing," she told him, "but information."

During the morning, messages were regularly relayed from the scouts. No sign was found of demons. The most skillful scout, a woman named Maud, was sent much farther ahead than was usual, specifically to search for the creatures. Garvin was pulled from his band to serve temporarily as her contact, at which Jann commented: "Now we're short. What a bother: I suppose it's Fletcher's talent for trouble, again." Orranyn's band had been moved up within the formation and was now dragging train. With Garvin absent, burly Merryk was both dragging train and carrying a pack.

Rowan was unable to tell whether Jann's observation was by way of complaint. "Surely it's better to find out about things before they cause problems."

The warrior sighed aggrievedly. "Of course it is. But the thing is," she said, glowering, "Fletcher's not a good warrior." Merryk shot her a cautioning glance; the bald statement was of the sort that caused Outskirters to take quick offense. Fletcher, however, was well out of earshot.

Jann continued. "You'd think that it would be the skillful warrior who finds danger first; we're trained that way all our lives. If there are strangers, or monsters, we ought to spot them. But we don't; a gangling fool like Fletcher does. It's like an insult."

"Perhaps," Rowan ventured, "it's because he has less ability with the usual Outskirter skills that he's developed—" She sought the word. "—more observativeness, perhaps. The ability to notice the incongruous."

"Or maybe his god protects him," Bel said, then knit her brows at Rowan's dubious expression. "You're too quick to deny the gods, Rowan," Bel admonished the steerswoman.

"I'm not quick at all," Rowan began, prepared to expand upon the subject; but Jann forestalled the explication that would have followed. She turned to Bel, speaking hotly.

"His god, ha! Did you hear what he said, that he found that egg by almost putting his knee on it? He kneels to pray, Bel; you should think of that. No warrior kneels to anyone. Not even to the gods." She trudged in silence for a long moment, then spoke as if to herself. "There are bad gods and better gods. You fight the bad ones and deal with the better ones. But any man who abases himself, even to gods, is no Outskirter."

Bel agreed easily. "That's true."

Rowan was taken aback. "Didn't you once say that one ought to respect other people's religions?"

"Yes. Because a person's religion is a part of his own way of honor. But this is different. When you belong to a tribe, the whole tribe is depending on you to do your part. You have to do it right, or someone could die. Your first honor is to protect the tribe." She thought long; high above, a pair of hawkbugs swooped, fighting for territory. Bel continued, uncertain. "I don't understand Fletcher's god; it doesn't sound right to me. If he were in the Inner Lands, I wouldn't think twice about it.

"But this is the Outskirts, and Fletcher is calling himself one of us. If he follows this god, then whatever he does, he does for different reasons than we do." She became decided. "In the Outskirts, it's Outskirter ways that succeed. If Fletcher wants to be an Outskirter, then he ought to be one completely."

They walked in silence for a while. "It seems to me," Rowan hazarded, "that whatever his motivations, Fletcher is doing more good than harm."

From behind them, Jaffry made one of his rare contributions. "So you say."

* * *

When noon meal was passed out, Rowan took the opportunity to drop back in the crowd, eventually falling in near Fletcher and Averryl.

She greeted them, then addressed Averryl. "How are you? Are you feeling fit to fight? And if that counts as an Outskirter insult, please accept my apology in advance."

Fletcher laughed out loud; Averryl did not, but his gray eyes crinkled. "It's no insult. And you'd have to do a great deal, steerswoman, for me to take any insult. I owe you and Bel my life." He still carried no load; but his steps were easier, his right arm swinging freely to their rhythm. His left arm he carried close to his body, occasionally flexing his hand unconsciously. The middle two fingers, slack, did not follow the motions of the others.

Fletcher was walking with his sword drawn, its hilt tucked under his right arm and its length braced along the forearm. He had a whetstone in his left hand and was idly honing the weapon. "A metal sword," Rowan observed, with surprise.

"Yes, indeed." He took a moment to study the edge. "Lovely thing, isn't it? Got it in Alemeth. Saved my pennies and commissioned the swordsmith three streets over to make it for me. Went and watched him at his work every day." He grinned. "Bothered him no end." He walked without looking at his direction, and the warrior in front of him threw wary glances at the exposed blade waving at her back. Fletcher ignored her, giving careful attention only to the maintenance of his fine weapon, as he strode along in his loose-legged lope.

All Fletcher's actions carried excessive movement: wide-armed gestures, turns of the body when a shift of the eyes would do—sloppy, undisciplined motions. It was impossible to imagine him being a superior fighter.

"Why have you never been challenged for your sword?" Rowan asked unthinking, then immediately regretted the statement. It contained an implied insult; that, if challenged, he would certainly lose.

He took no offense. "I was challenged about as soon as I arrived." The precision of his honing suffered as he warmed to his story. "There I was," Fletcher began, "settling into my first day in camp, and a huge strapping barbarian steps right up to me and starts complimenting me on my weapon. And I'm trying to thank him without thanking him, because my grandfather warned me about that. But if he'd warned me a little better, I would have known what this fellow was leading up to; it's all part of the form, see. So, I finally get the idea, everyone needing to explain it to me first, and I still wasn't all that certain they weren't just having me on."

"But you fought him and won."

"No," he replied. "I fought him and lost. Took all of about five seconds."

"But—" And she indicated the sword.

He looked down. "Yes, right." He resumed honing. "Well, I made such a fool of myself that it was pretty obvious to everyone that I was mostly useless, and not really a warrior at all. Then they all found out I hadn't gone walkabout, which meant that I was really a child. A little embarrassing. But the best thing, all around, really."

"And the warrior gave the sword back to you?" At this, Averryl snorted a laugh.

"Lord, no!" Fletcher asserted. "You don't waste a fine weapon like this on a child."

"But—"

He waved down her protest and indicated that she should let him finish his tale at his own pace. "So," he went on, getting back to work as he spoke, "the warrior who took my sword starts following me around, giving me suggestions, correcting my behavior when I do something particularly silly. He even offers me fighting practice sessions, and before I know it, he's become my mentor. Eventually I learn enough to try to become a warrior. Now, when a child is ready for walkabout—" He paused for the briefest moment, then continued. "When a child goes walkabout, it's customary for the mentor to give him a gift." And he smiled.

"Your sword."

"Right. It was—well, it's not usual to give something this fine. He was a good teacher, and now he's a good friend, and I'd be dead a hundred times over, if it wasn't for the things he taught me."

"A thousand times over," Averryl corrected.

"Really? That many?" Fletcher considered, with raised brows. "Well, you know best, I'm sure."

Rowan understood. "You were his mentor?" she asked Averryl.

The Outskirter shook his head sadly. "Someone had to be."

Fletcher spared a glance from his honing to look down at the steerswoman. "That's right," he said. "Averryl taught me, Averryl argued for me when I came back, and Averryl recommended me to Kree when there was an opening in her band. She thinks a lot of him; if she crosses the line before he does, I wouldn't be at all surprised if he took her place." At this, Averryl looked politely dubious. Fletcher continued. "She wasn't all that sure of me at first, but I've held up my end, well enough, I think."

"She speaks well of you," Rowan informed him.

He smiled and made an expansive gesture with the hand that held the whetstone. "It's my charm," he assured her. "Purely my charm."

Rowan spent the next morning among the goats, which traveled in two great streaming herds on either side of the tribe. As she was conversing with one of the flockmasters, she recognized the angular form and characteristic movement of Fletcher, on guard duty on the inner circle at position eight. He greeted her with a wide wave, which earned him a silent, energetic scolding from the relay, who had mistaken the gesture for a signal.

Rowan continued her discussion with the flockmaster, attempting to discover more about the specific differences between Outskirter goats and those living in the Inner Lands. She was considerably handicapped by a lack of knowledge of farm goats, which she had frankly never thought to study. Nevertheless, she thought she could discern differences other than appearance.

Outskirter goats seemed on the whole to be both more wary and more sociable than their farm cousins. On her arrival among them, they instantly converged upon her, then stood slightly back as she was submitted to careful inspection by one fat and lively female. The flockmaster, a mertutial named Kester, solemnly introduced the she-goat to her as "the Queen of Nine-side."

"She's a nice old queen," Kester told Rowan. "Doesn't mind stepping down to let me be queen goat, now and then."

Rowan was amused. "Can a human male be a queen goat?"

"Oh, yes. Have to be, sometimes. And sometimes I'm a king billy, and sometimes I'm a kid. Right now, I'm king; see the queen watching me? If she doesn't like what I'm doing, she'll come and stare at me, 'til I do something else."

Rowan and Kester strode along together, with the tribe moving on Rowan's right. She found she liked the sight; she liked movement, and travel. Here was the equivalent of an entire town, all of them doing exactly what she most enjoyed.

At first, walking among the flock, Rowan took pains to avoid the puddles of goat muck. In this she was frustrated: the animals seemed to defecate almost constantly. She soon gave it up as a lost cause.

"It's the redgrass," Kester informed her. "Runs through them, fast as anything. And it comes out not much different from how it went in. A goat'll eat a day, maybe two days before it's worked up enough to cud."

Rowan's scant knowledge indicated that this ought not to occur. "Greengrass would probably serve them better."

His hand swept the horizon. "Find some. They'll thank you."

Rowan laughed. "How does a goat thank someone?"

"By not crapping on your foot."

At noon a brief rest was called. Adults dropped trains and packs to sit in the dim sunlight that filtered through high, thin clouds. The children arranged themselves on cloaks and trains, and instantly fell asleep.

Rowan wandered along the edge of their area, eventually coming across two adults engaged in a homely, comfortable occupation: a woman, of about Rowan's age, was carefully combing out the long hair of an older man. The woman herself wore her hair short, and by this Rowan knew her as a warrior, and her companion as a mertutial. Warriors wore their hair short: men's hair routinely to the shoulders, although trimmed back from their faces; women's sometimes the same, but more often shorter still. When a warrior crossed the line, he or she ceased to trim the hair in a fighter's style. Length of hair was a good indication of how long a person had been a mertutial.

As Rowan approached the pair, the man looked up at her. Something in his eyes, in his posture, in the pure sunlit smile with which he greeted her, made her alter her intended manner. "Hello," she said with pronounced cheerfulness, as though to a child. "I'm Rowan. What's your name?"

"I'm Deely," he declared, leaning forward to tell her, as if it were an important statement. Then he leaned back with pleasure into the attentions of the woman with the comb.

The warrior introduced herself. "Zo, Linsdotter, Alace." Sister to Jann, Rowan noted.

"Oh!" Hearing three names prompted the man. He closed his eyes to think. "Delanno, Linson, Alace." He opened them again and smiled. "Zo is combing my hair." Although his pronunciation was perfect, he spoke with the careful separation of phrase common in the slow in thought.

"I see." Rowan sat down beside the pair. Both had Jann's straight brows and thick hair: Deely's a solid black, Zo's a warm shade lighter. "It looks like it feels good."

"It does," he said seriously. "It feels good." He squirmed a bit, to emphasize the point, and his sister said, "Stay still."

Taking the usual Outskirter conversational opening, Rowan asked, addressing Zo, "Whose band is yours?"

Deely replied for his sister. "No one's. Zo is a scout."

"That explains why I haven't seen her before." She exchanged a glance with Zo, then continued with Deely. "Scouts stay out a long time, don't they?" She became interested in him, and in his presence.

"Real scouts stay out a long time," Deely informed her. The statement saddened him. "It's very important." He was quoting someone, who had once spoken those words to him as explanation and reassurance.

"I see. But Jann and Jaffry don't have to. I see them around often." She hoped he could find solace from Zo's frequent absence by the presence of other family members.

"They're in Oro's band."

"Oro?"

"Orranyn. No one calls him Oro now." Deely and Orranyn were of an age; likely they had been childhood playmates. "Jaffry's funny."

"How so?"

"He doesn't talk." The idea caused him deep perplexity.

"I've heard him talk." In very short sentences, with the thoughts behind his words remaining unspoken.

Deely conceded the point. "Only a little."

The grooming was finished, Deely's hair a dark, rich fall of midnight lying across Zo's lap; should Deely stand, it would reach to his knees. "Shall I fix it?" Zo asked.

"I'll do it." He reached up and buried his fingers in darkness. Then, with astonishing speed, he quartered, subdivided, and nimbly braided.

The skill of his hands prompted Rowan's memory. "Of course! You're Deely, the weaver. I've seen your rugs. They're very beautiful." But, rapt in his work, he had forgotten her presence.

Zo watched him with pride, then briskly applied the comb to her own hair. "Deely makes rugs," she told Rowan, "and ropes, and boxes. Sometimes he helps Parandys with the dyeing."

"Your job keeps you away from him," Rowan observed. There was clearly much love between the siblings.

Zo nodded. "It's what I'm best at. But I do miss him. Jann doesn't understand him."

"Jann—" Rowan began, and stopped herself. Here was an opportunity to confirm her speculation about the source of Jann and Jaffry's dislike of Fletcher; but Zo, too, might share the feelings.

Zo finished the steerswoman's statement for her. "Jann is a very good warrior," she said, with a wry mouth and eyes that understood what Rowan had not said. "But she's not good at recognizing valuable things that come in odd packages."

"That's a good way to put it." In itself, the statement explained much. But Zo's frankness impelled Rowan to add, "Fletcher is an odd package, in his way."

Zo's reply was buried by Deely's. "Fletcher is back?" The prospect gave him joy.

"No," Zo told him carefully. "Kree's band went out to the first circle, remember?"

He nodded his disappointment, and his hands found their work again.

Rowan watched him a moment; Zo did the same.

"Fletcher's become a good friend to Deely," Zo said. "He wasn't, at first. He was well, he was a sillier person, when he first arrived."

Rowan chuckled. "Sillier than he is now?"

Zo's dark eyes caught the steerswoman's. "If you think Fletcher is really a fool, you're not very clever."

"I don't know him well enough to tell, for certain," Rowan replied with perfect honesty. "But his presence here does surprise me. I've learned that it's difficult to approach an Outskirter tribe. How is it that you let him in?"

"If you render a service, you can ask for a service in return," Zo responded. She shifted back a bit to give Deely more room; he had reached the center of one thin braid, stretching it out behind his body to work. "And if you can give the name of a tribe member, you can't be refused."

"Whose name did he have?"

"Emmary, Karinson, Gena."

Rowan hunted among her collection of names. "Merryk's brother?" Another connection emerged. "And Kammeryn's line name is Gena."

Zo nodded, her dark hair sifting forward and back with the motion. "Kammeryn's nephew."

Rowan laughed. "That's a good name to have."

Zo winced. "But a sad way to get it."

Deely had stopped braiding, becoming fascinated by the looping flight of a hunting hawkbug overhead. He laughed, found a stone on the ground, and tossed it clumsily into the air. It went nowhere near its mark; but astonishingly, the hawkbug dove for it, contacted it, then fluttered to the ground among the flock. Goats shied from the thrashing in the grass.

Zo caught Rowan's expression of distress and laughed. "Don't worry, it isn't hurt. It thinks it's caught something too heavy to carry. When it figures out it's just a stone, it will let go and fly away." It did so as Rowan watched. It was near enough for her to hear its voice for the first time: a high, exasperated chirring.

"A little over a year ago," Zo told Rowan, as Deely resumed braiding, "our tribe had a clash with another, over pasturage. We couldn't back off, there was another tribe too nearby, and nowhere else to go. We had to fight, and we did, and won.

"But Emmary had vanished in the fighting." She paused. "He was a warrior, but he had been planning to cross over soon. He had trouble with his eyes, and it was becoming worse. When the time came to move, Emmary was still missing, and assumed dead. We left." Deely had completed five thin braids and began weaving them close to his scalp.

"We learned later," Zo continued, "that during the fighting, Emmary had been cut off from our tribe. When the other tribe fled, he was forced to move ahead of them, in hiding. By the time he could get free of them, he had lost our position. He was wandering for weeks and never found us.

"He tried to steal a goat from the other tribe and was wounded, though he escaped. The wound turned bad, and a rot set in. He had almost nothing to eat for days. When Fletcher found him, he was dying."

"Fletcher couldn't help him?" Rowan tried to imagine it: alone, starving, sick, then found in the wilderness by a kindly stranger.

"Too late." Zo was silent for a moment. "He should have crossed before, really. I don't know what Berrion was thinking, keeping him on.

"Well. Fletcher gave him food and tended him as best he could. Before he died, Emmary told Fletcher how to conduct a proper Outskirter funeral."

Rowan's stomach gave a twist. "Casting?" She recalled Bel's description.

"That's right. And he brought back part to the tribe, for his war band to cast; that's proper. So, when Fletcher appeared with a tale of aid given, with Emmary's names, and with Emmary's own hand in a sack made of his cloak—no one could deny him. Fletcher asked to stay permanently, and the council was so moved that they gave consensus immediately." She stopped, blinked, and, astonishingly, began to laugh. "And they were sorry afterward!" Tragedy and hilarity wrestled on Zo's face; she quelled her laughter into breathy chuckles and struggled against the grin on her face. "Oh, Rowan," she said, "if you could have seen him! He was such an Inner Lander!"

25

Scouts habitually ranged beyond the outer circle: a group of loosely knit individuals, belonging to no war band, and answerable only to the seyoh himself. It was a position highly respected, owing to the degree of skill required.

Yet it was a strangely isolate respect; on matters internal to the tribe, the opinions of the scouts were rarely solicited. The scouts themselves seemed to prefer it so. All their skill, and all their attention, was directed outward to the wilderness. When required to remain in camp, a scout often seemed out of place, a visitor. He or she might wander the grounds as if observing the actions of strangers, or fall into long periods of musing that other tribe members rarely interrupted.

Only Zo, with her love for Deely, maintained what might be considered a normal connection in the tribe's social life. When not on duty, Zo traveled by Deely's side, on the edge of the small herd of children.

On one such occasion, one drizzling morning a week later, Bel and Rowan were walking with them, Bel and Zo discussing the geography of an area to the north, which Zo had scouted some days earlier; it had been passed over by Kammeryn, in favor of possibly better pastures farther east.

Rowan had begun the questioning, planning to add the information to her charts. But as Bel began to contribute questions of her own, Rowan asked less and less, and listened more. Bel, better informed on the nature of the Outskirts, found questions that were more astute, more revealing. By listening only, the steerswoman gained twice as much information: first from the question, then from the reply.

"There were plenty of brooks, but shallow," Zo replied to one of Bel's queries.

"Too much blackgrass, then?" Blackgrass thrived on damper land.

"It was a mix. If we'd camped there, we couldn't stay long." Goats could not digest blackgrass. What redgrass there was would be consumed too quickly to warrant a long stay.

"And hard work for the herdmasters." Goats enjoyed the flavor of blackgrass and would eat it despite its lack of nutrition. Herdmasters would need to watch the flock closely and discourage foraging in blackgrass patches.

"But safe from goblins. I didn't see a single sign of them, or their eggs." Goblins preferred dryness, and warmth; Rowan considered that their fascination with fire might constitute an extreme expression of instinctive preference.

Rowan was slowly learning the interconnections between the Outskirts wildlife and vegetation, beginning to see, through her incomplete information, that they followed the same rules of interdependence shown by life in the Inner Lands. "What eats goblins?" she asked.

She had been so long silent that Zo and Bel looked at her in surprise, as if she had just arrived. They considered the question. "Flesh termites," Bel supplied.

Zo nodded. "And nothing else."

Flesh termites ate any living creature—except goats and humans. Humans ate goats. "What eats humans?" In the Inner Lands it was wolves, and sometimes bears.

Zo made an indifferent gesture. "Nothing."

"Except where the Face People live," Bel amended. "There they eat each other."

They resumed their conversation; but Rowan had stopped listening. She was constructing in her mind a diagram of rising, interlocking lines: what preyed upon what, what needed which type of resource. There were too many empty spaces, where her lack of knowledge forced her to assume unknown interdependencies. And yet, even so, one side-branch seemed to stand almost isolated. Goats ate redgrass, humans ate goats and redgrass—"What else eats redgrass?"

She had interrupted Zo speaking, on a completely different subject, and received a perplexed look. "Other than humans and goats," Rowan amplified.

"Humans don't eat redgrass," Zo pointed out.

"They must do; where does your grain come from?"

Bel looked at her sidelong. "Humans can't eat redgrass grain."

"But from what else is bread made?" Every meal she had had in the Outskirts consisted of some combination of goat products and bread.

Zo found her ignorance puzzling. "Redgrass roots."

Rowan spread her hands. "But that's a part of redgrass . . ."

"Humans can't eat redgrass root," Bel said. "Not directly."

The Outskirter had spoken with such uncharacteristic delicacy that Rowan turned her a suspicious gaze. "Am I," she asked slowly, "about to hear something that I won't enjoy?"

Bel grinned, and explained how bread was made.

Redgrass roots were peeled and boiled in water, at least four times, using fresh water each time. A number of goats were killed, and the first stomach chamber of each, the rumen, was set aside. Next, the cook, cook's assistants, and anyone else who cared to help, took the roots, chewed them without swallowing, and spit the results directly into the severed rumens. When each was filled, it was submerged in cold water. The following day it was cut open, and the resulting paste and fluid was removed. The fluid was discarded, and the paste was washed and then prepared in any number of ways to become the various types of Outskirter bread with which Rowan had become so familiar.

The steerswoman listened silently. "Then," she said slowly, "all this time, I've been eating other people's saliva."

Bel was ostentatiously matter-of-fact. "That's right."

Rowan considered, then heaved a sigh of resignation. "It hasn't harmed me so far."

"The rumens are cooked, as well," Zo put in. She mused on the resulting dish with open longing. "There's never enough for everyone."

Outskirter culinary delights. Rowan rubbed her forehead. "I see." But the information only rendered her analyses more perplexing: humans and goats were even more isolated from the interdependencies of Outskirter life than she had thought. The goats, she thought; the goats are the link. "What else, of itself, eats redgrass?" she asked, then answered herself from the knowledge she had accumulated: "Nothing."

The tribe found a usable campsite two days later, and Rowan observed and participated in the same astonishing camp construction she had witnessed before. The finished camp struck her even more completely as a mobile village: the streets were the same, the courtyards and gathering areas exactly where they had been before. Rowan knew where each war band lived, and where to find her own adopted home.

Inside Kree's tent, Rowan and Bel assisted in laying the bright carpet and arranging the various bedrolls. A train-dragger paused outside while Kree's people retrieved a number of boxes of stiffened, patterned fabric, which they placed at the foot of each bedroll. These contained the personal possessions of each member of the band, those objects not carried while on duty; few, small, treasured.

The tent was empty when Rowan and Bel awoke the following morning; Kree's band had left before dawn, to serve on the inner circle. The two women rose at their leisure, risking the loss of a hot breakfast for the luxury of rest from the weeks of travel.

When they finally decided to rise, Rowan stepped out of the tent briefly to gauge the weather. As she gazed at the slanting sunlight and the hazy blue above, she felt something beneath her bare left foot and stooped to pick it up.

It was a long, woven band, such as was sometimes used to decorate camp clothing. Bright red, pale blue, and white, it showed a complicated pattern of squares overlaid with interlocking waves. The design was crisp, bold, and lovely to see, but by some difference of style Rowan knew it was not Deely's work. Unlike the other mysterious objects that had been left by the tent, this one had not been harmed.

She tied the tent flap open to admit the light and brought the band to Bel, framing a cautious question, designed to permit Bel to indicate whether or not the subject was one open to discussion.

Seeing the object, Bel spoke quickly. "Where did you find that?"

"By the door. And back at the old camp—"

"Did anyone see you take it?" the Outskirter demanded.

"I don't think so . . ."

Bel hurried to the entrance and cautiously peered outside. "No one in sight. Now, quick, put it back."

Rowan placed the band on the ground again just as Chess wandered into view, accompanied by Mander, deep in discussion. As Rowan stood by, Bel gazed about nonchalantly, pretended to notice the band for the first time, studied it with evident indifference, and then, amazingly, ground it into the dirt under her foot. The two Outskirters paused in their conversation long enough to watch the performance, then continued on their way.

Rowan waited until they had departed to speak. She abandoned any attempt at circumlocution. "And exactly what was that in aid of?"

"I should have warned you. But from now on, if you're the last person out of the tent and you find something left by the entrance, destroy it."

"What was it?"

"A courting gift."

It was the last explanation Rowan might have imagined. "A courting gift?" All her concerns became ridiculous. "Left by the tent door? Is that the custom?"

"Yes." Bel reentered the tent, Rowan following.

"But who left it? And for whom?"

"I don't know." Bel sat on her bedroll to don her boots. "But if someone saw you accept it," she said, "you would have been honor-bound to accept the person who left it."

"Some Outskirter man has an interest in me?" It seemed very unlikely.

Bel shook her head. "No. Well, probably not. But whoever it was meant for, it's someone who sleeps in this tent. Which means a member of Kree's band, or me, or even you."

Rowan thought. "The other gifts were all ruined by someone." She sat down on her bedroll.

"I know. If someone is leaving you courting gifts and you're not interested, you reject the gifts by destroying them. But if you don't want anyone to know that you realize you're being courted, you ignore the gifts." Bel completed lacing her boots, then sat back to explain. "That's what's happening here. If the gift isn't accepted by the time everyone else leaves the tent, the last person leaving has to destroy it. But that was usually you, and I knew you didn't know what to do. So I did it."

"If I'd taken it, whoever left it could . . . claim me?"

"That's the custom."

"That was rather a close call, then," Rowan commented. She leaned back on her hands, considering the situation with amusement. "Perhaps I should have taken it. I might like to learn about Outskirter lovemaking techniques."

"Ha. The giver might not admit he left it. Or she. They don't always." Bel looked at her, dark eyes laughing.

"What an odd way to manage things."

"I like it." Bel grinned in reminiscence. "There are a hundred ways to play it: you can be subtle, or daring, or cruel, or generous. You can even use it for revenge, by leaving presents for someone until they're accepted, and then never admitting it was you who left them."

"It sounds devious."

"Of course." The aspect pleased Bel.

"Then, whoever is being courted from Kree's band is not interested?" Rowan asked.

"Yes. Or it's too soon."

"Too soon?"

"You always reject the first gifts. Then they get finer."

Rowan spent part of the afternoon seated beside the fire pit, sketching various samples of Outskirts insect life. On her way to return her materials to Kree's tent, she passed through a small open yard where four sets of tents faced each other. In front of one tent, a number of warriors were seated, conversing. "Rowan!" Jann called from across the area. Rowan changed course to approach her.

Half of Orranyn's band was present, with two members of Berrion's, including Berrion himself. Jann jerked her chin up at the steerswoman. "I see you carry your weapon with you all the time. That's a good idea in the Outskirts."

Rowan's right hand went to her sword hilt, by way of assent; she had to shift her book to her left to do this. "I've heard that's the case. And I've experienced enough to agree."

"Let's have a look at it."

Rowan mentally juggled her still-unintegrated information on Outskirter custom and decided there was nothing that suggested she should not do as asked. She complied.

Jann held the sword, hilt in her right hand, the blade resting across her left arm, turning it to examine its structure. "It looks strong," she commented. "Well made."

Berrion leaned closer. "No ornamentation. That's not usual for Inner Lands swords."

"It's a soldier's sword," Rowan told him.

"How did you get it?"

Rowan gave a wry grin. "I'm afraid Bel stole it for me, at a time when I needed one."

"Ah."

Jann held it up to let the light play along its length. "I don't see any tooling marks, or any pattern in the metal."

"I'm afraid I don't know how it was constructed." Except, Rowan knew, that magic must have been involved.

"Plain, but sure," Jann said. "It's a good weapon."

Rowan came close to saying "thank you," but recalled that warriors did not thank each other; these warriors were treating her as an equal. "It serves me well" was the neutral reply she selected.

Jann rose and passed the weapon back to Rowan. "Let's see how well."

"Pardon me?"

The warrior gave a short laugh. " 'Pardon me,' now that's an Inner Lander phrase, to be sure. I don't believe that an Inner Lander can hold on to a sword like that."

Rowan was confused. "I've held on to it so far . . ." Then she understood. "Ah. I see." The expected sword challenge had come at last.

When Rowan first learned that only Outskirters who had gone walkabout were considered warriors, she had briefly believed herself immune to a sword challenge. Bel had disabused her of the notion, explaining that the rule was clear only concerning Outskirters. Rowan was an Inner Lander. Strictly speaking, her weapon could simply be confiscated; however, her acceptance by Kammeryn rendered such an act, at the very least, rude. But any warrior, by way of compliment, might elect to treat her as an equal—and Rowan carried too fine a sword for her to expect to be overlooked.

The other warriors had risen, and Berrion directed them back. "Let's clear a space." He turned to Rowan. "How much room do you need?"

She rapidly reviewed the new strategies Bel had trained into her. "Not much." She needed to keep closer than her natural instincts would direct her. A smaller fighting space would encourage her to maintain that proximity.

Not to the death, Bel had told her. At the worst, she would find herself equipped with a wood-and-metal Outskirter sword for the duration of her journey. Abruptly, the idea angered her. She preferred her own sword. She decided that Jann would have a difficult time relieving her of it.

Word was passed, and from elsewhere in the camp more people gathered. Bel appeared at Rowan's side as Jann took position. "I've seen Jann practice," Bel told the steerswoman quietly. "She's strong. She'll try to overpower you with sheer strength."

"She may be strong," Rowan said, passing her friend her logbook, pens, ink stone, and cleaning cloth, "but I know a few things she doesn't." She unstrapped her sheath.

"Take off anything else you don't need." Rowan was wearing an Outskirter fur vest over her blouse; she removed it, and carefully tucked her thin gold Steerswomen's chain into the neck of her blouse.

Between the tents around the little yard, spectators arranged themselves, shifting as they jockeyed position for a clear view.

Another voice spoke in Rowan's ear. "She'll lead with a sweep from her right to her left. She likes to surprise people straight off." Fletcher.

It was not the best first move for a right-handed fighter. Jann would need to leave herself open for an instant to gain a position with enough momentum. An opponent not aware of Jann's strength would try to take advantage of the opening, to be met by unexpected force. With enough speed and a proper accompanying dodge, Jann could gain an immediate advantage. "That's good to know," Rowan said by way of thanks; but Fletcher was gone, as was Bel, back among the observers.

Berrion paced off ten steps, then directed the fighters each to one end of the measurement. He pulled out a wooden field knife and held it before him; Rowan received one last instruction, called out by Bel.

"When it hits the ground, not when he releases it!" A starting signal. Rowan nodded, and assumed a ready position. Her eyes were already on Jann's, trying to read intent or the feigning of intent. Jann was doing the same. Neither woman watched Berrion, but waited for the soft sound of a knife falling on earth.

It fell point-down, which Rowan had not expected. She did not hear it at all, but saw Jann hear it, saw the expected opening about to appear, and swung into it, fully aware that it was the wrong move for any weapon but her own.

The force of her swing was met by the greater force of Jann's. But Rowan's sword was not pushed aside, as was expected, and Rowan was not thrown off balance. Her weapon absorbed part of Jann's power, flexing slightly. Rowan cooperated with it, dropping the point, and her blade slithered under Jann's in passing, hardly breaking Jann's momentum.

With Jann past her, Rowan swung fully around, angling a down-sweep at the warrior's now-undefended right side, desperately alert to the need to stop the blow before it actually contacted and killed Jann. But Jann stopped it herself, one-handed, the other hand bracing herself on the ground in the half crouch into which her first maneuver had collapsed. Rowan slipped her sword around and down, sweeping at Jann's arm and feet; the Outskirter escaped by executing an astonishing backward roll, miraculously keeping her sword free and arriving upright on her feet. Her face showed surprise and pleasure. "Ha!" Rowan saw Jann instantly reassess her opponent. Whatever advantage of surprise Rowan had possessed was lost.

Taking two steps forward, Rowan used the free space for a powerful overhead blow, with so much of her weight behind it that her right foot left the ground. Jann's blade met hers and tried to force hers aside. Rowan let it do so, let her blade move and recover, stepping right as her sword twisted around Jann's.

She was now on Jann's undefended left side, but in no position to strike. She dodged back as Jann recovered.

They began a cycle of sidesteps, circling, feinting. Each studied the other's stance and motion, seeking strategy. Beyond Jann's face, Rowan vaguely saw the faces of the watchers, each in turn, as she and Jann completed their circles. She ignored them, focusing on Jann's expression and the configuration of her body.

She saw the change in Jann's balance, reasoned which muscles would contract, knew the blow before Jann made it. Rowan did not try to escape it; she met it with full force, slid her blade up to Jann's hilt, twisted, disengaged, dodged back, spun, struck again, slid again, wrenching her edge against Jann's metal-edged wooden sword.

Jann recognized Rowan's strategy. She retreated, trying to protect her weapon's weakest point. Rowan pressed again. Three times they came face-to-face, hilts together, and Rowan's speed was such that Jann had no space to recover and reposition.

Jann was now completely on the defensive, stepping back and around, again and again, as Rowan dashed forward, struck, slid and twisted, slithered free, struck again. It was close fighting one instant, at sword's length another, in a pattern determined by Rowan's reasoning and her knowledge of both weapons, knowledge only she held. Rowan began to enjoy herself.

Backstepping, maneuvering, Jann twice left openings into which a quick fighter could insert a killing blow. Rowan did not trust her own ability to halt such a blow in time; she concentrated on destroying Jann's weapon.

There came at last one moment when Rowan struck and twisted, only to find her edge caught beneath the loosened metal edging of Jann's sword. She could not escape as expected and tried to change her motion to a scissoring slide that would free the metal from Jann's edge. But Jann did not try to pull back, or dodge out. She brought sudden power from below, forcing Rowan's sword up. Rowan's hands were thrown up, her entire body undefended; but at the high point of the motion she felt something give way, found herself released, fell back into a planned fall, ready to defend from the ground against the overhand blow that would follow—

"Yield!" Jann stepped back quickly, to the far side of the yard. She stood slack a moment, mouth dropped in amazement, then laughed a long laugh of warrior's delight. "Steerswoman," she called. "I yield!"

Rowan was on her back on the bare ground, sword at the ready, prepared to counter one blow, with no way to recover for the next. She could imagine no less defensible position.

Jann held up her own weapon and turned it in the sunlight: from hilt to point, one edge was bare wood. A battered curl of metal was attached to the point in a wide looping curve, springing ludicrously in the air.

Cheers filled the area. Hands appeared, helping Rowan to her feet: Bel's, Fletcher's, Averryl's, and, oddly, Jaffry's. Rowan's shoulders were clapped more times than she could count, as the crowd broke ranks to fill the yard.

Jann approached Rowan. "You're a good fighter, Rowan. I didn't expect that." She showed no regret at losing, only appreciation of her opponent's skill.

Rowan felt nothing but admiration for the Outskirter. "As are you," she said. "You certainly had me jumping!"

"You fight like a spring-hopper. I could hardly keep up." Jann shifted her sword to her left hand and offered her right to Rowan.

Rowan clasped it warmly. "I sincerely hope," she told Jann, "that I never find myself opposite you in a real fight."

Jann's glance moved past Rowan's shoulder; the steerswoman was aware of a tall presence behind her and knew it to be Fletcher.

In a flickering instant, Jann's open grin changed from genuine to formal. "Then," she replied, "be careful of the company you keep."

26

"*N*ow, put that down! Can't always be working, girl!"

Rowan looked up.

It was old Chess, her face wrinkled into the unaccustomed lines of a smile. "Saw the fight. You did good. Hoo, that Jann, she's a fine warrior! Never thought one like you would set her back. Just goes to show you."

Rowan was seated outside Kree's tent in the afternoon light, reviewing the notes she had made that morning. She looked around in startlement, disbelieving that all this sudden vivacity was directed at herself. No one else was present.

Chess held up her hands. "I brought something." Two small pottery jugs, one small-mouthed, one large.

Rowan set aside her book. "What is it?" she asked cautiously; it might be a gift, or something peculiar for a steerswoman to examine.

The old woman crinkled her nose roguishly. "Erby," she said, then jerked her head toward the tent. "Let's take it inside."

Rowan began to recognize a universal behavior. "Is it liquor? I didn't know Outskirters made alcohol." She gathered her materials and reluctantly followed the enthusiastic mertutial into the tent.

"Alcohol, ha! This is not just alcohol, young woman." Chess pushed aside a couple of bedrolls and settled herself familiarly onto the carpet. "This," she announced, "is the stuff, the stuff itself, of celebration!" Chess was being entirely too loquacious to suit Rowan; the steerswoman suspected that something was afoot.

The old woman set the jugs down and directed Rowan to a seat opposite her. When Rowan hesitated, she fussed. "Now, a good fight like that deserves celebration, don't you think? Come on, come on!" Her waving encouragement became ludicrous.

Not wishing to offend Outskirter customs, Rowan complied, cautiously. "What is it? How is it made?"

From somewhere within her clothing, Chess drew two shallow mugs. "Always the questions, I never stop being amazed! Well." She held up the small-mouthed jug, eyes sparkling in nests of wrinkles. "This," she announced, "comes from redgrass root, same as bread. You make it like you start to make bread, then stop, and let it sit for a good long time." She poured a measure into each cup: clear, colorless fluid.

"And this"—she took up the wider jug—"used to be goat milk." She waved one finger in a saucy negation, an appalling effect in one her age. "But it's not anymore!" She added the contents to both cups: pale white liquid, with small floating yellow clots.

Rowan peered into her cup dubiously. "There's something going on in there." The clumps were shifting, and more were visibly coalescing.

Chess emitted an Outskirter's "Ha." She took a sip. "Something going on, for sure, and it'll keep going on inside." She smacked her lips, then gestured at the steerswoman. "Now you."

"Well . . ."

"Come on, come on! A fighter like you can't be afraid of a little drink!"

Rowan took a very little drink. Her tongue was instantly coated with a sour, cheesy ooze. The fluid component of the erby converted to fumes before it reached her throat, and a cold, airy gap abruptly came into being between her mouth and the back of her head. She coughed.

Chess slapped her knee. "What a fight! I never saw anyone move like that!"

Rowan waited for her tongue to reappear. "Thank you," she said.

"Who was your mentor?" Chess drank again.

"Formally speaking, as you know it, I had none," Rowan began; at Chess's urging she took another cautious sip. It was necessary to pause and swallow the gooey clots separately from the liquid. "Specifically," Rowan tried to continue, then swallowed again to clear her mouth, "Bel instructed me in how to fight against Outskirter weapons." The airy space had spread to the floor of her brain; the top of her skull seemed completely disconnected from her body, a decidedly peculiar sensation.

"That Bel!" Chess enthused. "I never saw her fight, but I can tell, just from the way she walks, from the way she carries herself. No one should ever cross her. She'll slice you up and enjoy herself doing it." She drank again.

"I've seen her do exactly that," Rowan replied.

Chess waved at her. "Come on, do another. I did one, now you."

The regularity of the procedure disturbed Rowan; it definitely possessed a formal aspect . . .

Dubiously, she sipped again. There were more clots in her cup than had been there at first, and the liquid itself had become stronger. It survived long enough to pass down her throat, and began to define for her the specific shape and configuration of her stomach. "It's . . . it's very interesting . . ."

The entrance darkened as someone passed into the tent. Rowan was surprised at the difficulty she had in recognizing Bel. She greeted her friend with relief. "Bel, come in! Chess has brought some—Chess, what is it called?"

"Erby," the old woman supplied. "And you should join us."

"How far are you into it?" Bel asked.

"Three sips each," the mertutial replied, and Rowan's suspicions coalesced.

Bel shook her head. "I think I'll decline." She ambled over to her pack, began to rummage inside it.

Rowan blinked at the old woman, seeing her with difficulty through expanding and dispersing spots of blue light. Chess was smiling a thin, happy smile, perfectly content. "Bel," Rowan began. "Excuse me, Chess—Bel . . . what exactly have I gotten myself into?"

Bel turned back, suppressing a grin. "You've gotten yourself into Outskirter customs." She approached. "Pardon us, Chess, while I instruct this foreigner." Bel stooped down beside Rowan. "Drinking erby muddles your mind and puts you at a disadvantage. When people agree to drink with each other, they agree not to gain an advantage. If one person drinks, another has to, at the same time.

"If you're in a group, you pick one person, catch his or her eye, and drink; the other person has to drink, too. You make sure to pick a different person each time, and spread the effects. If it's just two people," and her grin escaped control, "you have to drink anytime the other person does. And she has to drink when you do. You stay even."

Chess ostentatiously took a large sip. Rowan hesitated, then did the same. The cheesy substance insulated her tongue from the effects of the alcohol, half of which ventilated her throat again; the other half found a new route to her brain, by way of her eyeballs. "I see," Rowan said, although literally, she could not, quite. Bel was a shadow against faintly blue light. "How does one ever stop?" She decided that the need for this information would soon be urgent.

Bel's form weaved in the air. "If one person doesn't take a sip, the other has nothing to match. If the second person also doesn't take a sip, the first has nothing to match. Then it's over."

"Ah." Experimentally, Rowan drank again, saw Chess do the same. "But," Rowan said, "but, what if one person never stops?"

"Oh, she will," Bel assured her, "one way or the other."

Bel seemed to vanish; Rowan watched as Chess charged both cups again, from each jug. "Why," Rowan asked, "don't you just put it all in one jug? Is it," she searched for the word, "a ritual?"

"Ritual, perhaps; a ritual of necessity," Chess replied. Rowan was amazed that the elderly mertutial could enunciate so clearly. "If you put it all together at once, it'll turn itself into cheese and vapors. Can't drink it then."

"Well," Rowan said. "Well." She studied her cup; her vision began to clear, although it acquired a liquid quality. The air on her body seemed tangible; her skin prickled. Her eyes possessed no bodily connection whatsoever to her face. "So this is how Outskirters celebrate?"

"Sometimes," Chess informed her, then gestured with her own mug, "when you're with a friend you can trust." She sipped, smacked her lips again.

Conforming to custom, Rowan drank. "Well," she said again, then forgot her planned statement: Chess, something about Chess. She found it. "I certainly can trust you, Chess. You cook everything I eat. If you wanted to kill me, you'd have done it by now." After the fact, she hoped the comment did not constitute an insult.

But Chess considered the statement seriously. "Yes, indeed I could have, Rowan the clever fighter! I couldn't fight you with a sword!" She blinked. "Not now, that is."

"You were a fighter," Rowan observed, "once." Of course she had been; all mertutials had been, once.

"One of the best, if you believe it."

Rowan was relieved to discover a basis for conversation. "How many people," she asked, "have you killed in your life?" She would be interested in the answer.

The mertutial let out a gust of breath. "Hoo. Plenty." She sipped; Rowan sipped. "By the time I was twenty," Chess continued, "I'd killed twenty. I decided then to make thirty by thirty; but by the time I was thirty, counting seemed silly. You can't kill people just to keep up a tally."

"No, indeed," Rowan said. "You might need to kill a friend, to maintain the numbers."

This was apparently the wisest thing Chess ever heard. She nodded, and tapped Rowan's knee. "True, true," she said. "You have to be careful who you kill."

"I'll keep that in mind."

"But twenty by twenty," Chess went on, "that's something. Because I didn't kill anyone at all before going walkabout. So, you see, that's twenty in six years."

"A truly remarkable achievement." Rowan was proud of the phrase. She drank again.

"I started off strong," Chess said, after matching Rowan. "I took down three when I went walkabout."

Walkabout. Rowan decided that she wanted to know about walk-abouts. "How did that happen?"

"Well." Chess arranged herself to tell a story. "It was me and Eden, two young girls, off alone on the veldt . . ." Rowan struggled to imag-ine it: Chess, with her remarkable collection of wrinkles, straggled hair and all, once a young, strong girl. Abruptly, an isolated corner of her mind, a calm and intelligent segment, caught up the concept and gifted her with a mental image brighter and clearer than the true one before her eyes: Chess would have been a small girl with wiry cords of muscles, quick of reflexes, determined of will. One little package of danger and death, never faltering . . . And Eden—

Chess began to recite:

> "Odd Eden, awkward and tall,
> Chess chided, cheering;
> 'Fear no foe, make no fault,
> We will be warrior women together . . .' "

Rowan listened, as Chess and Eden spent days crossing the fear-some wilderness: two children, alone in the Outskirts. They stayed within signal distance, but the signals passed were for recognition only: I am here. Each, alone, found and faced small, single dangers.

Until the day they crossed, unknowing, pastures held by another tribe. Eden sighted a guard, tried to angle away; the children had no quarrel with the strangers. But for reasons unknown, the guard de-cided to attack, and Eden found herself pursued. By the time she de-termined that escape was impossible, by the time she turned to face her enemy, Chess was at her side.

> "Hurrying, then holding, Chess halted.
> Eden must attack alone,
> And deliver death; but Eden was daunted,
> Faltering, failing, filled with fear . . ."

Chess stepped forward and dispatched the enemy, rescuing her partner. Then from the grass around the girls three more warriors appeared, intent on destroying their comrade's killer. Eden struck down one of them quickly, with a blow born more of panic than intent. Chess injured another, then assisted Eden against a woman who called out a name as she fought: the name of her beloved, dead by Eden's sword. When that foe fell, Chess returned to the man she had injured. She gave him the freedom to escape; he did not take it, but turned to face her, and was brought down by a fighter all of fourteen years old.

"Then Eden," Rowan said when the poem ended, "Eden failed the test. She didn't become a warrior." She was as breathless as if she had fought by the side of the children.

"Not that time." Chess refilled both cups. "She had to go again two years later, with Kester." She looked up in sudden surprise at the memory. "And she rescued *him*!"

Rowan clapped her hands together. "Good for her!" She found herself serious. "But walkabout, walkabout is dangerous." She drank again, thoughtfully: a toast to the bravery of children.

Chess nodded and took a contemplative draft. "You need good warriors. You need people who can face danger. If someone thinks he can't ever be a warrior, well, he can go straight to mertutial, and the tribe will thank him for his sense. Like Deely. Deely was born on the far side of the line—that's how we say it."

Rowan was following the tracks of some idea; she couldn't quite recall what idea it was, but the tracks seemed very clear. "People die sometimes." That wasn't quite it. "Children. When they go out on the veldt."

"Oh, yes." Chess was saddened. "Sometimes."

"When Fletcher went on his walkabout," Rowan began, then decided she didn't like the grammatical structure of her sentence: how did the Outskirters say it? "When he went walkabout," she corrected, "his partner—" She paused to recover the thrust of her statement. "Did his partner die?" The thought of the death of a child abruptly forced a false sobriety upon her. The wavering tent walls became suddenly stable, although the air remained murky. Rowan felt it was very important to pay respectful attention.

"Ah!" Chess nodded, slowly, with heavy deliberation. "Mai," she said. "Mai, Jannsdotter, Alace."

That was the idea Rowan had been pursuing: Jann's daughter, as she had suspected. "And Jann blames Fletcher."

"Jann and Jaffry do, yes. You see," Chess said, raising one finger, "he should have come straight back. He shouldn't have vanished, stayed away, then come trailing in months later. It looked bad, like he had run." She looked into her cup as if it held an answer. "Like he had run," she repeated.

Rowan considered long before asking the next question. "Did he?"

Chess weaved as she thought, a motion similar to Bel's character-istic movement. "Who's to say? I'm sure there was more to the story than he told." She took another sip.

Rowan forced herself to do the same, attempting to cling to her clarity of thought. "He didn't want to come back," she said, remembering Fletcher's comment in Kammeryn's tent.

"He was hurt," Chess said.

"Injured? How badly?"

Chess shook her head. She thumped her chest. "No, inside. In his heart. Because of what happened. I think he wanted to die."

"What did happen?"

Chess sighed, shifted, and uncrossed her legs, stretching them out straight; for its age, her gnarled body seemed remarkably flexible. "Now, I have this from my boy, who got it from Averryl, who filled in the spots where Fletcher didn't say much, which was most of it, except my boy had a few things from Fletcher himself, so he figured out the rest and it makes sense in the end."

Rowan was extremely confused by the sentence and became angry: at the state of her mind, at Chess for causing it, and at Outskirter cus-tom for enforcing it. She tried to remember who Chess's "boy" might be. Then it came to her: Mander. The necessary physical intimacy of healers with their patients often inspired commensurate emotional confidences under other circumstances. Between Mander's informa-tion and that of Fletcher's closest friend, the story that would follow was likely the most accurate version available.

"As Fletcher tells it," Chess continued, "they were coming up on a swamp, with a kilometer between them, Mai ahead, at about two by Fletcher. He didn't see her go down, but he heard her shout, and he started to go to her. And then she was screaming. And then she wasn't.

"He killed the creature—he called it a mud-lion"—Rowan nod-ded, remembering Fletcher's descriptions of the swamp creatures—

"after a bad fight, but too late for Mai. She wasn't dead, but she couldn't speak. And she didn't know who Fletcher was. She couldn't think anymore, my boy says, from shock. She should have died right away, but she didn't."

They drank again.

"Now, you know that I've seen plenty of blood, in my time. But my boy, he didn't like to tell it to me, how Mai died. Something about the way the beast's jaws worked—they don't tear, they squeeze and cut at the same time, sealing the wounds. The girl was in pieces, and there were plenty of pieces." She blinked at the image she created for herself, then dropped her head a bit and spoke more quietly, looking up at Rowan from under her grizzled brows. "She was cut through the middle, as well, still alive. So there she was, just a piece of a girl, most of the top half, in the mud, looking around, dying . . ." The old woman's eyes fell, her voice faded away, and she sat, looking blindly at the cup resting in her lap. It came to Rowan that the girl in the story had been a real, living person, known to Chess since her birth.

"I don't want to talk about it," Chess announced. She sat up, recovering a degree of animation. "We're supposed to be celebrating, and here I am telling sad stories." She ostentatiously took a long swallow.

Rowan pointedly did not do the same. "I want," she said, "the rest of this story. I like Fletcher. When I see him sad, I worry." A small, hazy corner of her mind was surprised at how true this statement was.

"I like him, too," Chess said. "He's peculiar, but I like that. When you get to be my age, you learn that peculiar is good. Young people don't understand that."

Rowan refused the digression. "The story," she prompted.

Chess shook her head. "That's all. Mai died, and Fletcher just put his face east and started walking."

"Planning never to return?"

"Planning nothing, I suppose. You've seen how he looks when he remembers it." Her voice became heavy. "Planning nothing, not even thinking. Just walking away."

Rowan tried to imagine it. It seemed like death. "But he came back."

"He came back." Chess paused. "Fletcher is a good warrior. Now, that is. I had my own doubts before. Since coming back . . . it's like he put more of his heart into being a warrior. He takes it seriously. We lost Mai, but we got a better Fletcher than we had before." She puzzled a moment, made to drink, then recalled that Rowan had not matched her. She waited, puzzling some more. "Fletcher's good now, but . . . but in a strange way."

"How so?" Rowan, conceding, drank; a smaller sip than perhaps was polite.

Chess gave further thought to the question; it rated yet another sip. "He doesn't look good," she said at last. "When you watch him walking, you think he's going to fall over his own feet. I've seen him practice, and he just barely holds his own, though he does seem to have a lot of stamina. But the thing is—" She leaned forward, tapping the rug for emphasis. "The thing is, and I have this from Eden who had it from her girl"—Kree, Rowan remembered—"that if you put him out on the circle, that position is damned well secure. If he pulls duty as temporary scout, he'll come back with good report, clear, full of things he wasn't asked to find out. He makes a lot of jokes, but don't let him fool you. He's got good eyes, and a sharp mind, and sometimes he just *sees* things, things other people miss—like your demon egg. He figures out exactly where to go, and what to do, to get results. If he's all alone and something happens, he can deal with it." She stopped, blinked. "Mind you, he'll just barely scrape by. But, see, that's it, that's it." She became excited by her discovery of the fact. "Any other warrior would be good straight off, or fail and die straight off, but Fletcher scrapes by—*all the time*. It's like you can always depend on him scraping by, all the time." She peered up at Rowan, at an angle. "That's useful. Do you see how useful that is? That's useful." She had begun to list to starboard.

Rowan took her delayed obligatory sip. "That's useful," she agreed. With the story ended, her self-enforced concentration began to slip. She felt pleased. She liked Fletcher. Fletcher was useful. "It's good to be useful." She decided that this was a deep observation; then decided that it was a statement inane to a positively puerile degree; and then, because it could hardly do more harm, drank again.

Chess did the same. "I like the boy," she said. It took a moment for Rowan to realize that she meant not her son, but Fletcher. "He makes me laugh."

Rowan sat amazed at the comment. She had absolutely never heard Chess laugh. The idea was worthy of examination. She paused to examine it at length, or at least seemed to: she was certainly doing something with her mind, although she could not quite identify what.

At some point she heard a sound and decided that neither she nor Chess had made it. She turned her head to look at its source, discovering that the action was very unwise indeed.

She acquired a tilted, unstable view of Bel, who was lying on her side on her bedroll, watching wryly. She had cleared her throat to gain Rowan's attention, and now indicated Chess with a lift of her chin.

Rowan turned back dizzily to find the mertutial fast asleep, head dropped on her chest. "Sleeping sitting up," Rowan observed. "A true Outskirter to the end." She blinked. "What do I do with her?"

"She'll have to sleep it off." Bel rose. "Let's put her in my place. I'll sleep in her tent."

Sometime in the night, Rowan was awakened by the sounds of Kree's band returning to their beds. "What is that racket?" Kree demanded. Rowan became aware of the sound: a raucous, buzzing rattle. Chess was snoring.

"Dragon, by the sound of it," Fletcher said.

"It's Chess," Rowan informed them, or tried to: she discovered that her face was muffled in her blanket. She cleared it and repeated the statement. It came out slurred, which annoyed her.

"If that's Chess," Averryl said, "where's Bel?" Rowan heard him undress and climb into his bedroll on Chess's far side.

She attempted to control her speech more precisely. "She's sleeping in Chess's tent. Because Chess is sleeping here tonight."

"No Bel?" someone asked, seeming amused by the concept. Four voices from various parts of the tent commented simultaneously: two "Ah"s, one "Oho," and one half-audible "Ha."

Rowan intended to ask what was meant by the comments, but fell asleep before the words reached her mouth.

She was shocked awake by swooping whoops, cracking cackles, a number of pounding stomps—

Rowan opened her eyes to dimness, her body heavy from the motionless sleep of the drunk. The tent was sweetly warm, her rough blanket comforting. She had no desire to move, and would be satisfied to stay in place all day—if only that impossible din would cease!

The sounds were joined by laughter and indecipherable comments pitched at a humorous level. Rowan rolled over and rose with difficulty; she felt that her brain consisted of viscous fluid possessed of a slow, independent momentum. She discovered that she was still completely dressed, and, resigned to action, she plodded out into the painful sunshine.

Outside: a crowd of laughing people, and more watching from nearby tents. Among them, a figure draped in a swirling cloak, turning and flapping with delight. "Oho," a voice declared, "someone loves me, and loves me true, that's for sure!" Rowan came closer.

It was Chess, lively and nimble despite the previous night's debauch. The cloak she wore was a delight to see, its patches, black and white, worked into a bold diagonal design, flashing before the eyes as she alternately spread and swirled it. It was clearly designed for campwear, and not for a warrior while on duty; it was eye-catching, immediately identifiable, from its clear pattern to its ties of bright blue braided wool.

Rowan found Fletcher nearby. "What's happening?" Looking up at his height caused her eyeballs to throb.

He grinned down at her. "Looks like Chess found a courting gift."

"But—" It certainly was not intended for Chess. "Can she do that?"

Fletcher assumed a wide-eyed, innocent expression. "I didn't see anyone else claim it." He laughed.

Chess's uncharacteristic sociability was explained. She had known, or suspected, that the next gift would be very fine indeed, and that it, too, would be refused. By spending the night in Kree's tent, she was technically as eligible as the gift's intended recipient. Rowan grinned wryly at the old woman's cleverness: Chess had acquired a lovely possession, prevented its likely destruction, and quite probably put an end to the clearly unwelcome petitions of the giver.

"You look awful." It was Bel, studying her with amused sympathy.

"Thank you so much," Rowan replied. "Far be it from a steerswoman to deny the truth. I feel exactly as bad as I look."

"She needs food," Fletcher told Bel.

"And fresh air," Bel replied to him. "Perhaps a little easy exercise."

"They're looking for people to hunt goblin eggs in the pasture."

"That's perfect."

"Actually," Rowan put in, "I thought of spending the day in bed."

They ignored her. "She slept straight through dinner last night," Bel said.

"So she did. I'll fetch her some breakfast. You walk her around a bit."

"To the cessfield and back should do it."

"Right." He loped off. Bel nudged Rowan's arm and led her away. Rowan, with a wry grin, permitted herself to be ushered.

As they walked, the steerswoman recalled something. "Bel, that cloak was meant for you."

The Outskirter stopped short, her brows went up, her wide eyes grew wider, and she weaved from side to side in thought; a total effect comical enough to make Rowan laugh out loud.

"How do you know?" Bel asked.

"By some odd comments in the tent last night, from Kree's people."

"Do you know who left it?"

Rowan smiled. "I have no idea at all. Have you?"

"None." Bel became satisfied; they resumed walking. "It's just as well that Chess took it, then. I hope it serves her well."

27

"Ask me why I'm following you around," Fletcher said. Four days had passed, and Rowan had already become restless. But the tribe would be in place for at least two weeks, and the steerswoman had no choice but to remain until they moved again.

On this day, she dealt with her restlessness by wandering among the flock in Fletcher's company, wading through the still-deep grass between the camp and the inner circle. The late-morning sky was bright, a cool clear crystal above the shifting, rippling red—a phenomenon still rare enough in Rowan's experience of the Outskirts that she intended to make the most of it.

She sauntered along in the sunlight, Fletcher beside her, or perhaps she beside him; the lengths of their strides did not match. Sometimes she was ahead, sometimes he.

She decided to humor him. "Why are you following me around?"

He paused a moment to apply his knee to the ribs of a browsing
goat, which was disinclined to give way. "Well, actually, I'm enjoying
it. But the fact is, I've been told to." He grinned down at her and
shook a finger. "Call yourself a steerswoman; you're supposed to notice
things. Haven't you noticed that you've had someone beside you every
minute today?"

"No, I haven't," she replied, bemused.

"Now ask me where Bel is."

Rowan stopped in her tracks. "Where's Bel?" Her companion had
risen before her. Rowan had not seen her yet that day.

Fletcher pointed north. "Last night one of the scouts found signs
of another tribe. Bel's gone to talk to them."

Rowan looked in the direction indicated: forty goats scattered
among the sweeping redgrass, some seen only by the disturbance they
made in the rolling pattern. In the distance, a single warrior at position ten.

Rowan resumed walking, annoyed. "I'd like to have gone with her."

Fletcher's eyes and mouth apologized. "Letting strangers stay
among us is one thing. Letting them wander off to talk to a tribe that
might be hostile, whenever they want to—that's dangerous."

"But Kammeryn let Bel go."

He raised a finger, amused. "But *you're* still here."

She stopped again, and her jaw dropped. "I'm a hostage?" It seemed
impossible, considering the friendship she had begun to share with
these people. Then she viewed it again, from the brutal perspective of
the Outskirts, and saw that it was entirely sensible.

"Let's just say," Fletcher told her, "that we're going to take very
good care of you, until your friend returns." He began walking again.
Rowan took half again as many steps as his, to catch up.

"I suppose it's to reassure the people who are bothered by Kammeryn endlessly extending your stay," he continued. "But if you really
want to talk to the next tribe yourself, you could probably reverse
things, next time. Bel could stay here."

"I don't know. I think Bel will do the best job of convincing other Outskirters. This is her work, really, and not mine." She watched her feet for a moment. "But I'd like to help her."

"From the sound of it, you have." He was momentarily distracted, as the man at ten signaled inward to the relay, then continued. "She wouldn't be doing anything at all, if it weren't for you. She wouldn't have found out about the Guidestars, or the wizards . . ." He acquired an uncomfortable expression.

"You still don't quite believe it."

"Rowan, there's nothing *for* a wizard here," he said, then thought. "Nothing I know about," he amended.

A small incongruous shuddering in the redgrass caught Rowan's attention: a handful of reeds, showing color out of pattern. She angled toward it.

Reaching the spot, she parted the grass and at first saw nothing, then saw a motionless irregular lump, brown, gray, and black. As she watched, the object shifted jerkily, then teetered.

Fletcher was stooping beside her. "What is it?" It was a mound, apparently consisting entirely of dead insects. Fletcher prodded it with one shaggy boot. "Stuck together?" The mass shifted, then suddenly trundled itself away, in a panicky amble. Fletcher laughed out loud, recognizing it.

Rowan stepped into its path, causing it to halt. "Is it a harvester? It seems too big." It bulked to half the height of her knee.

"Greedy fellow!" Fletcher stooped down to address his admonishment to the living insect buried beneath the dead. "Think you can get all that home? Think you can *eat* it all?" The load tilted up; a tiny black-and-white head turned glittering red eyes first on Rowan, then on Fletcher, then vanished; the entire mass rotated in place; and the ambling escape resumed, somewhat accelerated.

Fletcher noted the direction it took. "Ho, watch out," he advised the harvester. "That way's the cessfield!"

"I should think he'd find plenty of bugs to harvest there," Rowan said, as the grass closed behind the clumsily fleeing insect; then she abruptly realized that that was not the case. In retrospect, she could not recall ever having seen any insects in the tribe's waste area. "Insects, as well?" she questioned herself, aloud. In the Outskirts, human presence seemed to result in an inordinate amount of destruction. She turned to Fletcher.

She made to speak, then saw his head go up, like a listening dog's. He began to rise, stopped.

"What?" Rowan looked where he was looking, rising herself to see over the grass tops.

The guard at ten had just completed a signal and had turned away. Rowan prompted Fletcher again. "Motion on the veldt" was his distracted reply.

"Outside the circles?"

The guard signaled outward, turned, then signaled inward. Fletcher stood and looked back to camp for the reply. " 'Has it stopped?' " he read, then turned to see the guard again. A pause. " 'Yes.' "

"That's good," Rowan said.

He knit his brows, watching. "No . . . no, it isn't . . ." He startled; his hand made a movement toward the sword hilt at his shoulder, then paused.

"What?"

"The scout is gone."

"Gone?"

"Maud. She may have dropped into hiding." He stood quivering, head high, all attention outward. Rowan looked around. Nothing visible had changed.

The wind was from the north. A scout in hiding must move to remain concealed, else the grass waves would break around her, showing her position to possible enemies. Maud would be approaching the tribe.

In the windy quiet of the veldt, Rowan's heart beat hard, twice. She watched the guard at ten. There were no signals; he stood in Fletcher's pose, waiting. She watched Fletcher's face and learned more. A dozen possibilities were passing through his mind; his face showed each. His body wanted to move.

He made a sudden, quiet sound of shock, then a choked cry. His long arm flailed up to his sword.

"What is it?"

"Outer nine is down!"

"Down?"

"It's an attack!" And he took two loping strides away.

Rowan moved without thinking and found herself back at his side, her sword in hand. "Where do we go?"

"We—" He spared her a glance, then stopped so suddenly that he stumbled; he recovered, and stood staring at her, aghast.

Rowan grabbed his free arm and pulled. It was like trying to move a tree. "Come on! What do we do?"

He was a moment finding his voice. "Nothing."

"We have to help!"

"I have to stay with you." Then a motion back at camp caught his eye, and he spun, throwing out one fist in helpless rage. "Outer ten is down!"

Rowan looked back. The camp was unchanged, but for three warriors approaching at a run. She turned to Fletcher. "If I can't go to the outer circle, then you go." He looked down at her, speechless. "Go on, do what you need to," she reassured him. "I can take care of myself."

His mouth worked twice, and he made a small sound, almost a laugh. "I'm not here to protect you. I'm here to protect us—*from* you!"

Rowan said nothing. The approaching warriors passed, fanning out into separate directions.

Fletcher drew a shuddering breath and expelled it with difficulty. "You'll have to sheathe your weapon," he told Rowan. His eyes were wild, his voice was forced flat, and he trembled from the need to run to his comrades' aid. "Either that, or give it to me."

She looked at the sword in her hand, then looked up. "I don't understand." But he had stopped watching her; he was reading the relay, and she read its message mirrored on his face: that out on the veldt warriors were fighting and failing, and that enemies were working their way inward, toward the heart of the tribe. "What are they saying?"

He kept his gaze on the signals. "Lady, please don't ask me that." He slipped into the form, and the deference, of an Inner Lander.

"Fletcher—"

"I'm not supposed to tell you!"

She forced him around, violently. "Bel is out there somewhere!"

"I know. That's the problem."

A scout had found signs of strangers. Bel had gone out to talk to them. Now the tribe was under attack. "No," Rowan said. "No, she didn't bring them here."

"I know. I believe you." He could not meet her eyes. "But it doesn't matter. Put your sword away."

She did so. "If the enemy comes this far in," she said stiffly, "I hope you'll tell me in time to defend my own life."

"If they come this far in, I'm supposed to kill you myself."

They had been walking most of the morning, sharing observations, jokes, reminiscences. She stared up at him, appalled. "Would you actually do it?"

His pose shattered. "God, I don't know!" he cried out. "Don't ask me, Rowan, I don't know!" And behind him the wavering ripples of redgrass tops suddenly evolved three straight lines of motion, approaching fast.

"Eight, six, and five by you!" Rowan shouted, and shoved past him, running toward the endpoint of the nearest line, drawing her weapon.

The line on the grass vanished.

She stopped. Shaking with urgency, she stood. She thought.

Wind from the north; if the enemy was moving, it was at the wind's pace, in its direction. Angling now to the right.

She shifted, ran. There were sounds of pursuit behind: Fletcher, coming either to aid, or to carry out his duty.

Another line changed direction, doubling back toward her. A trap. They thought she would go for the visible target.

Fletcher called to her, cursing in the name of his strange god. There was a dip in the grass tops to her left: she spun, struck. The impact of her blade on bone sent a shock through her arm. The approaching second line arrived, and a figure burst from the redgrass, reeds chattering. She swept with her sword, high: a tanglewood club fell to the ground. The enemy dove for it. She struck down at his skull, sliced down his scalp, severed his neck.

She turned back to the first man. Her metal sword met metal and wood. She had wounded him before; he fought with his body angled away, his left side glittering red in the sunlight.

Nearby, Fletcher made a sound—a choked cry of battle. He was about to kill someone. She wondered if it was herself.

Her adversary fought with vicious speed, but clumsily. He gave her a dozen openings, recovering each time too quickly for her to use them.

Fletcher had not killed her yet. Someone else, then.

She disengaged, pivoted, took two steps, and struck again at her enemy's wounded side. He took the blow without a sound as her sword cut deep into him. He writhed and made a desperate sweep at her own undefended left, then changed direction to meet a second blade: Fletcher's. Sword stopped sword. He stood a moment so, with Fletcher's blade against his blade, and Rowan's inside his chest. Death overtook any further moves.

Fletcher turned away as the man fell, scanning the veldt for more action. Rowan pulled her sword from the corpse and did the same. Instinctively they halved the duty and found themselves back-to-back.

"At four by you, I've got three of ours against two of theirs, right by Sim's tent. And one more approaching from eight."

"I have five approaching at ten by me, some heavy engagement at twelve, too far to see clearly."

"Anyone heading for that five?"

"No."

"Let's go."

The enemy was making no effort at concealment; that time was past. Rowan did not know how to conceal herself like an Outskirter, did not know if Fletcher had that skill. They approached in the open. The two nearest adversaries first sped to flee, then wheeled about to engage.

Rowan's man had a club he hefted high to swing down; she struck beneath it, two-handed, waist-level, left to right, with as much speed and force as she could muster.

He dodged back, she dodged aside; both blows missed. She swung up to the left, grazed his head. He brought the club up, a weak move that struck her right forearm. Her arms were thrown back, right hand free of her hilt. With her left she swung down on the side of his neck. Her enemy choked, spraying blood from mouth and wound, and collapsed.

Fletcher was fighting against a metal sword, with difficulty. His enemy was half his size, twice his speed. Fletcher dodged back, trying to use his longer reach and greater weight. His opponent escaped each blow nimbly, recovered ferociously. Rowan moved to assist, but found a new enemy; she downed him with a fast low stab to the abdomen, then took on the next man who rose behind him.

He was less quick than the others; Rowan entered into Bel's drill. She slid her sword up his, twisted, pulled back, struck, slid, twisted. He lost his rhythm for the briefest moment when he saw what was happening to his weapon. She took the instant to gather force for one great blow that shattered his sword at the root. He stepped back in shock, staring at the hilt.

He was smaller than Rowan, wiry, his brown hair short as a woman's. His clothing was a tattered fur motley, his legs bare. He looked up in helpless horror. She drove her sword into his blue eyes, and his face became a thing of blood and bone.

She turned toward the ringing sounds of Fletcher's fight, found his enemy with his back toward her. She struck below one shoulder. Ribs broke; then she saw Fletcher's point swing high, trailing an arc of blood as the man fell back, his stomach and chest opened to his throat.

In the lull, the redgrass roared like surf. Fletcher and Rowan exchanged one wild glance, went back-to-back beside the corpse.

She was facing the camp, he the veldt. "There's something going on in camp, I can't tell what. Nothing between here and there." He did not reply. "Fletcher?" Silence. "Fletcher!" She turned to him.

He stood looking out. "Sweet Christ . . ."

A troop of figures, at least a dozen: a full war band approaching fast, with no other defenders between them and Rowan and Fletcher. And beyond, the rippling grass showed a complexity of contrary motion, lines too confused to be counted: a second wave moving below the grass tops, hard behind the first.

"We'll have to fall back," she said, then knew that there was no time. "We'll have to stand." They were two, alone. "Fletcher?" She looked up at him.

He had not moved. He stood with his body slack in shock, hilt held loose in his left hand, the point of his sword dropped to the ground, forgotten. His right hand gripped the Christer symbol on its thong, fingers white with strain. A dozen emotions crossed his face, each a separate variety of terror; then Rowan saw them all vanish, fall into a pit behind Fletcher's eyes, and he stood expressionless, empty, blank.

"Fletcher!" His face was the same as when he thought of his walkabout, of Mai, of death. "Fletcher, not now!" She pulled at his arm. He resisted. She tried again, harder, and swung him around.

He looked at her with dead eyes, then looked at her again; Rowan saw him see her twice. He saw, and Rowan felt herself being seen: a woman alone under blue sky, standing on crushed redgrass, a corpse at her feet, blood on her clothing and her sword, the home of Fletcher's people behind her, the enemies of Fletcher's tribe approaching, now near—

And it was in that direction that he turned, suddenly, and if he had not released his cross it would have been flung into the redgrass by the wild swing of his arm as he threw his body forward. He ran ten long strides and was on the first enemy, spun with his sword double-handed at the end of his long reach, and the first of the attackers dropped like a tree, the second fell back spilling entrails, the third stood howling with a sword deep in his abdomen—

Rowan hurried to join the fight.

Two men skirted Fletcher to rush toward camp. Rowan met them. The first raised a club to strike, and Rowan shattered his arm at the shoulder, continued across his throat, then abandoned him. The next man had a steel sword, and she used the force and moves that only her sword could take, slithering and pressing forward in seemingly impossible maneuvers, then with one singing flicker disarmed and slew him.

Across the veldt, from position seven, six warriors were approaching at a run; friend or foe, Rowan could not tell which.

She turned back in time to stop a club with her sword. She struck it again, sending black chips flying, dodged madly, took a step, turned, and severed her opponent's backbone from behind.

She stopped one more who had come around behind Fletcher, stopped another trying the same, and found herself at Fletcher's left side. He fought left-handed; she shifted to his right, met a wood sword, turned into her fight—

And then she and Fletcher were once again back-to-back, this time in battle. But Fletcher seemed unaware of her; he fought with such flailing fury that once her sword met his as he dropped the point low behind his head before delivering an overhand blow.

Beyond the remnants of the first war band, the redgrass erupted with warriors: the second band had arrived. Rowan shouted something, some words to Fletcher, the contents of which she could never remember afterward.

The new fighters seemed all to have swords, seemed all to be shouting, seemed to enter the battle with something like glee—
—attacking the first war band.

Rowan returned to her opponent, and when she looked back again, half of the remaining opponents had been downed; when she looked back at her foe, he was dead, by the sword of a huge, red-haired man, a stranger.

Fletcher was still in action, against a small, muscular man who defended himself wildly, stepping back with each blow, disbelief in his eyes. "No!" he shouted. Fletcher ignored his cry, and one of the man's comrades, a woman, made a sound of fury and started forward to assist.

"Fletcher, wait!" Rowan called.

One of the strangers cried, "Bel sent us!"

Fletcher fought on, oblivious. "Give us her names!" Rowan shouted.

And it was the man on the other side of Fletcher's sword who replied, desperately, "Bel, Margasdotter, Chanly!"

Rowan clutched the back of Fletcher's vest and pulled him back. He fell to a sprawling seat on the ground.

In the sudden quiet, Rowan looked around at the faces: a dozen strangers. "You're here to help?"

"That's right."

"Good. We need it."

The group who had been approaching from position seven arrived: half of Orranyn's band. Rowan recognized Jann and Jaffry and laughed with joy, thinking how like a warrior's that laugh sounded. "We have assistance," she called to them, "sent by Bel."

"Bel? Where is she?" It was Jaffry who asked.

One of the strangers grinned admiration for the absent Bel and shrugged eloquently. "Somewhere.".

"You're not dead," Jann observed, arriving at Rowan's side.

"Not yet." Rowan scanned the group, counted. "We're twenty." She turned back to Jann. "Where's the action? Should we split?"

Jann took a moment to consider the corpses scattered about: perfect evidence of the new war band's good intentions. "Split," she decided. She addressed the strangers. "Three groups, and each should have some of our own, so our people don't attack you by mistake. You split yourselves, you know best. Jaffry, Merryk, take one group, go to twelve. Cal, Lee, Lyssanno, take another the same way, then swing off to position three; we don't know what's going on there. Last group into camp with me, Rowan and Fletcher." She looked down at him, still on the ground. "Are you hurt?"

He was a moment replying. "No." He clambered to his feet.

They set off at a jog toward camp, where there were cries, flames. When they had crossed half the distance, Jann asked Rowan, "Why aren't you dead?"

The steerswoman felt a rush of Outskirterly pride and insult. "You fought me yourself," she said through her teeth. "You know how I fight. *That* is why I'm not dead."

It was only when they reached the tents that Rowan realized: Jann had been asking why Fletcher had not killed Rowan as ordered, why he had failed in his duty.

Then they found their battle and set to work.

28

*T*here were furious ambushes among the tents, sudden encounters; a force of six enemies made a stand by the fire pit and were coldly and systematically eliminated; wild-eyed mertutials, past warriors all, defended the children's tent, destroying would-be assassins before any younger fighters had time to assist; and at last the camp was secured.

Kammeryn took stock. "Who's still fighting?"

"Most of Kree's band is at twelve," he was told. "They have assistance. Last signal said they can hold."

"Good."

Another relay spoke. "There are single raiders spotted at four, about five of them. They made off with ten goats. Last report, maybe ten minutes ago."

"None since?"

"No."

"And Kester?"

"No report."

Kammeryn was pacing the edge of the cold fire pit. He stopped and scanned faces.

"Quinnan."

"Seyoh?"

"Go to four."

The warrior left, at a run. Kammeryn resumed his pacing, his tall, straight figure striding like an old soldier on guard, his eyes distant as he mentally assembled information. Across the pit, standing quietly by Mander's tent, Rowan did the same. What's happening at six? she wondered; and a moment later Kammeryn voiced that question.

"The band you sent is out of sight, no relay between."

"Fletcher."

"Seyoh?" Fletcher had been standing in an exhausted slouch, dazed. He came upright instantly, feverishly alert, breathing through his teeth.

"Go toward six. If they're near enough, relay. If not, find them, come back with a report. Don't join the fight, I want information."

Fletcher nodded, one quick jerk. "I'm off."

He was not: Jann stepped in front of him.

"Seyoh, I'd like to do that," she called, her eyes narrowly watching Fletcher's face. She did not trust him, or credit the trust her seyoh placed in him. Fletcher stared down at her as if he could not quite recall who she was.

The matter was trivial; Kammeryn gestured with annoyance. "Go." Jann departed. The seyoh turned away. "Nine?"

One warrior had just returned from there. "Secured. Half our people, half strangers."

The seyoh nodded to himself, then took a moment to meet the eyes of one of the warriors who had returned with Rowan: the small, muscular man. Kammeryn acknowledged his presence, and the help of his tribe, with another small nod. The man replied in the same fashion.

A girl, the one child near walkabout age, dashed into camp; she had been pressed into relay duty. "Twelve," she said. "Twelve is secure. Some of them are coming in."

"Have them move to ten."

"I can't, they don't know the signals."

Kammeryn glanced at the stranger again. "Go back to your post," he told the girl. "When they reach you, send them to me."

Kammeryn and Rowan each contemplated their respective images of the tribe's present defense: the circle was half secure, half uncertain.

The camp was silent. Kammeryn paced. Presently he asked, "New reports?"

There were none. "The children?"

"Safe," Chess called.

"Mertutials?"

"We lost some. Most of the rest are helping Mander."

"Wounded?"

Chess grunted. "Plenty. Warriors, mertutials, strangers."

The man at Rowan's side turned at Chess's words, then caught the seyoh's eye. He received a gesture of permission, and Chess conducted him to the tent where Mander was tending the wounded.

In the distance: voices, approaching from position twelve. Their sound was rhythmic.

"Who knows about the flock on nine-side?"

Rowan spoke up. "They ran from our fight, toward seven, or maybe six. Except for about twenty, who broke toward nine."

He mused. "No one has mentioned them. That's where the first strike was. We'll assume that twenty lost." He paused and looked again at the nearby faces: waiting mertutials and warriors, two relays. His eyes glittered. "Prisoners?" No one answered. "I'll assume none. If one shows up, tell me instantly."

The voices reached the edge of camp. They were singing. Kammeryn turned.

The song had no words, only a tune, simple, and a rhythm, repetitive: a song to march by.

Seven warriors entered camp, their swords sheathed. Three led. At left: a blond man, narrow-bodied, with a thin, foxy face. At right: a strong woman of startling height, her hair a short wild cloud of curls, her eyes black and laughing.

Between them, with one arm around each of their waists, their arms linked behind her shoulders, and half her face gory from a scalp wound: Bel.

She brought the troop to Kammeryn, where they halted. Bel stood a moment looking up at the seyoh. She grinned. "I think we can count the Face People as out." She unlinked from her friends and stepped aside. "This is Ella."

The tall woman turned to Kammeryn. "Seyoh," she said, dignity fighting triumph in her eyes.

"Kammeryn," he supplied, cautiously. First names only.

"My people tell me that they found ten goats in the company of some men who definitely didn't own them. The goats are on their way back. Please let your people know, so they won't kill mine before they can say Bel's names."

Kammeryn gestured; the relays went to pass the word.

Ella drew a breath. "What's your orientation?"

"You came from twelve."

"Right." She looked about, setting the configuration in her mind, then gestured. "We deployed two bands at your six. No report, but we know there was only one band of Face People there. I'd be damned surprised if it weren't secure by now. How many did you send there?"

He was watching her face, speculatively, with great interest. "One band," he said. "With yours, six is secure."

She raised her brows. "Might be some heavy losses. The Face People are a nasty crowd."

"I have a runner returning shortly."

"Good. We began with two bands at your six, one at eight, one at nine, and one at twelve. One more scattered along your three-side."

He became concerned on her tribe's behalf. "That's a lot of people to send out."

Her face darkened. "We had a grudge. We met that crowd before, and they did us damage. We wanted them dead."

Jann arrived, breathing heavily. "Six is secure," she reported. "The wounded are on their way in. Three of ours, and—" She caught sight of Ella and addressed her. "—and four of yours. And you've lost five of yours, I'm sorry to tell you."

"And ours?" Kammeryn prompted.

"None from six."

Kammeryn and Ella regarded each other. Kammeryn spoke. "When you return to your tribe," he said, "tell your seyoh that I am Kammeryn, Murson, Gena."

She studied his face. "Thank you."

*   *   *

Kammeryn took Ella and two of her people to his tent for more discussion. The rest of those who had arrived with her sighted their comrades by Rowan and Fletcher and went to greet them happily.

Bel approached and paused five feet away from Rowan. The two stood considering each other. Rowan's relief was too large for laughter, or embraces. She felt she needed something to lean back against.

Bel tilted her head. "How much of that blood is yours?"

Rowan looked down at herself. "I have no idea. And yourself?"

Bel fingered her scalp tentatively. "I should get this stitched. How many did you take down?"

"I forgot to count."

"Good. You should never count. It'll only make you conceited." She paused, then grinned. "I took fourteen."

And then Rowan could laugh.

Rowan's only injuries were a huge bruise on her right forearm, a smaller one on her left, and a number of badly strained muscles arranged in an annoyingly random configuration about her body. She stood by while Parandys, whose normal occupation was combing wool, spinning, and dyeing, trimmed Bel's hair with a knife and carefully sewed the wound with fine thread and a thin bone needle. After watching the procedure, Rowan went to Kree's tent and retrieved from her own gear the little packet of five silver needles. These she bestowed upon Mander, indicating that they were his forever. They were instantly put to use.

The steerswoman and her companion were set to work, carrying cloths and water, passing implements to Mander and his assistants, and doling out large and small drafts of erby, which served to rapidly numb the senses. Fletcher and Averryl were in and out, supporting or carrying wounded warriors; when the number of arrivals slackened, Rowan looked again and found Averryl working alone, Fletcher absent.

After a lull, more wounded arrived from position six: Ella's people.

One of their number had a thong tied around one forearm, twisted tight with a knife handle. Below the tourniquet, her arm was a chaos of bone and loose muscle, the hand a crushed ruin.

Two of her uninjured comrades posted themselves at her sides, as Mander waited for his implements to be cleaned and recleaned in boiled water. Rowan, feeling useless and helpless, urged the woman to drink from the cup of erby, which she refilled as soon as it was emptied.

Mander sat on the ground beside his patient, amiable. "What's your skill?"

The warrior replied through pain-clenched teeth. "Killing my enemies."

Mander shook his head. "Other than that." From this moment, she was a mertutial. Mander was asking what her new work would consist of.

The woman did not reply, so one of her comrades prompted her solicitously. "Goats . . ."

"Herding?"

"Diseases," the woman said, and Rowan administered another draft. "Diseases of the goat."

Mander was interested. "Ah. Well, now, diseases of the goat have much in common with diseases of humans, did you know that?"

"I could hardly care less." She spoke a shade more easily, and her muscles became looser: the alcohol's effect.

Mander directed her friends to position the arm on the ground away from her body, and the woman stiffened in anticipation. "Would you like to know how I chose my job?" Mander asked.

Her eyes were squeezed tight. "I would like you to *do* your job, and then leave me alone."

The healer continued. "It was like this—" He recounted, with great detail, an immense battle the tribe had faced some ten years before, and his own role in it. The tale was well delivered, and Mander depicted himself as a properly valiant warrior. The wounded woman began to relax, showing a certain amount of grudging interest in the drama of the fight. At the culmination of the story, Mander received a wound much like the one he now saw before him.

"The healer," he said, handing Rowan one of the silver needles to thread for him, "botched the job. A rot set in, and she had to remove more of the arm two days later. She botched it again, and had to take more. It was an outrage!" He adjusted his position, nimbly using his bare feet to brace the wounded arm, and applied pressure. "You can believe that I cursed her! I cursed her up one side and down the other,

down the river and back again. I wish I could remember all the curses I used; I'm sure I'd go down in legend as a true poet.

"Eventually she shouted back at me, 'If you think you can do better, do it yourself next time!'" He nodded briefly as Bel arrived with the tools on a cloth and set them down. "I said: 'Ha! I could do a better job with my *teeth*!'"

The warrior threw her head back and laughed out loud, helpless, her body completely slack; the laugh became a sudden scream, which silenced as she fainted.

Mander completed the rest of the job quickly and efficiently, then spoke quietly to the woman's friends as he rinsed his hand and dried it on the towel that Bel held for him. "She won't lose any more of that arm," he told the warriors. "I stole that old healer's job, and I'll keep it until the day I die." He clapped one of their shoulders in parting. "Because I'm the best."

It was full night when Rowan emerged from the infirmary tent. Bel had left sometime before; Rowan had not seen her depart. Rowan had remained at Mander's side, serving, as others did, as his extra hands, until someone had tapped her on the shoulder and curtly ordered her to get some rest. It was not until she stepped into the night air that she realized that the person who had dismissed her was Kree; that Kree had spoken exactly as she would have spoken to one of her own war band; and that Rowan had accepted the order as completely and instinctively as Kree's own warriors did.

The steerswoman wended her way among the tents by memory, only half-aware that she was guiding herself by a clear mental map of the camp, hovering in her exhausted mind. The map led her to Kree's tent; but her bleary perceptions did not notice the person who was standing outside its entrance, until he spoke. "Rowan?"

She paused. "Fletcher." She rubbed tired eyes, as if clearing them would dispel the night-dark itself. Aware that he was present, she now sensed him by hearing: his breathing, the creak of leather, small rustles of fur and cloth, all arranged and configured to the particular height and shape of his long body. He stood by, quietly occupying the air.

Before she could ask her question, he asked it himself, of her. "Are you all right?"

She enumerated her small injuries. "And you?"

He shifted. "A little slice down one side; that's minor. One of those weasels whacked me on the back. Maybe he cracked a rib; Mander wasn't sure. Someone stabbed me in the shin, but not deep." He spoke without gestures, and quietly. "A lot of people are dead."

Rowan nodded. "I suppose we won't know who, until the morning."

"There will be more in the morning than there are now."

Rowan thought of some under Mander's care who might not last the night. "Yes. But we gave better than we got, Fletcher." She remembered him in his blind warrior's fury, felling an uncountable number of Face People. Then another memory came unbidden: that frozen moment before the onslaught, when Rowan had not known if Fletcher would fight at all. It came to her that it was not fear of death that had held him in that instant, because when he did fight, it was with the wild and utter abandon of a man who knew he would not survive. What thoughts were in his mind as he watched the inescapable assault approaching, Rowan did not know; but at that moment, Fletcher had been faced with two options. He had chosen death as the preferable one.

But Fletcher always scraped by, Chess had told her. He had scraped by again, this time saving not only his own life, but the lives of many in his tribe. And it was his tribe, his own. He was no mere adopted Inner Lander. He was a warrior.

Rowan felt pride on his behalf. "You fought well," she told him. She said no more than that, but the tone of her voice said what her words did not.

When he replied, it was with a voice of quiet amazement. "After we cleared out that bunch by the fire pit," he said, "and everything got still, there I was, standing around in a daze. And Averryl, he steps up to me, looks me in the eye and says, 'You did good,' and wanders off again." There was no parody, no humor in his voice. "That's all. Just: 'You did good.' "

Rowan smiled. "Bel is much the same."

Fletcher stirred. "Well," he said, half to himself, "let's see what else I can do good." And he strode off through the quiet camp without another word.

29

ate the previous night, Bel had been awakened with the word that one of the scouts had discovered signs of another tribe. Before dawn, she had been escorted to the limit of Kammeryn's defended pastures, then left to continue alone. In speaking with the new tribe's council, her discourse on the wizards, the fallen Guidestar, and her mission were considerably aided by the poem she had composed. Their seyoh was impressed, and although she accepted Bel's information only as hypothesis, she guaranteed cooperation should the wizards' threat ever materialize. They parted on friendly terms.

But when Bel attempted to return to Kammeryn's tribe, she found herself approaching the rear of what was obviously an attack formation.

"I couldn't see a way to get around them to warn Kammeryn, not in time for it to make much difference," Bel told Rowan, as they lay on their bedrolls in the darkness. Despite her exhaustion, Rowan was unable to sleep; the battle continued to reenact itself behind her eyes.

Bel continued. "I went back to the other tribe. I was going to point out that these attackers probably would give them trouble after defeating Kammeryn's people, and it might be in their best interest to help us out now. But as it turned out, they'd met them before, and suffered fairly badly. They were ready to join forces with us, to get rid of them."

"We're lucky you arrived when you did."

"No, you're not." Bel turned over onto her stomach and rested her chin on cupped hands. "We could have arrived sooner. But the Face People would have seen us and run. We didn't want to chase them away, we wanted to kill them. We deployed so that they would be trapped between us and you. And waited until they attacked, so they were in the open, and off-balance."

Rowan sighed. "I would have preferred them chased away, if it saved lives." At last report, there were at least ten dead from Ella's tribe, and perhaps twenty from Kammeryn's. Many on both sides were wounded. Others were still missing, status unknown.

"Chasing them wouldn't have saved lives. They'd have come back later, when we weren't prepared. This way was best."

Rowan ran the strategy in her mind. "Of course. You're right."

Somewhat later, when her internal reenactment had progressed to the scenes in the infirmary tent, Rowan spoke aloud. "How often does this sort of thing happen?"

She received no reply; Bel was asleep.

The tribe lost seventeen people. Among those whom Rowan knew well: Kester, surprised among his flock on nine-side; Mare, of Kree's band, fallen in the furious battle at position twelve; Elleryn and Bae, of Berrion's band, which had been covering the outer circle on nine-side; Cherrasso, of Orranyn's band, who had been positioned at inner ten; and Dee, a mertutial relay who had maintained her post as the Face People struck the camp itself.

Also gone was Eden, Kammeryn's aide, but not fallen in battle. She had been assisting Mander through the long night, and near dawn had lain down to rest beside her son Garvin, who had been slightly wounded. In the morning Garvin could not wake her; age and exhaustion had taken her in her sleep.

Of the scouts: Zo was assumed lost until she staggered into camp the following day, suffering the effects of a blow to the head. She would be ill for days, but would recover. Of Maud, who had been ranging the area on nine-side, and whose disappearance had been the first sign of battle, there was no sign.

Rowan learned this over breakfast, which she took early. Kree's band had risen before dawn; they were scheduled to guard on six-side that day. Rowan had chosen to rise with them. Her dreams had been as full of visions of battle and blood as had been her restless hours before sleep. Rowan did not wish to prolong the experience.

An exhausted mertutial, one of Chess's assistants, told the news as he served them a cold breakfast. Kree thanked him, then turned to business. She counted heads. "Where's Averryl?"

"Here." He approached from the center of camp. Rowan had last seen him assisting Mander; presumably he had done so all night.

Kree disapproved. "I told you to get some rest."

"I did. For two hours, when things got slow. I'm ready."

"We don't know how many Face People are still out there. We might need to fight again."

"Good. I'm looking forward to it."

Kree made a sound of disgruntled resignation. "And Fletcher?" He, too, had not returned to the tent the previous night.

"He knew we were going out early. I expect he's off for some early prayers."

"Off and back again." Fletcher approached, his form a narrow shadow against star-dusted blue.

"Good." Kree settled down to give out assignments. "We'll be short on the inner half, with Mare gone," she began.

"No, you won't." Bel emerged from the tent, rubbing her fists against still-sleepy eyes. "It's been almost a year since I served on the circles," she said, and yawned, "but I think I remember how to do it."

Kree paused long. Someone commented, "She doesn't know our signals."

"That's true," Kree said. "Averryl, take her aside and show her some signals." No one protested when Rowan moved closer to watch.

The mertutial who had served them was gone. Rowan had not touched her breakfast. She passed it to Bel.

Light slowly grew, the flat pastel of predawn. People and objects seemed to wear the pale colors like paint on their surfaces and skins. The only tones that held any depth were the sea gray of Averryl's eyes; the rich earth brown of Bel's; and the fragmenting, shifting blue of the jewels on Bel's belt, glittering as she moved, testing the shapes of the signals she learned.

Pieces of the fallen Guidestar, Rowan thought. She found herself gazing up at the Eastern Guidestar, Averryl's lesson forgotten. The Guidestar stood in its assigned place in the sky, glowing brilliantly, reflecting the light of the unrisen sun.

It came to Rowan that Kree was taking rather long to get her band in motion. She looked at the chief, at the moment the chief herself glanced up, sighting something toward the center of camp. Kree stood.

"Fletcher." He glanced up. She beckoned, and he rose to follow her. The members of the band looked at each other in perplexity, then trailed along behind.

Kree led Fletcher to the fire pit, where Kammeryn stood musing over the fire tenders' preparations. The seyoh nodded once to her in greeting, and to Fletcher, then adopted a studiously casual pose that caused all within sight to drop conversation to watch. The interaction that would follow was clearly intended to seem personal, while constituting a public display.

Seeing this, Fletcher visibly shied, found an instant to send Rowan one bleak glance, then composed himself and stood waiting. Rowan became aware that Jann had joined the crowd and was watching with an expression that included a certain degree of anticipation of satisfaction.

The seyoh spoke. "Fletcher, at the time of the attack, you were assigned to watch the steerswoman. Her presence here was meant to serve as a guarantee that Bel would not betray us to another tribe."

Kammeryn's black eyes were carefully mild. Fletcher's sky-blue gaze was held by them as if at swordpoint. He nodded mutely.

"Your orders were that if we were attacked, you must kill Rowan, as payment for betrayal." Kammeryn glanced about at the watching Outskirters, then turned back to Fletcher. "My orders were based upon the facts that I had at hand. They were good orders.

"But when the attack took place, you were there. I was not. You saw what was happening. I did not. With what you saw, and what you knew, you decided to spare Rowan's life.

"Your decision was correct."

Fletcher's tense posture slacked, and he stood loose-boned and amazed. At the edge of her vision, Rowan saw Jann's face as a pale shape, her mouth a dark spot above a dropped jaw.

The seyoh continued. "Had you followed your orders blindly, the result would have been a pointless loss of life. Your judgment in this was more complete than mine. I would like to believe that all my warriors use their intelligence when faced with the unexpected, that they consider all the facts at hand. Thank you for proving my belief correct."

Kammeryn turned and wandered away, returning to his musing. A mutter of conversation rose from the watchers, and Averryl let out a loud and delighted "Ha!"

Kree clapped the still-gaping Fletcher on the shoulder. "Let's go."

As Kree led her band away, Fletcher turned to Rowan as he passed. "Do you believe that?" But he did not wait for her reply. She followed the band to the edge of camp.

As they were preparing to deploy, all the band members stopped short, almost simultaneously. "What's that?" Kree asked. Toward position six, Rowan saw a thick band of smoke rising from beyond the hills.

Fletcher spoke up. "I saw it when I was out at my prayers. I figure it's Ella's people burning their heroes." The phrase sounded odd in conversation, like a line from an Outskirter song.

Bel stepped forward and glowered at the horizon. "No. That's not where Ella's tribe is." She did not provide the other tribe's location; that information represented a trust granted to her.

Kree looked for and found a relay; although the man was within earshot, she signaled to him. Rowan recognized the gesture meaning "investigation."

Fletcher spoke up. "Send me."

"You've had no sleep."

"I'm fine. But I feel responsible. I should have reported it as soon as I saw it."

She studied him, then smiled wryly. "Very well—since our seyoh puts so much store in your intelligence." The compliment embarrassed him, and she laughed. "Take Averryl with you."

Two mertutials had been approaching across the pasture; arriving, they proved to be pulling a loaded train between them. An Outskirter cloak was draped across the load, concealing it from view.

As Kree's band departed, Averryl turned, indicated the train with a lift of his chin, and addressed the mertutials. "More dead?" he called.

The reply came back: "Maud."

The report was received before noon. Owing to the terseness of Outskirter signals, the news was equivocal, both reassuring and disturbing: Enemy discovered, no danger, position secured. Unsurprisingly, the report was followed by a request to debrief. Rowan was not present during the debriefing, but shortly thereafter word of the findings began to circulate through the camp.

Fletcher and Averryl had discovered what had once been the camp of the Face People tribe. It had been destroyed by fire in what must have been a surprise attack just before dawn. There were a great many burned corpses among the ruins, and a number of dead goblins who had been attracted by the fire; but no living Face People were found.

The opinions of Kammeryn's tribespeople, when they received the news, were mixed. No one was sorry to see the Face People destroyed; but the method of extermination was not considered quite honorable. Nevertheless, it seemed that Ella's people had completed their revenge.

Rowan herself was neither pleased nor distressed, but simply thought: More dead.

By late afternoon, there were few people about in the camp: the fire tenders; three cook's assistants; people carrying supplies to Mander, who was still at work; a few mertutials engaged in only the most necessary chores. All others were either on duty on the circles, out among the flocks, or participating in the events taking place around the edges of camp.

It occurred to Rowan that it might be useful for her to observe the casting rite, and that she might even be useful herself. She decided to assist. She wondered that she did not feel more disturbed at the prospect, or even pleased at the fact that she was not disturbed. She felt nothing at all. Even this did not disturb her.

And yet, some minutes later, she was still sitting where she had been, just inside the entrance to Kree's tent.

She sat in gloom. A shaft of sunlight slanted in through the entrance, carving from the shadows a single canted block of illumination, lying across the bright-patterned carpet. Colors glowed, brilliant: sharp planes, intricate cross-lines. There seemed to be two carpets: a shadowy one covering the entire tent-floor, and another, smaller one lying before her, constructed purely of colored light.

The carpet's pattern consisted of huge red squares, decorated within by borders of white. Thin lines ran between, dark blue on a light blue background. The steerswoman sat unmoving, gazing. When the colors began to pulse, she realized that she was forgetting to blink, and did so.

She decided then that she ought to be up and about her business. She remained where she was.

It came to her slowly that the blue lines defined a second pattern, ranked behind the first: a complexity of cubes shown in perspective, their true nature obscured by the red squares. She wondered how Deely had accomplished this design, if he had woven the cube pattern completely first, then overlaid the red. She wondered if, should she lift and reverse the carpet, the background pattern would become fore-ground; or whether she would see only the first design, with the cross-pattern revealed as illusion. She reached into the light and studied her own glowing hand on a square of glowing red, lines below defining dis-tant, possibly imaginary, forms of blue.

She rose and found her way to where the corpses were being pre-pared, directing herself by the smell of old blood and intestinal offal.

She arrived at the west edge of camp, where a group of mertutials were sitting quietly on the ground, around a recumbent cloak-covered form. Rowan hesitated. She wished to assist, but she could not tell whether or not the mertutials' attitudes indicated that solemnities had commenced and ought not to be interrupted.

Then Chess lifted her head and cocked an eye at Rowan. "Here to help?"

The steerswoman nodded.

"Got a good knife?"

Rowan's hand found her field knife; she displayed it. Chess saw, nodded, and beckoned with a jerk of her head.

Parandys shifted his position in favor of Rowan. "Here, take the arm, it's easier," he said quietly.

They resettled. Chess was sitting by the corpse's head. "Well," she said, then heaved a sigh. "Well," she said again, almost inaudibly, and wiped a sudden flow of tears from her eyes, using the heels of her hands, like a child.

Then she picked up her own knife; it was the same one she used to prepare food. With a gesture, she directed the others to remove the cloak. The form below was Eden. Chess leaned forward . . .

The steerswoman found herself far away, on the opposite edge of camp, on her knees in the dirt, coughing and choking in an uncon-trollable fit of vomiting. It continued for a long time.

Eventually she became aware that someone was supporting her shoulders. The arm across her back felt like ice through the cold of her sweat-soaked shirt, but it was steady, gentle, and patient. Rowan was weakly grateful for the assistance.

Finally, she could raise her own head and straighten her back. She turned away and sat shivering, looking into the camp. Behind her, Fletcher used the edge of one boot to shove loose dirt over the mess.

"Now, what brought that on?" he asked cheerfully when he had finished. "After-battle nerves? Chess's cooking?"

Rowan breathed slowly, deep breaths. "Casting," she managed to say. It was the first word she had spoken that day.

Fletcher's brows raised, and he pursed his lips around a silent whistle. He dropped to a seat beside her.

When she had regained control of herself, she found him watching her with complete sympathy and comprehension. She recalled that when Fletcher had found Kammeryn's nephew dying alone on the veldt, he had executed an entire Outskirter funeral rite, alone. "How did you do it?"

He understood her unspoken reference. "Wasn't easy."

She became angry with her weakness. "It's so foolish! I've seen dead bodies before; I've killed people myself. A corpse is just a shell, it's just . . . it's just matter."

"Not if it's someone you know." He shifted in thought. "Our brains think faster than our bodies, Rowan. You can look at Mare, or Kester, lying on the ground, and know for a fact that they're not really there at all, that they're gone, and you're just looking at where they used to be. Doesn't matter. If you watch them being cut up, you find your stomach has a mind of its own.

"I remember when I first came to the Outskirts, it took me forever just to *see* the land, clearly. My brain knew it all had to make sense, but my eyes figured differently."

Rowan nodded, remembering her own similar experience.

"Well," Fletcher continued, "you can figure out how things are, and tell yourself that's the way it is. But you can't always act the way you think you should, not right away. Sometimes you just have to live with it awhile first."

She shivered. The air was bright and empty. "Why casting?" she asked him. "Why do it *that* way?"

He thought long. "Casting . . . casting is the last victory."

"I don't understand."

"Outskirters fight," he began. "And there's plenty to fight against—but not only other people." He gestured at the quiet camp, referring to its present state, the result of specific enemies. "There's more to it, more than this."

"Goblins," Rowan suggested.

"And other animals, and insects. But, see, they're all part of the land, part of the Outskirts themselves.

"And the plants—we burn down tanglebrush, tear down lichen-towers . . ."

"Destroy the redgrass, with your herd and your waste."

"Right. We're fighting the land, in our way. The land wants to kill us. The whole of the Outskirts, with enemies, animals, plants, hunger, disease, even the shape of the land, with cliffs and ravines and too much water or not enough—it's all of it, all the time, trying to defeat us."

"And it wins in the end. Because, eventually, you die. Everyone has to die."

"But that's just it. You die . . . but then your comrades cast you . . ." He made a motion with his hands: out and around, spreading. "And there you lie. But the land, it can't stand to have you there. And it can't get rid of you."

Ghost-grass, Rowan thought. "Where you're cast, the land—it dies?"

"That's it, then; you've won. It's your last act, the last thing you can do—and you always win."

"But why cut up the corpse?" she asked, then answered herself. "To spread the effect."

"Right. The more you destroy, the greater the victory."

"But why does it kill the plants? In the Inner Lands, decaying mat-ter *helps* things grow." In her home village, the funeral groves were constructed far from the farms; years later, when farmland expanded, the people found green growth already in place, a fertile core about which the new farms could grow.

Fletcher shrugged. "Don't know."

Rowan considered the destruction each Outskirter tribe laid be-hind it, as it traveled eastward, always away from the Inner Lands. There should have been a huge lifeless swath across the land, from north to south, a dead barrier between Inner Lands and Outskirts. But she had crossed only occasional areas of such desolation, and recalled her journey so far as an almost-smooth progression: from old green forests to thinner green forests, to brushland, to green fields with an ever-greater proportion of redgrass, to the redgrass veldt. "Apparently, the damage isn't permanent . . ."

His mouth twisted. "Don't say that to a born Outskirter. Their belief is that it is. Casting conquers the land. They say it gives the land a human soul."

Victory even beyond death. She found she admired the idea. "I wish I could do something," she said. "Honor them, somehow, show the living the respect that I have for their dead . . . but I can't, not in the way they would wish."

He puzzled; then his face cleared. "Yes, you can. There's more than one way to do it." He rose and offered her a hand up. "Come with me."

He led her out of the camp, toward position twelve, where all day two lines of smoke had been visible on the veldt: funeral pyres, now extinguished.

At one of the sites, only two people were present, sifting ashes into goatskin bags: Quinnan and Gregaryn, scouts.

Rowan felt a rush of relief, and gratitude toward Fletcher. She could assist. She would need to handle no dismembered limbs, no segments of persons she had known in life; only clean ashes.

But Quinnan was reluctant: scouts considered themselves a group apart. "She's not one of us," he replied to Fletcher's suggestion.

"Well, she's no Outskirter," Fletcher replied easily. "So, yes, she's not one of us. But I think she's one of you."

The scout was puzzled. "How so?"

Fletcher spread his hands. "What do scouts do? Well, scouts live to find things out. Isn't that what a steerswoman does?

"Scouts travel alone. So do steerswomen. Scouts go and see what's out there, so that other people can know—just like a steerswoman. Scouts look at things from the outside. They try to figure out what's happening. That's what Rowan does, all the time.

"No good scout would ever give false information. No steerswoman ever, ever tells a lie.

"She isn't an Outskirter," Fletcher concluded, "but as far as I can see, she's as good as any scout."

Quinnan studied the steerswoman a long moment; then he took up one of the bags and told her what to do. Rowan listened closely to the instructions; but when she turned to Fletcher, to find some Outskirter way to express her thanks, she found he had gone.

Rowan stood alone on the windy veldt, waist-deep in redgrass a mile due north of the camp. Some twenty goats were browsing nearby, making their first pass at the grass. Later they would return again, to graze more closely, then again to crop the reeds to stubble. Rowan thought it a shame to spread the ashes where the animals would be eating and defecating. But she had been told to go no farther.

Halfway to the horizon, she saw a lone guard manning the inner circle. The warrior did not watch or acknowledge her, but attended to his or her own assignment.

Rowan opened the little bag cautiously. It contained small objects among the ashes: bones, she assumed, likely finger bones that had not had time or enough heat to incinerate. Through the bag's sides the ashes were cool, the bones slightly warm.

The steerswoman held the bag in both hands with the opening away from her, and put her back to the wind.

She passed the bag across the air; a fine white mist blew from it, caught by the breeze, vanishing instantly. "Maud . . ." she began, and tried to remember who Maud had been. Rowan had never met the scout, had only glimpsed her once, in the distance. She had no face, no form in Rowan's mind. A stranger.

Rowan moved her hands again. "Brinsdotter . . ." She looked among remembered faces for a woman, a mertutial or older warrior, named Brin. She found none. There was no living mother to weep for this warrior child.

A third time: "Haviva . . ." It was necessary to upend the bag to empty it completely. The small bones fell from the opening, disappearing among the chattering grass at Rowan's feet. Rowan knew of no other person in Kammeryn's tribe who carried the line name Haviva.

The steerswoman felt cold, empty. She looked about the endless wilderness: at the shimmering blades, at the cloud-crowded evening sky, and at the camp itself, lost on the veldt among its own shadows. The only sound was the voice of the grass.

Then she heard words. "Who is Maud?" She had spoken the words herself.

And she answered herself: Maud was no one; Maud was no face, no voice, no person; Maud was a road stopped before its destination. Maud, Brinsdotter, Haviva was three names, white mist, bones on the ground.

The steerswoman was tired by death. She did not know how to mourn enough for all the dead. But here was only one dead, one person gone, sent into the wind by Rowan's own hands.

Rowan felt she could mourn for one person; but she could not mourn for Maud.

She dropped the woolen bag, stepped over it, and walked back to camp.

She could not rest that night.

Eventually she rose and threaded her way in darkness through the sleeping warriors: past Bel, Averryl, Fletcher, who stirred uneasily in his sleep; past Chai, Cassander, Ria, and at last Kree in her position by the entrance. The chief sat up, instantly awake, asking softly, "Is that Rowan?"

How Kree had identified her in the dark Rowan had no idea. "Yes," the steerswoman said. "I can't sleep. I need to walk."

"The circles are undermanned. There may be more Face People out there."

"I'll stay in camp."

Outside, the night was cool and clear. Rowan walked down the alley between Kree's tent and Orranyn's toward the center of camp. The tents were faint shapes, difficult to discern; their black star-shadows seemed to hold more substance than they themselves did. Rowan passed in and out of those shadows, half expecting to feel their edges on her skin, like the touch of the water's surface on a rising swimmer's face.

The fire pit was cold, with the ancient, deserted smell of dead ashes. In the open center of the camp, Rowan looked up. Above were scores of bright stars; but she did not link them into their patterns, or give them their names. She left them solitary, each alone in the cold air. Among them, nearer to the zenith than ever she had seen it, stood the Eastern Guidestar. A wizards' thing, hung in the sky, she thought, and tried to be angry for the fact. She failed. Timekeeper, traveler's friend, she tried again; the terms had no meaning. Her beacon, urging her eastward forever, toward the place where its own fallen mate lay dead in the wilderness; the matter now seemed abstract, illusory.

As she watched, the earth's shadow overtook the Guidestar, and it vanished from sight.

Between two tents, in a patch of sky toward the edge of camp, five little stars, a canted parallelogram with a dipped tail: the tiny constellation of the Dolphin, caught in a joyous leap from the horizon into the sky. And because it was a dolphin, because it was of the sea that she loved, and because it named itself to her without her asking, she walked toward it.

From the edge of camp to the hills in the distance, the redgrass, bleached silver-gray by darkness, wavered and rippled like a sea that reflected more starlight than shone upon it. The night rattled sweetly with the voices of the grass. Stretched along the horizon, the Milky Way was a cold and glorious banner of light. Rowan rested her eyes on the sight.

During a lull in the light breeze, another sound came to her; not far to her left, someone was weeping, alone. Rowan turned to walk away, then turned back, because the voice was a child's.

Rowan found the child crouched among a stack of trains: a small form, ghost-pale in starlight. "Who is that?" A tangle of dark hair above a blurred, shadowy face. "Sithy?" The girl tried to compose her sobs into words, but failed.

The steerswoman came closer, hesitant. She had never learned how to comfort the sorrows of children. Stooping down, she put one hand on the small shoulder, then withdrew it instantly. The touch was faintly shocking; the child had seemed insubstantial before, only her voice real.

Sithy was clutching something to her chest: large, square, its woven pattern visible despite the dimness. It was a box, such as Outskirters kept by their beds to store small possessions, but too large to belong to a child. "Sithy," Rowan said again.

The girl's voice resolved into a word; but it was only her own name. "Sith . . ." Inside the box, something shifted quietly from a high corner to a low one.

With nothing else to say, Rowan said, "Yes . . ."

The sobbing ceased, held back for a long moment by sheer force of will; then words came from the girl, half-choked, half-shouted. "Sith, Maudsdotter, Haviva!"

Solitary Maud had had one small connection with the living tribe.

The weeping resumed, but silent, Sithy's little body shuddering violently. Rowan raised her head and looked past the child, at nothing. "I see," she said at last. And she sat down in the star-shadows beside the child, and remained until the sun rose.

30

"Zo gives it as a brook with a sharp bend around a big rock at four, a field of tanglebrush at twelve, three big hills in a line at seven, and the tribe back somewhere at nine."

"This with Zo facing north?"

"So she says."

"Good." Rowan took a sip of broth, blew on her chilled fingers, and took up her pen and calipers.

The tribe had been ten days on the move again, in the routine with which Rowan had become so familiar. By day: hours of travel, carrying packs, dragging trains, the changing of guard on the circles, the voices of the flock rising over the hiss and rattle of the veldt. By night: close quarters, in the warmth of buried coals rising from below the carpet. With the weather growing colder, Rowan had become an accepted fixture at each evening's fireside, using its warmth to offset the chill of sitting still, updating her logbook, amending her charts from the information relayed from the wide-ranging scouts.

She found the landmarks mentioned, triangulated from them, and noted Zo's position. "And Quinnan?"

The second relay squinted in thought, his old face becoming a wild mass of wrinkled skin, bright eyes glinting. "Facing east, he's got the land growing flat to the horizon at two, a brook running straight at his feet from ten to four, and at eight, three hills in a line."

The steerswoman repeated the procedure and found the second scout's location. From both sets of information, she calculated the location of the tribe itself, considered the significance of her results, then leaned back in deep satisfaction. "That's it then." She began to organize her materials. "Thank you both, and send my thanks to Zo and Quinnan at the next report. Is Kammeryn in his tent, do you know?"

"Consulting with the flockmasters, yes."

"And Bel?"

"Helping Jaffry guard the children; they're clearing lichen-towers."

"I'll tell her first, then."

Both relays were interested. "Tell what?"

Rowan slipped her charts into their case and capped the end. "It's time we were leaving the tribe."

"At its next move," Rowan told Bel as they watched the four children destroying lichen-towers, "the tribe will swing northeast. We should start moving southeast from this point. Now, or within the next few days."

"We'll need to prepare our supplies. Dried food, light, and probably as much as we can carry. How many days to the Guidestar?"

Hearing it said in words, Rowan felt her happiness transform into a thrill of anticipation. The fallen Guidestar was near; this would be the last leg of the travelers' journey. "Traveling hard, three weeks at the best. But we can't count on that; we have to skirt that swamp. And there's at least one large river to cross. If we can't find a ford, we'll need to build a raft." Rowan had tested and found that tanglewood did float. "And Outskirts weather isn't trustworthy. Call it five weeks."

Bel winced. "Short rations. Hardbread. Dried meat."

"A small price to pay."

The eldest child, Dane, emitted a warning cry. Creaking and crackling, a fifteen-foot lichen-tower arced across the sky. The wind of its approach blew the redgrass flat beneath it as it fell, changing the grass's constant rattle into a sudden roar, then into abrupt silence an instant before the crash. The tower settled, twice: once as its outer surface touched the ground, again when that surface collapsed to the accompaniment of a thousand tiny inner snaps. The breeze became damp and faintly sweet.

"What's that word Dane is shouting?"

" 'Timber.' It's what you say when you knock down something tall."

"I've never heard it used in that way."

Two people approached from camp, one of them dragging an empty train: Fletcher, easily identifiable from a distance by his height and his lope. When they arrived, the second person proved to be Parandys, come to collect lichen-tower pulp to make blue dye. "I hear you'll be leaving us," he commented, as the children attacked a fallen tower with their knives, competing to excavate the largest spine-free lump.

"The news has traveled fast," Rowan replied. "I was hoping to tell Kammeryn first."

"Well, he already knows. He's set Chess to making your travel provisions." Parandys examined one of Hari's offerings, chided the boy for leaving a spine in place, and stumped over to study the tower himself.

Fletcher cleared his throat tentatively. "I asked Kree if I could go along with you."

Bel was less than pleased. "Why? I thought you didn't believe in the fallen Guidestar."

"Maybe that's why. If I saw it, I'd have to believe." He gave a shrug, a gesture atypically small. "Kree said no."

"I think that's for the best," Rowan said, and on Fletcher's long face disappointment became so evident that she continued, apologetically, "because Bel and I are used to traveling together. We understand each other's limitations, and our natural paces are well matched. It's going to be hard travel, and we'll do it faster with only the two of us."

"I know," he admitted. "I just wish I could help somehow. But Kree said you don't need any help. She's right, I expect." He quietly watched the children at work for some moments. "But, look," he began, then seemed to think better of speaking, then decided to speak after all. "But look, Rowan, when you come back, Bel's going to leave you, isn't she? To talk to the other tribes?"

Bel replied before the steerswoman could. "That's right." She studied Fletcher. "But I'll bring her to a place she can reach her home from, first."

"Well . . ." He spread his hands, but without his usual flamboyance. "Suppose I do that?"

Bel did not quite approve. "You?"

"Well, me and Averryl, if you like. That way he and I would have each other for company, coming back to the tribe."

Rowan disliked the idea of parting with Bel at all, but recognized its necessity. She had hoped to delay their farewells as long as possible. However, she had come to respect Fletcher's skills, as unlikely and unexpected they might seem. "You would be free to begin spreading your message sooner," she pointed out to Bel.

"I was going to tell it to any tribe we meet, on our way to the Inner Lands. It won't delay anything if I go with you. And Jaffry wants to learn the poem, as well. He'll try to tell it to any tribe Kammeryn's meets. Word will be moving in two directions."

Fletcher's astonishment was extreme, and he became more natural. "Jaffry? On the other hand, what a good idea. It'll train him to say more than one sentence in a day." Then he thought. "Teach it to Averryl, as well. He'll do anything you or Rowan ask of him. Jaffry will spread the story east, Averryl and I will take it west on our way out, and you can go north."

Rowan became impressed. "That will cover a lot of territory."

Bel was still reluctant, but began to find the idea interesting. She looked up at Rowan. "You decide."

Rowan preferred not to. "No, you. I don't want to lose you; but it's to your own mission that this will make a difference."

Bel knit her brows, annoyed. "Not very much."

Exasperated, Fletcher threw up his hands. "Will one of you please decide to decide?"

Both women laughed; but afterward, Bel continued to wait.

"I decide," Rowan finally announced, "to think more about it. I'll tell you after we see the Guidestar. I don't yet know what I'll learn there; perhaps it will change my plans altogether."

Fletcher was satisfied. "Can't say fairer."

But as the group walked back to camp, with Fletcher trailing behind, cheerfully dragging the train and playing hilarious rhyming games with the children, it occurred to Rowan that as much as she might miss Bel, if she traveled with Fletcher she would be given, every day, reason for laughter. And she found that she liked that idea very much.

31

The dangers of the Outskirts did not merely inhabit the Outskirts; they constituted it.

Blackgrass grew in puddles beneath the redgrass: wiry tangles to trap the feet and send the traveler sprawling. Flesh termites scouted the tops of the grass, hunting the heat of breathing. Solitary goblin jills, exhausted and at the end of their lives after laying their last eggs, lay prone and half-hidden, to rise up suddenly in a last instinctive attack.

Even the damp redgrass itself snagged and sliced at the passerby. The surface of Rowan's gum-soled steerswoman's boots had become scarred to a fine network of white on gray and were now covered, thanks to the help of an inventive mertutial, with a pair of thong-tied gaiters of shaggy goatskin. Her trousers, torn with innumerable small cuts, were covered by rough leather leggings, and her gray felt cloak, its leading edges worn to the underbinding, had been left in the dubious care of Hari, who fancied it as a blanket. Rowan's new cloak, piebald in patches of brown and gray, was one discarded by Chess in favor of the appropriated courting gift.

As a result, the casual eye spying on the travelers would see not a warrior leading an Inner Lander, but two Outskirters, wading down the hills through rain-soaked redgrass toward the misty lowlands.

There were no casual eyes. There were only a convoy of harvesters, trooping along below the grass cover; a fleet of shoots sweeping the sky for gnats, bobbing behind slowly pacing trawlers; and a slugsnake, which had insinuated itself between Rowan's boot and gaiter, there to travel unnoticed for hours, comfortably coiled about her ankle.

There were also, somewhere in the nearby swamp, one or more mud-lions—and, quite possibly, demons.

"Fletcher never saw demons here," Bel replied to Rowan's speculation.

"I know. But Shammer said that demons need salt water." Rowan crumbled dirt onto her boot, covering the slime left by the evicted slugsnake. "And that the Inland Sea was the wrong sort of salt." She replaced the gaiters, knotting the thongs behind heel, ankle, and calf. "I was near the salt bog in the Inner Lands years ago, just after Academy. I'd like to taste the water here to see if it's the same."

Bel looked down at her sidelong. "You'd like to, but you won't."

Rowan sighed and straightened. "No. It wouldn't be wise." She had a sudden, vivid vision of the girl Mai being clutched by rough-scaled arms and torn by needle-studded jaws. In Rowan's mind, Mai was a younger, female version of her brother, so that it was calm Jaffry's familiar face that Rowan saw twisting in pain and terror.

"Good."

They skirted the marshier ground, keeping a course due east before swinging southeast past the swamp. Rowan found Fletcher's observations and landmarks invaluable. The weather had become uniformly gray and drizzling, the sun's direction difficult to discern even in full day, and the Guidestars remained invisible for long damp nights. Without Fletcher's information, Rowan would have had little idea of her true direction. She found reason, again and again, to bless Fletcher for his sharp observations; and a few moments, to her surprise, to miss him.

They paused for three days just before turning south. Bel had suffered from an attack of the stinging swarmers; she was mildly feverish, too dizzy to walk, and her sight was reduced to a deep red haze. Uncharacteristically, she dithered in frustration at the delay, behavior that Rowan attributed to the illness.

Rowan, stung only a few times, ignored the sparkling flashes at the edges of her own vision and arranged the rain fly in the most comfortable configuration possible, with redgrass reeds below and tanglebrush roots for uprights. By day she kept a fire burning, and by night buried the coals and shifted the rain fly over the spot, so that the women slept through the chill nights on heated ground.

The third night, the wind slowly picked up, rising at last to a monotonic, deep-voiced howl. Rowan began to worry about the sturdiness of her arrangements.

"It looks like a tempest coming up," Rowan shouted close to Bel's ear. "I think I need to batten down."

"I'll help." In the darkness, Bel's handicap was irrelevant.

"No. You stay dry."

By touch and memory she found the stakes and guys and tautened them. The wind pressed her cloak tight against her back, rattled its edges violently about her knees, and rain pushed down on her shoulders, suddenly hard, like hands urging her to sit. By shuddering lightning she saw the camp, in a series of colorless sketches: the fly white with reflecting water; the redgrass lying down, combed to the north and battered horizontal; the rain-dark stone where Rowan had sat in the gray afternoon, tending the fire.

Then blackness returned. The wind paused, veered slightly, backed again, paused again; and an instant before it violently veered once more, Rowan, with a sailor's instinct, turned and made a wild clutch at the open side of the fly.

The wind filled the shelter, belling the cloth like a sail; guys snapped, the uprights upended, one of them flying up to graze Rowan's face. She threw herself to the ground on top of the fly's free edge, trying to pin it down.

Bel sat up, began struggling against the cloth. "Stay put!" Rowan shouted. "I've got it!" The raindrops grew heavier, fell with more force.

Another flicker of lightning helped her find the broken, whipping guy lines. She grabbed at one and caught it as the thunder broke; the wind caught her cloak and whipped it over her head, where it streamed before her, booming about her ears. The raindrops were hard on her back, then harder, then became stinging, sizzling hail.

She ducked into the shelter, dragging the cloak in a tangle about her; Bel's hands found and removed the cloak. Rowan held down the tarp corner, forcing it to the ground with difficulty against the wind, as hail rattled on her head through the cloth. She finally solved the problem of securing the corner by pulling it under her and sitting on it.

She took a moment to catch her breath. The tarp was pressed down, propped only by the women's heads. The heat from the ground beat upward; Rowan felt as if she was breathing steam.

Bel spoke; her voice was buried in tumbling rolls of thunder. The cloak was between the women. Rowan groped at it, to arrange it. Its fur was soaking wet, crusted with tiny pellets that melted between her fingers. "Hail," she told Bel inanely. The Outskirter shifted, and a puff of cool air told Rowan that Bel had made an opening at the fly edge for ventilation.

Bel found Rowan's hand and deposited something in it, smooth, round, and so cold they were dry: three hailstones, each half an inch in diameter.

Rowan rattled them in her hand as their fellows rattled down on her head, only mildly cushioned by the tarp. She shouted over the racket of ice and thunder. "Rendezvous weather?"

Bel had doubled the cloak and was pulling it over their heads for more protection. It muffled the sound as well, and she replied into the relative quiet, "Nothing but."

The violence of the tempest had drawn the damp from the air completely, as often happened. Scudding clouds decorated the morning, and the sun rose yellowly before tucking itself behind a retreating cloud bank.

Rowan and Bel had spent the night wet: with no props for the rain fly but their bodies, condensation had soaked them wherever they had been in contact with the cloth. Their spare clothing was still damp from previous days; they spread everything in the sun to dry, and spent the morning huddled together under Rowan's cloak, the last heat of the buried coals rising against their bodies.

"How is your vision? Can you see?"

Bel peered about. "Well enough. No, it's getting darker."

"The sun went behind a cloud again."

"Then I'm all right."

There was a silence, which Rowan spent calculating. "The weather has been strange for over a month. Does that really indicate Rendezvous?"

Bel shrugged. "According to the songs and poems, yes." She sang a verse of a song describing a courting during Rendezvous; in the space of twelve lines, the weather was cold, warm, clear, stormy, hailing.

"That sounds like what we've been having."

"But now the weather is out of sequence with the years. It's odd."

Rowan shook her head in confusion. "Not to me. I don't see why it should be in sequence to begin with. What can be special about twenty years?"

"I don't know." Bel made a sound of feral amusement. "It will be interesting if some people think it's time to Rendezvous, and some don't. One tribe will set up an open camp, and another will attack it. The first will think that truce has been violated, and go for vengeance." Her amusement vanished. "It will make my job harder."

With Bel recovered, they left the lowlands behind, and the country began, almost imperceptibly, to climb. Clouds returned by night and remained, and a heavy fog appeared and disappeared intermittently, but the rain did not return.

The fifth night after the tempest, Rowan rose from sleep and stood in the darkness, with shifting clouds above opening and closing, concealing and revealing small starry sweeps.

Bel stirred on her bedroll. "What's the matter?"

"Wait." Rowan followed a particular gap as it ghosted across the sky: high above, the Swan. Then the opening sank east, to show the Hero, with one bright untwinkling star at his side, and Rowan took mental bearings from the Eastern Guidestar, her first sighting of it in many days.

"We've made very good time, considering the weather," she mused. "But where's the river?"

"The river?" Rowan heard Bel sit up.

The steerswoman nodded, then remembered that her friend could not see the motion in the darkness. "Yes. We should be only a few miles from it. We should be able to see its lichen-towers by now."

"Perhaps it doesn't have any."

Rowan nodded again, not in assent, but in thought. Above, the Guidestar vanished as the clouds closed in and opened elsewhere, more southerly. "The land isn't used to this much rain; it's normally dry. If there were a river anywhere near, the lichen-towers would be hungry for the water."

Bel was beside Rowan, scanning the sky as if she could read it as well as the steerswoman. "Then your map is wrong? The part you copied from the wizards? Or the river has shifted since they made the map?"

Rowan watched the skies with gaze narrowed in thought. "One of those reasons, perhaps . . ."

The women returned to their beds, and Rowan spent the night without sleeping; she brooded, and reluctantly began to recalculate, assuming a greater and greater eastern shift in the location of her final destination.

There was water, but transient water, little runoffs and rivulets caused by the overabundance of rain. Blackgrass thrived in standing pools, redgrass drooping and drowning around it. The women sloshed and slipped up the land toward a bare rocky field ahead.

They clambered among head-high boulders for more than an hour, then took a moment to rest among them. Rowan suppressed a desire to pull out her map and consult it yet again; it would serve no purpose. She sat in silence and internally berated herself at length: for having so untrustworthy a memory of the wizards' original map; for having waited so long before attempting to reconstruct it; and for what must certainly be a general and inexcusable slackness in her application of Steerswomen's techniques.

She called her complaint to a halt. She was neither slack nor forgetful. Circumstances had been beyond her control. Self-derision was a useless exercise.

She sighed and began to address Bel; but the Outskirter's expression stopped her.

Bel was gazing into the distance between the boulders in mild puzzlement. Then her face suddenly cleared, and she emitted a delighted "Ha!" and sprang to her feet.

"What?"

Bel slipped out of her pack and clambered atop an uneven boulder, motioning to Rowan. "I've found your river!"

Up beside Bel, Rowan looked out where the Outskirter indicated. "Where is it?" The jumble of boulders ended unevenly some thirty feet from where the women stood. Beyond was a rounded, featureless stretch of bare gray rock perhaps a hundred and fifty feet wide, which stopped abruptly, ending with nothing but air.

Rowan laughed. "It's a cliff! We're on top of it!" The river was near, but it was *down*. She saw another cliff facing her across the open, misty distance, a smooth gray-faced bluff. "It's two cliffs." Then, she said dubiously, "It's a ravine . . ."

Bel's pleasure had faded to suspicion. "That's a wide ravine."

"Let's have a look." They slid off their perch and threaded their way among the boulders toward the flat area beyond.

An instant before their feet touched it, both women stopped and stepped back, almost simultaneously. They exchanged puzzled glances, and Bel stooped to reach out and test the surface ahead. She ran her hand across it, then suddenly muttered a curse, drew her sword, and struck down.

There was a crunch, a crackling, and a faint, sweet odor, as the sword broke through, leaving a deep and narrow slash. Inside: white pulp, black spines. Bel stood, her sword dripping a faintly bluish fluid.

Rowan's mouth twisted. "And there's our lichen-tower."

Bel nodded, disgruntled, and pointed to where the gray ended and the air began. "That's not the cliff." She pointed at the jumbled rocks around their feet. "*This* is the cliff. This lichen-tower has grown up along its side, all the way to the top."

"Yes." Rowan studied the surface with vast distaste. Any person foolish enough to attempt to cross it would crash through, to be impaled below on thousands of the vicious internal spines. "We'll have to go around this. It can't be everywhere." She looked across the gap to the far bluff. It was over a mile away. "It's on the other side, as well." She looked around: standing boulders behind and around, the lichen-tower and open air before. "We need a better vantage. We can't see from here." Her eyes narrowed. "We have to get closer to the edge."

Bel grunted, annoyed. "This is the edge."

They scouted, tracing the true cliff, searching for a place where the rocks were not extended by gray growth. For more than an hour they paced, rounding crags recognized only by logic, disguised by the lichen-towers' surface. They found no free edge, and always a bluff stood across the wide gap; first one, then another, facing them, offering them a mirror of their own bland geography.

Rowan needed to stand at an edge, look down, look out. She could not see the lay of the land, could not determine where they must go.

They found one place where a sharp, rocky crag rose above the stone field, higher than the lichen-towers. Rowan shed her cloak, kicked out of her boots, and prepared to climb it.

Bel said, "Listen."

Silence.

"If the river were dry, the towers couldn't live." There was no sound of rushing water.

"It can't be dry, with all the rain we've had," Rowan said. "Perhaps they overgrew it completely?"

Bel shook her head, uncertain.

Rowan clambered up the rear of the crag, away from the cliff's edge and the treacherous surface of the lichen-tower. Bel watched from below, dubiously.

Presently she called up. "What do you see?"

Rowan pulled her attention from her handholds and looked.

It was a world of smooth gray, pale mist, white sky. Below: the bulge of the lichen-tower. Left and right: more of the same. Across the gulf of air: more, shoulder-to-shoulder with one another, crowding.

Up the wavering ravine, the winding, branching course of the un- seen river was marked only by gaps between undulating walls of fea- tureless gray. Rank after rank, until mist obscured sight, where barely seen shapes hinted at an endless complexity of mounds, curves, shapes . . .

There was no change, no end in sight. Rowan crouched, stupidly gape-mouthed, disbelieving. She pulled herself farther out, nearer the edge of the crag.

Downstream: the identical view.

"Can you see the river?"

Rowan was beyond speech. She looked straight down.

The pale sunlight lit the misty depths, growing whiter as it fell deeper. She saw somewhere below a tiny flash of silver and squinted, blinking, trying to discriminate one faint shade from another. There did seem to be a thin, wavering line below, barely discernible, but it couldn't be the water: to feed so many lichen-towers, and such tall ones, would require a very great river indeed.

Then she understood. It was a great river—and it was very far away.

"Gods below," she breathed. "It's over two miles straight down."

Bel could not hear her. "Rowan! Are you all right?"

The steerswoman pulled her gaze from the chasm. Bel was looking up at her, short hair falling back from her face, dark eyes worried.

Rowan reassured her. "Yes," she called, and gave a helpless laugh. "And I can see the river."

She descended and stood leaning against the base of the crag, breathless from exertion or from the impossible scene, she could not tell which. Bel watched her, waiting.

"It's two miles down, at the least," Rowan said when she recovered. "And over a mile to the other side. There are lichen-towers the whole length of the river, all the way up the cliffs. There's no way down, and no way up if we make it to the floor of this—I don't know what to call it—ravine, chasm." She shook her head again.

Bel thought. "None of the cliffs are bare rock?"

"None that I could see. And I could see far . . ."

Both were silent.

"We'll have to go around it," Bel said.

"Yes."

"North, or south?"

Rowan called her map to mind, and now she trusted it. "The river must run to the sea eventually, but I have no idea how far that might be. It ran to the edge of the wizards' map. And it may be even deeper farther south." Rivers sometimes cut deep beds for themselves as they flowed, over the years; but there was nothing like this known anywhere in the Inner Lands. "This must be the oldest river in the world."

Bel was not impressed. "North, then."

"North. We'll have to retrace our steps until we clear this." So much travel, wasted.

Bel leaned against a boulder, crossed her arms, and gave a wry half-smile. "Kammeryn's tribe will have gone east since we left them."

"Yes." In the midst of the eerie wilderness, Rowan felt amazement at the idea: that there were dear friends somewhere nearby, familiarity, a place to go. "If we travel due north, we can meet them again." And she wanted to, very much. "We'll stay with them until they've passed by"—she came back to her surroundings again and gestured—"all this. Then we can go south."

"It might have been worse. We might have had no one to meet, no way to find more supplies. And no one looking for us." Bel's smile became genuine. "It'll feel like going home." She straightened, clapped Rowan's shoulder. "Come on."

32

*E*ight notes of a jolly tune: an Inner Lands drinking song, whistled melodiously above the rattle of the redgrass. Rowan stopped short and turned around.

Fletcher stood behind, bouncing on his toes. "Wondered when you were going to notice me."

Rowan laughed out loud. "Skies above, it's good to see you!" Spontaneously, she threw her arms around his waist and gave him a bear hug, its momentum considerably augmented by the weight of her pack. Taken aback, he stumbled a bit.

Bel watched sidelong. "He's been walking behind us for an hour."

Fletcher disengaged himself and sent Bel a look of disappointment. "And here I thought my shiftiness was so improved."

"Oh, it is. I didn't notice you until you were as near as a kilometer."

"Well, that's better. Time was, you'd have known I was here the day before I arrived." He assumed an air of careful dignity and gave Bel a comradely clap on the shoulder, as formal greeting.

She responded with a poke in the ribs, which he attempted to dodge. "Where's the tribe?"

"Oof. Not where you'd think, which is why I'm here. Kammeryn's been sending scouts to the places we would have been. We keep moving, so there'll always be someone where you'd expect."

"You're a scout now?" Bel was frankly dubious.

"And thank you for your confidence. No, not really. But we're short, what with Maud gone, and Zo getting headaches. We're filling in with volunteers. That's me: volunteer, and I hope you appreciate it."

"We do," Rowan assured him. "Why did the tribe change route?" She considered possible reasons: land too wet to support redgrass; land too dry to provide enough drinking water; troops of goblins; demons; enemies.

"For the most pleasant of reasons." He spread his arms. "Ladies, to everyone's delight and amazement, it's Rendezvous."

Both women looked at the sky; it was clear, blue, and had been for days.

He held up his hands. "I know. Don't ask me. We came across an open camp in the midst of a tempest. The seyohs consulted, and decided that it was time. Another tribe joined us. Then another. Then it started to hail. The next day the weather cleared, and it's been like this since." He looked abashed. "Perhaps it's my fault. I prayed for a little sunshine."

"And did it arrive straightaway?" Rowan asked, amused. Bel weaved uncomfortably.

"Well, no," Fletcher admitted. "About a week later, really. But I also asked to be the one to find you two."

Bel spoke up. "Can your god tell you where you left the tribe?"

He laid a hand on his breast. "Just follow your scout."

They proceeded, ambling along a grassy ridge; a small brook crossed the land below, lichen-towers crowding its edge. One was so tall that Rowan looked across, instead of down, at it. She found she held it in disdain: she had seen the king of all lichen-towers.

Presently Fletcher said, "Oh, and one of the tribes at Rendezvous is Ella's."

Bel was delighted. "That's good!"

"And another," he continued, "is Face People."

They were four clear, cool, sunlit days traveling to Rendezvous.

On the night of the second day, Rowan dreamed that Bel stood above her in the darkness, listening to the night. Rowan's dream-self, aware that she dreamed, wondered if it was a real perception woven into the dream. It reminded her of the last time Bel had stood so, silent in the dark, and the memory struck her awake.

It was true. Taking up her sword, Rowan rose to stand by her companion's side and waited. She could see and hear nothing to prompt Bel's concern.

Eventually, the Outskirter said, "There's someone nearby."

Rowan moved to where Fletcher was sleeping and nudged his foot with hers. She dimly saw him shift. By Inner Lands reflex, he rolled over and burrowed deeper into his blanket; then Outskirts training assumed command and he was on his feet, his sword glittering starlight.

Silently, the three moved to stand back-to-back in a triangle.

Rowan studied her section of the landscape, with all her senses. The redgrass chattered, sending fleeing shadows of dark and greater dark across the view. The only breaks in the dim pattern were placed where Rowan knew, from the previous day's observations, that natural obstacles stood. No smell of human or animal reached her.

Presently Fletcher spoke, quiet words falling from his great height. "I think I've got him. Bel, you check, you're better than me."

The two traded positions. "At eleven by me," Bel confirmed.

"Nothing here," Fletcher told her from his new position.

"Nothing," Rowan added, "but—" She was ashamed to be so distrustful of her own perceptions, but the two warriors were better trained than she.

Fletcher touched her arm lightly. They traded places. "Nothing," he confirmed. Then he turned to stand beside Bel; Rowan followed his example. The three stood facing an enemy imperceptible to Rowan; and as they stood so, it came to Rowan how good a thing it was to have these two comrades to stand beside, in the dangerous, hissing darkness.

They waited long, and nothing changed. "I fight from the left," Fletcher eventually reminded Bel.

"Trade with Rowan."

They reconfigured. They waited. The wind died, and rose again. They were facing west.

Rowan risked a quiet question. "You're sure?"

"Yes," and "Yes," from the warriors.

She could not help from whispering, "*How?*"

"Listen."

She listened. The redgrass chattered in dithering waves. She tried to listen to it more closely, tried to hear each and every individual reed as it tapped against its neighbor. And she did hear them, sharper and more clearly than ever she thought she could, each tap like a tiny blow upon her ears. But there was no sound other than that.

Her heart became a fist, pounding her chest for escape. She waited until the strain of waiting became an agony in her bones. "Listen for what?"

"For silence."

Then she heard it: among the chattering of the grass, one place from which nothing emerged, one small pocket of silence where there should have been sound. She could almost hear, in that absence, the very shape of the person's body, although that might be illusion; but the shape seemed to her smaller than the average man.

Fletcher shifted, tense. "No attack?"

"He knows we're ready."

As Rowan listened, the pocket closed, filling from the edges. "He's going," she whispered.

"He's gone," Bel said.

They slept in shifts. They did not hear the stranger again.

33

"Skies above," the steerswoman said.

Fletcher beamed with pride. "And there it is," he confirmed.

The three travelers stood with the base of a high ridge to their left, an undulating valley before them, another ridge beyond. Down the valley, up and down the folds in the land and on both sides of a meandering creek, splayed a single mass of gray and brown tents.

"How many tribes at Rendezvous?"

"Six," Fletcher replied. He had told her before; nevertheless, intellectual calculation and immediate perception were two quite different experiences. There were well over a thousand people camped in the valley below. Rowan had never before seen one thousand people gathered together in one place.

The travelers descended, and as they approached the first outlying tents, Bel reminded Rowan, "You don't walk through another tribe's area unless you've been invited, or there's an emergency. There are paths between each tribe."

They found one: a broad straight avenue running from the edge of the encampment, sloping downward with the lay of the land. To the right, a scene both familiar and strange to Rowan: everyday camp life, with warriors lounging, conversing, practicing, mertutials bustling and drudging, children at play—but none of them people whom Rowan had ever seen before. She smiled at a pair of twin boys who had stopped a make-believe sword challenge to watch the newcomers pass; when she waved to them, she received a hearty wave from the bolder of the two, a shy one from his brother.

But along the left side of the wide path stood tents smaller than usual, and more crudely constructed. They were crowded close together with no access between, creating, in effect, a shabby wall guarding the residents from the eyes of passersby. The only sound from that direction was a muffled conversation, two voices speaking quietly in the distance.

Even the smell was strange. Over the right-hand camp, a familiar miasma composed of goat must, food smells, garbage, and human sweat hung in an almost visible cloud: strong, friendly, welcoming. The quiet camp on the left smelled only of the veldt: a faint scent like sour milk, cinnamon, and dust. The absence of the usual odors disturbed Rowan. It seemed to imply not cleanliness, but a lack of the normal and healthy adjuncts of human existence. It was a smell of poverty.

She turned to ask a question of Fletcher, but Bel asked it first and provided the answer simultaneously. "Face People?"

Fletcher nodded, then lifted one finger to covertly indicate the path ahead of them. On the ground, in the center of the avenue, sat a man.

He was small, with short dark hair. Cloakless, he wore a shabby goatskin tunic, a single garment with a hole for the head, belted around the waist, its hem ending well above the high tops of his boots. His sword was slung on his back, and his arms were wrapped around his drawn-up knees. The arrangement of his limbs left his genitals partially exposed; he was as indifferent to the fact as would be a dog. He simply sat, with his back to the lively camp and his face to the mottled walls of the quiet one, staring, neither blankly nor with hostility, but with infinite patience.

When the travelers parted to pass around him, he ignored them, gazing ahead stolidly. Rowan and Bel exchanged a disturbed glance over his head. Fletcher, however, remained irrepressible. "Morning," he called out cheerfully to the fellow in passing.

The man looked up, his expression unaltered; but a moment before Fletcher's glance turned away, he nodded, once, in acknowledgment. Then he returned to his study.

Out of earshot, Rowan asked, "Is he an outcast?"

Fletcher winced. "You'll have to ask him yourself; no one else wants to. He showed up about a week into Rendezvous; sits there for a few hours every day, then vanishes, no one knows where."

"Not into the Face People's camp?" Bel asked.

"Don't know."

They found Kree's tent, left their equipment within, and then proceeded to Kammeryn's tent to inform him of their return. But as they approached, Rowan noticed something lying across the threshold: two cloaks, one of them Kammeryn's, identifiable by the pattern on its bright woven trim.

The three stopped short, paused long. "Oops," Fletcher said eventually. Bel emitted a pleased "Ha!" Rowan blinked twice, then began perusing a mental list of the tribe's less decrepit female mertutials. Fletcher took charge of the situation and gazing at the sky with ostentatious nonchalance, led the women away. "Lovely weather," he commented.

"I didn't recognize the other cloak," Bel said quietly. She was suppressing a grin.

"You wouldn't . . ." He caught sight of Averryl, seated by Berrion's tent. "Aha! Just the man we were looking for!"

The warrior was repairing a break in his sword strap, braiding bits of leather between his fingers. "I see Fletcher found you. I thought he might. When you want something found, call for Fletcher. It's a genuine talent he has."

Rowan dropped to the ground, pulling her cloak under her. "Actually," she said, "Kammeryn is the man we're looking for, but it seems he's occupied at present."

Leaning forward, Fletcher spoke conspiratorially. "And when did that happen?" He tilted his head in the direction of the seyoh's tent.

"While you were gone. Not so surprising, when you think of all the time they've been spending together."

Rowan could restrain her curiosity no longer. "Who?"

Averryl exuded pride on his seyoh's behalf. "Ella."

Both women were taken aback. "The same Ella?" Bel asked.

"None other. Everyone knew she was being courted by someone. It turned out to be Kammeryn."

Rowan pointed out, "He could be her grandfather."

Averryl shrugged with the urbane air of one long accustomed to an unusual fact. He pretended to give careful attention to his work. "Actually," he said, "I believe he's some kind of cousin about fifty times removed. They're both of Gena line."

Bel had been considering; she reached her conclusion, tilted her head. "It makes sense to me. If Kammeryn courted me, I might think twice, but I wouldn't take very long to do it."

"There's no problem with her being of another tribe?"

Averryl shook his head. "We'll be at Rendezvous for another two weeks or so. It's enough time for a small romance."

"Then courting, and a romance, aren't necessarily a prelude to a more permanent arrangement?"

"No," Bel told her. "The rites are different for marriage. You have to be very certain and very serious. It's forever."

Rowan spent the next two hours plying the Outskirters with questions on the traditions and formal rites surrounding marriage and child rearing. Halfway through, Chess wandered by, listened a moment, commented, "Hmph. I see we've got our steerswoman back," and wandered off again.

34

"We had four days of tempest," Kammeryn told Rowan and Bel after they had described their journey and explained their return. "When the rain slackened, one of our scouts came back in, with an odd report.

"He had found another tribe of Face People, but pitched in open camp. I sent people to watch it, for two days; then I permitted one of our scouts to be spotted. The Face People responded with a request to meet."

He shook his head in thought. "It was the wrong season," he continued, "and twelve years too soon to Rendezvous. But I thought it might be a good thing, to gather now." He addressed Bel. "Under normal circumstances, it might take you eight months to deliver your message to four more tribes. But we have six tribes here, right now."

"They were all ready to Rendezvous? No one attacked?"

"I sent scouts to look for Ella's tribe, thinking that their seyoh, having heard your story, would feel as I did. They joined us. With three tribes together, no one would attack. And when scouts of other tribes sighted us, they could see that we were a genuine Rendezvous. They reported to their seyohs"—he gave a small smile—"and everyone was curious."

Rowan smiled to herself; curiosity, she knew, was a powerful force. "What did you tell them, when they came?"

"That, by the end of Rendezvous, two people would arrive who had seen a fallen Guidestar. And that all the seyohs must hear what they have to say."

"I can speak to them all at once," Bel observed.

"Yes. When would you like that to be?"

Bel thought. "Two days from now. In the afternoon. Tonight, we'll rest. Tomorrow, after dinner, when everyone will be telling poems and tales, I'll give my poem. The seyohs will have a night and the next day to think about it."

With a full day of waiting before Bel was to tell her startling tale to the massed tribes, Rowan found an afternoon's distraction for herself: she sat beside the fire pit, carving a bit of tanglebrush root with her field knife. Bel leaned against a cushion beside her, eyes closed, apparently half dozing. Rowan had attempted to converse with her, to be sternly told that Bel was adding new stanzas to the poem of her and Rowan's adventures in the Inner Lands, and that quiet was required. So the two sat silently, companionably, engaged in their separate occupations.

From one of the avenues of another tribe, Rowan noticed Dane, the eldest child in Kammeryn's tribe, emerge in the company of a strange boy. Dane caught sight of Rowan, waved, and approached; to forestall any interruptions to Bel's creativity, Rowan rose and went to meet the two young people.

"This is Leonie," Dane introduced the boy. He was dark, and broad of build, some four inches shorter than gangly Dane. He nodded greeting to the steerswoman. "When we leave Rendezvous," Dane continued, "he'll be coming with us."

"You're joining the tribe?"

"No," the boy replied. "I'll stay till after walkabout."

"There's no one in his tribe near his age," Dane explained. "And I'd have to wait three years for Hari. That's too long."

"I see." Rowan found appalling the prospect of these two children wandering the wildlands alone.

Dane's eyes were bright in anticipation. "We're working out signals. Because he can't tell me his tribe's, and I can't tell him ours. So we're making up our own."

Rowan searched for something to say. "Make the signals good ones," she told the children, "and learn them well."

By evening, Rowan was restless; but Bel declined to observe the evening's entertainment and remained in Kree's tent, contemplating her own presentation for the following evening. Rowan brought her dinner. "Why do you need to change your poem?"

When creating, Bel habitually wore an expression of utter serenity. Her face altered not at all as she replied, "To make it better."

"I don't see how that's possible," Rowan admitted honestly.

Bel began to eat, completely absorbed in her thoughts. Presently she said, mildly, "Go away. Find something to do."

The steerswoman smiled to herself and accepted the dismissal. She sought out Fletcher.

"Aren't you bored with my company by now?"

"Not at all," she assured him.

He offered his arm in exaggerated Inner Lands courtliness. "Then permit me to be your escort for the evening. Ho, Averryl!" he called to his friend, "I'm squiring the steerswoman tonight."

The warrior handed his empty bowl to a waiting mertutial. "What's 'squiring'?"

"Making sure she enjoys herself."

Rising, Averryl wiped his mouth on the back of his hand, and his hand on a cloth. "Get into another insult duel. That should be fun." He passed the cloth to the mertutial.

Fletcher acquired a fantastic glower. "I lost the last one. Miserably."

"Exactly."

The tribes were camped on a slope. Rowan, Fletcher, and Averryl walked down among the paths of Kammeryn's camp. They ended finally at the tribe's fire pit, skewed from its usual position. Not far to the right lay another fire, apparently belonging to another tribe, and to the left lay four more, all arranged to form a short arc. There were open-sided cook tents near each fire, each tribe ranging out behind its cook tent in a widening wedge. Rowan instinctively surmised a completion of the arrangement: a single central open area ringed around by fires, with the avenues between tribes radiating like the spokes of a wheel. The steerswoman calculated that it would take twelve tribes to complete the circle.

Averryl shook his head when Rowan commented. "No, that never happens. There are never twelve tribes near enough to each other to Rendezvous. The most I've ever heard of gathered is eight."

There was food at each fire pit, and all were apparently welcome to sample. Past the fires was a large flat area, where activities were in progress: dances with spinning sticks flung into the air, and impromptu groups of musicians with bone flutes, wooden clappers of various tones, banjos, and mandolins, the last amazingly constructed from the skulls of goblins.

They paused to watch a wrestling match, where a pair of muscular women contested, first one pinned to stillness, then both suddenly writhing and twisting, and the other now pinned to stillness. When the match was won, Averryl gave Rowan and Fletcher a sidelong glance, then wandered over to speak to the winner, saying something to her that immediately caused her to laugh out loud with delight.

Fletcher nudged Rowan; she nudged him back. Linking arms again, they left Averryl behind.

After dinner, a more formal gathering took place. People arranged themselves about the open area, on all sides, taking advantage of the natural slope. And one by one, each tribe was called upon for a song, or a poem, or a tale.

Rowan heard of a fierce battle for pasture; of a young warrior who presumed to court her own tribe's seyoh; of a haunting, where the spirit of an uncast man killed his tribe's goats, one by one, until his body was found and given proper rites.

But when the Face People were called upon, they did not respond. There was an uncomfortable pause, and then Kammeryn's tribe was called on, and Averryl delivered the tale of his rescue by Rowan and Bel.

When he finished, someone spoke out of turn. "I will tell," the voice called out. A small man approached from the back of the crowd and made his way down the slope to the center, walking stolidly, almost defiantly, as if to battle.

There came a slow rising, murmur of surprise, and within it isolated pockets of sharp comment, clearly disapproving.

"What's wrong?" Rowan asked, but when the man reached his position, she saw him clearly for the first time. "That's a Face Person."

He stood boldly in place, staring down each individual complaining group.

"Will they try to stop him?" Rowan asked.

"Don't know." Fletcher was squinting at the man. "That's our friend from the alleyway." The man they had seen, sitting alone, facing the Face People's camp.

When quiet came at last, the man announced, "This is for the one I love: Randa, Chensdotter, Luz."

"Should he say her names?"

"She must be dead."

The man drew a long breath, as if to shout; instead, he sang: "Who has seen her," he began in a harsh voice,

> "—Following the wind
> From end to end, long hills
> Winding, black and midnight, when her voice
> Comes shadowing down the sky? . . ."

"That's Einar's song," Rowan said quietly. " 'The Ghost Lover.' "

"One of Einar's songs," Fletcher corrected. "He wrote about a thousand."

The singer did not have a singer's voice: it was rough-edged and unmelodic, needing to be forced from note to note. But the song itself, somehow, did not suffer. It acquired a color far different from that which Bel had given it. It was no longer a song of sweet, eerie longing; it was a hopeless plea, a cry of pain.

> "From where she stands to where I stand
> Is but a hand, a link, and a lock,
> But there are doors, mine poor for being
> Always wide—"

Rowan thought it odd to hear of a door and a lock in a song sung by a tent-dwelling Outskirter. Tent entrances were sometimes loosely referred to as doors—but they had no locks.

All known Outskirter history began with the days of Einar, the first to use poem and song, easily passed on to later generations. She wondered what events lay lost before Einar's time.

> "I lose my days in days of days.
> I know my time by nights of yes or no,
> In going, stepping into dark,
> And standing, marking yes or no—"

Bel's home tribe believed that Einar, for the love of the ghost, never made love to a human woman, and thus left no descendants. Kammeryn's tribe believed that Einar did take part in normal romantic intercourse, but that his unnatural relations with the spirit-woman drained the power of life from his seed. Rowan found both versions credible: Einar's devotion to his mysterious love was utter, complete. Such an intensity could not exist without effect upon Einar himself, either emotional or physical. But Einar seemed not to care about the state of his soul, or, by implication, of his body. He only loved, totally; and hundreds of years later, the wiry, rough man now present held up that love for all to see, as the mirror of his own.

> ". . . And she will tell me, when she speaks again: the cry
> Of stars, the sweet of light, the secret tongue of numbers.
> When last I sang she smiled, and I will sing again

While all the world and winter rain complete,
Until fleeing has no home but her words,
Last known, last awaited, last spoken, last heard."

The song ended. There was silence. With no further ceremony, the small man immediately left the center, walked to the edge of the crowd, and vanished.

Rowan and Fletcher walked slowly back to camp together. Without looking, she was sharply aware of him as a long angular form of bone and muscle moving quietly at her side. She had instinctively lengthened her stride; he had shortened his. Their steps matched.

"He must have been a very strange man, Einar," Rowan said at last, thinking aloud.

"How's that?"

"His words work so oddly . . ." She struggled to express it. "They're beautiful, but so . . ." She found a word, but it was very unsatisfactory. "So imprecise . . ."

"You're thinking like a steerswoman," he told her. "Think with your heart."

She smiled. "People don't think with their hearts." But it was purely to her emotions that the song spoke. "You must have heard that song often. Do you understand it?"

He thought. "No. I can't deny it's beautiful. But I can't deny it makes little sense. 'The secret tongue of numbers—' " He stopped short. "Ha!"

"What is it?"

He grinned down at her. "Tongue, language. You know the secret tongue of numbers, don't you, steerswoman?"

She was taken aback. "In fact, I do." They resumed walking. "But Bel's home tribe says it 'the secret tang of numbers . . .' "

"Tang, tang," he mused. "How do numbers taste, Rowan?"

She did not hesitate. "Sharp."

They arrived at the tent. "Coming in?" he asked.

She paused. "In a moment."

When he was gone, she reached into the pouch at her belt and removed a small object. She stood regarding it for a moment, then stooped to the ground once, rose again. She remained awhile, smiling to herself, alone within the fading sweet of light, awaiting the first cry of stars.

At breakfast, Bel's preoccupation was no longer in evidence. "I see you've finished the new stanzas," Rowan observed.

Bel scooped bread gruel into her mouth with a folded slice of meat. "Done," she said around the food.

"What's in them?"

"You'll hear tonight."

Rowan spotted Fletcher, standing off to one side of the fire pit, looking very puzzled. He caught sight of her, glanced about, and surreptitiously gestured to her. Bel noticed his behavior. "What's Fletcher up to?"

"I think," Rowan said, setting down her bowl, "that he wants to speak to me, and alone." Fletcher was now standing in pretended nonchalance, simultaneously gazing at the sky and trying to see if the steerswoman had caught his signal.

When she reached him, he pulled her aside, out of sight behind one of the tents. "Here, come here, take a look at this." He showed her what he held in his hand.

A crudely carved bit of tanglebrush root. "Where did you find it?" the steerswoman asked.

"On the ground. But look, don't you see, it's a dolphin!"

Rowan examined it again. "It's not a very good one . . ."

He was agitated. "Yes, but it's still a dolphin. Rowan, there's probably not an Outskirter here who's seen or even heard of dolphins."

"I see. And where did you find it, again?"

"Just lying around." He seemed to consider her altogether too slow. "Look, don't you think it's significant? A dolphin? Out here?"

"I do indeed," she said. "And where *exactly* did you find it?"

Exasperated, he threw up his hands. "On the ground. Outside of the tent. No one around. But where did it *come* from?"

"On the ground," she clarified innocently, "by the entrance?"

"Yes—"

"Fletcher, in the Outskirts, there's only one sort of thing that gets left by a tent entrance."

He dismissed the idea with a wave of one hand. "No, I thought of that, see; but no Outskirter would know about dolphins—" And he stopped, his mouth still open on his uncompleted sentence.

"—and so that means that it wasn't left by an Outskirter," Rowan finished.

"But," he began, and several varieties of confusion and disbelief worked their way across his long face. Rowan watched until she could stand no more, then finally burst into laughter. "But," Fletcher said again, looking from the object in his hand to her face, over and over.

To stop laughing was impossible, and she laughed helplessly until she felt she needed support, found none from the tent beside her, and had to drop to a seat on the ground. Fletcher watched her, still gape-mouthed, and his disbelief slowly became amazement.

"Fletcher, you fool," she said finally, breathlessly, "you're supposed to reject the first gifts. Then they improve. Now you're stuck with just a rather bad wooden dolphin . . ."

"But," he managed again. Half of his mouth was shaping itself into a grin.

"Oh, no, you don't back out now! You picked it up, and you kept it. You'll just have to face facts, and do your duty; although, as we say in the Inner Lands, I believe you've sold yourself cheaply . . ." She sat, hugging her knees, grinning, looking up at him.

With a visible internal shift, he completely recovered his balance. "Sold myself cheaply, is it?" he declared, turning the dolphin over as if examining it for the first time, peering at it with one squinting eye. "Well. Well, we've got a saying in Alemeth that covers this, too, you know."

"And what's that?"

And he was down beside her, blue eyes inches away from her own, with a wise and canny look that did not quite cover the joy behind. In the space between their faces, he held up the carving: a crude, inartistic trinket, hurriedly made. He said, just before he kissed her, " 'You get what you pay for.' "

35

*T*hat evening, Kammeryn's entire tribe was present at the gathering for tales and songs. Warriors, mertutials, even the children, to the smallest who slept in its mother's arms: over one hundred and thirty people, outnumbering all those who had chosen to attend from the other tribes.

The others were puzzled, and there was a certain degree of glowering disapproval from the Face People present; but this was Rendezvous, at however unlikely a time, and no one believed that a threat was implied. Instead, a sense of anticipation appeared, grew, and slowly worked its way throughout the crowd: something important was about to happen.

Kammeryn had given his people no specific instruction, but when his tribe was called on, they passed one name along themselves, as comment, request, announcement. The words were like audible flickers, flashing across and around the slope: "Bel should speak," and "Bel has a good tale," and "Let Bel through!"

The Outskirter rose up from the seated ranks of other Outskirters and made her way to the fire's side. She gazed once at the sky, thoughtfully, then turned it a second, sharper glance, as if calculating the amount of light left to the day, and the time it would take to recite her poem. Then she shifted her stance to that formal yet easy posture she assumed when performing, scanned the crowd, and began.

Familiar now with the tale and the telling, Rowan watched the people, seeing more clearly the currents of emotion shown in their postures and their expressions. They listened first evaluatively, withholding judgment, waiting for Bel to earn their approval by her choice of story and her grace of language. This she did quickly, and they became rapt in the strange events surrounding the mysterious jewels.

When Rowan's own name was first mentioned, Bel made a broad gesture in the steerswoman's direction; to the other tribes, Rowan, dressed as an Outskirter, was merely another stranger in a tribe of strangers. Fletcher was at her side, half-reclining, his shoulder against her knee; now he sat up, and there appeared between them a three-foot distance, leaving the steerswoman separate and clearly identified. Rowan sat a bit straighter herself and acknowledged with a nod the gazes turned in her direction.

They turned to her at particular moments in the poem: puzzled, when first she was presented and defined; sympathetic, when the need for deceit required that Rowan resign from the Steerswomen; approving, when Rowan decided to abandon flight, to face and fight the wizards' men pursuing her; and full of a strange, feral joy when Rowan, a helpless prisoner facing two wizards in the heart of their own fortress, reassumed her order, and from that moment on spoke only the truth, even to enemies. Truth was the rightful possession of every steerswoman; and despite the differences between their lives and hers, her ways and theirs, each person present came to understand this, and approve, for the sake of Rowan's own form of honor.

But it was Bel who won their fullest admiration: one of their own, who had crossed a distant, incomprehensible country, survived fantastic dangers, and returned with a tale for her people, and a warning.

During the recitation, Rowan noted among Kammeryn's people a number of comings and goings, certain shiftings of position. She had attributed this to the people's familiarity with the events being related, assumed they felt no need to remain in place for the entire story. But halfway through the poem, Rowan recognized what had happened.

They had shifted around her. Now, all around, sitting closer to each other than was either casual or comfortable, were the warriors of Kammeryn's tribe, gathered together in a single body, with the steerswoman among them as one of their number. And slightly in front of Rowan, to her right, there was one empty seat in the heart of the warriors, awaiting the return of the teller of the tale.

Bel reached the end of the poem as Rowan had first heard it; but now came the new stanzas.

> "The call will come one cruel day.
> Outskirters will answer force with anger,
> Meeting magic. The might of wizards

Has never faced a fighter's fury.
Wizards' words and warriors' power
Never yet stood strength to strength.

"No one knows as a warrior knows
That the heart of humankind is held
By strength, by striving, striking down
Any and all who stand against us.
Foes and force, we do not fear them.
No one knows as a warrior knows."

Bel began to move, to pace, walking slowly, and one hand with one pointing finger swept the crowd, indicating each and every individual Outskirter.

"Who will hear," she asked of them,

"—or have the heart
To stand beside me, to stay, and strike?
Outskirters all now understand:
War will come. With weapons wielded
All as one must answer evil."

Bel dropped her arm and ceased pacing; and now it was only her face that challenged them.

"The call will come, and *I* shall call it.
The need will be known, by these three names—"

—and she stood alone before them all: small, strong, wise, and unafraid. "I am Bel," she said, "Margasdotter, Chanly."

36

"The tale in your poem has stirred the warriors' blood." The old woman shifted. "This may not be a good thing. Now they're eager to fight, but their seyohs have yet to decide if they may do so. You have caused us trouble."

"I am not causing trouble," Bel replied. "I am telling you of trouble on its way. When trouble comes, warriors want to fight; that's the way of things."

The tent was Kammeryn's own; the persons present were the seyohs of the six tribes at Rendezvous. Rowan and Bel once again sat within a circle of Outskirters; but on this occasion, none of the surrounding faces were near Rowan's age. The youngest person was a man of late middle years, nearly bald, with a beard braided to his waist. His right arm lay slack in his lap; at some time in the past, it had been rendered useless. The eldest person was a wizened woman, partially bald herself, with blind eyes gone blue-gray with cataracts. It was she who served as the meeting's moderator.

"If warriors look for trouble," she pointed out, "and do not find it, they sometimes create it."

"They'll find it," Bel assured her.

The blind woman tilted her chin up. "When?"

Bel drew a breath and released it. "That's what we don't know."

The steerswoman spoke up. "Wizards live longer than common folk, seem to age more slowly. The full course of Slado's plan may span five decades, or more."

"Or a century?" someone interjected, in annoyance.

Rowan turned to the speaker. "Possibly. But even so, we're not now standing at the beginning of things. I cannot yet determine with confidence when it was that Slado first began his work; however, when I started investigating the jewels from the Guidestar, Slado's response was quick. I don't believe he would act so immediately if the plan's completion lay far in the future."

"You both present all these things as truth; but we have no way of confirming anything you say."

Kammeryn suggested to the seyohs, "You must retrace Rowan and Bel's reasoning," and requested that the two women recount exactly, in narrative instead of poetry, the events they had experienced in the Inner Lands, and their analyses at each turn. The travelers did so, in detail.

Bel's jeweled belt was examined, as evidence of the fallen Guidestar's existence. Rowan attempted, in layman's terms, to explain the mathematics of falling objects, the calculations that had convinced her of the fallen Guidestar's existence, and the path it had taken as it fell.

"Did it burn?"

Rowan and Bel both turned toward the speaker, a small man, whose sparse fringe of hair was braided into a long, thin queue: the seyoh of the Face People. He was toying with the braid, weaving it through his fingers desultorily.

"While falling? I don't know," Rowan said. "Perhaps."

"Was such a thing seen?" Bel asked him eagerly.

He dropped his braid and adjusted his patched tunic. The boots he wore were very long, with his legs bare between their tops and the hem of his clothing. "It is in a poem," he said. "A burning thing in the sky."

Rowan leaned forward slowly and forced herself to speak calmly, trying to ignore the eerie thrill running down her arms and her back. "Will you tell us the poem? Or have one of your people tell us, if you can't?"

"No," he said definitely. "Our tales are our own. Their beauty is for us alone."

"If it really did happen," she persisted, "if it's not in the poem for— for artistic considerations"—she found herself fascinated by his inexpressive face, his veiled eyes—"it proves our facts. It would help us convince others."

He watched her cautiously, but said nothing.

Bel urged him. "Someone saw it happen, someone saw a Guidestar fall. You would be confirming everything we say: it's all true, if your poem is a true one."

He looked away, then looked back. "It is a true poem. It is set in the form of true poems."

"What form is that?" Rowan asked.

He seemed to regard her as a fool. "Alliterative, unrhymed. Caesura in each line." Rowan had not ceased to be surprised when she heard sophisticated terms from Outskirters other than Bel; coming from this most primitive of barbarians, the words were actually shocking.

While the steerswoman was recovering her balance, Bel suggested, "Tell us the events, without revealing the secret beauty of the words."

He tilted his head to study Rowan's companion, then the steerswoman herself. His eyes narrowed fractionally; the closest to an actual change of expression that he had yet displayed. Then he nodded. "There was a great battle for pasturage," he began; the other seyohs watched and listened. "The hero who led it was bold and fierce. But he sent his people back, caused them to retreat. This was because an omen appeared.

"As the attack began, a light appeared in the sky, over the enemy's position. It sped toward the attackers. It went over their heads, and away, leaving a line of smoke drawn across the sky. The hero believed that this told his people to go in that direction, to not attack the enemy. He spoke to his people, to explain the meaning of the omen. It was good. They went that way, and found free pastures."

"What was its color?" Rowan asked.

"Like fire. Burning. The smoke was black."

"In what direction was the line of smoke?"

"From northwest to southeast."

This coincided with Rowan's own calculations; she couched her next question carefully. "If I asked you to, would you tell us where the hero was when he and his people saw the object fall?" She wished to avoid placing any seyoh present under the Steerswomen's ban.

"I would not tell you." A statement of fact.

Rowan sat back, expelling a slow breath. "You don't need to. I can tell you; not precisely, but I can draw a line on a map, and know that somewhere on that line the hero and his tribe were located when they saw their omen."

She scanned the circle, meeting each pair of eyes individually. "It's true; someone saw it happen. A Guidestar fell, and the power of the wizards is real. Bel is one of the wisest people I know, and I sincerely hope you take her words to heart. You may face disaster otherwise."

By means of a subtle shift in his body, a calm gaze that indicating recognition and respect for each seyoh, and a careful, thoughtful pause, Kammeryn caused attention to turn to himself, and to remain there until he chose to speak. "I have been traveling with these women for some time," he told the seyohs. "I have come to know them, and have thought a great deal on the things they told me. I believe," he stressed, "that their ideas are correct in every particular. I am convinced that the wizards will soon turn their attention to the Outskirts—if they have not done so already."

The man with the braided beard protested. "There's been no sign of any such thing!"

Kammeryn addressed him calmly. "The wizards have magic. We cannot guess what form their actions will take, or how their attention might manifest itself. It is not enough to wait for some obvious sign of hostility. We must be on guard for events occurring now; any unusual event is suspect."

"Everything is unusual," one woman noted, speaking half to herself. "This meeting is unusual, this Rendezvous. The steerswoman is unusual." She jerked her head in the direction of the Face Person and addressed the group at large. "He's unusual. I've never seen his like before." The Face Person watched her with manifest disinterest.

Rowan had never before heard Kammeryn enunciate his position completely. It pleased her. "Kammeryn is correct," she said, and added to the woman who had spoken, "and so are you. All these unusual things may be connected."

"How can that be?" someone asked.

Rowan sighed. "I don't know. Not yet."

The moderator broke the pause that followed. "Bel, what precisely do you envision us doing?"

"I cannot be precise," Bel told her. "I don't know what, precisely, Slado will do, or his puppet wizards, or their minions, or their soldiers, if any. But the first thing we must do is make certain that every tribe knows what we've just told you. I'll do much of that myself; but it will help if each of your tribes passes the word to each tribe you meet."

The Face Person sat fractionally higher. "We do not meet with others, or speak with them. Only at Rendezvous. Other tribes are all our enemies."

"The more so if you steal their goats and kill their people," the bearded man pointed out, angrily.

But Bel continued. "The second thing we must do, when the time comes, is to cease being enemies. We will have to work together."

The bearded man spoke again. "I will not put my people at the service of another tribe. If I see advantage for my tribe, I will take it. If it causes another tribe difficulty, that's their misfortune."

"If the wizards try to rule us," Bel said, "or if they try to harm us, that's everyone's misfortune. If we join to defeat them, that's to everyone's advantage."

The third woman present spoke up for the first time. "But I see a difficulty," she said; and from her tone Rowan realized that she did not in fact see a difficulty, but spoke only to give Bel an opportunity to make some particular point. "When the time comes to act, how can all the tribes act with one purpose? Our seyohs may not agree."

Bel responded smoothly. "We will need one person in command." And before anyone could voice the question, she answered it. "Me."

Three seyohs protested immediately. Three did not; Kammeryn, who seemed to have expected the idea; the woman who had prompted the statement, who Rowan now realized was the seyoh of Ella's tribe; and the Face Person.

"I believe none of this," the long-bearded man declared. "Perhaps the wizards are causing trouble in the Inner Lands; perhaps something has fallen from the sky—but it has nothing to do with my people. Bel's concerns are imaginary. Unless this Slado acts directly against my people, my tribe, I will do nothing. No one will command me."

The woman who had earlier professed confusion had become definite. "This is counter to our laws. Each tribe lives or dies by its own skills. Each tribe answers to the seyoh, and the seyoh is alone."

The moderator leaned toward Bel, her blind eyes darting about in anger. "You have a young voice, and you are only a warrior. Can you think you know better than elders, than seyohs?"

Bel gave no ground. "In this matter, yes. I've met wizards, and dealt with them. You have not. I've been at the steerswoman's side throughout her investigation, and I'm still at her side. I know exactly what she knows. Only Slado himself knows more about his plans than we do. Even the wizard in Wulfshaven knew nothing until Rowan herself told him. The other wizards know even less.

"And I'm continuing with Rowan, until we reach the Guidestar. What she sees, I will see. I know more than any of you, and I'll soon know even more."

"You ask too much," the blind woman said.

Kammeryn replied, "She does not. I know her. She is wiser than you think, and stronger. If she calls me, I will follow."

The seyoh of Ella's tribe added, "It's true that Bel is only a warrior. But this will be a war—what sort, we cannot know yet, but war nevertheless. If we need to become like an army, we must."

The Face Person shifted, and all eyes turned toward him; but he did not speak.

A silence followed, and the moderator gathered her dignity. "We met in order to hear Bel and her companion speak. We have done so. This is something each seyoh must decide alone—"

"I have decided!" the man with the long beard announced.

The moderator made a gesture. "Then let us each take time to consider our decisions. Let us meet again tomorrow, to tell them to these two, and to each other."

37

The two women returned to Kree's tent, walking silently, separately considering the events of the meeting.

When they arrived, they discovered that the tent was not empty. Three people were seated inside, with three pairs of the little erby jugs on the floor around them; and one pair of jugs was already empty.

"Rowan!" Fletcher made a loose gesture of welcome. "Bel! Come in, sit down, have a drink. We've made a new friend."

Rowan was in no mood for celebration. "No, thank you," she said. "I'm afraid Bel and I have some things on our minds. And I've already had one experience with erby; I don't care to repeat it."

"Ah." He laid a finger aside his nose. "Ah, but you should. Wouldn't be sociable, otherwise."

Averryl spoke, with a shade of intoxicated precision. "You want to talk to our friend."

Rowan stepped further inside to see the stranger: a small man, hair cut short, dressed in a motley tunic with visible gaps, and bare-legged—

Bel said, "A Face Person." The same man they had seen sitting all alone in the avenue between camps.

"You wanted to know why the Face People are so far west," Fletcher said, nodding stolidly. "He told us he'd tell you."

Bel wavered, her thoughts clearly still on the meeting of seyohs. Then she nodded, at some inner observation. She strolled over to the group and joined them; Rowan followed, somewhat reluctantly.

Bel addressed the stranger immediately. "I'm Bel. I've fought some of your people. They were very good fighters."

"My people. My tribe," the small man said. His face, deeply lined, might have been carved from brown Inner Lands wood. He thumped his chest with one hand.

Averryl was interested. "Your own tribe? It was you who attacked us?"

"Yes," he confirmed. Rowan became disturbed by the direction of the conversation. By contrast, Averryl and Bel seemed deeply impressed, even admiring.

"If we hadn't had you outnumbered," Averryl told the Face Person, "if we hadn't joined forces with another tribe . . ." Apparently from the effects of the alcohol, he lost track of his thoughts. He paused to recover them.

Bel finished the statement. "And if I hadn't seen you in time to organize a resistance, we would have stood no chance at all. Your tribe was fearsome!"

Outskirter compliments, Rowan thought: We're very impressed that you almost destroyed us. Have a drink.

"You have to catch up," Fletcher announced. He stretched back and found two more mugs apparently set aside in anticipation of the women's arrival. "Here." He poured. "Four sips each."

They took their mugs, and the Face Person glowered across at them. "Women shouldn't drink. It is bad for the child in the womb."

"They're not pregnant," Fletcher assured him, then caught Rowan's eye and assumed an expression of panic. "Good god, you're not, are you?"

Rowan laughed. "No." She could hardly know so soon. However, she had carefully waited for the proper time in her cycle; additionally, Fletcher had introduced her to the use of a peculiar Outskirter device, coyly referred to as a "glove." She considered the eventuality extremely unlikely, and took a sip of the erby.

The small man still did not approve.

"Now," Averryl protested, "you wouldn't deny a warrior a drink, would you?"

"They are warriors?" The man was dubious.

Bel took a large draft and leaned forward to look him boldly in the eye. "I killed fourteen of your friends," she told him. He wavered, and his gaze flicked to Rowan.

"Perhaps that many, myself," she admitted. "I was far too occupied to keep a running tally."

The Face Person studied her. "Women shouldn't fight," he said.

"Yes, yes, we know," Fletcher said dismissively. "Bad for the child in the womb."

The stranger turned to him in surprise and, as if against his will, emitted one short laugh, like the bark of a dog. Then the wooden face split, and he laughed long and loud, pounding the ground with one fist.

Rowan exchanged an amused glance with Fletcher; he was, she decided, a very useful man indeed.

She spoke to the Face Person. "I'm Rowan." She took another sip; Bel did the same.

There was still laughter in his eyes. "Efraim. Fearsome women," he commented wryly. The humor had humanized him. He was no longer an anonymous danger, another depredation of the Outskirts; he was a small gnomish man of wiry strength and taciturn pride, who had survived the most dreadful battle of Rowan's life. "You are the steerswoman," Efraim said to Rowan.

"That's right." She and Bel sipped again; the liquor seemed to Rowan considerably less authoritative than it had been on her first experience. "Did Fletcher and Averryl tell you what that means?"

"You have questions?"

"Yes. I also answer any question put to me."

"And you tell the truth."

"Always."

Bel spoke up. "I hope you don't mean to ask anything that will help you attack our tribe after Rendezvous. If you do, we'll simply report it to our seyoh, and be prepared when you come."

"I have no tribe to tell it to. All are gone. From battle, from fire."

Remembering the destroyed camp Fletcher and Averryl had found, Rowan was suddenly sorry for the man. "All of them?"

"Yes."

Bel took a sip; Rowan did the same. And when Fletcher ostentatiously caught the Face Person's eyes, and both drank together, Rowan realized that she and her companion were now even with the men: from now on, each drinker would select a single person to match each sip, choosing a different person each time.

Efraim's draft was long, and when he finished, he sat looking into his cup.

"Why did your people come so far west?" Rowan asked him.

He looked up at her. "We were dying."

She looked at the small sad eyes in the weathered face. "Tell me about it."

38

"The land became cruel. Always the Face is a cruel place to live; but for many years, each time the tribe changed pastures, things went for the worse.

"At each moving, the redgrass grew less and less. The herd had not enough to eat in each pasture, and we had to move soon; but the next pasture was no better, and often worse. At last the land became like the prairie told of in legend, where only blackgrass grew. The herd could find no food, and could give little to the tribe.

"Now all tribes on the Face began to prey upon each other. But when they defeated each other, they had no one to prey upon. Many people died in battle, many more of hunger.

"Then strange creatures, and stranger ones, came to attack; creatures such as had not been seen before, nor told of in lore or song. The tribes did not know how to fight these creatures. And so the people grew ever fewer in number.

"At last all the seyohs understood that the land had won the battle of life, that it had defeated the Face People.

"And so we came west, seeking other people to raid: the rich, fat tribes west of the Face. But those tribes had good food, and were healthy and strong; we were poor and weak. The Face People most often failed.

"And then the weather began to say that it was time to Rendezvous. It had been long since the last Rendezvous, and by the count of years, and the season, the time was not right. But our law told what to do in time of Rendezvous, that we must meet and not fight.

"Some of the tribes of Face People listened to the command of the weather, and found a place to make open camp. But my tribe, my people, did not do this. Perhaps this is why all my tribe are now dead, why fate turned against us; it is punishment.

"Our seyoh was foolish. He told us that, because the great heat did not come, it was not a true Rendezvous."

The steerswoman leaned forward. " 'Great heat'?"

"Yes," the Face Person confirmed. "So the tales say: when it is time to Rendezvous, a great heat comes over the land, causing destruction."

Rowan looked to her friend. "Bel?"

"I've never heard of such a thing. Only Rendezvous weather," Bel told her. Averryl also expressed ignorance.

Efraim was not surprised. "It happened only on the Face. This is how our seyoh was foolish. We were already far from the Face; he could not tell if the heat had come there. But he did not want to Rendezvous, and so pretended more wisdom than he possessed."

"This heat," Rowan pressed him, "what was it like? What do you mean when you say it caused destruction?"

Efraim took a sip of the erby, requiring Rowan to match him. "All this happened long ago. I know only what I have been told, and what the tales say. It grew warm. People became ill. Then they fled the Face, knowing the heat would grow greater still, and that the land itself would die."

"The land, die?" Rowan grew appalled. "I don't understand."

"After Rendezvous, when the tribes returned to the Face, all plants were dead, all insects and animals." He drank again, Averryl with him. "It was a bad thing. No one was sorry when it stopped, when Rendezvous stopped, so many years ago."

Fletcher's face was a great wince of thought. "Everything was dead?" Belief was impossible.

But Bel said slowly, "I don't like this." Her dark eyes, growing darker, were focused on some far distance.

"Neither do I." Rowan was doing the same as Bel, and ignored her next drinking prompt. "Efraim, how do you mean this: dead in what way? From drought?" But Rendezvous weather brought rain. "By fire?" She imagined the grass and plants on the Face aflame, eventually quenched by rain . . .

He shook his head in apology. "I do not know. It was before my time, before my father's."

Rowan nodded abstractedly; she was calculating. "And how old are you?"

"I am twenty-two years old."

She broke from her thoughts to stare at him: she had assumed him twice that age. "I see." And before his father's time, as well . . . "How old was your father when you were born?"

"He was thirteen years old."

Thirty-five years. "And how long ago did the Face People last take part in a Rendezvous?"

"Long ago. Near to half a hundred years."

"Forty-eight years?" The Rendezvous immediately previous to the falling of the secret Guidestar.

"That long."

"It was the wizards doing it," Bel announced, then made an inarticulate sound: half a laugh, half a curse. "I come back to the Outskirts to rally my people against a coming threat—"

"—and the threat has been here all along," the steerswoman finished.

Averryl looked from one woman to the other, then to his friend Fletcher, who sat deep in thought. "The heat on the Face?" Averryl took a moment to consider, a process made difficult by alcohol. "But it stopped. That's good. The threat is over."

Bel struck the carpet with her fist, an action of helpless fury; only Efraim did not jump at the suddenness. "The wizards reached out from the Inner Lands," Bel declared, "out of their fortresses, and hurt my people. They sent their magic here. They can do it again."

"If what you call Rendezvous weather invariably follows the heat on the Face," Rowan said quietly, "it is being done again."

Bel turned a warrior's gaze to her. "Yes."

Efraim was puzzled. "Magic? Wizards?"

"Yes," Rowan said.

"Wizards are stories, they are fantasies. They do not exist."

Bel turned to him. "They're real. They hurt your people, they destroyed your pastures. They did it for centuries."

"But how can this be?"

Rowan shook her head. "I wish I knew." Only the sun and fire could emit heat to any great distance. "Efraim," she said, knitting her brows in thought, "was there any strange light visible when the heat arrived?"

"I don't understand."

"Light. Heat must have a cause, a source. Did anything glow, like a coal?"

"You confuse me."

"It might be mentioned, in a tale, a legend. Did the sun become brighter?" Could the sun grow brighter in one part of the world only? How immense a magical spell could this one be?

"No one stayed to see."

Of all the Guidestars, it was the Eastern that hung most directly over the Face. "Did the Eastern Guidestar become brighter?"

"Who can say? It happened long ago."

"Rowan," Bel put in, "if a Guidestar got brighter, everyone would see it. You'd see it in the Inner Lands."

"Perhaps . . ." Armies sometimes constructed beacons, shielded on all sides, except for the direction of the signal. But such a beam would spread, over enough distance. The Guidestars stood more than twenty thousand miles above the world. The light would be seen.

"It would be in the songs and legends of my own tribe, as well," Bel said.

"True." Sourceless heat: an impossibility. And the only source of impossible events: magic.

Rendezvous weather, then, followed the killing heat. The heat was caused by some wizard—or rather, a series of wizards across the centuries—in a twenty-year repeating cycle. A Guidestar fell, and the cycle ceased. The events were connected.

"The possibilities are two . . ." Rowan began, and her thoughts outpaced her words.

Either the fallen Guidestar's absence rendered the heat spell inoperable; or the event that caused the Guidestar to fall also caused the cycle to cease.

But Rendezvous weather had returned, or seemed to have, although out of pattern, so that the spell to cause heat still functioned, and was in use. Thus, it was not the Guidestar's falling that interrupted the cycle; rather, the falling and the cessation of the cycle had shared the same cause.

But what cause?

She had insufficient information. She was left with the same two possibilities she had begun with: either the causative event could not be prevented, or was initiated intentionally. It still came down to Slado. "Either he did it," she said without preamble, "or he did not stop it."

Efraim had been observing her lost in her thoughts, and now leaned forward into a dusty shaft of fading light from one of the sky flaps. "Did you have a vision? Are the gods speaking to you?"

"Yes," she said, "and no." She looked at him: strange, eager, simple. How much he understood, she did not know.

She attempted a smile of reassurance, forced herself to speak more lightly, and prompted him to join her in a drink. "A vision of a sort," she said. "Myself, simply trying to imagine how these events came about. As for the gods . . ." She attempted to trade a wry glance with Fletcher, who was looking aside and blinking over and over, as if trying to marshal alcoholic thoughts into some semblance of order. "As for the gods, I believe I'll leave them to people like Fletcher."

Efraim took her statement literally and turned to Fletcher in amazement. "The gods speak to you? Are you a seer?"

Fletcher abandoned attempts at cognition. "Seer, ha!" he said, catching Bel's eye, then draining his cup with a tipsy flourish even looser of elbow than was his habit. "I see things, that's for sure. As for my god speaking, well, mostly I speak to him. I often wonder how interested he really is." He took a moment to be puzzled by the question, during which pause Bel took her matching sip; then Averryl and Rowan drank, and the cups became empty. Averryl refilled them from the dregs of the jugs, moving with the careful overprecision of the deeply inebriated.

"The gods speak back," Efraim asserted. His voice had acquired a muzzy slur. "You must know how to listen. What do you listen to, when you listen?"

Fletcher seemed to have no good answer. "The air," he said vaguely.

Efraim took a deep breath, as if to steady uncertain internal processes. "The air is good to listen to. You must listen to the ground, as well. And the grass." Unanimously, everyone present paused, listening.

The wind across the sky flaps hummed two deep tones, rising and falling in tandem. Outside, the redgrass rattled, tapped, hissed. In her months in the Outskirts, Rowan had forgotten that the redgrass sounded like rain. Now it became rain again: the Outskirts themselves, daring to tell a lie to a steerswoman. False information, covering secrets.

Rowan shivered. "Do you believe that you know what your gods are saying?" The voice of the veldt grew perceptibly louder.

Bel's eyes narrowed. "They're saying 'Watch out.' "

Averryl listened with tilted head. "They're saying, 'We will destroy you.' " His drunken motions had steadied, and he sat balanced, intent, as if attending to the sounds of distant battle.

Efraim said, " 'Intruders. We hate you. You will never defeat us.' " He spoke quietly, heavily, as though in a trance, or half-asleep.

Rowan found her gaze locked with Fletcher's. "All in all," he told her sincerely, "I prefer my way of looking at it." They drank; the others did the same; the cups were empty once more. Fletcher leaned forward carefully and tapped one jug with a fingernail. It clinked hollowly. "Gone," he said. "Who wants more?" He blinked. "Please, nobody say, 'Me.' "

No one did. Averryl leaned back and stretched out his legs, preparatory to rising, then paused, perhaps thinking better of it. Bel sat brooding; then her glance fell on the Face Person. She sighed once, rose easily, and walked over to him.

Efraim had not moved, his lids drooping over unfocused eyes. Bel prodded his shoulder, and he brought his attention to her as if it were a weighty object, requiring great effort to raise. "Where are you sleeping tonight?" she asked him.

"On the veldt."

Bel's mouth twisted. "You can't sleep on the veldt in this state."

"I am very happy," he confirmed. But to contradict his words, a single tear rolled down from his left eye, to pause and remain unnoticed at the edge of his mouth. He was happy, because the erby and the company had permitted him to forget his solitude; but within, he remained aware that he was alone, tribeless, without family or comrades, and with his gods against him.

"A flesh termite will bite you as soon as the sun comes up," Bel said. "A harvester will drag you away in the night." This impossible scenario caused Efraim abruptly to bark his dog's laugh again. "Come on," Bel told him. "Let's find Kammeryn. I think he'll permit you to stay with our tribe tonight."

"Perhaps Mander has room in his tent," Rowan suggested.

Bel helped the Face Person to his feet. "That's a good idea. This fellow is going to feel bad in the morning. It'll be nice for him to have a healer right there."

Fletcher stirred himself. "When you wake up," he told Efraim, "please remember that we need Mander. So don't kill him, out of reflex." He blinked. "No matter how hungry you are."

"We'll see you get breakfast," Averryl added.

When the two had left, Rowan took a deep breath and climbed to her feet. She found to her surprise that she felt merely dizzy; the erby had had a considerably milder effect on her this time. She wondered if she had become acclimatized, then looked at her friends.

Fletcher seemed about to fall asleep where he sat. Averryl was studying his bedroll across the tent, fixedly, as if contriving a mathematical solution to the problem of getting himself from his seat to his bed. Neither moved.

"Come on, you two. The sun's gone down. Time to sleep." She took Fletcher's hand, attempted to pull him to his feet. In this she was frustrated: he offered neither resistance nor cooperation, but permitted her to pull his arm loosely into the air over his head, providing her no leverage.

Ignoring her completely, he addressed Averryl. "I feel sorry for that fellow."

Averryl abandoned his deliberations and turned his head slowly, speaking definitely. "He should join our tribe."

Rowan dropped Fletcher's arm. "Ours?"

Averryl brought his gaze up to hers. "Yes." He knit his brows. "He must be a good fighter, to have survived to now. We lost a lot of people. We don't have enough children to replace them."

"We lost a lot of people to *his* people," Rowan said. "Very likely he killed some himself. Mare," she said, Averryl's own comrade in Kree's band; "Kester," who had been mildly, harmlessly tending his flock; "or Maud." The unknown scout had come to symbolize to Rowan all Outskirters fallen in battle.

Averryl's expression did not change as he nodded. "In the service of his tribe," he confirmed. "If our tribe was his, we'd have that service from him."

"He'd have to change his diet," Fletcher pronounced blearily.

Averryl shifted attention back to him. "Then he'll change. If a man changes, I don't hold against him the things he did before the change."

Weaving a bit, Fletcher laid one hand against his own breast, over the Christer cross that lay there. "And they say *we're* kind."

Averryl eventually solved the problem of reaching his bedroll by approaching it on hands and knees. Once he had arrived, reflex and habit took over, and he undressed himself easily, although he closed his eyes to do it.

Fletcher presented greater difficulty. Rowan managed to half hoist him to his feet, where he was in immediate danger of falling. They stood so, unsteady, she behind with her arms around his waist. He looked about, unable to figure where she had gone, and found her by raising one arm and spying her beneath it. "You," she told him, "are very drunk."

"And you're not."

"No." She shifted her grip. "Take a step."

He straightened, then shifted one leg heavily. "And you're not," he repeated.

"That's right," she confirmed; then she stopped, and introspected.

She was slightly dizzy; her arms and legs felt heavy; there was a faint blue haze around the dimming sky flaps; and that was all. "Why aren't I drunk?"

Fletcher spoke with difficulty. "The second pair of jugs," he said, and thought, and continued, "and the third, had"—he winked; the expression, unfortunately, remained on his face as if frozen—"a lot of water in them."

She stared at him a moment. "Bel and I missed the first jugs entirely."

"Right." He nodded, and his features released themselves.

It became too difficult to hold him up. She pushed from behind, and he managed a pair of long staggering steps that brought him near enough to his bedroll for her to turn him about and permit him to fall to a seat. He rocked in place.

She brought her face close to his, to gain his attention. "Why was the erby watered?"

He spoke seriously. "Efraim . . . told you things. Maybe he wouldn't have, sober. Got him drunk. You were hearing things. Needed your brain. Couldn't be drunk."

With the first jugs at full strength, the Face Person had become comfortable and relatively talkative; after that, the reduced amount of liquor in the following pairs was sufficient to send him into inebriation. But Rowan and Bel, drinking only the weakened liquor, had been able to keep their wits about them. Fletcher had planned this.

She shook her head in reluctant admiration. "I would never have thought of such a thing."

"Of course not." He assumed a sloppily serious expression. "You're not devious. You're honest. I like that." Then he beamed with pride. "*I'm* devious."

Rowan began her preparations for sleep; but halfway through, she noticed that Fletcher was still sitting, weaving in place, brows knit over some deep thought that absorbed him completely.

"Do you need some help?" she asked him, and received no reply. She went to him and sat on her knees beside him.

He took a moment to notice her. His puzzled expression cleared, and he spoke as if pleased by his own reasoning. "I think," he said with careful clarity, "that he did it. On purpose."

"Who did what?"

"Slado. The Guidestar. Knocked it down."

One of her possibilities; and if wizards had once had the power to set the Guidestars in place originally, then Slado certainly had the power to bring it down. "What makes you so certain?"

"Hiding it. Not just from the folk. From the wizards."

"He might hide the fact for any number of reasons." She steadied his weaving form by one shoulder and began untying his vest. "He's the master wizard. If he's losing his power, he might not want it known."

"Maybe. But—" He paused to watch her hands working as if it were an action entirely new to him, and interesting. "But," he continued, "if something was making it, the Guidestar, fall down, and he wanted it to stay up . . ." It was too long a sentence for his inebriated mind. "Can't think." He put his hands on either side of his head, long fingers spread like spider legs. "Grinding like a mill in there. A few stones in the works. Noisy."

"Don't try to think," she advised him, and moved behind to pull off his vest. "Think in the morning." She pulled him down on his bedroll; he fell back in a spread-armed flop.

"Help," he said to the ceiling.

She had begun on his bootlaces, and now stopped. "What?"

"Slado. He'd ask for help."

She returned to her work. "Not necessarily." But it would have been the wisest course: if the loss of a Guidestar had far-reaching, negative results, as Corvus himself had speculated, then, for the good of all, Slado would ask the other wizards' assistance to prevent that event.

But Slado, she knew, was not concerned with the good of all. And so he kept his secrets.

The steerswoman had new facts, but facts only. She could not find, in that weave of facts, the one thread that would lead her to the reason why. Nevertheless, she tried, as the blue erby-hazed shadows faded toward darkness.

She came back to her surroundings to find herself sitting on her heels, Fletcher's boot still in her hand. She set it down and turned her attention to the other.

She had assumed him asleep; at the tug on his foot, he revived. He pointed one arm straight up and declared solemnly, "No fun tonight, Rowan!"

She dropped the foot to laugh. "I should hope not! We have company!"

Fletcher looked to his right and sighted Averryl, his arms crossed, composed for sleep. "Still here?"

"Still here," Averryl said.

"Lewd, s'what you are. Well, stay. Nothing's going to happen."

"Except you two talking all night. Shut up, or I'll beat you senseless. In the morning." He turned over.

"Can't talk," Fletcher complained as Rowan pulled up his blanket, "and can't cuddle. Rowan, I'm good for nothing."

"You are," she said, and kissed the end of his pointed nose, "good for more than you know."

39

"Before you speak," the steerswoman announced to the assembled seyohs, "before you give your decisions, we have new information for you to consider."

The moderator's unfocused eyes flickered in her face. "Tell us."

"Before I tell, I need to ask." She addressed the seyoh of the Face People. "Tell me," she said; then she remembered that the chairperson could not see to whom Rowan spoke. "I ask the Face Person, tell me about the heat that used to come before Rendezvous."

He had been toying with his braid. He stopped and gazed at Rowan, stone eyes in a wooden face. "How do you know of this?"

She took the most literal interpretation of his words possible. "By asking, and by being answered." She did not know if the Face People's habitual secrecy forbade Efraim to speak as freely with her as he had done. If asked directly, she must provide his name; but she would need to be asked directly. "In past times, when you left the Face and

Rendezvoused, you did it not only because your laws directed you to, but because if you stayed you would die."

He dropped his braid into his lap. "It is true." And there was a puzzled stir among the listeners.

"The heat," Rowan said, "and the weather that followed it both ceased when the Guidestar fell."

"The Face People last Rendezvoused forty-eight years ago." He carefully picked up his braid again and threaded it through his fingers; but now it was clearly a mannerism. "The Guidestar fell twelve years later, so you tell."

"And what was the heat like? Where did it come from?" She expected the questions to be refused; she did not care. Refusal, she believed, would only serve to convince the others of her conclusions.

But he did not refuse. "No one stayed to see. At the first sign of the coming of the heat, all tribes would flee the Face."

"What was the first sign?"

"It would grow warm. This was as it should be, when winter turns to spring. But it was a different heat, because although it was not strong, the people became ill, and the goats."

"Ill in what way?" The tent walls rippled in the wind, stilled.

"Pains in the head, and dizziness. The goats would vomit, and some weak people. If the tribe did not move soon enough, the ground became hot, and the air."

"And when you returned after Rendezvous, what did you find?"

He paused, a pause intended to seem merely contemplative. "We found all living things dead."

There was silence within the tent. Outside, a group of children shouted in laughter, passed by, and were gone.

Kammeryn spoke. "Dead by fire?" His voice was mild, his black eyes intent and unblinking.

The Face Person did not reply until Rowan repeated the question. "No," he told her. "No flame, no smoke." At this Kammeryn leaned back, and his gaze narrowed in thought.

"Dead with no marks on them?" Bel asked. He ignored her, studying the idle weaving motions of his hands. And it was a pose, Rowan understood; he was deeply disturbed and did not know how to conduct himself in this situation.

The chairperson spoke disbelievingly. "This is impossible. Can you truly mean *all* living things?"

The Face Person's only reply was a flat stare, which she could not perceive.

"Did nothing survive?" Rowan asked him.

"Nothing," he replied. "No plants. No insects. No animals."

Someone spoke in outrage. "How would your tribe support itself?" The tone implied that the speaker knew the answer.

The Face Person gazed at the man with an expression of indifference so complete that it constituted derision. But Rowan pressed: she wanted the facts, in words. "By raiding?"

"Yes. At first. Later, the land became alive again."

Rowan was confused. "The grass came back to life? And the animals?"

"No. New grass. Redgrass is strong, grows quickly. And new animals: the Face People themselves, and their goats, returning with the grass."

"I see. Then: every twenty years, an inexplicable, destructive heat; every twenty years, strange and violent weather; every twenty years, Rendezvous."

"Yes. This is what I was told. I saw none of it myself. It was before my time."

He looked Kammeryn's age; but Rowan was not surprised by his statement and merely asked, "And how old are you?"

"I am forty-one years old."

Bel stepped in smoothly. "Then you can't remember, as the other seyohs can, that the Rendezvous forty-eight years ago had bad weather."

The third female seyoh spoke. "Bad weather and Rendezvous don't always come together."

"But didn't they, before the Guidestar fell?" Rowan countered. She and Bel had discussed this with Kammeryn before the meeting. "If you search your memory, and your songs, you'll find that it's so. Likely your tribe didn't formally recognize the fact, as part of its tradition; but Bel's tribe, living farther east, did. I believe that the closer one was to the Face itself, the more severe the weather. The connection would be much more evident to Bel's people."

The man with the braided beard spoke true to form. "My people do not live on the Face. This heat is no concern of ours."

It was Bel who replied. "But the doings of wizards, that is. There's more." She addressed the Face Person. "The Face People have never come this far west before. Why are you here now?"

He turned his flat gaze on her and did not answer, and Rowan felt her friend began to seethe at his refusal. But when the steerswoman cautiously prompted him again, he did reply. His expression did not change, nor did he raise his voice, but his words and tone were so suddenly vehement that all present startled. "*I feed my people!*"

And Rowan nodded, and looked from one side of the circle to the other. "There is famine on the Face.

"The Face, from all descriptions, is the most difficult part of the Outskirts in which to live," she continued. "But people *can* live there, and have done, for centuries. Until recently. Until thirty-six years after a Guidestar fell."

"Thirty-six years later?" the blind woman asked. "If the Guidestar did cause it, why so long a delay?"

"Famine cannot happen overnight," Kammeryn pointed out.

"True," the steerswoman said. "But I don't believe it was the Guidestar's falling that caused the famine. Rather, the falling, and the famine, and the end of the killing heat all result from the same thing, from the choice of one person: the master wizard, Slado."

Now Bel took over, as planned. "The Face People can't live out on the Face any longer," she said. "There's not enough redgrass, no matter how hard they search, and strange and deadly creatures are appearing. The Face People stayed and fought as long as they could; then they moved west. They've come here.

"There have always been battles over pastures. But now there are *more* tribes, in the same pastures. The land can't support us all. We'll be fighting constantly; and our herds will dwindle from raiding. And we'll dwindle, too, from battle, and later from hunger."

"We'll recover," the woman who had disagreed before said. "The battles will end, eventually. The tribes that win the battle will recover, eventually."

Bel turned to look her full in the eyes. "But there's famine on the Face; what makes you think it will stop there?"

There was silence as the seyohs considered this. The moderator spoke, half to herself. "It would come here?" She was visualizing it; she did not like what she saw.

"But," the long-bearded man wondered, "why? Why would this wizard send a famine?" It was no longer argument, Rowan noted, but distress.

"The famine," Rowan began, carefully, "might not be intended; it might be a side-result—"

But Bel silenced her with a glare; and Rowan subsided. "Rowan is cautious," Bel told the seyohs. "She's a steerswoman, and she won't present anything as true if she isn't certain of it. I'm not cautious. I'm a warrior.

"I don't know why Slado should stop the heat on the Face, and I don't care. I care about this famine.

"Think of it: Why should Slado fight with a blade or with blasts of magic, when he can fight with hunger itself? He can save the blade and the spells for later, and attack his enemies when they are weak. And if he can get us to kill each other first, so much the better; fewer people, and weaker people, are much easier to defeat, and to control.

"Slado *did* send the famine on us, and it's having exactly the effect he wants it to. And he'll do more, and worse. We must not let him or his wizards come to rule us like Inner Landers. We must fight, however we can. And of all Outskirters, only I will know what to do."

There was more discussion, but to no good purpose. All information had been presented; no further relevancies could be discovered. Certain arguments already heard were repeated, but in a new tone: not challenging, but querulous.

At last, the seyohs stated their decisions, speaking in turn, around the circle.

The man with the braided beard spoke first. "Should it ever happen that the time comes to act, and Bel sends her names as signal," he said, "and if at that time I can see no clear proof that Bel is mistaken— then, I will do as she says."

Bel was satisfied. "I cannot ask for more than that."

The woman beside him said, "When Bel sends her names, I will put the matter to my tribe's council. I will take their wishes into consideration."

"It will slow your response," Bel pointed out.

"Perhaps. But I will promise no more than this."

The seyoh of Ella's tribe was next. "When Bel sends her names, I will answer."

The Face Person was next in the sequence; but he did not speak. He sat gazing inscrutably, not at Bel, but at Rowan. She became puzzled.

The moderator ended the uncomfortable pause herself. "I am very old," she said. "If Bel calls for me and my people while I live, I will answer. But I cannot bind my successor to my promise. I will tell my possible successors of my decision, but he or she must decide for the tribe when the time comes."

"I am also very old," Kammeryn stated. "But when the time comes for me to present my choices for successor to the tribal council, I will choose only persons who will keep my promise. When Bel calls, whether I live or not, my tribe will answer."

Now all attention was on the Face Person; his gaze passed once around the circle of faces and eventually settled on Bel. He took his time in speaking.

"Bel, Margasdotter, Chanly," he said, "I promise nothing to you." And without ceremony, he rose and left.

40

Bel spent the remainder of Rendezvous teaching her poem to four people, one from each of the tribes that had agreed to her plan. Instruction was conducted as a class, the students hearing and echoing first one line, then entire stanzas, in unison. Jaffry joined the class on occasion but, having the advantage of previous instruction, rarely joined the recitations. He spent his time watching Bel, possibly studying nuances of her delivery.

Rowan had never before seen her dangerous companion in such a role. The work was painstaking, detailed, and repetitive, but the Outskirter never showed boredom or impatience with the students. She corrected errors straightforwardly, berated no one, and simply repeated and corrected as many times as was necessary.

Rowan watched for a time, but soon grew bemused by the experience of hearing the events of her life endlessly repeated in a droning monotone by strangers wearing expressions of fierce concentration.

She spent most of her time with Fletcher.

Unable to discuss her aims and analyses with Bel, Rowan found herself doing so with Fletcher. His earlier dubiousness had vanished, and he was intensely interested in all aspects of the matter. The conversations and explanations were useful to Rowan; despite the fact that no amount of analysis yielded further conclusions, the act of explanation, as always, kept the interrelation of her facts clear in her mind.

On other occasions, they found other occupation, to their mutual enjoyment. Once the tribe was on the move, privacy would be impossible to find. Fletcher found several opportunities to remind her of this, with predictable result; and later, she took to reminding him.

On the last day of Rendezvous, Rowan and Fletcher, by unspoken agreement, left their cloaks across the tent threshold rather longer than was strictly necessary. They remained together, quietly, as the clouds that had gathered at noon blurred and misted above the sky flaps. Soon it would rain, and they would need to rise to close the flaps; for the moment, they enjoyed the quiet, the sense of distance from the tribe, and each other's presence.

Rowan was resting her head on one hand, observing the changing light, sensing the shift of weather, watching and appreciating Fletcher's face: his long chin, his narrow nose, his wide, wry mouth. It was a face made for laughter, and she saw that in future years laughter would come to etch itself in deepening lines across his forehead and around his wide blue eyes. It would be a process she could enjoy watching.

But she found herself under similar scrutiny, as Fletcher was studying her in turn; and the face made for laughter showed wistfulness, a trace of puzzlement, and a measure of sadness.

She had seen such an expression before and thought she knew the question that would follow, which she could answer only with the truth: She was a steerswoman, and steerswomen never stayed for long.

But Fletcher surprised her. "I wish," he said, running one finger down her arm, "I wish I could help you."

"You can," she said. His eyes met hers with blank surprise. "You'll have plenty of opportunity," she continued, "escorting me back to the Inner Lands."

Surprise became hope. "You mean you want me?"

Her reply, which contained no words, was definitely in the affirmative.

When Kammeryn's tribe left Rendezvous, Efraim accompanied them.

He traveled at Mander's side, sometimes pulling the healer's train. Mander watched him sidelong; he seemed to consider the man as a potential patient. Possibly with good cause: although the Face Person pulled a full weight and seemed never to tire, he was gnarled and scrawny, and looked as if he might at any time seize up in knots, or collapse in fever.

At noon meal, a brief rest was called, and Kammeryn took the opportunity to call Efraim aside and speak with him at length. Other tribe members left the two alone.

"Kammeryn wants to be sure that Efraim will fit in with the tribe," Mander explained to Rowan.

"He'll certainly have to give up some of his unusual habits," she commented.

"I don't think that will be a problem," the healer said, although his face showed less certainty than his words. "He seems stolid on the outside, but I think he's a lot more flexible than he seems." As they watched, the discussion ended, and Kammeryn, on departing, reminded one of Chess's assistants that Efraim had not been served yet. The woman nodded and took care of the matter; Efraim watched her askance as she approached, and stared after her, clearly astounded, as she left.

"He's still uncomfortable among women," the steerswoman noted.

Mander raised his brows. "He's not used to being with them all day, every day. His people keep their women apart."

"I wonder why?"

The healer made a disgruntled sound. "Safety, if you want to look at it that way. They can't risk their women in battle." He tapped his knee as he organized his thoughts. "I've been talking to him. From what he says, the average Face People woman becomes pregnant the same year her cycles first begin, is pregnant every year after that, and dies before she's twenty, in childbirth or miscarriage."

Rowan was shocked, then cursed under her breath. "Gods below, that's no way to live . . ."

"Most of the pregnancies end with miscarriage," Mander continued. "Most of the children born die in their first year. They need about five live births to get one surviving child. So it's keep the women alive, safe, or risk the tribe. They chose the tribe."

With these facts as given, the Face People's ways were merely a solution to the problem of survival. But the steerswoman struggled in an internal battle between recognition of necessity, and disgust. "Why so many miscarriages, and dying infants? Are the mothers ill?"

Mander indicated the Face Person with a jerk of his chin. "Take a look at our friend, there."

Rowan studied Efraim. With Mander beside her, she could not help but compare him to the Face Person.

Mander was tall and hale; Efraim, stunted and wizened. Mander was lean and smooth-muscled; Efraim's muscles stood in cords and knots directly beneath his skin. If not for his missing arm, Mander, at thirty-eight years of age, might have nearly fifteen years as a warrior ahead of him. Efraim, at twenty-two, looked to have less than ten.

"Now imagine a woman in the same state," Mander said, "and imagine her giving birth. Efraim has had a hard life, in bad conditions, and starting before he was born."

"The famine did this?" Rowan asked.

Mander shook his head. "Famine makes it worse. But his people have lived like this forever. Under the best circumstances, the Face is a terrible place to live."

"But how dreadful can it be, at the edge of the Outskirts?" the steerswoman asked; but Efraim's very body and spirit provided her answer. Efraim sat quietly watching the world about him, with the infinite patience and absolute physical alertness of a wild animal, waiting for danger to appear.

"Have you ever walked through a large stand of blackgrass," Mander asked her, "with it brushing against your skin the whole while?"

"No . . ."

Mander held up the back of his own hand, as if showing how it had once happened to him. "The skin gets red. If you wash it off, it's no problem, but there's an irritant in blackgrass. Get enough of it, and it's a poison. A little of it, every day, across your life, and it does a slow damage."

"There's more blackgrass on the Face . . ." And beyond lay the prairie, where no redgrass grew at all.

"Not only blackgrass," Mander went on, and held out fingers as he counted. "Mudwort; poison on tanglebrush thorns; any blue or yellow lichen—eat them and you die. The juice of lichen-towers irritates, but it can actually build up enough to kill you." He dropped the hand. "If the goats eat too much blackgrass, they get ill. They don't make enough milk, and the milk they have loses its fat; without enough milk and cheese, your bones get soft. Eat too much meat from those goats, and you grow weak. The goats' lives get short, your life gets short—you're both living just at the edge of starvation."

"The Face People eat their dead," Rowan said; and suddenly it seemed perfectly logical.

Mander nodded. "People are just another kind of meat."

It was three days later that Efraim was formally accepted into the tribe.

The tribe paused in its travel for one day, and Efraim removed himself from camp before dawn; he would remain alone on the veldt all day and return toward evening, symbolically entering the camp for the first time.

It was traditional that he should offer gifts to the tribe at this time, and under normal circumstances these would be provided by his home tribe, if the shift of membership met with his seyoh's approval. Efraim, with no home tribe, dug from the veldt two lengths of tanglebrush root, suitable for converting into swords.

Just before evening meal, with all the tribe gathered around the temporary fire pit, Efraim addressed the warriors and mertutials. Rowan and Bel were also present; no one protested, and the steerswoman understood that she and her companion, although outsiders, were held in very high regard indeed.

"I am Efraim, Krisson, Damita," the Face Person began. He paused, gazing about at the watching faces. "I came from Kriss and Alsander; my sibling is Evandar." Another pause. "Kriss came from Lan and Serranys; her sibling was Halsadyn. Lan came from Risa and Orryn; her siblings were Kara and Melannys. Risa came from Ren and Larrano—"

Rowan stirred; Bel stilled her with a gesture. "You mustn't stand up," the Outskirter whispered.

Rowan leaned close to Bel's ear. "To how far back will he recite his ancestors?"

"All the way to his first, to Damita."

"I should get my logbook. I should be writing this down."

Bel turned a glower on her. "No." Then she became less decided. "Ask Efraim to repeat it, later. But I don't think this should be written."

Efraim had reached the eighth generation previous to his own. He continued to recite, pausing after each generation, as Rowan listened, fascinated. Around her, each Outskirter was paying careful attention, some leaning forward intensely.

By the twenty-fifth generation, Rowan began to notice an increase in the number of siblings in each generation: one or two children had been usual before; three to six became more common.

At the thirty-first generation, Efraim recited, "Lena came from Genna and Klidan; her siblings were Jona and Dess," and in the pause that followed, Orranyn stood.

The recitation halted. The two men gazed at each other across the seated crowd, and Orranyn waited calmly. Efraim's face revealed that he knew he ought to have expected this, but had not dared to hope for it.

Rowan asked a question quietly, and Bel replied, "Orranyn is Damita, as well. His line must branch from this generation, from either Jona or Dess. From here on, all the way back, his lineage and Efraim's are the same."

When Efraim spoke again, Orranyn spoke, as well. They spoke the same names together: "Genna came from Koa and Dennys; her siblings were Chirro, Lana, and Tallin." And the two men continued, each generation a confirmation of shared heritage. Efraim's weathered face became tracked with tears, but he did not suppress them, and so kept his voice clear and steady.

Eight generations further along, far to the back of the crowd, Quinnan stood. Efraim turned his face of weeping joy to the scout; but when the reciting continued, Quinnan did not join, but only remained standing.

"Quinnan isn't of Damita line," Rowan said to Bel.

"No. But he found the name of a male ancestor as a mate in Efraim's line." Someone who had fathered children by more than one woman, so that his name would appear as a mate in both lines.

By the steerswoman's counting, Efraim had reached the forty-first generation previous to his own. Rowan became amazed at the man's memory.

She was not surprised when later, at opposite sides of the crowd, Mander and Chess stood simultaneously. The four Outskirters spoke together the names of their female ancestors, the ancestors' mates and siblings, for twenty more generations.

And at last Rowan heard the names of Damita, Damita's mate, their six children. Four voices finished, together: "And Damita was first."

Efraim looked about him, with eyes blind to everything but the four standing figures. He swallowed. "I am Efraim," he said again, his voice nearly escaping control, "Krisson, Damita."

Orranyn spoke. "Orranyn, Diason, Damita."

"Quinnan, Tilson, Sabine," the scout said.

Mander grinned. "Mander, Chesson, Damita."

Old Chess managed to grin and glower simultaneously. "Chess. Simsdotter. Damita."

Efraim looked at each, one by one. They were his family.

From his seat, Kammeryn spoke up. "Efraim is a warrior. Whose band will be his?"

Orranyn did not hesitate. "Mine."

And Kammeryn rose to stand beside the new tribe member. "This is Efraim, Krisson, Damita, a warrior of Orranyn's band, and our tribemate." Then he threw one hand in the air, and the people gave a single great shout of joy and surged to their feet, with glad laughter and cries of welcome. Those nearby came to Efraim to touch him, take his hand, or embrace him.

When Mander approached, Efraim wrapped him in a bear hug that caused the healer to laugh in pain. "Ho, don't break the arm!"

Chess received a look of amazement, and the comment "You are so old!"

"Ha. I'll get plenty older yet."

To Orranyn, Efraim said, as he looked up at the chief's great height, "I will serve you well."

"I know it," Orranyn replied, and offered his hand.

Standing at the edge of the crowd, with her good comrades beside her, Rowan suddenly felt sad and solitary. Her people, her true family, were her fellow steerswomen; but steerswomen traveled far, alone. Meetings were rare. Nevertheless, each chance encounter between steerswomen was like a homecoming, with these same joyful greetings and embraces. She missed her sisters.

She had not realized that she had leaned back against Fletcher as she thought; and he had wrapped his long arms around her. "You should have been here when they took me in," he said, from over her head. "Took all of about five seconds. 'Fletcher, Susannason,' I said. 'I came from Susanna and Davis,' I said. 'Susanna came from Luisa and Grennalyn,' which is a good Outskirter name, for all the good it did me. That was it. Everyone sat around, waiting for the rest."

In the center of the crowd, Quinnan had reached Efraim's side and asked him a question; Efraim replied, and they were soon deep in what appeared, from their gestures, to be a discussion of the techniques of moving in hiding.

"And one day," Fletcher continued, "I'll just be a name in some-one's line." He rocked a bit in place, musing, Rowan rocking with him. "Some poor fool will have to memorize me."

"Some fool or fools," Averryl amended.

Fletcher stopped in surprise. "Now, there's an idea. With some hard work, a little luck, and good timing, I could show up in twenty differ-ent lines."

The steerswoman interrupted his dreams of glory. "Please wait until I leave the Outskirts to begin your campaign."

He leaned down to her ear. "Ha. What you don't know won't hurt you."

She played along. "But what I discover could prove to be your un-doing," she said archly, then elbowed him in the stomach.

* * *

The next day, Rowan asked Efraim to repeat his line to her, so that she might copy it into her logbook. The steerswoman found it first necessary to explain to Efraim what writing was. She showed him examples and then explained that only persons who could read would be able to discern the names of his ancestors; and among Outskirters, only Fletcher and Bel had that skill. Then she pointed out that the book itself would ultimately return to the Inner Lands, where only steerswomen in research would study it.

He agreed; Bel remained disapproving, purely on principle.

But between time spent traveling, Efraim's new duties, and the impossibility of Rowan writing and walking simultaneously, it took several days for her to complete the written list of Efraim's line. During his dictation, Efraim was subject to not a few jibes from his new tribemates; generally, Outskirters only spoke their full lines when joining the tribe as a new member, as a new adult, or when comparing lineage with a person with whom they wished to have children. Seizing this explanation, Fletcher made a great pretense of jealousy, fooling no one but entertaining many.

" 'And Damita was first,' " Rowan finished one morning over breakfast. She paused, then continued writing: Chanly, Gena, Alace, Sabine . . .

Bel had been reading over Rowan's shoulder as she worked. "What's that?" The Outskirter's literacy was still tenuous.

"The line names. Those that I've heard."

"There are only ten or so in this tribe," Bel pointed out. "You'd have to ask every new Outskirter you meet for his or her line. It would take forever to get them all."

Rowan sighed. "Yes."

Efraim was interested. "The line names?"

"Yes," Rowan said. "The names of all the first ancestors."

"The foremothers." Efraim nodded and composed himself. "Alace, Amanda, Belinn, Bernadie—"

Rowan sat an instant with her jaw dropped, then dipped her pen, rushing to keep pace.

"Carla, Carmen, Chanly, Corrinn," Efraim continued. A few people nearby turned puzzled glances and shifted closer to listen. "Debba, Damita, Dian, Dollore—" When the list was finished, Rowan had in her possession the names of one hundred and twelve women, each the first of the line that bore her name.

Bel leaned toward Efraim, fascinated. "I've never heard that."

"It is ancient lore. We learn it with our lines."

"Will you teach it to me?"

"Bel," the steerswoman said, "look at this."

The Outskirter puzzled over the writing, her finger following the air over the wet ink. She paused, and smiled. "There's my line: Chanly."

"But can you see how it's organized?"

Bel shook her head.

"This list," Rowan said, "is in nearly perfect alphabetical order."

Bel traced along the list, singing under her breath a little tune Rowan had taught her, the one Inner Landers used to remind themselves of the correct order of letters. "Yes . . . I see it."

Rowan sat back, thinking. "When we first arrived in this tribe, Kester told me that at one time Outskirters wrote. I had decided that he was mistaken, or boasting." Kester was dead; Rowan resolved to ask other mertutials, at the next opportunity.

Bel's fingers had stopped. "What's that one?"

"Lessa. It's the only one out of sequence, in among the M's." She looked at Efraim, speculatively. "Is it always said that way? 'Marta, Maryan, Lessa, Mourah?' It seems more logical that Lessa begin with a different sound." She demonstrated: "Mmm . . ."

He repeated the noise, held it, and the name evolved. "Malessa," he said then, definitely. "There was a man of my old tribe, whose grandmother was brought from another tribe. He was of Lessa line, but always he said it 'Malessa.' He grew angry when we disagreed."

Rowan dipped her pen, then wrote the new name in the cramped margin above the old. Then she crossed it out. "It's still wrong . . ." With her eyes narrowed in thought, she wrote: Melessa, then crossed out again, rewrote it. "Melissa," she said. "That's a common name in the Inner Lands." She scanned the list again. Some of the names were already acceptable Inner Lands names; some became recognizable with slight alteration; others remained entirely strange. "Chanly . . ." Rowan mused. "I wonder what that used to be . . ."

Bel was not pleased. " 'Used to be'?"

"Yes." Rowan looked up at her companion and indicated the book with the blunt end of her pen. "Outskirters once wrote, perhaps a thousand years ago. And people's names from that time, given the natural alterations from being handed down orally across the centuries—those names are not much different from Inner Lands names. Long ago, your people and mine were one. You came from the Inner Lands."

Bel was definite. "No."

Rowan tapped the book. "Here's the proof. Writing isn't useful in the Outskirts; you need paper, you accumulate books. That's useless baggage to a wandering people. You keep books when you have a place to keep them, a home."

"We've always been in the Outskirts."

"The Outskirts were once much closer to the Inner Lands."

Efraim spoke up. "We are the first people."

"Outskirters were the first human beings," Bel confirmed.

"And how do you know that?"

Bel became even more annoyed at this doubting of her people's truths. She said, using the phrase Efraim had used, "It is ancient lore."

Rowan was too interested in the facts at hand to be concerned about insulting her friend. "Lore changes," she said, "across years, from mouth to ear, the way the names of your foremothers altered." She thought a moment. It was Outskirter lore that had provided her these clues; perhaps Outskirter lore could provide yet more. "How do you believe humankind originated?"

Bel was suspicious. "There are different legends. They don't agree, but they all say something true, in different ways."

"Legends such as?"

Bel thought. "The gods became lonely and created the first humans as company. But the humans wanted to be equal to the gods, so the gods turned against them."

Rowan smiled. "Fletcher would recognize that one; it's not much different from the Christer version. A legend from the Inner Lands. Tell another."

Bel was reluctant to cooperate in the undermining of her culture's beliefs. "Across time, some animals grew more intelligent, and eventually changed into people."

"I've heard that one, as well. Bel, think of the wood gnomes."

"Those horrible creatures that live around the Archives?" Bel's distaste was immense; and the wood gnomes had found her equally unadmirable.

"They stand halfway between humans and animals. They resemble humans more than they do other animals. They have their own language. And they exist only in the Inner Lands."

Efraim drew himself up to speak. "As the gods went about their doings," he said, "their power was such that it spilled over, spreading across the worlds. They did not care that this happened. But it caused much damage, and many strange things to occur. The spilled power entered objects, and they became alive: all the plants, the animals, and humankind. But of all living things, only humans could think and know. When the gods noticed this, they hated the humans for being aware, and seek always to destroy us. They tell us to lie down and die; but we will not. We fight them."

Rowan considered the life Efraim had previously led, and thought his legend not at all surprising. The Outskirts, indifferent and dangerous, showed no kindness to humans.

41

A week later, Fletcher's morning prayers were interrupted. The tribe was in fair pastures, planning to stay only a week. Fletcher had removed himself from camp, seeking a private place where he would be hidden from casual view, as was his habit. Rowan watched him depart, then turned to see about breakfast. She passed a relay on duty, but stopped when she saw the woman signal: "Understood." The relay then signaled wider, to a person farther distant: "Position seven," and the signal meaning direct address, and one requesting confirmation of previous information. While waiting for reply, the relay glanced away briefly and spoke to the person nearest, who was Rowan. "Get Kammeryn."

By the time Rowan returned with the seyoh, the relay was hard at work receiving signals from three different points. Fletcher was visible, wading through the grass toward camp. "Report," Kammeryn said to the relay.

"Fletcher spotted some movement on the veldt, far off, between positions seven and six. Shortly after, outer seven confirmed. Now outer six, seven, and eight have three sources of motion, one of them recognized as human."

The seyoh nodded curtly, then spoke to his aide. "Have the word passed to twelve-side. Take three people from Kree's band as extra relays." The aide went, at a run. Kammeryn gestured to a nearby mertutial. "Tell Anniss to gather the children."

Fletcher arrived at the camp, loping along in his usual gait. Rowan was not fooled by his nonchalance; his eyes were a shade wider, and when he reached her side she saw the tension in his muscles. He was nervous.

The news was now all across the camp. Warriors were assembling nearby, their chiefs waiting for the seyoh's instructions.

Orranyn's band and the rest of Kree's were nearest. Rowan heard Jann ask someone, "Where did he spot the movement?"

"Between six and seven," someone replied, aggrievedly, as if Jann had been told already.

"No, how far out?"

"Near the outer circle," one of Kree's band replied a bit smugly.

Rowan spared a glance from the signaling and noted Jann glowering in Fletcher's direction. But beside her, Jaffry was reluctantly impressed. "Sharp eyes," he commented.

"Fletcher, what do you say?" Kree's warrior called. "Did your god tell you where to look?" But it was a friendly gibe, almost a boast on Fletcher's behalf.

Fletcher ignored the man. He was reading the signals intently. He caught Rowan watching him. "I'm thinking," he explained. "Three people. Depending on how they're deployed, it might be three scouts from an approaching tribe. We'd see their outer line soon."

Bel joined Kree's people. "There's nothing on twelve-side," she informed Kammeryn. The seyoh nodded abstractedly.

Eventually, more signals: a fourth person was sighted, and a moment later, three more beyond. "It's a tribe," Kammeryn said.

And a moment later, his eyes narrowed. Bel translated the signal Rowan had missed: "They're making camp."

Under such circumstances, Kammeryn's tribe must move or fight. Rowan helped in the preparations around the camp for both eventualities, and the tribe waited for Kammeryn's decision.

Rowan's first clue that something new had occurred was the sight of Jann striding angrily by, hissing with fury to a comrade following her, who seemed perplexed by her anger.

Rowan watched them pass, thought, and returned to where she had left Kammeryn.

He was still there, with Kree and three more of her band, including Bel. "What's happening?"

Bel nodded toward position seven. "They sent one man in our direction, alone. It looks like they want to talk. Kammeryn sent Fletcher to meet him."

This was the source of Jann's outrage: Kammeryn's respect for the Inner Lander made even more manifest.

Fletcher was far beyond sight. His experiences were communicated by relay: outer circle, to inner, to the woman on duty beside Kammeryn.

The first signal was from Fletcher himself, stating that he had reached outer seven's position. Outer seven then signaled that Fletcher had passed and was approaching the waiting stranger, and that the two members of Kree's band who had accompanied him were moving into hidden positions.

Fletcher's next signal stated that the proper forms for approaching a member of a strange tribe were being observed.

There was a long pause as Fletcher conducted his conversation with the unknown person. Then came: "Meeting requested stranger. Approach to camp requested."

"For what reason?" Kammeryn said to the relay; and the question was sent across the veldt.

Reply consisted of that special signal which indicated that no existing signal corresponded to the requested information.

Kammeryn thought. "Is this man absolutely alone?" The signal went to seven, to six and eight, to a scout posted past eight, to the hidden guards. Confirmation was received from all except the guards, who would break cover only to reply in the negative. "Is there still no sign of more strangers elsewhere around our perimeter?" The question crossed the camp, spread outward in all directions. There was no sign of others. "Ask Fletcher for his own opinion."

The necessary terseness of the reply lent the distant Fletcher the illusion of authority. "Comply."

An hour later, Fletcher, the guards, and the stranger neared the edge of camp. The stranger was a Face Person.

When they arrived, Kammeryn stepped forward to meet the man; but Fletcher, with a wry expression, told him, "He's not looking for you, seyoh."

The small man stopped and planted his feet firmly. "I am looking for Rowan, called the steerswoman," he said.

Rowan exchanged a glance with Bel, then stepped forward. "I am Rowan."

The envoy looked up at her. "You must come and speak to my seyoh."

Rowan considered. "Why?" she asked cautiously.

"I do not know. He says to me, bring the steerswoman."

"I'm sorry," Rowan told him, "but I'll need a good reason. You must excuse me for being cautious, but I don't want to walk into some sort of trap."

"He promises no danger to you. You may come, and then you may go." He looked askance at Bel, Fletcher, Kammeryn, the many other watchers all around. "I wish to leave now. I do not like to be here."

Rowan turned to Bel. "What's your opinion?"

Bel addressed the Face Person directly. "Was it your tribe that we met at Rendezvous?"

"Rendezvous?"

"Yes." Bel became exasperated. "Two weeks ago."

"We were there."

Bel's mouth twisted. "I don't like it," she told Rowan, "but perhaps this means that their seyoh has changed his mind. He'd want to tell us personally."

"That may be the case . . ."

"All right, then. But let's bring some reinforcements. Kammeryn?"

The seyoh nodded, scanned the people nearby. "Fletcher," he said immediately, "and Kree—"

"No," the stranger said, brows knit. "Only the steerswoman."

There was silence. "Certainly," Rowan said to the man, "this concerns Bel, as well. And I'm sure you can understand that we'd be more comfortable with just a few of Kammeryn's people nearby."

"No. My seyoh says, only the steerswoman." He squinted at her. "That is you."

The steerswoman sighed, and thought. Bel watched her a moment. "Don't," the Outskirter said, definitely.

"Kammeryn?"

The seyoh shook his head. "I cannot command you. But I advise that you send this man on his way." Fletcher contributed no advice; but his eyes showed his evaluation of the idea.

"A hostage," a voice said, from behind Rowan.

She turned. It was Efraim. "You must ask for a hostage," he stated, "to guarantee the promise. Ask for a woman, or a girl child."

The envoy seemed to recognize Efraim as one of his own kind and gaped at him in outraged betrayal. "No!"

"They will never harm you, if we have their woman."

The threat decided the envoy. He thrust out his chin. "You refuse. I will leave now," he announced, and turned to depart.

"Wait," Rowan called. He halted, watching with narrowed gaze. The steerswoman said to her friends and to Kammeryn, "I think I should go."

"No," Bel said, all glower.

Fletcher was equally suspicious. "Why only you? Why can't you bring at least Bel, or me, or someone?"

"I don't know, and I don't think this fellow can tell me. But I'm curious; there's something about the seyoh of that tribe . . ." Trying to identify the source of her impression, Rowan reconstructed in her mind the meeting of the seyohs at Rendezvous. She had it. "At the meeting," she said to Bel, "he never refused my questions."

Bel considered the fact irrelevant. "And?"

"He refused yours, and Kammeryn's—everyone's at some point; but never mine."

"You're willing to trust him simply because he answered all your questions?" Bel clearly considered the notion mad.

"Well," Rowan said, "yes. Some of those questions were ones he wasn't pleased to answer; but he did, and only at my request. Why would he now, suddenly, wish me ill?"

Bel glared and planted her fists on her hips. "Now he regrets saying anything at all, and wants to kill you to keep his secrets quiet. You know that he and his tribe, and all the Face People have come out of the Face to prey on the rest of us. He doesn't want the news spread."

Rowan shook her head. "But you know it, and the other seyohs. That can't be his motivation." She spoke to the nervous envoy. "I'll come back with you."

But Kammeryn stepped between them and addressed the man. "We will send two warriors with the steerswoman," he announced. "They will wait outside your camp. They won't enter."

"No. Only her."

The seyoh set his mouth. "One warrior, who will stop and wait on this side of your inner circle."

"No." The envoy dismissed Kammeryn. "Do you come?" he asked Rowan.

She drew a breath and spread her hands apologetically to her friends. "Yes," she told the Face Person, "I come."

The Face People's camp looked deserted. The only signs of human presence were sounds: a few quiet voices, rising from somewhere beyond her sight, or perhaps from within the tents. The fire pit, when she and her escort reached it, was doused but still warm, cooking implements set nearby, as if abandoned the instant Rowan entered the camp.

At the seyoh's tent, she finally found more people: guards at either side of the entrance. Recalling her first meeting with Kammeryn, she relinquished her weapons to them without their needing to ask.

Inside were the familiar Outskirter furnishings: patterned rug and cushion, stiff fabric box, a bedroll folded out of the way against one wall. The decoration was simpler than in Kammeryn's tribe, and shades of blue and red predominated; Rowan surmised abundances of lichen-towers and flatwort out on the Face.

The seyoh of the tribe sat on the carpet, again toying with his queue, pretending nonchalance. He glanced up at her once, then gestured her to a seat.

Rowan searched for an appropriate opening statement to make under such circumstances; she failed, and reverted to Inner Lands politeness. "And how may I help you?"

"I will ask you some things," the seyoh declared, seeming to address the statement to his braid. He paused, then spoke less definitely. ". . . and you will answer with the truth, always?" He puzzled, studying the knotted end of the queue.

She found his habit annoying. "That's correct," she replied. "Because I require that people always speak the truth to me, I'm bound to always speak the truth to them. Because I require them to answer any question I ask, I must answer any question they should ask. It's the way my honor works, and the honor of all steerswomen."

He considered this. "You know that the names of all Outskirters are guarded. If I asked you the names of persons in the tribe with which you travel, if I dared to do such a thing, would you then answer me?"

The steerswoman sat quite still. If he did ask, and she supplied the names, he or one of his men could use the information to gain entry to the camp, under the deception that the owner of the name had trusted him and gave it freely. He could attempt to assassinate Kammeryn, or the children; or to signal his own tribe when conditions favored an attack.

Kammeryn's people were her friends; she would not willingly cause them to come to harm.

Years earlier, while she had been a candidate at the Steerswomen's Academy, there had been a rumor in circulation among the students: the tale of a steerswoman who had been captured by bandits and required to explain in detail the defenses of a nearby village. Since the steerswoman could not know if the person asking had previously lied to a steerswoman, she had no right to refuse and was faced with a choice.

The rumor had several alternative endings: the steerswoman answered, resulting in the town's destruction and causing her to take her own life in remorse; she answered, then escaped to warn the town; she answered with a lie, and on her release immediately resigned the order (or again took her own life, in yet another version); she refused to answer and was tortured and killed by the bandits.

The tale was generally regarded as apocryphal: there was no way to verify the events. Nevertheless, it caused a great deal of discussion among the students, as a hypothetical case, and they debated the options with the fierce, fresh, intellectual enthusiasm of the young.

But eventually, interest in the topic waned. It was an unlikely occurrence. Steerswomen meeting bandits were usually simply attacked, as would be any other of the common folk. They responded by fleeing or defending their lives by sword. In situations of smaller harm, such as personal intrigue, the steerswoman first told the questioner that all parties concerned would be informed of the entire conversation, and the question was usually withdrawn.

Rowan's own experiences had been more extreme, and she had responded to the wizards' threat to her life by resigning the Steerswomen, leaving her free to assume a false identity and deceive as necessary. But she had suffered during that period. While a steerswoman, she was a living embodiment of the principle she held highest; while not a steerswoman, the lack of that principle left a wound in her spirit, as sharp as physical pain.

She said to the seyoh, "If you asked for the names, I would first ask if you planned to use them to cause harm." A person intending harm would not be likely to admit to it; and she would catch him in an obvious lie, place him under the Steerswomen's ban, and be free to deny him the information.

He avoided the trap. "And if I did, and said so?"

She became angry. "Then," she said fiercely, "this is what I would do: I would answer your question, but I would delay my reply for the space of time it took for me to challenge you to a blood duel, and either win or die."

He raised his eyes and regarded her calmly. "A dead woman cannot answer. A dead man needs no reply. This is clever, but dangerous. You would do this to protect your friends?"

"No." She felt that she was thinking as an Outskirter, and that it was absolutely correct to do so. "I would do it as revenge against you personally, for daring to try and force me to betray my own honor."

And to her utter amazement, he smiled. "Ha," he said, and pounded the carpet with his fist, twice. He seemed to enjoy the action; possibly it served him in place of laughter.

Then he rose, crossed the tent, and returned carrying a box of stiff, woven fabric, somewhat larger than was usual. He placed it before her, opened it, and removed an object from within. He said to her, and it was a strange phrase to hear stated in such a prosaic tone, "Here is a wondrous thing." He closed the box, placed the object on the lid, and leaned back.

The steerswoman sat stunned. "Skies above," she breathed.

A squat cone on a short base, standing a foot and a half tall and perhaps two feet in diameter, made of tarnished, dented metal. Its surface was studded with smaller objects, some attached directly to the face of the cone, some placed on the ends of rods.

She forgot the Face Person, the tent, the fact that she was sitting in the middle of a possibly hostile camp. The object stood before her, startlingly incongruous, impossibly present.

Fascinated, Rowan moved closer, rising to her knees to do so. The seyoh spoke. "You may touch it; it is harmless."

She did so, hesitantly, then probingly. The rods and objects were attached securely, but four of the six rods were bent at an angle. She tested and could not straighten them. The objects on the rods' tips were damaged; one had glass shards where there must once have been a small glass boss.

She tilted the cone to see the base. The metal was cool on her palm, but it was not iron or steel, or brass; the entire thing shifted too easily, was too light to be constructed of those materials.

From the base hung a number of thick, stiff strings; and these she had seen before. When she and Bel had infiltrated the fortress of the wizards Shammer and Dhree, Rowan had managed by stealth to examine the contents of one of a number of wooden boxes being unloaded from a delivery cart: rolls of semirigid strands of a brightly colored, unidentifiable substance, with copper cores within, like magically coated jeweler's wire. These were the same. "This is wizard-made," she said.

"Wizards are legends, so I had always believed," the seyoh said. "I thought this merely made by men with strange knowledge."

She could not take her eyes from the thing in her hands. "We're both right," she replied distantly. "Wizards are men, with very strange knowledge indeed."

The connection between cone and base was crushed and flattened to one side. She peered up at the joining. It seemed designed to rotate. The base itself was hollow to a shallow depth, stopped by a flat surface etched with lines of copper. Not the pattern itself, but the intricacy nudged at her memory; it was vaguely reminiscent of the sort of decorations found on clothing made by the Kundekin, a reclusive craftspeople dwelling in the Inner Land. But more importantly, the spell that controlled the magical gate guarding the wizards' fortress had been activated by a wooden disk and a ceramic recess, both of which had lines not much different from these.

The magical gate had opened of its own accord; and Rowan knew that this was one use of magic, to animate the inanimate. Likely this object, as part of a Guidestar, did something, undertook some action; and as she had suspected, the Guidestars themselves somehow acted.

"I'm tempted," she said, "to try to take it apart."

"I have tried, myself, often. It does not admit my prying."

Rowan noted scratches and scorings on the surface. "Did you use a metal knife?" He had done. He showed it to her, and its edge was chipped.

The inner surface around the open base was of a substance something like very hard ceramic, bearing innumerable dark lines where the knife had been drawn across the material. She cautiously inserted her hand into the base; it was smooth on the sides, and the back of her hand was scratched by the copper-etched face, which seemed to have short bits of wire thrust through from the opposite side.

She removed her hand and looked inside again. The copper lines served to connect the short bits of wire to each other. The positioning of the wire ends suggested the placement of objects on the opposite side, tantalizingly; there were obvious sets of pairs, the outlines of rectangles and parallelograms. Using her fingers, she tried to feel the edges of the copper-etched face. The seyoh watched, then wordlessly passed his chipped knife to her. She inserted the blade and ran it around the sides, finding no purchase. "Have you tried to break it open?" A sledgehammer and anvil might have been useful.

"Yes. I failed."

The steerswoman stood the object back on its base, atop the Outskirter box. She drew away her hands and sat regarding it.

A piece of the fallen Guidestar. This thing had once dwelt in the sky, forever falling around the world, forever missing the ground, forever seeming to hang at one point on the celestial equator. And it now sat before her. "How did you get it?"

"I found it myself, as a young boy. There was more: a great hole in the ground where it had struck, and some more metal in the earth. I was tending the flock and discovered it, and ran to tell my seyoh.

"I thought straightaway that it was a piece of the light of omen, that it had fallen from the sky. My seyoh agreed, and saved this part of it. We carried it with us always." He made a small, disparaging sound. "He revered it, and said we were to do the same. I am no such fool. It is a only a thing. Wondrous, but still a thing."

"But you still keep it."

He nodded. "It is strange. It inspires strange thoughts."

She pulled her gaze from the object and turned to study the seyoh, speculatively. "You seem to regard that as good."

He smiled, slightly. "I thought long on it, as a child and as a warrior. I thought in a strange fashion. It is useful, to think strangely. You see the world in a different way, become hard to fool. It enabled me to rise among my people and become seyoh."

"I see." Inspiration from the sky; originality. "Why did you not mention this at Rendezvous?"

He grunted. "All Outskirters are my enemies. On the Face, to live is to cause someone else to die; by the sword, by hunger. And this is true elsewhere in the Outskirts; but it happens more slowly and is harder to see. I wish that among those living people shall be all the members of my tribe.

"Bel, Margasdotter, Chanly says to me that we must work together, and fight with all tribes side by side. To hear it, it sounds like a good thing.

"But if battle comes, or magical attack, perhaps Bel will see that three tribes will live if she sends one into danger, knowing it may die." His head jerked in anger, and he spoke vehemently. "That tribe will not be mine!"

"I see." Stated so, it made sense; but only from the one tribe's perspective. "But don't you understand," she went on, "that if the wizards, or Slado himself, come to the Outskirts themselves, that your tribe's help may make a difference to the outcome? And that if the other Outskirters' resistance fails, you and your tribe will suffer?"

He grunted. "So Bel has said. But she is an Outskirter. She will protect her own and let others suffer. I do not trust her. I promise nothing to her. But you—" Rowan found herself held in a gaze like deep, black water. "You are different."

"How so?"

He sat long in thought; and it came to Rowan that he would attempt to express a very abstract idea, and that the small words with which he was most familiar would prove insufficient tools.

"In the morning," he said hesitantly, "the sun comes up. This is good to know, for you must rise, and do things. But if you sleep in your tent, someone must come and tell you: The sun has come up."

"Yes . . ."

He became more sure. "To sleep or to rise, to do the work of your day or to wait—to decide this, you must first know one thing: that the sun is up. In life, this is always true. In order to do, you must know."

The steerswoman understood. "True." In order to choose between alternatives of action, or inaction, one must first possess the relevant information.

"But you do not always know what is needed for you to know. You must learn far more than you need to know."

"True." Once the choice of action was made, most facts acquired were revealed as superfluous to it, and unrelated to the subject; but one must first acquire those facts, in order to recognize that.

"You, steerswoman," the seyoh said, "you know a great deal."

"Yes . . ."

He looked down, then around, as if the walls of the tent had vanished and he could clearly see his tribe about him. "My people suffer. I wondered why. I did not have enough knowledge to say." He turned back to her, intent. "And then, at the meeting of the seyohs, you tell me. You know more than I."

"About this one subject, yes, I do . . ."

"Who is to say to you what is needed, or not needed, for you to know? And so you ask, always. Only foolish persons would not answer; because it is your way that once you understand, you give understanding to all who ask it of you."

"I'm a steerswoman," she confirmed.

"And you showed to me that you would rather die than serve as a tool for others to cause harm." His earlier questions had been a test.

He indicated the Guidestar fragment. "And so I show you this, and tell you what I know. Perhaps it will help you, and me, and my tribe. Perhaps not. Who can say? Only you, who know the most, can discover. And when you discover, you will tell all."

She left the camp in high spirits.

She was accompanied to the camp's limits by one escort, and to a distance of a mile out by a second: grim, small men, virtually indistinguishable from each other. Rowan found herself admiring them, for the sake of their seyoh.

When she was left to continue alone, she knew that there were other watchers hidden, somewhere in the nearby grass. The fact did not at all disturb her. And when a figure rose from the grass directly ahead, she expected no trouble whatsoever.

It fact, it was Fletcher. She regarded him, amused. "Have you been out there all along?" she asked.

"Hiding like a fool-you bug, up till now." He looked very nervous indeed. "Let's get out of here."

She smiled reassuringly. "It's all right. They don't plan any harm."

"So you say." He led the way back. "If they don't mean harm, why are they watching us so damn hard?"

Bel said, "Natural caution." Where Bel had appeared from, Rowan had no idea; but there she was, walking alongside. "If my tribe was so close to another, I'd have a full war band scattered in hiding, as well."

"Or two," Fletcher said, all attention fiercely on the surroundings.

Bel glowered. "I counted eleven; so I guessed twelve."

"I counted eighteen. I guess two dozen."

"Not that many." Bel was disparaging. "Your imagination is running away with you."

He spoke between his teeth. "I could hear the buggers breathing."

Rowan could not help but laugh; she could not ask for two more dedicated guardians. "Really, both of you, everything is fine. And I've heard and seen the most amazing things." She prepared to relate the entire experience, too excited to wait until they reached camp.

But Fletcher had come to a dead halt ahead of her and stood jittering. "Damn," he said under his breath.

Bel scanned the veldt. "What?"

He ignored her. "Look, you," he said to the redgrass ahead, "I understand. I sympathize with your, your natural caution. But if you think we're going to walk within two meters of you, you're damn well mistaken!" He made a wild gesture of dismissal. *"Clear off!"*

There was a pause, then a louder clatter among the chattering of the redgrass, and a line of motion, departing. Rowan and her companions continued on their way. Twenty feet later, Bel looked back, and Rowan did the same: the Face Person was now standing, looking after them with a bemused expression.

Bel said to Fletcher, "I hadn't noticed him."

"Spotted him earlier. Kept an eye on him." He drew a long breath. "Ladies," he said tightly, "please, let's just get out of here."

42

*R*owan filled four pages of her logbook with drawings and descriptions of the Guidestar fragment; the pages were growing few, she dared use no more than that.

She sat by the fire, upwind from the cooking smoke, intermittently pausing in her writing to hold up her palms to the warmth. Fletcher sat beside her, making a show of reading over her shoulder purely to annoy her; but Rowan thought that behind the joke, he was very much interested in what she was doing.

Someone spoke his name: "Fletcher."

He looked up. Rowan did the same; shading her eyes against the sun, she saw Jaffry, dark and still, standing above them.

The young man pitched his voice somewhat louder: all could hear. "Your sword needs a better master."

Fletcher sighed, but his reply matched Jaffry's tone. "And you think that's you?"

"I know it."

"Well." Unfolding himself, Fletcher stood. "Let's find out, shall we?"

"Who's to signal the start?" someone asked. The duty fell to a chief Rowan did not know well: Garris, tall and angular, with eyes like two straight lines behind high cheekbones.

People began to arrange themselves. Averryl spoke quietly to Fletcher. "You won't have your left-hand advantage." Jaffry also fought from the left.

"I know." Fletcher unstrapped his sword in its sheath and handed it to Averryl.

"Jaffry's a good all-around fighter, but you have a long reach, and more weight."

"Right." Fletcher untied his vest, removed it, and slipped off the wool shirt he wore beneath, passing both to his friend.

"Watch where you throw your limbs." At this, Fletcher grinned. "And you should take that thing off, too. It'll get in the way." Fletcher's cross.

Rowan had seen him without it only when making love. Fletcher paused a moment, and Rowan thought to see a quick flash of fear on his face. It vanished; he slipped the thong over his head, handed it to Averryl, and spoke without humor. "Please don't fuss with it. It's sacred." And he drew his weapon from the sheath Averryl was holding.

Jaffry had also shed most of his clothing. Rowan took a moment to study his physique. Each muscle was clearly defined, but of no great bulk. "Smooth moves," Rowan said to Fletcher. "He's probably a very fluid fighter, very controlled."

"I've seen him. He is." And Fletcher grinned again. "Perhaps I can make him angry." He put his right hand in the small of her back and drew her up for a kiss. "Wish me luck."

Rowan recalled Bel's response when Rowan had wished her luck, and provided it for Fletcher: "Ha."

But when the fighters took their positions, she felt less certain. Fletcher had fought and survived the attack of the Face People; but she had not closely watched him fighting, could not extract the memories from her own experiences in the wild heat of battle. She did not know if his skill, even with a steel blade, was sufficient to defeat Jaffry.

It would be a shame if Fletcher lost his fine sword; despite her wish to be confident in her lover, and her recognition of his very real skills, she could not dispel the suspicion that Fletcher needed every possible advantage to survive as an Outskirter.

The signal came, and Jaffry swung, then with a pivot of wrists converted to an overhand blow; Fletcher moved to parry the apparent maneuver, adjusting at the last second to meet the actual one. He let his sword be driven down, then slithered it from beneath Jaffry's, stepped left, and found his own blow expertly parried. His blade was pushed farther aside than one would expect for so long and strong a weapon; he was not surprised, but followed it, with a half step to clear himself for Jaffry's next swing. The action looked awkward, but achieved its purpose. His sword was in place to meet Jaffry's next thrust, and when it did Fletcher discovered a small, unexpected clear space to step into, at the last moment. It gave him a tiny piece of maneuvering room, for a tiny maneuver that sent Jaffry's weapon out of line for one brief moment.

But the young man recovered and compensated instantly, apparently without thought, without breaking his own rhythm. Fletcher had defended himself, but gained no advantage.

Near Rowan, Chess grunted once. "Look at him," she said around an expression of reluctant admiration. "He's doing it again."

"Doing what?"

"Scraping by." And it was true.

Jaffry moved with pure grace, with perfect oneness of body and weapon, his will and intellect directing the whole as a unit. Rowan could see as clearly as if drawn on a chart: lines of force, from mind to muscle, from muscle to weapon, the edge making flashing, clattering connection with his opponent's; and back from muscle to bone, from bone to earth. The young man stood in the center of two directions, the perfect pivot point, with the world on one side, the foe on the other. Jaffry's strength was in grace, in balance, in his unconscious comprehension of the physics of action.

Fletcher understood his sword, and what he wanted it to do—and nothing else.

He thought with the edge and the point of his blade. He sent his weapon where he wanted it to go, and his body followed or did not follow, depending on his stance and direction of motion, sometimes flinging wild counterbalances of arm, leg, throwing his weight into a blow, then with a dodging twist leaving both body and sword to continue of their own momentum, wherever that might lead—as long as the blade went where it needed to go.

And it did. It seemed too long a weapon to be directed so lightly, to move so quickly. But it did what he asked of it.

Fletcher, all odd moves, scraped by, again and again.

He took a wild step back, made a feint at the length of his reach. Jaffry saw opportunity to force Fletcher's blade down, and made his move; but Fletcher miraculously slipped his weapon free, spun it up and over, struck hilt-to-hilt, twisted his blade once, disengaged. And he repeated the maneuver, finding entry where there should be none—

Rowan saw the logic of the move and smiled a small smile of satisfaction: it was precisely what she would have done in Fletcher's place.

Rowan began to enjoy the fight. She studied the action, imagined the next moves, and saw them come into being as Fletcher again struck the weak point on Jaffry's blade before escaping easily from what ought to have been a perfect trap.

Jaffry entered a set drill, a holding maneuver. He was thinking, hard. Fletcher's strategies were obvious to the young man, their execution incomprehensible. Rowan realized with pleasure that she had an advantage over Jaffry in understanding Fletcher's style.

Then she realized of what her advantage consisted, and felt a sudden, cold shock. Unconsciously, she took a step forward. Bel pulled her back.

Jaffry set another trap, maneuvering Fletcher's parries inexorably toward a configuration that would permit one perfect flick of the blade to disarm him. Fletcher willingly entered the trap, springing his weapon free at the last instant.

Fletcher's move looked awkward, seemed impossible—but worked.

In the midst of a crowd of watching, enthusiastic people, in the center of a village of skin tents, out on a grassy plain in the heart of the wildest land—Rowan felt that there were two worlds present, separate but contiguous. One was a world of people, going about the living of their lives; persons known, admired, loved, two of whom were now engaged in a contest of skill. The other was the world of pure action: force, motion, mass, momentum. The worlds did not match.

Rowan stood dead still, staring in her mind's eye at the link between those two worlds. They did not match because the link itself was a lie.

She wished to deny the lie's existence. She wished to ignore the irrefutable world of fact and action.

She was a steerswoman. She stepped into the world of fact, holding the lie in her hands—and watched.

The fighters ceased to exist as persons; they consisted only of the actions they made. It did not matter who fought or why. She shivered, once, unconsciously, then gave herself to pure reason.

She saw that one fighter was slowly gaining advantage over the other, and that the other could wrest that advantage from the first, by using certain specific maneuvers. She saw some of those maneuvers become manifest. The opponent faltered, regathered. A moment later, in the midst of her calculations, she caught sight of one fighter's face.

For the first time in Rowan's experience that face, ever before calm and controlled, displayed a pure, unequivocal emotion. It was hatred. The steerswoman coldly added that fact to her analyses.

The fighter had been growing more angered throughout the contest. Now his anger had crested and broken, and its source stood clear: hatred. For the sake of hate, he was attempting to fight far beyond his own level of skill. He found the new level; he entered it; he inhabited it. He began to take brilliant risks. The risks paid.

The second fighter had noticed the hatred and faltered at the force of it. The first took that moment to shift his body, to change to a tight upstroke.

Just in time, the stroke was parried; but it was a stupid parry, too close, with no room to recover and respond. It was an utterly foolish maneuver, driven by panic. It was a move of reflex. It failed.

With cold clarity, Rowan reasoned under what specific alterations of parameters that particular parry would have been successful.

The steerswoman was vaguely aware of a rise of sound from the spectators. Beside her, Bel stiffened. "He shouldn't draw blood!"

Rowan had not noticed. "What?"

Bel relaxed somewhat. "It's only a nick. It can happen in a sword challenge, by accident."

What Rowan had noticed was a further disintegration of one fighter's style, an even greater focus in the other's. The blood had been no accident.

One of the fighters was failing; he was being driven back. The other man pursued, pressed, sending his opponent's sword into wilder and wider defenses.

And then they were close again; and the failing man ought to have pulled back. He was fighting in utter panic, Rowan understood. He had completely reverted to trained reflex; he possessed some instinct that told him that in this close situation he should move closer yet. He did so. The instinct was wrong. His opponent made one small, quick motion.

The fighters paused; a pause seeming offhand, innocent, held in an almost gentle silence.

Fletcher released his sword, and it dropped to the ground. He took a half step back, then turned away. In the crowd, someone cried out, then someone else. Fletcher took one more step, then fell to his knees, arms wrapped tight about his body, hissing between his teeth in a choked, rising tone, "*Christ!*" And Jaffry drew his blade back to strike again.

"No!" There was a hiss, a flurry of motion, a clash; and Bel stood between the two men, with Jaffry's sword stopped against her own. She faced him from behind the crossed blades. "Have you gone mad?"

Jaffry halted. Trembling, he stared at her with wild eyes. "I'll kill him."

"It's not a blood duel!"

"It should be!"

"Then call it as one—if you can justify it!" She stepped closer; he permitted it. "Justify it, Jaffry," she said. "Do you want revenge? Revenge for what?" Behind her, Fletcher was doubled over, gasping. Averryl broke from the crowd to rush to his friend; Jaffry pulled away from Bel and made for Averryl, who froze at the madness in the young man's face.

Bel interposed herself again. With a visible internal shock, Jaffry recognized her for the first time, and her face held him fascinated. He did not blink, did not move. He shuddered, rhythmically, as if to his heartbeat.

Averryl was at Fletcher's side, supporting him, calling out for Mander. Fletcher was making small, strange sounds and attempting to collapse.

"A blood duel for a wrong done," Bel said to Jaffry, "or for an insult too great to let pass: that's warrior's honor. But where's the insult? Or the wrong?" And she fairly spat the next words in fury: "*Justify!* Or call this murder." She tried to push his sword aside with hers; he resisted. She spoke more carefully. "You cannot murder a warrior of your own tribe."

Jann called out, "Fletcher's no warrior!" Jaffry's head jerked at her voice, but his eyes stayed on Bel.

"He is," Bel told her. "Your tribe named him so, and your seyoh. You can't have him fight and risk death for your tribe, then call him no warrior. Perhaps he's not the best warrior, but he is one, and he's yours." She turned back to Jaffry and looked up at him, dark eyes on dark eyes. Her fury melted. She said quietly, sadly, "Jaffry . . . there's no honor in this."

He was holding his breath. He looked down. Then he dropped his point and turned away.

Mander appeared. Fletcher had fainted; the healer tried to examine the wound that Averryl was pressing with bloody hands, laid his fingers against Fletcher's throat, and peered at his eyes. He called for help, and the wounded man was carried away.

Rowan watched them depart, noting the event as pure fact, mere information. She remained where she was.

Warriors muttered and mertutials cast sidelong glances at each other. Abruptly Jann stepped forward, reached down. "Here," she said to her son, and handed him what she had retrieved.

Fletcher's fine steel blade. Jaffry looked at it. "It's yours," Jann said to him.

He seemed not to want it; then he took it from her hand, and tossed aside his own weapon.

It fell three paces in front of Rowan's feet. It lay in the trod mud, its edging battered, its wood face nicked and gouged, its leather-wrapped hilt worn black from use. Amid the noise of the Outskirters,

Rowan stood as if in a small, silent room, gazing at the weapon, not seeing it.

There was argument: Garris, declaring that the sword challenge had been improperly conducted, that Jaffry's victory was void; Jann, disagreeing, calling for someone to bring Kammeryn to decide.

The steerswoman did not wait. Within her perfect, emotionless isolation, she had discovered a requirement, clear, airy, intellectual: a mathematician's need for completion.

She stepped over Jaffry's discarded sword, unbuckling her own weapon, unsheathing it, and dropping the sheath to the ground. "Jaffry," she said.

Discussion ceased. The young man turned. Rowan said, "That's a fine weapon you have. I'd like to see how you use it." She stood with her sword point-down, waiting.

Garris looked from one to the other. "Rowan, you should wait; Kammeryn will be here soon—"

"No."

Catching her empty expression, he ceased to protest, and stood watching her, with a warrior's respect.

Bel came to her side. "Rowan, are you sure of this?"

"Yes." The crowd was silent. Jaffry hesitated, confused; Jann was aghast, and then anger slowly reshaped itself on her face.

"Is it against custom," Rowan asked Bel, "to challenge him so soon after another fight?" She did not look at her friend, nor at her opponent; she could not move her eyes from the steel sword in Jaffry's hand.

Bel glanced back once, to where Fletcher had been taken, then took a step away from the steerswoman, studying her. "No," she said slowly. "Not unless Jaffry were wounded, or exhausted." He was neither. "But you're using the wrong words. For revenge, for a blood duel, you should say, 'Stand and die,' or 'Face me, if you dare,' or something of that sort."

Rowan's face was unchanged. "No blood duel. Call it another sword challenge." The spectators became perplexed, disbelieving. She ignored them. "Jaffry," Rowan said. She did not shout; her voice was mild, empty of emotion. "Use your sword, or I'll take it from your hand." She took five steps forward, leaving Bel behind.

Jaffry looked at his new weapon, then at the steerswoman. Jann's expression was narrow, suspicious.

"She's a fool," Jann said. "Her sword is as good as Fletcher's. There's no point to this." She slapped her son's shoulder, to urge him forward. "Go ahead. It hardly matters who wins."

They assumed their positions and waited for the signal. Then they began.

It was no contest.

They fought at first wide, Rowan striking at Jaffry's sword between its midsection and point, over and over, backing and circling to maintain her chosen strategy. She saw Jaffry's surprise at the first blow, saw him falter at the next, try to recover at the third. It was no use. He could not send his strength down into his new blade: its flex dissipated his power, its faintly vibrating recovery confused him. He began backing himself and twice lost his rhythm. Rowan used the advantage to press him.

She entered a drill, like a dance to the singing and hissing music of the steel. Jaffry knew the steps with his body; but his sword wanted other steps.

He had practiced before with borrowed steel swords; he knew how to change strategy from that required by wood-and-metal. Rowan watched him using exactly the correct maneuvers for fighting with a metal blade, and against metal. Again and again, he tried to unify his actions to his familiar perfection. He failed. He worked wildly, but he was divided: his body constantly seeking balance, his blade constantly refusing it.

Jaffry's grace of violence had vanished.

The steerswoman needed neither grace nor violence. There was nothing in her but intellect, mathematics, logic, proof—and memory. She recalled the moves Fletcher had made in panic and reflex, the moves that had failed him. At the right time, in a moment of close fighting, she used one, copied exactly from Fletcher's final, losing maneuver. At that close instant, she stepped closer still—into a space that should not have existed.

She found it: exactly twice as much free room as the flex in her own sword would have provided.

The blade seemed to leap from Jaffry's hand, of its own accord. It spun away, toward one side of the crowd; the spectators on that side scattered.

Jaffry stood looking at his own left hand. He made a single sound, the closest to a full laugh that Rowan had ever heard from him. He gestured at the weapon. "It's yours." Someone near it picked it up, to pass to her.

Rowan found it difficult to speak; her proof was achieved, further action meaningless. She forced a word from her lips. "No."

"What?" Jaffry was puzzled. The man who had retrieved the fallen weapon paused with it half held out.

"The winner," Rowan said with painful slowness, "gets the choice of weapons." She reversed her grip on her own sword and held it up, hilt first. "I choose this one." She turned and walked away.

The shocked crowd was disinclined to part before her. She shouldered her way through.

Someone put a hand on her arm as she passed—a member of Kree's band. "Rowan . . ."

"Let her alone," Bel said, close behind. Rowan ignored both. The hand vanished. She continued walking away.

But the next touch was a grip of iron that clutched and spun her around. She was face-to-face with Jann. The warrior's eyes were small with fury, her brows a straight black slash. She spoke through her teeth. "If your intention was to dishonor my son, you've done it."

That had not been the intention; but Rowan could not reply. She was empty. Words had fled; there were none left in her. The steerswoman stood silent, looking out through her eyes, from behind her face.

Jann's grip faded, and her expression altered. She read something in Rowan's eyes—what, Rowan had no idea. The warrior grew puzzled. She looked as though she felt she ought to pity Rowan, without knowing why; she became confused and dropped her hand.

Rowan turned and walked away.

Reaching the edge of camp, Rowan wished not to stop, wished to continue out onto the veldt. She was moving, and there was relief in motion. She was walking away from something, something better abandoned. There was no place to go, and nothing ahead; and she liked that very much indeed.

Her body was wiser than her heart; she stopped at the edge of camp.

She heard Bel following behind, pausing as she paused. Rowan remained, looking at nothing. Eventually, after some minutes had passed, she heard Bel drop to a seat on the ground.

An uncounted measure of time later, Rowan did so herself.

Much later, Rowan decided to speak. She drew a breath and turned to Bel.

The Outskirter was seated on redgrass stubble, a mottled gray-and-brown tent rising at her back. There was anger on her face, but not anger at Rowan; it was a fury deferred, a waiting hatred.

Rowan released the breath and did not speak after all. Bel's mind was as quick as her own. Bel did not need to be told.

The Outskirter said, "Fletcher is a wizard's man."

"Yes."

43

"*I* didn't see it when you did," Bel continued, "when he was fighting Jaffry; but when you used your sword against his, then I saw . . ."

"Yes."

"That's a wizard-made sword Fletcher was carrying."

"Yes." Rowan's own sword was of wizard make. When Fletcher fought well during the duel, he used the same techniques that Rowan would have used. But more than that:

When a fighter became panicked and desperate, when he lost the ability to think clearly, he would most often revert to instinctive maneuvers, imbedded in him from his earliest training. When Fletcher had reached that point, he used, again and again, moves that assumed his opponent possessed a weapon with the same virtues as his own.

Not only was his sword of wizard's make; all of Fletcher's training in swordsmanship, before entering the Outskirts, had been against a sword of the same type.

It was Fletcher's undoing. The moves he had used were not suited to fighting against an Outskirter weapon.

And that was the test Rowan had made, the equation of action that had provided her final proof: when Rowan fought Jaffry, when it was wizard blade against wizard blade, those same maneuvers succeeded.

Fletcher was a wizard's man.

"He told me," Rowan managed to say, "that he had had the sword constructed for him, by a swordsmith in Alemeth."

"That's a lie."

"Yes." If, by some miracle, the swordsmith had known and used wizards' methods, Fletcher would have learned his skills against a common blade only. He would not have been betrayed by his training. Fletcher had acquired his weapon by no such innocent means.

"What's he doing here?"

What would a wizard or wizard's minion be doing in the Outskirts? "He was sent."

Bel nodded, fractionally. "By Slado himself."

"Quite likely."

"What do you think his plan is?"

"Plan?" Rowan had not thought so far.

"He's here in the Outskirts. And you show up, the very steerswoman that Slado tried to kill. He gains your confidence—"

No emotion reached Rowan's awareness; but of itself, her body shuddered, and her arms wrapped themselves tightly about her, and she doubled over where she sat, shaking in unfelt hatred. Lies, she thought. She had been fed lies, had trusted lies, had built a world of joy on lies.

She was a steerswoman; Fletcher, who had known this, and claimed to care for her, had given her lies. Fletcher himself was a lie. She had given every part of herself to a lie. No part of her body or spirit was untouched by the lie.

Eventually, she stilled. She sat up and drew a breath of cold air— and cold air pressed like ice everywhere upon her.

Bel eyed her. "Are you all right?"

"Yes."

The Outskirter nodded. "Then, what's his plan?"

"Not to kill me. He's had endless opportunity." They had been alone together often: out on the veldt; among the flocks; in Kree's tent, under the most intimate of circumstances.

Bel was considering the same events. She said, hesitantly, "Perhaps he really cares about you."

"No." Rowan gave a short, harsh laugh. "Wandering in the Outskirts, I happen, by purest coincidence, to bump into a wizard's man— no. He knew I was coming. This was intended. We should tell Kammeryn—"

"No."

"Why not? This concerns him, and the tribe—"

"But what is Fletcher doing here at all?"

Rowan forced herself to think, rubbing her forehead with her fingers. "He's been here for over a year."

"That's right. He wasn't sent here after you. But once you were here, he found you."

"How?" She was still rubbing her forehead; she took her hands from her face and interlaced the fingers in her lap to keep them still. "How could he find me? How would he know I was here at all?"

The Outskirter threw out her arms. "He's a wizard! Wizards can see things far away, sometimes; Corvus told people that he saw us die in Donner."

And Corvus's information had been only slightly inaccurate. "It's called scrying," Rowan began inanely.

"But why is he here?" Bel was urgent, insistent—and was repeating herself. From this, Rowan understood that her own mental processes were slowed, stalled.

She was behaving like a person who had witnessed the shocking, gruesome death of a loved one. And she understood that, in a manner of speaking, she had.

She separated her hands carefully and placed one on each knee. She sat up straight, only now realizing that she had not been doing so before. "Very well. What is this wizard, or wizard's minion, doing in the Outskirts?"

Bel did not reply, but only watched her.

"He can't have caused the famine on the Face," Rowan began,

"that's been building for years. Perhaps he caused the return of the killing heat to the Face; that's more recent."

Bel continued to wait.

"But there's no way for us to know that, for certain. Other factors may be at work."

Bel said nothing.

Rowan sighed. "We need more information."

"Exactly. How do we get it?"

"Certainly not by asking him. Nor by telling the tribe that there's a wizard's man in their midst. They might act against him. He might be forced to strike back at them . . . At the least, he would flee, and we'd learn nothing."

"We watch him," Bel told her. "Now that we know, we have the advantage. We keep our eyes on him; sooner or later, he'll do something that will only be explainable in one way—and that'll give us our clue. Enough clues, and we'll know something of what Slado is up to."

Rowan did not reply. Bel, aggravated, rose and came to her side. "Rowan, this is a chance to find things out. Don't you want that?"

Rowan looked up at her. "How bad is his wound?"

"I don't know," Bel said. Her mouth twisted. "Let's go and see."

"You go."

"Rowan—"

"Do you think he'll die?" Rowan asked mildly. "I rather hope that he does."

Bel stood silent a moment, studying her friend's face. "I can't say I blame you. In your place, I might kill him myself. But what's important now is that he doesn't suspect we know what he is."

"How can we prevent him suspecting?"

"He'll have to think nothing has changed."

"I'll need to lie."

"That's right." Bel nodded, then caught the steerswoman's expression. The Outskirter was briefly angry, then immediately, reluctantly, sympathetic. "Rowan, I know it's hard for you to lie—"

"For a steerswoman, impossible."

"Then resign!" Bel dropped to a seat close beside her. "You did it before, for perfectly good reasons. It was the only thing you could do. This is the same. Rowan, you have to do it again."

The steerswoman said carefully, "I have to make him believe that absolutely nothing at all has changed?"

"Yes—" Bel began, then broke off as she realized exactly what would be required of the steerswoman to maintain the deception. Despite her acceptance of deceit as an often-useful tool, Bel's honor balked at the concept. She continued, but with the greatest reluctance. "Do you think you can?"

"You know me," Rowan said. "What do you think?"

Bel studied her for a long moment, then turned away to think for a longer one. "Not you," she said at last, with a wry expression. "If you resign the Steerswomen, yes, you can do things like give a false name, pretend you're some other person, refuse to answer a question, answer a question with a lie. But when it comes to how you act, and the look on your face—you can only deceive when the lie fits in with your natural reactions."

"In normal, daily activities, perhaps I could fool most people, or even Fletcher. But even if I did manage to force myself to make love to him, he could not fail to notice some difference in me."

Bel's mouth twisted one way, then the other, as she considered. "End the romance."

"I'd need some explanation. Everyone will wonder."

"No one will wonder." The warrior gave a short laugh. "In fact, they'll think better of you."

Rowan puzzled. "How so?"

"When you watched Fletcher fight," Bel said, "you knew what you were seeing. No one else did. What they all saw, and what I saw, was this:

"Fletcher began by fighting badly, but managing by some trick or by luck to hold his own; Jaffry got angry and fought worse, and Fletcher gained some ground; then Jaffry became furious, fought better, and Fletcher got frightened, lost all control, and made the stupidest, most ridiculous errors possible, doing things any idiot could see were useless, and proving that he was entirely incompetent."

Rowan considered. "And?"

Bel threw up her hands. "Who would want a man like that? Not me."

"You're thinking as an Outskirter."

"Yes. And so will everyone else. You fought Jaffry not for Fletcher's sake, but for the sake of your own honor. Even if Fletcher wasn't worthy of you, he was your lover at that time. Jaffry dared to injure your lover in what should have been a bloodless competition. So you fought him, but you didn't call it a blood duel, you named it a sword challenge; then you defeated him so easily it was laughable, and refused to take his sword, proving that you weren't interested in it in the first place. You did it to shame Jaffry, and it worked. No one will blame you; he *should* be ashamed for losing control as he did."

"People will accept this?"

Bel was definite. "Yes."

"Not Fletcher himself," Rowan pointed out. "He doesn't think as an Outskirter. And he won't believe I do."

They were quiet a moment. "Can you have an argument with him?"

"Now, while he's lying wounded?"

"Well, no, you'll have to wait. But can you think of something?"

"I don't know." And they both pondered the problem, silently.

A voice spoke from behind. "Rowan?" She turned.

Averryl was standing between two tents, seeming hesitant to come nearer. "He's awake. He's asking for you."

Rowan was reluctantly impressed by Fletcher's skill at deceit. He had been told to watch her, or deal with her, or prevent her from accomplishing her mission; and yet, even wounded, he still remembered to maintain the illusion that she was important to him personally.

Quite suddenly, Rowan saw what she could do. And it required no lies on her part, no need to resign her order. Instead, it required that she remain, perfectly, a steerswoman—and that she have a small degree of sympathetic assistance.

Rowan said to Averryl, "I am not coming." The warrior gave her a long gaze of disappointment, but he did not protest. He departed.

Bel tilted her head in his direction. "See?"

Rowan nodded. "Just as you said. Now, listen: this is what I need you to do."

44

Fletcher's wound was not deadly, but it was two days before he regained the strength to rise. He immediately sought out the steerswoman.

"Where have you been?" He was pale, faintly unsteady. "Averryl told me some story," he said, and half laughed, "I couldn't believe it! Why didn't you come?"

It was a question. No steerswoman was permitted to answer a question put to her by someone who was known to have lied to any steerswoman. Rowan did not reply. She returned to her study of a small Outskirter handloom that one of the scouts was practicing on, watching the tiny bone shuttle being carefully threaded through the warp.

Fletcher knelt beside her, turning a puzzled gaze at the scout, dismissing him, and turning back to Rowan. "Rowan, please, what's wrong?"

He had told her countless lies. Her refusal to reply was justified. But he was not aware that she had caught him in any falsehood. It was necessary for her to do so, visibly, and in a fashion that did not hint at the true extent of her knowledge.

They had been lovers; now they were not. By asking one specific question, Rowan could insure that the entire matter would be perceived as merely a lover's quarrel.

"Fletcher, what do you feel toward me?" she asked, and sat calmly looking up at him, waiting for his answer.

With the question posed in such a way, under such circumstances, he could give only one reply. He gave it, appearing properly confused. "I love you."

She smiled at the words, and he warmed to the smile, mistaking its meaning. "That," she said, with the deepest satisfaction, "is a lie." And she rose and walked away.

He stayed where she had left him, looking after her; then abruptly he threw himself to his feet and hurried after her. "What do you mean?"

She continued walking.

"Rowan, you can't be serious!"

His second statement had not been a question. She said, "I am perfectly serious." She provided the fact as volunteered information.

"But why? What's wrong?"

She did not reply. She continued walking; he continued following.

They passed Bel, who was occupied in repairing her sword strap. Fletcher turned to her. "Bel, why won't she answer me?"

Bel pointed out, with careful indifference, "Steerswomen have to answer any question put to them. Usually."

"But," he said, then stopped short; his face underwent a series of expressions, apparently designed to reflect an internal sequence of arguments and confusions.

He was supposed to be an Inner Lander, and to know well under what circumstances a steerswoman may refuse to answer. The obvious inference came to him. He spun back to Rowan, throwing up his long arms. "But it wasn't a lie, it's true!"

Rowan turned back to look him in the eyes. She could not feign emotion; but she could prevent emotion from showing in her own expression—completely.

The face she presented to Fletcher was one of impassivity, utter disinterest. It was not a face he had ever seen on her before.

His hands dropped, and he stood slack in apparent disbelief. Once more, Rowan turned and walked away.

He watched her, then suddenly said, as if to himself, "Bel." He looked about, found the Outskirter still beside him, and pleaded with her. "Bel, she won't refuse you, ask her why she doesn't believe me—"

"No." Bel was adamant. "This is between you and her, and I'm not about to get in the middle."

He gazed down at her, aghast, then looked around again. The wool-weaving warrior was nearby. "Gregaryn—"

"No." Gregaryn gathered up in his equipment and rose. "You can do your own dirty work," he announced, then departed, shaking his head.

Fletcher stood completely still. He blinked, then scanned the camp. All eyes were on him, all embarrassed at his behavior. Fletcher shook his head as if to clear it of a bad dream, and went after the steerswoman again. He stopped a mertutial in passing, asked her to ask his question of Rowan, and was again refused. He tried a warrior and was refused, and then another—no one would assist him.

During the two days Fletcher had lain weak from his wound and from blood loss, Bel had carefully explained to every tribe member that Rowan had terminated her romance with him; that she was deeply upset about it and wished to be let alone on the subject; that it would be extremely unkind for anyone to abuse the laws of the Steerswomen to force Rowan into discussing the matter against her will; and that Fletcher, as a mere Inner Lander, would be unlikely to face the disappointment with a proper degree of warrior's dignity, or with honorable respect for Rowan's own decision.

Fletcher now confirmed Bel's evaluation.

He ranted, raved, railed; he brought into use all his skill, all his expressiveness of body, face, and voice. He stormed about the camp, following the steerswoman, asking and then begging for reply. Then he was shouting, first at her, then at anyone nearby, and then, finally, to the universe at large.

Rowan thought it rather an impressive display.

Eventually he exhausted himself and dropped abruptly to a seat on the ground, shaking and gasping from the exertion. Mander, who had been drawn from his tent by the noise of Fletcher's carryings-on, examined his stitched wound angrily, then gave him a stern lecture, delivered with scant sympathy, on the necessity of rest and recuperation.

Fletcher sat listening dizzily, seeming dazed. Possibly he was; the difference at this point was immaterial. Rowan and Bel left him sitting by the fire pit, Mander at his side, mertutials giving the pair a very wide berth as they moved about, preparing dinner.

Rowan gathered her belongings together, wondering where to move them. While she was at work, Jann provided the answer.

Rowan was surprised, and then was not. "But how does Jaffry feel about it?"

Jann's wide mouth tilted wryly. "He'll get over it. Things got out of hand, and he deserved what you gave him." And she hesitated, then continued with some reluctance. "I got out of hand myself. We're both lucky it got no worse."

"Well." Rowan set to rolling up her bedding. "Perhaps I understand things a bit better now. I have no real grudge against Jaffry. He's a fine young man, and a fine warrior."

"That's well said." Jann clapped Rowan's shoulder, then helped her carry her belongings outside. "Fletcher isn't worth your attention," the warrior assured her as they crossed the camp. "He fooled you for a while, that's all. He's fooled a lot of people." And they walked past Fletcher himself; he was in an argument with Averryl. Seeing them, the wizard's minion stopped in midsentence and watched Rowan pass, with apparent sorrow and longing, until she was out of sight.

By evening, Fletcher had descended to the low tactic of sending Deely as his go-between.

The weaver stood outside Orranyn's tent and waited, undecided, apparently uncertain of the propriety of his own mission. The steerswoman went out to speak to him.

He addressed her without preamble. "Rowan, don't you like Fletcher anymore?" He seemed relieved to have gotten the sentence out.

She responded with the truth, spoken gently for Deely's benefit. "No, I don't."

He shifted on his feet and looked down, sorrowful and uncomfortable. "But why not?"

"Because he lied to me. You're not supposed to lie to a steerswoman."

This had been explained to him several times in the past, by several people. She wondered to what extent he understood or accepted the custom.

Rowan attempted to forestall further questions. "Deely, you know that sometimes people who are in love have fights."

"Yes . . ."

"Well, it's very sad, but it's also very hard on the people. Sometimes it hurts them to talk about it. I don't love Fletcher anymore, and I want him to leave me alone. Please don't make me talk about this, Deely—I really don't want to."

He thought very hard, then reached out and patted her on the shoulder with clumsy sympathy. "I'm sorry. I won't do it again."

His concern was total, and sweet in its simplicity. Rowan wished she could comfort him. "Promise?"

"I promise."

Three days passed, with the only unusual event being the departure of Dane and Leonie on their walkabout. The two children slipped away before dawn, following Outskirter custom. Any rites or celebrations would wait for their return.

Rowan spent the days in camp, going about her usual business, covertly studying Fletcher's behavior from a distance. Bel stayed close beside the wizard's minion when not on duty herself, watching for signs of evil intent.

Neither woman noticed anything amiss.

"He's not very active," Bel told Rowan over breakfast one morning, at a moment when no one was paying them attention, "but Kree ordered him to stay put, so he can recover. He hasn't been able to go out on the circles with the rest of the band."

"I haven't seen anything." Rowan paused when Chess approached, waiting as the old mertutial passed mugs of broth to the two women. Fletcher had been staying in camp, in Kree's tent. The weather had been fine, and on all three days the wizard's man had rolled up the sides of the tent, so that he might rest in the sunshine. He had been completely visible to any passerby.

He now sat with the rest of his band, picking at his breakfast with little interest. He seemed to sense Rowan's attention and looked her way. She removed her gaze an instant before he caught it.

"Well," Bel said, "Kree's putting him back to work today." The statement was innocent enough to permit Chess to overhear.

The cook grunted. "He must be feeling better," she said, and jerked her chin once in Fletcher's direction. "First time he's done that in days, too. But he's late today. Hope his god doesn't mind."

Rowan glanced back. Fletcher had abandoned his food and was walking away, out between the tents, toward the edge of camp. "Off on his prayers," Rowan said without thinking; and it was suddenly necessary to restrain herself from clutching at Bel to gain her attention.

Bel had noted Rowan's sudden tension. When Chess was gone, she said quietly, "What is it?"

Rowan leaned very close. "Fletcher is certainly no Christer."

"And?"

"Then, what's he doing, Bel? What's he doing right now?"

Bel's wide eyes grew wider, and she clearly wished to look back in the direction Fletcher had gone. "Not praying," she said.

"I sincerely doubt it." They finished their breakfast in silence, and after, with careful nonchalance, strolled to the edge of camp.

Fletcher was nowhere in sight; it was his habit to tuck himself behind some natural obstruction or another when attending to his presumed devotions.

"He goes off alone, almost every single day," Rowan said, studying the single stand of tanglebrush that likely provided Fletcher his present privacy. "And he has done, all the time he's been in the Outskirts. If he's not a Christer, why would he need to be alone?"

Bel smiled thinly. "He's doing something other people shouldn't see."

Rowan was angry at herself for not suspecting this peculiarity long before. "Can you get close enough to see him, without him spotting you?"

"Yes." Bel scanned the sky, gauging the wind. "I'll have to swing around from the north." Then she winced. "Sometimes he's fantastically good at seeing people in hiding. And sometimes he can't see past his own nose."

Rowan frowned in thought. "Magic," she said at last. "When I went to talk to the seyoh of the Face People tribe, and you and Fletcher followed me, Fletcher knew where the watchers were hiding, even when you didn't, despite the fact that you're a better Outskirter. But earlier—" She paused in her speech, waiting for a pair of water-carrying mertutials to pass. "But earlier, when Efraim's old tribe attacked us, Fletcher had no idea at all that anyone was about."

Bel nodded, eyes narrowed in thought.

"What was the difference between those events?" Rowan asked her.

Bel replied immediately. "The first time, you were standing right next to him. The second time, he was hiding in the grass, and so was

I. We couldn't see each other. Whatever he does, he only does it when no one's watching."

"And no one can see him right now." Rowan's mouth twisted in dissatisfaction. "I don't think you'll be able to get close to him."

"I'd like to try."

Such an attempt might be dangerous; but the only destructive magic Rowan had ever witnessed had been loud, visible, and required hours of preparation.

Perhaps Fletcher's abilities differed from those of the boy Willam. But if Fletcher had access to a more quickly acting destructive spell, he certainly would have used it when the Face People had attacked Kammeryn's tribe. The wizard's man had been clearly and obviously in a state of terror at that time. Had he been able to summon magic to insure his survival, he would have done so. The only options open to him had been to fight by sword, or to run; he had fought.

The steerswoman drew a breath. "Do you suppose, if he notices you by magic alone, that he'll be able to actually recognize you?"

"Who can say?" Bel thought. "I'll put together some excuse to be there. Practicing Efraim's Face People techniques, perhaps, using them to play a joke on Fletcher."

But when Bel returned, she reported only failure.

"I got to within three meters of him," Bel told Rowan much later in Orranyn's tent; the band was on duty on the outer circle. "All I saw was him kneeling, with his eyes closed and his hands folded. Looking—" She searched for the proper word, then supplied it with distaste. "—humble."

Rowan made a dissatisfied sound. "He knew you were there." She gave herself to thought. Very little was known about the functioning of magic spells in general, and less of magical means of perception in particular. She considered, instead, natural perception, and animals with particularly sharp senses: cats with their vision; dogs with hearing, smell; frogs, which could capture small, rapidly moving insects . . .

"Perhaps," she ventured, "he sensed you approaching."

Bel caught the idea. "Then tomorrow, he won't. Because I'll already be in place, waiting for him."

The next morning, Rowan was awakened at dawn by hands shaking her. She flailed out in startlement. "What?"

"Get up," Jann told her urgently. "Get your clothes, and your sword, and get outside!" And the warrior was gone.

The tent was already empty. Rowan threw herself into her clothing and hurried outside.

War bands were congregating by the dead fire pit; Kammeryn was in place, with relays nearby. Rowan read the reports as they came in, all of them the same, single gesture: negative, negative, negative . . .

She looked about for Bel; the Outskirter was nowhere in sight. The rest of Kree's band stood near Kammeryn, all of them seeming intent and prepared. Among them was Fletcher, his face as grim and determined as his comrades', standing with his muscles twitching, like a frightened horse.

Rowan found Jann and sidled over to her unobtrusively. "What's going on?"

But it was another warrior who replied. "Fletcher says he saw someone, hiding. He says"—the woman was dubious—"that the stranger is *inside* the inner circle."

Now Jann spoke. "I don't believe it. Our people are too good for that. It can't happen." Her eyes were not on her chief, or on her seyoh; she watched Fletcher.

Orranyn thumped her on the arm. "Pay attention, you!" Rowan knew from the tone it was not a sudden anger but exasperation of long standing.

"Orranyn, it can't happen—"

"Fletcher's been too right too often for us to ignore him. If you can't bear to lose a little sleep for safety's sake, then think about crossing over." The war band stood shocked by the statement. Orranyn pretended indifference to their reaction; he was reaching the limit of his indulgence of Jann's obsession.

But Jann was not the only person watching Kree's band. "Where's Bel?" Jaffry asked, and as he spoke, Rowan watched Kree, across the fire pit, put the same question to each of her warriors. When the question reached Fletcher, he reacted with surprise so extreme that he seemed to have been struck. Then he spoke to Kree, pleadingly; she interrupted him, sternly, clearly indicating that he should be most concerned with the duties immediately at hand. When Kree turned away, Fletcher's eyes sought and found Rowan, and he looked at her in seeming distress, spreading his hands in a gesture intended to communicate helplessness. It was very eloquent, and very clever, and Rowan hated him far worse than she ever had yet.

Rowan might easily have been too conservative in her estimation of Fletcher's power. Bel might already be dead, by magic; she might be cast to sleep forever under an evil spell; she might have been transformed into some strange creature; she might be crouched in hiding out in the pastures, unable to move for fear of attracting attack, with all Kammeryn's tribe convinced that she was an enemy, and Fletcher's magic insuring that all eyes would see her as one.

"What's happening?"

The steerswoman spun, dropped her weapon, and threw her arms about Bel, pulling the small woman completely off the ground in an embrace of utter relief.

The Outskirter pretended amazement at the reception, extracted herself, and repeated the question.

"Where were you?" Jaffry demanded.

Bel regarded him with fists on hips. "Can't a warrior visit the cessfield without the tribe falling apart behind her back?"

But as she left to join her war band, she quickly pulled Rowan aside and forced the steerswoman down to hiss in her ear, "I'm never doing that again!"

It was not until much later, after the guards had determined that Fletcher had been mistaken, after Kree's band had served their rotation on the outer circle, after evening meal, that the two women could meet, alone at the edge of camp.

"Well, for what it's worth, I did see something," Bel said.

Rowan found herself almost indifferent; it was far more important that Bel was unharmed. "What was it?" she managed to ask.

Bel thought, then shook her head in confusion. "I'm not sure . . . perhaps you can make sense of it.

"When he settled down, he had his back to me. I was disappointed, because I thought I might not see anything . . . I shouldn't have worried. Because, all of a sudden, there were things in the air."

Rowan was taken aback. "Overhead? Someone would have seen them."

"No, not up. Just in front of him. Floating things, like they were trapped in a trawler's shoot—but flat." She held her hands before her, delimiting an invisible vertical surface. "They went no higher than the grass tops, and all the way down to the ground. The things were small, like insects, bright colors. But they didn't move, they just hung. And they glowed."

Rowan had not expected anything quite so dramatic. "Glowed? Like fire? Was there any heat?" There could not have been, or the grass would have caught—

"No. More like stars: cold light. Blue, red, yellow, all colors. It was strange. The colors were bright, but the light didn't seem to be . . . It's hard to describe."

"Just spots of light, hanging in the air in front of him?" Rowan tried to imagine it, but failed. "Not . . . scenes from far away, or writing, or a pentagram?"

"Some of them might have been arranged in something like a pentagram . . . it's hard to say, I didn't get to look for long. Fletcher sat down, the lights appeared; then he shouted, the lights vanished, he jumped up, drew his sword and turned around—" Bel leaned closer, spoke more quietly and more intensely. "—and he came straight at me!"

"He knew you were there."

"He knew *exactly* where I was."

The magic lights had somehow told him. "What did you do?" Rowan was aghast.

The Outskirter leaned back, tilting her head. "I moved. And he went for exactly where I used to be."

Fletcher's magical perceptions were limited to the moments when the spell itself was active.

"I tried to stay put after that," Bel continued, "but he started flailing around in the grass, at random, and I had to dodge. Then he stopped and signaled to six; a reply, I think. He must have been seen carrying on. He told six that there was an intruder in the inner circle, and then he took to his heels, back to camp."

"Was there any indication that he knew it was you?"

Bel shook her head broadly. "But I don't dare try it again. So that's all we're going to learn about Fletcher's prayers."

Rowan's mouth twitched in dissatisfaction. "We have to wait," she said grimly, "for him to do something more obvious."

They did not wait long.

* * *

It happened over breakfast. Fletcher was late from his prayers.

And then Rowan heard someone calling his name, wondered why, then saw him enter the center of the camp at a flat run, ignoring the voices that asked why he ran.

Bel's eyes narrowed. "What's he up to?"

Rowan rose slowly. "I don't know."

Fletcher stopped and stood by the fire, arms splayed out as if he had forgotten them. He was glancing about, wide-eyed, as though desperate, and blind to everything but what he sought. "Where's Kammeryn?" he called out.

All were now watching his performance. "In his tent," someone supplied. Fletcher rushed to Kammeryn's tent as the seyoh was emerging. "Seyoh, the tribe has to move."

Kammeryn was bemused. "What?"

"We have to move," Fletcher insisted. "We have to go east. We need to do it now!"

Kammeryn put a hand on his shoulder and studied his wild eyes. "Calm down. What are you trying to tell me?"

"I had—" Fletcher drew a great breath. "I had a vision. We have to move. We have to go east."

Someone had fetched Kree; she came up to them, all confusion. "Fletcher, what is wrong?"

He turned to her, saw her, dismissed her. "A vision," he repeated to Kammeryn.

"What sort of vision?"

The wizard's man seemed to find no appropriate words, settled for vague ones. "Something terrible is going to happen. It's coming here. I don't know what, a tempest, a monster—*something*. We have to go away."

Kree made to protest; but Kammeryn gestured her silent. He paused long. "Perhaps . . ." he began, and he was watching Fletcher's pleading face closely. "Perhaps we ought to do it. But I'll send scouts around first, have them report what they find—"

"No! We won't have the time." In his urgent act, Fletcher dropped all form, all deference to the seyoh. "Send a scout ahead of us if you like, but let's start moving *now*."

The Outskirters were stirring with discomfort at hearing their seyoh spoken to in this fashion by a mere warrior. Rowan and Bel stood among them, quiet, intent.

Kammeryn must not do anything Fletcher required.

"Very well." The seyoh became decisive. "Karel, relay to Zo and Quinnan that I'll shortly have new directions for them. Everyone, prepare to pull out. Fletcher, come with me and tell exactly where the tribe is to move. Kree, with us." He walked to his tent and entered, with Fletcher hurrying behind. Kree watched an instant, amazed, then rushed to join them.

Dumbfounded, the watching warriors and mertutials stood speechless until someone broke the spell with an outraged, inarticulate, disbelieving cry. The yard became a chaos of arguing voices. Rowan and Bel looked to each other silently, and silently agreed. As one, they turned and walked, passing through the yard as if it were empty.

They entered the tent without ceremony. Kree broke off some comment to Kammeryn; Fletcher startled, the panic he had painted on his face now overlaid with confusion and annoyance. Only Kammeryn remained undisturbed.

"Do you two have something to add?" the seyoh asked. The sunlit sky flaps threw rectangles of light at his feet.

"Yes," Bel said. She was standing with feet apart, a pose of challenge. "Whatever Fletcher says, don't do it. Whatever he wants, it's the very thing you mustn't do."

Rowan said, "Fletcher is a wizard's man."

Kree spun to Fletcher. "What?"

Fletcher stood as if alone, looking at Rowan from the light-split shadows. "No." He mouthed the word, too shocked for speech.

She held his gaze, impassive. "Or a wizard himself."

He found his voice. "I'm not a wizard!"

"One or the other," Bel said.

"It's not true!" Fletcher tore himself from the accusing eyes and turned to Kammeryn, throwing his arms wide, speaking quickly. "Seyoh, I don't know why they're saying this—I don't know, and I don't care. Rowan has some grudge against me, I don't know why. Now she's gotten Bel into it, but for Christ's sake—" His body twisted as he beat one fist on his thigh, his voice risen to a desperate-sounding cry. "—for Christ's sake *none of that matters*! This is what matters, this is what I know: There's something terrible coming, it's coming here, and you've got to get the tribe away!"

Rowan could almost believe him, so expressive, so seemingly urgent and intense was he. "It seems to me," she said, her voice quiet and reasonable, "that if a wizard sends you away from a place, then there's something going to happen that he doesn't want you to see."

Bel grinned tightly. "Let's stay and find out what, shall we?"

Fletcher ignored them and spoke to Kammeryn alone. "Seyoh, I know you don't believe in my god, but you do believe in gods. I saw this thing, and if my god didn't send me the vision, then some other did. What can it hurt, to go? If I'm mad, if I've dreamed the whole thing, then I'm a fool and more than a fool, but what can it hurt, to go? Seyoh, take us away from here!"

"I have never met any Christer," Rowan observed, "who would admit even the possibility of other gods than his existing. You're not even a Christer, are you, Fletcher?"

Kree spoke up at last. "Rowan and Bel," she said, and her small, diamond-sharp eyes were steady on them, "Fletcher is my man, one of my warriors. Anything you say against him, you had better have good reasons to say. Or it's me and my people who you'll have to face."

"Fletcher carried a wizard's sword," Bel told her, "until Jaffry took it from him."

"A sword of wizard's make," Rowan clarified.

"How can you know?"

"Because I carry one myself. His is like it. I realized that when I saw him fight Jaffry, and confirmed it when I fought Jaffry myself." She turned to Kammeryn. "Perhaps you think we ought to have told you immediately, and perhaps you're correct; but it seemed to us that if you knew, you'd make some move against him. We didn't want that, not at that time. We thought more could be learned by seeing how he behaved, while he thought his deceit was still intact. We've been watching him."

It was Kammeryn's composure, his dignity, his calm demeanor, that held Kree and Fletcher silent as he considered Rowan's statements. Then he nodded minutely. "I know," the seyoh said. "I've been doing the same."

45

The steerswoman was speechless; but Bel spoke, eyes narrowed in suspicion. "You knew he was a wizard?"

"I've known since Rendezvous."

"I'm no wizard!"

Bel spun on Fletcher. "Minion, then," she spat. "Servant. Property. Slado's hands and eyes in the Outskirts."

"No—"

"Be silent, both of you."

Bel subsided; Fletcher did the same, assuming the appearance of the dutiful warrior, waiting for his seyoh to command.

Kammeryn gazed at him, and more than anything else, his expression was one of deep disappointment. He spoke to the three women. "Please draw your weapons. Now that he is revealed, we cannot predict his behavior."

Bel did so instantly, and Rowan, surprised by the force and speed of her own motion. It was a relief to draw a weapon on this creature.

Kree hesitated. "Kammeryn—"

"Do it."

Kree complied, slowly. She drew a breath. "Fletcher, give me your sword."

He looked at his chief, shocked. "It isn't true." His voice was small, his body inexpressive. Her response was a jerk of the chin; he did as ordered, drawing and passing the wood-and-metal sword slowly, as if the weight of it was too great for his hand.

"And your knife," Kree said.

"It's not enough," Rowan said. Her grip on her sword tightened, and its point rose. "We don't know what magic he can call down on us."

"Fletcher," the seyoh said, "you must make no sudden moves, speak no magical words, or you will die instantly."

Fletcher looked at his two empty hands. "Seyoh, I can't do any magic . . ."

But Kammeryn had turned away, and he stepped around Rowan and Bel, to the tent entrance. He spoke quietly to his aide outside. "I want Orranyn's entire band posted around this tent. At any disturbance, they are to come in, fighting." And he closed the flap on the astonished face.

Fletcher attempted his arguments again. "Seyoh, please, we're wasting time. The only thing that matters is that we get away from here, now."

Kammeryn made a show of puzzlement, faintly mocking. "Must we?"

"I am not a wizard."

"Aren't you?" He walked calmly back to his position. "Then listen to this:

"At Rendezvous," the seyoh began, addressing the women, "I met Ella again. When I saw her, I took a moment to congratulate her for her tribe's destruction of the Face People's camp.

"She had been about to say the same thing to me. It was not her people who destroyed the camp. Someone else did it. I wondered who that might be.

"No third tribe could have been near without my scouts or those of Ella's tribe seeing signs of them. It was just possible that one very skillful person might be nearby, in hiding, but no single person could possibly destroy an entire camp—"

Rowan had a sudden memory of the boy Willam, standing in the shifting light of fire with a mighty fortress blasted to ruins behind him.

"—unless that person possessed powers beyond those of other human beings," Kammeryn said.

"Because of Rowan and Bel's missions," he continued, "I had wizards on my mind. Perhaps a wizard, I thought, might easily destroy an entire tribe, by magic.

"But why that tribe, and no other? The wizard, if he indeed existed, had harmed neither my tribe, nor Ella's. He had acted to our benefit.

"But suppose . . ." The seyoh began to pace the length of the tent slowly, long strides, like a soldier on guard. "Suppose the wizard were hidden, not out on the veldt, but within one or the other tribe? Then, to defend that tribe would be to defend himself. And he would steal away to do it in secret, because he would wish his power to remain hidden. Neither Ella's people nor mine would know he had done this thing.

"I asked Ella about the movements of her people during that time; but even as she answered, I was asking the same of myself, and finding my own answers."

He stopped and faced the listeners: Rowan, fascinated; Bel, suspicious; Kree, confused and disbelieving; and Fletcher.

"The smoke from the Face People's camp," Kammeryn said, "was first sighted by Fletcher, who had gone out early to say his daily prayer—and had gone out, as ever, alone.

"When Bodo discovered the broken demon egg, and Rowan wished to know more, it was Fletcher who, the very next morning, discovered another, intact—and did it alone. And it was Fletcher, with his small skill at arms, who had survived the stealthy attack of a skillful Face Person raider—alone; and Fletcher who sighted the approach of another Face People tribe, before even the outer circle saw them— and did it while alone.

"Fletcher, who, when he meets the unexpected, can always deal with it—alone. Fletcher, who looks and speaks like a fool, but who always seems to see more than better warriors—

"Fletcher, who always, somehow, survives.

"But I could not judge against a man simply because he possessed skills useful to my tribe. I began to watch him. I saw only what I always saw: an odd man, a cheerful and friendly Inner Lander who for some reason chose to live out his life in the Outskirts. I doubted myself.

"When Rendezvous had begun and the tribe stopped moving, I had ordered volunteers to the positions where Rowan and Bel might expect to find the tribe. They would meet these scouts only if some problem forced them to return before the end of Rendezvous. I did not know of any problem they might encounter. The order was a precaution only.

"But one day Fletcher, who had shown no previous interest in the duty, volunteered to go out. And I thought: He has some foreknowledge.

"I permitted him to select his own position to cover. I ordered Zo to feign a headache and follow him in hiding, lest he have some plan to injure you. And I told myself: If Fletcher, of all the ones I sent out, is the one to meet Rowan and Bel as they return unexpected, then I will know."

Rowan recalled the unseen follower in the night, and that she had thought the person smaller than the average man. "We knew we were being followed. It was Zo?"

"Yes. I didn't think the wizard would harm you, as he had had many opportunities before. But, in case I was mistaken, you had one unseen protector."

Fletcher said quickly, "I could never harm Rowan."

Kammeryn's sad gaze met his. "So you say."

"I don't believe it," Rowan said.

Fletcher turned to her. "It's true."

"Don't talk to me of truth, damn you." Her voice was level, her face blank with hate. "In the Inner Lands the wizards hunted me. I come to the Outskirts, where there are no wizards, and suddenly one of their minions is right beside me." Her gaze narrowed. "I know that you were already in the tribe before my troubles began in the Inner Lands. But, somehow, Slado passed a message to you: that, being here already, you were to come after me."

"No—"

"You somehow caused the tribe to come to where Slado thought I would be—"

"No! I didn't know about you, or any fallen Guidestar, or any-thing!"

Rowan held her breath. It was not an admission; but there were implications in his words:

He did not know about any fallen Guidestar: Fletcher had been in the Outskirts before Rowan began investigating the Guidestar. Of the other wizards, only Corvus knew about it, and only because Rowan herself had told him. If Fletcher were the mere servant of some wizard other than Slado himself, then he would be doubly unlikely to know.

He did not know about Rowan herself: Isolated from the Inner Lands, he would not have heard of the events surrounding the wizards' hunt for Rowan. And she had left that country quietly, drawing no at-tention to herself. If all her care taken had been successful, then Fletcher's own master would have had no reason to alert him to her arrival.

"I believe you," she said to Fletcher, studying his expression. "You didn't know. But, perhaps, you feel you ought to have been told. Have you told your master that I'm here?"

He stood before her like a startled animal, a deer surprised by a hunter, too frightened to flee. "Kammeryn," he said, and the speaking of the seyoh's name freed him to turn from Rowan's eyes. "Kammeryn, you know I've never done you any harm. I've *helped* the tribe." He became again pleading, desperate. "I just want to help again. You've got to believe me, we have to get away from here."

Kammeryn was impassive. "Answer the steerswoman's question."

The wizard's man had three swords pointed at his heart, a dozen warriors waiting outside, an entire camp of fighters all around. He opened his mouth to speak, stopped, began again, stopped again. He stood with his long arms loose at his sides, and his gaze went far away, then returned, very slowly. He said, "I've told no one."

Bel hissed at the confirmation. "Wizard's man!" She spat, and her grip tightened on her sword, so that its tip became level with Fletcher's wide blue eyes.

He stared at it, frozen; then his eyes shifted beyond it, to Rowan's face. He spoke to her directly, as if explanation was due only to her. "It's not a tempest," he said levelly. "It's the heat that Efraim told us about, the one that used to come before Rendezvous. It's coming down from the Eastern Guidestar, it's coming here, and we need to get away."

"Can't you stop it?"

"Me?" His surprise was extreme. "No."

Rowan thought. "Then we'll wait for it to begin, as proof of what you're saying."

"There's no time!"

"Efraim's people had time," Bel said.

He turned to her. "This is different. There's no buildup, it's coming all at once."

"How do you know about it?" Rowan asked him.

His mouth opened and closed three times as he tried to answer. "I don't know how to explain it."

"Then don't explain," she spat. "Describe."

He struggled to organize his words, then surrendered to the impossibility. "I checked old schedules for repeating events in a twenty-year cycle, and found something called 'routine bioform clearance.' The last one recorded was forty-eight years ago. But this morning, it showed up on the upcoming schedule, same code, same label. I wouldn't have known what it was if I hadn't been looking before."

Bel was in total confusion. "Looking where?" But Rowan's mind was tearing at the words Fletcher had spoken, pulling them apart and finding the meaning she needed imbedded in his three short sentences.

Schedule: she had reasoned correctly. The heat was a planned thing, initiated by the wizards.

Routine: it was usual, expected—until it stopped after the Guidestar fell.

Checking, finding, looking: one could look at a schedule only if it were written down; could check it, find something on it. But Fletcher carried no papers.

The magic that warned him when there were enemies nearby could also show him objects even more distant, or permit him to speak with someone who had the schedule at hand. He could scry. Scrying was done by means of an enchanted object. "Fletcher, where is your cross?"

Of itself, his hand went to his breast; the cross was absent. "I destroyed it."

"Why?"

The hand dropped. "So Slado couldn't find me."

Bel looked to Rowan for explanation; but the steerswoman was thinking too quickly to stop. "Could he see you even when you weren't scrying at that moment?"

"Scrying?"

"Using the cross to find things out."

He was startled by her comprehension, almost frightened. "Yes. The link, the cross, it has, it's like, like a flag, or a beacon." He stopped to compose himself, then spoke more calmly. "Anyone who knows how to look, can find me."

"But they can't see you now?"

"No," he said. "Well, yes, but they can't tell it's me. They can't tell me from anyone else anymore—there's no flag."

Rowan thought of him carrying an invisible banner with an invisible sigil, declaring to all who had the means to see: Wizard's Man.

If Slado could see Fletcher, he could see him run, and perhaps see the tribe run with him. Slado would know that Fletcher knew of the heat and had told the tribe. Slado would realize that they all knew far more than they should.

But Fletcher had dropped the banner.

He wanted to help, he had once told her. He had used his magic to destroy the enemies of the tribe, used it to watch for danger.

Rowan wondered what other abilities Fletcher possessed with his link destroyed, what unknown powers of attack and protection.

She looked into his familiar face, so clever, so expressive, and saw it now naked, open, desperate. She read her answer there: he had none. He was without magic, without even a sword. He had made himself helpless, in order to help.

Rowan turned to the seyoh. "Kammeryn—"

How much of the conversation Kammeryn had understood she did not know. But he had understood what mattered to the tribe. "Yes," he said to her, then spoke to Fletcher. "Where must we go? And how quickly?"

Fletcher gasped, almost sobbing with relief. "Due east. The heat will be in a band, north to south. We're near the eastern edge. It'll come three days from now. We can get out, if we hurry."

"How wide a band?" Rowan asked him. He provided the area, with longitudes and latitudes of the limits; she had not known he was familiar with the terms. With this information, she saw that escape was possible.

If the tribe moved now. "Kammeryn, we can't wait."

"Yes." And with three steps he was at the tent entrance, throwing the flap aside.

His aide and Orranyn were outside, with faces of confusion. "Take down this tent," Kammeryn commanded Orranyn as he exited, followed by Fletcher, the Outskirters, and Rowan. Kammeryn strode into the camp, urgent, leaving his followers behind. "Reyannie!" he called. An old man hurried up: the mertutial in charge of breaking camp. Kammeryn turned to him. "How soon will we be packed?"

"An hour . . ." The old man was perplexed.

"Why have you been so slow?"

"We were confused . . ."

"Stop being confused." The seyoh stopped and scanned the camp, once. "Abandon half the tents." He walked away, around the fire pit.

The mertutial's jaw dropped. "Seyoh?"

"We'll take four warrior's tents," Kammeryn announced to the tribe at large, "and two mertutial's. That's all." He called back. "Orranyn!"

"Seyoh?"

"Forget my tent. Fletcher!"

Fletcher's head came up, hopeful. "Seyoh?"

For an instant Kammeryn hesitated; then he became decided. "Stay exactly where you are. Orranyn, I want half your people watching him, with their swords drawn, and the rest in reserve. You, Berrion! Take your band to twelve-side; I want four lines of guards ahead of us when we move."

Orranyn was still standing aghast. "Fletcher is a prisoner?"

"Yes." Kammeryn turned back toward him, impatient. "Do it now."

Orranyn assigned the guard, and Fletcher was circled by armed warriors. Among them: Efraim, stolid and unquestioning; Jaffry, intent; and Jann, watching Fletcher with eyes of glittering black ice.

Rowan said to the seyoh, "You don't need guards—"

But Kammeryn was still in motion. "I want Lonn." Chief herdmaster. Someone was sent for her. "Relay!" One appeared. "New reports?"

"None."

"How many scouts on duty are within range?"

"Gregaryn, at ten."

The herdmaster arrived.

"Have your people pull their flocks into a tight formation," the seyoh told her. "We'll be moving quickly. Once we're moving, if any animal can't keep up, *leave it behind.*"

"I'll need more people."

"Take any mertutial. Except Anniss," he added, naming the woman in charge of the children. Kammeryn's movements had brought them to the cook tent. "Take Chess."

The cook stopped her packing. "Someone needs to do this."

"We're leaving the cook tent."

"How will we pull the food?" The cook tent converted to a train.

"Abandon the food. All of it. We'll slaughter fresh when we need it. Someone, kill this fire!" The nearby mertutials were leaving with the herdmaster; Hari and Sithy rushed to obey their seyoh's command.

Kammeryn spoke to the relay as they continued around the fire. "This is a forced march. Pass the word outward. Have Gregaryn cross forward and find Lona at twelve and pass the word to her, then head back toward ten. Lona will find Amarys at two, and tell him. All of them are to double their distance from the tribe; other people will be sent to their old positions. Go." The relay went.

"Kree." Kammeryn was once again beside his tent, where Fletcher stood slack-limbed among the warriors, with Rowan, Bel, and Kree nearby.

"Seyoh."

Kammeryn paused, and Rowan thought, A wizard's man has served over a year as a warrior in Kree's band, and Kree has reported nothing amiss.

But Kammeryn's tone was reassuring. "I need three of your people to serve as extra relays. Send the rest as extra scouts, to cover twelve-side between the outer circle and the regular scouts' new positions. Make one of those people Averryl." Kammeryn wished to keep Fletcher's closest friend out of sight, away from any influence the wizard's minion might effect.

"Yes, seyoh," Kree replied with relief.

Behind the seyoh, and all around, the camp was partly collapsed, only those tents to be abandoned still standing. People shouted instructions to each other, and urgent words. Trains began to appear, and pack carriers.

"Bel, Rowan."

"Seyoh?" Bel answered.

"Kammeryn?" Rowan found herself waiting for command, as completely as if she were one of his own.

He gazed at the two a moment. "Stay by me." Then he strode off again, Rowan on one side, Bel on the other.

They stopped by the dead fire. "Scouts on hand?" Kammeryn called.

"Here, seyoh!" Zo approached.

"Quinnan is the only scout on six-side?"

"Yes, seyoh. He's out of contact."

"Take enough food for yourself and for him, for six days."

The scout blinked in thought. "He's only a day away, seyoh."

Kammeryn nodded. "You and he go northwest. Find Dane and Leonie."

Rowan gasped: she had forgotten the children on walkabout.

Fletcher made a noise, a wild cry of horror. "The children!" He stood with his arms splayed. "My god, it's too late, they'll never get out in time!" His voice was high, uncontrolled.

Kammeryn ignored him. "From Quinnan's position, you and he will have two days to find Dane and Leonie. Travel as fast as possible, by night as well, if you can. If you don't find them in that time," and he put all the force of his command into the words, "*you will turn around and come back*, Rowan—"

"Seyoh?"

"Tell Zo what to expect."

The steerswoman provided the information quickly: a concise desription of the effect, to the extent it was understood, the time factors, and the distances. Zo listened wide-eyed, nodding sharply at each sentence. Behind them, Fletcher was speaking, saying over and over, "My god, the children . . ." His ring of guards watched silently.

Kree came up, with two of her band. "We're your relays, seyoh."

"Take your positions."

Rowan felt a bump at her knee and looked down. Hari had brought her pack and was giving Bel hers. Goats began crossing the camp, escaping from the new herders driving them inward. Train-draggers and pack-carriers were ranged about the fire pit, waiting.

"Seyoh," Hari said, "I'll pack your things for you."

"I need nothing." Kammeryn looked about and signaled; the signal was caught by the relays and sent outward. The seyoh was already walking, along with Rowan and Bel. With a surge like a wave, the tribe followed.

46

"Kammeryn, I don't think you need to keep a guard on Fletcher," Rowan said.

The seyoh did not reply. Bel sent Rowan a narrow glare, but said nothing.

"He doesn't mean us harm, not now. I'm sure of it," Rowan continued. "Whatever he did before, whatever his original purpose for being here at all—it's changed. He's helping us."

"Helping himself," Bel said.

"He could have run!" Rowan said. "Only he knew, and he could have simply gathered a few supplies and taken to his heels."

"And been alone. With no way to replenish his supplies. No friends to help him fight goblins. He's using us; we're just damned lucky that we can use him back."

"Now is not the time to discuss this," Kammeryn said. He looked at neither woman; his eyes were focused directly ahead, but with a distant look, as if on an internal vision far more urgent than the real. "Save your breath for walking."

And they had been walking, all that cool, bright morning, traveling eastward, with a south wind rattling the redgrass across the land before them. High, small clouds chased each other across the sky, and the breeze carried an iron scent of water from somewhere beyond sight, and the sweet odor of lichen-towers; and over all, the dusty cinnamon-and-sour-milk smell of the redgrass itself. A typical morning on the veldt of the Outskirts; and a tribe, typically, on the move.

But this tribe was fleeing.

As noon approached, Rowan remembered that the tribe had brought no prepared food. She checked the figures that Fletcher had given her, checked them again, and was distressed. The time the tribe had in which to escape was barely sufficient. Preparation of a meal, including the slaughtering of goats, would lose the tribe some three hours of travel.

But noon arrived, and passed, and no halt was called.

From behind, Rowan heard a slow murmur of conversation, heard it work its way back toward the last walkers, leaving in its place a spreading silence.

She glanced back to where Fletcher traveled, still within his ring of grim guards. The faces of persons nearby had lost their perplexity at Fletcher's confinement; Fletcher's true nature was now known by all, and the reason for the tribe's forced march. Rowan tried to catch Fletcher's eye, to exchange some recognition or offer some reassurance. But he was looking elsewhere. She returned to comparing her calculations with the passage of land behind the tribe.

There was no meal that day. Only one person complained, a child, who was silenced with a sudden, brutal blow. By that act, the other children immediately recognized the urgency of the situation. No child of speaking age complained again for the rest of the march.

Throughout the day, reports were received from the warriors ahead, the doubled inner and outer circles, the augmented, distant scouts. They held more information, and more precise, than was usual; and by afternoon Rowan realized that the reports had evolved to such a degree of precision that they were now expressed in meters, with every rock and rill and gully described and located exactly among all other features.

Rowan began to wonder at the necessity of this; but even as she wondered, her trained instincts began unconsciously to use the information, constructing for her a mental map of her surroundings. It consisted of a kilometer-wide band, extending ahead to a distance of fifty kilometers, the location of the farthest scout. The map shifted as the tribe moved, coming into existence with the report of the point scout, amended and expanded by the warriors that followed.

As the map grew clearer in her mind, Rowan became more interested, and then fascinated, staring blindly ahead. The map was like a living thing, moving, even breathing, in waves of information. With knowledge of this detail, she felt she could walk the veldt blindfolded.

She emerged from her absorption to see Kammeryn beside her. He walked confidently in his usual measured pace, but his eyes looked only inward. Rowan realized that he was doing the same as she had been, but doing so completely, with all his attention and concentration. It came to Rowan that the information, and its detail, were of desperate importance.

When night fell, and darkness ended further reports, she understood. The tribe slowed slightly, but did not stop.

Now Kammeryn began to speak, quietly, constantly: specific directions and warnings to guide the steps of those who walked behind. No tribe member questioned his instructions, or the need to risk travel in the deadly night. Each sentence the seyoh spoke was repeated by those walking behind him, passed back to the rear of the tribe, out to those walking among the close-packed herd; in star-spattered blackness, the tribe was a single, murmurous animal, surging across the veldt.

One ancient mertutial toward the center of the tribe stumbled and fell, breaking her hip. People supported her, half carrying her as she wept in pain, while word was passed forward that she asked to be left behind. Kammeryn was long in replying to the request; he was still issuing his instructions. But a few minutes later, between a warning of a large boulder at the tribe's left and the exact number of meters to a marshy sink, he inserted the sentence "Send Chian my farewell."

At last the sky began to lighten, and the entire span of the mental map had been crossed. The night's march was done.

But now the tribe could see to walk. There was no rest. They continued on.

During the night, the tribe had caught up with most of the guards ahead, who had been forced by the darkness to wait. Now, as the sun rose, the scouts themselves were sighted; but they were rested, and begged permission to move ahead immediately, informing the seyoh that the point scout had done so already, daring to walk step by careful step, out into the unknown land. Permission was given, and the scouts set off at a flat run, the lines of guards reconfiguring more slowly.

Kammeryn was now silent, often walking with eyes closed. Rowan understood that he was resting his thoughts from the night's efforts; and from this, that he was preparing to receive the next reports, for the creation of another map; and from this, that he intended the tribe to continue traveling throughout the next night.

Kammeryn's aide walked close beside him, holding his elbow, occasionally speaking to warn him of objects underfoot. Her instruction was insufficient, and Kammeryn stumbled once. On his other side, Rowan reached out to assist, grasping him by the arm.

The touch sent a shock through the steerswoman. The seyoh's arm was thin, the skin loose, the muscles slack. His bones seemed light as a bird's, and as she helped him regain his balance, she felt his weight almost not at all.

Kammeryn was an old man. She had forgotten.

Kammeryn always stood tall and straight, striding about his camp with a firm step; his dark eyes were clear, his comprehension deep, his authority unquestioned. He was a man of power.

But his wisdom was the wisdom of years. The years were marked on his face, and the years had long ago wasted the mass from his body. His power came from his tribe's recognition of his wisdom; his strength was strength of spirit and intellect.

But it was not his spirit alone that had now walked twenty-four hours with no rest. It was his body. And he was an old, old man.

Reports slowly began to come in again, briefly interrupted as the outer line paused to deal with a number of goblin jacks. Back in the tribe, another mertutial succumbed, falling in exhaustion, and died where he lay. His body was carried to the front of the tribe, segmented by mertutials as the tribe passed around it, and cast by warriors in the rear positions of the outer circle.

The herdmaster reported that twenty-three goats had escaped in the night. The seyoh's mind was already occupied; he nodded indifferently.

Rowan's own thoughts began to be claimed by the new information from the warriors ahead; and before she grew too completely involved, she slowed her steps and dropped back within the tribe.

Orranyn and his band, with Fletcher within them, were traveling some thirty feet behind and to the left of the seyoh's position. Rowan crossed to them and caught Fletcher's attention; but before she could speak, Jann interposed herself.

"No," the warrior said.

"I just want to talk to him."

"No. Kammeryn said, keep him apart."

The night's march had been hard on Fletcher. It was only a week since he had been wounded, and his reserves of strength were not great. He was pale, panting in effort, and limping slightly. He watched the two women speaking, his bright gaze flickering between them.

"I'm sure Kammeryn didn't intend to keep me from speaking to Fletcher," Rowan said.

"No."

"Jann, he knows things we might need to know!"

And Fletcher called out to her. "How far have we come?"

And it shocked her to recall: Fletcher was under the Steerswomen's ban. Rowan could not reply.

Orranyn came around the guards and joined Jann. "Rowan," he said carefully, "do you want to ask Kammeryn if you may speak to the prisoner?"

Her mouth moved once in realization; then she said, "No." She dared not distract the seyoh from his work. She drew a breath, expelled it. "Orranyn," she said, "you might be interested to know that, by my estimation, the tribe has traveled one hundred and twenty kilometers." And she hurried forward to rejoin Kammeryn.

Up front, Bel had slipped off her pack and was carrying it below one arm, while she rummaged inside with the other hand. "Here," she said to Rowan, handing her something.

Rowan looked at the object: a box wrapped in silk cloth. "Your cards?"

"And here." A spare knife. "Put them in your pack. And these." The three remaining handleless knife blades the travelers brought from the Inner Lands.

"In my pack?"

"Yes. I'm losing mine; it'll slow me down." Bel indicated the land ahead with a jerk of her chin. "I'm moving up to work as a scout. They lost the point man overnight."

Rowan groped back over one shoulder to thrust the items into her pack. "I'll feel much better knowing it's you out on point," she said.

"Ha," Bel said, still rummaging. "I'm not going to be point. I'll take someone else's place; *they'll* move to point."

Kammeryn spoke. "Relay."

"Seyoh?"

"Bel is point scout."

The relay gave Bel one appraising glance, then sent the signal forward. Bel grinned, thumped Rowan on the shoulder, and was off, moving at a tireless jog, her pack still in her hands. Thirty feet away, she swung the pack three times over her head and sent it flying off over the redgrass, then disappeared among the brushy hills.

Kammeryn was not yet so occupied as to be unaware of conversations nearby. Rowan hazarded addressing him. "Seyoh, you might be interested to know that I can do the same as you. I can interpret the reports coming in, I can visualize the landscape, and I can keep track of the tribe's progress."

"Are you current on the reports?"

"For the most part."

"Tell me about the brook we're approaching."

No brook was visible. "It's now ten and one half kilometers away, oriented northeast to southwest. At the point we'll meet it it will be too deep to wade, unless we change direction now. We can't change direction because of that hill ahead of us at position ten, five kilometers away. We must go to the brook, and travel along it for one and one half kilometers, where the water is just over a meter deep. We'll know the place by the young lichen-towers the scouts crushed to mark it."

The old man smiled into the distance. "Stay by me. Keep up with all the reports."

"Yes, seyoh."

Just past noon they came to a doused fire pit, with slabs of half-cooked goat meat hung across it. The fire had been started by members of the far outer circle, checked by the following circles, doused by the innermost. Kammeryn called a halt. The tribe settled down to eat, the stronger ones bringing food to those more exhausted; and for the most part it was now warriors serving mertutials, and mertutials thanking the warriors for the service. Rowan brought the partly raw goat meat to Kammeryn herself.

The tribe rested for four hours, and most people slept; but Kammeryn did not, nor Rowan. When the tribe prepared again to march,

Rowan noticed that five warriors had lost their packs and were instead carrying small children strapped to their backs. Asleep, the children stirred fitfully as they were hoisted up on the warriors. Some fell back to sleep; two began weeping continuously but softly, too tired for louder complaint.

By midafternoon, hazy clouds climbed in from the south, crossing and then filling the sky. The clouds deepened; horizons dimmed, then vanished. A fine drizzle more mist than rain began.

Soon, no further reports could be received, and well before nightfall, the tribe was again traveling by night tactics—without stars by which to check true direction.

Kammeryn was again issuing instructions continuously to the tribe. Rowan listened intently, matching each word against her own knowledge, constructing her own version of the imagined chart. The work was difficult, and soon absorbed her completely. All her concentration was required to maintain the clarity of her vision and her route. Other considerations faded; her very identity seemed diminished.

The situation struck her as oddly familiar, but she had not the freedom of thought to analyze the impression. She gave herself to the work, and it owned her, utterly. In her mind, the tribe slowly inched its way across the land.

When they reached the last known position of the innermost line, they encountered one warrior of Berrion's band, waiting alone in the hazy light. The woman fell in with the tribe, as expected. But when, only one kilometer farther along, they found another single waiting warrior, Rowan understood that a different tactic was being used.

The warriors ahead had stationed themselves along the route Kammeryn had selected. For the rest of the evening and partly into the night, the tribe met them, hailing from the darkness, one after another, at approximately one-kilometer intervals.

But later, after fifteen warriors had been met, the tribe walked over a kilometer without meeting anyone.

Kammeryn called a halt; everyone behind sank immediately to seats on the ground, drawing up their hoods against the soft rain. The seyoh, his aide, and Rowan remained standing.

Kammeryn called for a volunteer. Garris sent one of his warriors forward.

The woman was given careful, precise directions, and alone walked ahead at a slow pace, step by measured step, into the wet darkness. While the tribe waited, word came forward to Kammeryn that another mertutial had succumbed to age and exhaustion, and one infant. The mertutial was cast, the infant buried.

An hour later, the volunteer returned; she had found no one. Kammeryn issued new instructions and sent her off at a slightly different angle.

She was never heard of again.

The tribe slept, waiting for the dawn. Rowan and Kammeryn spent the night speaking to each other in strange, short sentences, consisting purely of measurements and the names of natural features, as they mutually reconfirmed their understanding of the land ahead.

The rain stopped shortly before sunrise, and in the morning light Kammeryn recognized that the tribe had wandered north off its route. He and Rowan amended their information, and the tribe slowly resumed travel.

The waiting lines of guards ahead were met, slowly, and sent ahead again. The new reports began.

Eventually the scouts began to be heard from, and at last the point scout herself. Rowan accepted the information provided and integrated it; and somewhere within, a small part of herself recalled that it was Bel whose words she now heard. That small part of Rowan found a moment to be pleased, and grateful. Bel was ahead, discerning what dangers the tribe must avoid; Rowan was behind, observing, integrating, planning, waiting for her own wider knowledge to be called upon. The configuration struck the steerswoman as perfectly natural, and correct.

They traveled until noon, when they found food again. They ate, and rested briefly. They walked on again, people shambling, stumbling in exhaustion. When night came, their seyoh permitted a three-hour rest.

Kammeryn did not sleep; Rowan wished to, desperately, but followed his example, realizing that once she released her detailed understanding of the invisible land ahead, she would be hours, perhaps a full day, regaining it. Kammeryn did not dare to slack his attention, for the sake of his tribe; Rowan refused to rest her own.

She found she must stand, or fall asleep. She and the seyoh walked together in the dark, pacing back and forth on a twenty-foot line they both knew to be flat.

After three hours they woke the tribe; and through the rattling redgrass, across the rolling veldt, under a thousand stars and the two bright, untwinkling beacons of the Guidestars, Kammeryn led his people on through the remainder of the night.

Just before first light, Rowan stopped short, realizing that she had walked the last ten paces alone.

She turned around, unconsciously adjusting the map in her mind to take that fact into account. She walked back, forcing herself to see and hear what was immediately present.

The leading edge of the tribe had stopped, the rest slowly easing to a halt. There was a clot of activity directly before Rowan.

Kammeryn's aide was stooping to the ground, speaking to someone. "Give us a name." Rowan could hear Garris shouting for Mander. She stepped closer.

Kammeryn was half-prone, attempting to rise; his aide would not permit it. "Mander's coming," she said. "Seyoh, give us a name." Kammeryn attempted to speak, but failed. Behind, the tribe members, helplessly, one by one, dropped to seats on the ground.

The healer approached, Chess following close behind him. By starlight, Mander looked into Kammeryn's face and said immediately, "He's going no farther." Kammeryn no longer tried to rise, and was breathing in long breaths, slow but shallow.

Rowan looked at her mental chart, triangulating from known landmarks, comparing distances.

"Seyoh," the aide repeated, trying to get his attention. Rowan stooped down beside them and cautiously permitted herself to be aware of Kammeryn's face.

The seyoh saw and recognized her, and Mander bending over him, then looked past the healer's shoulder. "Chess," he said.

The cook grunted in surprise. "Right." She heaved herself erect and looked about in the dim starlight. "You!" she called, and pointed.

"What's on that train? Never mind, clear it off! Mander, Jenna, get him over there." They hurried to obey, raising the seyoh between them. He spoke weakly; Rowan could not hear his words.

Chess did, then turned to the steerswoman. "He says you know where we are."

Rowan checked her figures, checked the time by the stars.

"Where do we go now?"

She looked at the route ahead and became briefly confused; she thought there was one number that she had neglected to take into account . . .

"Rowan!"

The map glowed in her mind, as if lit by a fire behind it. And then a second chart overlaid itself: Fletcher's information, longitude, latitude, area. The features of both charts merged, matched.

They vanished. Rowan stood shivering with cold, shuddering in exhaustion, redgrass chattering around her, with Chess's gnarled face before her, dim in starlight.

The steerswoman swallowed. "No farther. We make camp here."

47

"Chess, I need to speak to Fletcher."

It was now full light. The tribe had slept, struggled back to wakefulness, and set to work.

The old woman pulled her attention from the rising tents and eyed Rowan. "Sounds like a good idea to me." They passed together through the standing and sitting tribe members.

Fletcher was seated on the ground, looking down, weaving in place. Half of Orranyn's band was seated in a circle around him, watching him with eyes feverish from exhaustion; the other half sat leaning against their comrades' backs, asleep. One of them was Orranyn.

Chess kicked his foot. "Wake up. We're going to talk to him."

Orranyn came awake with a violent start. "Kammeryn said—"

"Kammeryn's asleep. He put me in charge. Stand up when you talk to me, boy."

"Chess—"

"If I can stand, you can stand, and I'm standing, so stand!"

He stood.

"We've got a captive wizard here," Chess said, "and we want to know some things. Move aside." And she led Rowan into the circle, which shifted at their chief's gesture to make more room within.

Fletcher looked up at the two women. One side of his mouth twitched. "Shall I stand?" He looked too weak to do so.

"We'll sit." They did. Chess jerked her chin at Rowan. "You ask. I don't know what to ask."

"Rowan—" Fletcher said.

She put up her hand. "Fletcher, just don't ask me anything. Answer." He nodded, jerkily.

"Girl, your laws are stupid," Chess said.

"Yes," Rowan said without thinking, "sometimes." And if the survival of these people she loved, and her own life, had depended upon breaking those laws at this moment, she would have done so, on the instant. But that was not necessary.

She said to Fletcher, "Rendezvous weather."

He nodded. "We're safe from the heat, but we'll catch the weather that follows it."

"How soon will it come, and how bad will it be?"

"I'm not sure." He rubbed his face. "Before, when I was looking back at the twenty-year cycle of routine bioform clearance, the weather started reacting about two weeks after the start of the heat. But looked at another way, it came one day after peak."

She shook her head in annoyance; she was too weary to puzzle through his language. "Peak being a high point? The moment of greatest heat?"

"Yes. And there's no buildup this time. It's coming all at once. We might have as little as twelve hours from the moment the heat starts."

"At nightfall, today?"

"Yes."

Chess leaned back and shook Jaffry awake. "You. Go to Steffannis." One of the cook's assistants. "Tell him to start a fire, slaughter twenty goats, and start cooking them now. And to set a crew to making bread."

The young man made to protest in confusion, but Orranyn sent him off with a gesture.

Chess turned back to Fletcher. "How long will it last?"

He spread his hands. "The heat? Twenty-four hours. The weather, I don't know; weeks, months, perhaps, altogether. But it will be worst for a much shorter time. Days, perhaps."

"What do you mean by the worst? What exactly happens?"

He moved his shoulders. "Winds, to start. On the Face, they reached over a hundred miles an hour."

This was incomprehensible; she had expected him to say "very high winds," or "gales" or "hurricane," if he knew such terms. But miles an hour was a measurement applied to the movement of objects. The wind was no object. Rowan tried to imagine an object caught in such a wind; but its speed of motion would depend not only upon the wind force, but on the size, shape, and construction of the object. Perhaps the greatest danger would come from loose objects, such as bushes, or bits of lichen-tower, flying at high speed. She thought of ships' sails, when a sheet gave way from stress. The loose end moved suddenly free, and powerful, like a great thrashing hand, smashing everything before it—

Sails. She stood up suddenly. "This is wrong."

"What?" Chess asked.

Rowan looked around the camp, at the tents now almost all erected: vertical walls of skin, with no great masts, no yards to brace them. The lines and poles would never hold. "We have to dig in."

Chess had stood up beside her. "Wind'll knock all this down?"

"Yes."

Chess called out. "Stop everything! You, you, and you, over here!"

Rowan looked down at Fletcher. "Where will the wind come from?"

"At first, east to west, toward where the heat was. A few hours later, northeast to southwest. Sometime later, southwest to northeast."

Rowan spoke to Chess. "We dig into the ground, wide holes, and erect the tents' skins as roofs over them, with a low peak, running northeast to southwest. Cross-lines for bracing, inside and out."

The mertutials whom Chess had called over stood by, weaving, bleary-eyed. Chess's face lost all expression. "The people can't stand digging like that," she told Rowan. "They've been walking for three days. They're at the end of their strength."

"I know."

Chess chewed her lip. "I'll divide the tribe, and assign each group to the tent it'll be using. They'll dig at the best pace they can manage, for as long as they can. Erect the roofs at sunset."

"That sounds like the best we can do."

Chess jerked her head at those waiting. "Come on."

Rowan watched them depart, then scanned the skies above, blinking blurred eyes. The sky was decorated with small clouds slowly shifting east. The blue between them was as cool and pure as a jewel.

She turned back to Fletcher. "Other than wind, what else?"

He had been watching intently; now he moved his hands in a vague gesture. "Rain, hail; maybe even snow, I don't know."

She knit her brows, thinking; her mind seemed not slow but vacant, airy and empty. Information entered it, to be used and then to vanish into some underground chamber. Ideas appeared seemingly from nowhere. "Hot air expands," she said. Sealed, heated bottles burst. "Why would the wind move *toward* the heated area?"

"Don't know." And he looked up at her, plaintive, helpless.

Directly behind him, silent throughout the whole conversation, sat Jann.

The tents were down, with groups of people gathered about each of the previous locations. At each site, a handful of people were digging, with knives, swords, their hands. Others watched. More slept.

She found Chess sitting beside a group of diggers. Kammeryn was nearby, asleep or unconscious, Rowan could not tell. His aide dozed close by. "Assign me to the same tent you put Fletcher in," the steerswoman said to Chess.

The old woman pointed to the ground. "Right here. And we're in with you." She spotted movement off at the edge of the camp. "Ha. The inner circles are coming in."

An old man digging stopped, gaping up at her. "The inner circles left position?"

"At my order. You don't like it? Do you want to take over? Do you think anyone will listen to you?"

"But—"

Chess heaved herself to her feet. "The inner circles are coming in," she announced, and people stopped to listen. "And the outer, and the scouts. Everybody's coming in. When this wind hits, any tribe nearby will be too busy to think about attacking us." And she sat down.

When the people returned to their work, she spoke to Rowan quietly. "There's another tribe spotted, just southeast of us. Your friend Bel went to warn them."

Bel's last reported position was some eighteen miles away. "But she doesn't know what to warn them of."

"Rendezvous weather. We knew that. Just didn't know how bad it would be."

48

*R*attling, tapping, hissing—and Rowan thought: The rain has started.

She tried to turn over and rise; something seemed to press down on her, heavily. She struggled, and gasped at the pain of movement.

"Hush, girl." It was Chess, nearby.

"What?" The weight holding her down was the weight of her own body; the pain was of muscles pushed past their limits of strength by days of walking, now locked into knots by the hours of exhausted, motionless sleep.

Rowan was curled on her left side. She tried to straighten, slowly. "What's the hour?"

"Must be near dawn."

Rowan managed to roll up to a sitting position. The tent roof was close above her head; a bare earth wall behind her sent waves of cool-

ness against her back. "I need to move a bit." She opened and closed
her hands; even they were stiff, from digging.

"Not in here." There was no room. Nineteen people were sleeping side by side; and at one end of the tent, six more warriors were
sitting upright, in an inward-facing circle. Along one wall of the
shelter, and complaining intermittently, ten goats lay on their sides
with their legs trussed. The light was barely enough for the steerswoman to see.

"Where's the door?" There was one, she knew; she had suggested
its location herself. Now she could not recall where it was, or where
in the tent she was.

Chess reached out a dim hand, and Rowan used it to get herself
into motion. She crawled over the two sleepers between herself and
the mertutial. "Over there," Chess said, and pointed her on.

A triangle of gray light above, just this side of the goats. Rowan
made her way painfully across to it. None of the sleepers she clambered over were disturbed by her passage.

At the entrance, she pulled herself erect, hissing in annoyance
at her body's complaint. Standing, she had not the flexibility to
climb out.

It was not raining; the sound had been only redgrass. Above, the
sky was too light for most stars, but still a deep blue too dark for day.
It seemed ominous, as if purposely emptied of all but the twin
Guidestars, and waiting.

The Eastern Guidestar looked no different from the Western.
Rowan considered its angle. The magic heat, if it came from the Eastern Guidestar, must certainly pass above the camp to reach the area
west. And if there were heat crossing the sky above, surely the area
immediately below must also become warm.

And yet it was cold outside, quite cold.

All around, lying close to each other within pockets of crushed
grass, were scores of goats. Some began to stir and stand, shaking their
flop-eared heads, the weight of their horns lending a ludicrous drunk-
enness to the motion. Among them, only slightly taller than the redgrass, were the low peaks of the other shelters.

And one standing figure. She waved it over. "Help me out, please."

"Is that Rowan?" It was Averryl. He gave her a hand, then two,
pulling her from the ground purely by his own effort.

"How long have you been up here?"

"Hours. Since just after midnight. I slept some, then I couldn't any longer. I wanted to see. And . . . and it's not comfortable in there . . ." He nodded toward one of the shelters, presumably his own.

"Comfortable?" she echoed. His voice had lent the word a meaning beyond the merely physical.

He was a moment answering. "They're saying that Fletcher caused all this." The forced march; the deaths while traveling; hours of digging into the ground; close quarters; discomfort. Fletcher was resented, perhaps hated; and Averryl, his closest friend, was conveniently at hand.

Rowan became angry. "All this," she said, "is intended to save our lives. And if we do survive, then yes, Fletcher will have caused that."

He nodded silently.

She scanned the horizon. Nothing appeared unusual; it was simply a late-autumn morning in the Outskirts. "If you've been watching, have you seen anything odd?"

He was gazing westward, and nodded again. "Just before first light. The stars along the horizon—" He stretched out one hand and trembled it as demonstration. "—they twinkled, harder than I've ever seen before. And some of them seemed to move."

She was appalled. "Move?"

"Up and down, back and forth. But only right on the horizon, in a space just the width of two fingers. If we didn't have a clear horizon, I wouldn't have seen it." There was a clear horizon due west, and southwest; north, a ridge blocked the view.

"Heat," she explained. In the Inner Lands, she had often watched stars writhing through the heat rising from a campfire.

Heat properly should rise; heat should not come down invisibly from the sky. Nevertheless, it was doing so, even as she and Averryl stood together in the cool morning, waiting for the sun to appear.

Averryl looked straight up. "What's that?"

Above, a faint gray haze. "I don't know." Unconsciously, she took two steps forward, as if by walking she could move closer to the sky itself. The haze was thickening. "Fog?" And high beams of the still-unrisen sun cleared the eastern horizon, washing the gray to pure, pale, breathtaking gold.

It was high vapors coalescing, creating themselves as Rowan and Averryl watched, evolving into a faint line of cloud that stretched up from the southwestern horizon, crossed the sky above, and vanished behind the ridge to the north. Sunlight glowed upon the cloud, and it stood strange and glorious, spun gold against the lightening blue dome of the sky.

"It's beautiful," Averryl said, in a voice of wonder. Rowan thought it impossible, and horrible.

Jaffry emerged from the shelter at her feet and caught sight of her and Averryl. "Chess says—" He began. He stopped, stared above. "Oh . . ."

"What does Chess say?" Rowan asked him. The cloud-sweep was growing deeper, more defined.

"Is that the heat? It's running the wrong way . . ."

"No, it's not the heat. Whatever this is, it's parallel to the area that the heat is striking. What does Chess say?" The cloud was thickening visibly, beginning to look uncomfortably like a squall line coming into existence from nothing, directly above their heads.

The young man pulled his attention from the sky and addressed Averryl. "That no one should worry about the goats outside. I'm supposed to tell each tent."

Averryl nodded. "I'll tell the people in mine."

"Is Bel in with you?"

Averryl had been about to leave; he stopped, and hesitated before replying. "Bel isn't here."

"What?" Jaffry's face was suddenly blank with shock.

Rowan was puzzled by the intensity of his reaction. "She was serving as point scout, and sighted signs of another tribe to the east. She went to warn them."

He spun on her. "When?"

"Yesterday morning. She hadn't made it back by nightfall, and she couldn't travel in the dark. But if she went to the first scouts of the other tribe, told them, and turned straight around, she must have been near here by sunset. It's light now; she'll arrive soon."

"Jaffry," Averryl said, and the young warrior turned to him. "There's nothing that you can do."

Jaffry stood staring at him for a long moment, then abruptly turned and hurried away toward the next tent, on his errand for Chess.

Rowan framed a puzzled question to Averryl; but before she could utter it, it answered itself:

The courting gifts left for Bel had appeared the first morning she and Rowan were in camp, a very short span of time for the appearance of romantic feeling. Only two men of the tribe had been acquainted with Bel for longer than a day: Averryl, who was too ill to make and leave gifts; and Jaffry. Rowan wondered why she had not seen this before.

Rain began to fall. Rowan looked up. The line of cloud was heavier. A cusp of sun appeared on the eastern horizon, and Rowan instinctively turned her back to it to look for a rainbow. She found one in the western sky: bright, high, complete across its entire length, and triple in form.

The cloud was now pure white in the sunlight, and roiling with abnormal speed. Averryl watched it with jaw dropped. "We should go inside," he said presently.

"Not yet." The light breeze that had been stirring the grass tops hesitated, then ceased. The redgrass silenced. Rowan and Averryl stood waiting.

Far to the west, under the arc of the rainbow, the shadowed land seemed to shimmer. Movement of some sort—then Rowan understood. The redgrass at the horizon was flattening under the force of a distant wind. The area's nearer limit visibility approached, swiftly. The steerswoman braced herself.

But the air nearby, all around her, already calm, now semed somehow to still even further, to grow almost thinner. Rowan felt a sudden, sharp pain in her ears—

Then all the air was in motion, the edge of flattened grass arrived and swept past, and Rowan stumbled forward at the force of the wind at her back—a wind not from the west, but the east. She turned into it, and recovered her balance.

It was strong, storm force; had Rowan been on a ship, she would have been hurrying to shorten sail. But there was no danger to this wind; the tents would easily hold.

The wind did not gust, nor swirl. It ran, steadily east to west, seeming almost perfectly horizontal and coming from no storm, but the sweet sun-glared horizon. Leaning harder into it, she considered that the tent slopes might have aligned better; but Fletcher had said that the wind would later shift.

She stepped back to Averryl and leaned close.

"Let's get inside," he said over the rushing noise.

She shook her head. "You go on. This isn't bad. I want to wait for Bel." A dead tanglebrush rolled up the slope and caught against a goat, which started bawling, dancing away from it. Other goats bawled response, and those standing shied about, then made their way to the lee of the low tent peaks. The tanglebrush, now free of its obstacle, spun in place crazily, upside down on its mazy dome.

"You're being stupid!" The words were not angry, merely louder to carry over the wind.

Rowan laughed. "Do you know," she said, close to his ear, "I'd hate to have to count the number of times an Outskirter has said that to me."

The wind increased; soon, it was better to sit on the ground, back to the wind. Averryl gave her one edge of his cloak, and she wrapped herself close to him. They steadied each other as the force against their backs grew.

The wind should have dispersed the line of cloud. No such event occurred. The cloud had ceased to spread, but it stayed in place, and its face was roiling faster. The cloud built higher, lower, and its western edge was now shadowed from the sun, black and threatening. The top, along its entire visible length, was forming into the familiar anvil of a thunderhead, made weird by infinite extension north and south.

At the first sign of lightning, they would have to take shelter. Rowan thought of Bel, alone on the wind-driven veldt. She looked over one shoulder.

The shimmering redgrass had vanished. In its place: a single featureless expanse of dull brick red. The grass was lying completely horizontal, driven by the solid, sourceless gale. Rowan swept water from her eyes as she tried to see if she could discern a single, approaching figure. None was visible. Rowan imagined the gale wind catching Bel's cloak and lifting her, to send her spinning away into the sky like a lost sail. But Bel, although short, was in no way a light person. Rowan found the vision amusing; and then, quite suddenly, appalling.

Movement above caught her eye, and she twisted about again, looking up. The top of the squall line was sending out wild streamers, swirling out without diminishing the whole, speeding away east.

The ground wind blew east to west. The wind above was west to east. Rowan could not explain it.

It was now full morning, with white sunlight casting her and Averryl's shadows before them, rain falling at a sharp, windy slant from above, and the triple rainbow, a trifle lower in the sky, even brighter than before. But behind the rainbow, below and past the squall line, over the presumed area of the magical heat, the western sky was as clear and blue as the eastern.

From one of the shelters, a figure half-emerged, looking about, short red hair wild in the wind: Kree. Rowan nudged Averryl. "Go on, she's looking for you," she told him; she had to repeat it, louder.

"Are you going in?" he shouted back.

"Soon!"

His expression was stubborn. "I'll wait!"

There came a thump on Rowan's shoulder; she turned into the wind.

Bel: glaring, leaning down to shout her words an inch from Rowan's nose. "What are you doing out here?"

Rowan grinned. "Waiting for you!"

"You're a lunatic!"

"Yes!" the steerswoman replied with enthusiasm. And Averryl instantly made off, with obvious relief.

Rowan and Bel helped each other to the shelter's entrance, struggling against the wind, bracing their arms on each other's shoulders.

"Where's your cloak?" Rowan asked when they were inside.

"I lost it."

Bel slept, promising to relate her experiences after her rest. The report was delayed further: three hours later, the wind noise even in the shelter became an unchanging roar, too loud, too steady, for conversation.

There was thunder, intermittent, and then almost constant. Lightning became a continuous flicker, outlining the shelter roof, the crack in the door; someone hurried to secure it tighter. The rain was heavier, seeming to fall like stones. The air shook, constantly, as if the shelter were a drum continuously ruffled, with the humans trapped within. It was not far from the truth.

Outside, heard only in the short gaps between thunder peals, the goats cried out in their weirdly human voices, seeming quiet and distant against the roaring wind. The animals tried to hide behind the tent peak, crowding, shoving each other onto the tent itself. The ceiling sagged, writhed, and threatened to collapse. Rowan and three others quickly stood to push up from below, spilling the animals off; and they did the same again moments later, and again; more helpers joined the work. At last there were nine people standing with bent backs, supporting the laden roof against their shoulders.

One of Garris's warriors, at his own initiative, tied a safety line about his waist, handed its end to his comrades, and exited the shelter. There was a tense half hour of waiting; then, one by one, the weight of each goat on the roof vanished. When he returned, exhausted and rain-drenched, the word made its way slowly across the shelter, from shouting mouth to noise-numbed ear: "He killed them."

Rowan wanted to know what else he had seen; whether the inhabitants of the other shelters had done the same as he; whether the other shelters were still intact.

Such detailed communication was impossible. Rowan returned to a seat beside Bel, who was now awake, looking about with a sharp gaze, thinking, waiting for an opportunity for useful action.

There was nothing to do but wait. More people slept than Rowan thought possible amid the noise: they were still too spent to do otherwise. Others sat, huddled, as if the sound of wind and rain were itself wind and rain, as if it were necessary to brace and protect oneself from the mere noise. With painful slowness, the hours passed.

Kammeryn had awakened briefly. In the near-blackness of the shelter, it was impossible for Rowan to evaluate his condition. He attempted to sit up; Chess did not permit him to do so. He acquiesced so quickly that Rowan was concerned.

Chess tried to fill him in on the situation, shouting each sentence near his ear. Eventually the seyoh was made to understand that all persons within the shelter were currently safe; that the condition of others was undetermined and indeterminable. He nodded at the information—weakly, it seemed to Rowan—and gripped Chess's shoulder once in response. Then he closed his eyes and lay quiet, possibly asleep; and Rowan assumed that Chess was still in command.

Rowan's own weariness began again to overtake her. She did not want to sleep. She wanted to observe, to notice every detail of experience—but not for the sake of a steerswoman's endless search for information.

It was not her being a steerswoman that made her want to know; she had become a steerswoman because of her own need, the need to know and understand. And at this moment, she merely wished, for herself, to be aware, and could not bear the thought of being otherwise.

Hoping to husband her strength, she braced her back against the bare earth wall. The contrast between the shuddering air around her and the utter stability of the earth against her back confused her senses; she was immediately, horribly nauseous. She leaned forward, away from the wall. The conflict vanished, and she was instantly more at home, in the midst of every sailor's proper element: motion. She sensed it on her skin and behind her eyes; it gently trembled her bones. She reached back and groped along the earth face, finding one of the internal guy lines where it dove into the dirt. She wrapped her fingers about it, and it was like a living tendon in her hand. The taut tent skin above spoke to her through the line, through her fingers, and she listened with her body to the tale of wind, force, and power driving across the land above.

She felt the wind slowly shift, slowly veer to the northeast, then felt it start to slack, even before its roaring voice began to fade.

She tapped Bel's knee to gain her attention and alerted Chess. In the growing quiet, amid the cries of relief from the huddled people, the three women made their way across the shelter.

They entered the circle of Fletcher's guard and settled beside him. He was fast asleep. Rowan gently shook him awake.

He came to awareness slowly, swinging his head about in the gloom, confused. Rowan spoke his name, her voice small in her noise-deadened ears.

He became alert, peering about in the gloom as if amazed to be alive. "Is it ending?"

"You tell us," Bel said.

"How long was I asleep?"

"All morning. It's past noon, now, at a guess," Chess supplied.

The hope on his face vanished. "Then it's just begun." As if to put the lie to his words, the rain ceased drumming overhead. On one side of the shelter, someone was keening, continuously, and possibly had been doing so unheard all morning.

"How do you know?" the steerswoman asked him.

He flung an arm out in frustration, nearly striking one of his guards. "I *don't* know. The track from forty-eight years ago showed high winds and storm, on both sides of the print. I don't know how long it will last this time, but—more than one morning. There's more coming."

Rowan let out a pent-up breath of frustration. Track, print—he had again begun to use words almost completely incomprehensible to her, words that only hinted at meaning, that relied upon knowledge and understanding outside of her experience.

She turned to Chess. "If you want reports from the other shelters, this may be your only chance to get them." The old woman nodded, then clambered off, calling to her dazed warriors.

Rowan turned back to Fletcher, thinking, Track, like the track of an animal, left behind for hunters to follow—does the weather leave tracks, and by what means can one possibly see them? "Forty-eight years is a long time ago," she began. Could any marks made still be visible? "Didn't you look at the recent track?" Behind her, someone threw open the entrance, and a wash of pale light entered the shelter, painful to dark-adapted eyes. Voices complained reflexively, and people began to shift stiff limbs. "The Rendezvous weather, the mild version we had, that caused the Face People's tribe to think it was time to Rendezvous; that was quite recent, by comparison. There must have been heat on the Face then; did that make a track?"

His blue eyes were wide on hers. "I looked for one. It wasn't there."

"There was no track?"

"None."

She thought. "But it must have occurred . . ." How were tracks eliminated?

A clever person who wished not to be followed would obliterate his tracks by dragging branches over them, like sweeping chalk marks off a slate . . . "It was erased?"

He looked at her in quiet amazement. "Do you know," he said in a small voice, "sometimes you frighten me. Yes, that's exactly it. The information was erased. And there's something else." He held his hands out, then moved them together, defining a small space. "The gap, the time span—it was little. It wasn't as long as the time it used to take for the heat, when it came before, every twenty years. I think . . . I think it might have been a test; someone seeing if the heat still worked, if it was worthwhile to use it for . . ." He dropped his hands and looked around, up. "For this."

One covered one's tracks when doing something one wished kept secret. "It was Slado himself who erased the information?" She used Fletcher's own turn of phrase; it seemed properly abstract, and apt.

"It must have been. Any number of people know how to do it; but none of them would bother to. It doesn't matter to them. And I don't even know why it matters to him . . ."

"He didn't tell you?" It was Bel who asked.

"Tell me?" He seemed to find the idea incomprehensible.

"Yes, you," Bel said, tightly. "He was getting messages to you, somehow, wasn't he?"

He leaned back, confused. "No—"

"He sent you here!" And the warrior's eyes were full of fury. "He put you in the Outskirts, for reasons of his own. Didn't he tell you why?"

"Bel, I've never spoken to him—"

"And when he heard that Rowan and I were in the Outskirts, he sent you to find us—"

"No!"

"—and do what? Follow us? Gain our confidence? Stop us? Kill us?"

"Bel, I never meant you or Rowan any harm; I didn't even know you exist—"

"You're a wizard's man. You showed up, right where we were. It's too big a coincidence."

He stopped short and made one small sound, half a helpless laugh. "You don't know. It *is* a coincidence—but not a big one. I'm not the only one in the Outskirts." He gestured with one hand, indicating the whole windy wilderness. "You come out here, wandering all over— one way or another, sooner or later, you would have met one of us."

"How many? How many of you wizard's dogs are there in the Outskirts?" Bel sat straight; her dark eyes glittered. "How many exactly?"

He looked to Rowan, perhaps for reassurance. But she, too, wanted an answer. "I don't know," he said to Bel, "not for sure. I think they started with fifteen, years ago. And then they lost a couple, no one knows what happened. It could have been anything, disease, a battle, an assassin . . . It was before my time.

"But when they lost another person, two years ago, I heard about it, and I did some checking. I could see that they were short; but nobody seemed to care. No one wanted to take the job. But when I heard about it, I wanted it. I was in logistics." He looked suddenly weary. "I hate logistics," he said quietly. "I'm so bad with numbers." He became exhausted. He stopped speaking.

Rowan wished she could let him rest. She did not. "Why did you want this particular work?"

He looked up from his lap: a child's look, a dreamer's. "It was a hard job. It would be life and death, every day. I wanted . . . I wanted to do something big."

She heard a sudden echo of the old Fletcher, the bored young baker who had wanted a life of excitement and had found something he loved more than he had expected.

Fletcher's gaze dropped again.

Half of Orranyn's band had taken the opportunity to step outside. Now they returned and traded places with their comrades. From the corner of her eye, Rowan noticed a silent argument between Orranyn and Jann. The woman warrior did not wish to leave. Her chief physically pulled her from place, angrily directing her outside. He took her former position himself.

"And of what precisely did your duties consist?" Rowan asked Fletcher.

"Looking," he said. "Reporting."

"Passing on information?" Fletcher had been able to dispatch messages, she knew. "Using your cross?" she asked, then recalled the term he used; "Your link?" A link: a connection, as if the cross had been magically joined to something else. She thought of the guy line in her hand, telling her the stress on the tent above her, the direction of the wind outside—information at a distance, through a physical connection.

"That's right."

"That's all?"

"For the most part."

"We don't want to know the most part," Rowan told him. "We want to know the least part. Everything."

He stirred himself. "I was supposed to report everything I found out about the Outskirts, every detail. When Bodo found the demon's egg, I reported that. Then I called up a trace of large animals for that sector and ran it back. Some things don't read well, like goblins. I always reported goblins, and their eggs, when we found any. But something big and warm always shows up. I ran the record and watched a large creature passing through that area two months before. I followed along part of its path, and found the egg."

Both women were a long time considering these statements. They were incomprehensible. Rowan grasped at one small fact among the confusion: "You could see into the past?" Outside, the wind's low tone altered, ascended.

"No . . ." Fletcher began. "Well, yes, in a way . . ." He struggled for analogy. "It's like your logbook. You write things down, and years later people can come and read it. So they're seeing into the past."

"Who writes it down?"

"No one. I don't know how to explain it, it happens by itself . . ."

"A spell?"

He accepted the term. "Yes."

Rowan imagined a room filled with books, where a pen moved across an open page, as invisible hands recorded everything seen by distant, invisible eyes.

"Where are the eyes?"

"What?"

But she was already thinking: to see the movements of animals over a long period of time, to see Fletcher's invisible banner, would require a very high point of vantage indeed . . .

"The Guidestars," she said. "The Guidestars are watching us." She was hardly surprised.

"Yes."

"And the Eastern Guidestar sent down the heat?"

He nodded.

"And it's stopped now?" she continued.

"Unless the schedule was changed again."

"Why didn't we *see* it?" Her voice was desperate in confusion, at impossibility. "Something so hot, why didn't it glow, *burn*? It was going on all last night; why couldn't we see it?"

"I don't know."

A voice spoke close behind the steerswoman. "Rowan?" It was Jaffry, crouched close beside her. "Chess says come outside. And bring him." He jerked his chin at Fletcher.

"What's happening?"

He paused. "There are slugsnakes in the sky." The wind was now keening.

Bel was incredulous. "Slugsnakes?" But Rowan instinctively reached up to the tent roof, feeling for the external bracing lines outside the skin. Despite the sound, touch told her that the wind was nowhere near strong enough to send animals flying through the air.

Jaffry's expression did not alter. "Big ones."

Rowan clambered out of the shelter and crouched on the ground beside Chess. The wind was no longer steady, but gusting wildly, and the air was filled with a continuous distant rumbling, overlaid by a sourceless high-pitched scream. The sound was uncanny; it seemed to enter Rowan's skull, move through her body, and exit through her skin, leaving it crackling with warnings of lightning to come. She looked east.

Directly ahead, far out on the brick-red veldt: a slugsnake in the sky.

It was small in the distance, huge in fact. It hung below churning clouds that were lit by internal lightning that writhed in colors such as she had never seen: bright, glowing green, orange, red, an evil pink that pained her eyes. From the sky to the ground, the body of the thing swayed slowly, its top merged with the clouds above, its lower end obscured by a moving brown haze. The haze, she suddenly knew, was earth; the thing was tearing at the earth itself.

"Fletcher!" And he was right beside her, beside Chess, beside Bel. Orranyn was with him, still uselessly on guard; Rowan thought it stupid. "Fletcher, what is that thing?"

He looked to be in shock. He answered, but could not be heard above the rising noise. The slugsnake was stretching, swaying, approaching. Fletcher repeated, "A tornado!"

"What?"

His hands made a shape: two curves, as on each side of a cylinder. "Like a hurricane!" he shouted, then closed his hands, collapsing the shape into a single narrow funnel.

A small hurricane; it sounded like no dangerous thing. But then she thought of the vast force of a hurricane's winds; thought of that force channeled, tightened. The force would multiply, into a power far beyond her scope of comprehension.

"Inside!" she called; but none could hear. She clutched Bel's arm, and Fletcher's, and tugged at them. The five people struggled together back toward the shelter. But when Fletcher was about to duck into the entrance, he suddenly stopped, looked up and past the low tent peak, then stood. Rowan shouted to him; he could not hear. She rose to pull him down—

Past the tent peak, out to the west, dim in the gray storm light, seeming silent against the shriek and roar of wind: more tall shapes, slowly tilting and shifting. There were three of them due west, two more south beside them, and diminishing southward in the distance, masses of cloud that seemed to touch the ground, seemed to be churning and spinning into more distant funnels . . .

They were lined up along the western horizon, swaying like drunken soldiers. And over the ridge that obscured the northwestern sky, Rowan could see flickering, burning colors within the clouds; and she knew there were more behind the ridge.

And then she was inside, and the others with her. Someone struggled to secure the entrance. Rain rattled, and then rattled harder; Rowan thought it was hail, then thought it was earth, then knew it was, by the choking dust that suddenly filled the shelter. Something heavy fell on the roof; the tent skin sagged, dropping, and then rose again, and Rowan knew that whatever the weight was that had struck above had been taken back into the sky.

The roaring was continuous; whether thunder or the wind itself, she could not tell. But over it all, that impossible screaming, shaking her brain until she thought her ears would die from the force.

Light dimmed further. Only Bel was clearly visible, crouched beside Rowan, watching the shuddering ceiling with wide eyes. With no words able to pass between them, Rowan reached out one hand to the

Outskirter's wrist and held it. It was the most basic of human statements: I am here, you are here, we are both alive.

Bel twisted her hand around and clutched Rowan's desperately, with fingers strong from years of wielding a sword. She turned her gaze on Rowan, and the steerswoman saw the look she had seen only once before on the Outskirter's face, when she and Rowan had sat helplessly silent, listening to the approach of a demon: terror.

And Rowan understood that here was the only thing that her warrior friend feared: helplessness. When the demon had approached, Bel could do nothing; she could not attack or defend, but only wait for whatever fate would occur. And she could not strike at these tornadoes. She could do nothing. Her skills were useless, her will impotent, her own life, and the lives of her comrades, completely out of her hands.

It became difficult to breathe, and Rowan gasped through her open mouth. Her ears popped. The roof belled up, taut against its braces. Light vanished—

—and returned. Rowan found herself braced against the wall, her fingers driven into the earth. Against her back, the wall itself was shaking.

And rapidly, so rapidly she could hardly believe it, the scream faded.

The air became still. People slowly raised their heads, gazing at each other in disbelief.

Chess pulled at Jaffry's arm. "Check outside." She had to shake him to get him to heed; then he recovered himself suddenly and hurried to obey.

Across the tent, Fletcher was seated upright, shaking his head slowly; he was saying something, apparently one single sentence, over and over. Rowan felt just as dazed and wished she herself had something coherent to say, that perhaps could bear infinite repetition. Beside her, Bel sat leaning slightly forward, very still, and seeming very small. Rowan gripped the Outskirter's shoulder. "Are you all right?"

Bel looked from side to side. "I'm alive," she began, as if it were the start of a longer statement; but no other words followed.

Rowan waited, then nodded. All about, people were stirring, tentatively, calling to each other, reassuring themselves that they lived.

Ignored, Fletcher sat alone, repeating his sentence. Rowan crossed over to him.

Fletcher's guards had abandoned their duties, more concerned with each other. Efraim was still huddled into a ball, rocking; Garvin was holding him in his arms, stroking his back, his own eyes squeezed shut tight. Orranyn was moving about, checking the state of each of his warriors.

When Rowan reached Fletcher's side, he seemed relieved to find someone to whom he could say his words. "I didn't know."

"You've done what you could," she told him. "Fletcher, you did everything you possibly could, and if we live, it's entirely due to you."

He seemed not to hear her. "I didn't know," he repeated. Then, with a visible effort, he regathered himself, speaking more cogently. "Rowan . . . I thought I was just collecting information. I didn't know what it was used for, who needed it. I didn't know it was for—for this . . ." And he looked at the ceiling.

"You tried to help," she said. "To help Kammeryn, the tribe, me. You watched when you could, warned when you could, joined the warriors in defense . . ." She abruptly recalled what Kammeryn had said: that the tribe of Face People who had attacked Kammeryn's tribe had later been killed by Fletcher, alone. "And . . ." An entire tribe, destroyed. It seemed an act of typical wizardly cruelty; she could not reconcile it with her recovered understanding of Fletcher's character. "How did you destroy the Face People's tribe?" she asked.

Fletcher found the memory distressing. "The link has a weapon in it . . ."

"A destructive spell?"

"Yes."

Rowan had had experience with destructive spells. "Why didn't we hear it?" In the Inner Lands, the boy Willam's destructive spell had made a sound like a thousand thunders.

"It's silent." A different sort of magic. "It spreads a sort of fire . . ."

"You burned them to death."

"Yes . . . I didn't want to . . . But they would have attacked again. They had almost no herd. And they couldn't leave, they were boxed in, and they didn't even know it. Ella's tribe to the east, ours to the south, another northwest . . . They would have hurt my people again;

I couldn't let that happen." The roof began to shudder, silently, then snapped and settled into rhythm as the wind began to rise.

"You saw all that through the Guidestar?" Rowan thought it strange, very strange that she should care at this moment about any such distant thing as a Guidestar.

"Yes," Fletcher replied.

"Why didn't you see them before the attack?" Just at the threshold of hearing, there came a distant rising tone, joining the sound of the wind.

"I did." Thunder rolled briefly, distantly. "That morning, during my report and reconnaissance. But I didn't know who or what they were then; they just looked like a small tribe. You don't understand, I can't " He amended his words. "With my link, I couldn't actually see them, not as if I were a bird. I saw . . . notations, like on your charts. I could tell that they were people, because they were arranged like a camped tribe, but they weren't deployed like attackers, not when I looked. That happened later . . ."

Rowan thought long; and as she did, the rising tone became a far-off, approaching scream. "But this magic weapon . . . You could have used it to stop the battle."

He closed his eyes. "Yes. And given myself away. Anyone who saw would know I had magic. They'd assume I was a wizard. I couldn't know how they'd react. And in my training . . . the rules said to protect my cover, at any cost. If people see you using magic, the simplest thing to do is kill the witnesses."

How many people might have been looking in Fletcher's direction, Rowan could not guess. But she herself had been at Fletcher's side.

He would have needed to kill her; and any nearby warrior; and any relays watching; and any person to whom the relays spoke. Kammeryn. Perhaps the entire tribe.

In that frozen moment, with the Face People bearing down on him, with his link in one hand and his sword in the other, Fletcher had been faced with a choice. And he had abandoned his magic powers, taken up his sword, and thrown himself into a battle that he was certain he could not possibly survive.

He had been willing to die rather than harm Kammeryn's people. "That's why you didn't use the spell to help your walkabout partner," she said.

He turned toward her; but his eyes were blind, his face suddenly, shockingly empty. His mouth moved once. "Mai," he said, but too quietly for her to hear the sound.

It was the expression she had seen before—emptiness, a silence of body and mind. But now she understood it. "Fletcher," she said, and of itself, her hand reached toward his shoulder.

But he pulled back violently, twisting away from her hand as if he could not at that moment bear a single touch. The mask of emptiness writhed on his face, shattered, and fell away, and for the first time Rowan could see what he had kept hidden behind it: it was horror.

"Dear god, Rowan," he said. "It happened so fast." The terror on his face was so great that it drained all emotion from his voice, his body, so that he was sitting perfectly still, speaking almost inaudibly, and rapidly, without will or control. "I heard her shout," he said in that quiet voice, with that face of horror, "and I ran to her, and then—"

"Fletcher, don't . . ." She reached toward him again, but slowly. "That's past, you couldn't help it."

He did not hear her. "And then she was screaming, and when I cut down that *thing*—" His voice came alive again with the saying of the word, with the force of the memory, and his body twisted, as if trying to escape the very words he spoke—

Rowan froze.

"And then," he went on, his voice becoming wild, "and then it was thrashing on the ground, burning, between us, and she was standing there, blood all down one arm, *looking* at me, and the look on her face, and she was saying, over and over, '*What are you?*' " He jerked once, as if from a sword thrust, and wrapped his arms about himself. "She was shouting at me, '*What are you?*' "

He quieted, slowly, shuddering. Rowan tried to speak his name, failed; she could make no sound.

"And I," he continued, in the empty voice again; and she wished that he would stop, stop now—"and I didn't know what to do . . . I just, I couldn't think, and it happened so damned *fast* . . .

"And then, after . . . when I saw . . . I wanted to die. And I thought, I'll just go away, I'll just walk away and die . . ."

Rowan spoke at last; but now it was against her will. "You killed her."

He looked up at her, into her eyes, and he seemed puzzled. "And I walked. I think I walked forever. I didn't die. And then, somehow, I was walking back." He reached out and clutched her wrist, held it tight. "Mai was gone. But if *I* died—Rowan, don't you see that if I died, it would be like losing them *all . . .*"

"Fletcher." But it was not Rowan who spoke. Fletcher was slow in comprehending, slow in turning to the speaker.

Jann was a shadow, a quiet voice. "Fletcher," she said, "your life is mine."

And it was done quickly.

49

*T*he tornadoes in the west did not strike the tribe but slowly worked their way northeastward and dissipated.

The tribe lasted through two tornadoes that writhed toward them from the east, through hail, debris, and through three full days of trailing high winds at mere hurricane force.

The weather never ceased; but there came a time at last when it slacked, when the boiling clouds above emitted no lightning. And hesitantly, cautiously, small groups of people emerged from the shelters to make their reports to Kammeryn. Chess stayed at his side, urging him to eat when he forgot to, to sleep when necessary.

The tribe had lost one shelter. Rowan herself went out to view it. It had become a hole in the ground, with a ten-foot length of lichen-tower core wedged inside. The tent skin, the poles, the internal and external bracing wires, and all the people who had been in the shelter were gone. Rowan stood gazing at it, wondering stupidly how Outskirters would handle funerals in which the corpses had already been cast across the land by the wind itself.

There were other dead. A warrior had been killed when a stave was pulled by its line out of the earth behind her, striking and crushing her skull. A mertutial had died at the height of the first tornado, apparently from terror. One young boy succumbed to exhaustion and pneumonia, contracted after one side of the children's shelter tore, letting the driving rain soak all the inhabitants.

And there was Dane.

Zo and Quinnan had returned two days after the last tornado; they had been sheltering among the rocks in the ridge to the north. They were wet, half-starved, and at the end of their strength, and they were carrying the girl between them.

Dane was unable to walk, could not control her own body. She trembled and spasmed constantly; she recognized no one.

Zo and Quinnan, going against Kammeryn's command, had dared to enter the near edge of the zone of heat. But the air was not hot, not even warm. Instead, they began to feel ill, first Zo, then Quinnan; nausea, fits of trembling, blinding pains in the head. They struggled onward and found Dane, crawling toward them; of Leonie there was no sign.

Dane's hands and knees were raw and blistered. When Zo and Quinnan bent to raise her, they found that it was the ground itself that was warm, some of the stones hot, and that the grass was almost brittle, as if drying from within, in a slow, flameless heat.

Dane lasted one day in the camp; Mander could do nothing for her. Zo's headaches did not abate, and she sat huddled in pain, Quinnan caring for her, never leaving her side.

And with the weather slackened, the people had time to deal with their dead.

Rowan and Bel stood out on the slope, gazing across the land. The wind was stiff and steady, southwest and northeast. "Fletcher said it would change," Rowan said. The weather was following the course he had predicted. It felt strange to her, as if his remembered words somehow controlled instead of reflected events, as if he were perhaps still present, waiting to tell her more, his long form standing just behind her, just past the edge of her sight.

"He's gone," Bel said.

"Yes . . ."

Bel took three aimless steps, looking down, looking at the sky. "We need him and now he's gone." Her voice was expressionless.

Rowan understood that Bel's distress had a different source from her own. She roused herself from her thoughts. "He helped us, yes. If he were here, he would keep helping us . . ."

"He knew magic. We need magic."

"Perhaps not . . ."

"We're useless without it." Bel suddenly took five strong paces forward, spun back to the steerswoman, and stretched her arms out to indicate the entire visible world. She stood so, with the rolling roof of clouds above her; with the earth torn in freakish lines from horizon to horizon, where tornadoes had riven it; with fragments of lichen-towers, fragments of goats, splintered bushes, redgrass crushed flat, all about her, a hole that had once contained human beings at her feet. "Look at it, Rowan!" she shouted. "Look!"

Rowan looked—at all of it. Bel dropped her arms as if she had not the strength to hold them up, sat as if she could no longer stand. Rowan went to her side.

"If Slado sends soldiers," Bel said quietly, "we can fight them, face-to-face. And if he sends too many soldiers to face, then we can fight them from behind: hiding, sneaking.

"If Slado sends wizards, we'll face them until we learn the limits of their magic; and then we'll vanish into the landscape, strike when they're not looking, or bait them until they fall into some trap."

She raised her hands, made them into fists, and drew them down as if forcibly, to rest on her knees. "If they build fortresses," she said, "we'll break them down. If we can't, then we'll infiltrate. If they take up residence, we'll become their servants and their lovers and murder them in their sleep . . ." The rain returned, spattering, hissing. Bel ignored it.

"Rowan," she said, water trailing down her face, "I can fight people; any people that he sends here, I can find some way to fight. Any wizard who comes here, despite magic, despite guards—if they come, I can strike them. Anything that I can touch, I can fight . . ."

And she gathered her strength and shouted, as if it were the last shout of her life: "Rowan, *I cannot fight the sky!*"

And the warrior sat silent on the torn earth. She dropped her head and closed her eyes.

The steerswoman gazed down at her. "I can."

Bel looked up.

"One person has caused this, Bel," Rowan continued. "One single man: Slado. And I can fight him.

"I'll find out what this is all for, what it's meant to accomplish. I'll find out how it's done—and put a stop to it." She dropped to her knees beside her friend. "I need to know more. I need to learn, to learn everything I can. And when I know enough, *then* will come the time to act."

Bel gazed at her. "Can you learn where Slado is?"

The steerswoman nodded. "Eventually. Yes."

"We'll find him, and kill him."

"If that's what it takes."

"If it's not what it takes, it's still what we'll do. I'll slit his throat myself. He's a murderer, Rowan. Murderers die." And the steerswoman could not argue.

A voice spoke from behind. "Rowan?" She turned.

Averryl was there; and behind him, Kree, and the rest of the band. There was something in their midst. Averryl said, "We're going to cast Fletcher."

Rowan looked at the shrouded form lying among the warriors; not standing invisibly behind her, not waiting to speak, not one moment away from touching her shoulder.

"Cast him?" she said uncomprehending. An Outskirter rite of honor for a wizard's minion, a man who had been sent for Slado's purposes, to aid in a plan which had caused only horror and death?

A man who had taken up Outskirter ways, Outskirter life; who had come to love the world he lived in, and each person who had stood beside him, for their beauty, for their strength, for their honor. A man whose every word was a lie, but whose every chosen action was driven by only truth, the truth that was his love of the life; who had declared, with laughter, with joy, his love of a tribe's old cook, of a hand-woven rug, of a rough pottery bowl, of a steerswoman. A man who had discarded unimaginable powers and accepted the simple sword, striking at the enemies of those he loved, knowing he could die in the attempt and believing it worth his death.

A man who had stood by his tribe, by his seyoh, by his chief. A warrior of Kree's band. Fletcher.

Outskirter rites for an Outskirter. Rowan stood, rain on her clothing, her hands, her face. "Yes," she said. "Yes, of course. I'm coming."

50

Dust Ridge was appropriately named.

They saw it first as a smoky line on the horizon. Rowan took it to be a low cloud; but it did not follow the rest of the weather. It grew larger as they approached, and at last they could see that it was a long cliff, with winds from above spilling dust from drier land beyond, over the edge. Rowan worried about climbing up into that dust, but it was only with the wind from the east that the phenomenon occurred. When the wind faded, or changed, Dust Ridge stood bare and calm.

They had traveled with Kammeryn's people for two months as the tribe slowly recovered. The Outskirters had survived by replenishing their flock with goats strayed from tribes that did not survive the tempests and tornadoes. But when they reached land too grim to support the tribe, they paused to wait, and Rowan and Bel went on alone.

Dust Ridge should have been out on the blackgrass prairie; the report of Bel's father had placed it so. It was not. It was on the Face.

Rowan wondered at her own surprise. The Outskirts moved, she knew, shifting forever eastward. The Face moved as well, she now saw, staying always ahead of the Outskirts themselves. When Bel's father had been here, it had been prairie; now it was the Face.

Rowan had before given little thought to the fact that Bel's father had been to Dust Ridge; the steerswoman had not before fully comprehended the nature of life in the Outskirts, on the Face, on the prairie. Now she wondered at his interest in a land so inhospitable. But Bel could provide no good answer: it had been her father's way to always travel, she told Rowan, often alone, and often to places that did not much interest other people. Bel found it not at all surprising that he should have seen fit to take himself out onto the blackgrass prairie, for no other reason than that it existed.

But there was no blackgrass at Dust Ridge now, nor were there goblins. The heat had come to the Face for the first time in decades, earlier that year, and had destroyed all life then present, leaving the tanglebrush bare and brittle, the lichen-towers weirdly desiccated, their internal spiraled spines bare and dead against the sky.

But there was new life: redgrass, spreading in from the Outskirts, meeting no natural competitors at all. Rowan and Bel walked across dried mulch composed of dead and rotted plant and insect life, merged and mixed by the intervening rains. Here and there were small and larger stands of redgrass, rattling sweetly, promising pastures to come.

Rowan's calculations of the location of the fallen Guidestar had a limit to their accuracy: she could not narrow the possible area to anything less than twenty miles. But Rowan had no plan to scour the face of the ridge for the Guidestar.

Instead, she and Bel made their camp on the plain below the cliffs and waited.

At sunset, Rowan stood facing the ridge; and as the sun fell behind her, illuminating the cliffs with gold and rose, she saw a streak, a smear of white glints on the raw face of the ridge, glowing brighter as the light changed, then fading when it disappeared. She marked the place in her mind, and sat staring at it long after dark.

They found a path up to it, certainly the same path Bel's father had used; there was no other. It was rough, and switched back and forth. They left their equipment below, taking only Rowan's logbook, pens, ink, and a waterskin, in an otherwise empty pack.

Rowan and Bel stood at last at a place where a thousand glittering blue jewels lay at their feet, in the shadow of a huge, shattered shape that thrust out from the cliff itself.

It was as large as a large house, and had once been larger; they could see that one side was torn, and open. Inside, there might once have been a chamber; but the body of the Guidestar was itself crushed, and that possible chamber was collapsed, extruding trusses, beams of metal, blackened with the heat of its burning fall.

Rowan clambered over it, probing, peering. She found more wires, their coatings melted like wax from the copper cores; more mysterious surfaces etched with copper on one side, black with soot, brown with corrosion. She pried one loose and saw for the first time its opposite side. It was festooned with tiny objects, partially melted, like square insects with their metal legs thrust through to contact the copper on the other side.

Most of the Guidestar was metal; some was ceramic, and Rowan found something like a wide, broken ceramic plank, wedged under one edge of the body of the Guidestar. Bel helped her tug it out. It freed by breaking, leaving most still under the hulk.

The plank was some four feet wide, perhaps six long. When it was freed, Rowan saw that one edge was hinged. She and Bel pried at the opposite edge, and the plank opened like the cover of a book. Inside, both faces were coated with perfect, unbroken jewels, their opalescent colors fracturing the light within them, their surfaces crossed by a grid of tiny, silver lines. Rowan knelt beside the plank for many minutes, running one hand across its eerie surface.

"Rowan! Take a look at this!"

Bel had wandered off to one side and made her own discovery: a large rectangle of metal, once flat, now twisted like taffy. Rowan went to it and sat beside it, bracing her legs against a boulder to keep from sliding downslope.

Bel was wedged on its opposite side. "Look at this." She had wiped dust from is surface with one palm, showing only corrosion beneath. Now she wiped again, widening the clear area. "Isn't that writing?"

Rowan would not have recognized it as such at first glance; it was too different from the forms she knew. But Bel, perhaps because she was new to writing, had recognized it as belonging to a category: shapes designed to communicate.

Rowan cleared more dust from it. The letters were an inch tall and consisted purely of deeper areas of corrosion lined up below a hole in the object itself. She puzzled out the shapes, compared them with known forms, found similarities, and guessed at the words.

" 'Turn left,' " she read, " 'and latch.' "

Bel looked at her. "Latch? Like a door?"

Rowan inserted her fingers into the round hole and felt the works within. "Exactly like a door."

Rowan settled down on a flat rock with her logbook, laying her pens and ink stone carefully beside her, to sketch and describe the Guidestar. Above her, Bel leaned back against the hulk itself, warming herself in the sunlight, with sun-warmed metal at her back.

Rowan filled the final pages of her book. The sun slowly shifted.

At last she set down her pen and paged through what she had written, moving forward and back, helplessly. Then she closed the book.

What she had written and drawn was mere description. Even standing beside the Guidestar, even touching it, she could not wrest from it the secrets of its magic, of its purpose, nor the reason it had fallen from the sky.

All she knew, she had learned earlier: the Guidestars sent down killing heat, at the command of wizards; and they watched the world from high above.

Rowan herself was high, halfway up a cliff, with sun-drenched air all around. She looked out, down.

Far to the west, the wild colors of the distant veldt merged into a single mass of brick red. Ahead, to the north, the land was gray and earth brown, with the sparse stands of redgrass discernible only directly below. To the northeast, just at the limit of sight, the line of the cliffs disappeared into a sudden blot of darkness: the near edge of the blackgrass prairie, where humans could not survive.

Blackgrass poisoned human skin. The goats could not live by eating it. Blackgrass was stronger than redgrass; where blackgrass was established, redgrass would not thrive. There were demons, goblins, other stranger creatures, beyond the Outskirts, beyond the Face.

"The Outskirts move." She had always assumed that it was the growth of the Inner Lands themselves, the cultivation of green life that pushed back the redgrass, the spreading of farms and towns that pushed back the barbarians themselves. But the Outskirters could only be pushed so far, to the Face, where there was more blackgrass than redgrass. Movement would be stopped there.

But then came the killing heat. The blackgrass, the poisonous plants, the monsters, were destroyed. And with no competitor, redgrass, always quick to grow, spread into the dead area. The Face people followed it, even as the living prairie sent new blackgrass back, eventually meeting and intermingling with the red, creating the mix of life common on the Face. And twenty years later, the cycle repeated.

But if the Face itself moved, then the zone of heat must move. Each time it appeared, it must appear farther to the east; destroying, clearing the way for the expansion of the Outskirts.

And the western edge of the Outskirts also shifted east, as the Inner Landers claimed new fields for cultivation. But as blackgrass was stronger than redgrass, so redgrass was stronger than greengrass. Farmers always needed to pull any redgrass that appeared, or it would choke their crops. But at the edge of the Outskirts, there were no farms, but young forests, bramble, greengrass fields. Green life spread of its own power.

She realized with a shock that it did so because it was free to do so. The Outskirters themselves cleared the way.

The goats ate the redgrass to the roots, their feces killing what they did not eat. The Outskirters themselves destroyed more, with their waste, offal, corpses. They pulled down lichen-towers, they hunted goblin eggs, purely for the sake of destruction.

Goblins, blackgrass, lichen-towers, insects: these were native to the Outskirts, and to the prairie beyond. Humans and goats were not. The redgrass stood between; and it was the only thing that stood between, the only link.

As if from a Guidestar, Rowan saw the world spread below her. She saw a band of heat destroy the Face and a portion of the prairie; and redgrass fill and spread into the dead area; and Outskirters using the redgrass, clearing it behind them as they moved east; and sweet green life following their path, feeding on the fertilization they left behind.

The Outskirters were the destroyers, and the seed. They conquered the evil land, used it, and made it ready for better life to come. They gave the land a human soul.

"And then killing heat stopped," Rowan said to the blot of black on the horizon.

"What?" Bel leaned forward to look down at her.

The Face People had been stopped against a barrier, constructed of life that could not support humankind. They had tried to push into the prairie, and could not. They starved. And then they doubled back, to prey on the inhabitants of the Outskirts proper.

"It's the end of the Outskirts," Rowan said.

"What do you mean?" Bel scrambled, slithered down to stand beside Rowan.

The Face needed the heat; the Outskirts needed the Face. Rowan looked up at her. "Slado is destroying the Outskirts. That's his plan, or part of his plan . . ." But such a process might take centuries; even wizards did not live so long.

How might the process be made to move faster?

Don't wait. Destroy the Outskirts directly. Test the heat spell, see that it works, and then move its aim away from the Face and into inhabited lands.

Outskirters would die in the path of the heat, and from the weather that came after. Those who survived would have a harder life—

And would turn in on the Inner Lands. "It will be war," Rowan said. "Your people against mine."

"How soon?"

"I don't know." The Outskirts was huge; even if Slado continued his accelerated destruction, years might pass before the situation became critical.

"We'll have to find Slado," Bel said simply, "and stop him before it happens."

But who could win such a war? The Inner Landers? And what then?

With the Outskirts destroyed, the Inner Lands would continue to grow as before; but there would be no intermediary zone between it and the deadly life beyond the Face. Eventually, expansion must stop. And as the people increased in number, there would be shortages, hunger. They would prey on each other. "Slado will destroy the Inner Lands . . . How can he possibly want that?" She scrambled to her feet. "Bel, what can possibly be the point?"

Bel had her own answer. "Slado is mad."

"No." Madness was the inability to recognize and deal with reality. Madness could not control, could not be so clever, so powerful, as to design and execute a plan of this scope. "I must be wrong. He can't mean to do this."

Rowan turned back to the shattered Guidestar, went to it, and laid her two hands against its sun-warmed surface. She had learned nothing from it, nothing. It was the Outskirts that had given her what knowledge she had, and the Outskirters, with their traditions, poems, their very names. But there was one answer they could not provide. "Why did this Guidestar fall?"

Then she remembered an answer provided, perhaps unwittingly, by a wizard's man. At Rendezvous, after plying Efraim with erby, Fletcher had said of Slado: "I think that he did it. On purpose."

Guidestars made it possible for humankind to spread to new lands. This Guidestar had hung over the opposite side of the world. It had been planned that humans would one day live there. Now that would never happen. Rowan said, "He's stopping everything. He'll destroy us all." She thought of her home village and her family; she thought of the Archives. She thought of Kammeryn and his tribe waiting for her and Bel's return, friends and comrades all, two weeks' travel away across the Face.

All would die.

She turned back to the open land, where far on the horizon, a small blot of black stood. And now it seemed to her that it was not retreating, but advancing, moving in to swallow the Outskirts, the Inner Lands—all the world she knew.

People could not survive in the world that the world would become.

Rowan picked up her pens, her ink stone, her books. She thrust them into the pack.

"Let's get out of here," the steerswoman said. "This place was never meant for human beings."

© DEB MENSINGER

ABOUT THE AUTHOR

Rosemary Kirstein makes her living in information technology, having variously served in programming, user training, tech support, and technical writing. She has also worked as a field-laborer among migrant workers in tobacco fields, as an airport security guard, as a wielder of the "green" brush in a hand-painted watercolor factory, as a truck loader for UPS, as a dish-washer in a nursing home, and as a waitress. She is also a singer/songwriter/guitarist who, early in her career, was involved in the folk-music resurgence centering around the Musicians' Cooperative in New York's Greenwich Village, and was a con-tributor to and sometime associate editor of the *Fast Folk Musical Magazine*, a monthly magazine/vinyl LP. Back issues of FFMM are planned to be reissued in CD format, and will include some of Ms. Kirstein's music. She lives in the Boston area with two cats.